# HERITAGE
## BOOK I: THE FLAME OF FREEDOM

by Adrienne Ramsey-Harris

Copyright © 2009 by Adrienne Ramsey-Harris

All Rights Reserved. No part of this publication
may be reproduced, stored in a retrieval system,
or transmitted, in any form or by any means, electronic,
mechanical, photocopying, recording or otherwise
without the prior permission of the copyright holder.

Self-published by Adrienne Ramsey-Harris through
Createspace.com

ISBN-13: 978-1481877138
ISBN-10: 1481877135

Illustrations by Rex E. Davis

## Dedication

*To Tony, who believed in me,*
*To Jonathan, who loved me,*
*To Leonard, who inspired me,*
*And to Wynn, the wind beneath my wings,*
*This book is dedicated, in*
*loving memory of those who*
*have gone ahead, and in*
*gratitude to those who yet remain.*

# HERITAGE
# BOOK I: THE FLAME OF FREEDOM
### by Adrienne Ramsey-Harris
<u>Table of Contents</u>

| | |
|---|---|
| Author's Foreword | vii |
| Personal Acknowledgements | viii |
| Historical Acknowledgements | xi |
| Genealogy | xiv |

## PART ONE: BEGINNING – THE SEED IS SEWN

| | | |
|---|---|---|
| Chapter 1 | Sigismund Square: September 30, 1861 | 3 |
| Chapter 2 | Prison Without a Gate | 15 |
| Chapter 3 | Death and Birth | 24 |
| Chapter 4 | Revelations | 40 |
| Chapter 5 | Renunciation | 47 |
| Chapter 6 | Love and Death | 55 |
| Chapter 7 | Private Tragedy, Public Unrest | 61 |
| Chapter 8 | August, 1862: Blood and Politics | 67 |
| Chapter 9 | September, 1862: Leave-taking | 76 |

## PART TWO: COMING OF AGE

| | | |
|---|---|---|
| Chapter 10 | Flight | 86 |
| Chapter 11 | Uprising | 104 |
| Chapter 12 | Plaz Marjzendiak | 119 |
| Chapter 13 | A Time to Laugh and A Time to Weep | 132 |
| Chapter 14 | Choices | 144 |
| Chapter 15 | Sweet Sorrow | 156 |
| Chapter 16 | Music Hath Charms | 163 |
| Chapter 17 | Chance Encounters | 171 |
| Chapter 18 | Loose Ends | 178 |
| Chapter 19 | Lovers and Friends | 188 |

## PART THREE: FRUITION

| | | |
|---|---|---|
| Chapter 20 | A Time for Tears | 198 |
| Chapter 21 | Before God and This Company | 209 |
| Chapter 22 | The Rigors of Reconstruction | 218 |
| Chapter 23 | Contradictions and Consequences | 226 |
| Chapter 24 | Aftermath | 234 |
| Chapter 25 | August 30, 1868 | 241 |
| Chapter 26 | Problems and Solutions | 250 |
| Chapter 27 | 1869: Growth and Evolution | 266 |
| Chapter 28 | Fall, 1869 | 274 |
| Chapter 29 | 1870: A New Decade Begins | 284 |

## PART FOUR: NEW DIRECTIONS

| | | |
|---|---|---|
| Chapter 30 | Hope and Fulfillment | 294 |
| Chapter 31 | Contrasts and Compromises | 303 |
| Chapter 32 | Love and Transition | 312 |
| Chapter 33 | Courtship and Controversy | 322 |
| Chapter 34 | Warsaw: 1873 | 331 |
| Chapter 35 | Widening Horizons | 341 |
| Chapter 36 | Changing Perspectives | 350 |
| Chapter 37 | Plot and Counterplot | 358 |
| Chapter 38 | Truth Laid Bare | 370 |

## PART FIVE: ALL THAT GLITTERS

| | | |
|---|---|---|
| Chapter 39 | Resolution | 384 |
| Chapter 40 | Growth and Conflict: A Backward Glance | 393 |
| Chapter 41 | Conspiracy | 409 |
| Chapter 42 | Assassination | 421 |
| Chapter 43 | Inferno | 431 |
| Chapter 44 | The Tides of Turmoil | 439 |
| Chapter 45 | A Dream Realized | 461 |
| Chapter 46 | Drawing Room Diplomacy | 472 |
| Chapter 47 | Street Politics | 480 |

## PART SIX: THREADS IN A TAPESTRY

| Chapter 48 | The Shape of Things to Come | 500 |
| Chapter 49 | Against All Odds | 510 |
| Chapter 50 | Tightrope | 520 |
| Chapter 51 | New Beginnings | 535 |
| Chapter 52 | Politics and Presentiments | 542 |
| Chapter 53 | Three Departures | 552 |
| Chapter 54 | The Tides of Change | 565 |

## PART SEVEN: DENOUEMENT

| Chapter 55 | Turning Points | 582 |
| Chapter 56 | Grief and Desolation | 593 |
| Chapter 57 | Life Goes On | 601 |
| Chapter 58 | The Ending of An Era | 615 |
| Chapter 59 | Homecoming | 629 |
| Chapter 60 | Exodus | 648 |
| | Bibliography | 661 |

### *Illustrations by Rex E. Davis*

| *Ephraim Marjzendiak at age 48* | *2* |
| *The Marjzendiaks flee the uprising in Mira's coach* | *104* |
| *The Assassination of Isaak Marjzendiak* | *582* |
| *Ephraim Marjzendiak at age 88* | *614* |

## Author's Foreword

Based on the record preserved in Genesis, centuries ago, God formed a covenant with a desert people in a world where every other nation in creation worshipped a multiplicity of deities. They often fashioned their images from stone, wood or clay. This God of the desert tribesmen was a very different sort of deity. He came to them through his prophet Abraham, and He forbade them to make graven images and to worship them. He would not even tell them His name, so they called Him by a term in their language meaning "He who is and has no name," Yahweh.

God made a promise to Abraham, that He would make his descendents more numerous than the sands of the seashore, uncountable as the stars in the heavens. In return, they must worship no other god but Him, Yahweh. For this, He would make of them a light to the other nations, the model and the symbol of the covenant between the people and their one God. These people were the Jews. God caused them to endure many hardships and even slavery in order to test and strengthen their faith, just as a metal smith tests his steel to strengthen it for the purpose it is meant to fulfill. Yet God never abandoned them; never allowed them to be totally overcome or destroyed.

I am a daughter of that Covenant, but only by adoption. I am a convert to the Catholic faith. To me, as a matter of logic and reason, the church that Christ founded using the "rock" of Peter's faith and zeal as its earliest foundation, according to historic record, must be the Catholic Church. No other formalized Christian religion dates from that time. But that church has a heritage that has been denied, ignored or distorted for far too long. It was left to the papacy of John Paul II to acknowledge and to embrace that legacy. He recognized the Jewish people as the "elder brother" of Christianity. He described Judaism as "the very root of Catholicism." When asked what he had done to help his Jewish brethren in Poland when the Nazis invaded and overwhelmed that nation, which had only two decades earlier reclaimed its independence, the pope replied sadly, in effect "Not enough."

In one context, none of us can ever do enough to assuage the horror and the shame of that incredibly vile event known as the Holocaust. For that matter, we of the Catholic faith bear the burden of guilt for a much earlier similar atrocity, the Inquisition. Nonetheless, in writing the history of a Jewish family of which this novel is Volume I, I have endeavored to make a small contribution to the effort that Pope John Paul II initiated when he visited the Yad Vachem Memorial and the Western Wall of Solomon's Temple, vowing that "Never again must such a horror be possible – never again." Thus he echoed the phrase that so profoundly embodies the conviction of the Jewish people in response to the ultimate genocidal cataclysm to which anti-Semitism – indeed any form of racism – if allowed to flourish, will irrevocably lead.

-Adrienne Ramsey-Harris

June, 2013

# Personal Acknowledgements

Truly, no man (nor woman) is an island. We are all interconnected by such intricate and often tenuous bonds. Our lives impact one another in circuitous ways, some positive, others negative in their effect.

Certainly, few if any undertakings of stature or value are ever accomplished solely by one person. God plays a major role in the process. On rare occasions He intervenes in obvious and unmistakable ways. More often, his methods are more subtle; He utilizes human instruments His wonders to perform.

Experiences that we perceive as painful, negative and profoundly disappointing in the short term may, with the ever forward progression of time, prove to be positive, constructive influences that help to shape our lives in a most positive way. Certainly, I feel that God has led me to the mission that this literary work represents; He has called me to carry out this assignment, sometimes in ways that defied understanding and that tried me almost to the breaking point. Yet, like Job, I have always trusted Him, and He has never failed me.

Twice I was engaged to be married. On each of those occasions, I found myself dressed in black, attending my affianced bridegroom's funeral. The first time that happened I was age eighteen, and thanks to having a teacher for my mother, I was already in college. The young man's name was Antonio, but everyone including myself called him Tony. Tony never returned alive from South Korea. He died trying to rescue the children of a South Korean family from a house under attack. The house exploded and all inside were killed. In the church I sat between his mother Gloria and my own mother Vijaya, listening to the eulogies that extolled his virtues, and there were many. Some, no one truly understood except me. Tony and I had first met when I was a four-year-old girl who, thanks to a nearly fatal accident at age two, narrowly escaped electrocution and afterwards could scarcely talk. Yet, with Tony, I could communicate fairly clearly, and he was patient enough at age seven, to hear me out and to feel I had something inside me that was worth saying and was worthy to be heard.

Because we had both planned to be doctors of medicine, I went on to accomplish that goal, partly in tribute to his memory, and partly because of my wonderful mother's early training, guidance and support of me. She it was who taught me to speak clearly again after my accident by making me play notes on the piano with every word I tried to say. She it was who had me reading Shakespeare at age five and committing his immortal lines to memory. Thanks to her, I was able to give my valedictory address at my high school graduation.

Much later, while I was in Medical School, a friend invited me to a piano recital presented by a young Jewish musician. It was there that I was introduced to my second fiancé, Jonathan. Our time together, first as friends and then as a betrothed couple was woefully short – only one year. But in that year he taught me the meaning of unconditional love – the kind of love that gives itself without reckoning on expecting any return. He did not want me to convert to Judaism for his sake. He would only accept my doing so if I truly believed in that faith. His career was just beginning, and he showed tremendous promise. He had amazing technical skill, and with it an emotional power and interpretive genius that was mesmerizing. In a concert hall filled with people, he could make each one present feel that he was playing just for that person, speaking to them through the composer's notes. Tragically, an airplane crash silenced his genius before it could become widely known.

Still, despite these tragedies and sorrows, my life continued and so did my medical career. In due course, I met colleagues and acquired friends whose families had been intimately acquainted with the horrors inflicted by the Nazi regime that engulfed Europe during World War II. And Jonathan's family had also been included in that company. I later met another creative Jewish artist whose family was fortunate enough to have left Russia before life there became unbearable because of World War II.

In the course of my residency training, I met my distant English cousin Wynn. She was a nurse who had formerly been a ballerina with the Sadlers Wells company, later the Royal Ballet of London. She was on stage when the German bomb fell that destroyed the Sadlers Wells Theatre. That bomb also ended her dancing career, and led to her entering training to become a nurse. She became like a sister to me, and we were very close until she died at the age of ninety-two.

The effect of all these people on my life ultimately coalesced into the irresistible compulsion to write this multi-faceted, multigenerational, multi-volume family saga. All my life, from childhood onward, I had written poetry, essays, short stories, even novels, though none were published. But never before had I even imagined such an undertaking as this was destined to prove. It would require, I knew, far greater skill and technique than I then believed I possessed, even at the age of fifty-one.

For this reason, I began to spend my weekends taking courses and seminars in creative writing. That is, those weekends that I wasn't taking professional seminars for continuing medical education, a prerequisite to renewing one's license to practice as a physician. By far, one of the most influential of those writing courses was one I took from Paul Gillette, a writer and psychologist probably best known to the general public for his award-winning film script PLAY MISTY FOR ME, the book he later wrote based on the script, and for his Pulitzer Prize nominated novel DIVA. Paul taught creative writing for some years at USC and he soon asked me to join the writer's workshop which he hosted in his home on a weekly basis. Paul took me under his wing, taught me several "tricks" of the writing trade, and brought my manuscript to the attention of a prominent literary agent in New York City. Unfortunately, Paul died years before the first volume was completed, but I owe him a great debt of gratitude for setting me on the right path.

In the course of the extensive research required for me to complete this work, I became well acquainted with nearly every member of the staff and reference department of the Glendora Public Library. This included Caroline Hernandez, Carolyn Thomas, Ted Taylor, Sandy Krause, Carlos Bafiggo and Rebecca Simjian. The help, encouragement and advice of these individuals was invaluable in enabling me to ensure a firm historical grounding for my series of novels.

And since I write the old fashioned way, in longhand, before transferring the text to a typed format, as most modern authors do to begin with, I cannot fail to mention my dear friend Sally Wiger. Her tireless work in bringing this epic to a presentable form, often without adequate compensation, kept me from giving up in frustration over a period of twenty years. I must also thank her husband Marty for his patient understanding throughout that time. During those years, another close friend took an interest in my work. His name was Phillip Townsend Sommerville. He was a friend of my English cousin, Wynn Wilson, and he took a copy of the voluminous manuscript (all four volumes as then they were developed) to England in search of a prospective publisher. Three different publishing houses were attracted to the work; however, at least at that time, no foreign publisher could purchase and publish a manuscript by an American author until it was first published in the United States of America. Alas, Phillip's efforts on my behalf were in vain. He knew books. He specialized in buying and selling rare antique volumes. Sadly, he died before the manuscript was completed.

Later, when Sally finally moved miles away, I was left without transcription support, but the cavalry came to the rescue in the person of another dear friend, Eric Magallon. Eric is the son of a medical colleague and friend of mine, Richard Magallon and his beautiful wife Dorothy. He and his partner, JJ Jackman, have brought this work to its finished form, its present form, transcribing, proof reading, and making constructive suggestions without which <u>Heritage</u> would never have seen the light of day.

As for the many friends who have contributed moral support, encouragement and unselfish dedication to helping me realize my goal, I can scarcely even name them all. Prominent among them are Rabbi Henry Kraus, himself a survivor of the infamous death camp at Auschwitz. Then there are Laurel and Timothy Bullara, who are like a daughter and son to me as well as my closest long-term friends. They and their seven children have been my cheering section for many years. Then there are Laurel's mother, Elfriede Webb, Nancy Updegraff, Sylvia Brister, Dr. Michael Borkin, his mother Dr. Joy Borkin, who has told me repeatedly that she "loves the way I write." Also, I must mention Dr. Mark Anapoell, who not only encouraged me and referred me to Rabbi Kraus, but who also serves as the model for the surgeon who saves the life and career of my principal character in Volume IV of <u>Heritage</u>, entitled <u>An American Virtuoso</u>. And certainly I must acknowledge the debt of gratitude owed to father Frank Cassidy, the former associate pastor of my church who, though now retired in residence there, remains an active, even dynamic force in the parish community and beyond because of his increasing involvement in the ever growing force of Christian meditation. Since he introduced me to this powerful entity, my life and my literary efforts have been transformed and spiritually uplifted in a manner that defies description. This new focus has enabled me to bring my work to fruition and to finally complete first Volume I, and then, to a major degree, the remainder of this family saga.

Last but certainly not least, I must thank the very creative and talented artist who contributed the illustrations which illuminate this volume and some of the subsequent volumes. His name is Rex E. Davis. We met through the intervention of a mutual friend, and Rex offered to attempt to create some suitable artwork to illustrate a few of the dramatic high points of the narrative. We subsequently lost contact with each other, but I remain immeasurably grateful for his artistic contribution to my literary endeavors.

My heartfelt thanks to all of you, even those whom I may have inadvertently failed to mention by name.

-Adrienne Ramsey-Harris

June, 2013

## Historical Acknowledgement

The following text is a work of fiction; fact-based fiction, fiction that draws upon the rich and colorful resources of history, but fiction nonetheless. Literary license has been exercised in those instances where it was essential in order to enhance the appeal and the vividness of the story. But for the most part, historic facts have been adhered to and set forth essentially in the manner in which they occurred.

History, since it represents the life experiences of our species, should present to us lessons that inform us of our future and prepare us to meet the challenges which the future embodies. Yet those among us who study history as an academic discipline frequently lament the fact that mankind consistently fails to learn from past mistakes. Of course there are and have been notable exceptions to that unfortunate rule. Sadly, those exceptions are rare. Certainly, the Romanov family, the ruling dynasty of the Russian Empire for a period of 304 years from 1613 to 1917, illustrate the rule rather than the exception. Those outstanding monarchs among them who exercised admirable statecraft and laudable concern for the future of their empire and their subjects were, after all, only mortal. They were not able to bequeath either their savoir faire or their foresight to their successors. And in the hands of those successors, the dynasty and the empire inevitably came to ruin.

As in all historical novels, fictional and historical characters interact and the threads of their lives are interwoven into a literary tapestry that serves to illustrate and illuminate the course of historical events and their impact upon humanity. It staggers human imagination to contemplate the disastrous fate of millions of people. One can be appalled by tragedies of such magnitude, but one can scarcely internalize them in terms of personal experience.

Instead of attempting to work upon such an expansive canvas, I have presented herein a condensed but very human family whose members are both flawed and ennobled by their faith, their beliefs, their personal integrity and by their encounters with the relentless force of destiny. It is my hope that by this means, the reader will be enabled to relate to their story and to understand the mechanisms at work in bringing about the fate that overtakes them but that cannot totally destroy them.

In the current context, I have used original dates rather than those recorded following the conversion in 1912 of the Julian Calendar to the Gregorian Calendar. That event moved all historically recorded dates ahead twelve (12) days in the 19th Century and thirteen (13) days ahead in the 20th Century.

<u>Heritage: The Flame of Freedom</u> constitutes the first installment of a four volume historical saga that chronicles the triumphs, trials and tragedies of a fictional family having the challenging (to pronounce) surname of Marjzendiak. They are descended from Ukranian Jews who migrated to Poland in order to escape Russian anti-Semitic oppression.

Ironically, following the three "Great Partitions," which effectively terminated the existence of Poland as an independent nation during the late 1700's, the family finds itself once more living under Russian domination and the constant threat of recurrent pogroms. (The Great Partitions of Poland occurred from 1782 to 1795.)

This fictional family is really a composite of four separate Jewish families who lived in and near Warsaw, Poland during the time frame depicted in the novel. From a literary standpoint, it is virtually impossible, and certainly unwieldy, to manage the telling, in compellingly affecting terms, of four separate narrations involving separate casts of characters. However, by combining the major characters into one family structure, the task becomes more readily accomplished.

The question of course arises – why tell the experiences of this family in a narrative content at all? Because so doing allows them to interact with real flesh and blood historical figures as the individual families actually did.

Archbishop Melchior Fijalkowski truly was the archbishop of Warsaw. He was banished from that city because of his nationalistic sentiments and patriotic activities. He was allowed to return only when Tsar Alexander II, referred to as the "Tsar Liberator" because of his emancipation of the Russian serfs, ascended the throne in early 1861. In less than a year, the Archbishop, known to be on friendly terms with Dob Baruch Meisels, the city's leading rabbi, was killed under circumstances that closely parallel the events described in the early chapters of this novel.

The Russian administration of Congress Kingdom Poland did indeed use conscription into the Russian military service as a means of controlling revolutionary activities among the area's young male subjects. Following the 1863 rebellion, harshly enforced methods of compulsory Russification were brought to bear on the subject population there.

By contrast, the Austrian-controlled section of partitioned Poland enjoyed a much more liberal administrative policy. And yes, the yellow six-pointed star that the Jews were compelled to wear on their outer garments in order to facilitate immediate recognition of their origin dates back, not just to the years of the Nazi subjugation of continental Europe, but to the 17th and 18th Centuries, and in Eastern and Central Europe, to even earlier times.

Prior to 1850, when most of the gates of Europe's ghettos were finally removed, except for those in Rome, the vast majority of European Jewry resided within confined spaces – ghettos, behind high walls and iron gates. Those gates were locked at night, usually by 9:00pm which was the prevailing time of curfew. Any Jew found outside the ghetto after curfew was subject to fines, imprisonment, and occasionally even death. In response to this inhumane treatment, the Jews as a group learned to be self-sufficient, to educate their children, secure and supply the goods and services necessary for survival, to construct synagogues as places of worship and cemeteries to bury their dead. The resulting close-knit communities were called shtetls, and life within the shtetl, while confining, could also be rewarding on several levels.

The assassination of Tsar Alexander II in 1881 was employed as an excuse to vilify and persecute the Jews throughout the Russian Empire, despite the fact that only one provably Jewish member of the People's Will was involved in the conspiracy. And she was not a key figure among the members of that group who actually carried out the regicide.

As regards the Polish patriot, soldier and statesman Jozef Pilsudski, a man who, viewed in retrospect through the lens of history, seems larger than life, he truly did survive an assassination attempt. This would-be political murder was foiled by an associate and friend of Pilsudski's who, alerted by the sight of a firearm being aimed, stepped in front of Pilsudski, took a bullet for him, and died in his place. That man's identity remains a mystery, and I have taken the liberty of identifying him as the second son of my fictional patriarch. And since Pilsudski later became the first Prime Minister of the newly resurrected and united Polish Republic, after World War I, this sacrifice on the part of a relatively young Jewish politician forms a logical basis for Pilsudski's liberal attitude towards Poland's Jewish subjects during his administration.

The Alfred Dreyfus trial in France was precisely the travesty it is represented to have been within these pages. It was a blatant and deliberate miscarriage of justice, perpetrated against a man whom his associates in the French Army disliked because of his social aloofness and because of his Jewish origins. For those reasons, he was considered expendable, and despite his rank and his achievements as an officer, was convicted on trumped up evidence of spying and treason despite the fact that the identity of the true culprit was known. The culprit was a member of an important aristocratic family, and so he was protected. Even after he had confessed, Dreyfus was still not acquitted, but was held under appalling circumstances in the government prison on Devil's Island. Only international public outcry belatedly brought about a retrial based on new evidence. When a guilty verdict was again rendered, the judiciary and the military were so savagely attacked in the press that the verdict was finally reversed and Dreyfus' rank and honors restored.

That event led, at least indirectly, to the convening in Basel, Switzerland of the First Zionist Congress in the year 1897. That historic gathering and the subsequent Zionist Congresses formed the basis for the founding of the State of Israel in 1948. Ironically, they also provided an excuse for agents of the Russian secret police based in France, the Okrana, to produce the infamous and totally fictitious Protocols of the Elders of Zion. This libelous document was plagiarized in part from a fictional scene in a Gothic novel entitled Biarritz, written by a former postal service worker named Hermann Goedsche. However, the main body of the work was lifted almost verbatim from an obscure political protest novel by Maurice Joly, published in Belgium and smuggled into France to denounce the tyranny of Emperor Napoleon III under the title Dialogue in Hell Between Machiavelli and Montesquieu. The resulting Protocols have been repeatedly exposed as a fraud. Yet they remain in print to the present day. Adolf Hitler had the text reprinted and distributed throughout Nazi Germany and in all the European nations conquered by the Axis military forces. The book has been translated into numerous languages from the original Russian Compilation published in 1905 by the eccentric Sergei Nilus in the third edition of his puzzling tale The Great Within the Small. The work has been adapted by organizations as divergent as the Ku Klux Klan and the Jihadist Muslim fundamentalists, and always for the purpose of inciting anti-Semitism. The work has no basis in fact; this has been shown by articles in the London Time and by an official pamphlet published by the Committee on the Judiciary of the United States Senate as well as by a ruling by the Supreme Court of Basel. And still it survives.

Indeed, mankind has not readily learned from past mistakes. On the contrary, in several instances, man has persistently repeated some of his most odious errors, thus causing the inestimable suffering of many of his fellow men. Yet history does not desist in its efforts to instruct and to warn and guide us away from the paths of self-destruction. History continues to furnish the literary imagination with engrossing materials from which to construct engaging and illustrative historical fiction. When such fiction is painstakingly researched, cross referenced, verified and then carefully presented in an appealing, involving and entertaining story, more fulfilling intellectual fare can rarely be found. Contained within these pages is an abundant repast for those who relish such fare. Enjoy!

-Adrienne Ramsey-Harris

June, 2013

# The Marjzendiak Family

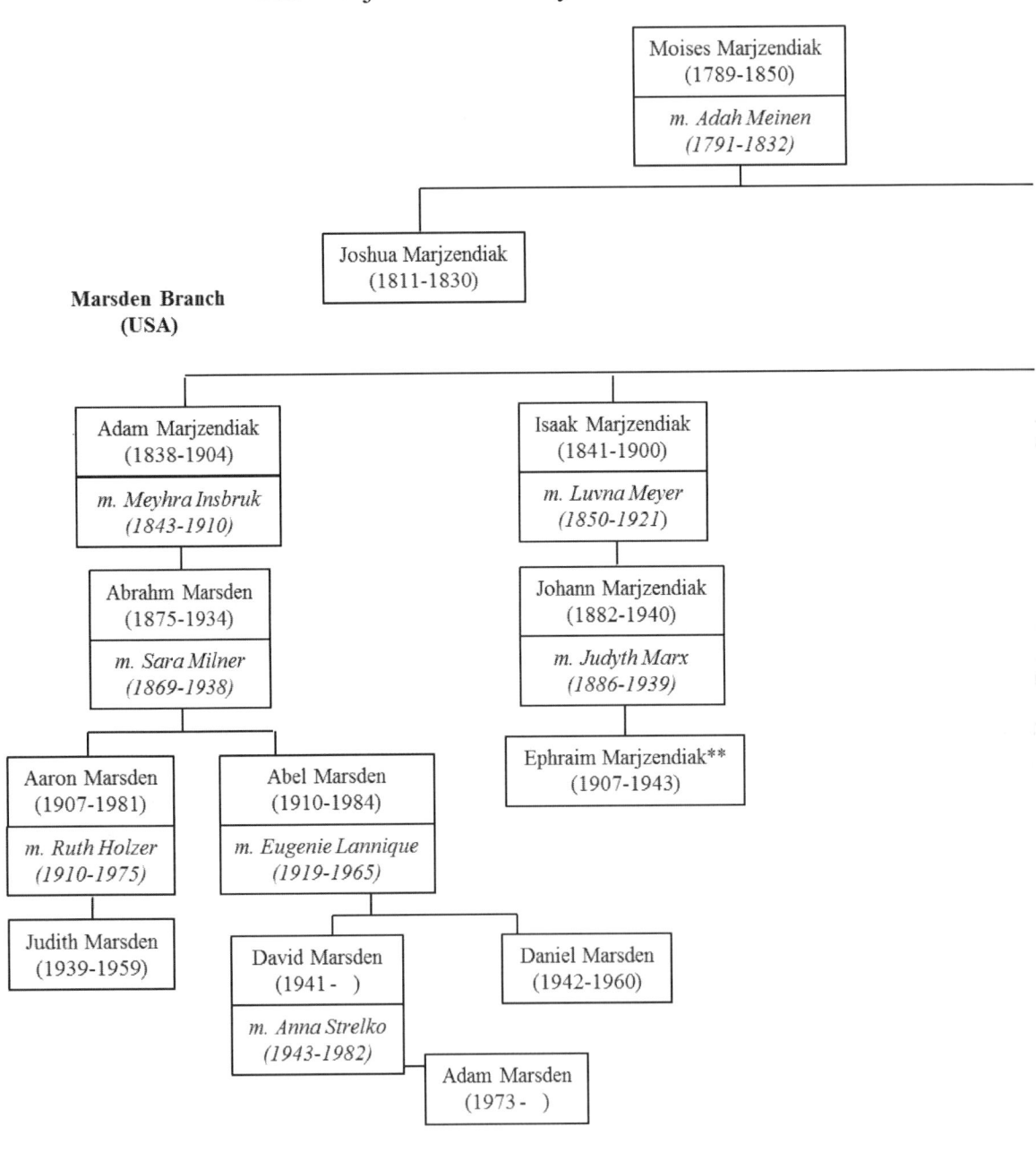

- **Moises Marjzendiak** (1789-1850)
  - *m. Adah Meinen* (1791-1832)

  - **Joshua Marjzendiak** (1811-1830)

**Marsden Branch (USA)**

  - **Adam Marjzendiak** (1838-1904)
    - *m. Meyhra Insbruk* (1843-1910)
    - **Abrahm Marsden** (1875-1934)
      - *m. Sara Milner* (1869-1938)
      - **Aaron Marsden** (1907-1981)
        - *m. Ruth Holzer* (1910-1975)
        - **Judith Marsden** (1939-1959)
      - **Abel Marsden** (1910-1984)
        - *m. Eugenie Lannique* (1919-1965)
        - **David Marsden** (1941- )
          - *m. Anna Strelko* (1943-1982)
          - **Adam Marsden** (1973- )
        - **Daniel Marsden** (1942-1960)

  - **Isaak Marjzendiak** (1841-1900)
    - *m. Luvna Meyer* (1850-1921)
    - **Johann Marjzendiak** (1882-1940)
      - *m. Judyth Marx* (1886-1939)
      - **Ephraim Marjzendiak**\*\* (1907-1943)

## Marjak Branch (Germany)

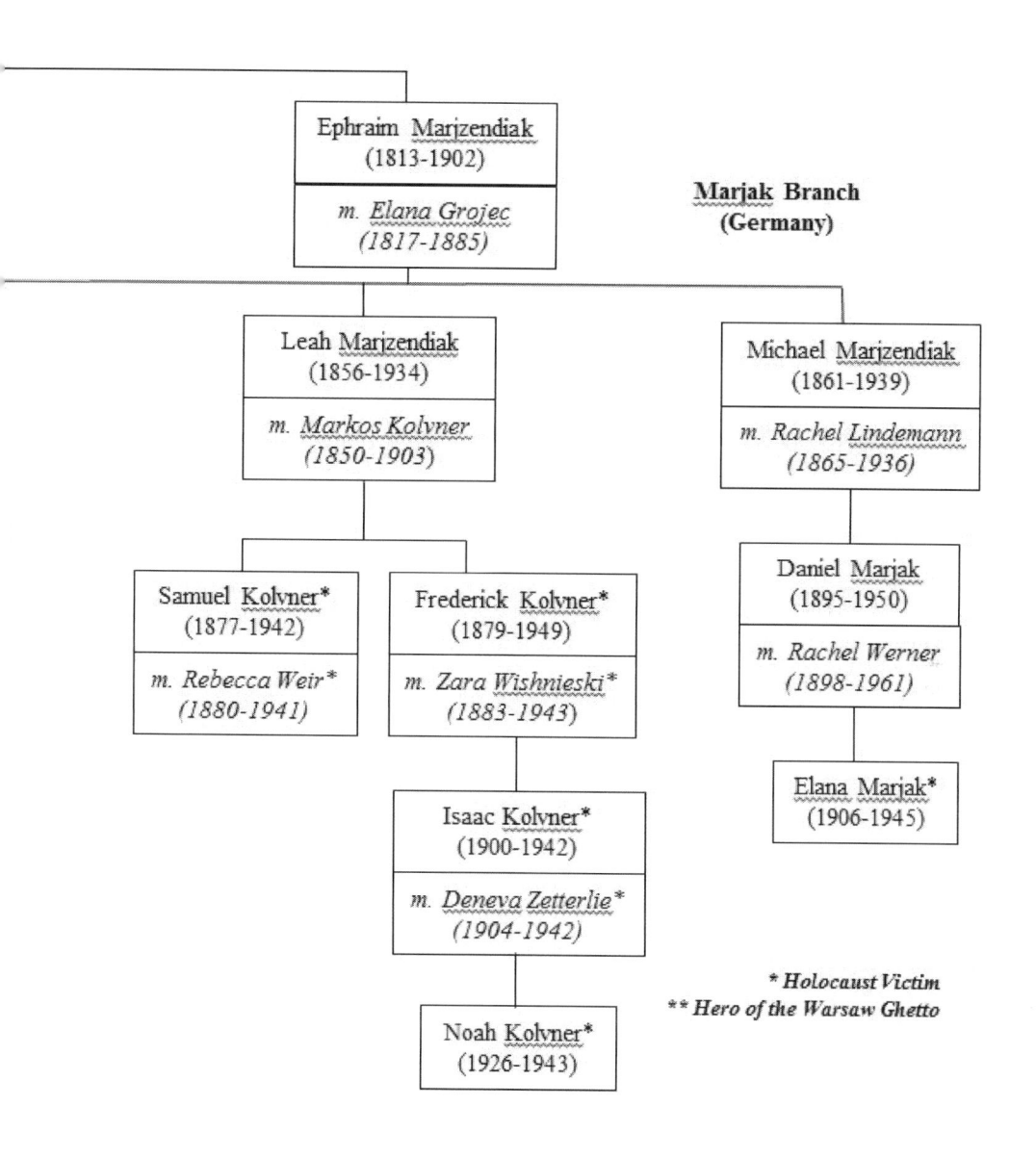

**Ephraim Marjzendiak** (1813-1902)
m. *Elana Grojec* (1817-1885)

### Children:

**Leah Marjzendiak** (1856-1934)
m. *Markos Kolvner* (1850-1903)

**Michael Marjzendiak** (1861-1939)
m. *Rachel Lindemann* (1865-1936)

### Children of Leah and Markos Kolvner:

- **Samuel Kolvner*** (1877-1942)
  m. *Rebecca Weir* * (1880-1941)

- **Frederick Kolvner*** (1879-1949)
  m. *Zara Wishnieski* * (1883-1943)
  - **Isaac Kolvner*** (1900-1942)
    m. *Deneva Zetterlie* * (1904-1942)
    - **Noah Kolvner*** (1926-1943)

### Children of Michael and Rachel Marjzendiak:

- **Daniel Marjak** (1895-1950)
  m. *Rachel Werner* (1898-1961)
  - **Elana Marjak*** (1906-1945)

\* *Holocaust Victim*
\*\* *Hero of the Warsaw Ghetto*

# PART ONE: THE SEED IS SEWN

Remember the days of old;
Consider the years of many generations.
Ask your father and he will inform you,
Your grandfather and he will declare unto you…

(Deuteronomy 32:7)

Ephraim Marjzendiak at age 48

# CHAPTER ONE

## SIGISMUND SQUARE: SEPTEMBER 28, 1861

An unseasonably cold wind swept through the streets of Warsaw as the late-afternoon sun struggled to penetrate dense, steel-gray clouds. There was precious little warmth in Sigismund Square[1], where several thousand people massed before the Royal Zameck Castle, the seat of government in the Polish Congress Kingdom.

The throng began assembling shortly before noon, led by Melchior Fijalkowski, Archbishop of the Roman Catholic Archdiocese of Warsaw, and Dob Barush Meisels, chief rabbi of the city. The archbishop wore his usual red-trimmed black cassock and scarlet skullcap, the rabbi his customary black suit and yarmulke. The caps, identical in shape though of contrasting colors, seemed to symbolize that the two faiths, despite their abundant differences, shared a common origin.

The religious leaders brought a petition to the square. They and their followers sought to persuade Poland's Russian rulers to restore political rights that were withdrawn several years earlier, under the brutally restrictive Tsar Nicholas I. Now that Tsar Nicholas had been succeeded by the infinitely less tyrannical Alexander II, the petitioners hoped that reason would prevail. After all, earlier in February of that same year, the Tsar signed the Emancipation Act, freeing, at a stroke of his pen, hundreds of thousands of serfs throughout the empire, and allotting to them modest parcels of land. Nothing in the current petition asked for modifications of imperial policies anywhere as far-reaching as that. And one year before, in 1860, the Archbishop had presented a petition that met with a moderate degree of success. Hopefully, God would smile on this current effort.

As the chilly afternoon wore on, the crowd continued to grow. Students, just finishing the day's classes, made their way through the narrow streets that funneled into the square. They were joined by workingmen, some accompanied by their wives and children. Chants of protest rose from the throng, led by the archbishop and the rabbi, who stood on wooden benches immediately before the castle. After a time, the archbishop began reading loudly from his petition. "We, the people of Poland," he quoted, "demand a voice in the election of local representatives and a clarification of the term of obligatory conscription for our sons who are called to serve in the tsar's army."

From a window on the second floor of the castle, beyond the sound of the archbishop's voice, Count Charles Lambert wordlessly surveyed the scene. Lambert, a tall, slim, and extremely handsome man in his early fifties, had been appointed several months earlier as viceroy of the Polish Congress Kingdom. In that capacity, he was, in effect, the head of state of Poland, the vice-roi, as it were; the "under-king" who, by virtue of the powers vested in him by the Tsar, held the fate of all Poles in his hands.

Lambert was a Russian whose paternal great-grandfather was French, an accident of heredity that the count exploited at every opportunity. Imperial Russia worshipped France and the French, equating that nation and its people with everything that was elegant and beautiful. The viceroy's detractors in the court of the new young tsar contended that were it not for his decidedly non-Russian surname, he might still be but a court clerk, despite the

---

[1] Sigisimund Square, named for several polish monarchs, was also known as Castle Square because the royal castle was its main feature. Over the last years of the 19th century, the square was expanded as were the streets leading into it.

title he inherited from his father. Lambert was aware of this assessment of him and recognized it as accurate but did not let himself be troubled by it. So long as he enjoyed the favor of the tsar, the opinions of others did not matter. Happily for Lambert, Alexander II, perhaps even more than other Russians, was enamored of all things French.

Standing beside Lambert was the Marquis Alexander Wielopolski, his chief minister and the next-most powerful man in the Congress Kingdom. Wielopolski was a Pole and the embodiment of everything that Lambert disliked about the nation and its people. A broad-shouldered and muscular man of Lambert's own age, Wielopolski, though an aristocrat, somehow looked as if he would be more at home on a farm than in a governmental office. He seemed to the viceroy never to be appropriately dressed: inevitably his suits were outmoded, his ruffles not properly pressed, and his accessories ill-chosen. He also had the habit, infuriating to Lambert, of noisily clearing his throat, a nervous affliction that Lambert himself unknowingly provoked.

As the two officials observed the rapidly expanding crowd, a frown creased Lambert's elegant brow. Gesturing toward the square, he asked, "What do you suppose they expect to accomplish by this?" His disdain was absolute; he might have been speaking of a band of urchins.

Wielopolski cleared his throat as he nervously fingered his collar. "In time, Your Excellency, they will realize the futility of opposing the tsar."

Lambert's lips rose slightly at the corners. At first, Wielopolski could not be sure whether the viceroy was smiling or wincing. After a long pause, Lambert said, "Minister, I did not ask you to look into the future. I asked you what they expect to accomplish."

Wielopolski again cleared his throat. "I believe, Excellency," he said, "that they expect to persuade us to accept their petition."

Once again, Lambert's lips rose at the corners. "I believe," he replied, "that they are on a fool's errand."

\* \* \*

Half a kilometer from Sigismund Square, on Senatorska Street, a Jew named Ephraim Marjzendiak struggled to concentrate on his ledgers. The office of Ephraim Marjzendiak, chief cashier of the head office of the Bank of Poland and one of only three Jews currently in its employ, overlooked the street. Throughout the afternoon he could not avoid noticing the many people who were making their way to the square, presumably to participate in the demonstration called for by Rabbi Meisels and Archbishop Fijalkowski.

From the very start, Ephraim was opposed to the demonstration. He was not unsympathetic with its ultimate goal; however, he felt certain that the demonstration could not achieve that goal. If anything, it would make matters worse, as the new viceroy, known for his arrogance and imperiousness, felt forced to show the Poles and the tsar back in Russia that he was firmly in control.

Ephraim, as a seventeen-year-old, took part in the Revolution of 1830, in which his nineteen-year-old brother Joshua was killed. Having served a prison term of a year and a half for his participation in the uprising, Ephraim soon came to appreciate, amazed that he had not done so earlier, that revolutions must be fueled by more than mere ardor. Unless the revolutionaries can claim clear superiority of manpower, initiative and arms, their cause is doomed to failure without help from an outside source, or a foreign power. In 1830, such help was not forthcoming from any of the nations of Europe.

In the intervening years, Ephraim rose from clerk-teller at the Bank of Poland to the high rank of chief cashier. He did so because he had learned to cooperate with people whose values he did not necessarily share and whose methods he did not wholeheartedly endorse. He did so because he was, above all, determined to survive, determined to protect his family and the interests of his family.

Now, at age forty-eight, Ephraim sat at his desk and worried about his own sons: Adam, who was twenty-two, and Isaak, twenty. They worked at a flour mill while Adam awaited consideration for one of the precious few slots allocated to Jews at the Warsaw Akademy of Medicine and Isaak waited for the reopening of the University of Warsaw, an event that, according to the tsar's promise, would soon occur.

If Viceroy Lambert reinstated conscription, the boys could be sent to Russia for an indefinite period as soldiers in a foreign army, perhaps not returning until they were well into middle-age, if ever they returned. Meanwhile, if violence broke out locally, there would be danger also to the other members of Ephraim's family: his wife, Elana; their precocious five-year-old daughter, Leah; and the child that Elana now carried in her womb, likely to be born three weeks hence. It was not so long since the last pogrom[2] that Ephraim Marjzendiak could forget the destruction visited on the ghetto by marauding thugs.

Frightening as these prospects were, there was even another, of more proximate concern. Ephraim knew that Isaak was a passionate partisan of the Nationalist cause now being represented in Sigismund Square by Archbishop Fijalkowski, Rabbi Meisels, and their followers. Adam, who shared Ephraim's conciliatory approach, would not dream of venturing into the square during the demonstration. But Isaak might well be in the thick of it. Nearly a year earlier, a similar gathering presented a petition to the previous viceroy. Thanks to the intervention of Wielopolski himself, the situation did not get out of hand. However, circumstances now were different: Lambert was a known reactionary, marginally liberal on occasion, but jealous of his own prerogatives, snobbish by nature, and he apparently hated the Polish people even more than they hated him. If things turned ugly in Sigismund Square, Isaak could be arrested, conscripted, deported to Siberia, or even killed.

Ephraim looked out the window. On the streets, the crowd moving toward the square grew more dense. Ephraim wished that there were some way he could persuade the demonstrators of the futility of their approach. The solution to Poland's problems lay not in confrontation but in negotiation. One could not negotiate with the Russian conquerors through simple force of will. One had to be in a position to offer an incentive, a benefit that the opposition desired to possess. The people of Poland were not currently in that position, but future circumstances might hopefully change that situation.

Ephraim bent over his ledger, trying to push political thoughts from his mind. After a moment, he became aware of someone behind him. He turned to see his employer and close friend, Franz Pietrowski, assistant commissioner of the Bank of Poland, a man ten years his junior. It was Pietrowski, a Polish Catholic, who hired Ephraim as a clerk-teller, Pietrowski who sponsored his various promotions, Pietrowski who jeopardized his own standing at the

---

[2] Pogrom: a vicious riotous assault directed against jewish persons and their property.

bank by being <u>protecteur</u> and mentor of a man who every day was forced to wear on his coat the large, gold Star of David that identified him as a Jew.

"It doesn't look very good out there," Pietrowski remarked.

Ephraim nodded. "Wielopolski has accomplished so much. He has the young tsar's favor. If only the people would give him more time."

Pietrowski's eyes met Ephraim's. "Perhaps you should leave early today. Get a head-start on the Sabbath. Get home before the crowds grow worse."

Ephraim knew that Pietrowski sensed what he feared most, that Isaak was involved in the demonstration. Ephraim wanted to embrace his dear friend. Instead, whether through natural reserve or in deference to their business relationship, he felt compelled to offer a token protest. "The day's tally is complete, but there still is so much work to do."

Pietrowski smiled. "I'm sure it will wait patiently for you until Monday morning."

* * *

From the second-story window at the Royal Zameck Castle, Marquis Alexander Wielopolski watched the still-growing throng in the square. Only last month he assured Tsar Alexander that his program of reforms would put an end to such incidents. Now, here was the largest demonstration in more than a year, and the viceroy himself was a witness to it.

Wielopolski was keenly aware of the viceroy, who paced nearby, the heels of his boots resounding sharply on the highly-polished marble floor. Wielopolski knew that the viceroy's irritation was mounting. Worse yet, Wielopolski was completely at a loss as to how to pacify the man.

Lambert disliked him from the start, owing in large part to the fact that Wielopolski was appointed by the tsar himself and granted far-reaching powers in the local government. Though neither Wielopolski nor any other Pole stood a chance of supplanting the viceroy, Lambert could not fail to see Wielopolski as an adversary. If the programs initiated by Wielopolski proved successful, Lambert could claim no credit for them. However, if they failed or were discontinued before they had an opportunity to succeed, Lambert could argue that he solved the problems that Wielopolski only exacerbated.

In any event, from the point of view of the viceroy, Wielopolski's approach to the management of the Polish Congress Kingdom was an open invitation to further attempts at revolution. Wielopolski had not learned from the revolts of 1817 and 1830, let alone from the more recent Decembrist rebellion in Russia, or those almost a century earlier in France and the United States, one unarguable fact: there are certain people who are not content with limited amounts of freedom; either one must keep them under heel, or one is faced with anarchy. Had Wielopolski not persuaded the tsar to overturn a ban on Jews venturing outside the ghetto except to travel to and from jobs cited on their work permits, the Rabbi and his followers would not be here today, adding fuel to the fire being fanned by the seditious archbishop.

Heels clacking loudly on the marble floor, Lambert returned to the window. "Well," he said to Wielopolski, "they seem to have lost none of their energy."

Wielopolski made a show of looking at his pocket-watch. "Your Excellency, there are not that many more hours of daylight. Soon the rabbi will have to begin preparations to celebrate the Sabbath. Give things time, and they will move in our favor."

"The Jews," Lambert hissed, ignoring the reply. "They're ever in the center of things. Even in St. Petersburg, they're at the heart of every conspiracy. When will they cease to plague us?"

"Here in Warsaw," Wielopolski replied softly, "most Jews are law-abiding subjects. You'll see relatively few star-shaped badges in that mob. The majority of the dissidents are Polish laborers and impressionable students."

"Led by that doddering archbishop. I warned His Imperial Majesty that releasing him from exile would be a mistake. You supported his release, as I recall."

"He has many followers, Your Excellency. They could become more dangerous had he remained in exile and died there."

Lambert appeared not to have heard. His voice grew more shrill, his anger more intense. "Give them time, you say! Time, Marquis Wielopolski, is something of which we have very little. Despite the tsar's nobly worded sentiments, he is a man of little patience. Perhaps you do not know him as well as you think. In the days ahead, excuses will not serve."

Wielopolski, after an instant's thought, permitted himself a show of strength. "I make no excuses, Your Excellency. My accomplishments speak for themselves." He did not venture to enumerate, aware that Tsar Alexander had already informed the viceroy of the minister's reforms.

Lambert gestured furiously at the people in the square. "And for whom do they speak!?"

Wielopolski replied levelly, "For the forces of dissent, Your Excellency. They are a distinct minority. And soon they will grow tired and hungry. When they see that their leaders have failed to accomplish anything tangible, they'll return to their homes."

For a moment, Lambert seemed about to indulge himself in yet another diatribe. Then, abruptly, he turned and strode away.

Wielopolski watched him, not knowing quite what to expect or to do.

Hands clasped behind his back, Lambert went to a table at the opposite end of the room. From it he took a short walking-stick of the sort favored by military officers. Returning his hands behind him, he began slapping the stick noisily against one palm, clutching and then releasing it.

Wielopolski continued to watch as Lambert resumed his pacing. The viceroy changed direction several times for no apparent reason, then went to the fireplace, where he gazed at the painting above the mantel as if seeing it for the first time. Wielopolski considered following him, then decided that the wiser course would be to stay where he was.

After a time, Lambert turned from the painting and smiled, seeming strangely refreshed. Wielopolski allowed himself a tentative smile as Lambert returned to the window.

Out in the square, Archbishop Fijalkowski stood facing the crowd, apparently giving instructions of some sort, but his words did not carry to the window from which the viceroy and his minister watched. Lambert spoke softly, as if reflecting on a matter that was wholly academic. "Between them, Fijalkowski and that rabbi give the radicals a false air of respectability that appeals to the masses and further misleads the idealists. That cannot be tolerated."

Wielopolski was about to offer a reassuring rejoinder when the windowpane shattered, showering glass into the room. The viceroy leaped back, as if trying to evade an attacking animal. The projectile that did the damage, a large stone, lay near the count's feet.

Wielopolski, pale and shaken, asked, "Are you all right, Excellency?"

Lambert ignored the question. "They throw stones at me? These peasants dare to throw stones at their viceroy?" He strode to the door, shouting "Guard! Guard!"

Wielopolski permitted himself a hesitant look out the window. The crowd seemed under the archbishop's control. Apparently the rock was thrown by an isolated member of the throng and was not precursor to a host of similar missiles.

A gray-and-red-clad militiaman wearing the bars of a captain responded almost instantly to the viceroy's cry. He was, by Wielopolski's estimate, in his mid-twenties, a well-trained and fearless officer who could not have earned his rank so quickly had he not unflinchingly entered situations of peril and emerged triumphant.

"Station two men at that window," Lambert ordered. "If anyone seems about to throw something, have them shoot to kill. Then disperse that crowd immediately."

The captain disappeared as swiftly as he had arrived, and, within moments a pair of rifle-carrying guards was at the broken window. Lambert returned to the window, Wielopolski at his heels.

"That rabble will learn," Lambert said with cold fury, "that a subject of Imperial Russia does not throw stones at his rulers."

\* \* \*

Ephraim Marjzendiak went to Sigismund Square directly from the bank. He walked twice through the crowd, hoping to happen conveniently upon his son, but did not find him. Then he positioned himself in the archway of a building laterally across the street from the castle. From this vantage point he could see the faces of those at the front of the rabble.

As his eyes methodically traversed row after row of impassioned demonstrators, he felt himself growing relieved: he had underestimated Isaak's good judgment; the boy obviously was not part of this crowd.

Just then, Ephraim was jarred by the sound of shattering glass. There was a stir through the crowd, a movement, accompanied by a sort of mass murmur. Then the archbishop raised his hands, apparently trying to keep his followers under control. His voice echoed across the square:

"No! No violence! This is a peaceful mission. Violence will not sway these men; it will only incense them. We must prevail upon them with reason and the justice of our cause."

Though Ephraim agreed with the archbishop, he saw little hope that the clergyman's words would be heeded. His impulse was to flee, but he was not fully satisfied that Isaak was not present. Then, as he continued to search the faces in the crowd, a platoon of militiamen stormed from the palace. These were not the regular, green-clad Polish guardsmen, who were positioned around the square when he arrived. These were the feared Russian unit that comprised Count Lambert's personal guard, the equivalent of Caesar's Praetorian Guard. These were soldiers known to fire with little provocation, confident that their superiors would support them no matter what they did.

\* \* \*

The young captain of the militia led a platoon of soldiers onto the square from the main entrance of the castle. The detachment moved in perfect military formation, trotting at double-time, boots thudding in unison on the cobblestones of the square. The young captain and his charges carried their rifles in the "ready" position, at "port arms."

The troops, following their captain's cadenced commands, came smartly to a halt, with the captain standing in front of the archbishop. "Your Eminence," the captain said loudly, his rifle still at the ready, "this assembly is unlawful. Already royal property has been damaged and the viceroy's life has been endangered. You and your people are ordered to clear the square."

A few at the periphery of the crowd fled instantly at the sight of the dreaded militia, but most held their ground. Those in the front ranks had no direction in which to flee.

"Captain," the archbishop replied, "we are a peaceful assembly. We wish to speak to the viceroy."

The captain pointed up at the broken window behind him. "That hardly looks like a sign of peace! The viceroy narrowly missed being struck by the rock that broke that window. You have heard the order," he said. "Clear the square!"

More members of the crowd, located at the periphery near the side streets left the scene, but the archbishop held fast. Rabbi Meisels was no less firm.

"All we ask," said the rabbi, "is that we be permitted to present our petition to Count Lambert. We need no immediate answer from him. We simply want to place our petition before him."

In support of that declaration, the archbishop held up the petition.

"The viceroy is not interested in your petition," the captain said. "For the last time, I order you to disperse or suffer the consequences."

\* \* \*

Ephraim Marjzendiak, if he were to live for another hundred years, would never forget what he saw that day in Sigismund Square. Instead of dispersing, the crowd pressed forward. Perhaps there was no intent on anyone's part to defy the militia. Perhaps the people in the square were merely trying to get closer to the captain and the archbishop so that they could better see and hear what was happening. In any event, the people, like slivers of steel drawn by a magnet, drew more closely together and pressed more tightly toward the center of activity.

The captain obviously was flustered. He yelled, "Disperse! Disperse!"

He did not realize that, given the configuration of the square and the magnitude of the crowd, the people were unable to comply even if they wanted to. Those in the rear of the crowd, unable to hear the captain's order, were pressing against those at the front, who, with few exceptions, had nowhere to move except even closer to the captain and toward the castle.

Ephraim, huddled in his archway barely a dozen meters from the captain, could see and understand what the captain, intent on carrying out his orders, apparently could not. He watched in impotent horror as the spectacle unfolded.

The captain again demanded, "Disperse!"

The crowd, as if an independent organism, continued to press forward. The archbishop and the rabbi raised their arms, gesturing to the people to back away, but to no effect.

Once again the captain commanded, "Disperse!"

And the crowd continued to press forward.

The captain ordered, "Fire over their heads! Over their heads! Fire!"

His troops fired into the air, and, for a moment, the crowd was motionless, the organism frozen in place. The archbishop and the rabbi continued to gesture to the crowd to back away, to disperses, but still without effect.

Finally, the archbishop resignedly shouted: "Do as he says! Disperse! Go home!"

At the archbishop's words, a wave of disappointment but also of resignation swept through the assembled citizens. Most seemed ready to withdraw. And then, from within the crowd, a stone was hurled at the captain. With uncanny accuracy, it struck him on the cheek.

The archbishop's voice rang out hoarsely, "No! No!"

The rabbi's voice was an echo of that cry as he gestured futilely to the crowd to back away and follow the captain's orders.

The captain, pressing his hand to his cheek and finding blood, yelled to his soldiers, "Fire! Fire for effect!" After a moment's hesitation, he repeated in a much louder tone, "Fire for effect! Shoot to kill!"

The militia began firing into the crowd indiscriminately and repeatedly. These troops, Ephraim found himself thinking, were mere boys, many of them younger than his own sons. But they were armed with rifles, and there were bullets in those rifles, and the bullets were being fired into people. They were tearing into human flesh, smashing human bone, blotting out human life without concern for age or gender. And the captain, himself barely half Ephraim's age, was able to command them to shoot those rifles, the bullets from which were entering the bodies of the people assembled in Sigismund Square wounding and killing these people.

One target, a beautiful young Jewish girl with dark, wavy hair, holding tenaciously to her mother's hand, was trying to comply with the captain's order. She was trying to move quickly with her parent to safety. Alas, it was not to be. A rifle bullet ripped mercilessly into the back of the young girl's head, traversed her skull and tore away most of her face as it exited her cranium. The corpse stiffened, the hand jerked from the mother's grasp. The mother, surprised, glanced back at her child and screamed in anguish as her eyes beheld the horror that but a moment before had been a vision of almost ethereal loveliness. The features of the girl's face were obliterated, leaving only a ruin of jagged bone and torn flesh. The waves of cascading brunette hair were covered with blood. Transfixed with horror, the mother watched helplessly as the corpse, impelled by the bullet's momentum, staggered blindly forward, the limbs jerking convulsively, and fell prone in the street. The mother sank to her knees and bent over her mutilated child, crying out in anguish and weeping pitifully.

Throughout the square, other cries of anguish rose from the crowd as more bullets struck home, as more human targets, blasted indiscriminately or cruelly singled out, were shot and fell bleeding and dying in the cobbled street.

And the firing continued.

Ephraim, paralyzed with fear, watched awe-stricken as a bullet entered the head of a woman whose hair was the same titian color as that of his wife. The bullet penetrated the woman's forehead near the left temple, opening a large, irregular hole and releasing a fine pink spray as the woman's head jerked backwards. Her body seemed almost to leap into the air, like a poorly manipulated marionette. Then it went slack and fell to the ground, twitched spasmodically for a few seconds, and lay still in death, a pool of blood spreading around it on the pavement.

And the firing continued.

A cloud of smoke began to fill the square, the product of so much rifle fire. It hardly seemed possible that the noise of the rifles firing and the rising smoke that resulted could come from no greater number of weapons than those of the men who had first followed the captain from the palace.

Surely, Ephraim thought, more militia must have joined the fray. Through the smoke, he saw a boy, no older than twelve or thirteen, struggling to escape from the organism that was the mass of demonstrators. A soldier took deliberate aim at him as he ran, allowed him to come close to achieving his escape from the area, then fired once, twice, a third time in rapid succession. The bullets tore into the boy's back, stitching his jacket with red, and propelling him forward, faster than he was running, causing him to pitch forward onto his face. His body twitched on the pavement and then went still, no less slack, as it lay with its limbs splayed out in a pool of blood, than that of the red-haired woman whom Ephraim saw die just moments earlier.

And the firing continued.

A man dressed in the blue shirt and coveralls of a laborer and standing near the front of the crowd began to back away, as did many others, seeking protection from the hail of bullets being directed into the crowd. Those at the front were particularly vulnerable. The laborer stood out because the cap he wore was trimmed with a red stripe around its crown. He suddenly raised his arms as if in a signal to someone. His movements seemed to make no sense, but they were precipitated by the force of the bullet that had just struck him savagely in the abdomen immediately below and to the right of his navel. His hands went convulsively to the wound as if they could somehow magically undo the lethal damage. Blood shot out between his fingers as if from a garden hose. He grimaced, his mouth contorted, and he fell screaming to the ground, clutching at his midsection, his cries mingling with the staccato crash of gunfire. Blood, urine and bowel contents seeped from his torn abdomen and puddled around him as he lay in his death agony. His screams sank to the level of sobs and moans. The anguished thrashing of his limbs subsided; he grew quiet and finally still.

Ephraim, still paralyzed with fear, astonishment and horror, could not take his eyes away from the devastation in front of him. He watched as more bodies fell and were trampled by stampeding people attempting to escape the brutal carnage that engulfed them. He desperately wanted to do something, anything, to help. But he was one man, alone, unarmed and as helpless as those he saw being attacked, wounded and murdered. There was no way he could help, nothing he could do but stand there in the archway, pressed back as far as possible against the closed door, praying that this senseless butchery would soon end.

Out in the square, the two clergymen retreated from their wooden benches. Rabbi Meisels was tugging at the archbishop's arm, apparently pleading with him to withdraw toward one side of the building, away from the fray, thus setting an example for the other surviving demonstrators. It was to be hoped that his example might also inspire the militia captain and his troops to cease firing and to withdraw.

Abruptly, Fijalkowski yielded to the entreaties. The two clergymen turned and moved in the direction of the archway where Ephraim stood. At that moment, a slender, golden haired woman moved closer to the archbishop and reached out to him. As he bent toward her, a bullet sped past his head downward in a slightly oblique trajectory. The bullet tore brutally into the left breast of the blond woman, essentially demolishing that breast and the vital structures of heart, lung and major blood vessels that lay behind it. The woman's shoulder blade splintered as the fatal bullet breached her back. She shrieked, clutched vainly at the gaping cavity where her breast had been, and fell lifeless to the pavement, blood gushing from both the entrance and exit wounds.

Archbishop Fijalkowksi blanched; his face was a mask of mixed sympathy and horror, as he stooped beside the dead woman. He saw her ravaged breast, her sightless, staring eyes, and the pool of her blood around her. He shook his head sadly, helplessly, and tears streaked his face. He realized that he recognized this woman. She was one of his parishioners, a faithful attendee at Sunday mass. She had on several occasions made a point of coming to him at the close of the service to praise and thank him for his sermons over the past year since his return to Warsaw. She had come to him now in the midst of the chaos in the square, reached out to him in supplication, and was instantly struck down.

He had led her and many others, far too many others, to their deaths. He had misjudged the extent of Wielpolski's influence and fatally underestimated the scope of Lambert's arrogance, the quickness of his temper, and the unbridled bestiality of the Russian militia.

He made the sign of the cross over the woman's corpse and closed her eyes. Then, as he sought to rise to his feet, he suddenly cried out in agony as a bullet ripped into his side, knocking him downward onto the dead body.

Rabbi Meisels crouched over the archbishop as if trying to shield him from further injury. Then, with strength born of desperation, the rabbi half-dragged and half-carried Fijalkowski out of the line of fire and toward the archway where Ephraim stood.

Panting, the rabbi laid his wounded companion supine in the relative safety of the arch. Then, with a handkerchief, he attempted to staunch the bleeding from his wound.

The archbishop, semiconscious, moaned softly and whispered brokenly, "My fault, all my fault."

"No!" Rabbi Meisels protested. "You couldn't have known, nor could I, that they would do anything so terrible."

The gunfire in the square was at last diminishing, its purpose having been accomplished. Most of those who were not killed managed to flee. As sporadic shots continued to ring out, the young captain gave the order to cease firing.

Ephraim stared unbelievingly at the scene of wanton destruction. Hundreds of bodies, perhaps close to a thousand bodies, lay dead in the square. Here and there, people huddled protectively over their fallen friends and loved ones. Some struggled to move the wounded to safety. Ephraim took particular note of an elderly Jewish man, straining to carry on his shoulders the lifeless body of his wife. Nearby, a young man paused in his flight long enough to kneel and close the sightless eyes of a fallen comrade. What could be seen of the pavement, the portions of it not covered with the dead, was slick with blood. Ironically, the archbishop's petition, the central purpose of this disastrous assembly, lay intact in the street. A young man fleeing from the scene, stooped and snatched it up, stuffed it inside his jacket and ran down a side street.

As if only now becoming aware of the other two men on the porch, Ephraim knelt next to Rabbi Meisels. "May I help?" he asked, ashamed for not having offered sooner.

The rabbi nodded expressionlessly. After a moment he said, "His church is scarcely a block from here. Will you help me carry him to his rectory?" Ephraim nodded, speechless. He was overcome with horror and outrage. Together they improvised a stretcher by tying together their coats. Then they slowly made their way through the blood-spattered streets.

At the rectory, a stunned monsignor, Fijalkowski's assistant, produced scissors and gauze. As Ephraim and the rabbi cut away the archbishop's clothing, the monsignor prepared to dress the wound. However, when the archbishop's flesh was exposed, all three men could readily see that the wound was far too severe to yield to their amateur efforts. Quickly, they applied a bandage, but it was almost as quickly soaked with blood.

The monsignor said, "I must go to the infirmary and bring back a doctor."

"That may take too long," the rabbi responded. "The Akademy of Medicine is on the other side of the city. Doctor Jedewreski's office is much closer." He was referring to the most revered Jewish physician in Warsaw. This doctor practiced in the Stare Miasto, the city's oldest section, which housed the Jewish ghetto, but was not far from Sigisimund Square.

The monsignor's voice was hesitant. "Would he treat a Catholic?"

"He's a doctor," the rabbi snapped. "Let us hope he has no emergency cases that would prevent his responding immediately."

"I'll go for him," Ephraim volunteered, already on his way to the door.

Outside, he swiftly made his way to the network of side streets behind the cathedral. Thanks to Marquis Wielopolski's reforms, Jews could now walk the city's main streets without fine or detainment. However, today was not a day to flaunt controversial privileges. By using only side streets, he could avoid drawing attention to himself, even if running.

Soon, the Stare Miasto rose before him in the hazy twilight, its centuries-old walls mottled, cracked, and scarred by the ravages of time. The ancient quarter had long been for him both a place of welcome and yet the symbol of his captivity. His ancestors settled here when they first arrived in Poland, fleeing Russian oppression. Now the Russians ruled in Warsaw, too, expanding their Pale of Settlement, the boundary beyond which Jews were forbidden to migrate. From its confines had risen the ironic colloquialism, "Beyond the Pale." [3]

---

[3] This term has two derivatives. One refers to the ancient boundary markers of the Roman Empire that inspired townspeople to cite the behavior of those considered acting outside the boundary of moral decency as deserving of exile. The other later origin was coined by the Russians to denote the boundaries beyond which aliens or non-citizens were not allowed to venture or settle.

Glancing over his shoulder, Ephraim noted with relief that there were no militiamen following him. He hurried through the open gateway of the wall and ran at full speed to the office of Doctor Samuel Jedewreski. The waiting room was full, but Jedewreski's nurse, recognizing Ephraim's urgency and seeing the spatterings of blood on his clothing, brought him immediately to the doctor.

Barely able to catch his breath, Ephraim told of the archbishop's injury and the apparent seriousness of his condition. Jedewreski, who had been applying salve to the lacerations on a young man's face, asked his nurse to finish the job. Hurriedly removing his white coat, he donned his street coat and seized up his medical bag.

"I'll return with you," Ephraim said.

"No," Jedewreski protested. "I know the shortest route to the Catholic Cathedral. Once or twice I've treated men who sought sanctuary there. There's really nothing you can do to help me. At a time like this, your family needs you, and you need them."

# CHAPTER TWO
## PRISON WITHOUT A GATE

As Ephraim neared the building that housed his modest apartment, he broke once again into a full run. The urgency in getting help for the archbishop had distracted him temporarily from his concerns about his own family, but now his anxiety returned with an intensity that increased as he drew closer to home.

Bounding up the stairs, he saw the door open as he neared it. His wife, Elana, stood there and suddenly went ashen-faced on seeing him. Instantly, his sons Adam and Isaak appeared behind her and seemed no less horror-stricken. It took him a moment to remember that his hands and clothing were covered with the archbishop's blood.

"I'm not hurt," he blurted out, then explained that he had been assisting an injured man.

Elana and the boys demanded details.

"Soon enough," Ephraim replied, enormously relieved at finding all three of them safely at home. "First I'm going to wash and change."

This chore he accomplished quickly, anxious to remove the physical signs of the horrors he had witnessed from his own person. He gratefully changed into other clothing, and glanced in passing at a mirror to ensure that he had washed away all the blood. If only, he thought, he could wash from his mind the bloody images recorded there. What he had observed horrified him, made him tremble even here and now, in the relative safety of familiar surroundings. The thought of what he might yet be compelled to encounter appalled his imagination. For his own sake, and for the sake of his own family, he must try to dispel those images and the fears that they engendered from his mind. Instead, he must prepare to welcome Shabbat, the Sabbath, the Queen who, at the end of every week, visited the homes and hearts of Adonai's chosen people, reminding them of His many blessings and most of all the blessing of creation.

When he returned, Elena and their sons were waiting in the living room with five-year-old Leah. "Hello, Papa," she said, running to hug him. "I've been helping Mama with dinner."

He lifted her above his shoulders, then hugged her and covered her cheeks with kisses.

"What a grown-up girl you've become!" He was relieved that she had been in the kitchen when he arrived; he could imagine how horrifying it would have been for her to have seen him covered with blood.

"Perhaps," Elana said, "we should have our Sabbath meal a little later than usual tonight. Perhaps we should all relax for a while first."

Ephraim agreed. Sitting on the couch next to Elana, he lovingly placed his hand on her swollen abdomen. As if in response, the baby inside kicked, creating a slow, rolling movement that Ephraim was thrilled to feel.

Unprompted, Adam went to a cabinet and poured small glasses of the traditional Sabbath wine. Then, as Ephraim and the family sipped the delicious beverage, he told them of the massacre in Sigismund Square.

Elana and his sons had learned something of it from neighbors. Ephraim expanded on what they had been told, emphasizing the sequence of events while omitting the gorier details.

"Father," Isaak said, "how did you, of all people, happen to be there?"

"I was," Ephraim hesitated, "running an errand."

Adam looked to Isaak, and Ephraim perceived accusation in the older boy's glance.

Isaak instantly got the message. "Father, were you afraid I'd be there?" His eyes met Ephraim's.

Ephraim looked away.

"Father, I wouldn't dare jeopardize our family or myself in that way." He seemed genuinely contrite that he had caused Ephraim to imperil himself by thinking otherwise. Quickly he added, "I may sympathize with the Nationalist cause, but I'm also a realist. Now that Count Lambert is viceroy, nothing useful can be achieved by petitions and demonstrations."

"I'm very glad to hear you say that, Isaak." Ephraim stood and gestured to both sons to come to him. Hugging them at the same time, he continued, "Adonai has blessed me with the two of you. We will face some very trying times in the days ahead. It comforts me to know we shall face them in unity and mutual understanding." Softly, he added, "Now let's put this subject aside and speak of something more suitable for the dinner hour."

The boys spoke of their workday at the flour mill, Elana and Leah of the way Leah had helped prepare that evening's roast chicken. Listening to them, Ephraim looked from one to another, his joy in them undisguised.

Adam, at twenty-two, had lost the boyish roundness of early youth. He had grown lean and wiry, like his father, and was slightly taller. He had the same gold-flecked brown eyes of Ephraim and the same abundance of straight brown-black hair, a wayward lock of which tended to fall across his forehead.

Isaak, at twenty, was slighter of build though equally tall, and his face was fuller and softer. He was crowned with dark chestnut hair that had a slight hint of curl, and his intense hazel eyes reminded Ephraim of his own brother Joshua, slain in the revolution of 1830.

Leah was small and fine-boned; she possessed curly auburn hair and the grey-green eyes of her mother. The whole of her being seemed to be infused with an energy that bespoke ambition and high intelligence.

And then there was Elana, the extraordinarily lovely Elana, whom Ephraim had met almost a quarter century before, when he had gone to the neighboring town of Grojec looking for work. Her sparkling eyes and vivacious smile had gone straight to his heart, even before he had noticed the star-shaped badge on the bodice of her dress. Before the day was out, he was determined to ask her father for her hand in marriage.

Now, as he sat with his family in the living room, Ephraim Marjzendiak told himself, as he so often did, that he was a very fortunate man: he had suffered much, and he and his family doubtless would suffer more; yet, together, they were blessed with the strength to endure and the capacity to find delight in each other.

At the dinner table, Ephraim's Sabbath blessing was especially meaningful to him. He prayed aloud that his family would remain safe and intact despite the growing turmoil between the tsar's forces and the Nationalist rebels. He prayed also that Rabbi Meisel's participation in that afternoon's tragic confrontation would not lead to retaliation against Warsaw's Jews. And he prayed for the baby who in but a few weeks would be one of them.

Adam silently poured more wine while Elana served the soup. Ephraim once again thought of how fortunate he was. And yet, the afternoon's events continued to haunt him. He was alert for the sound of booted footsteps on the cobbled streets just outside. He dreaded the prospect of an authoritative knock on the door that could mean arrest and detention. He had, after all, been seen with the rabbi and the archbishop. Surely there would have been someone present who recognized him. Might he have been identified to the authorities? Might he soon be?

Elana eyed him worriedly, reading his thoughts. The last pogrom remained fresh in her memory. The horrors of the assault by Polish ruffians had been followed by the descent of the militia upon the ghetto. This led to unexplained arrests and unprovoked attacks, inflicting injury and death. No Jew who lived through it could ever again recall that event without an acute sense of terror.

Furthermore, every Jewish parent of sons felt the always-looming threat of the cantonment, the former tsar's special brand of conscription. Jewish boys aged twelve to eighteen faced being confined in camps where they would be forced to attend Eastern Orthodox services and be subtly tormented until they accepted "conversion" to that Christian faith. Afterward, the conscripts would be subject to twenty-five years of military duty on whatever front the Russians were currently engaged in war. Most of the Jewish youths taken in the last raid would not have come home for another decade had not young Alexander II abolished the hated cantonment at the time of his coronation. That imperial proclamation had been hailed throughout Russian Poland with public tributes, parades, and religious celebrations by Christians and Jews alike.

And now? Now, under the local tyrant Lambert, there was little to celebrate. The liberties that had been given were, one by one, being taken away or made ineffective by new enactments. The Nationalists were growing increasingly restive, the Russians ever more determined. Where would it all end? Wherever it ended, the journey there would be painful for Congress Poland and especially for its Jews.

When the family retired that night, Elana lapsed into exhausted slumber, tired out by her ordeal of worry over her husband's prolonged absence. Ephraim, however, could not sleep. In his mind, he still heard the dreaded boots on the cobblestone streets, the authoritative knock on the door. Surely, he told himself, the Russians would not come this late: early evening had always been their preferred time to launch a raid, since families would still be awake and there would be no need to waste time rousing them and waiting for them to dress. But in his mind, the tramp of the boots and the knocking on his door persisted.

He thought of his many years in the shtetl, the Jewish settlement within the ghetto. Through most of that time, conditions had been far more severe than at present. Until several years ago there had been a strict curfew; that meant a harsh fine or imprisonment for any Jew found outside the locked gates of the ghetto walls between sundown and sunrise. There also had been oppressive taxes, assaults and robberies by local thugs, and the always-dreaded visits by the militia. Yet, the Jews managed not merely to survive but to thrive.

The community had learned quickly to be self-sufficient. Jews have long been skilled artisans and merchants: in the shops and stalls of the shtetl, one could purchase garments, tools, leather goods, and every conceivable variety of foodstuffs. A bride could obtain fabric for her wedding gown, an expectant mother could buy blankets for her soon-to-be-born infant and, in certain less-frequented corners, the superstitious could avail themselves of talismans and potions to ward off fancied evils. In the modest store adjacent to the Great Synagogue on Tlomacki Street, a boy could select the tallit, or fringed prayer shawl, for his Bar Mitzvah, and a housewife could find a siddur, or prayer book, to suit her taste and means. Meanwhile, elders could explore at their leisure the literature and lore of the Midrash, the ancient exposition of scriptural tradition.

In the shtetl, even during the worst of times, young people could achieve, if they chose, the equivalent of a college education without ever venturing outside the walls, so dedicated were the leaders of the community. A student with an interest in painting or music, physics or mathematics, could find an accomplished teacher. Many local leaders in the various educational disciplines had studied outside Eastern Europe, then returned to share their learning with their fellow Jews.

The Community Council met to arbitrate conflicts between employers and employees or disputes over the ownership of property. In all such arbitration, rabbis played a dominant role. Meanwhile, well-trained physicians attended the ill, while midwives presided over routine births. Groups of elders called Chabrah Kaddishah, ritually designated and specially trained for the task, took charge of preparing the dead for burial and led the prayers of mourning. Land had been set aside and consecrated as a cemetery, so that even the sad necessity of burying the dead could be met within the precincts of the shtetl.

By the enforced dual confinement of ghettoization and the curfew, the European Christians compelled the Jews to fall back upon their own resources. The Jews responded by utilizing to the full their potential not only to survive but to enjoy and take pride in their own ingenuity in transforming mere survival into a rich and rewarding lifestyle.

Seven years ago, the curfew had been lifted and the ghetto gates removed, but Ephraim knew that the curfew order could be reinstated at any time at the pleasure of the provincial governor. For all practical purposes, Warsaw's Jews, indeed most of the Jews of Eastern Europe, were still confined, not so much by the physical walls of the ghettos but by the social and cultural isolation which those walls symbolized.

And yet…

And yet, as richly rewarding as life in the shtetl could be, Ephraim still suffered a gnawing discontent. No, not merely a discontent, but a passion and a hunger. There burned in his brain the flame of freedom, the fervent wish to have the same liberties and opportunities as those who were not Jews.

He remembered an autumn afternoon when he had traveled in Franz Pietrowski's carriage on an errand to a nearby branch of the bank. The sun was obscured by dense clouds, and the wind held a hint of rain. In the distance, the slopes of the northern plateau wore gossamer-thin, iridescent crowns of early snow. At the foot of the plateau was a broad expanse of rich farmland, rare in this region of northeastern Europe.

As a boy, Ephraim had dreamed of owning some of that fertile land. His soul ached with anger when, at age ten, he learned from his mother Adah that no Jew in Poland could own real estate. Even when he was that young, the prohibition seemed the most fundamental of injustices. Had not societies through the ages considered land the ultimate measure of wealth? Well, to Ephraim's mind, soil was the ultimate measure of man's abilities. In order to survive and flourish, one must adjust to its rhythms; one must learn to coax food from it, learn to build with it or with its products. Ephraim wanted desperately to test himself against soil that was his own, to tend it and to cherish it.

Yes, he wanted to own property, if he proved resourceful enough to earn the money to buy it. And he wanted to wear the Star of David, whether on his clothing or on a chain about his neck, because he chose to wear it, not because someone decreed that he must. He wanted his sons to have the same opportunities as every other man's sons to study in the best universities, to take a place in the professions or in business, to pursue the highest level of achievement that each one's abilities and ambitions would permit. And for as long as this flame of freedom burned in Ephraim's brain, he might know joy with his family, he might know pride in his children and in his work, he might even consider himself, as he did, a happy man, but he would never, he could never, consider himself a complete man.

As he tossed in bed, the imagined sounds of boots and of a knock on the door continued to haunt him. And then he remembered one of the women he had seen shot that afternoon in the square, the woman with hair the same titian color as Elana's. He looked at his sleeping wife and shuddered. He could picture what the other woman's family must be feeling at this moment, while Elana lay beside him warm and alive, nurturing their child within her. The recurring memory of the red-haired woman he had seen die in Sigismund Square tormented Ephraim. Resolutely, he tried to shut out that tragic sight and the others that had accompanied it from his mind. He must focus his thoughts on his own life, his own family. His mind went back in time to a day almost a quarter of a century earlier.

He had gone to a neighboring town to seek work and had lost his way. Considering the turmoil of his thoughts that day, it was not surprising that he had become confused. He had just ended another argument, the most recent of many, with his father, Moises. The conflict arose from his refusal to serve as his father's apprentice. Moises Marjzendiak was the estate-clerk for one of the local landowners. To the senior Marjzendiak, that post represented an ancient and honorable service which the Polish Jews had fulfilled for many generations. Ephraim, however, aspired to greater goals than a job that was viewed as "fit only for a Jew."

That divergence of opinion was not Ephraim's only point of difference with his father. Ephraim, the younger of Moises' two sons, was always made to feel guilty because his birth had been the cause of prolonged illness for his mother. She never fully recovered, and following the ordeal of so traumatic a childbirth, she had never again been the ardent wife she once was. Ephraim at that early age was too young to understand his father's bitterness toward him, but it poisoned their relationship.

When the 1830 rebellion broke out, the seventeen-year-old Ephraim joined its ranks. His nineteen-year-old brother Joshua followed his example mainly to guard the impulsive Ephraim from danger. As fate would have it, Joshua had been killed doing just that; that event served to provide Moises with another grievance against his younger son.

After the conflict ended, Ephraim served a term of imprisonment for his part in it. Then he returned home only to find that he and his father disagreed more than ever. After the death of his wife Adah Marjzendiak, Moises became a lonely, brooding, embittered man, prematurely old though still efficient in his clerical duties.

Angry and hurt, Ephraim left his father's house in the Warsaw ghetto and set out to make his own way. He began inauspiciously by getting lost and having to stop to ask directions at a cottage which was set in a wooded glen. The cottage was part of a larger estate dominated by an imposing mansion, surrounded by lush fields of grass and grain.

Ephraim's knock was answered by a beautiful young girl at least eight centimeters shorter than he. Fine-boned and delicate-looking, she was the most beautiful woman he had ever encountered.

She greeted him pleasantly. "Are you here to see my father?"

Ephraim was puzzled by the question but thrilled by her rich alto voice. "Your father?"

"Most of the strangers who come to our cottage want to consult him. He's considered very learned and wise," the girl answered proudly.

"Who is your father?"

"Matthew Grojec. I'm his eldest daughter, Elana. "

"Mer Grojec has a beautiful daughter," Ephraim commented. "That may be an even greater blessing than either his learning or his wisdom."

"Thank you for the compliment, sir," Elana said with a warm smile, "but there is no greater blessing than a broad knowledge of Adonai, and men." She was instantly drawn to the tall, handsome young man who stood before her.

"Your father has a wise and beautiful daughter," Ephraim amended, admiring the girl openly. She blushed under his appraising gaze. Only then did he recall why he had stopped here. "Do you know the way to the brewery?"

"Which one?"

"The one that's advertising for workmen."

"That would be the Grijalski Brewery. It's owned by the family that holds this estate. You'll find it on the other side of the property just at the end of that road," she said, pointing back the way he had come.

"Thank you." Wishing he could find a way to prolong the conversation, Ephraim added. "By the way, is your father at home?"

"He's at the manor house. He manages all Mer Grijalski's business affairs for him."

"In return for which Mer Grijalski provides this cottage for your family." Ephraim considered that fact for a moment. "What time is your father expected back from the manor?"

"It varies. Usually, before night fall."

"When he returns, tell him that I envy him his beautiful daughter, and that I wish to speak with him." Ephraim paused, suddenly uncertain. "You're not already promised, are you?"

Elana stared at him, momentarily surprised that a stranger should ask that question. "Not yet," she answered smiling, "much to the annoyance of my sisters. By the way, I can only convey your message if I know your name."

Looking closely at her, Ephraim saw the flashes of darker green fire in her eyes. He sensed that there was a hidden reservoir of passion behind her circumspect demeanor. He longed to tap that reservoir, to arouse and explore that hidden passion. "I'm Ephraim Marjzendiak from Warsaw," he replied, and silently promised himself that this was the girl he would one day make his wife.

The job in Grojec proved to be quite a temporary one, scheduled to last for only a few weeks while the peak-season orders were filled. Ephraim made the most of his opportunity there. He demonstrated to the brewery's foreman his skill with figures and his ability to determine the quantities of ingredients necessary to fill each respective order.

In so doing, he succeeded in prolonging his employment for several additional weeks. At the end of that time, he learned of an opening for a clerk-teller at the local branch of the Bank of Poland.

The suggestion that Ephraim apply for the post was actively promoted by Elana's father, Matthew. Having by then promised his eldest daughter to this young man, Matthew wanted to see him well-situated. At the same time, having noted Ephraim's intelligence and ambition, he did not want Ephraim as his assistant. Such an assistant, he suspected, might one day aspire to his own position, which could conceivably lead to conflict within the family. With so much conflict surrounding them, Poland's Jews labored to maintain peace among themselves.

Ephraim could remember even now his conversation with Matthew on the eve of his wedding to Elana in October of 1837.

"I am relieved to know my Elana has found a husband who will provide well for her," Matthew said to him. "You are intelligent, ambitious, and independent. I have no doubt you will be very successful, Ephraim."

"I'm grateful for your faith in me, sir. I will make your daughter a good husband, I assure you."

"I have no doubt you will try," Matthew acknowledged, "but there is one thing I advise you to remember. On whatever road you choose to travel through life, remember to take Adonai with you. All the decisions will not be yours to make."

Ephraim murmured an appropriate response to his future father-in-law's admonition, somewhat puzzled by its underlying meaning. Of course Adonai was always there watching out for His chosen ones. However, the prophet, Moses, had made it clear long ago that a man must utilize his skills and avail himself of every opportunity in order to be worthy of Adonai's choicest blessings.

While not ostentatiously religious, Ephraim had always followed the major principles of his faith and relied on his own abilities to achieve the advancement he sought.

Ephraim's wedding day turned out to be the major turning point in his life. Within six months, he was promoted to the position of senior teller at the bank in Grojec. During this time, he and Elana lived in her father's house. Ephraim resented every day of that period, although he tried not to show it for Elana's sake. Nonetheless, he rejoiced when the day finally came that they moved into a place of their own, a recently vacated peasant dwelling that they were able to sublease. Despite the fact that he had to awaken at four o'clock in the morning to perform farming chores before going to his job at the bank, he was truly happy.

The fact that part of the fruit of his toil had to be paid as a fee to his landlord did not lessen his joy in tilling the soil. One day, he promised himself, he would till his own soil.

Adam was born late in 1838. With his birth, Ephraim had begun to perceive the beginnings of fulfillment of his far-reaching ambitions. He eagerly learned all he could, both about banking and about farming methods, in order to prepare himself for the day when he might be able to acquire a parcel of land of his own.

Two years later, he was promoted to the Bank of Poland's head office and returned to Warsaw. He brought with him a radiant young wife to help him establish his own home and his own place among his fellow Jews in the Stare Miasto. The fact that he also brought with him not one but two fine sons to carry on the Marjzendiak name finally cemented the ruptured relationship between Ephraim and his father. At last, Ephraim felt that his father had ceased to blame him for Joshua's death.

In his years away from Warsaw, Ephraim learned the value of patience, humility and self-sacrifice. Now, gazing lovingly at Elana's beautiful features, serene in repose, Ephraim was thankful to Adonai for letting him lose his way that day many years ago when he had gone to nearby Grojec looking for work. What, he wondered, would his life be like now if he had not found Elana to share it with him?

He placed his hand gently on her swollen abdomen.

She stirred restlessly. "Ephraim," she whispered.

He reached out and embraced her. "I'm here, my love."

She smiled and, with a contented sigh, went back to sleep, cradled in her husband's arms.

# CHAPTER THREE
## DEATH AND BIRTH

Despite the best efforts of Doctor Samuel Jedewreski, Archbishop Melchior Fijalkowski died a few days after the massacre in Sigismund Square. His parishioners, having already buried so many loved ones, were numb with grief. For three days, the Archbishop's body lay in state in the Church of the Holy Ghost. While Warsaw's Catholic population came to pay their respects, the militia stood guard both inside and outside the church, charged by Viceroy Lambert to maintain order and observe all that took place. The Nationalists, in their underground newspaper, Liberty, seized this occasion to publish several editorials stating that the beloved clergyman's death was nothing less than murder and that the presence of the militia defiled the sacred confines of one of the city's main Catholic churches. The newspaper called for the retaliatory assassination of the viceroy, reminding readers that it had been only two decades earlier that one of his predecessors had met that same fate.

On his way home from work, on the afternoon of October 10, 1861, Ephraim Marjzendiak approached Sigismund Square by way of the Krakowskie Przegmiescie, Warsaw's main street. The ancient clock in the tower of St. John's cathedral tolled the hour, three o'clock. The bells of the smaller but more ornate Church of the Holy Ghost chimed in answer.

Turning a corner, Ephraim caught sight of the imposing cathedral, Warsaw's principal Roman Catholic church. The blood-stained pavement of Sigismund Square still bore mute witness to the ruthlessness of the Russian militia. The "official" count of those killed in the September demonstration was twelve. The popular assessment, however, was at least two hundred killed, possibly more, and nearly five hundred wounded.

As he drew near the church, Ephraim was surprised to find an immense crowd blocking his passage. Thousands of people filled the square, many kneeling in prayer. The liturgical chants of the Archbishop's Requiem Mass, being held inside the cathedral, could be heard clearly in the street. Those outside the stately old building sang in answer to the chants within. Ephraim, who had once served in his synagogue as assistant cantor, listened appreciatively to that harmony.

The doors to the cathedral were left open so that the chants of the Solemn High Requiem Mass could be heard in the street. The mourners kneeling outdoors sang the standard responses to the chants within. Significantly, there were several slight deviations from the usual liturgy: the celebrant of the mass, Auxiliary Bishop Cosmo Elevski, interspersed portions of patriotic Polish songs, among the standard Kyrie, Gloria, and Credo. He did this in order to fulfill the last request of the dead archbishop.

Ephraim turned away, searching for a path through the crowd. At that moment, he unexpectedly encountered his friend, Samuel Jedewreski.

The doctor greeted Ephraim affably. "Good day, Ephraim. How are you?"

"Frustrated." Ephraim gestured toward the crowd. "I was hoping to get home early. I didn't know that the Archbishop's funeral would be today." Ephraim paused. "I was sorry to hear of his death despite your efforts, Samuel."

Jedewreski answered dispiritedly, "I was too late. There was really very little I could do."

"Another black mark against the Russians," Ephraim commented bitterly.

"Not in their eyes. The Viceroy accorded the officer responsible for that butchery a special commendation."

Ephraim stared at his friend in dismay. "A commendation for wholesale slaughter?"

"For a show of force calculated to keep the rebels subdued."

"If they think such tactics can succeed, they don't know the Polish people," Ephraim observed. "But what a change of policy this new Viceroy has brought."

"Indeed, the petition the Archbishop presented a year ago went as peacefully as one could hope. And now, he's dead." Disheartened by the discussion of such depressing events, Jedewreski shook his head and changed the subject. "By the way, how is Elana?"

"She's very tired of late, Samuel. I'm worried about her. This latest pregnancy has truly taken its toll."

Samuel clasped Ephraim's shoulder encouragingly. "Stop worrying, Ephraim. Elana's a strong woman. In a few short weeks, the two of you will have another child."

"I hope you're right, Samuel. But this is not a comfortable world in which to contemplate bringing a new life, especially a Jewish one."

Their conversation was abruptly interrupted by the staccato footsteps of approaching Russian militiamen. The major who was in charge of the detachment of militiamen at the church was of the Orthodox faith and unfamiliar with the Roman Catholic liturgy. Thus, he did not realize that he was hearing anything other than the traditional funeral service. Eventually enlightened by a Catholic subordinate, he sent a messenger to the Royal Zameck Castle. Within minutes, Ephraim and the doctor were heedlessly brushed aside by a new detachment of armed soldiers marching in double-time toward the cathedral. Kneeling mourners were jostled and cast aside as the men in gray and red uniforms, weapons at the ready, forced a path through the crowd to the stone stairs leading to the main entrance.

Ephraim and Jederewski watched as a young captain, the same man who had ordered the shooting in Sigismund Square, trotted briskly up the stairs, drew a document from his tunic, and handed it to the waiting major, who read it quickly then instructed the captain and several nearby guards to accompany him inside. Having ordered a guard posted at each door, he strode up the aisle, his boot steps echoing loudly through the cavernous chamber.

By this time, the Requiem Mass was concluded, and Auxiliary Bishop Elevski and his fellow priests and deacons began the final blessing of the coffin. They looked up in astonishment at the intruder, who now stationed himself directly in front of the coffin and turned to face the worshippers as if the officiating clergy were not even present.

Unrolling the document, the major read it loudly in Russian to the assemblage:

"By order of His Excellency, Count Lambert, the Cathedral of St. John and Warsaw's other Catholic churches are being ordered closed, effective immediately. Moreover, if the current unrest continues, all Catholic churches in congress Poland will be closed permanently. Further communication with the Vatican in Rome is forbidden."

Meanwhile, everyone in the Cathedral was instructed to leave immediately and go directly home. Anyone who disobeyed would risk the same necessary force that had been employed twelve days before to quell the disturbance in Sigismund Square.

Most of the people in the church could not understand Russian, but this mattered little to the major. Russian was the official language of the Empire, and the better-educated members of the community could take the responsibility of translating the directive and the verbal instructions to the others.

A loud murmur surged through the church as the decree was translated. Meanwhile, Auxiliary Bishop Elevski, who spoke Russian fluently, came around to the foot of the coffin and stood before the major.

"In the name of God," he pleaded, "permit us to complete the service! Surely the tsar does not condone interference with the exercise of religious duties!"

"Religious duties," the major replied evenly, "are not our concern. It has come to the attention of the viceroy that this church, under the guise of religious assembly, is a meeting-place for those who would incite revolution."

"This is a funeral, for heaven's sake!" The Auxiliary Bishop could not suppress the anger in his voice. "These people have come to pay their final respects to their spiritual father, who was killed by your troops! Do you now intend to provoke further bloodshed?"

The major remained calm.

"No, father, and that is why I have ordered your parishioners to disperse. If you are wise, you will urge them to obey." When Elevski did not respond immediately, the major continued, "You mistake my motives, father. I am here to keep order. Once your parishioners have left, you may complete your ceremony at leisure, and then my troops and I will escort the funeral procession to the cemetery and ensure the peaceful conclusion of these rites."

Elevski hesitated, then turned to face the crowd, which remained in place. "Our dearly beloved Archbishop," he said, "would have no wish that any of you be injured or killed on his account. I urge you to obey the major's order and return peacefully to your homes." As yet another angry murmur rippled through the crowd, Elevski raised his hands for silence. His eyes misted as he said, "My heart is with you, my children, but take strength from the words of Christ: turn the other cheek."

There was more murmuring, and then the parishioners slowly began to file from the cathedral. When the last of them had gone, Elevski, the other three priests and the four deacons completed the ceremony. Then, seven of the eight clerics acting as the pallbearers took their places alongside the casket, with Elevski at the front of the procession.

Suddenly the major all but leaped from the nearby pew where he had been waiting for the rite to end. All of the pallbearers were priests or deacons, except one: Rabbi Meisels. The major strode to him and stared closely at him, as if he could not quite believe what he was seeing.

"Well, well," he said, affecting a chuckle, "what have we here, a crow among the pigeons?"

Meisels was silent and expressionless, hoping to avoid provocation.

The major brought his face closer to the rabbi's. "What is a Jew doing participating in a Catholic funeral?" Without awaiting an answer, he turned away and stared, one by one, at the other members of the funeral party. "Or is this more than just a funeral? Is there perhaps a cache of firearms concealed beneath the body? Arms and ammunition for the revolutionaries?" He approached the coffin as if to see for himself.

Elevski stepped in front of him. "Please, major! Spare us this indignity! Surely the pallbearers would not be able to lift the coffin if it also contained weapons and arms in addition to the Archbishop's body."

Meisels came quickly to Elevski's side. "Major, I'm unaware of any statute forbidding men of different faiths to pay respects to one another, either in life or in death. I can assure you that Archbishop Fijalkowski would brave the precincts of my synagogue to pay his respects to me."

The major hesitated, then turned away. He had not exactly grown tired of the game, and he certainly was not intimidated, but he suddenly had an idea that he was certain would give him more satisfaction than his continuing harassment of the funeral party. "Very well," he said softly, "my troops and I shall escort you to the cemetery." He paused for effect. "Afterwards, I may have further questions for you."

The pallbearers complied with the captain's unsubtle invitation and the procession pursued its course out of the cathedral and along the main street. Behind them, the sound of heavy metal chains clanged harshly against the cathedral doors. Iron locks were secured in place to close the city's main Catholic house of worship.

The crowd of mourners was still in the process of dispersing. Ephraim Marjzendiak, troubled by the implications of what he had just seen and heard, hastily bade farewell to Samuel Jedewreski. He gathered his cloak around him against the penetrating chill and started home. As he went, Ephraim wondered what further outrages would be heaped upon the people of Poland in the name of "keeping the peace."

Even for a well-intentioned ruler like young Tsar Alexander II, reform in such a large and sprawling empire as that of nineteenth-century Russia was an impossibly difficult task. The implementation of many of the sovereign's programs had already proved very different in practice from his original conceptions, sometimes with tragically divergent results.

* * *

That evening in the Marjzendiak household, Elana Marjzendiak, still possessed of an elegant grace despite her advanced pregnancy, lighted the candles for evening prayer before dinner. As she did so, the golden flame of the taper illuminated the white veil she wore over her radiant red-gold hair. Her face was serene and, despite the hardships inherent in her life, still smooth and fine-textured. Her most striking features were her gray-green eyes, endowed with warmth and humor. Ephraim often said her eyes smiled even when her lips did not.

As she, Adam, and Isaak joined Ephraim in the recitation of the prayers, Elana's thoughts were ones of thanksgiving. Their home was modest but sturdy and the three men of the family were able to provide for their basic needs. On rare occasions, Ephraim surprised her with some small but treasured luxury. As she felt the stirring of the precious new life within her, she gave thanks for Adonai's beneficence.

At dinner, Ephraim recounted his experiences of the day, mentioning the funeral and the delay it had caused him.

Five-year-old Leah asked ingenuously, "Was the Archbishop a good man, Father?"

Ephraim thought for a moment. "Yes, dear," he answered finally. "I believe he was. Certainly. Rabbi Meisels thinks so."

Adam looked concerned. "It was dangerous for the rabbi to attend the services," he said. "He shouldn't have gone."

Isaak bristled. "Why shouldn't he? He and Archbishop Fijalkowski were friends for many years. They corresponded all the time the Archbishop was exiled in Siberia. Naturally, he'd pay his final respects."

"Enough," Ephraim said. "Enough talk of death and funerals. Now is the time to think of life and of hope." He smiled and lifted his wine glass in salutation. "May the Lord bless us and prosper his chosen people." He took a drink of the wine as did all the others at the table, even Leah. "Today," he added, "the Assistant Commissioner granted me a raise. Although he never mentioned the subject, I think it was in anticipation of the little one to come." He glanced proudly at Elana. "He asked about you, my love. Mer Pietrowski has grown quite mellow since his own promotion."

"I only wish the foreman at the flour mill would grow mellow," Isaak said a trifle bitterly. "I do my work quickly and well, yet he does nothing except complain."

"It's a personal thing," Adam remarked. "He doesn't treat me that way."

"That's because you never open your mouth. Anyone who expresses an independent opinion becomes his target."

"The moral is clear, brother," Adam observed. "Keep your opinions to yourself."

"What good is an opinion if you can't express it freely?"

"For us," Ephraim said, entering the dispute, "discretion is the wisest course. We are conspicuous enough as it is. Our dress and the badges they insist we wear set us apart from others."

"So much the better," Isaak said.

"Yes, of course," Ephraim agreed. "But that does not mean we should engage in conflict on every point of difference. As bravely as Rabbi Meisels acted today, I still do not agree with all his views. Encouraging Nationalist philosophies can only lead to disaster for us."

"I agree, father," Adam asserted. "The Russians are too strong. Now is not the time for revolt."

"We are all in agreement there, brother," Isaak answered. "We must bide our time."

"Good," Ephraim said with relief. "Before the discussion progresses any further, I suggest you two philosophers assist your mother by clearing the table."

"I can help too, Papa," Leah announced, rising from the table.

Elana shook her head. "No, Leah, you cannot reach the sink yet," she said. "All the dishes your grandmother treasured would end in broken pieces. You can help by drying the silver and putting it away."

*  *  *

While the Marjzendiak family enjoyed dinner that evening, Rabbi Baruch Meisels and Auxiliary Bishop Cosmo Elevski were roused from their meals by teams of militiamen. The clergymen were taken to the citadel, the ancient military prison. In the basement, they were pushed roughly into detention cells.

Meisels was left alone in his cell for more than two hours. There was no water, and there was nowhere to sit except on the cold cobblestone floor. An overpowering stench, issuing from the open-hole floor-toilet in one corner, made him want to vomit.

He wondered, of course, what was in store for him. He tried to reassure himself that he would not be tortured or murdered because neither act would serve a reasonable purpose. And yet, neither did it serve any reasonable purpose for the militia to interrupt Archbishop Fijalkowski's funeral. Viceroy Lambert might indeed have decided that with the archbishop out of the way, now would be the ideal time to eliminate the rabbi also, thereby defusing the leadership of the opposition in two quick strokes.

He speculated that he was being kept waiting while Auxiliary Bishop Elevski was interrogated. If the interrogators were spending so much time with Elevski, who, after all, was merely Fijalkowski's assistant, how much more severe might they be with Meisels, a leader of the demonstration and a Jew, the rabbi most revered in Warsaw, its chief rabbi?

The longer he was left alone, the more anxious he became. Because he was Jewish, he presumably was hated even more intensely by the viceroy than the archbishop had been. At the cathedral on the morning of the funeral, the major's hatred of him had been virtually palpable. Might such hatred prompt them to torture him before they killed him? Would he be able to resist the torture? Would they demand some sort of confession, something that could justify a public execution?

Finally a guard opened the cell door, bound Meisels' wrists, and roughly escorted him to an office with a sign on its door identifying it as that of the commander in chief of the citadel. At a desk sat a squat, hefty man in his forties who wore the epaulets of a colonel. Seated to one side was the major who had confronted the rabbi at the archbishop's funeral. The guard forced Meisels to his knees on the stone floor in front of the desk.

For the better part of a minute, the commander stared at the rabbi in silence. Then, affecting a smile, as if inviting the rabbi to share in a private joke, he said, "You devious Jew, what were you doing today with all those Catholics?"

The rabbi measured his words carefully, hoping not to create additional problems for himself. "I was attending the funeral of my friend."

"There can be no friendship between Gentiles and Jews."

The rabbi could not resist a mild sarcasm. "Is that an opinion, or is it a statement of official policy?"

"I'm asking the questions, Jew." The commander continued to smile, as if certain that Meisels at any moment would join in on the joke by confessing his nefarious purposes.

"I only wish to be certain of your meaning, sir, so as to answer the question accurately."

The commander's smile vanished.

"That funeral was a travesty," the commander pronounced, pounding the desk for emphasis. "Revolutionary songs and slogans were clearly heard by the officers who later closed the cathedral."

"The old Polish National Anthem was played in honor of the Archbishop's wishes. Likewise a Chopin Polonaise. These were his favorite melodies," the rabbi answered. "Christians, I have observed, tend to play and sing the favorite songs of their dead during their last rites. Our own customs regarding such matters are much more strict and formal, Your Excellency."

The commander rose from his desk, almost knocking over his chair. "Are you now mocking me, Jew?"

"No, sir."

"Do not address me as 'Your Excellency!' That is the viceroy's title."

"Forgive me. I meant no disrespect to either the viceroy or yourself. Please tell me how you wish to be addressed."

The reply was a shout. "Commander!" Pausing for effect, the commander added, "Now what I want from you is a detailed account of all the seditious statements and speeches that were uttered at that mock funeral."

The rabbi was silent for a moment, his face revealing his perplexity. "I'm afraid that will be impossible, commander. The only words spoken were in Latin, the language of the Roman Catholic Mass. I do not understand that language."

The commander's smile returned. "Then perhaps you can tell me some things you've learned in languages you do understand. I have a list of questions." He took a sheaf of papers from his desk. The major, who had sat silent and motionless through the entire exchange, remained silent but now took paper and a pen from the desk.

Over the next hour, the commander interrogated Meisels about events leading up to the demonstration, frequently repeating questions in paraphrase several times, as if to test the rabbi's memory. He demanded the names of the organizers of the various groups of students and workingmen who participated. He also demanded that the rabbi identify Nationalist sympathizers within and outside the Jewish community. He sought information about the funding of the underground newspaper, Liberty. Sometimes he asked the questions in a friendly fashion, at other times with obvious hostility. The rabbi, for his part, revealed nothing of consequence: in the interest of appearing to cooperate, he occasionally identified people who already were very well known as Nationalists, but he said nothing that would compromise anyone. Through it all, the major silently took notes.

Eventually, the commander returned his list of questions to his desk and the major put away his notes. Looking at Meisels with an expression of contempt, the commander leaned back in his chair and said, "You people call yourselves the 'Chosen of God.' But wherever you go, you do the work of the devil. You have been heard preaching rebellion in your own synagogue. This will not be tolerated any longer. You saw what happened at the funeral. No priest will dare preach further disruption in Warsaw now, nor will you and your fellow rabbis, lest your synagogues also be closed. Do you understand?"

"Your meaning is quite clear, sir."

The commander gestured to the guard. Meisels feared that this interrogation had only been preliminary and that he now would be turned over to the major or some other officer for torture. However, as the guard grabbed hold of the ropes on his wrists and yanked him to his feet, the commander said, "My meaning had better be clear! Now go, Rabbi, before I change my mind and lock you away where none of your followers will find you."

The rabbi left, amazed that they had let him go and totally perplexed as to why, if they wanted nothing more of him, they had bothered to take him into custody in the first place.

\* \* \*

On the evening of October 14, Count Dmitri Lambert, the viceroy of the Congress Kingdom, summoned Marquis Alexander Wielopolski, his Minister of Education and Commerce, to the Zameck Castle. The viceroy received the Marquis in his study. The ornate desk behind which Lambert sat was stacked with newspapers.

"Come in, Alexander," Lambert said affably. He laid an expressive hand on the stack of periodicals before him and asked, "Do you know what these are?"

Wielopolski recognized the publication at the top of the stack immediately. Paradoxically entitled Liberty, it was one of the underground tabloids devoted to reporting the latest acts of oppression and reprisal committed by the Russian overlords. Wielopolski nodded solemnly. "If they are all of a kind, Your Excellency, they are publications of the so-called 'Free Press.' They're hardly worth your time."

"Quite the contrary, My Lord Minister. I have spent many profitable hours reading these. I advise you to do the same."

"As you wish, Your Excellency."

Lambert's mirthless smile broadened as he picked up the publication atop the stack. "Arise, sons and daughters of Poland," He read aloud. "Let us honor our heroic dead on the anniversary of the death of one of our greatest heroes. Let us fill the streets. Let our oppressors know no peace."

Replacing the publication atop the stack, he asked, "Do you know, my dear marquis, the date to which these flowery patriotic exhortations refer?"

"Not offhand, Your Excellency. I don't even know when they were published."

"They refer, Alexander, to tomorrow, October fifteenth. Do you by chance recall the significance that some of your fellow Poles attach to that date?"

Wielopolski turned pale. The date was the forty-fourth anniversary of the death of Tadeusz Kosciuszko, one of Poland's most revered heroes, who had fought in the battle of 1796 to forestall the third and final partition that deprived Poland of nationhood. He was wounded, captured and imprisoned, but survived. It had been during the later rebellion of 1817 that the famous hero actually died in Switzerland where he was trying to raise funds for the war effort.

Lambert seized his walking-stick from his desk and banged it furiously on the stack of papers. "Had you been more attentive to your duties, Marquis, you would not need me to inform you that tomorrow I shall face insurrection!"

Wielopolski knew that Lambert was accusing him unjustly. Monitoring the rebels and their publications could not have been farther removed from the duties of the Minister of Education and Commerce. However, Wielopolski also knew full well that there was no arguing with whatever position Lambert took, no matter how unreasonable.

Lambert began pacing behind his desk. When he resumed speaking, it was in the same affable tone with which he originally had greeted Wielopolski. "I warned you more than once that your efforts at conciliation would only fuel the rebels' resolve. Now I must deal with the situation in my own way. Beginning in the morning, there will be no public assembly numbering one hundred people or more, not even in churches. The rabble is lucky I've allowed the Catholic churches to reopen. The banks and stores will be closed until further notice, and the militia will keep the main streets clear. There will be a general curfew beginning tomorrow evening."

Wielopolski wanted to warn that the viceroy's edict could only worsen the situation, adding even more strength to the rebels' already firm resolve. Instead, he remained silent.

Lambert smiled acidly at Wielopolski. "If I were you, Alexander, I'd go home and re-evaluate my future plans. This farce you called your ministership is over." He picked up the stack of revolutionary publications and threw them at Wielopolski. "Take these with you and see what they have to say. You may learn what your compatriots think of your efforts."

Later that night, Alexander Wielopolski sat in his study, reading the newspapers which Count Lambert had forced on him. The Nationalist press had been scathing in spelling out its opinion of his efforts to right the wrongs done to the Polish people. Too little and too late was their assessment, but how, Wielopolski wondered, could open insurrection accomplish any more?

The heterogeneous elements of Russian Poland's current population were not united as they had been in the uprisings of 1817 and 1830. The landed aristocracy, mostly Roman Catholic, opposed the goals of the predominately Eastern Orthodox middle class. The peasants, most of whom were members of the Uniate Catholic Church, mistrusted both groups. The militant youth were the most vocal and actively defiant of Wielopolski's opposition and they ran the free press. It was little wonder that he had been so severely castigated in the Nationalist newspapers.

The Nationalist leadership had planned its largest and most flamboyant demonstration to coincide with the emotion-charged anniversary of Tadeusz Kosciuszko's death. In the current period of partition and subjugation, the famed patriot, statesman, and military strategist who had fought not only for Polish but also for American independence, seemed a larger-than-life hero, an appropriate inspiration and rallying point for the youth of the once-great Polish nation.

Thoroughly frustrated, Wielopolski wearily cast aside the periodicals. He took up quill and paper and wrote a letter of resignation to the tsar. In the letter he stated his regret at having failed his Monarch and expressed his sincere wish that his successor would prove more successful. As for himself, he planned to retire to his family estate near Lodz. There he could find respite from the pressures of public life.

The next morning, as Wielopolski was packing for the journey to Lodz, his preparations were sharply interrupted by the staccato reports of rifle fire. The menacing sounds seemed to come from several directions at once. So it has begun, he thought. He rested his head in his hands and wept for his divided nation.

*  *  *

Early in the morning in the streets throughout the city, the militia was out in force, dispersing any citizens who attempted to assemble and arresting those who resisted their orders. The militia's instructions were to prevent the scheduled demonstration from getting underway. Extra troops were assigned to guard the viceroy's palace. Armed patrols were stationed at public buildings and along major thoroughfares. The viceroy was expecting trouble on a grand scale, and the men who patrolled Warsaw that day required only the slightest provocation to react violently.

Ephraim Marjzendiak pushed against the imposing double doors of the Warsaw office of the Bank of Poland, surprised to find them locked. As a Jewish resident of the Stare Miasto, and therefore situated beyond the perimeter of the Viceroy's announcement, he had not received news of the bank's closing.

The church bells had long since chimed the hour of nine o'clock. There could be no mistaking that. Ephraim had felt a twinge of guilt because the patrols in the street had caused him to be late. Yet he found himself alone. If the bank was merely late opening that morning, where were its other employees? Was he the only one not informed? Puzzled, he went to the rear entrance and was relieved to find it unlocked. He was about to enter the bank when he was unceremoniously seized from behind by a uniformed man armed with a rifle.

The militiaman shook him harshly. "What are you doing here, Jew?"

Ephraim was momentarily startled. "I work here, sir," he answered respectfully.

"A likely story," the soldier snapped. "The bank is closed today. Everyone who works here was aware of that."

"I was not informed."

"I have orders to arrest anyone found in this area without authorization. Show me proof of your employment," the militiaman demanded.

Ephraim searched the pockets of his coat, praying all the while that he had his papers on him. He dared not guess at his fate if he had inadvertently left his work permit and identity badge at home in his other coat. Relief spread over his face as his fingers found the stiff cardboard badge and the folded rectangular certificate of employment. He handed them to the soldier.

The soldier examined Ephraim's identification card. Ephraim thought with a flash of panic that the Russian might pocket the document and arrest him anyway. Such events were not uncommon. The militiaman peered closely at the certificate, comparing the name printed there with that on the badge. "Mar-zen-jak," he said haltingly. "What sort of name is that?"

"A good honest name," Ephraim replied.

The militiaman gestured toward the bank building. "What do you do here?"

"I supervise the clerk tellers."

The Russian eyed Ephraim curiously. "Indeed," he remarked. "Well, you'd better get your head out of the clouds, Jew, and keep in touch with what's going on. The banks are closed today by order of the Viceroy. It was announced last evening."

"Where?"

"All over the city."

"No announcement was made in the ghetto."

The Russian militiaman smiled. "I guess it was considered unnecessary. Few Jews work in this area."

At that moment, the door of the bank opened and a tall, aristocratic-looking man stepped out. "Ephraim," he said, "I wondered if you'd heard the news."

The Russian stepped importantly between Ephraim and the other man. "Who are you?"

"I am Franz Pietrowski, the Assistant Bank Commissioner." From his coat pocket he produced his identification papers.

The militiaman saluted, obviously impressed. "You shouldn't be here, sir," he said. "The radicals have planned a demonstration today. Already, there have been several confrontations."

Franz Pietrowski turned to Ephraim. "I apologize that you weren't notified, but I'm glad you're here. I need your help. Please come inside."

"You'd both better be out of here by noon," the Russian warned them. "From then on, Senatorska Street will be closed. Anyone found here will be arrested."

"But, Captain," Franz answered respectfully, deliberately according the man a far superior rank than the one he held, "if the streets are closed, my carriage may not be able to get through."

The Russian's tone was gruff. "What does the carriage look like?"

"It's a closed carriage, gray with black trim."

The militiaman held out his hand. "For a consideration, I can make sure it gets through."

Without speaking, Franz took a silver coin from his pocket and handed it to the Russian.

The soldier inspected it distastefully. "Only one zloty from the Assistant Bank Commissioner?"

Ephraim started to protest but Franz silenced him. He reached into his pocket and took out a second coin.

"Very good, Commissioner," the Russian said expansively, pocketing the money. "I'll see to it personally." He saluted Franz, glanced derisively at Ephraim, then strode away, proud as a peacock.

Franz clenched his fist angrily. "We are reduced to bribing foreigners to insure our safety in our own land. I don't believe we're in any danger whatsoever from the demonstrators."

"Danger wears a Russian uniform," Ephraim answered, remembering the sight of the wounded and dying outside the Viceroy's palace only two weeks before.

Despite the extreme efforts of the militia, the anniversary celebration took place as scheduled. Revolutionary placards appeared mysteriously on walls and fences, and were replaced more quickly than the Tsar's soldiers could tear them down. In bars and coffee houses, patriotic songs were sung and speeches made. In the secret precincts of the underground, the leaders of the Nationalist movement addressed those citizens brave enough to come out to hear them speak. A special deputation of students defiantly gathered in Sigismund Square, inviting arrest and imprisonment.

Count Lambert fumed at the sight of them but wisely ordered his guards to take no action. At intervals throughout the afternoon, groups of ninety-nine assembled in the reopened churches, knelt silently in prayer and then dispersed, scrupulously adhering to the dictum that not more than one hundred citizens could gather in any public place on that day.

* * *

On the evening of that eventful day, the Marjzendiak family gathered together for their evening meal, once again discussing the disturbing events of the past few days.

"Lambert," Isaak said exultantly, "wasn't really able to avert the demonstrations in tribute to Kosciuszko. They went right ahead anyway."

Ephraim regarded his second son with sudden suspicion. "What role did you play in those demonstrations?" he asked sharply.

"None whatsoever," Isaak answered. "I was at work all day from early morning until late afternoon." He turned to his elder brother. "You can attest to that, can't you, Adam?"

"For once, I can." Adam responded. "He never left the premises, not even for lunch. We ate together."

Ephraim nodded approvingly. "I'm relieved to hear it" he said.

Elana let out the breath she had been holding in anticipation and dread of where this exchange might lead. "So am I." she said, then she gasped and bent over suddenly, obviously in pain.

Ephraim was instantly at her side. "Are you all right, Elana?" He put his arms protectively around her. Elana smiled up at her husband.

"It looks as though for once in his life, Samuel was wrong," she said half-apologetically. "This little one of ours is anxious to be born. Now."

Ephraim picked up Elana in his arms. "Isaak, go and bring Zorah," he said urgently as he carried Elana toward the bedroom. Zorah Lupinska was the midwife who usually carried out the deliveries that Dr. Jederewski had determined were likely to be uncomplicated. Those expectant mothers who harbored complicating medical conditions or were pregnant for the first time, the doctor customarily delivered himself.

As Ephraim laid his wife on the bed, she reached up and smoothed back a thick lock of brown-black hair from his forehead.

"Don't look so worried, Ephraim," she whispered. "All will be well. Zorah is an excellent midwife, and I have had plenty of practice."

"I know, but I can't help feeling helpless at times like this," Ephraim answered, kissing her gently.

"Don't fret, my love," Elana reassured him. "Before morning, we'll have another fine, healthy child. A son."

Ephraim smiled indulgently. "How can you know that?"

"Trust me. Mothers know these things."

Leah Marjzendiak had been put to bed shortly after dinner. Now, three hours later, she emerged from her small room and rejoined her father and brothers in the living room.

Ephraim cradled her in his lap as they waited for word that his and Elana's fourth child had been brought successfully into the world.

"You're aware," he chided gently, "that your mother would be displeased to find you up at this late hour."

"But, Papa, who can sleep at a time like this?"

Ephraim chuckled softly. "You're right about that, little one. Major events in one's life are hard to sleep through."

"Did Adam and Isaak stay awake when I was born?"

"You bet we did," Isaak said from across the room.

"But," Adam added, "we were much older then than you are."

Ephraim hugged her. "Your mother often says that Adonai shows His wisdom and power most openly in the miracle of birth. Each individual is like a new book, not yet opened, full of promise and hope. Each is a limited edition, unique unto himself."

Just then, a tiny cry issued from the bedroom, and at three minutes before midnight on October 15, 1861, Elana Grojec-Marjzendiak gave birth to her fourth child.

In the future, Ephraim would remember his youngest son's birthday in terms of opposite extremes. Fifteen days ago, Ephraim had witnessed a massacre. Five days ago, the archbishop had been buried. And now Ephraim had just become a father again. Birth and death, he reflected, were two faces of the same coin, twin portals through which flow the tides of life.

After the delivery, Elana was tired but exhilarated. Zorah placed the infant in her welcoming arms, and Elana cradled the newborn against her high, small breasts. She studied the tiny face and thought back on her previous deliveries. She savored the joy and exultation she had experienced each time she had participated in the miracle of birth.

After several moments, she handed the baby back to Zorah. "Take him to Ephraim so he may bless him and give him the name we have chosen."

Zorah flinched, her cabalistic superstitions surfacing abruptly. "In times such as these, you named a baby before he was born?" She was one of the Eastern European Jews who believed that to name a child before birth was a presumption that might incite divine anger. "Suppose the child had not lived?"

Elana merely smiled.

Zorah wrapped the baby boy in his swaddling blanket. "Gentile parents may do that," she muttered as she left the room. "Not Jews. What's so terrible about waiting until afterwards?"

In the living room, she handed the newborn to his father and spoke the ritual words of their faith. "Ephraim, Adonai has favored you, for you have begotten a son. May your name be blessed in Him."

Ephraim took the child from her and embraced him. Then he opened the blanket and admired the boy's tiny body. Ephraim had indeed been blessed: yet another of his children had been born whole and perfect, with fine, straight bones and well-proportioned limbs.

Ephraim went to the table where the siddur, the timeworn book of daily prayer, lay open. He read from it, then turned to the others in the room and concluded the prayer, "This is Michael, meaning, 'who is like unto Yahweh[4]. I am truly blessed in him."

Leah stretched to her full height as she strained to see her new brother's tiny face. "Are we blessed in him, too, Papa?"

"Yes, Leah," Ephraim replied reverently, "we are all blessed in him."

Despite the dangerous and uncertain world into which his new son had been born, Ephraim had faith in the truth of those words.

*  *  *

The Jewish High Holy Days came late that year. By many it was felt that their timing was auspicious. Rosh Hashanah, the celebration of the new year, was greeted with an extra measure of welcome. It seemed appropriate that those fortunate enough to have survived the September massacre and the tumultuous period that had followed should doubly rejoice to be entered into the book of life for yet another year. Adonai's blessings were hailed and the shofar sounded outside the synagogue doors, symbolizing yet again the substitution of the ram in place of Abraham's son Isaac, as a sacrifice to the divine king of kings.

The Marjzendiak family was jubilant on this High Holiday. They had much cause for celebration. The family remained intact. All had survived the terrible events of late autumn, and now there was a new family member, Michael, who seemed to symbolize Adonai's promise to preserve His chosen people. In a time of death and destruction, birth brought new hope.

Ten days later, on the event of Yom Kippur, Rabbi Meisels stood before the congregation of Warsaw's devout Jews in the Great Synagogue on Tlomackie Street to invoke the ma'ariv as the last strains of the thrice repeated Kol Nedre sung by the cantor echoed into silence.

Everyone present felt the gravity of this night. It was less an event than a process, a culmination of all that had happened around and within the Jewish community. The sufferings, the conflicts, even the deaths of loved ones, friends, and neighbors were embraced and accepted as part of the process of atonement embodied in this ritual of prayer, confession and self subjugation to the laws and will of Yahweh.

Leah and Michael were too young to be present here, but Ephraim, Adam and Isaak were there, wrapped in their tallits and kittels. Elana, with the other women, stood in the balcony, close to Zorah. They, too, wore white garments made especially for this purpose, but less ornate than the many-pleated kittels of the men. The mood of solemnity, of humility and awe was all pervasive.

Adonai, the king, the covenant maker, the judge, the absolver, the just, the merciful reigned supreme and absolute, and His presence and power were a tangible entity in this place and within the hearts and minds of all His people gathered here in witness and acknowledgement of His existence in defiance of all secular powers that strove to stand and act in opposition to Him. Tonight there were many more than one hundred people

---

[4] Yahweh and Adonai are synonyms for the Jewish concept of God. Yahweh is Hebrew, and is more formal in its convocation. Adonai is a more personal form of address between the worshipper and his or her creator.

assembled in worship. There were close to a thousand. And for them, on this day of prayer and atonement, the tsar's military governor and his ministers did not exist.

* * *

Tsar Alexander's reaction to Wielopolski's resignation was one of frustration. He had relied heavily on the Marquis' ability to implement his program of reform. Yet, despite Wielopolski's efforts, insurrection and dissent not only persisted in the Russian Polish territories, they grew worse. Alexander's plans for a centralized and peaceful empire had suffered a crucial setback.

The tsar reacted by sending to Warsaw as military governor General Nicholas Sukhozanet, a career soldier. Leniency, the tsar concluded, provoked only greater dissension. Perhaps strictly enforced obedience would put a stop to the demonstrations and restore an atmosphere of quiet, if not of peace.

Upon assuming his duties as military governor, Sukhozanet's initial act was to extend indefinitely the temporary curfew initiated by the viceroy Count Lambert. All Roman Catholic churches, while not padlocked, were forbidden to hold any services including marriages and christenings at which there were more than one hundred persons present. These measures were to continue pending "normalization of conditions," a term which was not clarified by the Governor. Punitive taxes were levied against both individuals and businesses suspected of actively supporting the revolutionary movement.

The Council of State was ordered adjourned for ninety days. Conscription, the primary issue that had precipitated the earlier demonstrations, was accelerated. The militia was instructed to hunt down and destroy clandestine printing presses. The younger men engaged in producing the underground newspapers were conscripted and the older ones imprisoned. In this atmosphere, the year 1861 drew to a close.

The winter of that year was the most destructive which the Congress Kingdom had endured in more than a decade. Travel was seriously hampered, and since the harvests of the preceding autumn had been scant compared to recent years, food was in short supply for rich and poor alike. An atmosphere of silent desperation descended like a shroud over Warsaw. Only the approach of the holiday season promised a respite from the combined impact of physical and psychological suffering. Presents were made and bought, and the air was sweet with the aroma of breads and cakes baking in countless ovens.

Ignoring the edict limiting the assembly of more than one hundred people at any gathering, the newly-appointed archbishop, Sygmund Felinski, celebrated Christmas Eve Midnight Mass at St. John's Cathedral. The gathering of the faithful all but overflowed the ancient edifice. No reprisals were exacted by the Russian authorities. Even the military governor knew when not to press an advantage.

Hanukkah, the festival of lights, fell four days after Christmas that year. Elana Marjzendiak, her health and strength fully recovered after her difficult pregnancy, was in good spirits. Despite the hardships imposed by food shortages and the harsh winter, she felt exultant. Her baby son, Michael, was healthy and her supply of milk was abundant.

The Jewish custom of giving presents, known as Hanukah gelt, varied widely. In some areas, gifts of increasing value were presented on each successive day. In others, gifts were given only on the first day of the eight-day holiday, while still others favored the last day for gift giving.

At two months of age, Michael Marjzendiak did not appreciate the symbolism of the Hanukah celebration. However, the warm blankets and leggings which Elana had woven specially for the occasion appeared to delight him.

Leah, older and more attuned to the holiday mood, welcomed literally with open arms the blue and white ruffled frock that Ephraim and Elana presented to her. To complement her new dress, Isaak gave his sister a necklace of blue and silver beads which accessorized the gown perfectly.

Adam gave Leah a treble recorder which he had haggled for a week to obtain from the proprietor of a nearby antique shop. Leah was instantly enthralled by it, especially after Adam showed her how different sounds could be evoked by covering various windows or stops. As she mastered the technique of playing it, the recorder would become her favorite possession. The instrument's silky wood finish, its tone, and the feeling of satisfaction it gave her when she played it were destined, over time, to become one of the chief joys of Leah's life.

The Bank of Poland had given Ephraim a holiday bonus for working overtime to ensure a timely closing of the year's books. From that bonus, Ephraim gave each of his children, including Michael, five zloty. His only stipulation was that each child spend the gift wisely.

Leah questioned such an arrangement. "What about Michael, Papa? How can he spend the money wisely? He's still a baby."

"When Michael is bar mitzvahed," Ephraim replied, "I will give him this money to spend as he likes. Meanwhile, it will be held in the bank for him and earn interest." This seemed to satisfy her.

Later in the evening, after the children had gone to bed, Ephraim and Elana lingered before the fire, clasped in each other's arms, enjoying the warmth and the play of lights emanating from what had become lately a luxury.

"Do you remember," Elana asked, fitting herself more closely into her husband's arms, "when we sat before the fire like this at my father's house on the last night of Hanukah?"

A small smile played on Ephraim's face, lighting his dark eyes and making him seem for the moment years younger. "I told you that I had asked your father for permission for us to marry."

"As I recall," Elana said with a smile, stroking his cheek fondly, "you were more concerned about his answer than you were about mine."

Ephraim laughed. "As if a daughter had much to say in such matters. Besides, I knew your choice paralleled mine."

"How did you know?"

"You were my destiny," Ephraim answered. "I knew it from the moment I saw you standing at the door of your house. When you looked into my eyes, I knew that whatever it took, I would make you my wife."

"How could I have refused? Besides, my younger sisters would have killed me. They were all three waiting for me to leave home so it would be their turn to marry."

Ephraim stroked Elana's bright red-gold hair, removing the pins which held it confined. He sought thus to distract her from the painful memory. "Have you ever regretted your choice?"

For a moment, Elana said nothing, but she moved to fit more snugly into Ephraim's arms, and to wrap her own about him with an almost jealous protectiveness. "With our latest child lying in the next room, does that question really need an answer?"

There was a smile of joy and quiet triumph on Elana's face as their lips met. Almost as if on cue, the fireplace darkened as the final embers of the subsiding fire flickered and went out, leaving the room in shadow. Ephraim drew his wife even closer, cradling her in his arms. He kissed her face, then her neck and breasts, igniting in her a growing flame of desire that matched his own.

A short time later, Ephraim lifted Elana in his arms and carried her into their darkened bedroom. Neither felt the growing chill as the winter night settled on the Stare Miasto. The warmth of their lovemaking was sufficient barrier against the cold.

# CHAPTER FOUR
## REVELATIONS

In January of 1862, Isaak Marjzendiak went to work for the Wishnieski lumber mill, the largest mill in the Warsaw district. Isaak's natural aptitude for things mechanical soon brought him to the attention of the mill's foreman, Joseph Skiljret. Joseph listened with interest to Isaak's suggestions for making the mill operate more efficiently. Pleased by the recognition thus accorded him, Isaak's ambitions soared.

Elana Marjzendiak was concerned for Isaak. His enthusiastic descriptions of the machinery used in the lumber processing business made her fear that some crippling or fatal accident might befall him. Isaak, on the contrary, entertained no such worries, and Ephraim was proud but not surprised to see his son achieving recognition. Isaak had always been more extroverted and gregarious than his elder brother Adam, but in the past his aspirations had seemed unfocused. Now, although only twenty, Isaak was demonstrating a maturity and sense of purpose which put to rest Ephraim's earlier misgivings.

Adam, two years older than Isaak, was still employed at the flour mill. Nevertheless, he continued to pursue his dream of being admitted to the Warsaw Akademy of Medicine. Under the tutelage and encouragement of Dr. Samuel Jedewreski, Adam was preparing to sit for the entrance examination to the Akademy. Until recently, such a step would not have been possible for a Jew. Now, thanks to the Tsar's program of liberalization, Adam and other aspiring qualified Jewish candidates could now compete for a coveted place in the freshman class.

On a February evening in 1862, Isaak sat with his father and elder brother after dinner, discussing his plans for advancement in the lumber mill. To Isaak's obvious enthusiasm, Adam voiced a rare note of doubt.

"You really think," Adam asked skeptically, "they'll promote you to assistant foreman as early as this Spring? You've only just started. You're still learning the routine."

"More importantly," Ephraim added, "the owner, the managers, everyone of influence there is Polish. The few of us they hire are held to low-level jobs with meager pay."

"And no protection, either," Adam said with a flash of anger. "I've heard that the non-Jewish mill-hands are guaranteed pensions for life if they're disabled, and a maintenance fund is kept for their families if they're killed. Do you have that guarantee?"

"Not yet, Adam," Isaak answered defensively. "There's a trial period before any new worker can join the Guild. That's where the pension comes from, not from the owner. The workers contribute a percentage of each month's pay to replenish the fund. The monies are held in the Warsaw office of the Bank of Poland."

"The banks! That's the real seat of power," Ephraim said emphatically. "It's the logical place to begin. After all, the Rothschilds have set the example," he concluded referring, as he often did to strengthen an argument, to the Rothschild family's meteor-like ascent from the oppressive Frankfurt-on-Main ghetto to the Royal courts of every major European capital.

"The Rothschilds have a genius for investment," Isaak replied, "and the proper setting in which to exercise it. Not an easy example to follow here in Poland, Father. Especially now."

"Human ingenuity can always find room to express itself," Ephraim said sagely, indicating that the discussion was closed.

* * *

Markos Wishnieski, in addition to having three fine sons, none of whom was as devoted to the mill as their father, had a lovely daughter named Mariska. She had just turned nineteen and was a true beauty with wavy ash-blonde hair and a slim but curvaceous womanly figure. Her eyes were a clear pale blue and her skin had the translucency of fine china.

As Mariska stood before her mirror on an early spring day in 1862, a mood of expectation, even of impatience, pervaded her spirit and accelerated her movements. She deftly fastened a shawl about her shoulders, checking her image in the mirror to make certain she had achieved just the right touch of delicate, seemingly natural color at lip and cheek.

The use of makeup in these times was sparing among women of the rising middle class who took their fashion cues from the ladies of the aristocracy. Abundant artifice was left to women of the lowest social strata.

Reassured by her reflected image, Mariska hurried from the room. She ran lightly along the upstairs corridor and down the stairs. At the front door she paused and looked about, feeling a trifle guilty and clandestine. Then, opening the door she stepped out into the early afternoon sunlight.

Mariska felt exhilarated but somewhat apprehensive; she was meeting her lover as she had done on several occasions since mid-winter, but this time she had urgent and serious news to impart. As she recalled the blossoming of their friendship and its ultimate ripening into a deeper relationship, she was keenly aware that the course it was now pursuing was attributable primarily to her own efforts. But, Mariska rationalized, she was in love and all was therefore forgivable, all was permissible. Even members of the Eastern Orthodox clergy were allowed to marry, a sharp contrast to the priests of the Western Roman rite. Nevertheless, she had to admit that Father Mouzworski, her father-confessor, would have frowned upon her choice of a love partner. Not only was Isaak Marjzendiak not a member of the Orthodox Church of Poland, he was a Jew and therefore of the lower class, a resident of the ghetto section of the Stare Miasto.

Mariska, hurrying towards her rendezvous, stopped by the kitchen door to pick up a basket which Kara, the Wishnieskis' cook, had lovingly packed for her. Mariska had told Kara that she was going on a picnic with some school friends. Feeling a pang of guilt for having deceived the servant who had cared for her since childhood, Mariska took the basket from a table just inside the door and swept out of the family grounds, her thoughts now centered upon her meeting with Isaak.

As she walked along the northward path that led out of the city, the sky was colored in pastel blues and pale lavenders. The heights of the northern plateau were crowned with frozen snow awaiting the spring thaw. Mariska thought back to the day last winter when she and Isaak first took this road, hand-in-hand, and wandered to the sheltered place where they had met many times since in recent months.

They were dressed warmly, but as the wind grew stronger and colder, they clung closer together, two children enjoying an outing in an enchanted wonderland of snow-draped trees and earth carpeted with iridescent white. They found a clearing ringed by foothills, landscaped by boulders. They played in the snow, pelting each other with snowballs, laughing and chatting aimlessly. They were glad to escape from the harshness of reality into this world of fantasy where Orthodox Catholic and Jew were only words with no power to divide them.

The swiftly rising wind whipped the gently falling snow into a blinding curtain of stinging ice. Isaak found a cave behind the largest boulder and they crawled inside to keep warm until the storm subsided.

There was no dry wood to build a fire, only a tiny mound of brush which Isaak ignited and before which they both knelt, warming their hands. All too quickly, however, the small fire burned out. The cave, with its stark rock walls, provided shelter from the worsening storm, but no real warmth. Isaak and Mariska huddled close together, trying to keep warm by close proximity, each sharing the heat from the other's body. However, as the snow melted, they found that their clothing was sufficiently damp to absorb their body heat, leaving them chilled and shivering.

Isaak, gazing out of the cave entrance, his lips faintly blue as he spoke, remarked "It's getting worse. We'll have to stay here until it's over. We'd better get out of these wet clothes."

Mariska looked at him in horror, but with the passage of time, the validity of Isaak's suggestion became only too apparent. They had both grown steadily colder crouched on the cave floor, and Mariska began to cough.

"Take those things off and come over here again next to me," Isaak insisted. As Mariska hesitated, he urged her further. "Hurry, you little goose. You're as cold as I am. No one's going to see us in here, but if you go home with pneumonia, your parents are going to be furious and then I'll be blamed."

Half persuaded, Mariska still hesitated. Finally, however, she capitulated. "I'll hang up our garments so they'll dry faster," she said. Then she joined Isaak in the furthest corner of the cave, as far from the icy drafts coming in through its entrance as they could get. Their initial embraces, clumsy and companionable, were initiated mainly to protect them from the cold. However, Isaak was young, Mariska was beautiful, and both were inexperienced. Soon they progressed to unplanned intimacy, kissing, embracing and exploring one another with child-like curiosity born of unaccustomed close proximity, mutual affection, and suddenly awakened desire.

Afterwards, they clung to each other, feeling ashamed but thrilled that they had found pleasure in each other's bodies. With the new experience had come a special communication between each other's minds as well. Shocked by the enormity of what had passed between them, they nevertheless gloried in what they had found together.

As spring emerged from the cold shadows of winter, the easy companionability of the relationship Isaak and Mariska shared earlier had quickly evolved into something far deeper, more compelling and even frightening in its intensity.

Mariska thought yet again of Isaak's gentleness as he made love to her, of his concern for her feelings, and of his deep sensitivity. She loved his ready wit and expansive knowledge. She was deeply stirred by his deft grace and dark masculine beauty. Isaak's looks were a total contrast to that of all the members of Mariska's family and this added to his physical charm. This was the man she loved, and despite all obstacles, this was the man she would find a way to marry. Naturally, her father would object; probably, Isaak's father would object as well. She hoped that the shock of what she now knew for certain had developed would soon be forgotten in the joy of both families over the prospect of a new member.

There could be no doubt of that any longer. She had missed her last two periods, and she had never been late before. Nor had she shown previously the changes in her bodily contours nor the slight darkening of her nipples that she had noticed over the past two weeks.

Mariska counted on her father's confidence in and reliance upon Isaak to turn the tide. After all, thanks to Isaak's suggestions and sketches, portions of the mill had been redesigned to utilize a new process in curing the wood for distant transport. Wishnieski had also heeded Isaak's suggestion that when trees were cut down for lumber, it was wise to plant other trees in their places. This would ensure that the famous forests of north central Poland would not be ravaged beyond their power of self-restoration. Surely, Mariska thought as she went to meet Isaak, her mind on the revelation she must make to him, her father would see the value of having Isaak as his son-in-law, especially since his own sons had no interest in operating the mill.

Thus absorbed, Mariska was unprepared to encounter one of the watchmen from her father's mill coming toward her along the road. His name was Wilhelm Droski and on several occasions, much to Mariska's distaste, he had shown an amorous interest in her. She had tried repeatedly by her coldness to make him aware that his aspirations were in vain, but since she worked after school in her father's office at the mill, she had not been able to completely avoid him.

Droski approached with a self-assured swagger that reminded Mariska of his unwelcome advances and provoked her resentment.

"Well," he said affably as he drew near her, "what a pleasant surprise." His eyes lighted on the basket Mariska carried. "And how thoughtful," he added, lifting the checkered cloth that covered the basket.

Mariska slapped his hand away. "This food is not for you," she snapped.

"How disappointing." Droski said with his heavy German accent. "Who is this fortunate picnic companion? Do I know him?"

"I'm meeting with my girlfriends from school," Mariska answered impatiently.

"I see," Droski answered. "Well, surely your girlfriends won't object if I sample a bit of lunch."

"They surely will object! And so will I."

"I could change your mind," Droski said suggestively.

Mariska shivered at the implication. "Hadn't you better hurry? You don't want to be late for work. My father wouldn't like that."

Droski bowed to Mariska with exaggerated politeness.

"I shall not give him cause for concern," he promised. "We shall meet again though, I'm sure, Fraulein Wishnieska." He smiled and continued down the road.

When Mariska was certain he was out of sight, she hurried toward the meeting place she and Isaak had made their own, the small clearing above the base of the north plateau. From this vantage point, the roof and upper story of her father's mill were clearly visible. Today, she was disquieted by that thought. She did not wish her meeting with Isaak to be seen by anyone at the mill, most especially by Droski. It was Sunday and most of the laborers would be at home, but the watchmen her father paid to safeguard his investment would be on duty.

Suddenly, a movement off to her left caught her attention. She turned and Isaak was standing there, the sunlight creating an aureole of pale golden light around his wealth of dark, wavy hair. Her heart beat rapidly at the sight of him, as it always did, and she ran to meet him. As Isaak threw his arms around Mariska, she stood on tiptoe so that their lips could meet.

"I've missed you," Isaak said, gazing at her lovely face.

"And I, you," Mariska replied.

Isaak glanced at the basket Mariska carried. "What have we here?"

Mariska smiled enigmatically. "You'll see." She uncovered the basket and began setting up the luncheon. Spreading a bright plaid cloth upon the fragile early spring grass, she placed the basket at one corner and its lid at another. Isaak gathered small rocks to weight the remaining corners as Mariska brought out plates, cups, and cutlery. She carefully arranged the fresh bread which Kara had baked, the variety of cheeses from her father's estate, the home-grown vegetables and tree-ripened fruit. Last of all she brought out the heady Polish ale produced in the local brewery.

Isaak was uncertain how much of this sumptuous feast he owed to Mariska herself and how much to the family's beloved cook, Kara, of whose culinary skill Mariska often boasted.

"It all looks good enough to eat," Isaak said mischievously.

As they ate, Isaak surveyed the Wrepz River, already swollen by the melting snow. Soon, he knew, the thaws would begin in earnest and then the river complex would start to overflow its boundaries, posing a threat to the mill's foundations. Isaak had seen the river's destructive floods in previous years. Last winter had been particularly harsh. He made a mental note to discuss with his foreman, Josef, the proper procedural safeguards in the event that the thaw produced too rapid a rise in the water system.

As he looked at Mariska, these thoughts retreated into the background of Isaak's mind. The ambivalence which he experienced with her confused him. He sensed a deep tenderness within her, yet underneath her facade of softness, he was keenly aware, was a will of iron.

Mariska looked up into Isaak's face. Her hand brushed the curve of his chin and the shallow cleft that divided it into two perfect halves. Prompted by a romantic whim, she stretched upward and kissed him at precisely that spot.

"Isaak," Mariska whispered softly, "there is something I want to discuss with you."

Isaak nodded. "What is it, love?"

Mariska laid her head against his shoulder.

"Something important to us. I've been meaning to tell you for almost a week now, but we've had no time to ourselves lately." There was a slightly sad, reproachful note to her voice.

"Well, you know I'm working double shifts," Isaak said defensively.

"I know," she agreed. "I know how anxious you are to succeed, to advance in my father's business."

"It's more than just that," Isaak said. "My family needs the money. And I need some money for myself. I want to set something aside for the future."

Ah, she thought, the future! She too had plans for the future, plans that included social prominence, wealth and luxury for herself and this ingenious and handsome young man on whom she had centered her hopes.

"That's what I wanted to talk with you about," Mariska said. "The future. Our future!"

"Our future, Mariska? Why not enjoy the present and allow the future to fend for itself?"

"I can't do that, Isaak. We can't. Sometimes, the future won't wait for our convenience." Suddenly, she found that she could not look at him directly. Now that the moment had come, she was intimidated by the audacity of her plan and the heavy odds against its success.

"What is it," Isaak asked earnestly, "that's bringing the future suddenly so close? Tell me," he persisted, taking her face in his hands. "Whatever it is, you've been leading up to it all afternoon. I've felt it leaning over us like a shadow, a ghost."

Mariska laid a finger gently on his lips.

"No," she said softly. "Not a ghost, Isaak. It's very real, very much alive. Oh Isaak, can't you guess? I'm speaking of our child that's due to be born next fall. We'll be married, of course, by then, and I'll have our house beautifully decorated and the nursery furnished and waiting." She paused at Isaak's expression of terror-stricken shock. "Don't look so frightened, Isaak. It's joyous news!"

Isaak stared at her. "Are you sure? I've heard my mother say that many things can throw a girl off her schedule. "

"Your mother discusses such things with you?" Mariska asked in disbelief.

"Not with me, no. But I've heard..." Isaak's voice trailed off.

Mariska smiled at him in a manner she hoped was supremely seductive.

"Of course, I'm sure! Would I tell you if I weren't? After all, I'm not an imbecile. It's not as if I planned it to happen." A tone of petulance crept into her voice, even though in her heart she admitted that she had done precisely that. After their first time together, it was she who had planned their subsequent meetings. She had gently seduced Isaak, all the while excusing her actions with the motive of love. Totally ignoring the utter impossibility of the situation she was thus creating, she had refused to recognize that she was placing them both in an untenable position.

"I didn't say you planned it, Risch," Isaak said, using the diminutive pet name he had coined for her. "It's my fault as much as yours. We should both have been more careful."

Mariska's mood of exultation vanished, replaced by disappointment, then by anger.

"Careful? Careful, is it? When we made love together nothing was said of being careful. How dare you," Mariska asked, incensed, "say that to me now?"

Isaak took hold of her shoulders trying to soothe her anger.

"I apologize, Riskch. It serves no purpose to talk about being careful now." He shrugged resignedly. "The thing is done and neither your family nor mine is going to give their blessing to our marriage."

"What is that to us? We can slip away to Praga and be married there. After that, there will be nothing they can say that will make any difference."

"And would you be satisfied with that sort of hole-and-corner wedding? I wouldn't. It goes against everything I've been taught to believe. It would be a hurried, shameful ceremony. I would never feel married after such a travesty. Worse yet would be our expulsion from the community; you without dowry, me without employment, and both of us without the support of our respective families. That's no solution to the problem."

Mariska faced him almost defiantly. "Do you have a better solution?"

"Going to your father and confessing the whole situation seems the most honest approach," Isaak answered.

Mariska knew that her father was a highly emotional man, and that she was his pride and joy. Nothing would convince him that her deflowering had been achieved other than by force. He would never consent to her marriage with her despoiler, especially if he were identified as an underling in his own employ.

"That's no good," Mariska protested. "If we just go to him and tell him, he'll find a way to keep us apart and you'll lose your job. I couldn't stand that." Mariska began to cry and Isaak put his arms around her, attempting to console her. "I suppose I could go to one of the hillside villages," she went on, "and find a midwife who could get rid of the child. I hate the thought of that, but it may be our only alternative."

"No! You mustn't even think of such a thing," Isaak objected. "Life is precious, and it's not ours to destroy. That right belongs to Adonai." Isaak sat there rocking Mariska gently in his arms, seeking vainly for a viable answer to their awful dilemma. Suddenly, an inspiration came to him. "Why not go to your mother instead of your father? Surely she would understand and try to help."

Mariska considered that suggestion, tempted but hesitant, trying to anticipate her mother's reaction. Eva Wishnieska's Hungarian background prejudiced her against Jews. Revealing Mariska's pregnant state to Eva might require careful preparation. "I have a better idea," she said. "Let's talk to your mother."

"My mother?"

"You've told me often," Mariska argued, "that she has great sensitivity and perception. She'll know what to do."

Isaak hesitated. He knew that whatever her feelings, Elana Grojec-Marjzendiak was a woman of wisdom, understanding, and compassion. She would not berate him pointlessly after the fact. The more he thought of Mariska's words, the more favorably he considered them. Elana was the logical confidante for them both.

# CHAPTER FIVE
## RENUNCIATION

A decidedly subdued Isaak and a pseudo-brave Mariska sat facing Elana in the kitchen of the Marjzendiak home. Over the steaming cups of coffee which Elana provided, the two young people, hardly daring to look at one another, poured out to her their problem. Much was said of guilt by each of them, but little was mentioned regarding love. This troubled Elana deeply.

"It's no good regretting the past," Elana said at last. "It's the present that must be dealt with. If it's Adonai's will that this child enter His world, so be it. What you must both decide is what sacrifices you are prepared to make for the child's sake and for each other."

"We know that, Mama," Isaak said solemnly, "only too well."

"Then tell me," Elana said, "what you want to do." Isaak and Mariska looked at each other for several seconds. Finally, Isaak spoke.

"I love Mariska," he said. "I want her and our child with me."

Mariska's eyes, large and round with wonder, met his. "You mean that?"

Isaak stared at her in silence, his eyes more eloquent than his lips.

"He means it, my dear," Elana replied for him. "I know my son. He doesn't say a thing unless he means it. And do you, Mariska, love my Isaak?"

"Oh yes," Mariska answered exultantly. "Isaak loves me and I love him."

"But Mariska, are you willing to embrace Isaak's faith as freely as you have embraced Isaak? Can you give up your fine home with all its luxuries to live confined within these walls with your Jewish husband?"

"Oh, but Isaak would move out of here once we're married," Mariska answered, her words ignoring the harsh reality of the life the Jews led under Russian law and Polish prejudice.

"Where would he move, Mariska? Where in this city can a Jew move outside the ghetto? To prison perhaps, or to Siberia if he comes to the notice of the Russian authorities. Even in death, we must remain here. Indeed, the burial grounds allotted to us grow crowded." She paused thoughtfully, then went on.

"Love can be a brutal taskmaster. For centuries our God has shown us His love in the most inscrutable, often painful ways. But we are still His chosen people. "

Mariska stared at Elana. "You really believe that, don't you?"

Elana nodded, smiling. "That belief has kept us alive, literally, through centuries of pain and strife. It has given us hope, and the will to survive."

Mariska turned to Isaak. "You never talk about what you believe. Not the way she does. She makes it all sound so simple, so real."

"It is real for us," Isaak answered. "It is often for us the only reality. The one unchanging thing in our lives."

Elana looked approvingly at her son and then at Mariska. "Whatever decision is reached, the child will be assured a home with our family, if that becomes an issue," Elana advised. "I would suggest, however," she added, turning to Mariska, "that you seek your mother's counsel just as you have sought mine. Mothers are more understanding in such matters as a rule. Once she realizes how you and Isaak feel about each other, I'm sure she'll want to help in every way she can."

* * *

For as long as Mariska Wishnieska could remember, all her problems, large and small, had been brought to Eva Wishnieska for solution. It was only because of her love for Isaak and her sense of guilt at having betrayed her mother's trust that she had not gone to Eva in the first place.

Three days had passed since Mariska and Isaak had met with Elana. In that time, Mariska had repeatedly asked herself if she were strong enough to face a future such as Elana had painted. The thought of its bleakness frightened Mariska; losing Isaak frightened her more.

Eva was engaged in embroidering an altar cloth as Mariska entered the solarium of the Wishnieski home. Eva was very proud of her skill with needle and thread, especially when it came to making church linens. Father Mouzworski had often commented on her talents in this regard.

As Mariska knelt by Eva's chair, she kept her eyes on the pattern of the embroidery, not daring to look into her mother's eyes.

"Mother," she began, "we need to talk."

Eva put down her needlework and patted Mariska's cheek. As she did so, she was reminded of how much like Mariska she looked in her youth. She realized that, because of her many social and religious activities, she had failed to devote sufficient time to this beautiful young replica of herself and she was assailed by a small qualm of guilt.

"We don't talk much of late, do we, dear?"

Mariska shook her head.

Eva said wistfully, "You're growing up so quickly."

"That's what I want to talk to you about," Mariska responded and then paused to gather her nerve.

Eva stared at her daughter fixedly.

"Mother, I've fallen in love," Mariska confided gravely.

Eva sat back, obviously relieved. "My dear, I can assure you that the first love always seems serious at the time, but then..."

"It's more than that, Mother," Mariska interrupted.

"Is it?"

Mariska nodded.

"Who is he?"

"You don't know him, mother. He's, he's a student."

"Why don't you bring him here so that your father and I can meet him?"

"He's Jewish, Mother," Mariska said quietly. "Would you and Papa welcome him here?"

"Mother of God!" Eva crossed herself devoutly. "A Jew? You're in love with a Jew?"

"Yes, I am, and I'm going to have his child." She had meant to put it more gently, more carefully, but her mother's reaction shocked the truth out of her abruptly.

"I don't believe it. You're saying that to test me. You've taken a fancy to this boy and now you concoct this story to see if you can have him accepted in the family."

"It's not a story, Mother," Mariska said levelly. "It's true."

Eva looked as though she had been struck. "My God! We'll never live down the disgrace."

"But if we get married, there won't be any disgrace."

"They're outcasts. Don't you realize that? They're ostracized from polite society."

"I know. They live in the ghetto. I've been there."

"You're not to go there again," Eva snapped. "Not ever." Eva seized Mariska by the shoulders. "Do you realize what you've done? It would be bad enough with a Catholic boy, but a Jew!"

"Yes, a Jew," Mariska said defiantly. "A brilliant, gifted, beautiful young man who will have a fine future one day. The Tsar has eased restrictions against the Jews. It's only a matter of time until they'll be able to own property."

Eva's tone was derisive. "Did he fill your head with that nonsense?"

"It's true, mother. It's in the popular press. The Tsar has promised ultimate equality to all his subjects."

"Ultimate, indeed," Eva remarked in exasperation. "That will scarcely happen in our lifetime. You cannot plan on that."

"But, Mother, we want to get married," Mariska said pointedly.

"Never! No child of mine will ever marry a Jew. But marriage _is_ the answer. The question is to whom?"

\* \* \*

Later that night, Mariska, devastated by her mother's lack of sympathy and understanding, tried to pray before the statue of the Madonna in her bedroom, but the statue's disturbing facial resemblance to her mother only upset her more.

'Do you, too, Holy Mother,' she thought, 'condemn me for loving a Jew?' She began to cry, burying her face on her arms across the bed.

Moments later, she heard a knock on her door. She quickly dried her eyes.

"Come in."

The door opened and Eva Wishnieska entered the room.

"I've spoken with your father," Eva announced. Her voice was calm, almost cold. "He feels exactly as I do, as I knew he would. You're to have nothing more to do with this Jew!

If you do, your father will find out his name and have him expelled from school. Do you understand?"

Mariska was shocked. Thank God, she thought, she had not told her Isaak's name or the fact that he worked at the mill. To have done so would have exposed him to grave danger. Mariska knew she must protect Isaak, for both their sakes. She further realized that she must renounce her love for Isaak, conceal her true feelings, and discourage his love for her for his own safety.

"I understand, Mother," she said bleakly. "I won't see him again."

* * *

Josef Skiljret was seated in his favorite spot on the rear porch of the Wishnieski lumber mill overlooking the Wrepz River. Now that he was foreman, Josef made a habit of retiring here when he wanted to be alone, and since it was outside the building, it was the quietest part of the mill. It was more private than the office which he shared with his employer, Markos Wishnieski. None of the men who worked under Josef ever sought to share it when he was there unless they were invited.

Josef's origins were obscured by centuries of wandering and upheaval. His grandfather, also named Josef, had been born in Lithuania, the illegitimate son of a local magistrate by his housekeeper's daughter. At nineteen, after his mother's death, he had gone off on his own, anxious to leave the town which had ostracized him for as long as he could remember.

His migrations had brought him to Praga, on the outskirts of Warsaw. There he had set up a profitable carpentry business. His son, Alfred, Josef's father, had also become a carpenter. However, young Alfred Skiljret had lacked his father's business acumen and, despite his skill as a carpenter and cabinetmaker, had failed to prosper. The family business had been sold and Alfred had undertaken work in one of the smaller lumber mills upriver.

Josef's earliest memory was of visiting his father at that lumber mill. The love of wood had united father and son, and even now, years after his father's death, Josef remembered him with great affection.

Now Josef felt he had found another man who shared that love of wood: Isaak Marjzendiak. For most of the mill workers, the sole reason for working at the mill was the paycheck they received at the end of each week. With Isaak Marjzendiak, Josef sensed, it went far beyond that. Josef had noticed the young man's interest in the complex process by which the wood was preserved and cured. Isaak's innovations in the processing resulted in wood that was more resistant to weather and insects, and thus more valuable in the marketplace.

Josef and Isaak quickly formed a close friendship, based not entirely on their love of wood. Josef, though not politically active, was a keen observer of the affairs of men. He watched with interest the Marquis Wielopolski's reform programs and their effect on the various factions of the citizenry. He seldom discussed his observations with his wife Petra or with his two daughters Myrna and Jalah. His son Friedriech was far too young to share in such discussions. But with Isaak he felt free to express his thoughts. Today, not for the first time, he asked Isaak to join him.

While the two men ate their lunch, they spoke of the latest political developments within Congress Poland.

"Strange how this governmental game of cat and mouse goes on," Josef remarked. "The names change but the strategy remains the same."

"I thought the Marquis would be able to make a difference," Isaak replied.

"In some quarters, he has," Josef allowed. "Frankly, I agreed with several of Wielopolski's policies, especially equalization of rights for all segments of the people. But neither the conservatives nor the Nationalists gave him much support."

"The Nationalists support no one who cooperates with the Russians," Isaak observed, taking a bite of his sandwich. "Yet what other course is there? Open rebellion has only resulted in bloodshed and tragedy for the Polish people." Isaak glanced soberly at his friend. "Austrian Poland seems to have the best arrangement of all. Self-determination and self-government."

"But to accomplish that," Josef observed, "one must accept the fact that this is a partitioned nation and no longer an independent state. Even the old Archbishop, for all his patriotic zeal, realized that. Unfortunately, many of our wild-eyed young hotheads are still reliving the glorious days of 1830."

Isaak scoffed. "Glorious? They were defeated and then slaughtered. Those who survived were either imprisoned or banished to Siberia."

"You quote facts, Isaak. We're speaking here of emotions."

"I quote history," Isaak replied heatedly. "Are we not to learn from our past mistakes?"

"One would hope so," Josef agreed, "but we seldom do."

"I've heard that the Tsar has emancipated the serfs of Russia," Isaak stated. "If that's true, it will serve only to inflame the peasants here, and outrage the landowners."

"If you're right, this will not endear the Tsar to the aristocracy," Josef added. "While the peasants, hungry as they are, feel that their only hope is for the whole house of cards to come tumbling down so that they can snatch what remains in the resulting chaos."

"What if this Tsar really wants to change things? If nothing comes of his efforts at reform, won't he give up in disgust and conclude that his father and his grandfather were right?"

"That's a distinct possibility," Josef answered.

"Then we'll all be worse off than ever," Isaak said, disheartened.

"Maybe not," Josef interjected. "The Council of State has been busy of late. They've granted a little of what each faction asked for in that petition of a year ago. Just a little. Enough to encourage them to ask again."

"Instead of resorting to open insurrection," Isaak observed. "But the latest petition ended in a massacre. Will such a strategy work?"

"Perhaps," Josef answered. "For a time it will polarize the various interest groups, setting them against each other. For example, the Agricultural Society is petitioning to reinstate Wielopolski, and the factory owners want repeal of the higher taxes. But does the Council address either of those matters? No!" Josef paused dramatically. "Just before lunch, I heard from one of the midday shift workers about a declaration just issued today. It was being posted as he came to work. It seems the Council, by order of Tsar Alexander, has granted the right to own property to those Jewish families with annual incomes above two hundred zloty. Not that many will qualify. But it is a long-awaited step forward, isn't it?" Josef looked into his friend's eyes, his own twinkling with sympathetic understanding.

"Yes," Isaak said breathlessly, half-fearful that somehow there might be some mistake. "It is, if it's true."

Isaak was overjoyed. Adonai had moved in one of His mysterious ways. This was the answer to his and Mariska's prayers. Now, if the declaration truly stated what Josef described, with the help of his family he could purchase land and build a home.

As soon as his shift ended, Isaak hurried to the mill office to talk with Mariska. Entering the office, he scanned the room warily. Adonai was indeed favoring him. Mariska was alone.

Isaak quietly stepped inside and closed the door, causing Mariska to look up from her desk. She wore a strange expression.

"Well, there you are at last. It's been a week since we went to see your mother," Mariska said coolly.

"A very eventful week," Isaak said, thinking of the news he had just heard from Josef.

"For me as well. My mother thinks she's found an answer."

Isaak was confused by the strangeness of Mariska's mood. "An answer?"

"There is a young man here at the mill," Mariska said lightly. "He's a watchman at present, but he's ambitious, and not lacking in education or connections. It seems he's the youngest son of a Prussian aristocrat who's willing to settle a sum of money on him if only he'll agree to marry respectably."

"He's fortunate," Isaak said, "But that's no concern of ours." He reached to take her hand but she drew away, and turned to face the window. Isaak could not see the misery etched on her young face.

"Indeed it is. My mother says my marriage must take place at once."

"Then she consented! And your father?"

"He could wish for a more suitable match, but with advancement and tutoring…"

She got no farther. Isaak was beside her, turning her to face him, embracing her tenderly. "Oh, I'll study anything he wants," Isaak said. "I'm very quick. You'll see."

Mariska struggled against him, escaping his tender but awkward embrace. "You haven't heard a word I've said," she protested.

"Of course, I have. And you must already know my news," he responded hopefully, still puzzled by her seemingly hostile mood.

Mariska stared at him, uncomprehendingly. "What news?"

"The declaration! Jews have been given the right to buy land." He did not have the opportunity to elaborate, to fill in details.

Mariska turned away again, struggling to keep the tears from her eyes as Isaak continued.

"We can have our own home," Isaak exulted. "We can choose where it will be." Already in his mind's eye, Isaak could see that home, its land productive and prosperous.

"We can do no such thing," Mariska said, regaining control of her emotions. "I followed exactly what your mother suggested. I pleaded with my mother to intercede for me with Father. I said I loved a Jewish student, that we had been foolish and careless but that his intentions were honorable. The only thing I didn't tell her was your name." Mariska paused. "My mother listened to what I had to say, and her solution was that I should marry as quickly as possible whatever acceptable suitor can be found among my peers."

"Whatever suitor?" Isaak began to understand.

"Yes," Mariska said distinctly. "Whatever suitor will have me. After all, I'm damaged goods now. I can no longer pick and choose. It seems that Wilhelm Droski is less than fastidious about how he finds a wife so long as she comes from a family of means."

"Wilhelm Droski? You can't mean you intend to marry him!"

"Why not? He's very enthused about the idea." Mariska said in a matter-of-fact tone. "It fits perfectly with his plans."

"His plans! What about our plans?"

Mariska's heart seemed to miss a beat. How ironic it seemed to her that now that her secretly nurtured plans for the future had become Isaak's dream as well, it had been placed effectively beyond their reach. She held back the tears that threatened to betray her true feelings. She swallowed the sobs that rose in her throat. Somehow, she must play a role for Isaak's benefit. To prevent his revealing himself as the father of her unborn child, she must appear to spurn him. She must turn him against her and pretend that her own feelings for him were dead.

"Our plans were based on a childish fantasy," Mariska said flatly. "It would never work between us, Isaak. There are just too many differences."

Isaak turned away, refusing to let the tears in his eyes spill down his face. Pride and anger were instantly forged into an armor to mask his feelings. "You're right," he said at last, his tone bitter. "Marrying Droski would provide a convenient answer for you."

"It does seem the most logical solution to everyone's problem," Mariska said, struggling to maintain her facade of aloofness.

Isaak nodded miserably, all his joy quenched, his excitement and enthusiasm hurled brutally back in his face.

"No doubt, you're right," he answered hollowly. "Your mother's a wise and worldly woman. I'm sure she has your best interest at heart. I wish the best for you, and your bridegroom," he added. Without another word, he turned and hurried from the mill office, closing the door behind him. Mariska stood trembling, tears falling unchecked down her cheeks. She held her left hand over her mouth while with her right hand she groped for the chair at her desk. Finding it, she collapsed into it and laid her head upon her desk. It was all she could do to keep from crying out, so great were her anguish and despair.

Isaak's own tears lodged in his throat like lead as he descended the stairs leading from the mill office. He had dreamed that somehow the social ban forbidding Jew and Gentile to marry could be set aside in his case, and that Poland could somehow become a land of equal opportunity and status for all its citizens. That still might one day occur, but not in time for him.

His hopes for the future had been crushed. He now had to face bitter reality and cast aside those hopes. Now he must put all thought of Mariska from his mind. His child would be claimed and raised by another man. Somehow he had to find the strength and resolve to endure that burden, just as his people had endured countless burdens throughout the centuries since the time of Abraham.

* * *

Markos Wishnieski was in an expansive mood. His mind was relieved of a terrible burden. So grateful was he to Wilhelm Droski for providing a respectable solution to Mariska's shameful situation that he promoted the watchman to Chief of Security of the lumber mill, a management position for which he would not ordinarily have been considered in the foreseeable future. Wishnieski, furthermore, granted major concessions to the Workmen's Guild, including higher wages and extra pay for overtime worked. Josef Skiljret was promoted to personnel manager, and Isaak, in fulfillment of the expectations he had voiced earlier to his father and elder brother, was advanced to Josef's former position of foreman.

Under the circumstances, the promotion brought Isaak no joy, though the increase in pay provided a welcome lift to his family's fortunes. Despite his best efforts to banish her from his consciousness, Isaak's mind was constantly on Mariska. Day and night, he thought of her and his unborn child. Nevertheless, when he, like the other management personnel of the mill, received an invitation to Mariska's wedding, he tore it up on the spot, vowing yet again to forget that he had ever known her.

# CHAPTER SIX

## LOVE AND DEATH

Mariska Wishnieska sat in the front pew of the ornate Eastern Orthodox Cathedral of the Trinity. She was watching her prospective bridegroom rehearse the details of the wedding ceremony with her closest friend and maid of honor, Magda Sokorska.

The late afternoon sunlight shone through the stained glass windows behind the altar, transforming the sacristy into a vision of ethereal beauty. For an idyllic moment, bemused by the magic of that aberration of lighting, Mariska fancied she saw Isaak standing there. She caught her breath and rose quickly to her feet. With the resultant change in visual perspective, the cold light of reality showed only Wilhelm Droski.

Her mood darkened instantly. How differently she would have felt if what she had momentarily imagined were actually true. How different would the prospect of her future life appear to her if she could look forward to spending it with the man she truly loved instead of this Teutonic boor puffed up with his own self-importance. Even as Mariska watched, Droski leaned towards Magda and whispered to her with a wicked leer. Magda blushed and drew her head away, her expression one of decided embarrassment. So this man who sought Mariska's hand and her dowry could not even wait to finalize the wedding vows before he began to flirt openly with other women. Mariska almost regretted the superstitious custom that precluded the bride from exchanging vows with the bridegroom prior to the actual wedding ceremony. Much as she dreaded going through that empty ritual even once, she would have preferred to spare her friend the ordeal.

Afterwards, at the rehearsal banquet, as Droski imbibed freely of his future father-in-law's champagne, Magda leaned towards Mariska. Droski, on Mariska's other side, was too absorbed with his own conversation with his best man, Heidrich Reinke, to pay attention to the somber exchange between his bride-to-be and her friend.

"My dear," Magda whispered solicitously, "I hope you're not making a tragic mistake."

"If I am, it's too late to correct it," Mariska remarked.

"It's never too late," was Magda's reply. "In your place I think I'd rather die than face the prospect of life with…" She shrugged significantly and rolled her eyes heavenward.

"Don't say that," Mariska warned half mockingly. "I might take you up on it."

"Couldn't your family have done better by you?"

"There were reasons, my friend," Mariska answered. "Compelling reasons."

"Yes," Magda whispered. "I know," she alluded to the as yet unannounced pregnancy, still too early to be readily apparent. "But still, it does seem awkward."

Mariska nodded in silent affirmation.

At the close of dinner the orchestra began the evening's entertainment. Droski asked Magda to dance with him.

"I'd suggest you practice dancing with your bride," she answered. "There's no custom against that even at the wedding rehearsal."

"I have the rest of my life to dance with her," Droski remarked. "Besides, at present her state of health is a trifle delicate." He seized Magda's arm and drew her to the dance floor, forcing her to accept his invitation or create a scene. Reluctantly, she complied.

Droski's intent in asking Magda to dance went deeper than light flirtation. Magda's brother Viktor worked at the lumber mill and there was talk that he was the leader of the Nationalist sympathizers among the workmen there. Magda kept aloof from political matters and she seldom discussed her brother. She had learned it was safer that way.

"You're an attractive young woman," Droski remarked as they danced. "But I seldom see you at parties. Why don't you have your brother bring you to some of the social events? You're far too pretty to stay at home."

"I go out socially," Magda replied evasively. "Besides, what girl wants to ask her brother to escort her?"

"Is it a matter of feminine pride, or is brother Viktor too busily engaged in political agitation?"

"I don't presume to pry into my brother's personal affairs," Magda said levelly. "If they are of such interest to you, Mer Droski, I suggest you ask him about them yourself."

Droski smiled and shook his head. "Never mind. I have other ways of finding out what I wish to know, and then your brother had better beware." He smiled grimly and bent towards her. "Perhaps I'll find that you're not so innocent in all this either." As the music died away and Magda strained to escape his embrace, Droski held her firmly. "I suggest you warn Viktor to confine his political activities to his off-work hours."

"I've told you I don't pry into my brother's affairs."

"No need to pry, my dear," Droski responded. "Just a warning. From those gentle lips of yours, I'm sure he will accept it with good grace."

"You're insufferable!" Magda whispered angrily.

"We'll see. As my wife's friend, I'm certain you'll grow accustomed to me, even as she will."

As the evening progressed, Droski's arrogance, coarseness, and fondness for drink all grated upon Mariska's sensibilities, but she said nothing. She simply observed the man in silence, more apprehensive than ever regarding what her future life would be.

That night Mariska could not sleep. She could see no solution to her dilemma. She must not disgrace her parents. She owed them that. They had raised and cared for her all her life, and though her opinions differed markedly from theirs, they were, nonetheless, family.

Her mother's origins were Hungarian. In that land, the prevailing sentiment regarding Jews was that they were 'inherently inferior' while here in Poland, the Jews were frequently viewed as inherently untrustworthy and devious. Mariska knew from personal experience that both those views were erroneous. They failed to recognize individual variations or cultural distinctions. And her father's total rejection of the unnamed Jewish student was the more perverse in view of his reliance upon his Jewish foreman.

As the night advanced, she heard in her mind the echo of Isaak's incredulous words: "Wilhelm Droski? Surely you don't intend to marry him!" Furthermore, Magda's cautious warning also haunted her thoughts.

By morning, Mariska's level of frustration had reached the point of desperation. It was now three days until the wedding. How, she wondered, could she endure those three days, to say nothing of the years that stretched ahead?

Plagued by these thoughts, Mariska was in no mood to receive her husband-to-be when he called upon her the following afternoon, his day off from the mill. He was dressed meticulously, his manner was conciliatory, almost unctuous.

"I hadn't expected to see you," Mariska responded in answer to his greeting as she handed the flowers he had brought to Fedya, the housekeeper. Droski's attempt to embrace and kiss her she skillfully avoided.

"So much the better," he responded undaunted by Mariska's aloofness. "Consider my visit a pleasant surprise." He paused momentarily. "Aren't you going to ask me to sit down?"

"Forgive me," Mariska said distractedly. "Sit down, of course."

Droski seated himself, obviously at ease, his eyes coolly assessing the young woman whose person and dowry would soon be his.

"You look as slim and virginal as ever," he said at length. "How much longer until the happy event?"

Mariska cringed inwardly. "I don't know for certain," she answered.

"Nonsense," Droski responded. "I've always heard that women know these things."

"In approximate terms, yes, but no one can know exactly. Not even Dr. Plotz." She referred to the Wishnieskis' family physician who had attended her mother in all but her first pregnancy. For a family of the Wishnieskis' status, the services of a midwife were considered unacceptable.

"A pity such things are so uncertain," Droski remarked. "Still, there may be some advantage to that." He patted the sofa cushion next to him. "Come, my dear, sit here beside me. We must talk."

Instead of joining him, Mariska sat in a chair opposite him, as distant as circumstances would permit.

"What is there to discuss?"

"Coyness doesn't become you, Mariska. Not with me. After all, we understand each other."

"Indeed," Mariska answered coolly.

"I have been very generous with you," he said, "very considerate of your tender sensibilities."

"You didn't come here bringing flowers just to tell me that," Mariska observed.

"You're quite right," he said. "I had another motive."

"Oh?"

"Now that our interests will be united, I'm sure you'll wish to assist me in my efforts to advance. As you must know, your father has invested considerable trust in me. I fully intend to justify that trust."

"An admirable intention," Mariska commented, "but how does that involve me?"

"Last night I tried to learn from your friend Magda the details of her brother's involvement in the revolutionary movement," Droski explained.

"I know," Mariska said. "She told me."

"She did not tell me what I wanted to know," Droski said.

"I gather she doesn't know anything about it."

"I doubt that," Droski commented, shaking his head. "But what she was reluctant to reveal to me she would readily disclose to you."

Mariska leaped to her feet, aghast at the implications of Droski's words.

"You're suggesting I should entrap my best friend into betraying her brother?"

"I'm advising you to place the concerns of your father and his business ahead of your girlhood ties with this insurgent's family. For all we know, they may all be working with the Reds. If the girl's brother should be found out later, the Russian militia may go so far as to close down your father's mills. They have already temporarily closed the Roman Catholic churches, and now their services are limited with regards to attendance."

"They'd hardly go that far because of one employee," Mariska scoffed.

"One match can light a large and highly destructive fire if properly placed. Men such as Viktor Sokorski spread disaffection and sedition." Droski paused briefly. "It wouldn't surprise me in the least if this student who seduced you turned out to be another of their agents working in the school. He may even have been assigned to attract your attention."

"I've never heard anything so ridiculous in my life," Mariska said disgustedly. "That new position at the mill has gone to your head."

"Why else would a Jew scheme to consort with an Orthodox Catholic whose father just happens to be one of the leading industrialists in Warsaw?"

"Don't pursue this, Wilhelm," Mariska warned him. "I won't listen to another word."

"If you're wise, you will," Droski insisted despite her warning. "Or do you flatter yourself that this Jew actually cared for you?"

"Stop it! Stop it this minute," Mariska said harshly, putting her hands over her ears in an effort to shut out the hated sound of Droski's voice.

Unabashed, he took her hands away and insisted on putting his arms around her. "My dear, you are so naive. It's fortunate that from now on you'll have me to guard you, to guide you." Droski smiled in a manner he intended to be reassuring. "Think of it. Only three days and then you are mine." Elated by the prospect of becoming lord and master of this alluring child-woman whom he had admired and coveted almost from their first meeting, Droski kissed her, pressing her pliant young body firmly against his own.

Instead of yielding to his ardor, Mariska bit his lips, lips she had grown almost to hate in the weeks since the publication of their marriage banns. Her strong well-groomed nails slashed at his face as she fought to free herself from his embrace. Crying out in pain, Droski released Mariska. The two stared wild-eyed at each other, she in shame and outrage, he in frustrated passion and jealous anger.

"All this passion you display," he said angrily. "It's a pity it's not for me. Who is this secret lover of yours?"

Mariska glared at him, trembling with fury. "A better man than you!"

"Then why does he not show his face or stake his claim to you? He takes his pleasure and then disappears." Droski paused momentarily as Mariska opened her mouth to protest. He raised his hand imperiously, warning her to silence. "I was willing to accept his leavings and claim them as my own, and what did I ask in return? Honorable marriage. You could have found no better bargain than that."

Mariska blanched as the meaning of his words dawned upon her. His renunciation of the marriage agreement would bring shame upon her family. Her voice was strained as she echoed his words. "Could have found?"

"I've decided I want more. In fact, I demand more."

"What more?"

"A larger dowry," Droski said, looking at her menacingly, "and an advance on my investment from you." His meaning as he reached for her was only too evident.

Mariska drew back, abandoning any show of diplomacy. "You'll get nothing! Not from me or my family. Get out! I never want to see you again."

Droski smiled at her wickedly and applauded.

"Bravo! A fine display of outraged innocence. Totally false, but impressive. When you have gotten over your fit of self-indulgence, send me word. I'll be waiting, but not too long." With that, he turned and was gone.

Mariska, still trembling with outrage and revulsion, attempted to collect her thoughts. She realized that regardless of the consequences, she could not give herself to Droski. She could not meekly accept a lifetime of catering to his whims and submitting to his arrogance. Certainly, if today had been a sample of his approach to romantic lovemaking, she could not surrender to him as a lover, not after having known the exultant joy of physical and mental union with Isaak.

Mariska quailed to think her parents were so inordinately proud of the marriage they had arranged. True, they had saved the family's good name from disgrace, but it now dawned upon Mariska that life could hold far worse terrors than disgrace.

As she walked upstairs to her bedroom, Mariska tried to determine an alternative course of action. She was a sheltered, inexperienced young woman with no resources other than those of her family. Without money there was nowhere she could go. Her close friend Magda, though sympathetic, was similarly situated. Elana Marjzendiak had offered to shelter the child, but if Mariska went to her, that in itself would betray Isaak as the child's father. The conflict between her parents' wishes and her own basic instincts seemed irresolvable.

Magda's words came to her mind: "In your place I think I'd rather die than face the prospect of life with…" Such a life, she realized sadly, would be no life at all.

"Mother of God," she prayed aloud as she threw herself on her bed, "What am I to do?" When, hours later, she at last arrived at a desperate answer to that question, she knelt before the Holy Mother's shrine and silently asked her forgiveness.

* * *

The next morning, Isaak was early for work. He paused at the last curve in the road below the mill, stopping to watch the majestic swirl of the Wrepz River as it curved around the promontory on which the lumber mill stood. As Isaak admired the beauty of his surroundings, he was joined by Josef Skiljret who had approached the mill by way of the opposite road leading from Praga.

"Many people," Josef said between puffs on his pipe, "extol the beauties of sunset, but this is my favorite hour. It's the time of beginning, the time of utmost promise in any day."

Isaak nodded in silent assent. It was refreshing to permit himself this rare moment of pure pleasure. As he gazed at the river, appreciative of its graceful flowing rhythm, the glint of something metallic in the water caught his eye.

"What is that?"

Josef turned, his eyes following Isaak's pointing finger. "I don't see anything."

"Just there at the river's edge," Isaak said, moving nearer to the water with Josef close behind him. Isaak removed his boots and slipped off the wooden decking. Wading into the cold water, he reached to retrieve a shiny, strangely familiar object clinging to the rocky outcropping at the edge of the mill's foundation.

As he closed his fingers about the object, he recognized it as a pendant he had seen before. At the same moment, his hand touched something else, something soft yet rigid. Grasping it, he discovered the slender fingers of a human hand. For a moment that small, slim hand seemed to wrap itself around his own, almost beckoning to him.

Josef leaned forward curiously. "What is it, Isaak? What's wrong?"

Isaak could not answer him. Horrified, he grasped the hand and pulled. Encountering resistance, he pulled harder, finally succeeding in dragging a waterlogged body from under the rocky ledge. A cascade of dark blond hair draped the face of the drowned victim, concealing it from view.

Isaak knew instinctively whose corpse it was even before he drew the strands of hair away from her face. He knew the slender, pouting lips, the pointed chin and gently curving jaw, the narrow brow and tilted nose.

Josef gasped in horrified recognition. He took his pipe from his mouth and the color drained from his face. "I'll go and summon help," he whispered, although for Mariska Wishnieska, there could be no help. Still, he felt compelled to do something. As Josef turned and hurried toward the mill, Isaak wondered how his friend would break this tragic news to Markos Wishnieski.

Crouched there, cradling her cold wet body in his arms, Isaak mourned for his dead love, realizing that for this brief moment Mariska was his alone, as she had never been before, as she would never be again.

# CHAPTER SEVEN
## PUBLIC UNREST, PRIVATE TRAGEDY

A sudden spring storm prevailed in Warsaw on the morning of Mariska Wishnieska's funeral. The somber setting matched Isaak Marjzendiak's frame of mind. With the mill closed, the workmen had agreed that the entire crew would attend the services in order to pay their respects both to the unfortunate young girl and to her father. For the Christian lumber mill workers, that decision involved no conflict. However, for Isaak, the announcement that he was going to an Eastern Orthodox cathedral provoked a sharp family controversy.

"I can't see why you're so determined to attend this funeral," Adam objected. "You can't participate in the service."

"We were friends, Adam," Isaak replied. "Close friends."

Ephraim's eyes narrowed at this last comment. "How close?"

"Mariska worked in her father's mill," Isaak answered. "We saw each other almost every day. We talked. We communicated. Besides, all the mill employees are planning to attend to show their respect to Mariska's father. The mill will be closed. If I don't go, it will seem a pointed insult."

"That could jeopardize your employment," Ephraim observed. "I do not expect you to take that risk, Son. But I do expect you to remember who you are."

"I can never forget that, Father," Isaak said levelly, and then added softly: "nor do I wish to."

Mariska's funeral Mass was held in the Eastern Orthodox Cathedral of the Trinity, the church that was to have been the site of her wedding. It was a long and solemn ceremony, with many liturgical readings and hymns chanted in Greek and Polish. Elana accompanied Isaak, explaining to the puzzled Ephraim that she could thus assure that their son did not, in any thoughtless way, prompted by emotion, participate in the religious proceedings.

Speculation and rumor were widespread regarding the circumstances surrounding Mariska's death. The official version put forth by the Wishnieski family was that Mariska had returned late to the mill, most likely to retrieve some forgotten personal possession, had missed her footing in the darkness, and had fallen into the river. Never a skillful swimmer and quite sensitive to cold, she must have been unable to pull herself up onto the slippery rocks that ringed the promontory. Unable to attract the attention of any passersby, the poor child had succumbed to the combined effects of chill and exhaustion and had drowned within a few yards of safety.

Neither Elana nor Isaak believed this fabrication. They knew the dead girl's situation and now strongly suspected that the hastily arranged marriage had been sharply counter to her wishes, a grim capitulation to the demands of expediency. Isaak was plagued by remorse. He reviewed in his mind the last words that had passed between himself and Mariska in the mill office. Vainly he tried to pinpoint what she had said that should have warned him of her desperation and her fatal intent. He was certain that her death had not been accidental but a deliberate flight from the sad reality he had mistakenly thought she favored. He blamed himself for not seeing through her façade of aloofness, so sharply in contrast to her normal behavior towards him. He realized, belatedly, that she had sought to protect him, had withheld his identity from her family, and had submitted to the wedding plans in desperation, in surrender of her own desires, that he might be spared.

In any case, the prevailing acceptance of the "accident" theory operated in the dead girl's favor. It assured her the full rites of the Orthodox Catholic Church which would have been denied if she had been proven a suicide.

Throughout the service, Isaak held Mariska's pendant clasped tightly in his hand, its slender chain twisted around his fingers. That diminutive gold pendant, wrought in the shape of a heart framing an early-blooming rose, would be counted among his personal effects for the rest of his life.

\* \* \*

Ephraim Marjzendiak, encouraged by the decisions of the Council of State regarding Jewish property rights and ownership, began quietly to investigate the price of various parcels of land in and around Warsaw. The nearby town of Wola, with its wooded terrain and rich farmland, was the main focus of his search. He was strangely attracted to that area without realizing that it was similar to the Ukrainian village that had been his family's place of origin. At that time, Ephraim's family had had no surname. His grandfather had taken the name of Marjzendiak when the family immigrated to Poland. Its meanings were somewhat obscured by ancient linguistic customs, but that it meant strong, assertive and protective of rights and possessions he felt certain. It definitely suited his personal philosophy and objectives.

Ephraim was determined to acquire a home site for his family to which succeeding generations of Marjzendiaks could feel free to return, to draw the support and nourishment of the spirit which can only derive from having one's own land.

At the close of business on June 7, 1862, the clerks and tellers of the Bank of Poland departed, leaving the bank's officials to review the day's tallies. After even these had departed, Ephraim sat with Franz Pietrowski, the bank's Assistant Commissioner, discussing the political climate.

Pietrowski was a political conservative of the landed aristocracy who could trace his lineage to Sigismund Augustus on the maternal side of his family and to Casimir the Just on his father's side. Yet, having married a wife from the industrial middle class, he entertained an inherent sympathy for the struggles and sufferings of the Polish people. Being a banker and possessed of an orderly mind, he shunned the thought of rebellion and felt that the law was the best course to follow in any controversy.

"These demonstrations are sheer madness," Pietrowski remarked. "The revolutionaries cannot possibly hope to win. When will it end?"

"When Poland is departitioned," Ephraim responded. "And that will only happen as a consequence of international war."

Pietrowski was shocked. "You think it will come to that?"

"I think international war will erupt eventually," Ephraim answered candidly. "When it does, that will be Poland's chance to seize her independence, if she can. Even then, it will remain to be seen whether she can maintain it."

"Yours is the most pessimistic view I've heard yet," Franz responded, wiping his brow nervously.

"I didn't always believe this to be so," Ephraim answered soberly. "But in view of what is happening around us, it's clear that Poland needs a strong army before she can hope to achieve independence. One segment alone can never succeed. In order to prevail, Poland must be united under one leadership, and even then, she will need support from other nations."

"That seems a virtual impossibility," Franz remarked, "but as I have learned, Ephraim, you're usually right about such things. Perhaps that's why I like you."

At that moment, without warning, a low-pitched rumbling echoed through the building from the ground floor, followed immediately by a stunning explosion. Franz was hurled violently backwards against a file cabinet, striking the side of his head. He staggered and would have fallen had not Ephraim moved quickly and effectively to prevent it.

As Ephraim helped Franz to a chair, the deep wound on the Commissioner's forehead began to swell ominously. Ephraim applied pressure to the wound, stopping the flow of blood.

"That is a nasty gash," he observed. "It needs to be attended to by a doctor," Ephraim advised. "I think it needs to be stitched."

"Absolutely not!" Franz exclaimed. "When I get home, my wife will attend to it."

Despite the violence that had damaged the town hall and the bank, the Pietrowski carriage stood unharmed near the rear exit. The two men left the building and walked rapidly to the carriage, Franz leaning upon Ephraim for support.

Public volunteers were already engaged in extinguishing a blaze at the town hall, where black smoke poured forth from a break in the wall. Russian militiamen were busy subduing and dispersing the crowd, several of whom were being arrested and taken into custody.

Throughout the journey toward Wola near which he lived, Franz was restless, dozing fitfully, and then waking uneasily. He said nothing. Sensitive to his condition, Ephraim, too, was silent. His mind, however, was actively attempting to assess the probable impact of this latest violence upon his own people. Ever the favorite scapegoat caught between opposing factions, Jews throughout Eastern Europe viewed any disruption of public order with justified apprehension.

Depressed by this train of thought, Ephraim turned his attention to the surrounding countryside, the details of which, until now, he had known mainly as squares and rectangles on maps and charts. As he gazed eagerly around him, the sheer beauty and grandeur of the scene filled him with a hushed reverence which he likened to the rapture Joshua of old must have experienced upon first beholding the Promised Land.

This fertile terrain, well-irrigated and richly endowed, was bordered by foothills and an evergreen forest. Agriculture was a natural pursuit here and several prosperous farms graced the district.

Seeing this verdant acreage, Ephraim could envision it as the site of the home and sanctuary he desired. In the midst of violence and upheaval, Ephraim, gazing enraptured at the surrounding scenery, began for the first time truly to believe in the possible fulfillment of his dream.

Mira Pietrowska, a well-educated woman of the rising industrial middle class, had attracted the aristocratic Franz Pietrowski as much for her quick mind as for her physical beauty. She could add a column of figures in her head without benefit of quill and paper; she could accurately assess human motives and sincerity on rather short acquaintance; she was an excellent hostess and a supportive help-mate. These qualities became of great benefit to the ambitious Franz and certainly aided him in his ascension through the hierarchy of Russian-Polish banking.

Mira was in the garden of the Pietrowski estate, overseeing the placement of newly-acquired ornamental plants when Ephraim brought Franz home from the bank. Seeing her husband's carriage approaching, Mira cut short her instructions to the gardeners and came forward to meet him. As Ephraim Marjzendiak helped Franz Pietrowski from the carriage, the gash in Franz's forehead began to bleed again. Franz was overtaken by a siege of dizziness which caused him to nearly fall into Ephraim's arms. Mira cried out in alarm as she moved quickly forward to assist her husband, excitedly pushing Ephraim aside.

"What's happened to him?"

"There was an explosion at the bank," Ephraim answered.

"An explosion?" Mira's voice was harsh with shocked apprehension.

At this point, Franz roused himself sufficiently to try to put his wife's mind at ease. "It's the demonstrations, my dear," he said soothingly. "The agitators never seem to rest." He put his hand to his head as another wave of dizziness assailed him.

Together, Mira and Ephraim helped Franz to one of a pair of elegant stone and wrought iron benches by the driveway. Mira then knelt before her husband, examining the wound on his forehead and trying to ensure his comfort. Distractedly, she turned to Ephraim. "You should have taken him to the infirmary," she lashed out at him, "instead of bringing him home. Can't you see he needs medical attention?"

"I quite agree with you, Madam Pietrowska," Ephraim answered, "but he insisted on being brought home. He wanted to be cared for only by you."

"It's not his fault, my dear," Franz interjected in Ephraim's defense. "I did insist on coming home. With the turmoil taking place in the city, I felt safer in your care."

"But Franz, I'm not a doctor." Mira protested. "You've suffered a serious injury; left unattended it could lead to a disfiguring scar and perhaps a dangerous infection."

"That was my thought, too," Ephraim agreed.

"We must get you to a doctor as quickly as possible," Mira stated firmly.

"No, it's too dangerous," Franz objected. "There are still likely to be demonstrations in the streets."

"I don't care about the demonstrations," Mira said firmly. "We're going right back into Warsaw and get your injury taken care of."

Fortunately, the Medical Akademy Infirmary was located on Arzulai Street at some distance from the center of the demonstrations. By the time that Franz, Mira and Ephraim returned to the city, most of the demonstrators had been dispersed by the militia. Remnants of the earlier mob still roamed the streets but there were no further acts of overt violence.

When Franz was examined at the infirmary, his injuries were pronounced minor. However, as a precaution it was decided that he should remain at the hospital under observation at least until the following day. With the week almost at an end, Franz acquiesced, putting his trust in Ephraim to complete the process of closing out the bank's work week. When he had been put to bed, Mira rejoined Ephraim in the waiting room.

"I'm glad to know he's not suffering shock," she said in a strained voice.

"The doctor feels certain he'll be all right, then?" Ephraim's voice also sounded strained.

Mira nodded and hurriedly sat down, at last betraying her fatigue. The last two hours, with their compliment of anxiety and concern, had depleted her normally inexhaustible energy.

Noting through the curtains the red glow of sunset, Ephraim experienced a different form of concern. "I wish there were some way I could contact my wife," he said. "It's the beginning of our Sabbath and I'm quite late. She'll be worried."

"I'm terribly sorry about delaying you," Mira replied graciously. "I have not thanked you properly for saving my husband's life. Forgive me. You too might have been injured or killed. I'm truly very grateful to you. Franz and I are both in your debt."

"Your husband has been and is my friend as well as my superior. I could have done no less. I had not, however, your powers of persuasion. He was determined to come home to you rather than pay a visit to a doctor."

Smiling, she answered. "I know Franz is very stubborn even when it endangers his own interests. I confess even I was surprised when he agreed to come back to Warsaw against his own convictions, but as you say, it's late and your wife will be worried. I will see you home."

"That's hardly necessary, Madam," Ephraim replied, not wishing to inconvenience her.

"Nonsense," Mira answered. "Besides, I can hardly let you walk home with the streets as they are at present." She shook her head. "I find myself at odds with my countrymen," she went on. "I cannot see that any good will come out of all this turmoil. It will only lead to reprisal, with the Polish people as the victims."

"And my people as the scapegoats," Ephraim said with resignation. "Because of these riots, we may lose all the small gains we have made, including the right to own land."

"You own a plot of land then?" Mira's eyes were speculative as she looked at him.

"Not yet, and perhaps not ever, if the authorities are persuaded that the Jews have taken part in what transpired today."

"Let us hope they won't come to that conclusion," Mira said encouragingly.

"I hope not," Ephraim observed. "It remains to be seen."

"Don't worry," Mira stated with conviction, "my husband is your friend as you have said, and as long as he is Assistant Bank Commissioner your position is safe. As for the land you desire, do you have a particular parcel in mind?"

Ephraim was silent, surprised at the accuracy of her evaluation and the forthright boldness with which she stated it. He determined to match her directness.

"Yes," he answered enthusiastically. "There is a certain piece of land I admire. In fact, it's quite close to your own property. The Zielinski estate. Do you know it?"

"Indeed I do," Mira said in answer. "I know it well. The executorship passed to the bank last month with the death of the owner's attorney. The last owner was the Marquis Michail Josef Zielenski. I was acquainted with him." Her eyes hardened and she grew intensely business-like. "The taxes in that area are exorbitant. How much capital can you raise?"

"A sizeable amount, possibly the entire sum, before the end of the year." The speed with which Mira Pietrowska was moving both pleased and surprised Ephraim.

"I'm sure that will suffice," Mira answered. "I'll see to the matter personally for you. It's the least I can do to show my gratitude for your kindness to Franz."

"You are most gracious," Ephraim said, pleased by this unexpected turn of fortune.

"I am in your debt, sir," Mira responded, smiling enigmatically. "You will find that I pay my debts, promptly and with interest." She said the last with studied emphasis.

As he took his leave of her at the entrance to the Stare Miasto, to which she had graciously insisted on taking him, he felt a certain apprehension. She was too intense, too overwhelming for his liking. Undoubtedly she could be a valuable ally, but she could also be an implacable enemy. He promised himself that he would make every effort to remain in her debt no longer than was absolutely necessary.

As Mira's coachman drove her home in her husband's carriage, her mind was busy with plans to implement her promise to Ephraim Marjzendiak. At present, she felt herself in his debt. Despite the admirable attributes he displayed, perhaps even because of them, she did not wish to remain in that position. Better he should be obligated to her than she to him. Her husband had stated that he expected great things from Marjzendiak. Having met him in person, Madam Pietrowska found that she was inclined to share her husband's convictions.

Furthermore, Ephraim was an intensely attractive man, tall, slim, and dignified of bearing. He was not at all what she had pictured when Franz had spoken to her about him. It would be a fascinating enterprise to explore the effects of her charms upon him without betraying her own feelings.

Mira Pietrowska was almost legendary for possessing one of the most perfect figures in Warsaw. It was a reputation she owed in large part to her having made the acquaintance of Marie Doussoult, an excellent dressmaker of French-Polish ancestry. These two women had formed a firm, enduring friendship, and Mira had profited ever since from Marie's unquestioned skill. She glanced down and smoothed the skirt of her striped pink and lavender gown, conscious of her unquestioned appeal.

Then, too, Mira thought wickedly, it would add a certain spice to the project if she were to aid her husband's Jewish protégé to acquire the very land that had once belonged to the arrogant, supercilious, openly anti-Semitic Marquis Zielinski. More than once he had made Mira feel inferior and put-down because of her middle-class origins. In fact, he had dared on one occasion to question Franz's reasons for marrying beneath him. That memory strengthened her resolve. She would do all in her power to ensure that the former Zielinski estate ultimately became the property of the Marjzendiak family.

# CHAPTER EIGHT
## AUGUST 1862: BLOOD AND POLITICS

The Marquis Alexander Wielopolski, supported by the moderate and conservative political elements of the Congress Kingdom, was re-appointed by the Tsar to the post of Minister of Interior Affairs in the second week of June, 1862. At the same time, the Tsar appointed his brother, the Grand Duke Constantine, to the post of Viceroy, having recalled Count Lambert the preceding week. Wielopolski's supporters were encouraged by this appointment. They hoped the Marquis' return to power and the appointment of the Grand Duke, a member of the Imperial family, would serve to restore order and enhance public confidence in the Tsar's commitment to reform.

At first it seemed their hopes might be realized. For the first few days of June, a mood of calm prevailed despite the intermittent publication in the underground press of inflammatory editorials and articles that incited Nationalistic sentiments. With the exception of the Senatorska Street demonstration, the overt conflict seemed to have subsided.

One of these editorials, accompanied by a derogatory caricature of the Viceroy, was circulated at the Wishnieski mill. It came to the attention of Wilhelm Droski who, taking advantage of his new authority as head of security, attempted to identify the workman responsible. Although he had no evidence on which to base his assumption, Droski intended to place the blame on the new foreman, Isaak Marjzendiak. He had no valid personal quarrel with Marjzendiak, but the foreman's Jewishness combined with his agile intellect, his creativity, and his obvious ambition aroused in Droski a jealous antagonism. Furthermore, despite his best efforts, he had been unable to unearth any concrete evidence against Viktor Sokorski. Having failed in that endeavor, he decided to move, instead, against the young Jew

He summoned Isaak to the mill office where he had laid out the newspaper article on his desk. He began his interview on an interrogatory note, calmly stated but intended, nonetheless, to intimidate.

"What can you tell me about this? Is it familiar to you?"

"In a sense, yes," Isaak answered truthfully.

"In what sense?"

"I've seen it before."

"Where?"

"Here in the mill," Isaak answered.

"Was it being circulated among the workers?"

"It was tucked under a work bench, as I recall."

"What did you do about it?"

"Such things are best ignored," Isaak replied. "To accord them too much importance only serves to fan the flame. That's exactly the goal of the people who write these."

"You disclaim any knowledge of how this newspaper was brought into the mill?"

"Absolutely!"

"Why should I believe you?"

"Because I'm telling you the truth," Isaak replied levelly. "I totally disagree with the sentiments expressed in the newspaper editorial. Why would I bring it into the mill?"

"Precisely my question," Droski answered. "Why did you?"

"I didn't," Isaak answered. "To my way of thinking, it serves no useful purpose."

"But it does provoke controversy and heated discussion," Droski persisted.

"And thus diminishes efficiency," Isaak pointed out. "That makes me look inept. Obviously, it would be against my interests to circulate such a stimulus among the men under my supervision."

"True," Droski was forced to admit. "Whom, then, do you suspect?"

"I've no idea," Isaak replied, shaking his head.

"Have you made any effort to find out?"

"I thought my efforts would be better utilized in diffusing controversy and focusing the attention of the work crew on the job at hand," Isaak answered.

"Very well," Droski said coldly. "Continue your efforts. Meanwhile, if you should learn the identity of the guilty man, notify me at once."

"Understood," Isaak responded. "May I get back to work now, Mer Droski?"

"Yes, of course," Droski said, but in his own mind he had already dismissed the foreman. He was determined that somehow he would find a means to trip up this arrogant Jew.

\* \* \*

In late June, the Grand Duke Constantine, while attending a theater performance, narrowly survived an assassination attempt perpetrated by a brewery workman named Klas Jaroszyriski. The Viceroy wisely publicly proclaimed that the reform policies would proceed despite the Jaroszyriski incident. However, despite his proclamation, the conscriptions which had temporarily been suspended, began anew.

In July, Adam sat for the qualifying examination to enter the prestigious Warsaw Akademy of Medicine. Although it had been in existence for only a few years as compared to the far older Krakow Akademy of Medical Sciences, its reputation was already well established. From all across Congress Poland and beyond, applicants came to Warsaw to compete for a chance to enter the freshman class.

With Dr. Jedewreski's help, Adam was able to complete a course of study equivalent to the premedical curriculum formerly taught at the University of Warsaw prior to its closure. Upon completion of the test, Adam felt confident of success, but as time passed with no notification of his standing, doubt began to plague him. He grew silent and reclusive, fearful that he had perhaps been over-confident. When at last the letter of notification came, bearing its official seal and blue-edged borders, Adam could scarcely bring himself to open it. Instead, he handed it to Isaak who for once was home early from the lumber mill.

Isaak opened the letter and on reading it, smiled and embraced his brother. He then handed the letter to Adam. "Here, read it yourself," he said heartily. "It's good news, but then I was certain all these weeks that there could be only one outcome."

As Adam read the letter, he confirmed Isaak's words. He had passed. He was one of the fortunate few Jewish students in Russian Poland in this year of 1862 who qualified to enter the study of medicine. To Adam, there could be no greater thrill than to some day be addressed as "Doctor." He longed to follow in the footsteps of men such as Aesculapius and Hippocrates, names that for Adam were magical, touched with greatness, seemingly only a little lower than the angels named in the Torah.

"I passed! I passed," Adam said, repeating it like a prayer. And seeing the depth of his emotion, Isaak was happy for him. Both men laughed and wept simultaneously.

For Isaak it was a bittersweet moment. If he and Mariska had been able to wed, he would have reacted in just the same way.

\* \* \*

Near the end of the work shift on a particularly hot and humid August day, Wilhelm Droski stood outside the mill office enjoying the cool crosscurrents that emanated from the turning of the semicircular saws. He was grateful for a respite from the confining office and its oppressive heat. The landing on which Droski stood afforded him a panoramic view of the mill floor. As he contentedly surveyed the men and equipment, Droski noticed Isaak Marjzendiak coming up the stairway.

Droski smiled unpleasantly and asked, "What are you doing here?"

"Mer Wishnieski has sent for me," Isaak replied evenly.

"Indeed!" Droski eyed Isaak. "Transact your business, then, and be on your way."

"I'll be on my way when Mer Wishnieski has finished with me." Isaak's voice, face and stance reflected an attitude of challenge.

"Next to Wishnieski," Droski said, "I'm the highest ranking manager in this mill. You'll do as I tell you, you upstart pig."

The metaphor was deliberately chosen. Droski knew that pork was a defiled and forbidden meat to the Jews.

"You're very free with insults these days," Isaak said coolly. "One would think you really were Mer Wishnieski's son-in-law."

Droski reacted with a start. His frustration at having been cheated of his bride and her dowry had left him a bitter man. He seized Isaak by the lapels of his shirt, unbuttoned at the neck as a compromise with the hot and humid weather. Isaak stepped back, sensing an impending blow and wanting, if possible, to avoid open conflict.

Droski, struggling to retain his hold on his quarry, was thrown slightly off balance as he stepped forward, raising his fist toward Isaak's face. Isaak side-stepped the blow, just at the last moment. Droski, thrown further off balance by this unexpected move, lost his hold on Isaak's clothing and his own footing almost simultaneously.

The landing gave very little maneuvering space for Droski to recover his equilibrium. With a sudden, stifled cry of terror, he catapulted headlong down the stairs. His cry was cut off abruptly as his head struck the edge of one of the lower steps. The dull thud of his body striking the hard, rock-like surface of the mill floor below seemed to reverberate in Isaak's mind with the stunning force of an explosion. In shock, Isaak turned as the office door opened behind him, and found himself face-to-face with Markos Wishnieski.

Wishnieski looked from Isaak to the immobile figure at the base of the stairwell. "What happened here?"

Isaak struggled to speak. He raised his hands helplessly, then dropped them. "My presence seemed to anger him," he answered haltingly as he tried to recall the events of the preceding moments. "He made some remark that made no sense and then came at me as if he would strike me. I backed away as he reached for me. His hand caught at my shirt and then he fell. I would have fallen too, if I hadn't grabbed the handrail. I could feel the momentum of his fall dragging me down with him. Luckily for me, the rail held."

The mill owner nodded, satisfied if not pleased with this explanation. What lay between the two men Wishnieski did not know, nor did he care to. Despite his relief when Mariska's marriage had been settled, he felt little liking for the Prussian.

Down on the mill floor, Josef Skiljret knelt by Droski's body and felt for a pulse. He turned Droski's head gently, then stood up and looked at his employer and shook his head.

Wishnieski glanced at Isaak, his expression one of civil dismissal. "We'll talk later," he said. "I'll have to attend to this tragedy now."

Isaak turned and walked slowly down the stairs, his movements stiff and jerky like those of a mechanical toy. He was filled with apprehension, although he knew he was innocent of any wrongdoing. What he did not realize was that there had been a silent witness to the tragedy. Josef Skiljret had been waiting for Isaak to finish his interview with Markos Withnieski and had seen the entire event from the bottom of the stairs. On his testimony, the incident was dismissed as an unfortunate accident, and Isaak had yet another reason to be grateful to Josef.

\* \* \*

As summer moved toward fall, conscriptions became more intense. Having been granted most of the rights of Polish citizens, the Jews were not exempt from such conscriptions. Ephraim and Elana lived in fear that any day one or both of their elder sons might be forcibly inducted into the Russian Army.

When Adam was notified of having passed his examination, the family, pleased at the news, was nonetheless apprehensive, wondering how this might affect his conscription status. When Isaak announced the tragic accident at the mill, they prayed earnestly and frequently that this would not lead to the loss of his employment. Unemployed young men were the earliest conscripts.

On August 7, 1862, another assassination attempt took place, this time directed against Marquis Wielopolski. His initial response was to discontinue temporarily all public appearances. The Grand Duke advised against this tactic as a show of cowardice. On August 15, a second assassination attempt was made, this time upon the life of the Grand Duke himself. Though neither of these efforts succeeded, they were much better planned and carried out than the earlier action taken by Jaroszyriski. Wielopolski determined that the perpetrators of the attack on the Viceroy must be executed to discourage any further acts of violence.

The men in question were students from the University of Warsaw, the recent re-opening of which Wielopolski had personally engineered. Of the four would-be-assassins involved, all had escaped but one: Josef Wishnieski, the mill owner's youngest son.

Markos Wishnieski was in a state of shock.

Tragedy seemed to be stalking his family. First his daughter Mariska, he believed, committed suicide, though the family staunchly denied the rumors that had arisen to that effect and had successfully persuaded the clergy of the Eastern Orthodox Church that the girl's death was an unfortunate accident. Then Droski died from yet another tragic accident.

Initially, his son Josef's decision to come home when the reopening of Warsaw University was announced seemed the answer to his family's prayers. This was especially true in view of his mother's illness and depression over Mariska's death. Now it turned out that the young man had allowed his misguided patriotism to embroil him in the activist cause. This had finally led to the attempt on the life of the Grand Duke, Tsar Alexander's own brother.

Count Wielopolski had no choice but to make an example of the one assailant the militia had been able to apprehend.

The day before the scheduled execution, Markos Wishnieski was summoned to the Citadel. Eva Wishnieska was too ill to make the effort. Josef was brought to an interrogation cell to meet with his father. Markos Wishnieski scarcely recognized his son, so altered was his appearance. Gaunt, unwashed, exhausted from repeated questioning, Josef Wishnieski's suffering was clearly evident in his face.

Father and son stood facing each other, both at a loss for words. They embraced, overcome with conflicting emotions.

Josef knew why his father had come. He also knew that his mission would be in vain. "I'm glad to see you, Father," he said, "despite the circumstances. I'm grateful for this opportunity to say goodbye."

Markos interrupted him. "It doesn't have to be goodbye, son. All you need do is tell the authorities what they want to know and you'll be freed."

Josef shook his head and turned away. "I won't betray my friends."

"Josef, these people are not your friends. If they were, they wouldn't have left you to be captured. They'd have fought for you as you are fighting to shield them."

"We share the same beliefs, father. That makes us kindred, as much as any blood tie. We are Poles. This land is ours. We cannot see it end as a Russian province. If blood must be spilled to accomplish that, even mine, I say so be it."

"Josef, my son," Markos Wishnieski pleaded, "you are filled with patriotism. But what have all these demonstrations accomplished? Your friends are only bands of undisciplined, poorly-armed youth. Emotions are a poor substitute for military strength."

Even as the father spoke, his son shook his head resignedly.

"Listen to me, Josef! You say you share kinship with these dissidents. What of your family, what of your mother?"

"Leave Mother out of this!"

"You came home to be with her, so you told us. Now it seems you came home to conspire with your fellow traitors."

"We're not traitors! We're patriots. And I love Mother. But I also love my country."

"She's dying, Josef. This thing you have done will kill her."

"No! She was ill all summer. She was ill before I came home."

"But now she has no will to survive. She has lost her only daughter. If she also loses you, she will give up. She will die! Is that what you want?"

"Of course, not," Josef replied bitterly, "but there's nothing I can do. It's out of my hands."

"No," Markos insisted, desperation in his voice. "The Marquis has given me his word. If you tell him the names of the others involved with you in this terrible act, your life will be spared."

"Spared? I'll be exiled to Siberia and I won't last one winter there. It is one death sentence exchanged for another. Even if I did what you ask, the "Reds" would seek me out and kill me as a traitor to their cause. Don't you see? It's all the same. I'm a dead man, Father. Accept it as I do. Go home. I cannot bear any more."

With that the young man turned away. He knocked loudly on the locked door to summon the guard, anxious to end this futile interview and escape from the pain it had brought to both himself and his father. He needed to be strong now. To face death, a man must be strong.

"Josef! Josef!" His father called after him in vain as the guard unlocked the door and led Josef away. Markos Wishnieski wept, realizing that the situation was hopeless.

As the trap door was opening beneath his feet and the noose was being tightened about his throat, Josef Wishnieski would still hear that anguished cry ringing in his ears.

On the morning of August 23rd, Josef Wishnieski was hanged. His mother Eva died late that same night. Her illness did not respond to the medications which her family doctor had administered. Markos Wishnieski sat by her bed, holding her hands, too stricken to speak in answer to her frenzied queries about her youngest son. She knew what his fate must be even as Josef had known. Helpless to alter its course, she followed him within twelve hours.

The joint funeral service took place two days later on August 25th. The Wishnieski mill stood silent and vacant, its machinery stilled for that day of mourning.

Markos Wishnieski, exhausted by grief, was a broken, defeated man. He watched the dry, heat-baked earth being shoveled into the twin graves, his mind numbed, his heart filled with pain and bitterness. He leaned heavily for support on the arms of his two elder sons, Zoltan and Friedrich. The three of them were all that remained of the family.

* * *

In the years that Ephraim worked at the Bank of Poland, Isaak had never visited him at work before. Therefore, his father was somewhat surprised one September afternoon when the door of his office opened to reveal Isaak, standing there indecisively. The young man was obviously impressed by the air of understated grandeur that surrounded his father. It pervaded the paneled walls, the dark rich draperies, and the highly polished furniture. Watching the ease with which his father moved and functioned in this setting, Isaak saw Ephraim with new eyes.

As a good son, Isaak had always loved his father, had revered him as the head of the family even when their opinions differed, as they frequently had in recent months. But he was unprepared for the imposing man of business who stood before him now.

"What a pleasant surprise," Ephraim said warmly. "Is this a social call, or a matter of business?"

Isaak looked searchingly into his father's sensitive face, seeking vainly for a way to begin. He stretched out his hands toward his father but could find no words to frame an answer to his question.

Ephraim took the young man's hands in his own.

"How can I help, Son?"

"I need your advice," Isaak said at last. "I'm uncertain as to what I should do. I have been made an offer. If I accept it, I'll be bound here, perhaps forever."

Ephraim smiled and nodded, motioning Isaak to a chair. He took an adjacent chair, deliberately avoiding placing the desk, of which he was justifiably proud, between his son and himself.

"At your age, Isaak, forever seems a very long time. Choices are painful but necessary. Tell me the offer. Perhaps then I can formulate a suggestion."

"When I changed jobs last fall, and went to work in the lumber mill, I felt as though I had found a place in life. I learned all I could about wood, how it's processed, preserved and shipped. I thought when the University reopened, I could still work odd shifts and move upward. Being a mill worker is not my life's ambition, but it is an income until I can complete my studies." Isaak stopped, uncertain how to relate the next part of his narrative.

"Go on," Ephraim said encouragingly.

"Well, if Mer Wishnieski had made the offer then I would have felt no conflict about it, but he wouldn't have wanted to sell it then. The mill, I mean."

Ephraim was shocked. "Wishnieski has offered to sell you his mill?"

Isaak nodded but looked at his father dejectedly. "I don't have sufficient capital."

"We'll consider that aspect in a minute," Ephraim said thoughtfully. "I've heard Markos Wishnieski is building a second mill several kilometers north of Warsaw. Is that why he wants to sell this one?"

"He wants to sell them both," Isaak answered, his voice rising. "He wants to leave, wants to try to forget everything that's happened here."

Ephraim could now perceive the motive behind Wishnieski's offer. "I sympathize with his loss," he said.

"It's partly my fault," Isaak said sadly.

A puzzled frown creased Ephraim's brow. "Your fault? In what way?"

"Mariska and I were very close." Isaak struggled for words in which to convey his long overdue confession. He could not in good conscience ask his father's help without acquainting him with the facts. On the other hand, he could hardly expect to receive that help once the confession was made.

"I know you were determined to attend her funeral," Ephraim said and waited for Isaak to proceed.

Isaak stood up and walked toward the window, too embarrassed to face his father. "I was in a way responsible for her death. I should have shown more strength. I should have resisted temptation. Instead, I, I made love to her, more than once. In my heart I knew it was hopeless, and yet I couldn't stop myself." His voice grew fainter. "I came to love her, even before I knew about the baby, but I didn't dare hope she could love me."

Ephraim had a mind for figures; it was just as agile in dealing with facts. His memory was faultless. Rumors regarding the suddenness of the Wishnieski heiress' wedding plans had reached even the Stare Miasto and had been related in whispers by clerk tellers and others at the bank. Ephraim now had his answer to questions of his second son's behavior that had mystified him for some time. In the silence that ensued, the father joined his son at the window.

"There's not much to be seen from here, Son," he said quietly. He touched Isaak's sleeve and then gently turned him so that they faced each other. "All of us encounter temptations. They are part of life. A man must do his best to uphold the laws of God and, whenever possible, those of man that do not compromise his honor. But none of us is perfect. Not Moses, nor Elijah, nor Isaiah. And certainly not you or I."

"I loved her," Isaak said, the tears he had long withheld falling at last. "I loved her, but her father would never have accepted me as his son. And you would never have welcomed her as a daughter. Her family chose a husband for her instead. And now she's dead. They're both dead, Mariska and the baby. Even Droski's dead. She never told him my name, but he hated me anyway. Now her father offers me his mills."

There was a sense of unreality about the situation that called forth a bitter blend of tears and hysterical laughter which Isaak could not restrain.

Ephraim embraced his son as he had seldom done since Isaak's childhood. "It is not a recompense of equal value," Ephraim said. "Nothing is as precious as life. But perhaps it is Adonai's way of showing His forgiveness, and of granting you a means to make atonement."

Isaak raised his head and stared intently at his father. "Atonement?" Isaak's voice was hushed.

"You said you were uncertain, undecided about what path to take. You wish to leave Warsaw, but you wish also to accept Mer Wishnieski's offer. Why?"

"Because I know how he must feel. Everything at the mill, at his home, everywhere, reminds him of his family, the ones who are no longer there. I hate going near the office at the mill. It was there I saw and spoke with Mariska that last time before I found her dead. Did you know that? It was I who pulled her out of the water."

Ephraim shook his head sadly. "I didn't know that, son," he said. "I'm sorry." He turned and walked over to his desk. "How much does Wishnieski want for the mills?"

"The price is fair, fifteen hundred zloty. One hundred zloty would be an acceptable down payment. I've saved seventy zloty. I had hoped to use it to finance my studies at the University of Krakow."

"What you did was wrong, Isaak, but very human," Ephraim said warmly. "I regret we did not have this conversation sooner. Nothing can alter what's past, but the present is open to suggestion. You know how your employer feels," Ephraim continued, "because his feelings parallel your own. That is the basis for understanding. In order to ease his loss, you are willing to stay and be reminded of your own; that is noble. However, you are not willing to stay indefinitely and give up your dream of Krakow. That is realistic." Ephraim guided Isaak back to the chair he had left and sat down again himself. "Perhaps I can help you to accomplish those goals. I, too, have money saved for a dream of my own. I will lend that money to you, but by the year's end, I will require you to repay the loan. Without interest," he added smiling.

"No, Father," Isaak insisted. "This is business. I will pay the fair interest rate. That way, you will benefit from helping me. And the atonement will be more effective."

Ephraim smiled, then Isaak. The two men shook hands.

"Agreed," Ephraim said approvingly.

After Isaak left, Ephraim uttered a silent prayer of thanksgiving. Isaak, despite his activist political sentiments, did not, like Josef Wishnieski, allow his patriotic zeal to involve him in any criminal acts against the prevailing government. There was still a chance, if the conscription did not accelerate, that both his adult sons might be spared. With Isaak owning and managing the Wishnieski mills, his work might be considered crucial to the economy. Adam, on the other hand, was scheduled to become a student shortly. Students, as Ephraim knew, formed the backbone of the radical movement.

Ephraim was well aware that Isaak had always desired to study in Krakow, which, unlike Warsaw, had no restrictions or quotas barring Jewish students. More importantly, with the borders of the Polish nation having been constantly redrawn with each successive partition, Krakow was now just across the border in Galicia under Austrian rule and, therefore, not subject to Russian authority. It well might be the ideal place for both his sons.

# CHAPTER NINE
## SEPTEMBER 1862: LEAVETAKING

In early September of 1862 the final confrontation took place between the Marquis Alexander Wielopolski and Count Andreai Zamoyski. The Count was a leader among the Polish landed aristocracy and an ardent supporter of Polish autonomy. Throughout both Wielopolski's terms of office, he had personally favored the Marquis' reforms. He had also labored to preserve his own role as a Polish patriot, an image that would have suffered considerably from whole-hearted support of a program openly cooperative with the Russian autocracy. Calling upon the rapport that had formerly existed between the two men, Wielopolski sent for Zamoyski. Reluctantly, Zamoyski came; patiently he listened to Wielopolski's efforts to convince him that the reactionary measures he had enacted were in accord with the reforms which Zamoyski favored.

The Count remained unconvinced. "What of the conscriptions?"

"They must continue," Wielopolski replied insistently. "They are our only effective means of thinning the ranks of the radicals."

"And the hangings? Are they also effective for 'thinning ranks?'"

Caught off guard, Wielopolski stared at Zamoyski, recalling the hanging of Klas Jaroszyriski, Josef Wishnieski, and the others who had been subsequently apprehended. "The men who were hanged were all involved in assassination attempts."

"In fact," Zamoyski said, "we can expect no revision of currently prevailing policy in this office."

"Not while the acts of violence and vandalism continue."

"You know my views on that subject," Zamoyski said. "Even the Grand Duke himself pleaded for leniency. And he was the intended victim. When you've given the matter more thought, I shall be willing to discuss it further with you."

As the door closed behind Zamoyski, Wielopolski could scarcely believe his ears. The interview had terminated almost before it had begun. On September 4th, Joroslow Dubrowski, leader and treasurer of the City Committee, the Nationalist political organization, was summarily arrested and imprisoned. On September 7th, Count Zamoyski was served notice of his banishment from Poland for an indefinite period.

It could be argued that controlling measures were being undertaken against both the radical and conservative factions. In any event, by mid September, a major exodus of Polish males of conscriptable age had occurred.

Many families were divided by the abrupt departure of their sons to destinations in eastern and western Galicia, Silesia, and Lithuania. Once there, they could vanish into anonymity, helped by sympathetic citizens who had once been part of the proud Polish nation.

Other families were polarized, as was the Congress Kingdom itself, by conflicting political and ideological convictions. The Wishnieski family represented a significant minority. Already deeply touched by tragedy, the family's remaining members were anxious to escape the scene of such unpleasant memories.

Faced with conscription into the Russian Army on the one hand and chaotic civil upheaval on the other, Adam and Isaak Marjzendiak faced the same dilemma that gripped the entire Congress Kingdom. Adam had become acquainted with several of his future fellow students only to see them called up to serve their Russian overlords on a distant frontier. The Akademy was now viewed by the Minister, the Viceroy, and the Council of State as a center for dissident gatherings. The student body's ranks were being rapidly depleted.

Isaak had committed to acquire the two Wishnieski lumber mills. Deeds of trust had been signed and money delivered. The lumber mills were closed for the inventory that had to be presented at the time of formal transfer of property. For the time being, however, the new owner dared not rejoice since he could be inducted into the Russian army at any time.

Adam, preparing optimistically to begin classes in the fall, had finally resigned his post at the flour mill. He had, however, agreed to work partial shifts throughout the spring and summer of the following year.

Early in the second week of September, Mira Pietrowska sought out Ephraim at the bank. She knew that the pressures of increasing responsibility now prevented his going home every day for lunch. As a consequence he had lost weight and was leaner and even more distinguished looking. Mira still harbored a secret curiosity regarding Ephraim. She knew he was married with grown children. She, too, was a matron and a mother. However Ephraim, with his Jewish mystique and his aura of polite aloofness, represented in her mind an intriguing challenge.

Mira regarded Ephraim Marjzendiak with speculative eyes as she accepted his invitation to sit down in his office.

"I have news for you, Mer Marjzendiak," she began dramatically.

"I see," Ephraim answered, keeping his voice neutral. "Favorable or the converse?"

"Something of both," Mira replied, her smile inscrutable. "Which shall I tell you first?"

"The bad news," Ephraim answered instantly. "Save the good for last."

"Very well." Mira said. "I take it you are aware of the drastic decline in property values."

"I've heard the general cries of doom and gloom," Ephraim replied. "Nothing specific."

"Our property, Franz's and mine, will scarcely fetch the price we paid for it on today's market," Mira said somewhat grimly.

"I'd say that was specific," Ephraim remarked. "Intriguing news, indeed. So much for the unfavorable aspects. And what is there to counterbalance that, Madam? "

"Property values and taxes tend to parallel one another," Mira replied.

"Naturally," Ephraim responded, following her line of reasoning. "The taxes on your lands and those of your neighbors have all declined."

"Naturally," she echoed.

"To what extent, then, Madam Pietrowska," Ephraim asked, beginning to guess to what Mira was leading, "is your tax burden lightened?"

Mira considered a moment before answering. "At least twelve percent."

"That renders the property of which we spoke some weeks ago much more readily available," Ephraim remarked candidly, sensing her eagerness to see him acquire the land.

"Indeed it does," Mira agreed. "to a great many prospective buyers."

Ephraim looked anxiously at Mira. "Do you think there are many?"

"For such a choice piece of land, I'd be surprised to find no takers," she replied. "But so far as I know, the required commitment has not yet been paid."

"Good." Ephraim responded. "However, there is still one obstacle."

"I had thought, Mer Marjzendiak, that you were a man who overcomes obstacles."

"Whenever possible, I do, Madam Pietrowska," he answered. "The current difficulty is a family matter."

"Nothing serious, I hope."

"It involves my son, Isaak," Ephraim explained cautiously. "He was made an offer too unusual and too favorable to refuse. In order for him to take advantage of it, I've had to lend him a considerable sum. It has depleted the funds I had reserved to defray the taxes on the Zielinski property."

Mira briefly and silently considered this information. "What is the offer that was made to your son?"

"To buy the Wishnieski mills. Both of them."

"Wishnieski? Ah, yes. The hanged son and the drowned daughter," Mira mused, recalling the catalogue of tragedies that had overtaken the family.

"And the inconsolable mother, all dead," Ephraim added.

"Yes," Mira said, nodding, "a tragic chain of events, but not without its positive side. The senior Wishnieski has offered to sell your son his business?"

"That's correct," Ephraim answered.

Mira's eyes narrowed. "For what consideration?"

"For one hundred zloty as a down payment with installments of fifty zloty until the sum of fifteen hundred is paid," Ephraim responded.

"Can your son manage such a financial burden?"

"Yes, with my help," Ephraim said softly.

"And so you would risk losing the land you desire in order to help your son own lumber mills?"

"My son needs my help, Madam," Ephraim said. "And I need yours," he added, swallowing his pride.

Mira Pietrowska suppressed the question she was about to ask and substituted another. "Isn't that precisely why I'm here?"

"If you are the chosen instrument of Adonai, Madam, your visit is well-timed," Ephraim remarked, half seriously and half in jest.

Mira Pietrowska smiled warmly. "Does your God sometimes use Gentiles to do His will?"

"Adonai has uses for all those whom He has created, Madam," Ephraim answered in the same vein. "We are often unaware of how we are to serve Him."

"And just how is it you wish me to supply this help?"

"If you were to entail the property in exchange for interest in the mills," Ephraim suggested, "we could arrange an agreement whereby the taxes will be repaid on a quarterly basis. You would retain your interests until your monies were fully repaid."

"Fair enough," Mira pronounced. "And thus you become a property owner on a grand scale, Mer Marjzendiak. I see you're an even more formidable businessman than I had thought." She rose and shook hands with him. "I congratulate you. I hope your son appreciates your help."

"I'm sure he does," Ephraim responded.

Mira Pietrowska left Ephraim's office that afternoon convinced that he was a shrewd and devious businessman. She sensed his compulsion to own real property and was convinced he would buy out his son's investment to enlarge his own holdings.

Nevertheless, she was vaguely disappointed at seeing this new aspect of his character, a strain of cupidity that seemed to override even family feeling.

Her opinion would have been quite reversed had she been present that evening in the large sparsely furnished room that served the Marjzendiak family as living room, family room and parlor. Elana, perceptive as usual, had left the main room of the house to the men of the family and was imparting to Leah, now aged six, a lesson in weaving.

Ephraim convened a council of strategy with his two elder sons. It was the eve of the Day of Atonement, Yom Kippur. In deference to his protégé, Franz Pietrowski had graciously accorded to Ephraim the two-day leave he had requested in order to fulfill his religious obligation. During this time, it was Ephraim's objective to carry out a course of action that would effectively minimize the dangers facing his family.

Standing before Adam and Isaak in the main room of the house, Ephraim placed two leather pouches, fastened with thongs, upon the table before them.

"I have considered with great care what I'm about to say to you," he began. Isaak started to speak, but stopped when his father raised a hand for silence. "I know that both of you have plans and dreams of your own that you have cherished for some time. As a father, I have hoped to see those plans fulfilled, those dreams realized. That is still my hope, but I can no longer imagine that fulfillment taking place here in Warsaw. In order to survive, we must yield to the external pressures around us. The family cannot remain together at this time, much as I would like it to be so."

Now it was Adam who interrupted. "Father, are you saying the family must move?" His voice was strident with shock.

"Not all the family, though that might be preferable," Ephraim answered. "No, I am saying that you and Isaak must leave Warsaw. And not only Warsaw, but Congress Poland for the time being. Both of you are under the age of twenty-five and therefore subject to conscription. Conscriptees from Warsaw and the surrounding districts are being sent furthest from home, to Russia and the Turkish frontier. I do not wish that fate to be yours, and I can see only one remedy."

"But the mills," Isaak protested.

"I am to begin classes within the month," Adam said with a hint of desperation in his voice.

"I'm aware of that, my sons," Ephraim answered.

He picked up the larger of the two pouches and offered it to Isaak. "This includes a sum more than equal to what you have paid Markos Wishnieski for the lumber mills. I propose to buy them from you, Isaak, for the present. Admittedly, I know little about the lumber industry. However, your friend, Josef Skiljret, is over the age of thirty and is no longer subject to conscription. He has agreed to remain and manage the mills for me in your absence. When you return, they will again be yours. But you will need funds for the present to live on, to finance the education you wish to pursue. There is no other way I can assist you in making that possible. This sum should leave you free to make your own decision as to where you will stay. However, it is my hope that you will stay with your cousins in Krakow."

Having learned from Elana of the property Ephraim wished to acquire, Isaak was keenly aware that his father offered the money at great personal cost. He did not know of the offer put forth by Madam Pietrowska.

Isaak was overcome with emotion. "What can I say? I never expected this."

"Good," Ephraim replied with ironic humor. "Then we are both surprised."

Ephraim now turned toward Adam whose gloom was profound. Adam's dream of studying at the Warsaw Akademy of Medicine had been almost within his grasp, but he knew the validity of his father's words and his father's fears. Adam, too, was a realist. He squared his shoulders and stood taller as he awaited Ephraim's next words.

"Adam," Ephraim said, "you are my first born. I need hardly try to explain what that means to me and to our people." He paused, trying to gain control of his feelings. "Your portion is slightly smaller, not because your value to me is less, but because I feel certain you will be staying with family. My cousin Jada and her husband Zachareus, who live in Krakow, will welcome you warmly. Your presence in their household will help to ease their grief over the death last year of their son, Jacob." Ephraim picked up a sealed envelope from the table where it lay beside the pouch he had indicated as Adam's. He handed the letter to Adam. "Dr. Jedewreski left this in my keeping for you."

Adam took it solemnly and stared at the envelope for a few moments. Finally he broke the seals and removed two sheets of paper. He instantly recognized the small neat characters of his friend's handwriting. The first sheet of paper Adam read was a letter addressed to him.

"Dear Adam,

As you know, I was fortunate to be one of only a handful of Jewish students to graduate from the Medical Akademy of Krakow. Knowing your ambition to become a doctor and the unlikelihood, despite your exemplary showing in the qualifying examinations for the Warsaw Akademy, that you will be permitted to begin classes there, I have presumed to suggest an alternative.

Your father has shared with me his fears for your future and that of your brother Isaak. I share his concerns as any thoughtful man must in times such as these. Out of that concern I have written to the Medical Akademy of Krakow recommending you for acceptance on the basis of my knowledge of your qualifications and the records of your examination results, which speak for themselves.

Your score was among the highest ten percent of all the applicants this year. You can feel justly proud of such an achievement even as I am proud for you. I know you will make a fine physician, Adam. And although I know Ephraim will help you financially in every way possible, I have enclosed with this letter a bank draft redeemable at the Bank of Poland's Krakow office. It is but a small token of my love and regard for you.

May Adonai bless and preserve you always,

Samuel."

Adam stood speechless when he finished reading his friend's letter. It went so far beyond his most fantastic expectations. This was indeed a night of surprises, first Ephraim's unanticipated generosity, and then Samuel Jedewreski's equally unexpected recommendation and financial support.

Isaak and Adam came forward and embraced Ephraim.

They were both deeply moved. Words seemed inadequate to express what they felt.

"Every father knows he must one day see his sons leave home to seek their fortunes. But the circumstances of this leave taking seem extremely sorrowful, extremely hard to bear," Ephraim said solemnly. "Who knows when I will see either of you again?"

"Soon father," Isaak answered encouragingly. "I feel certain it will be soon. The conscriptions cannot last forever. When they are abolished, we will both come home. By that time you just may be in charge of the bank."

It was a needed touch of levity, a family jest based on Ephraim's often-voiced admiration of the Rothschild family's achievements a century earlier. The laughter between the three men was as heartfelt and genuine as were the tears of leave taking.

One thing remained to be done. When the sun set the following evening, the Day of Atonement, the most solemn and revered of the High Holy Days, would begin. However, instead of spending that day in the synagogue in prayer and contemplation of their transgressions, Adam and Isaak would be in flight. Ephraim had, therefore, arranged for Rabbi Janowski to visit the family this evening and lead them in prayer. In this way, Adam and Isaak could join the family in partaking of the rite of Yom Kippur.

For this observance, Elana and Leah rejoined the men of the family. When Rabbi Janowski arrived, the entire family gathered in the parlor. Only Michael, already fast asleep in his lindenwood cradle, would not participate. For him there would be other Holy Days. At present he had little for which to atone.

Normally this night would have had no special significance other than that of preparation for the Holy Day to begin the following evening. Elana and Leah would have spent this time preparing additional food for the next day, cleaning the house, and making ready fresh linens for the ritual feast at the end of the day, with its prescribed twenty-four-hour fast. Ephraim and the two older boys would have spent the evening in Talmudic study.

Inwardly, Ephraim felt a surge of deep resentment that the normal rhythm of their religious traditions and practices had to yield to geopolitical and civil forces beyond their control. That the Russian militia would certainly take advantage of the Jewish Holy Day, neither Ephraim nor Rabbi Janowski doubted in the least. Indeed, the occasion provided an ideal opportunity to surprise and detain young Jewish men whose names appeared on the conscript list while they were gathered in the synagogue in observance of the Atonement ritual.

In order to fulfill the need for a quorum in any gathering for prayer, Rabbi Janowski had brought with him his nephew Aaron, Josef Semerdjiak, a cloth merchant, Aaron Sokolov, who now worked as a clerk teller at the bank, Samuel Kapeski, a teacher at the shtetl school, and the Koppel brothers, Abel and Eli, friends of Adam's from the flour mill. These men were unaware of the real reason for the special service, but they were supportive of the family, nonetheless, and came to join them in prayer.

Adam and Isaak realized that it might be a long time before they gathered together once more to pray with the rest of their family. They were impressed by the preparations Ephraim had made and deeply moved by the significance and solemnity of the occasion.

Rabbi Janowski began by asking them to banish all secular concerns from their thoughts and to direct their attention towards prayer and reparation. The rabbi then continued the private unofficial ceremony with the Order of Capuroth; in place of the traditional sacrifice of a rooster for the men and a hen for the women of the family, Ephraim offered a small purse of coins for each family member to be afterwards donated to the poor. Because he offered atonement for male and female family members, Ephraim spoke the words suitable for both. "A soul instead of a soul; the price of sacrifice for the sacrificial fowl."

At the conclusion of this portion of the reading, Ephraim continued in the specified ritual words, "This is our charge, this is our compensation, this is our redemption. May this ransom serve as sacrifice for our transgressions while we shall be admitted and allowed a good, happy, and peaceful life."

The rabbi accepted the sacrifice offered and blessed it solemnly. He then intoned: "Magnified and sanctified be His great Name in the world He hath created according to His will. May He establish His kingdom in your life-time and in your days, and in the life-time of all the house of Israel."

The quorum responded, "Let His great Name be blessed for ever and ever."

The readings continued with each member of the quorum reciting one portion of the responses including Elana and even Leah who had been promised this distinction as part of the family observance. The long catalog of sins and transgressions were recited and regretted. Finally the most inspiring passages of the Tephilat Zakkah were recited. "Let the words of my mouth and the meditation of my heart be acceptable before Thee, O Lord, my Rock and my Redeemer. Amen. May thus be Thy will!"

Rabbi Janowski closed the ceremony as he had begun it, with the Kol Nidre, the time-honored main prayer of the Day of Atonement for which only one melody has ever been known for a thousand years. The rabbi chanted the cantor's segments while Ephraim's rich baritone led the "choir".

"All vows, oaths and promises which we made to Yahweh from last Yom Kippur to this Yom Kippur and were not able to fulfill - may all such vows between ourselves and Yahweh be annulled."

"May they be void and of no effect, may we be absolved of them and released from them," Adam added.

"May those vows not be considered vows, those oaths not be considered oaths, and those promises not be considered promises," Isaak concluded.

With the culmination of the prayers, the quorum adjourned and the family and their guests shared a repast of light refreshment, preceded by the traditional blessing before meals and followed, upon its conclusion, by the customary grace after meals.

# PART TWO: COMING OF AGE

Hear, O Israel, the Lord is God, the Lord is One.
And you shall love Yahweh, your God with all your heart,
With all your soul and with all your strength.

(Deuteronomy 6:4-5)

## CHAPTER TEN
## FLIGHT

Early the following morning Adam and Isaak, dressed in work clothes, left the Marjzendiak household. The packs which each carried contained several changes of clothing into which their precious stores of money and valuable documents had been carefully wrapped by Elana. Josef Skiljret demonstrated the scope of his friendship for Isaak by providing both men with cleverly forged identity papers which would assure their passage from Congress Poland into Galicia. Despite their authentic appearance, however, Isaak was particularly desirous to avoid too thorough an inspection of their identification documents and travel permits.

Each time he looked at them, checking to ensure that they were safe and intact, he breathed a silent prayer of thanks for Josef Skiljret and his selfless loyalty. Any other long-term employee of Josef's seniority might have resented being passed over when Markos Wishnieski decided to sell his mills. But Josef, recognizing Isaak's abilities, had encouraged him to accept the offer and congratulated him when he took possession of the business.

In order to avoid detection, the brothers were advised by Skiljret to leave Warsaw with the construction workers who were currently engaged in building a new bridge. The time-honored but now dilapidated one near the north boundary of the city had been further undermined by the force of the spring thaw. The foundations and supports of the picturesque structure had been so weakened that the Council of State had been obliged to close the bridge until repairs could be effected.

Considering the negative impact of this closure on Warsaw's economy, workmen assigned to the project were allowed to pass freely through the gates of the city, even in this critical period of civil rebellion.

Without challenge, Adam and Isaak left their home city. Both brothers experienced ambivalent sentiments at the moment of departure, but for Isaak, the commencement of this journey was a prelude to the fulfillment of his dream.

As soon as they reached the bridge, they detached themselves from the group of itinerant workmen in whose company they had left the city. Adam could feel rather than see the foreman watching them with frankly curious eyes. Followed closely by Isaak, Adam walked confidently to the far end of the bridge.

Taking a measuring rod from his pack, he spanned the distance from the upper end of the worn anchor post to its base. Then he leaned down as if to get a better view, beckoning Isaak to join him. Seconds later, both of them disappeared over the edge of the bank. The puzzled Russian foreman watched for several seconds, then started toward the spot where he had seen them vanish.

In the next moment, a loud altercation claimed the foreman's attention. The thought of the unfamiliar workmen left his mind, banished by more pressing concerns. On a project staffed by a crew ranging from Lithuanians to Silesians, peace on the job site was more important than the idiosyncratic behavior of two workmen.

Krakow lay approximately 360 kilometers from Warsaw. With winter approaching, a journey on foot between the two cities was potentially as perilous as a pilgrimage to the Holy Land and nearly as unlikely to succeed. Nonetheless, apprehension regarding the fate that awaited them should they turn back drove Adam and Isaak onward.

Isaak, the more outgoing of the pair, was naturally selected to be their spokesman. Adam took responsibility for the majority of the funds and resources. On that first day, the brothers traveled mostly on byroads and footpaths. They were fortunate in obtaining a ride from a merchant for several hours. By nightfall they had traveled fifty kilometers and came upon a roadside inn. It immediately drew Isaak's eyes and stimulated his hunger pangs. Adam, wary of attracting the attention of fellow travelers, urged caution in approaching the sumptuous, attractive public house for fear that Russian conscript agents might frequent such an attractive gathering place.

Less than two kilometers down the road, the brothers found a more rustic-looking inn. It seemed likely to offer less expensive lodging and was doubly recommended by the pungent aroma of homemade vegetable soup and freshly-baked bread coming from the kitchen. The worn sign in Polish and Russian could be interpreted as Wayfarer's Rest or Wayfarer's Haven, depending upon the liberality of one's translation.

To Adam and Isaak, the modest inn seemed haven indeed. The unpretentious atmosphere, the fire in the main dining room, the hearty openness with which the innkeeper's wife greeted them, all these served to reassure them. More reassuring still were the patrons - native Poles, not Russians.

Adam was particularly pleased since it was his intent that they remain in this comfortable dwelling until the following night. In the quiet serenity of their own room, he and Isaak could recite the obligatory prayers and perform the meditations of Yom Kippur. To avoid suspicion, they would plead 'traveler's indigestion' as the reason for their refraining from food for the next twenty-four hours.

* * *

Once they were on the road again, Adam and Isaak traveled cautiously and mostly at night. Their workmen's clothing proved helpful to them on more than one occasion. Shortly after they had passed through Redom, Adam helped a farmer repair his cart while Isaak, taking charge of the money they received for this service, visited the local market and obtained provisions sufficient to feed them for the next two days. On the road to Kielce they found shelter in the barn of an abandoned farm. They fell asleep wondering uneasily what had become of the farmer and his family.

At Sandomierz they had a very close call. By now their beards had grown abundantly. There had been neither time nor opportunity to trim and shape them as they customarily did at home. As a consequence, they looked older than they were and as they entered Sandomierz, Isaak developed a limp that further contributed to their more mature appearance.

"You never complained of an injury on the way here," Adam observed. "Why are you limping now?"

"It helps our image, brother," Isaak replied. "We mustn't seem too young and able-bodied or we'll never make it across the border."

"You've a point," Adam agreed. "And should I develop a disability also?"

Isaak shook his head. "One of us disabled is enough," he said. "Two would make them suspicious."

"And have you thought of where we'll spend the night?"

"We'll find something," was Isaak's cheerful answer.

Something proved to be a large, homey, and moderately priced inn. Once they had gone inside, it became apparent that it was being used as a headquarters for the conscript agents. A squad of militiamen were congregated in the dining room and despite their hunger, Isaak declined the host's offer of a meal, pleading that after their hard day's work, sleep was the more pressing need.

Isaak waited until he had locked the door to their room before he turned to Adam and asked: "Did you see the Tsar's constables?"

"More to the point," Adam responded, "did they see us?"

"They don't miss much."

"Then we don't dare stay here the entire night," Adam said.

"I agree. We'll sleep lightly and leave well before dawn."

"If we leave by the usual route, that may seem even more suspicious."

"Maybe. But if we can slip away unnoticed, it won't matter who suspects what in our absence. We'll just have to make certain to cover our tracks."

"There was a construction site on the north end of the city," Adam recalled.

"I noticed it," Isaak said. "What do you suppose they're building?"

"I suggest we go there and find out, just before dawn."

That proved to be easier said than done. When Adam and Isaak left the room they had shared, they noticed armed guards in the lower hall. Quietly retreating back to the room, they managed to pry open a window and climb down an ancient Cyprus tree that grew adjacent to the wall. Concealed by its bristly foliage, the two brothers watched as militia officers led away five hapless young men obviously attempting to avoid conscription. Only their resolve to arise and depart early enabled Adam and Isaak to evade the militia's net.

Later that morning, two new workmen presented themselves to assist in the repair of the Church of the Resurrection. Insurgents protesting the conscription had severely damaged the structure which was one of the oldest and most revered of the Eastern Orthodox houses of worship. In addition to damage to walls, one of the elegant stained glass windows was also broken. The glass was just being cleared away from the wall where Adam and Isaak were assigned to work. Once more luck was with them. The church stood against the northwestern wall of the city. By nightfall, the construction crew had already lost its two newest members.

* * *

Southwestern Congress Poland in the early 1860's was an area of flourishing farms scattered amid rural hamlets and forests. Here grew plentiful crops of rye, oats, wheat and barley. The local marketplaces abounded with the produce of the area's rich farmlands and among the favorite items of commerce was the almost constant supply of honey furnished from the hives of the district's beekeepers.

Just as they came within twenty kilometers of the Russian-Austrian border, a sudden storm overtook Adam and Isaak. Searching, now wet through, for a place to wait out this unexpected event, they took refuge in the barn of one of the dairy farmers. They were as quiet as possible, slept very little as a result of the pounding rain on the roof of the barn, and resolved as soon as dawn broke to depart unseen and to leave the cost of a night's lodging nailed to the gate.

Unfortunately, they found themselves unable to fulfill this last intent. The rain continued until well past daybreak. Finally, it did subside, the sun broke through the clouds, and the day began to offer brighter promises. As they were about to depart, a swarm of bees descended upon them and Adam was badly stung on the right arm. Within minutes, he had gone into shock and his condition so frightened Isaak that he was compelled to seek help from the dairy farmer's family.

Through a parlor window, Isaak observed a young lady diligently occupied at her spinning wheel. For a moment, he found himself at a loss for words. Then, she looked up directly at him and arose to her feet, startled. He beckoned her to come around to the door so that he could speak with her. Isaak met her there as she cautiously opened the door a few inches.

"Please," he said with a note of urgency. "My brother is in your barn. He's been stung by a bee. I can't seem to remove the barb and I'm afraid he's running a fever."

Without taking time to inquire further, the girl gathered some bottles and jars in a basket along with an oddly-shaped instrument. She followed Isaak to the barn. He stood by and watched while she extracted the barb from Adam's arm, bathed and dressed the wound, and then roused the patient sufficiently to coax him to drink a few spoonfuls of liquid from one of the bottles.

When Adam awoke, his right arm was bandaged and he lay on a pallet of clean straw covered with a warm blanket. The girl kneeling beside him gazed anxiously into his face.

"My brother," Adam began.

She smiled. "He's fine," she answered. "He's asleep just now. He sat up with you all night."

"What happened?"

"Have you ever before been stung by a bee?"

Adam nodded. "When I was very young, about age three or four," he replied.

"When your brother was a baby. That explains why he doesn't remember. There's always a prior time whenever it makes a person as ill as you've been," the girl said sagely.

"Was I so ill?"

"Your heart was racing and you could hardly breathe. It's fortunate there are herbs and plants that can help in such cases."

"And you know these plants?"

"We grow them. Even though this is primarily a dairy farm, we also keep bees and sell honey. When you've done that for several generations, you learn about what to do in case one of the bees stings someone who's extra sensitive to their toxin."

"One of them must have decided I was trespassing," Adam observed sheepishly.

"And weren't you?" Despite her smile, the girl made the question sound like a challenge.

"I suppose I was," Adam said. "But not intentionally."

"Who are you?" It was the inevitable question, and one Adam did not dare to answer without first consulting Isaak to know what had already been said and what withheld while he had been asleep. Adam stared at the girl who had been his nurse and benefactress. She seemed if anything to grow more beautiful as he looked at her. Her deep rich auburn hair cascaded down her shoulders, unrestrained except for a slender turquoise ribbon that matched the laced bodice of her full-skirted dress. Her eyes were pale brown flecked with green and a hint of blue, the latter reflected from her bodice. Her skin was as smooth and creamy as the milk from her family's cows. But the mind behind that lovely facade was sharp and clear and growing wary and suspicious of these two young intruders.

"How beautiful you are," Adam whispered as though he had not heard the question. "I thought I must either be dreaming or dead when I first awakened."

"No," she replied, shaking her head. "You're very much alive."

"What's your name?" he asked, wishing Isaak would awaken and rejoin them before the girl's insistent questions forced him into an awkward corner.

"Marja," she responded absently. "Marja Miatowska. And you are...?"

Adam gazed at her blankly. "I'm, I," Adam put his hand to his head and sighed. "How long did you say I've been here?"

"I thought you would know that better than I," Marja said with undisguised exasperation. "The fever must have affected your wits."

Adam allowed his head to sink back against the cushion that she had provided. His arm throbbed under the bandage. He reached toward the injured site with his other hand but Marja drew it gently away.

"No," she cautioned. "You mustn't scratch at that. You'll only make it worse. Just rest. The foxglove extract I've given you will work better if you don't try to be too active. Perhaps your brother will be more informative when he wakes up." With that she drew the blanket closer around Adam and watched as he lapsed back into sleep.

When her brother Jan came back from delivering the milk later in the morning, Marja would discuss with him the matter of these mysterious lodgers. He would decide what was to be done with them. Meanwhile she went about her chores with only half her mind on what she did. The other half was on Adam.

By lunchtime she had finished her work. Jan had not as yet returned so Marja went to check on her patient. She found both brothers engaged in a whispered conversation which she tried with little success to overhear.

"If we can just get to Cousin Jada's, you'll have plenty of chance to recover," Marja heard Isaak say. "We're nearly there. It can't be more than twenty kilometers to Krakow from here."

"The longest twenty kilometers of the entire journey," Adam said solemnly. "It tires me just to sit up."

"Don't even mention my going on without you," Isaak warned. "I wouldn't hear of it. We go together or not at all."

"And just how long do you think our pretty young hostess is going to shelter us here? She's curious about us now and the longer we remain, the more questions she'll have."

"But we've done nothing wrong. Not by our standards. Not by any standards," Isaak insisted. "As far as we know our names are not on any conscription order. We've committed no crime. We're only seeking an education, and work if we can find it." He added the last words as his keen ears detected a muted footstep on the wooden ladder leading to the loft. A moment later a head of auburn curls lifted itself over the edge of the hayloft and two hazel eyes peered at them.

"Both awake, I see," Marja observed. "Perhaps now I can get some answers from both of you."

Isaak turned to face her, his manner serious. "What are the questions?"

The girl climbed into the loft with practiced ease. With a faintly wistful smile she glanced about her. "This is my special place," she said. "I come here whenever I need to be alone or to think." She looked at Isaak. "Sooner or later I'd have found you up here even if you hadn't come looking for me to help your brother. All that little worker bee did was speed up the process." Her eyes traveled from one face to the other. "Would you, I wonder, have come and told me you were hiding here if that hadn't happened?"

"If that had not happened," Isaak answered, "I doubt we would still be here."

"We'd be in Krakow by now if it weren't for my clumsiness," Adam said ruefully. "It's all my fault you were disturbed. Forgive me."

Despite her misgivings she was disarmed by his manner. "And you really are going to Krakow?"

"As soon as I can move," Adam replied.

"We have relatives there who expect us, have been expecting us for several days," Isaak added. "We were delayed."

"I don't suppose you're willing to tell me your names," Marja said.

"Polewski," Isaak answered promptly. As he hoped, the name meant nothing to Marja. If questioned, she would not be able to link them to their family in Warsaw. And once they were across the border, the militia would have no authority over them.

"Abel and Erik Polewski," he continued. "We're on our way to Krakow to study and to find work," Isaak continued. "If you will let us stay here one more night, I'm certain my brother will be able to travel by morning. We are both grateful for all you've already done."

"And you're not fleeing the authorities?" Marja was certain they would not confess it to her even if they were.

Isaak shook his head. "I can assure we have done nothing wrong. We are simply poor. We have traveled a long distance from Vilno. An expensive journey by public transportation. More than we could afford. We've had to travel much of the way on foot."

"And if the militia find you, you'll be conscripted," Marja finished for him.

"I might be," Isaak replied. "My brother is already twenty-six. He would be exempt," Isaak lied smoothly.

"The militia came once for my brother Jan, but he had papers to prove his age. They have not come back." The way she said it spoke volumes. Throughout Congress Poland the Russian militia was hated and feared.

"That is fortunate," Isaak remarked.

"On that occasion, they questioned my entire family, even my father, although he was quite ill. He died soon afterwards." The memory brought tears to her eyes.

Isaak went to her, placed his hand upon her shoulder and with the other gently wiped the unbidden tears from her cheeks.

Madam Irina Berioslowska Miatowska was aged forty-five, widowed and without children of her own. Her world was composed of her niece Marja, her nephew Jan, the dairy farm, and the Uniate Church.

Irina insisted on presiding supreme over her own kitchen. Marja might regulate the running of the remainder of the household and Jan was the head of the family in matters of finance and commerce, but Irina would brook no interference with the planning and serving of meals. She knew by heart every item of supply in her larders. And only she had the authority to dispense them.

Isaak insisted on paying for the food Marja sympathetically provided for their breakfast. However, bread and cheese enough to quench the hunger of two six-foot men in their twenties was sufficient to be missed, and missed it was.

As the two women were preparing a late lunch, Isaak could hear their voices raised and suspected instinctively that he and Adam were somehow the cause of their controversy. Despite a natural reticence to interfere with a domestic altercation, he felt in all fairness he must go to Marja's defense if she was under attack by her aunt on his behalf. As he approached the kitchen, he could make out their words.

"I told you, Aunt Irina, they paid for the food."

"Show me the money," the older woman challenged. "Who are they? What are they doing here anyway hiding in the barn like thieves?"

"There has been no theft," Isaak said firmly as he entered the kitchen. "I have paid for the food with good Polish zloty. Probably more than it would fetch at market."

"Exactly what I tried to tell her," Marja remarked indignantly.

"And who are you?" Irina queried coldly.

"Erik Polewski," Isaak answered levelly.

"And what are you doing here?"

"If you recall," Isaak answered, "it rained heavily last night." Irina nodded, confirming that she indeed remembered the storm. "My brother Abel and I were caught on the road without shelter. We sought sanctuary in your barn. We were planning to leave the price of a night's lodging nailed to your gate. When we were leaving, we noticed that some of your bees were massed near the gate. Before we could find another exit, my brother was stung by one of the bees."

Irina looked unimpressed. "Why are two young men out on the road to Krakow from Vilno in times like these? The conscription details have seriously depleted our young men. Those who are left are ill, injured or working with the insurgents. You look neither ill nor injured." There was a cold menace in the woman's voice which made Isaak nervous.

"My brother is very ill, Madam," he replied hesitantly.

"And you? You are healthy and very smooth of speech. Too smooth to be the workman that your mode of dress proclaims. You are a stranger here. And strangers are suspect in times of turmoil."

"I realize that, Madam," Isaak responded. "But we are laborers, nonetheless. Both my brother and I have worked as mill hands. I have done carpentry."

At this, Irina came forward, seized both his hands, and looked at them expecting to prove him guilty of falsehood. She was greatly disappointed to find them the hands of a workman, roughened and calloused though scrubbed clean of soil. She nodded and looked deep into his eyes as though she could read in them an answer to the puzzle he posed.

"Your hands speak in your favor," she said. "They tell of honest toil. And my niece showed me the money you gave her in exchange for your food. And yet, despite this, there is something about you that I cannot trust."

"I mean no harm to you or yours, I assure you," Isaak answered.

Still doubtful, the woman nonetheless bade him join them at lunch. While Marja set the table, Irina sliced bread and cheese and ladled clover honey into a cruet. Isaak was assigned the tasks of carrying in a can of recently drawn milk and of pumping some water from the well.

As Isaak returned with the milk, Marja, who had just finished setting the table, turned to him with very real concern.

"Jan has never been this late before. What can be keeping him?"

"Perhaps there was some delay in his route," Isaak suggested. "Perhaps he picked up an additional customer."

Marja shook her head, totally unconvinced. She went to the window and peered out hoping to catch sight of her brother's milk cart. As she was about to turn away in frustration, her search was rewarded. She turned to Isaak, jubilant. "He's here, finally." With that she ran from the kitchen calling out, "Aunt Irina, Jan is back."

Jan joined the family in the kitchen and then stopped abruptly, surprised to see a stranger there with his sister and his aunt.

Marja, seeing her brother safe and sound, ran to embrace him, overcome with relief. She had experienced serious misgivings due to his delayed return. "Thank God you're safe," she exulted, still hugging him enthusiastically.

"Indeed," Irina commented, "we began to fear you were lost."

"I was nearly something worse than lost," Jan said with a slight shudder. "I was stopped and questioned by the militia at the border. My cart was searched and then the militia commander questioned me at length. He acted quite suspicious." Jan turned to Isaak, his expression one of concerned inquiry.

Marja hastened to answer the unspoken question in her brother's eyes. "This is Erik Polewski, Jan," she said.

Isaak extended his hand in greeting to the tall fair-haired young man so like Marja in feature and build. "A pleasure to meet you," Isaak said respectfully. "I am in your debt and that of your sister. I truly believe she saved my brother's life."

Jan extended his hand in greeting but continued to look puzzled.

Marja attempted to explain. "His brother was stung by one of our bees. They were caught in the storm and stayed in our barn."

"As I explained, we were planning to leave money to compensate for a night's lodging. I regret that events determined otherwise."

"I hope your brother is much better by now," Jan said earnestly. "Some people are sensitive to bee stings and they can rarely even be fatal."

"Your sister is an excellent nurse. She seems to have done everything necessary."

"Good," Jan responded. "Why don't you and your brother join us for lunch? I'm certain there's more than enough." He looked significantly at his aunt whose angry stare fell before the determined expression of her nephew.

"My brother is asleep at the moment," Isaak answered. "Perhaps I can take him something later."

When they sat at table it was Irina who led the grace before the meal. The three Uniate Catholics crossed themselves as was their custom. Isaak bowed his head and prayed in silence, uncomfortably aware of Irina's eyes riveted upon him.

"You do not make the sign of the cross like a good Christian," she said accusingly.

"Customs differ, Madam," Isaak replied, meeting her accusing stare. "But only God can judge the sincerity of prayer."

"Well said, sir," Jan remarked approvingly. "The Russians try to make every people they govern fit into their mould. They outlaw our language, disallow our customs, and deprive our teachers of employment unless they learn to teach our children in Russian. Individual difference has almost become a capital crime."

"Silence," Irine commanded. "Would you bring their wrath down upon us? Who knows what ears may be poised to catch an unwary word and report it to the authorities?" Irina's glance darted furtively toward Isaak as she spoke. He instinctively felt her hostility and sensed that it would be even more openly expressed if she suspected that he and Adam were Jewish. Isaak wondered if their forged papers would be of any value in that event.

The meal continued for some minutes in an atmosphere of strained silence. Finally Isaak excused himself from the table, saying that he wished to share his portion with his brother.

It was just at sundown that Marja came to the barn. With professional objectivity she unwrapped Adam's bandage and inspected the site of the sting wound. Thanks to her earlier ministrations, much of the redness and swelling had subsided. Adam's breathing had returned to normal and he seemed measurably stronger than be had earlier in the day. After completing the re-bandaging, Marja asked Adam: "Do you feel well enough to get up and walk about?"

"I think so," he responded.

Isaak helped him to his feet and stood by as Adam tried a few tentative steps, ready to come to his aid if he should falter.

"That feels much better," Adam remarked. "My legs seem like legs again instead of butter." He turned to Marja. "It's all thanks to your generosity and care. I cannot thank you enough."

"Don't thank me just yet," Marja said. She glanced at Isaak questioningly and then went to pick up the tray of food she had brought. "You've no idea the controversy you two have provoked between my aunt and my brother," she remarked. "Aunt Irina is all in favor of handing you over to the Russian authorities to show them what good citizens we are. Especially after what happened to Jan this morning." As she spoke, she distributed bread, cheese and sausage. Each brother, Marja noted, enthusiastically consumed bread and cheese, but carefully avoided eating the sausage.

Adam, puzzled, asked, "What happened to Jan?"

"The militia searched him and his delivery cart," Isaak answered.

"What were they searching for?"

"Whatever incriminating evidence they could find," Marja answered. "Anything from subversive pamphlets to arms for the insurgents. I don't think they really knew for certain."

"More of the same harassment," Adam said heatedly. "They arrested students in Warsaw for singing patriotic songs." He was immediately silent, wondering how much he had inadvertently betrayed.

"Yes," Isaak agreed quickly. "We got that far by train before we realized that our funds were low and that we'd never make it to Krakow unless we found a less costly means of travel."

"So," Adam said, "we joined a work crew and helped repair a bridge for a while."

"You're very adaptable and clever," Marja noted. "You're also Jewish, aren't you?"

Adam looked up from his meal and stared at the beautiful girl seated in the hay before him. She took the slice of sausage from his plate and held it up.

"Is it important?" Isaak asked.

"Isn't it to you? Isn't that why you're trying to get out of Russian territory?"

Adam paused thoughtfully. "Our family is still _in_ Russian territory," he answered.

Marja looked at the two young men with new understanding. She could sympathize with their hardships, especially after the treatment to which her brother had been subjected.

Isaak turned to her urgently. "Has your aunt sent for the militia?"

"Not to my knowledge," Marja replied. "Besides, my brother is violently opposed to it. And he's the head of the family now that my father is dead. I don't think she'd openly defy him."

"But she might do so underhandedly. We'd better not risk it. If you can walk," Isaak said, turning to Adam, "we'd best leave now while we still can."

Marja stood up. "My brother knows of some caves quite near here. That might be a safer place for you to spend the night. I'll talk to him."

When he heard of Marja's proposal, Jan enthusiastically agreed. In fact, Marja's suggestion to transfer the two brothers to the partially subterranean caves at the boundary of the farm property anticipated his own plans. After the confrontation with the militia, he was prepared to expect anything.

As soon as Adam and Isaak were relocated, Jan drew Isaak aside. "I suggest you two stay put tonight. No matter what you may hear outside, don't return to the farm. And don't wander about. It's easy to get lost in here. Marja or I will come and tell you when I can come back for you and your brother."

Isaak nodded. "The sooner we're out of Congress Poland, the better."

\* \* \*

The Russian militia descended upon the Miatowski farm before dawn the next day. Everything but the bee hives was searched. Even the militia commandant was not willing to risk inciting a colony of bees to swarm in anger.

"If you'll tell me what it is you want," Jan offered helpfully, "I'll try to help you find it."

"If it's here," the commandant answered gruffly, "my men will find it. And when they do, all of you will have some explaining to do!"

"Here, sir, you will find nothing but a dairy farm," Jan said calmly.

"If that's true, you have nothing to fear," the commandant promised serenely. His serenity vanished when his men, after a two-hour search, could find nothing suspicious anywhere on the premises.

The displeased senior officer closely questioned his second-in-command. "You're certain there is nothing?"

"Everything has been searched and searched again, Commandant Muhailovich. There is nothing and no one. All is as the young farmer stated. There are only his sister, his aunt and himself besides the dairy livestock and two dogs." The man saluted his senior officer nervously.

"And yesterday there was nothing in the cart but milk," Jan said vehemently. "Just as it was the day before that and the week before that. Just as it always is. I'm a dairy farmer, nothing else."

"We have owned and worked this farm for five generations," Irina added, glaring malevolently at the commandant. "This family's honor has never been questioned before." Marja, beside her, nodded.

"That may be," the Commandant responded. "We shall see." The tall dark-haired mustached commandant bowed slightly to each of the women, then turned and strode smoothly off to join his men. Only when they were out of sight did Jan dare to give vent to his innermost feelings. He spat upon the ground where the commandant had stood.

Irina turned to her nephew. "They did not find our two guests," she remarked significantly.

"Which means they are no longer our guests," Jan responded with an enigmatic smile. "You two go back to the house."

"I'll help you load the cart," Marja offered.

Jan nodded, embraced his aunt and escorted her to the veranda.

When he and his sister were alone, he said to her, "Never mind the cart today. I'll see to it. Go and tell our guests to stay where I've left them at the end of the main passage. They are not to move about the cave. Tell them not to show themselves until they hear my cart coming. When I whistle the first several notes of Chopin's Revolutionary Etude and then repeat them, they are to come out. Only then. Is that understood?"

"Yes, Jan," she replied, "but why such elaborate precautions?"

"I don't want the location or the extent of those caves divulged to strangers," Jan answered.

Something in his tone of voice filled Marja with dread. "Jan, you're not a part of this rebellion, are you?"

"Marja, what are you saying? In times such as these, a quick means of escape across the border that is known only to us and our dead ancestors is an invaluable asset, one I do not wish jeopardized by our two Jewish lodgers. How and when they left will remain our secret, little sister."

Jan began the arduous task of transferring to his horse-drawn cart the tall heavy milk cans, used for the transport of large quantities of milk, that Marja had filled before the Russians' visit. He was proud of his delivery cart which had been purchased less than a year ago to better meet the orders of his growing roster of customers. His brightly painted cart was well known throughout the community, on both sides of the border. Why, he wondered, this sudden interest in his activities on the part of the Russian authorities? He had been more than careful, taking no one into his confidence, contacting only those known to the 'City Committee' network throughout Congress Poland. They were a select group, scrupulously trustworthy. Yet, might one of them, under duress, have betrayed him? He tried to push those thoughts from his mind as he finished his preparations.

He was doing a favor for people whom few Poles would have helped under similar circumstances. He meant to ask one in return.

Jan took from his pocket a note he had written to his contact in Krakow. He placed it with a packet of documents he had received from his contact in Luow earlier in the week. He secreted the packet in a leather pouch and placed it between the double layer of floor boards he had had constructed at the bottom of his cart. That done, he finished loading the milk cans, mounted the driver's box, and set off into a glorious late fall sunrise.

As he drove, his thoughts were disturbed. For almost a year, in addition to managing and working his father's dairy farm, he had acted as a courier for the Nationalist cause. This second career he had kept from his sister and his aunt, but it was becoming progressively more difficult to maintain that secrecy. He knew that his aunt would not approve. She might even feel tempted to betray him to the authorities although, from a practical point of view, that would be an unrealistic course of action for her to follow. She and Marja alone could not take care of the dairy business.

The visit of the militia that morning had filled Jan with apprehension. Coming on the heels of his interrogation the preceding day, he was sure the visitation did not bode well for him or his family. Despite the beauties of the morning, the future looked bleak indeed to Jan Miatowski as he went about his milk deliveries.

Two hours later, having completed his local itinerary, Jan approached the Galician border checkpoint. He waved as the familiar faces of the guards came into view. He was expecting an answering smile despite yesterday's incident. Instead, the expressions he met were uniformly grim. As he approached the lowered barrier, Commandant Muhailovich, the officer in charge, stepped out of the guard's lodge. He greeted Jan with a show of warmth.

"I see we meet again, young sir," Muhailovich said in greeting. "Is that the milk you deliver each morning?"

"Part of it, Commandant," Jan answered levelly.

"Some has already been delivered?"

"Yes, sir," Jan responded. "As we discussed earlier today, these remaining cans are the ones I deliver on the other side of the border."

"You're running late, aren't you?"

"Thanks to your visit this morning, sir," Jan answered resignedly, "but if I hurry, I think I can make up the time."

Jan was careful not to glance at any of the guards lest he betray the one who was his confidant and coconspirator.

The commandant looked Jan over appraisingly, then stepped back. "Check the milk cart," he ordered over his shoulder.

Two soldiers approached the cart, but a grizzled sergeant stepped forward and intercepted them. "I'll handle this," the sergeant said gruffly, motioning for the soldiers to turn back. The sergeant began shoving the cans briskly back and forth. He struck the sides of each can to check for a hollow compartment, then loosened the lids and looked inside a few of them. Only Jan noticed the small canvas package which the sergeant dropped surreptitiously into the cart between the displaced cans.

The sergeant then walked over to the commandant, saluted briskly, and reported. "Only milk, sir. Nothing more."

"Good," the commandant said smiling. "Perhaps your neighbors just envy your prosperity, Mer Miatowski. Who knows? These are troubled times. One cannot be too cautious."

"Of course, sir," Jan replied. "May I go now?"

"You may, but remember what I said about caution."

The commandant slapped the milk horse smartly on the flank and set him off at a trot.

Jan fully expected to be followed. When he heard the sound of horses' hooves behind him on the Krakow road, he didn't turn around. Moments later, Muhailovich and a contingent of militia pulled him off the road.

Jan smiled. "Have you forgotten something, Commandant?"

Muhailovich pointedly ignored the question. Instead he directed two soldiers to once more search the cart. The sergeant walked over to where the commandant stood waiting impatiently, and saluted.

"Commandant," he whispered. "He knows we're watching him now. He's been warned. He wouldn't dare transport anything today."

The commandant nodded and walked over to where Jan sat. "You are either very naive or very clever, young man." He signaled to his men. They mounted their horses and rode back the way they had come.

Jan drove onward, well past the far end of the caves which were hidden among rocks and brush growth. As he drove, he "accidentally" dropped a small pouch of coins. He proceeded slowly until he was well out of sight of the foothills.

Nearly a half hour later, Jan drew rein. He turned the wagon about and doubled back. This time, however, he followed a different course through the foothills that enabled him to observe the road below and the heights above. A few minutes later, he stopped and waited. Presently, he saw the commandant leading his small party back along the lower road towards the border checkpoint where they had stopped him earlier.

Then he heard a whistled signal. He was intrigued to see two more parties of militiamen join the commandant's group from other points along the road, one from the mountain path above and the other from a break in the foothills further on. The contingent reassembled and rode back the way Jan had originally come that morning. Still Jan waited. He was taking no chances. He hid the horse and the cart in a small clearing ringed by boulders and continued along the path on foot.

When he reached the cave entrance, he paused to be certain he was alone, then pushed aside the sheltering bushes, knelt down, crawled inside and whistled softly the prearranged signal, stopping abruptly and then repeating it. Isaak came out of hiding first and when he saw Jan he beckoned for Adam to join him.

Signaling for silence. Jan crawled out first.

Satisfied that all was clear, he motioned for Adam and Isaak to join him. Crouching and crawling through thick brush and shrubs, they made their way to the clearing where Jan had left the wagon.

Jan quickly emptied the contents of two of the largest milk cans into the brush. Adam and Isaak climbed into the still-wet containers, crouching to conform to the height of the cans. Once they were inside, Jan reset the lids in such a way as to allow for the passage of air.

Then, Jan drove the wagon back to the place where he had dropped the purse of coins. When he reached that point, near the junction of the side route he had followed and the main road to Krakow, he halted the wagon. He got out and pretended to search about for a few brief moments, then retrieved the purse and attached it to his belt, shaking his head. He jumped back into the wagon as if anxious to make up for lost time. He never stopped again until he crossed the border.

A short distance from the east gate of Krakow, Jan Miatowski stopped his cart. He climbed down and opened the lids of the two milk cans containing the Marjzendiak brothers.

Adam raised his head cautiously. "Is it safe to come out?"

At the same time Isaak emerged shading his eyes from the bright sunlight. "Is this Krakow?"

Jan laughed and nodded his head. "Yes," he answered, "to both questions. We've crossed the frontier. There is Krakow." He pointed toward the city's ancient walls that had stood for nearly six centuries.

Adam and Isaak stretched, gratefully relieving their cramped muscles. Isaak's pulse quickened with excitement as he viewed the city around which his hopes had long centered.

Krakow in 1862 was an ancient city in transition. Once capital of Poland, it had been the center of the sovereign Republic Of Krakow confirmed by the Congress of Vienna in 1812 and abolished in 1845. It had long been a cultural and educational center. In Krakow's buildings and monuments, the city's heroes from Casimir the Great to Copernicus were commemorated and honored. Here, the politically advanced theories of Andrezez Frycz Modrzereski and the poetic masterpieces of Jan Kochanowski had come into being.

As Jan, Adam and Isaak presented their passes and were waved through the gates by the uniformed Austrian guard, Isaak grinned broadly and clapped Adam on the shoulder.

"We made it, brother," he chortled. "We're truly in Krakow!"

Adam smiled in agreement. "It hardly seems possible." He turned to Jan. "We wouldn't have made it without you and your sister," he said warmly.

"Our pleasure," Jan answered. "It is not the first time I've assisted someone who wanted to leave Russian Poland. It probably won't be the last."

"Judging from this morning," Isaak warned soberly, "you're in for a perilous future."

"I'm afraid you're right," Jan agreed ruefully. "The border is tightening more every day. Still, one must continue to try."

Isaak shook Jan's hand vigorously. "If I can ever return the favor, it would be an honor," he said.

Jan studied Isaak for a moment. "As a matter of fact," Jan said finally, "because of all the delays this morning, there's an errand I won't be able to carry out." He reached into the back of the cart and retrieved the leather-bound packet he had hidden earlier between the double floor boards. "I wonder if you could deliver this for me. The location is less than a kilometer from here." He pointed to the address written on the label of the packet.

"I'd be glad to oblige," Isaak answered, "but unfortunately, I'm not familiar with the city."

Jan readily explained the directions and, a short time later, guided by Adam's unfailing sense of direction, the two brothers reached their destination. Isaak knocked on the door and within a few moments was greeted by a tall, slender young man whose manner was pleasant, but distant.

"Can I help you?"

"A friend asked me to deliver a package to this address," Isaak replied. "There's no name so I don't know to whom it's to be given. I trust you'll know for whom it's intended."

The man glanced up and down the street, then nodded to Isaak and took the package from him. "Thank you," he said and closed the door.

Isaak rejoined Adam at the end of the street. "I wonder what was in that package."

"The matter is best forgotten. We've done our good deed," Adam commented. "I think now we'd better find Jada and Zaccahreus."

"Well spoken, brother," Isaak agreed. "We've kept them waiting long enough."

Adam withdrew from his pocket an address which Ephraim had given to him on the morning of their departure from Warsaw. "Our cousins Jada and Zaccahreus live at seven-two-nine Stanislaw Street," he read, then looked at Isaak. "Which way do we go?"

Isaak grinned lopsidedly. "Why ask me? You're the scout on this expedition. One thing I can tell you," he added. "since there is no ghetto here, Krakow doesn't have a true shtetl. The Jewish community isn't strictly geographically defined."

"Cousin Jacob was attending the university when he died," Adam pointed out. "It seems unlikely that the family would have lived too far from the campus."

"You're probably right," Isaak agreed. "Even if they had to move, I think they'd make every effort to make things as accessible for Jacob as possible. According to Father, they were extremely proud of him."

As the two brothers walked together toward what seemed to be the center of town, a church bell sounded the hour, nine o'clock. As the last echoes of the bell faded into silence, a bugle call sounded from the church tower.

Adam looked at Isaak questioningly. "What is that?"

Isaak smiled knowingly. He had read everything he could find on Krakow, its background, its history, and its politics. Savoring the sweet notes of the bugle, he answered, "That must be the heynal. It sounds hourly from St. Mary's church just after the bell."

Just at that moment, the bugler suddenly stopped playing in mid-note.

Adam waited for the music to continue, then turned to Isaak, confused. "Why did he stop playing?"

"The bugle call is played in tribute to a legendary bugler of the thirteenth century. The city was under attack by the Tartars. The bugler played the heynal to warn the people. His throat was pierced by a Tartar arrow at that point. Ever since, the bugle call stops on his last note." Adam shook his head in amazement at such a custom.

Within a few minutes, the brothers had reached the University of Krakow. The Jageillonian architectural style, a contribution of early Polish kings, was preserved in the buildings of the imposing compound. Both Adam and Isaak felt a sense of energy and excitement as they walked through the campus.

Adam stopped near a fountain, his breathing rapid and somewhat ragged. "Wait up for a minute, Isaak," he said. "I need a little rest."

Remembering the bee incident and its devastating effect on Adam, Isaak was immediately concerned. "Of course you must not exert yourself too much, Adam," he answered. "You're probably still feeling the effects of that sting." He looked about the campus, trying to gain some clue to how close they might be to their destination. "We're probably fairly near to Cousin Jada's now," he said encouragingly.

At that moment, two young students, engrossed in earnest conversation, walked by. Isaak beckoned to them. One stopped, the other, apparently younger, moved closer in answer to Isaak's signal.

"Yes?"

"We're new in town," Isaak began. "Could you direct us?" Isaak showed the young man the address.

The student glanced at the paper, then nodded. "I know that area," he said reassuringly. "Go down this street," he continued, pointing off to his left. "Stanislaw Street is two streets down. Turn right. That address will be on your left."

"Thank you," Isaak replied. "And one more thing. Can you tell where the registrar's office is located?"

"It's in the administration building, the tall building at the end of the quadrangle." He pointed towards a majestic edifice towering above its companions at one end of the square.

"Thanks again," Isaak said as the student hurried away. "I hope we shall meet again."

* * *

As Adam and Isaak drew near the home of Jada and Zaccahreus Polewski, they could hear the notes of a pan pipe coming from the rear of the building. Ephraim had told his sons that Zaccahreus Polewski prided himself on being a self-taught virtuoso of that instrument. The sound of the pipe was an auditory beacon guiding them the final steps to their new home.

Jada and Zaccahreus, an engaging couple in their early fifties, greeted their cousins warmly. They still felt keenly the untimely death of their only son Jacob who had been a student at the University. As Ephraim had predicted, the arrival in their home of not one but two young men quickly brought the sunshine back into their lives.

As Jada prepared breakfast, Isaak recounted their adventurous crossing of the Russian-Austrian frontier.

"We're delighted to have you here safe and sound," Zaccahreus said. "From what you've told us, it sounds as though it can be only a matter of time until the militia catch your friend Jan delivering something more than milk."

"Thank God they didn't catch him delivering you," Jada said prayerfully.

"We've been worried about the two of you," Zaccahreus admitted. "We expected you over a week ago."

Adam was genuinely surprised at this news. "You were expecting us for that long?"

"Ephraim wrote to us on the eve of Rosh Hashanah," Zaccahreus explained. "He said two near relatives had promised to look in on us on their way back to school."

"We knew it must be you," Jada added.

Adam smiled at Isaak. Each knew what the other was thinking. Ephraim never left anything to chance. He always double checked every item in the ledger.

By the end of the following week, both Adam and Isaak were deeply immersed in their studies at the University. Adam was attending the Medical Akademy; Isaak, the Institute of Advanced Akademic Studies. Although they were fulfilling their ambitions, both were homesick. They wrote to Elana and Ephraim but were uncertain whether the letter would truly be delivered.

In late December, Adam and Isaak received the following letter from Ephraim:

"My dear sons,

I trust this letter finds you well and happy. Needless to say, we miss you both. However, we are glad you are safe from harm and beyond the reach of the Tsar's authority.

No doubt by now word has reached you of the tragedy that befell the Stare Miasto on Yom Kippur. The conscription agents came just before sundown and surprised us in the synagogue. I am unable to accurately report how many were taken. Those who resisted were beaten and chained. One of that number, Morris Cohen, died of his injuries. Finally, after more than a week, his body was returned to his family.

Most of the young men have been sent away to distant places on the Russian frontier. It is ironic that this is the one way large groups of Jews are permitted to venture beyond the Pale of Settlement.

In the midst of so much anguish and uncertainty, perhaps it is wrong of me to rejoice on behalf of my own children when those of so many of my friends and neighbors are forced to fight on distant battle fronts. But I do rejoice, as does your mother, that you are safely pursuing your studies. She is well and sends her love, as does Leah.

Be well, my sons. Study and prepare yourselves for the future, for it will come despite the adversities of the present.

My love to your cousins Jada and Zaccahreus.

May Adonai bless you always,

Your Loving Father,

Ephraim."

Ephraim's letter made no mention of the fact that the day after the Yom Kippur incident, conscription agents had come to the Marjzendiak home seeking Adam and Isaak. Ephraim, knowing his mail would be monitored, was careful not to write to Krakow until he received word from his cousin Jada that his sons were beyond the reach of Russian authority.

## CHAPTER ELEVEN

## UPRISING

The Hanukah holidays which the Marjzendiak family celebrated that December were sharply in contrast to the festivities of the year before. With part of the family absent and with the mood of foreboding and unrest that dominated Warsaw, there seemed little to celebrate. Nonetheless, Ephraim and Elana did all in their power to make the holiday a joyous one for their two younger children.

All the traditional foods that were normally prepared to celebrate the season were in evidence. The potato latkes that were Leah's favorite at this time of year were prepared and served with apple sauce and Elana even managed to obtain a supply of soft cheese, which she crumbled and served with the latkes. No meat was served at this meal. Instead, there was a variety of vegetables, and for dessert there was a kichlen frosted with sugar and further sweetened with currants.

Of course, dinner was preceded by the lighting of the menorah. There was the lighting of the shamash candle and then the candle representing the first of the eight days on which the lights burned in the temple were duly commemorated. Elana wore her new fringe-bordered white veil for the occasion, and Leah, following her mother's example, wore the blue velvet dress that her parents had given her the year before, and the blue necklace, Isaak's gift, that accessorized it so charmingly. She was pleased to note that although she was a year older, the garment seemed to fit her better now than it had before, a testament to Elana's wisdom in cutting the garment along generous lines to allow for her daughter's growth and to prolong the usefulness of the present. Leah helped Elana clear the table and then after dinner she and Michael played dreidel games. Ephraim and Elana sat by the fire, watching them. Tonight, the gifts had been simple tokens, cookies and coins for the two children, a chain bracelet for Elana and for Ephraim, a black silk hand-sewn yarmulke his wife had made herself.

It was clear that none of the family felt like indulging in extensive festivities with two of its members far away from home. They all went early to bed on that first night, though only Michael went promptly to sleep.

*  *  *

As had been widely anticipated for months, an insurrection erupted in Congress Poland on January 22, 1863. The conscription, initiated by the Russian military governor and ratified by the Marquis Wielopolski, had ultimately precipitated the very result it had been implemented to avert. The Nationalist elements were driven to open conflict by what they viewed as intolerable repression. However, unlike the large-scale conflict of 1830, this uprising was poorly organized and essentially uncoordinated, a conglomerate of guerilla attacks which was doomed to failure from its inception.

In March of 1863 the confrontations between the insurgents and the Russian military forces moved into the streets. The main streets were soon converted to a no-man's land into which only the courageous or the desperate dared to venture. Business came to a virtual standstill. The economy of Congress Poland suffered accordingly.

Meanwhile, the various factions of the population became further polarized as the puppet Council of State enacted sweeping agrarian reforms which effectively transferred large parcels of land from the aristocratic landowners to their former tenants, the peasants. The blatant bribery worked quite efficiently. Not only did the peasants fail to support the revolution, in some instances they even served as Russian agents and informers.

The desperation of the revolutionaries was further aggravated by the failure of England, France, Sweden, and Holland, all of whom had expressed support for the rebels' cause, to exert either diplomatic, economic or military pressure on the Russians.

Even at the head office of the Bank of Poland, the forces of war were making their influence felt. At one o'clock on an afternoon in mid-March Ephraim Marjzendiak and Franz Pietrowski stood in the bank's central foyer, surveying the lobby, empty except for the bank personnel and the two guards on duty.

"We may as well close for the day," Franz remarked to Ephraim, "and maybe for the duration. Who is going to brave that street out there to attend to something as mundane as money?"

"Only the favored few who have money enough to attend to," Ephraim responded. "The old rules don't seem to apply anymore, as our former First Minister has learned to his cost," Ephraim continued, keenly aware that the Marquis Wielopolski, following the outbreak of rebellion, had been recalled from his post and had permanently retired from public life. This man, with his intense Polish patriotism, had proved to be a friend of the Polish Jews and Ephraim was saddened by his fall from power, although, with the course events had been pursuing, that had been the inevitable outcome.

"This whole thing is beyond belief," Franz remarked. "It's as though the revolutionaries are bent on destroying themselves and all the rest of us with them."

"Every afternoon when I leave here," Ephraim noted gravely, "I wonder if I'll manage to get home alive!"

Franz Pietrowski glanced at his assistant, his eyes reflecting both surprise and admiration. "And still you return?"

"I return because it's my obligation," Ephraim said simply. "You do the same."

"I'm the Commissioner," Franz said with dignity.

His promotion to Senior Commissioner had conferred upon him both greater prestige and heavier responsibilities. "Of course I come and go by carriage which may or may not be safer than traveling on foot."

"Nothing is safe under the present conditions," Ephraim remarked.

As Ephraim and Franz spoke, two well-dressed men entered the bank's main lobby, followed by a middle-aged woman. The men approached the teller's window opposite which Ephraim and Franz were standing. The woman hesitated briefly, then stopped at the patrons' counter where deposit and withdrawal requests were kept in narrow wooden slots. Moments later, two more men, dressed in workman's attire, entered by another door.

Ephraim turned to Franz. "That decision to close may have been premature," he said.

"So it seems," Franz answered, obviously gratified at the sudden surge in business.

At that moment, one of the well-dressed men began to berate the clerk teller who was serving him, accusing her of slowness and ineptitude. Franz stepped forward to intervene but was intercepted by one of the workmen.

"Who's in charge here?" The man's voice was cultured and well-modulated, in marked contrast to his mode of dress.

"I'm the Bank Commissioner," Franz answered.

"Good," the man said and then drew a pistol from inside his clothing. "Then you can be depended upon to maintain order."

The two guards, one stationed near the door, the other near the tellers' block, immediately drew their guns and trained them on the workman. Simultaneously, they moved toward the little group at the center of the foyer. "I advise you to drop that, sir," one of the guards said politely but firmly, as he came within ear shot of the workman.

"Drop your weapons!" The voice was so sharp, it seemed impossible that it could have emanated from the woman at the patrons' counter. Nonetheless, as Ephraim's and Franz's attention was directed toward her, it was apparent that she held an extremely threatening-looking firearm, apparently a large pistol, clutched in both hands. It was pointed meaningfully toward the guards who, taken by surprise, instantly complied, aware that they had no backup. The militiamen usually assigned that duty were engaged in controlling the uprising.

Checking to make certain that no other guards were present, the second workman drew out a small hand gun and pointed it at the terrified clerk.

Franz, obviously frightened by the turn events had taken so rapidly, gaped at the man holding the gun on him. "What do you want?"

"To survive, the revolution needs funds," the man said sharply. "We are here to obtain them."

Franz protested, "You can't do this!"

"Watch carefully and you'll see that we can," the man said with amusement.

Ephraim studied this young man, certain he had seen him at the mill during one of his infrequent visits there. Josef had mentioned his name, but Ephraim could not immediately call it to mind.

The two well-dressed men began to systematically empty the tellers' drawers, while the other workman and the woman stood guard. The man holding the gun on Franz and Ephraim was the obvious leader of the group. He pressed the muzzle of his pistol into Franz's side. "Now, Mer Commissioner," he said in a distinctly authoritative tone, "you will open your vault and hand over the gold reserves."

Franz looked at Ephraim who nodded his head imperceptibly. Franz shrugged helplessly.

"Follow me," he said.

"You, too," the revolutionary leader said to Ephraim.

At the rear of the bank was a stairway leading down to the vault. The three men descended it wordlessly, their footsteps echoing hollowly in the narrow space.

At the bottom of the stairs, the heavy metallic door of the vault shone with a dull luster. Franz spun the dial of the lock a few times and opened the door. He stepped back.

The insurgent leader shoved him forward roughly.

"Start stacking the bars and put them on the floor," he ordered.

Franz Pietrowski stood frozen.

"Do as I tell you," the rebel leader demanded, "or I swear I'll kill you."

"You'd best do as he says," Ephraim warned Franz. "I'll assist him if you like," he said to the rebel leader.

Franz looked at Ephraim as if he felt betrayed.

"Let's get started." he said flatly. As he moved forward to enter the vault, his foot pressed a small button concealed in the pattern of the floor's tile work. The button controlled an alarm which could not be heard in this portion of the building. Ephraim saw this and exchanged glances with Franz as they entered the vault together.

Franz, unaccustomed to physical labor, worked slowly and clumsily. Ephraim's pace was quicker and soon he had built a much larger stack of gold bars than Franz.

"Take these bags and drop the money into them," the leader ordered, pushing two coarse sacks into their hands. At that moment, gunfire erupted from the upper floor of the bank. The rebel leader, realizing that Franz must somehow have triggered the alarm, turned upon him angrily. "I warned you," he snarled, leveling his pistol at the commissioner.

Franz held up his hands in supplication.

"Please," he pleaded.

Ephraim moved behind the rebel leader. In his hand was a gold bar. The metal bar collided with the side of the rebel's skull just as he fired at Franz, partly deflecting his aim.

Franz fell almost in unison with his assailant.

Ephraim rushed to Franz as the militia officers descended the stairs.

"Mer Marjzendiak," the commanding officer of the detachment said, addressing Ephraim, "are you all right?"

"Yes," Ephraim responded, "but Commissioner Pietrowski is wounded and needs medical attention urgently."

The officer signaled two of his men to assist Ephraim, then gestured toward the rebel leader. "Who is this man?"

Recalling belatedly the name Josef had mentioned at the mill, Ephraim answered distractedly: "His name is Viktor Sokorski. Apparently, he led the robbery."

The militia commander kicked Sokorski in the ribs.

"Scum," he said, spitting on the fallen man as Ephraim shuddered at this senseless violence. Together, Ephraim and the two militia men carried the unconscious Franz up the stairs and out of the bank to a waiting militia carriage. This time, Ephraim thought ironically as he transported his friend to the Academy of Medicine Infirmary, Franz was in no condition to refuse medical treatment.

* * *

In a desperate attempt to keep the revolution alive, the young rebel leadership had resorted to robbing stores, private businesses, and even banks. Outraged, the middle class, whose members had never been overly enthusiastic, turned totally against the revolution. The movement also lost the emotional and intellectual support of the aristocracy, partially as a result of the increasing violence and also because of the punitive legislation directed against the upper class landowners.

For the next several weeks, Franz Pietrowski hovered between life and death. Finally, his condition stabilized and he embarked upon the slow road to recovery. Throughout this period, Ephraim was put in charge of the bank, directing repairs resulting from damage occasioned by the fighting in the streets, and managing the daily operation, once the repairs were completed and the bank was reopened for business.

By June, Franz was able to leave the hospital and return home. His first visitor was Ephraim. Franz received him on the veranda of the Pietrowski estate, Mira at his side.

"I can't tell you how good it is to see you looking so well, Franz," Ephraim greeted his superior.

"That's thanks to you, Ephraim," Franz answered enthusiastically. "That was very brave of you, overpowering that rebel, Sokorski."

"I wish I had struck him sooner," Ephraim said regretfully. "I was certain I recognized him, although at first I couldn't remember who he was or why he seemed familiar."

"Sokorski," Franz repeated sadly. "They're an important family. One doesn't expect a member of such a family to be involved in anything like that. But then, there was the Wishnieski boy in that attempted assassination."

"One hardly knows what to expect these days," Mira remarked. "People I thought I knew well I've come to look upon almost as total strangers. And family names are no assurance. This rebellion has split families apart, turned brothers against each other, parents against children. Even among our own servants, Fedya Borovska, who came to us from the

Wishnieskis when they moved away, has turned in her son Peter to the militia. I can scarcely believe it."

Franz looked pained. "I know," he said. "Has she given any reasons?"

"She won't discuss it," Mira answered, "and I don't pry into the servants' personal affairs. But her own son! The thought makes me shiver."

Ephraim asked, "Has the young man been tried?"

"He's already been sentenced," Franz replied. "Exiled to Siberia at hard labor for ten years."

Ephraim was shocked. "Such a harsh sentence!"

"These are extraordinary times," Franz commented. "You realize what a considerable risk you take every day just going to the bank. And yet I depend on your doing just that."

"We are both dependent upon you," Mira added, "and very grateful." She nodded to Franz and the two exchanged knowing smiles.

"It's time we demonstrated that gratitude, Ephraim," Franz said expansively. "How does the title Deputy Bank Commissioner strike you?"

Ephraim considered the question for a moment. "Pleasantly," he answered thoughtfully, "but I think you know that titles are not a major objective for me."

"Yes," Franz replied. "I know that. Perhaps that's why it's taken me so long to properly reward your services to me and to the bank. The title is simply a way of giving credit where credit is due. You have acted as Deputy Bank Commissioner throughout my illness. Why not call those endeavors by their proper name?"

Mira rose from her chair. "Precisely! It's long overdue." She reached out to Ephraim. "Come with me," she said. "I have something to show you."

She led the way to the other side of the broad, columned veranda and pointed towards the neighboring property. "From here you can just see the upper floor of the house and a portion of the grounds. Workmen are refurbishing the house completely."

Ephraim blinked. "Madam," he said, "I'm not quite certain I understand."

"It was the least we could do," Mira responded, smiling. "I know I had promised to attend to entailing the taxes. But, after all you've done, Franz and I wanted to help with the repairs as well. The house was in a deplorable state, vandalized beyond belief. There were very few pieces of furniture left, and of course nothing's been done about the grounds. But it's a beginning."

"I hardly know what to say, Madam Pietrowska," Ephraim said humbly.

"Mira," she corrected. "And you needn't say anything." She smiled mischievously. "Besides, this way, Franz and I will always know where to find you."

* * *

As summer advanced, the Nationalists were no nearer their objective of Polish independence than they had been in January when hostilities had first broken out. The common Polish people, caught between opposing forces and faced with food shortages and a stagnant economy, found it increasingly difficult to maintain a passion for national autonomy. Nonetheless, the Marjzendiak lumber mills continued to prosper. Lumber was essential for fortifications and barricades, as well as for rebuilding what the conflict destroyed.

The Bank of Poland was protected from further assault by a special detachment of militia. Each day when Ephraim reached his workplace, he felt as if he had successfully forded a dangerous flood and arrived at a place of safety. The knowledge that Elana's passionately expressed farewells to him each morning were prompted by her fear that she might never see him alive again wounded Ephraim deeply. Nevertheless, he did not outwardly acknowledge either her concern or his own apprehension lest these feelings undermine them both. Instead, the love and devotion which they shared found its expression in the nights that followed those days of trial and terror.

Each evening when Ephraim reached home, Elana would greet him with tender enthusiasm. The mere sight of her elicited in him an intensely pleasurable excitement.

As the hostilities had intensified, Elana had economized in many ways in order to set aside a store of supplies in case of shortage. Lately, she had made a practice of rationing the number of candles on the table at night, thus unintentionally creating a romantic effect.

One evening in late June of 1863 after Leah, supremely mature at age seven, had cleared the table and undertaken the task of putting her twenty-month-old brother to bed, Elana and Ephraim remained seated at the table, their eyes focused on each other. It was a perfect moment set apart in time, an oasis of peace in a desert of disharmony. Silence was prolonged since neither was willing to disturb the fragile balance of thought and feeling which bound them together. Ephraim reached out and gently touched Elana's fingers, outstretched on the table, intertwining them with his. She smiled and turned and laid her head against his shoulder.

"You grow lovelier with every passing year," he whispered. "Every morning when I leave for work, I carry your image in my heart. All day I look forward to seeing you again. Each night I thank Adonai for once more granting me that privilege."

Elana pressed the fingers of her other hand to his lips, alarmed by his words that echoed the dread of her own thoughts. "Adonai is gracious! He will watch over us all. We shall grow old together. And one day you'll look at me and see gray in my hair and lines on my face and wonder how you ever thought of me as lovely."

"Never," Ephraim insisted, shaking his head. "To me you will always be beautiful, just as you are now." He drew back and gazed at her, thrilled by the seductive picture she presented. Then he picked her up in his arms, amazed yet again at how slight she was.

When he laid her on the bed in their room, he carefully removed the pins that held her hair so tidily in place, releasing a bright cascade of reddish gold that fell about her shoulders.

Elana surrendered willingly as Ephraim undid the ties that held her bodice demurely in place. He swept the fabric of her dress downward to reveal her naked breasts.

"When we move into the home I've acquired for us, I'm going to have your portrait painted just like this," he said teasingly.

"What a scandal that would cause," Elana noted wryly. "No, my love, this is the private me solely for your consumption." She reached out and embraced him with both arms, her insistent mouth seeking his. Then she grew thoughtful and serious. "I've gained a bit of weight since you last carried me off to bed," she said.

"I don't notice any difference," he replied, as he drew her into his arms.

"You should!" She lifted her firm, gently pointed breasts in her hands and held them closer to Ephraim, who gazed at them admiringly. "The nipples are darkening now. It's about the time the changes become most visible." She leaned back against the pillow, smiling triumphantly. "Can't you guess what I'm trying to tell you, my love? Soon we shall be blessed with another child."

Ephraim could scarcely contain the sense of wonder and elation that filled him. It overflowed in an excess of erotic hunger that seemed to defy fulfillment. He covered Elana's face and throat and breasts with kisses. She responded eagerly. The ever-present threat of danger, separation, and death accentuated the poignancy of their mutual desire. They clung to each other with an almost desperate hunger, striving in the most intimate terms to communicate the depth of their love and the totality of their mutual commitment.

* * *

By mid July, Senatorska Street had become an armed camp. Nationalist guerrillas, the Reds and the Whites, faced the Tsar's militia in pitched battle. The bank, reopened for less than four months, transacted almost no business. Neither aristocrat nor peasant dared brave that bristling gauntlet on a purely monetary errand. Gunfire punctuated every hour of the day; the rumble of nearby explosions and the acrid aroma that accompanied the blasts lent an air of unreality to the mundane world of banking.

At noon on July 15, Ephraim decided that the risk to both the patrons and the employees under his charge was too great. He closed the bank, advising the employees to hasten to whatever safe quarters they could find. The bank, he announced, would remain closed until the current confrontation was resolved.

After the last employee had departed, Ephraim locked the main doors of the bank and returned to the sanctuary of his own office. Only then did he discover that Mira Pietrowska, whom he had encountered and greeted much earlier that morning, had remained within the bank ever since. He felt certain he had seen her walking toward the rear door. Nevertheless, there she sat behind Ephraim's desk, engrossed in an assortment of documents, a model of calm amidst a sea of storm and turmoil.

Mira smiled and beckoned Ephraim to join her.

"Come and see," she said eagerly. "You and I make an excellent partnership. Behold how our investments prosper."

Ephraim crossed the room and joined her at his desk. He remained standing, not out of servility but because he wanted to maintain an element of distance between them.

"The mills have done extremely well despite this brainless rebellion," Mira said with deep intensity of feeling. "That man Skiljret is a genius at management and he tells me that this uprising favors production rather than undermining it. The demand for top grade wood has more than doubled during the past year. Can you believe that?"

"I can believe that, Madam. In the wake of the madness surrounding us, I can believe almost anything," Ephraim said.

"Truly," Mira remarked. She rose from the chair and moved closer to him. "Nothing can surprise you then?"

She looked up at him, still smiling. Her motives, she told herself, were centered in safeguarding her own and her husband's interests. Still, if a little wayward pleasure could be gained as a corollary to the major objective, so much the better.

Ephraim looked steadily at her for a long moment.

"I believe I said almost anything, Madam Pietrowska," he replied without smiling.

"I've told you before," she chided. "My name is Mira. We are partners, remember? When this madness ends, as it soon must, you and I will have gained a fortune."

"But how many lives will be lost in order that this fortune can be won?"

"Ephraim, lives are going to be lost in this uprising," she said, a hint of exasperation in her voice. "Nothing we do will alter that fact."

"True," Ephraim admitted. "But to profit from the misfortune of so many others seems immoral, even obscene."

As he spoke these words Ephraim recalled some of the scenes he had witnessed lately in his daily journeys between the Stare Miasto and the bank. In 1830 he had been too young to truly understand the nature of the uprising that had claimed the life of his elder brother Joshua. The revolution had seemed to him, until that tragic event, a chance to escape from home. Captured and imprisoned by the Russian forces soon after Joshua's death, the conflict had ended too quickly for Ephraim to become closely acquainted with the full spectrum of horror inherent in battle. However, in the current controversy, Ephraim had grown painfully aware of the devastating physical realities of war. In the present conflict, he had seen men, women, even children lying dead in the streets, their lifeless bodies torn and dismembered by the impact not only of bullets but of exploding bombs.

Mira Pietrowska's words recalled him abruptly to the present. "There are always misfortunes, Ephraim," she said, "and there are always those who profit from them. That is the way of the world. Instead of being a victim, one must learn to take advantage of favorable circumstances when they present themselves. That is the only way to avoid being overwhelmed by misfortune."

Mira's middle class background had shaped her personal philosophy of objectivity and perseverance. She knew, too, that Ephraim Marjzendiak had benefited from seizing opportunity as it offered. However, although she now felt she knew him quite well, she had as yet failed to perceive the basic differences in their outlooks on life.

Ephraim deftly changed the subject, directing his attention to the problem at hand. "How did you come to the city today, Madam?"

"Our coachman brought me most of the way," she answered. "The last few blocks of Senatorska Street are barricaded. We couldn't drive through."

"Is the coachman waiting for you?"

"No. I told him to try to come back at four o'clock as he normally would for Franz. He will wait at Sigismund Square. The militia are letting some traffic pass through there with proper identification."

"Proper identification?"

"I have Franz's passport to enter and leave the city by coach. I take it your papers permit you to travel through the city on foot."

Ephraim nodded in assent. "I wasn't aware there were different sets of papers for different modes of travel," he said.

"From what I can understand, they change the passports from time to time. It's supposed to be a safeguard against infiltration of certain parts of the city by the rebels."

"As you can see, Madam," Ephraim said, "that policy seems to have proved fruitless. The rebels are certainly in the heart of the city at present."

"That's why I came back here. It seemed a safer place to wait 'til Tetrov comes back, about four hours from now." With that she turned back toward the desk, moving gracefully to collect her papers. Her pose, her smile, her tone of voice as she handed them to Ephraim all offered a subtle challenge that was not lost on him.

"You're certain the driver will have no difficulty reaching the Square?"

"So far, he's had no problem," Mira replied. "With this new outbreak of hostilities, one can't be sure of anything."

"Four hours is a long time," Ephraim commented. "How do you propose we spend that time, Madam Pietrowska?"

"I thought I might leave that to you," Mira said, the taunting smile never leaving her lips. "I've heard that Jewish men must always be the dominant force in a relationship."

Alerted by the choice of words, Ephraim moved away from her and toward the window. It afforded him a less than reassuring view of events taking place outside and offered no real answer to the question she had asked.

"If by that you refer to the fact that the Jewish man is the head of his household, Madam, you are quite correct. If I thought we could reach my home in safety, I would offer you its hospitality. As it is, I do not think either the militia or the rebels will let us get that far unchallenged. On the other hand, I do not believe we are totally safe here."

Mira looked about her, somewhat alarmed by his words.

"Judging from the thickness of the walls and those metal bars at the windows," she said, attempting to reassure herself, "I should think this would be our safest refuge."

"Both times your husband has suffered injury since I've known him, it has occurred within this building," Ephraim said.

"What course do you suggest, then?"

"You are Christian, Madam. Do you know if both factions respect the doctrine of sanctuary in the Christian churches here?"

"To my knowledge, none of them have been attacked as yet," Mira replied.

"Which church is nearest to the place where your coachman is to meet you?"

"The Church of the Holy Ghost, I think," Mira said after a moment's consideration.

That name provoked a nightmarish memory for Ephraim. Nevertheless, he responded in a tone that told Mira the matter was decided, "We will wait for your driver there."

Minutes later, Ephraim led Mira out through the exit near Franz's office. Amid sporadic gunfire, they darted down alleyways and side streets on a circuitous route that led toward the main square.

\* \* \*

Throughout the city of Warsaw, the insurgents battled with the Russian militia forces. Meanwhile, the peasants, taking advantage of the breakdown of social order, were looting public buildings and private dwellings, many of which had been vacated in the wake of erupting hostilities. In instances where the trespassers found little to reward their efforts, windows were smashed, furnishings destroyed and the structure set afire. The peasants cheered enthusiastically as the hungry flames devoured the buildings.

Inspired by Rabbi Meisels' Nationalistic sentiments, which he freely expressed in his public speeches and confrontations with the Russian authorities, many Jewish youths had joined the rebels in their frantic and violent efforts to turn the tide in their favor. While the battle raged throughout the city, the militant Rabbi Meisels was at prayer in the Great Synagogue on Tlomacki Place, leading a service of worship and supplication for the success of the rebellion. The service was attended by many of the older residents of the Jewish quarter who supported the rabbi's ideals in principle but lacked the initiative or the energy to venture into the streets in open conflict.

"Remember the days of old," Meisels recited reverently, intoning the words from Deuteronomy designated for that day in the Jewish calendar. "Consider the years of many generations. Ask your father and he will inform you, your grandfather and he will declare unto you." Moses had spoken those same words in his final farewell to his people.

As Rabbi Meisels recited the moving passage, Russian soldiers, sweeping through the Stare Miasto in an effort to eradicate the Jewish rebels, forcefully entered the building.

The quorum of Jewish elders assembled in prayer was at first too stunned to speak out or to resist. Several soldiers roughly seized the rabbi and the two men assisting him. As the soldiers hastily bound the startled men's wrists, the sacred scroll of the Torah was knocked from the rabbi's hands.

Momentarily stunned by this violent desecration, the other men gathered in the synagogue quickly converged upon the Russian intruders. A struggle ensued during which several of the older men were jostled and knocked down. One, the cloth merchant Josef Sumerdjiak, was trampled to death.

Rabbi Meisels called out to his followers to return to their seats and implored the soldiers to free his hands until he could attend to Sumerdjiak who lay prone and bleeding at their feet. The Russian commander ignored the request, and ordered his men to take the three prisoners outside.

More soldiers entered and several other of the Jewish men were also seized. When the Rabbi's cousin, Samuel Baruch, resisted, he was shot to death where he stood. In less than five minutes, two men had been killed and several injured.

While the militia conducted a door-to-door search for insurgents and rebel sympathizers, the raggle-taggle band of Polish peasants that had followed the troops into the

Jewish quarter enthusiastically pursued their own objectives, looting and destroying what property they did not appropriate. Any resistance by the residents of the Stare Miasto was met with swift and violent reprisals. The terrified residents soon filled the narrow streets of the quarter. The acrid odor of buildings being put to the torch added measurably to the peoples' anguish. The Gentile citizens of Warsaw fared no better. Many of their homes and places of business were simultaneously being looted and destroyed.

In the Church of the Holy Ghost, Mira Pietrowska knelt at the communion rail, her head bowed. Nearby, standing in prayer after the custom of his people, Ephraim Marjzendiak tried to close his consciousness to the unaccustomed surroundings. Adonai may be sincerely worshipped, he reminded himself, in any setting. Any place of devotion, even one dressed in unfamiliar trappings, was worthy of respect and deference.

It had taken Ephraim and Mira nearly an hour to travel the half mile from the Bank of Poland on Senatorska Street to this church fronting the main square of the city. Throughout that perilous journey, through side streets and alleyways, dodging sites of conflict and gunfire, Ephraim had been torn between his obligation to protect Mira Pietrowska and a desire to be with his family and friends in the Jewish quarter.

The barricades which he and Mira had seen had been draped with lifeless bodies, some still bleeding. For perhaps the thousandth time, Ephraim had offered a silent prayer of thanks for the inspiration that had caused him to send Adam and Isaak to Krakow.

The waiting seemed interminable, more so to Ephraim than to Mira, who found solace and a sense of belonging in her current surroundings. The combination of uncertainty as to the fate of his loved ones and the sense of being even now an outsider, a stranger in a place of sanctuary, stretched the three-hour wait to an eternity for Ephraim.

Much to Mira's dismay, she and Ephraim had gained access to the closed church by breaking and entering through a rear window. She was relieved, however, to find that thus far the church premises had remained inviolate from the opposing forces.

Ephraim's keen hearing translated every sound outside the church into a potential threat. For this reason, it was he who first noted the metallic clang of horseshoes on the cobbled pavement. He moved quickly but cautiously to the side door and peered out into the street.

Mira reached his side within seconds and gazed out in the direction which he indicated, recognizing both her carriage and driver in one brief glance. She started out the door, but her forward impetus was checked by Ephraim who placed a restraining arm across the doorway.

"We must move with caution," he warned. "The square is far from safe despite the absence of barricades here. I noticed snipers on the walls of some of the buildings as we passed."

Mira shivered at the thought.

"I will see you safely to your coach," Ephraim said. "Then I will try to find a way home." He hoped there were no barricades at the Stare Miasto.

Mira studied Ephraim, her glance a strange blend of cool speculation and compassion. "I'll have Tetrov take you there. By carriage it will not take long. Franz' passport will get us past the military roadblocks."

"Passports may be of no value in the present circumstances. It depends on who has possession of which streets," Ephraim said. "I'll find my way. Don't worry."

"I won't allow you to take such a risk," Mira began, but she stopped in mid sentence, pointing ahead of them. Ephraim's eyes followed her pointing finger to a wall that stood near the church. An armed man stood glaring down at them, his rifle poised to fire. Ephraim pulled Mira back inside the church.

Seconds later, they heard a burst of rifle fire. Impulsively, Mira peered out. Their would-be assassin lay dead in the street. Mira crossed herself.

Ephraim, equally aware of the impersonal aspects of the fortunes of war, felt a kindred sense of pity, but it was tinged with relief. Now there was one less danger to be faced.

Ephraim stepped into the street, waited, then took Mira's hand. They ran across the square to the concourse where her carriage waited.

Ephraim quickly assisted Mira into the coach. As he was about to close the door, Mira seized his arm.

"Get in," she said. Ephraim shook his head. Mira repeated heatedly, "I said get in!" Reluctantly, Ephraim complied.

"Take us to the old town," Mira shouted at Tetrov.

"But that's north of here, Madam," the driver protested. "That's where the fighting is most fierce!"

Mira saw the look of alarm in Ephraim's eyes. "Then we'd best start," she answered the coachman curtly, as much to speed them on their way as to forestall further disturbing revelations.

Mira Pietrowska's driver, Tetrov, reluctantly applied the goad to the horses and set off. As they neared the Stare Miasto, they began to smell the acrid scent of smoke. Turning a corner, they discovered its origin.

In the distance the Citadel had been set afire and dark silhouettes were working hastily to extinguish the flames. Closer at hand, several smaller fires raged unchecked. Clusters of desolate refugees huddled together in the streets outside the Stare Miasto.

Ephraim was devastated. These were his neighbors and his friends. The carriage was within sight of the main entry to the quarter when the sound of gunfire rang out from inside the ancient walls. Ephraim stiffened as though the shot had struck him.

Tetrov pulled to a halt at Mira's order. Immediately, Ephraim was out of the coach at a run. He saw that the Great Synagogue was intact, but that the group of elders standing before the main portal seemed agitated and distressed. The rabbinical library next door was the site of frenzied activity, the purpose of which he took no time to assess.

He was unaware of Mira running close behind him, her flowing skirts gathered up to facilitate her movements. At one point, she was nearly knocked to the ground by a shower of falling masonry as one corner of the roof of the Yeshiva School on the other side of the synagogue, set aflame by the peasants, collapsed into the street.

A short distance inside the Stare Miasto, Ephraim stopped in front of what had been a modest but attractive home. The front door stood open, and Mira continued to follow Ephraim inside. Furniture and clothing were strewn around the entry hall.

Ephraim rushed into the house, shouting, "Elana!" Silence answered him. "Leah! Michael!" Still there was no answer. His terror grew as he moved from room to room and beheld the wanton destruction. Most of the family's prized possessions lay scattered and broken. Ephraim searched the house frantically, finally going to his and Elana's bedroom.

Here, the furnishings were more intact though disarranged. In the dim light, he glimpsed a flash of reddish-gold as Elana, hidden behind a chair in the furthest corner of the room, raised her head briefly, then quickly lowered it.

"Elana, it's Ephraim," he said breathlessly, relieved to know his wife was still alive.

At the sound of his voice, Elana peered over the back of the chair, a smile of love and recognition lighting her tear-stained face.

Ephraim moved quickly to her, pulled aside the chair and lifted her into his arms. The two younger children, hiding with her, wrapped their arms fiercely about his neck. The family clung together in silent relief.

Mira Pietrowska, standing at the bedroom door, realized that between Elana and Ephraim existed a bond of love that, even if she ever set for herself such a goal, she would never succeed in breaching, even if she were to seriously try.

Ephraim gently brushed a smudge of dirt from Elana's cheek. "What happened, my dear?" His voice was hoarse with emotion.

"The militia came," Elana answered brokenly. "They searched through everything, throwing things on the floor, smashing them in their haste. And then…" Her voice broke off.

Ephraim turned to Mira. "Would you please take the children to the front room, Madam?"

Mira smiled at both children reassuringly; she took Michael by the hand and reached for Leah's hand as well. Leah hesitated, then ran to retrieve the family prayer book from where it had fallen to the floor. It was the one possession from the family's past that linked them with the entire ancient tradition of their people. She clasped it to her chest, unaware at that moment that her mother's single strand pearl necklace had been stitched inside its soft leather cover. She ran back to Mira's side, and Mira took both children and led them from the room.

"Tell me what happened," Ephraim said as soon as they were gone.

"One of the soldiers seemed to find me attractive." Elana began to cry.

"Did he touch you?"

Elana nodded reluctantly. "He threw me on the bed and began to embrace and kiss me. He would have raped me, but one of his officers yelled at him in Russian. I couldn't tell what the words were. I was just grateful that he stopped."

Ephraim held her closer, soothing her fears, trying to shut them out. "Never mind, my love. You're safe now."

He lifted Elana carefully in his arms, cast one parting glance about the room in which they had spent so many happy hours, and then carried her out of the house into the hazy sunlight. Mira followed with the two children in tow.

The narrow, cobbled streets were crowded with milling residents. Most of them had lost homes or property. Even those whose homes had escaped damage had temporarily vacated them in panic.

As the Marjzendiak family and Mira approached the Pietrowski's carriage outside the front entrance of the quarter, Tetrov, Madam Pietrowski's driver, sat at attention on his box. Mira, incensed that she alone had to assist Ephraim in getting Elana into the carriage, spoke sharply. "Move, Tetrov! Quickly, man!"

Her commands met with inaction. Ephraim looked up at the driver from the other side of the carriage and froze momentarily in horror. The right side of Tetrov's head and face had been demolished by a barrage of bullets. Ephraim leaped from the coach.

"Ephraim," Mira shouted, "get back inside! Think of your family!"

"That's exactly what I am doing," Ephraim replied as he mounted the driver's box. He laid Tetrov's battered body on the floor of the platform. Mira, belatedly realizing the true state of affairs, crossed herself devoutly.

Ephraim took the goad from the dead driver's hand and stung the horses into action. He turned the coach in a tight, smooth arc and swiftly headed the carriage away from the Stare Miasto. There was no necessity for words to define their destination; there was only one place to which they could go.

## CHAPTER TWELVE
## PLAZ MARJZENDIAK

At the north gate, Madam Pietrowska's passport once more worked its magic, and soon they were outside the city. The countryside about them was lush and green, its beauty, after the terror and ugliness they had just left behind, as intoxicating to the senses as wine.

Less than an hour later, Ephraim caught sight of the Pietrowski estate. It had been many weeks since he had last seen the adjacent Zielinski property which he now owned. The rest of the family had seen it only in their mind's eye, painted in vivid colors by Ephraim's enthusiastic descriptions.

It was nearly twilight when Ephraim ushered his family into their new home. There were few pieces of furniture in the house. Fortunately, the bedrooms and kitchen were, for the most part, furnished.

The children were enthralled, and slightly intimidated. Even in their wildest fantasies, they had not imagined that the house and grounds would be quite so large or so elegant.

Ephraim picked up Elana in his arms and carried her like a bride across the threshold. Mira went before them, enthusiastically explaining details about the house as they passed through it. As Ephraim placed his beloved wife on the postered bed, she opened her eyes and glanced confusedly about her.

Ephraim smiled reassuringly at her. "We're home, my love," he whispered.

Elana smiled and nodded, then nestled her head in the curve of his arm and promptly fell asleep. Ephraim sat at her bedside, whispering reassurances which somehow seemed to reach her submerged consciousness.

As Ephraim recalled Elana's halting description of the abortive assault upon her by a Russian soldier, anger welled up in him.

He tried to turn his thoughts to the more positive aspects of this day's perilous events. Against highly unfavorable odds, he had been reunited with his wife and children. Despite the actions of the Russian soldier, there would soon be an addition to the family. Finally, through the foresight of Mira Pietrowska, their new home had been ready to receive them in their hour of need.

When Elana was stronger and was fully recovered from the horrors of the experiences she had suffered today, Ephraim would show her the grounds and the secondary buildings of their estate. He would obtain from his own factory the furniture needed to complete the restoration of the main house. Before long there would be crops ripe for harvest, livestock to keep and to sell at market, even, Adonai willing, bee hives brimming with honey. He and Elana would share all this, and would keep it in trust for countless unborn generations of Marjzendiaks.

While Ephraim sat dozing fitfully beside Elana, Mira fed and bathed Leah and Michael and put them to bed, noting with indulgent amusement Leah's insistence on keeping her prized recorder, worn on a cord about her neck by day, close by her bed even at night.

Ephraim awoke with a start to find Elana awake and restless. She was moaning softly and was obviously in distress. He felt her forehead and thought she seemed feverish. Yet, when he sought to question her, she simply shook her head from side to side. Alarmed, Ephraim got up and went in search of Madam Pietrowska.

As she was preparing to return to her own home after tidying the Marjzendiak kitchen, Ephraim intercepted Mira on the stairs on her way to bid the family good night. He was obviously agitated.

"Ephraim," Mira said, concerned, "What's wrong?"

"Elana is ill," Ephraim replied, nervously ushering Mira into the main bedroom.

Elana was breathing heavily, perspiration pouring down her face. Mira drew back the bed clothes and examined Elana critically, then turned to Ephraim. "Her water has broken," she said matter-of-factly. "I'm certain her labor has begun."

Ephraim shook his head. "I had thought there were about two months remaining." Ephraim felt himself at a loss.

They both realized that premature labor could be fatal for the child. Ephraim gave Mira instructions on how to contact Dr. Jedewreski, then returned to Elana's bedside, dreadin the worst.

*　*　*

Ephraim was deeply grieved but not truly surprised that despite his physician friend's best efforts, the child, a daughter, did not survive beyond a few hours after birth. She was given the name of Rachel and Ephraim hastily constructed a makeshift coffin from strips of wood he found in the stable. He dug a small grave in the Zielinski family cemetery at the boundary of his new estate. Contrary to custom, there would be no Chabrah Kaddishah, no ritually assigned elders, to take charge of the tiny body and prepare it for burial, and no holy women veiled in black to mourn with the family at the grave site. With the turmoil and upheaval that had suddenly erupted within the Stare Miasto, there was also no rabbi available to say the holy words. Rabbi Meisels had been imprisoned and Rabbi Janowski was overwhelmed with countless responsibilities resulting from the raid.

Early the next morning, Ephraim carried the coffin to its resting place and read the stipulated passages from the worn family prayer book, which Leah had rescued from their abandoned home. Samuel Jedewreski recited the mourner's Kaddish while Leah, standing near him, wept. Michael was as yet too young to truly comprehend the meaning of the ceremony.

Gently laying Rachel's coffin in the earth, Ephraim scattered the first handful of soil over it in traditional symbolic commemoration of the soil of Israel. Then he and Samuel completed the interment. When they were done, Ephraim knelt to smooth the earth over his infant daughter's grave with his bare hands. He remained there kneeling on the ground, his head bowed in silent, unassuagable grief for this child of his mature years who would never grow to adulthood. In the throes of that grief, Ephraim tore the lapel of his black coat, the one he normally saved to wear only at the bank. It was the mark of profound mourning.

Later that day, Ephraim stood alone on the terrace, watching the late afternoon sunlight bathing his property with its golden hues. The time-honored words of Job echoed in

Ephraim's mind as they had earlier that day when he had read them from the siddur over Rachel's grave:

"The Lord giveth and the Lord taketh away. Blessed be the name of the Lord!"

* * *

In the months following the raid on the Stare Miasto, Ephraim's investments prospered. In addition to the now-fully-productive Zielinski estate, his two lumber mills continued to operate at peak capacity and he began construction on a third.

Ephraim assisted a number of his fellow Jews in acquiring property outside the Stare Miasto just as he had been assisted by Mira Pietrowska. When, because of bank standards, he had to turn down Jewish applicants whose merits he knew personally, he would often lend them the money they sought from his private funds, at a lower rate of interest.

True to her word, Mira had paid the taxes on the Zielinski property. As soon as he had paid her back, Ephraim erected a wrought iron fence at the boundary of his estate, its gate surmounted by an iron frame with large bronze letters spelling out the words: PLAZ MARJZENDIAK, meaning the place of Marjzendiak.

In July of 1864, Ezra Pragawitz, the stonecutter, carved and transported the metzivah, the grave marker, to the Marjzendiak compound and helped Ephraim to set it in place above the infant Rachel's burial place. The family members gathered at the grave site with the rabbi of Wola, Eli Olnitz, to intone the sacred words that marked the end of the year of mourning. True, the child had not reached viability in either the Gentile or the Jewish custom of practice, but she had been born and had at seven lunar months attained the age of potential viability and so was entitled to the customary formalities of burial and mourning, and the celebratory aspects of yahrzeit, the observance of the anniversary of death of a loved one. Since neither of her older brothers could be present, the minyan on that occasion was composed of Ephraim, Rabbi Olnitz, Dr. Samuel Jederewski, Ezra Pragawitz, Emmanuel Skolnich, the cloth merchant; Saul Kolvner, the importer; Teyral Insbruch, the jeweler; Aaron Meinert, Ezra's assistant; Samuel Marks, a cousin of Ephraim's, and Ira Grodnitz, a tutor in Hebrew Studies from the newly repaired Yeshiva Shul of the Great Synagogue in Warsaw. They were joined by Elana and Leah, of course, and Mira Pietrowska came, as the ceremony was beginning, to pay her respects. She had been present at Rachel's birth and death; it seemed only fitting that, though a gentile, she should be present on the occasion of the anniversary of those events. She brought with her a package which she presented to Ephraim. He put it in his pocket surreptitiously while the others were preparing to begin the prayer ritual.

The mourner's kaddish was recited by Leah as the only child present, following the opening prayers of the rabbi. Ephraim recited from memory the appropriate Torah reading for the day. Samuel Marks read a passage from the family siddur. Then, finally, Rabbi Olnitz concluded the proceedings with these words:

"All who weep for the dead are forgiven their sins because of the honor they have given the dead. May the pure spirit of this innocent child, as it ascends to the height of the blessed, serve as a guardian and a source of blessing from Yahweh upon the living members of her family from this time forward."

Then the canvas covering was removed from the metzivah, revealing the name and data of Rachel's short span of time, with the words "Beloved Daughter" carved beneath.

Elana had prepared a light collation for those who had come to participate in this brief memorial. She now led the minyan back to the house. Ephraim, however, explained that he, Samuel and Ezra had a few final chores to carry out before joining the rest of the group.

Beneath a second canvas cloth, larger than the one that had covered the grave marker, a second grave had been dug the night before, illuminated by a bright full moon. This cavity was only slightly larger than Rachel's grave, but it was much deeper. In it, Ephraim had placed a heavy stone chest lined with lead. A second similar chest stood in front of it. Ephraim now took from the voluminous pockets of his long coat a packet of documents that Mira had brought at Franz' direction, sealed in a coarse gray envelope such as those used to file court and bank records.

"These," he said, "are duplicates of the title and transfers of this property to the Marjzendiak family from the Pietrowski family in perpetuity for services rendered. They prove our right of ownership of this land under Tzar Alexander II's mandate. Other certificates and bank notes are also included. They will be buried here against future need in time of peril, if not for our use, then for that of our descendants." He placed them in the empty chest. In the second chest he placed several coins and gold and silver bars, and then the three men shoveled soil into the cavity, smoothed it over, and erected over it a second marker, not new-looking nor clearly marked like Rachel's, but weathered, worn and ancient in appearance, as if belonging to a youthful but long dead ancestor. Only a few half-obscured letters marked its surface, and the few numbers visible suggested a date a generation earlier. No one, noticing this grave, would ascribe it to the Marjzendiak family without knowing its history.

*** 

Now, fourteen months after she had first come here, Leah Marjzendiak stood on the front terrace of her family home, gazing contentedly at the formal rose garden that spread before her. This garden, a pleasing array of patterns and colors, was Leah's favorite place. Its serene beauty reminded her of her mother, who had personally planted every flowering bush that grew here. The project had been part of the therapy that Dr. Jedewreski had prescribed for Elana after the death of Rachel.

At first deeply depressed by the knowledge that she could not have another child, Elana had eventually grown resigned to Adonai's will. She occupied her time with domestic duties, of which there were many in so large a house. The home, with its numerous rooms and expansive lands, had become her child, an almost living entity which she and Ephraim would nurture and preserve for future generations of Marjzendiak children.

For Leah, her own childhood seemed to have ended abruptly in her eighth year. It was almost as if a great conflagration had swallowed up much she had treasured from her earlier recollections, along with all the material possessions that represented home and family to her. The only exception was the family prayer book that she had salvaged after the looting of her old home in the Stare Miasto. That prayer book had symbolized, in her child's mind, the historic legacy of her family and her people.

Leah's earliest remaining childhood recollection was of winding her fingers through the vastness of her father's beard. It was a pleasant memory, largely because she associated with it a feeling of protection and welcome. Later, she had felt a similar pleasure when her mother allowed her to brush her lustrous, red-gold hair. It was as though each of her parents had instinctively known that the most meaningful avenue of communication with her was through her intensely perceptive sense of touch.

As she stood reviewing these things in her mind, Leah remembered that early one morning last fall, Elana had been working in the garden, digging shallow basins around the roots of some newly-planted rose brushes, and Leah had been helping her. They had both heard the sound of an approaching coach even before it appeared around the curve in the drive. Glancing at her grass-stained apron and dirt-smeared hands, Elana had felt an impulse to run and hide but there had been no time. The elegant Pietrowski carriage had come to a stop right in front of Leah and Elana. Mira had alighted, arms laden with coarse sacks. Over her full-skirted, uncharacteristically plain cotton gown she had worn a broad apron.

"Good morning," Mira had said joyously. "I've brought you some gifts for your garden."

Obviously puzzled, Elana had responded, "Gifts?"

"Cuttings from my rose bushes. They're a real treasure. Some of them are direct descendants of rose bushes in the garden of the Empress Josephine." Mira had smiled conspiratorially at Elana. "You know how famous her roses were!"

Elana, unfamiliar with the Empress's roses, had nodded noncommittally.

"I've brought some vigorous root stock as well. With careful planning, your garden can be just as lovely as Josephine's, if not as famous."

While Leah had looked on in awe, Mira had assisted Elana, not only with planting the bushes but in planning their surroundings and in choosing the proper accessories such as the porcelain jardinières now that graced the veranda.

When the newly-planted bushes had come into bloom the following spring, the carefully-grafted deep reds had blossomed next to blue-reds and soft pinks, all concentrically arranged to achieve a breathtakingly dramatic effect. In a similar manner, the whitest roses had been encircled by cream-colored old-fashioned ones, then pale yellows, and finally rich gold and apricot-colored blossoms.

Viewed as a whole, the Marjzendiak rose garden was reminiscent of an artist's palette, displaying nearly all the colors of the spectrum. The flower beds themselves, large diamond-shaped affairs, had been laid out according to Elana's original design but with lavish embellishments contributed by Mira Pietrowska who had also, upon occasion, lent to Elana the services of her head gardener.

Leah smiled as she remembered how she and Pola, Mira's daughter, had first met. Mira had extended an invitation to Leah to play with Pola, and Mira herself had served the girls tea with small sandwiches and sweet cakes, much in the manner of an English high tea. Once Leah had mentioned how much she loved music and how greatly she admired the famed pianist, Marie Pleyel, Pola decided to entertain her by playing the piano for her. The selection Pola chose was a Beethoven Sonata which she executed with a flourish on the Pietrowski's majestic grand piano. As she listened, Leah fingered the recorder which she always carried with her, much as another child might fondle a favorite toy. Leah always kept the small, slender instrument with her, fastened about her neck on a woven cord, as though it were a pendant made from a precious stone.

Delighted with Pola's rendition, Leah suggested that the two of them play a simple duet, Pola at the piano and Leah accompanying her on the recorder. Leah's ear for pitch was unerring, and she easily followed Pola's lead. Soon, the two girls were playing together almost like veteran musicians, transposing tunes from one key to another. Impulsively, Pola offered to teach Leah the rudiments of piano technique and Leah responded with delight to that suggestion.

Impressed by Leah's talent and enthusiasm, Mira had encouraged Pola by all means to make good on her offer to teach Leah piano. Mira had also persuaded Ephraim that Leah should study academic courses with Maria Boroska, the tutor she had hired to teach Pola and her brother, Erik. Maria, a displaced Polish school teacher, had lost her position when, after the rebellion, the Russians had taken over the administration of all the Polish schools. The courses she was teaching the Pietrowski children included geography, mathematics, Polish literature, and Polish and French grammar. Leah was also motivated to study Polish history and was mystified that Maria steadfastly refused to address that subject. However, as soon as Leah realized that mathematics was closely related to music, she approached that discipline with enthusiasm. Soon, mathematics became her favorite area of study second only to her piano lessons. Eventually, it became apparent that Leah was learning piano at so rapid a pace that she would quickly exhaust Pola's store of knowledge. At Mira's request, Maria Boroska took over Leah's piano lessons directly as well as tutoring her in academic subjects. For Leah, this situation was destined to prove quite beneficial.

Considering the strictly-enforced quotas applied to Jewish students even in the primary schools, Leah would have been denied the opportunity to receive a formal education had it not been for Mira Pietrowska's generosity. The child valued this chance to expand her knowledge without reference to gender or undue emphasis on her expected role of wife and mother later in life. After all, that was far in the future. The intervening time span would have seemed barren indeed without the stimulus of learning which, Leah now realized, fulfilled a hunger from which she had suffered from earliest childhood. The opportunity to satisfy that hunger, Leah mused, had come about because her mother had turned to her garden for solace and Mira Pietrowska had decided to further involve herself in the Marjzendiak family fortunes.

Leah was so engrossed in these reminiscences that she did not hear Elana come up behind her. Elana smiled at her daughter's depth of concentration.

"Leah, dear," she said softly so as not to startle her, "it's time for your music lesson."

Leah looked up and smiled at Elana. "Already?"

Elana nodded and said, "Madam Pietrowska's coach is waiting."

Leah glanced once more about the garden. "I suppose now that I'm older," she said, "time passes faster than it used to." She turned obediently and entered the house, Elana following closely in her wake, barely able to restrain her laughter. She knew Leah was not deliberately joking, but her words in a child's mouth were undeniably humorous.

As she came into the hall, Leah saw Ephraim talking with Dr. Jedewreski. She ran to Dr. Jedewreski and asked timidly, "Is Mama sick again?"

"No, child," the doctor answered reassuringly. "Your mother's in fine health. This is a social visit, not a medical one."

"Good," Leah said happily. "Then I shall go and take my piano lesson. Perhaps I'll see you when I come back."

Ephraim smiled at Leah's remark. "Some day, dear, we'll buy you a piano of your own."

"That would be wonderful, Papa." Leah took her portfolio from a nearby table, and then kissed first Elana, then Ephraim. Finally, she turned to Jedewreski. "It was nice to see you, Doctor, on a social visit." She waved and went running out the door.

"That child is growing up awfully fast," Samuel Jedewreski remarked.

Ephraim shrugged. "The fortunes of war. Even Michael seems older than his age."

"Pola and Erik Pietrowski show it, also," Elana added thoughtfully. "They each display a maturity that would normally belong to a much older child."

Dr. Jedewreski nodded in assent. "Thanks to this accursed revolution, the generation that's growing up now will bear many scars, even more than their parents. No matter what good comes to them later in life, they will always be children of adversity. It is not a happy heritage. Too bad the political leaders don't think of that before they start these things."

"Well, at least the revolution is over," Ephraim commented. "The Russians have declared hostilities officially terminated."

"Unfortunately, that declaration hasn't put an end to the fighting," the doctor said somberly. "The rebels refuse to concede defeat. The guerrilla attacks and the bombings go on while more lives are lost to no purpose."

Elana led Ephraim and Jedewreski into the small intimate breakfast-room. As soon as they were seated at the table, Elana poured coffee and served apple-filled knishes spiced with cinnamon and cloves.

Samuel Jedewreski smiled. "You know, Ephraim," he said warmly, "it's a real pleasure to see you the settled man of property."

"A man with some property, perhaps," Ephraim corrected, "but hardly settled. None of us, Jew or Gentile, can feel safe until this conflict is truly ended."

"It can't go on much longer," Elana said with conviction. "There's too much controversy in the rebel ranks. I've heard they're killing each other almost as rapidly as the Russians are killing them."

"I wish I could dispute that," Dr. Jedewreski said. "Unfortunately, I am personally aware of hundreds of such assassinations. It's no wonder Poland can't successfully fight off her oppressors when there's so much internal fighting going on between factions in the revolutionary forces. They've seldom agreed on any matter of consequence since the beginning of the uprising eighteen months ago."

"It seems longer," Elana remarked. "Every day since it began, I've lived in fear that some harm might come to Ephraim on his way to and from work. But you know Ephraim, Samuel. He has no concern for himself."

"I merely do my duty, Elana," Ephraim answered.

Jedewreski shook his head. "If that's true, why did the Banking Commission appoint you, a Jew, as one of its members? Obviously, it's because of the courageous way in which you have fulfilled that duty, Ephraim."

"The Commission was most generous," Ephraim said with humility.

Elana's eyes flashed. "And where would Franz Pietrowski have been when he was shot if it weren't for you?"

"On that occasion," Ephraim answered, "we were both extremely fortunate."

"Speaking of fortunes," Jedewreski observed, "you've used yours to help others prosper as well. Our community is deeply in your debt." He paused uncomfortably. "That's why it's hard to ask yet another favor from you."

Ephraim's eyebrows rose slightly. "What favor, Samuel?"

"It's well known that you've opposed the rebellion from the first. Obviously, you and the other conservative voices among us, including my own, have been proved right. However, that is no longer an issue. With hostilities hopefully drawing to an end, we need now to close ranks and heal the wounds of the past. "

"I agree," Ephraim said.

"As you know, the Russians have repeatedly rejected our petitions for Rabbi Meisels' release," Jedewreski continued.

Ephraim nodded. "A most regrettable consequence of his involvement in the uprising. But what can I do that the Synagogue Council cannot?"

"You are known to have opposed Rabbi Meisels' Nationalist policies publicly," Jedewreski asserted. "You have no political bias on his behalf. Your voice added to ours will show our unanimity. Furthermore, you have powerful friends, Gentile friends, whose pleas are less likely to be ignored."

"You would have me trade on those friendships?"

"The Bank Commissioner owes you his life!"

"That is not a debt one calls in, Samuel. You of all people are well aware of that. Half our community and many members of the Catholic population of Warsaw owe you their lives. You have never sought to capitalize on that."

"There is a difference, Ephraim. I deal with life and death every day. Those are the conditions of my profession. But what you did went far beyond the call of duty. Not only did you save your superior's life, you also salvaged the majority of the bank's assets." Jedewreski looked at Ephraim pleadingly. "The Synagogue Council does not expect miracles, Ephraim. Rabbi Meisels' imprisonment has lasted for more than a year. Immediate success is hardly a realistic expectation. All we ask is that you try."

Ephraim glanced from Jedewreski to Elana. "I will try," he said finally, "but it will take time."

"Rabbi Meisels is no longer a young man," Jedewreski observed. "His health is fragile, and certainly the atmosphere of the Citadel has not improved it. Perhaps that argument will sway your associates to act quickly to bring about his release."

"The Russian authorities will hardly find it in their interests to render him a martyr," Ephraim observed.

"I daresay Rabbi Meisels' imprisonment serves a symbolic purpose for them," Jedewreski noted. "After all, he has supported Polish autonomy for years. Now, with everything Polish being abolished, it's possible they fear that releasing him now will only reactivate the struggle."

Ephraim shook his head. "Whatever purpose the rabbi's imprisonment may have originally served, to continue to hold him now is simply a pointless cruelty."

Elana nodded in agreement. "Pointless indeed," she said, "to civilized people, but who would argue that the Russians are civilized?"

While her parents discussed Rabbi Meisels' fate with Dr. Jedewreski, Leah was happily immersed in a Chopin Etude. As she played, her teacher, Maria Boroska smiled approvingly. Chopin, the patriotic Polish hero of the concert stage, was Maria's favorite composer.

"Excellent, Leah," Maria said enthusiastically at the completion of her rendition. "Your strength and skill are rare in one so young, particularly a girl."

"Girls can be strong, too," Leah asserted. "Their fingers are more flexible than those of boys, so they should be more skillful."

"Nevertheless," Maria remarked, "only a handful of women musicians have ever achieved recognition."

Leah looked crestfallen.

Madam Boroska realized that although she had praised Leah, her reference to the small role of women in music was a blow to the child's feelings. Hastily, she added, "But what a glorious handful! Clara Wieck Schumann and Marie Pleyel, to name but two."

Leah shook her head. "I could never hope to be classed with them!"

"But, child, that's exactly what hope is all about."

"Hope has no value without talent," Leah said thoughtfully.

"You have talent, Leah," Maria asserted. "It is a gift like a rare jewel, but diligent effort is necessary to develop it to its full potential."

"I can be very diligent, Madam," Leah responded, studying her teacher with intensely serious eyes.

Maria Boroska said with equal seriousness, "My little one, a teacher of music waits many years to find a promising pupil. You are such a pupil. You have talent and passion. If you persevere, you have the makings of a true artist."

Leah leaped up from the piano bench and threw her arms about the unsuspecting teacher. "Oh, thank you, Madam," she said enthusiastically. "You've no idea what it means to me to hear you say that."

Recovering from her surprise, Maria Boroska patted the radiant auburn curls of her diminutive pupil. "Perhaps I have," she said warmly. "Perhaps I have a very good idea."

* * *

A week after Samuel Jedewreski's meeting with Ephraim, the conservative leadership of Warsaw's Jewish population, led by Rabbi Jacob Janowski, Ephraim Marjzendiak, and Dr. Samuel Jedewreski, petitioned yet again for Rabbi Meisels' release. The petition stressed the disruptive effect of Meisels' imprisonment at a time when efforts were being made to restore order and quell unrest.

Joining in the petition were Franz Pietrowski, the Senior Bank Commissioner, Josef Walenski, former Chief Minister of the Council of State, and Francysk Oblitowski, the titular Mayor of Warsaw.

Following the filing of the petition, Ephraim went to visit Rabbi Meisels at the Citadel. Meisels' initial instinct was to decline Ephraim's visit. In the past, Meisels' encounters with Ephraim had usually been the occasion for heated arguments because of their differing philosophies regarding the Nationalist efforts. At present, Rabbi Meisels was in no mood for conflict. Nevertheless, curious as to the reason for the visit, he agreed to see Ephraim.

When two burly guards brought Rabbi Meisels into the visitors' room, Ephraim rose immediately to his feet. "Shalom Aleichem, Rabbi."

"Aleichem, shalom," Meisels replied. He signaled for Ephraim to resume his seat. The guards moved away a few feet and stood near the door. Seating himself, the rabbi asked, "To what do I owe this honor?"

"To the deep concern <u>all</u> your people feel for your welfare," Ephraim answered.

"I have not been aware of such unanimity of opinion among my people these past few years," Meisels said off-handedly. His point was not lost on Ephraim.

"Nevertheless," Ephraim responded, "we are all one in the covenant we share with Adonai. Compared to that unity, our differences of opinion are meaningless. The main issue now is to get you out of this dreadful place."

Meisels glanced about him. "There are walls, floors, and ceilings here, as in many other settings," he observed.

"There are also guards, poor food and dampness," Ephraim said. "We must have you released from here as quickly as possible. We are making some progress now in that direction. A new petition has been submitted to the provincial governor. We await his decision with great hope."

Meisels placed his hands on Ephraim's shoulders in a gesture of benediction and acceptance. "I will be released when Yahweh wills it."

Over the next few months, Warsaw's Jewish citizens prayed for the success of the petition. Ephraim visited Rabbi Meisels frequently, bringing him news of any progress in the effort to gain his freedom.

Finally, in December of 1864, Rabbi Dob Baruch Meisels was released from the Citadel of Warsaw. He had been imprisoned for nearly seventeen months, and his health and strength had suffered immeasurably. Nevertheless, he greeted his followers with a flourish and a lightness of spirit that was inspiring to witness. He reminded them cheerfully that the scriptures reveal that the Lord Yahweh[5] created everything out of formless chaos. In that

---

[5] Yahweh is the scholarly religious designation for the one true God in the Hebrew language. Adonai is the more commonly used terminology employed by most Jewish people.

case, the rabbi reasoned, disorder should be viewed as the place of beginning. Although the Jews had lost many battles in their long history, their faith and their covenant, Meisels assured them, guaranteed that they would ultimately prevail.

\* \* \*

The weeks and months that followed the end of the rebellion brought more hardships for the people of Congress Poland. The Tsar's reforms had failed, and in their wake stood an implacable determination to convert the former Congress Kingdom into a totally subservient Russian colony. The universities were once more closed and the Polish language was forbidden to be taught even in the primary schools.

Much of the property of the Roman Catholic Church was confiscated and many of its monasteries were closed. The Church and its administration were placed under the Ministry of the Interior. The Council of State, the nation's legislative body, was 'temporarily' adjourned and its functions assumed by an Administrative Council of Russian appointees. All government functions were directly subject to the joint authority of Viceroy Prince Viktor Cherkassi and the new Governor-General, N.A. Milyutin. Under this joint administration restrictions were harsh and even minor infractions were severely punished. The ensuing winter months were a time of hardship and oppression for the vast majority of Poles and for the Polish Jews in particular who were singled out and treated as subversives even though numerically their role in the uprising had been relatively small. Taxations, unwarranted reprisals, and arbitrary injustices seemed to conspire with the worsening weather conditions to render life a bitter and unending struggle for survival.

\* \* \*

By the spring of 1865, Adam felt overwhelmed by homesickness. His studies no longer excited him and, unlike Isaak, who still romanticized Krakow, he had lately become disenchanted with the city, primarily because he sorely missed his family. He wrote a letter to Ephraim, asking permission to return home. The letter he received in reply surprised him:

"My Dear Adam,

I read your letter with joy. It pleases me beyond words to know how well your studies are progressing. I would have expected no less, knowing the determination and dedication that are your dominant attributes.

Isaak has also written and conveyed a similar report of his studies. I am proud of both of you.

After more than three years, I long to see you, but your desire to return home comes at a bad time. Warsaw is not the city that you once knew. A state of martial law prevails, and the entire city is under curfew. Punitive taxes have been imposed, and one need not even commit an offense to be taken into custody and questioned. In addition, both the University and the Akademy of Medicine are closed, as well as the Music Konservatory.

It would be unwise for you to return at present. Perhaps in a few months, the forces of reaction will have run their course and the normal rhythm of life will have resumed. In the meantime, my advice, indeed my earnest request, is that you remain in Krakow where you are safe and secure.

The family is well. Leah is growing up rapidly. She is studying music with a new-found friend, Pola Pietrowska, and seems to take to it naturally. Michael insists he will become a writer and make the family name well-known through his journalism. I hope I shall be able to help the younger children achieve their goals in life as well as I have managed to help you and Isaak.

Your mother and Leah send their love, although Michael scarcely remembers you. I pray that soon we can be united once more as a family.

I shall answer Isaak's letter separately. Meanwhile, please inform him that his prophecy has been fulfilled. For a few months, at least, I was indeed in charge of the Bank of Poland in Warsaw.

My love to you and your brother always,

Your Father Ephraim"

*　*　*

In the late fall of 1865, Ephraim wrote to Adam and Isaak inviting them to come home for the Hanukkah season, which that year coincided with their winter break from school. Their replies surprised him. Isaak wrote:

"Dear Father,

This year is proving to be a major challenge for me. I have entered upon the world of political science in earnest. As I had expected, it is a vastly interesting world, but as I had not anticipated, it entails an extremely difficult and intricate course of study. In order to complete my thesis on time, I must spend the winter recess in the library.

Much as I wish to see you, Mother, Leah, and Michael, not to mention the new home that is to you no longer new, I feel certain that you will agree with this decision and appreciate what it costs me to make it.

All my love to you and the family. Happy Hanukah.

Your devoted son,

Isaak"

Adam wrote:

"Dear Father,

After my disappointment earlier this year when you advised us to remain in Krakow, I feel ridiculous in declining your offer to share the Hanukah celebration with the family.

The truth is I have met the girl with whom I hope to share my life. We met here at the Medical Akademy. No, she is not studying to become a doctor, though with her excellent mind and powers of concentration, I don't doubt that she could. Unfortunately, the medical curriculum is not open to women, even in Krakow.

She is studying biology, and I have promised to tutor her over the winter recess to help her prepare for her oral examination in the spring. With my own studies, that's the only opportunity I will have to keep the promise. So you see, it is a matter of obligation and honor. But what a happy obligation, what a delightful honor!

The spring term will end in early June and then, I promise, I shall come home. Perhaps Sarah, that is her name, will be able to come with me.

Love always to you, Mother, Leah and Michael, and a joyful Hanukah to you and all our friends.

Your son,

Adam"

The disappointment which Ephraim felt at this dual rejection of his invitation was tempered by the knowledge that his two elder sons were, indeed, maturing. They had embraced life fully and were enjoying the experience. He could scarcely begrudge them that, even if it deprived him and the rest of the family of an opportunity to be reunited with them after such a prolonged separation.

# CHAPTER THIRTEEN
## A TIME TO LAUGH AND A TIME TO WEEP

Isaak spent the first evening of the Hanukah celebration with his cousins Jada and Zaccahreus. Adam, however, had been invited to spend the evening with Sarah's family, and he was loathe to decline the invitation.

The young woman who had attracted Adam's admiration was named Sarah Krakowska. Her father Abel owned a textile mill famed throughout the city for the creation of fine fabrics; silks, wools and many cloths of mixed fibers useful in the making of garments, linens, even carpets. The family name of Krakowski was an example of a common practice among lower-class European families and Jewish families of all ranks, taking the birthplace of their first recorded male member as the family name.

Sarah's mother had died when Sarah was twelve. Since then Sarah had assumed the role of homemaker and mistress of her father's house. For years she had overseen the running of the Krakowski household. Moreover, she had acted as confidante and advisor to both her brothers; Reuben, her elder by two years, and Jakob, five years her junior.

The meal that Sarah prepared for the opening night of Hanukah could easily have rivaled Jada Polewska's for its diversity. The menu contained an abundance of the specified cheese dishes traditional for the holiday. Fried potato latkes supplied the "oils" decreed to commemorate the miracle of the single vessel of oil which had, according to tradition, lasted the eight days of the rededication of the temple in Maccabean times. That period of joyful celebration, following the triumph of the numerically inferior Hebrew forces over their more numerous and better-armed Greek adversaries, was the origin of the Hanukah holiday.

As he helped Sarah carry the dishes to the table, Adam was filled with genuine admiration. "You never cease to amaze me. I've been impressed for some time by the Sarah of the laboratory and the library. But the Sarah of the hearth and home is every bit her equal. I believe you could do anything well."

Sarah smiled as she set a plate of knishes in Adam's outstretched hands. "From time immemorial, women have been called upon to play many roles. It is expected of us. You shouldn't be surprised."

"But I am," Adam replied. "Perhaps I'm most surprised at myself and at the way seeing you like this makes me feel. I want to ask your father for your hand right away." He suddenly set down the platter on the table and took Sarah in his arms. "I want us to be together always."

"I do, too." she answered shyly, "but if dinner grows cold, my father will be in a temper, and then you won't be able to ask his permission for us to marry."

Adam smiled and took the platter into the dining room. Before the family and their guest began dinner, they observed the ritual of the lighting of the menorah.

Sarah recited the prescribed words in lieu of her deceased mother. "Praised are You, Lord our God, Ruler of the universe, who has sanctified our lives through His commandments, commanding us to kindle the Hanukah lights." She took the shamash candle and lit the first of the eight candles. Then, with hearts filled with the sentiments of the celebration, the Krakowski family and Adam sat down to enjoy Sarah's sumptuous meal.

After dinner was completed, Reuben began to distribute the Hanukah gifts. While the exchanging of gifts was a customary part of the celebration, the gifts themselves were for the most part simply tokens, their significance more symbolic than literal. The gift-giving custom varied from community to community and sometimes from family to family.

Knowing this, Sarah had warned Adam in advance. "So," she had teased him playfully, "what token will you get for me?"

"Something appropriate," Adam had answered solemnly. "You'll see."

The packages which the Krakowskis exchanged were wrapped in the traditional colors of blue, gold, and silver. Abel gave Sarah a length of finely woven white fabric which he hoped would one day be used to make her wedding dress. Recalling Adam's words in the kitchen, Sarah responded to the gift with both tears and laughter.

To Adam, Sarah gave a scarf and gloves which she had made herself.

"These, my love," she whispered tenderly as she presented the package, "will keep you warm when I'm not around."

Adam feigned embarrassment as he opened the gift.

"I hardly know what to say," he commented. "They're so elegant. They far outshine what I have to give you."

Sarah smiled tentatively, but her lower lip quivered slightly.

"Whatever it is," she said, "I'm sure I'll treasure it."

Adam's eyes sparkled as he reached inside his coat pocket and brought forth a tiny blue parcel tied with an unpretentious silver cord. He handed the box to Sarah who cradled it in her hands, postponing opening it.

"Shall I guess what's inside?"

"Why not simply open it and find out?"

"Because," she answered, "anticipation makes it more exciting, more special."

"It certainly adds to the suspense," Jakob remarked.

"My little sister loves games," Reuben commented, watching the wordless interplay that was now taking place as Sarah and Adam gazed at each other longingly, using the present as a convenient excuse.

Abel Krakowski stared at his daughter and the young man with whom she was obviously smitten. "Well, Sarah, do you accept the gift?"

Sarah glanced at her father with a start and was abruptly recalled to the reality of her surroundings. For a few moments, she had strayed into an exhilarating future with Adam, borne on the wings of imagination. "Oh, yes," she answered, blushing.

"Then open the package and put an end to the family's suspense," Abel admonished her kindly.

Sarah carefully untied the delicate silver cord that secured the tiny box. When she lifted the lid, Sarah's eyes shone with profound joy. She held up a gold star of David on a delicate golden chain.

"Put it on for me, Adam," she said, drawing him close.

Sarah had made her father a present of an illuminated siddur which she had found in a small antique shop. She watched with anticipation as he opened the package. To Reuben and to Jakob, she had also given books. Each expressed his heart-felt appreciation for the presents. Reuben and Jakob had jointly purchased a seed-pearl-trimmed prayer veil for Sarah which she accepted with delight.

After the gift-giving was concluded, Adam and the Krakowskis played Dreidel games, traditional holiday contests using ancient lots marked with Hebrew letters, each assigned a monetary value much as modern dice are marked with numbered dots.

Shortly before it was time to say good-night, Adam took Abel aside and the two conversed seriously for several minutes. As Sarah watched, Abel shook his head determinedly several times during the conversation. Sarah's heart sank.

She waited in the front hall for Adam. When he finally joined her there she said, "I'll walk with you as far as the gate."

When they were outside, Sarah waited impatiently for Adam to speak, but he was unusually quiet. When they reached the front gate, she could stand the suspense no longer.

"He said no, didn't he?"

Adam paused for a long moment before answering. "No," he said.

Sarah nodded. "I thought as much. Did he say why?"

"Why?"

"Why I can't marry you." Her voice rose with exasperation and disappointment.

Adam shook his head. "He didn't say 'no', Sarah. He said 'yes'."

"Yes?" Tears of joy sprang to Sarah's eyes.

"Yes!" Adam took her gently in his arms and kissed her. She surrendered happily to his embrace. "Mind you," Adam added, "he didn't say we could marry right away. We must wait until after I graduate and am able to earn a living."

Sarah grew serious. "How long is that likely to be?"

"At least two years."

"As long as that?"

"I'm afraid so," Adam replied, "but not a moment longer."

"Oh, Adam, I'm so happy. We'll be married in the main synagogue. Your parents will come to the wedding, won't they?"

"Of course they will." Adam assured her.

"I want everything to be perfect for us."

"I think everything is perfect now," Adam said as he took Sarah once more in his arms.

The next day, Isaak confronted Adam with Jada's reaction to his absence from the preceding night's family celebration. Jada had treated both brothers with such motherly concern and affection that Isaak felt obliged to transmit to Adam the depth of her disappointment.

"You know she thinks of us now as sons," Isaak said, "and you shouldn't have stayed away from our home on the first night."

"But Isaak," Adam responded excitedly, "this was special. I had to go! It was my opportunity to ask Mer Krakowski for permission to marry Sarah."

"You mean that it's gone that far and still I haven't met this paragon?" Isaak's tone was taunting.

"I never met Mariska."

"That was different," Isaak responded stiffly. "I couldn't bring her home."

"Forgive my mentioning that, Isaak," Adam apologized. "That was thoughtless of me."

"Forget it," Isaak said distractedly. "I'm glad for you." He paused thoughtfully. "I wonder if I'll ever meet the right girl."

"Of course, you will," Adam assured him with a brotherly pat on the back. "By the way, I'm invited back to Sarah's for the last night of Hanukah. Inasmuch as her father agreed to the marriage, I really felt I couldn't refuse."

Isaak nodded in answer to his brother's pleading expression. "All right, Adam, I'll make your excuses to Cousin Jada. But don't make a habit of this. Sooner or later, even I shall run out of excuses." Noting the grateful look on his brother's face, Isaak offered a silent prayer that all would go well for Adam and his future bride.

\* \* \*

Adam arrived early at the Krakowski home on the last day of the Hanukah celebration. It was also the beginning of the Sabbath, and he wanted to spend as much time with Sarah as possible. Sarah, however, had not yet returned from classes. Abel and Reuben were still at the textile mill; only Jakob, Sarah's younger brother, was at home.

Like his sister, Jakob was fascinated by matters biological, especially those relating to botany. Jakob knew every shrub, tree and flowering plant in his father's garden by its common and botanical name as well as by its distinctive characteristics.

The wind was brisk and penetrating and the winter sun shone down from an almost cloudless sky. To Adam it seemed a perfect day, and with Jakob showing him about the garden, explaining the distinctive characteristics of the winter-blooming plants, the time he waited for his beloved Sarah seemed to pass quickly.

"These are Euphorbias," Jakob said while Adam gazed in wonder at the profusion of plants and their varied range of foliage. Strangely, none had any fragrance, not even the lovely red-hued plant at the center of the group. "That is Euphorbia Pulcherina," Jakob said, pointing toward the large red-leafed plant. "It is the queen of the genus, the poinsettia. The red leaves that form the base for the flowers are thought by some to be the flowers. But they are only leaves, the bract on which the flowers bloom. And there," he said, pointing to another plant, "is Euphorbia Fasciolata, the 'fan maker', or so it will appear if properly pruned and trained." The leaves of the unusual-looking plant seemed to grow in the shape of a fan, or rather a family of fans, surmounted by little yellow flowers.

Adam stood transfixed, impressed by Jakob's memory for details. "Are you saying that these are all one genus?"

"Precisely," Jakob answered, pleased to explain to a truly interested observer the wide variety of his living treasures. "They are my favorites because there are so many different kinds. The ones with thick prickly leaves are classed as succulents, but all are related. You can tell them by their blossoms. If you prick them, they all 'bleed' the same thick white milk. They are like our people, Adam, endlessly different and yet, at heart, very much alike."

"A perceptive observation, Jakob," Adam remarked, still more impressed. "A truism one would hardly expect to find so vividly illustrated in a garden."

"Ah, but this is no ordinary garden," Jakob answered. "I've tended it since I was ten years old. I've studied every kind of plant and shrub there is. I've even managed to get cuttings of some that are very rare and hard to grow. This collection," he said proudly, "is a botanist's dream."

"I can see that," Adam responded appreciatively.

He leaned close to a tall stately tree that grew near the center of the garden. Even in winter, devoid of foliage, the trunk and branches seemed regal and imposing. At its base was a label: Ficus Religiosa.

"That tree is of an ancient lineage," Jakob explained. "There are hundreds of varieties of Ficus. This one originated in the Orient, but it can be adapted to grow in most temperate climates. Legend has it that it was under one of these trees that Buddha sat until he became 'enlightened.' In India, it is called the 'Bo' tree, in Japan, the 'Bodesai'. It's greatly revered by Buddhists."

"You certainly know a great deal about botany," Adam remarked.

"Some day, I hope to teach at the university. I want to instill in my students a love and respect for plants. If people could learn to live in harmony with the rest of their environment, the world would be a better place."

"That's quite profound," Adam said. "I can tell you've given this matter of co-existence a great deal of thought."

"One has time to think, working around a garden."

Adam noted the slowly lengthening shadows. "Perhaps we should go in now."

Jakob nodded. "This is the night we make music and dance. Each of us plays an instrument, and Sarah sings. She has a lovely voice."

"I'm sure she does," Adam responded. "I shall be looking forward to the family concert."

"In our family," Jakob said enthusiastically, "the celebration of religious festivals has always been filled with joy. Even Yom Kippur has its joyous side. Adonai forgives us. From Him we learn to forgive one another."

"You have a wonderful philosophy of life," Adam remarked warmly. "I plan to make your sister my wife. I hope you and I will also be friends." He clasped Jakob's hands in his own.

Jakob smiled. "I'm sure that we shall."

In the early spring of 1866, Adam read in the campus newspaper that Marja Miatowska, the girl from the dairy farm who had helped him and Isaak to reach Krakow, was getting married at St. Mary's Church. The best man, the editor of the campus paper, was also the younger brother of the bridegroom.

Adam was eager to see Marja and her brother Jan once more. However, in view of the differences in their respective beliefs, he did not feel free to attend the wedding without a formal invitation. Instead, on the morning of the ceremony, he waited outside the church with other well-wishers who had gathered to pelt the newlyweds with rice.

Adam had found the perfect wedding gift in an artisan's market place. It was a collection of crystals and gilded wires contrived in the shape of a bee emerging from its hive. It was set on a carved and polished wooden stand. The artisan's wife had wrapped it for Adam and garnished the bow with a sprig of rosemary. She had explained to him that the herb, when given to a bride, represented the remembrance of past joys.

As he waited impatiently for the nuptial services to be over, Adam mingled with the rest of the guests in the courtyard under the canopy of blue skies and arching trees. He felt self-consciously alone. Isaak, plagued by a recent bout of influenza, had been unable to accompany him.

When the bridal party finally came out of the church, Adam saw Jan Miatowski, but hesitated to come forward. After all, he had not sat at table with him as Isaak had done. However, toward Marja, to whom Adam owed his life, he felt no shyness. He walked over to her and her new bridegroom. "A wedding gift for the beautiful bride," he said, presenting the gaily decorated parcel to Marja.

She glanced at the proffered present, then studied the face of its bearer. Her smile of welcome faded to a look of puzzlement, then of fear.

"It is also a token of gratitude for saving my life," Adam added in an effort to allay the sudden apprehension so nakedly displayed in the girl's eyes. "When you open this, you will remember," he promised, smiling.

The groom, Everard Michelowski, extended his hand in greeting to Adam as he asked Marja, "Who is your friend?"

Marja's beautiful face was creased with a frown as she strove to call to mind the name of the young man before her. "Abel Polewski," she finally managed, turning to Everard. "This is my husband; Abel, Everard Michelowski. He owns the largest newspaper in Krakow," Marja boasted proudly.

It was Adam's smile that had made Marja remember him. She had often wondered what had happened to the two young men who had left their farm in milk cans four years before. "Abel is an echo from the past," she added, embracing him. "Jan," she called, turning to her brother, "look who's here!"

Jan walked over to where Marja stood with Adam and took his hand. "Polewski," he exclaimed excitedly, "it's good of you to come." Jan Miatowski glanced about them. "Isn't your brother with you?"

Adam shook his head. "He's not feeling well."

Jan's eyes probed Adam's deeply. "Give him my regards. I owe him a debt of thanks," he added. "Will you join us for the reception?"

"I can't," Adam answered hesitantly, uncertain whether he was really expected to accept. "I have final exams tomorrow morning. I have to get back."

Jan Miatowski nodded and gave Adam's hand a parting shake. "Good luck," he said.

"I'm certain you'll do well," Marja added.

"Thanks," Adam responded as a host of well-wishers converged upon the bridal party.

* * *

Later that spring Jakob Krakowski began manifesting bizarre changes in behavior and mood. His symptoms were initially attributed to fatigue, and to apprehension regarding his final examinations. With his phenomenal memory and passion for detail, Jakob had always been looked upon as a prodigy. Lately, however, he had noticed difficulties in remembering names and facts which before had come to him with amazing ease.

One day, Adam ran into Jakob in the science library. It was now only a few weeks until the summer recess, and all the students were studying feverishly as courses moved toward conclusion. Jakob looked flustered and turned away, as if to avoid Adam. Adam went over and tapped Jakob gently on the shoulder. "That's a fine way to treat a friend." he remarked pleasantly as Jakob turned around. "How are things going with you?"

Jakob looked pained. "Not too well. Lately I can't seem to remember anything."

"You're just tired," Adam responded reassuringly. "We all get to that point at times. I suggest you take it easy for a day or two. Take your mind completely off studying. You're just getting a bit stale. It'll pass. "

Jakob smiled wanly, but he was not reassured. He knew himself too well. Adam's well-meant remarks, instead of making him feel better, only served to emphasize the growing deficiencies of which Jakob was increasingly aware.

In the next few weeks, Jakob became prey to nightmares, which gradually began to creep into his daytime thoughts as well. He grew nervous, irritable, and finally withdrawn. Even with Sarah, he found it difficult to communicate.

The week prior to final exams, Jakob went to see his faculty advisor, Professor Andreus Tcharnowski. The professor was shocked at his prize student's appearance.

Jakob, usually the epitome of neatness, seemed bedraggled and unkempt. He was unshaven, and his gait, as he walked into the office, was slightly unsteady.

"Sit down, Jakob," the professor instructed him. "What's wrong?"

Jakob took the chair that was offered, but he seemed at a loss for words. For a long moment, he sat silently staring at the professor. "I had to see you," he began finally. "I can't go on."

Professor Andreus Tcharnowski was overcome with surprise and concern. "What is it with which you cannot go on?"

Jakob looked up at him in anguish. "School," he responded. "I can't seem to study anymore. The more I try, the more I seem to forget. I've noticed problems for weeks, now. Lately, it's grown much worse." Jakob got up abruptly from the chair and began nervously to pace the room.

"Are your final exams troubling you?"

Jakob nodded. "I can't pass them," he said.

"But of course you can," Professor Tcharnowski reassured him. "You're one of my brightest students."

"Professor," Jakob said, turning determinedly to face his friend and advisor, "I've decided to withdraw from the course." Once he had succeeded in saying these words, Jakob seemed immensely relieved.

Professor Tcharnowski, on the contrary, was greatly distressed. "You can't mean that!"

"I do mean it, sir. I can't go on."

"What you mean, I think, is that you can't take the final exams now," the professor said. "Finals seem an insurmountable obstacle to many students," he observed. "Once they're over, things come back into perspective. But, if you feel strongly about it just now, why don't you take the summer off and then take the examinations?"

Jakob shook his head determinedly. "You don't understand, sir," he said impatiently. "It's getting worse and worse. If I don't take them now, later it'll be impossible."

Tcharnowski was devastated. He knew Jakob Krakowski to be a brilliant and dedicated student. The Jakob who stood before him now, however, alarmed and terrified him.

Jakob began to pace again when suddenly he stumbled. He reached out to a nearby chair in a futile effort to steady himself, but with a stifled cry, he fell at Tcharnowski's feet. Before Tcharnowski could reach him, his body began to jerk spasmodically.

"Jakob," Tcharnowski cried out, kneeling beside him. "In God's name, what's the matter?" For about two minutes the spasms continued.

Finally Jakob lay still and silent, his face pale and sheened with sweat. Tcharnowski felt for a pulse and was relieved when he found it strong and only slightly irregular. The professor got to his feet and ran from the room, calling out for help.

Within a few minutes, Jakob was in the student infirmary. Sarah had been located in class and notified of her brother's sudden illness. She hurried to the infirmary, where she found Professor Tcharnowski waiting outside Jakob's room.

She ran up to the professor, breathless and concerned. "What's happened? How is he?"

"My dear," Tcharnowski answered, "I'm not really certain what happened. Jakob seemed to have a seizure of some kind, but even before that, he seemed agitated and depressed." Even now, Tcharnowski could not quite master his own amazement at the unexpected turn of events. "He actually asked to withdraw from his curriculum."

"Jakob would never do that," Sarah exclaimed.

"So I would have thought," Tcharnowski echoed, "until today. But he came to my office saying he couldn't take his final exams."

"Why?"

"Exactly the question I put to him. He had no answer. He simply repeated that he had to withdraw. Then he collapsed on the floor in a convulsive seizure." Tcharnowski looked earnestly at Sarah. "Has he ever had anything like this before?"

Sarah shook her head distractedly. "Never," she said, beginning to cry.

The young physician who had attended Jakob assured Sarah and Tcharnowski that he was resting comfortably. The professor had another class to teach and could remain no longer. Sarah, abandoning all thought of her own studies in this crisis, stayed with Jakob.

She watched him as he slept, first quietly, then fitfully as though he were tormented by painful dreams. Finally, he opened his eyes. When he saw Sarah, he began to weep.

"Jakob," Sarah asked anxiously, "how do you feel?" Jakob turned his face to the wall, sobbing pitifully.

"I've sent for Father," Sarah commented, hoping to establish communication, but these words provoked only more tears and sobs.

Sadly, Jakob faced her. "I'm sorry you sent for him," he said.

"Why?"

"Because I don't know what to say to him."

Sarah didn't know either.

Jakob was still silent and withdrawn when Adam came to visit him that evening. As part of his medical training, Adam and his fellow students in their third and fourth years of study took turns serving in the student infirmary. Adam elected to take over Jakob's care.

"Hello, Jakob," Adam said, taking a chair beside the bed. "Are you feeling better?"

Jakob looked at Adam for several heartbeats before he attempted to answer. "I'm still confused." he finally said. "I lost consciousness, didn't I?"

"Only at the end," Adam answered. "Can you tell me what you felt before that?"

"How long before?"

"As far as you care to go."

"It started several months ago," Jakob began softly. "I guess it began with a series of bad dreams."

"Everyone has nightmares, Jakob," Adam said carefully.

"Not every night," Jakob answered emphatically. "Certainly not such horrible ones that they're afraid to go to sleep."

"What did you dream about?"

"At first, there were the usual imaginary creatures pursuing me, the weird fantasies one expects in bad dreams. But then I began to dream about myself, about <u>my</u> behaving like those nightmarish creatures, doing terrible things." He began to cry.

"Perhaps," Adam said encouragingly, "they only <u>seemed</u> so terrible because they were happening in your dreams."

Jakob shook his head vehemently. "No," he insisted. "These were really terrible things, things I'm ashamed to talk about."

"You can tell me," Adam said reassuringly.

Jakob looked at Adam with pleading eyes. "Have you ever imagined yourself inflicting torture on a helpless living being? Have you ever watched helplessly while you committed a brutal act of murder and then dismembered the body in order to conceal the crime?"

Adam shook his head, barely managing to conceal his own horror. "Were you always aware that it was only a dream?"

"Yes," Jakob responded. "At first I knew, but I couldn't control it. I couldn't seem to turn those horrible images off."

"Dreams are like that," Adam remarked. "They tend to take on the guise of reality, if we let them. But that may have nothing to do with what happened today."

"I'd like to believe that," Jakob said earnestly. "For weeks, I told myself those same encouraging lies. But then the nightmares began to affect my waking hours. I found myself actually doing some of the things I had dreamed, things like stealing or destroying other people's possessions. I'm not like that," Jakob all but shouted, "but I couldn't help myself. Those nightmares began to be part of my waking life. It got to the point where I couldn't tell the difference." The tears were falling freely now. "Not long after that, I noticed that I was having difficulty contracting my muscles. I started dropping things because I couldn't hold on to them. I also started forgetting things I knew well. Sometimes I couldn't even remember the names of my friends. That day I saw you in the library, I turned away because I'd forgotten your name."

"How long had that been going on?"

Jakob considered for a moment. "I've lost track. A few months now."

"Have you ever had a seizure before like the one you had today?"

"There've been jerks and spasms before," Jakob recalled, "but today was the first time I've lost consciousness." Jakob stared helplessly at Adam. "Tell me, what does it all mean?"

Adam felt a shiver of apprehension course down his spine. "Before I can say with any degree of certainty, Jakob," Adam said hesitantly, "I'll need to examine you and perform some tests."

"Do you think it's something serious?"

"I really can't say," Adam answered carefully, "until I've examined you."

Adam began his examination, checking Jakob's reflexes and coordination. With each test, Adam grew steadily more alarmed as the tally of abnormal findings mounted.

In 1866, the study of neurological diseases was in a relative state of infancy. The mechanisms of the various disease entities had not been clarified. It would be years before medical science understood La Fora Body Familial Myoclonic Epilepsy, the disease from which Jakob suffered, a progressive storage of an abnormal glucose polymer in the brain, muscles, and liver. Adam, concerned for his friend and in a state of panic because of his love for Sarah, tried to find out as much as he could about the symptoms Jakob was manifesting and what they might mean.

A few nights later, Adam was in the library doing research on Jakob's illness when Sarah appeared at his side. Sarah quietly sat down beside Adam, trying not to disturb his concentration. She recognized the names of some of the books he was studying. For a few minutes she watched as Adam turned page after page of the various volumes.

Finally, Sarah could not restrain herself any longer. "Have you learned anything." she whispered, "that might help Jakob?"

Adam shook his head. "So many causes can precipitate the same symptoms." Almost in desperation he asked, "Have any of your other relatives ever been ill like Jakob?"

"Are you implying that my family's blood is tainted?" Sarah's voice rose shrilly as Adam sought to quiet her.

Adam looked shocked and dismayed. "I meant nothing of the kind, but any clue could be the key. We don't have much time. Jakob's growing worse each day and he knows it."

"That's the worst of all," Sarah said and began to cry.

Adam put his arm around Sarah's shoulder and led her outside where they could talk freely without disturbing their fellow students. Unfortunately, though they felt closer for having communicated on this difficult subject, they were no nearer to an answer to Jakob's illness and the problems which it presented for them.

By term's end, Jakob was much worse. He was given permission to return home, but he declined. That, he knew, would place an enormous burden on Sarah just when she was preparing for her final examinations. He did not want to jeopardize Sarah's chances for passing those rigorous tests.

Adam had completed his exams the week before. He was gratified but astonished to learn that he had placed in the top ten percent of his class. Elated, he went to the hospital to share his joy with Jakob.

Jakob embraced Adam warmly when he heard the news.

He shared vicariously in Adam's enthusiasm and sense of achievement, especially since he now knew he would never experience that flash of triumph in response to his own accomplishments.

"I'm happy for you," Jakob said earnestly. "I knew you would do well. You're smart."

"Brains have nothing to do with it. I owe my success to hard work," Adam answered laughing. "Studies don't come easily for me."

"So much the better," Jakob replied. "You wouldn't value your success as much if it had come easily."

Adam studied his friend for a moment. The abrupt involuntary movements of his limbs were quite evident. The disease was advancing rapidly. "You're right of course," Adam said. "Nothing of value is ever easily won. Neither love nor laurels."

Jakob mocked him gently. "So now you write poetry as well as hand out pills?"

Adam shook his head. "I read that somewhere, but I can't remember where. Still, it's true. We have to strive and struggle before we can permit ourselves to enjoy. "

"And now you're about to enjoy the pleasure of a journey," Jakob said, changing the subject. "When are you going home?"

"Tomorrow," Adam answered, perhaps a shade too enthusiastic at the prospect. "I can't believe that it's been four years! I'll hardly recognize Leah and Michael. And I've never seen the new place. I'll know it, though. My mother's letters have described it in detail."

"You're lucky, Adam. You have everything, even your mother." Bitter, angry tears suddenly coursed unchecked down Jakob's face. "I think you'd better go now," he said. "You'll have a lot to do between now and tomorrow. I'm tired just thinking about it. So tired." The long searching glance from Jakob's huge, pain-filled eyes pierced Adam like twin swords.

"How thoughtless of me," he said, chagrined.

"No! I'm glad you came. Who knows what you'll find when you come back?" His hand trembled as he held it out to clasp Adam's hand. "Good-bye, Adam," he said haltingly.

In Adam's absence, another student physician would take over his role, working under the supervision of an attending senior staff member. The ominous meaning of what Jakob had just said troubled Adam deeply. The tremor grew more intense as their hands locked together. Adam grasped Jakob's hand more firmly and continued holding it until Jakob fell asleep.

# CHAPTER FOURTEEN
## CHOICES

Ephraim met Adam's train at the Warsaw railway station. He seldom visited the station and was fascinated by the bustling activity. As he waited for Adam's train, Ephraim thought of the changes that had occurred since his sons had left Warsaw. The family fortunes had certainly prospered and Poland, though partitioned and devoid of statehood, was also prosperous and flourishing with the cessation of hostilities, bitter though the transition had proved to be.

A train pulled into the station amid the raucous clamor of whistle and engine and the stench of acrid smoke. Ephraim moved closer to the train, propelled by the sea of humanity at his back. Disembarking passengers began filing off the train to be met and greeted by waiting friends and relatives. Many of the passengers, Ephraim noted, were around Adam's age. How many of them, like Adam and Isaak, had fled Congress Poland to avoid the conscriptions?

Ephraim searched the vast array of faces, strange to him and yet familiar. They were the hope and the spirit of Poland, the generation that would have to lift the country from its present state of subjugation if Poland were ever to stand again among the company of nations.

Adam emerged from a car near the end of the train. He and Ephraim recognized each other simultaneously. Their eyes locked and for a moment they stood regarding each other. Then they embraced, eager to satisfy the yearnings of four years of separation.

Adam was impressed with the carriage to which Ephraim led him, and even more so with the confidence and expertise his father displayed in driving it. The countryside passed by swiftly, and within half an hour, they came to the main gate of the family estate.

Adam stood up in the carriage. "Stop, Father!"

Surprised, Ephraim obeyed. "What's wrong?"

Adam smiled. "Nothing. It's just that this is the first time I've seen it. It's like a wonderful dream suddenly come true."

Ephraim nodded. "That's exactly the way I feel."

As the carriage approached the main house, Leah came running out. "Mama, Adam's home!"

Moments later, Elana appeared, leading Michael by the hand. At the sight of his mother and siblings, Adam began to cry. The family was soon entwined in a huddled embrace.

For Adam's homecoming, Elana had prepared all his favorite dishes including his favorite dessert, peach strudel. The flow of conversation around the dinner table was animated and ongoing, and none of the family could seem to hear enough of Adam's stories and experiences.

By late afternoon, an aura of quiet had returned to the household. Adam, "talked out," sat quietly in a corner, absorbing the atmosphere of his new home. When Elana asked him if he wanted anything more, he shook his head, then smiled and kissed her hand.

Nevertheless, an hour later, Adam grew restless. Digging his hands into the pockets of his jacket, he announced that he was going for a walk.

Leah joined him on the terrace. "Would you care for some company?"

Adam smiled at his sister and nodded. "Come along," he said.

They walked among Elana's roses and beyond the formal garden to the neatly-manicured lawn. Leah showed her brother the kitchen garden with its herbs and spices, its ripening vegetables, and its border of ornamental onion and garlic to discourage pests. She led him to a portion of the grain fields and finally she showed him the cemetery and Rachel's grave.

During their walk, Adam acknowledged Leah's comments but, uncharacteristically, volunteered little original commentary of his own. Leah knew instinctively that her favorite brother was nursing some private pain. "If there's anything I can do for you," Leah told him confidentially, "you have only to ask."

Adam smiled, but shook his head.

"Maybe not now," Leah said sagely, "but one day there might be."

"You'll be the first to know," he said warmly.

"After Papa," Leah said with a knowing smile.

Adam looked surprised. "How do you…?"

Leah put her fingers to his lips for silence. "I tell Papa all my secrets, too," she whispered. "I love Mama and she loves all of us, but Papa understands!"

"So he does," Adam answered, impressed that one as young as Leah should be so astute.

The next morning, Ephraim had business to transact at the lumber mill with Josef Skiljret. Adam went along with him for company. While Ephraim and Josef toured the building discussing various modifications in the operation, Adam made his own inspection. He noted with pride the neatly inscribed placard his father had set in place above the main entrance proclaiming the mill the property of Marjzendiak and Sons.

When Skiljret and his employer shook hands on the rear porch of the mill, their thoughts were already diverging. Ephraim was reliving his first tour of the property after he had purchased it from Isaac so that his younger son could be free to leave Warsaw. Skiljret's thoughts were also of Isaac, but were of a more sorrowful nature, for he was remembering the horrifying morning on which together they had found Mariska's drowned body in the river.

Thoughtfully, Adam waited for his father, silent until the day's business was concluded. When Josef Skiljret went inside to see to the closing up of the mill for that day, Ephraim took a seat on the porch, his manner open and receptive.

"And now," he said to his eldest son, "come and sit with me, Adam. Since the moment you arrived, I've sensed there was something you've wanted to say to me, but somehow the time has flown, and we've had little chance to really sit and talk. Soon your visit will be over and you'll be heading back to Krakow." He looked inquiringly at Adam as the younger man took a seat on the bench nearby. "You've scarcely mentioned that lovely lady whom you hope to make your bride."

"Sarah," Adam responded reluctantly. "Sarah Krakowska." He was unable to say more for the moment.

"She's beautiful, of course," Ephraim prodded, keeping the conversation going.

"Very beautiful," said Adam, "and remarkably learned. Her intellectual accomplishments are amazing, and so are her skills as a homemaker. She runs her father's house. He's a widower."

"In short, she's the ideal candidate for my son's wife," Ephraim offered, smiling indulgently.

Adam's eyes fell before his father's steady gaze. Ephraim waited in silence, his concerns mounting as the silence was awkwardly prolonged.

"Yet there is more to this narrative than you've mentioned," Ephraim finally said. "What is there that stills your tongue and clouds your eyes? Have you and Sarah quarreled?"

"No," Adam answered. "We love each other deeply."

"Then what is wrong? For something surely is."

Adam looked at his father, his eyes filling with tears. "It's her brother, Jakob," His voice trailed off into silence. "He's very ill," he managed to say between sobs. "He's going to die."

"That's a great sorrow for the family," said Ephraim. "I'm sorry to hear that. Your Sarah must be very distressed."

"Jakob's illness," Adam murmured, "is hereditary. One of their uncles suffered from it as well. It's a form of epilepsy that's progressive, degenerative. The nervous system is gradually destroyed. The mind withers and decays. It's awful!" Here he broke down completely, weeping brokenly.

"Oh, Adam, I had no idea!" Ephraim rose from his seat and went to sit by his son. He embraced Adam tenderly. "I'm so sorry," he said comfortingly, but for Adam there was no comfort.

"I know what this means," Adam said. "I've asked her father for her hand, and now I can't." He could not say the words at first. "I can't marry her."

Ephraim was silent for a long moment.

"Son," he finally said, "You are a grown man. I can no longer tell you what to do. That's not my place. This is a decision that you alone must make. But one must think of one's children, and their children, and their children's children. Would you willingly condemn them to a fate you would not choose for yourself, had you the choice?"

It was a question to which there could be but one answer.

* * *

Throughout the railway journey back to Krakow, Adam's mood was one of deep sadness. He had read extensively about neurological disorders since Jakob's first seizure. He knew that his friend's malady was not the usual form of epilepsy but instead an insidious degenerative neurological disease that was currently making its presence known with devastating effect.

Before he had left for Warsaw, Adam had discussed with his friend and faculty advisor, Dr. Helmut Lindenmayer, all he had read regarding Jakob's symptoms and the rapidly downhill course the young botanist's illness was pursuing.

Dr. Lindenmayer had summed up his opinion by saying, "I cannot give you a name for your young friend's malady, Adam. I can only tell you that I've seen and heard of other similar cases. These patients do not live long and that is probably a blessing. Invariably, when you search and question, you find that other family members have died in the same tragic way. It's like a curse."

Adam had argued futilely and finally tearfully that other causes might produce the same symptoms, but in the end he had been forced to admit the truth of Lindenmayer's words. Jakob was fatally ill and the same fate might lie in store for any children Adam and Sarah might have if they were so rash as to ignore the implications of Jakob's illness.

Ephraim's words on the porch of the lumber mill came back to Adam's mind repeatedly during the first days following his return to Krakow.

"One must think of one's children, and their children, and their children's children. Would you willingly condemn them to a fate you would not choose for yourself, had you the choice?"

According to ancient rabbinical law, a serious physical or mental impairment in the bride or her family, known but undisclosed to the prospective bridegroom, was grounds to withdraw a proposal of marriage. Between Adam and Sarah, no marriage contract, or ketubah, had been drawn up. Adam, filled with love and youthful enthusiasm, had asked for Sarah's hand in marriage. Abel had consented, imposing conditions of time and economic stability.

Now, everything had changed. As the firstborn son, Adam's obligation to his own family demanded that he withdraw his request and make known to Abel his reasons. Adam felt deep remorse over this necessity. He knew well that Sarah, well educated and already in her mid-twenties, would find it difficult to attract another husband. Once the nature of her younger brother's illness became known, and such information would be difficult to suppress indefinitely, even if the Krakowski family in shame and anguish attempted to conceal the truth, no young man from the Jewish community of Krakow would want her. Furthermore, once Sarah acknowledged the true meaning of the tragedy that had befallen her family, she would not accept any future marriage proposal.

Perhaps the most awkward aspect of Adam's dilemma was finding a way to discuss with Isaak, with whom he had lately shared so much, the imminent dissolution of his engagement to Sarah.

Adam had loved Sarah almost from the moment he had first seen her. Now, he would have to put aside his love for her, faced with the necessity of renouncing any hope of a life together for the two of them. Furthermore, he would sooner or later have to acquaint Isaak with the reasons for his decision. Reluctantly, Adam remembered the joyful occasion on which he had introduced Sarah to his brother Isaak at the time of the Biology Department picnic in the spring of 1866. He could still recall the expression on Isaak's face as he beheld Sarah and reached out to take both her hands in his.

"So here, at last, is Sarah. I've looked forward to meeting you. Adam has told me so much about you, and now I see that it's all true." Isaak had turned to Adam with a mischievous smile and had nudged him playfully. "You're lucky I didn't meet her first."

\* \* \*

By the time Adam had summoned sufficient courage to carry out the painful errand which honor and duty imposed upon him, the Sabbath had begun, and he decided to postpone breaking the news to Sarah and to Abel until the conclusion of that ancient and honored rite.

When the occasion for his visit drew near, Adam's gloom deepened. As he approached the Krakowski's front door, his legs felt leaden. His impulse was to turn and run from the confrontation before him, but he knew he could never face his own family again if he were to commit such an act of cowardice. Steeling himself, he knocked at the door.

Abel Krakowski opened it and seemed pleased to find Adam standing there. "You're back," he said affably. "Sarah will be delighted to see you." He stepped aside to admit Adam, obviously unaware of the young man's reluctance to enter the house.

Adam, as he stood in the entrance hall, contrasted the earlier joyous visits he had paid to the Krakowski home with the ominous significance of his present errand. As Abel closed the front door, Adam felt trapped. Sarah, having awaited with mounting anxiety Adam's first visit upon returning from Warsaw, ran lightly down the stairs and came forward to greet him eagerly, arms outstretched. Adam was shattered. This was the woman he loved, he reminded himself. Until very recently, he could not envision his future without her. Now he could hardly bear to think of the future at all, and the present had abruptly become a waking nightmare. Once more, his father's prophetic words echoed in his mind.

"One must think of one's children, and their children, and their children's children. Would you willingly condemn them to a fate you would not choose for yourself, had you the choice?"

"Adam," Sarah exclaimed excitedly, "at last you're here! I've missed you!" Her loneliness during his absence, her fears and uncertainties regarding Jakob's illness were nakedly apparent to him as their eyes met.

"Sarah," Adam responded, taking her in his arms, "how are you?" When she made no answer but simply gazed longingly into his eyes, Adam felt compelled to ask, "How is Jakob?"

"He's home, finally. He waited until my exams were over so he wouldn't be a burden."

"How like him!" Adam felt genuinely concerned, yet terribly awkward.

"I'll leave you two to visit," Abel said benevolently. "Come to my study afterwards, Adam. We have things to discuss."

"Yes, sir, we do," Adam agreed as Abel withdrew.

"Sarah," he added, unsure how to begin, "you and I must talk as well."

Sarah led him to the parlor and seated herself on the divan facing the over-sized front window, with its panoramic view of the garden. She patted the cushion beside her. "With Jakob's illness and then final exams, you and I haven't talked much of late, have we?" As Adam remained silent, Sarah plunged desperately onward. "Then you were away in Warsaw and," Sarah's eyes met his, and her own became shadowed with dread. "Did something happen when you went home, Adam?"

Adam looked away, unable to meet her eyes. He knew he must follow the course of duty and family obligation, but he dreaded hurting Sarah. "I had a long talk with my father," he said at last. "He put certain things in perspective for me."

Sarah's voice was a hushed whisper as she asked, "What things?"

"Personal choices. Responsibilities. Family loyalties."

Sarah nodded in understanding, and tears gathered in her eyes and coursed slowly down her cheeks. "He told you that you can't marry me," she said dully.

She had given Adam an easy way out; he could blame the painful decision on his own father, but that would not be either truthful or fair. Ephraim had shown Adam where duty lay, but had left the fulfillment of that duty to Adam. Ephraim had thus demonstrated his complete confidence in Adam's maturity and wisdom. It was a heavy burden, one Adam would have preferred to lay aside; but the specter of future generations of his descendants, flawed as now Jakob was, deterred him.

"He told me what marrying you could mean for the family," Adam answered honestly. "He reminded me of the jeopardy our people constantly face, having no homeland and repeatedly subjected to restrictions, pogroms, and expulsions. As the eldest son, I owe it to the family to ensure the survival of its name and its heritage."

Sarah understood the truth of Adam's words, the gravity of his obligation, but she could not help but ask, "What about us?"

"There's no future for us, Sarah," he answered sadly. "There can't be." He gazed at the beautiful face that he loved most in the world, now stained with tears. "I love you," he said softly. "I don't think I'll ever stop loving you, but…"

"But you don't love me enough," she said accusingly.

"I can't simply forget about our children and their children." He paused, unable to go on.

"I love you, Adam," she exclaimed passionately. "Enough to forget everything else! I thought you felt the same."

"That's not fair," Adam answered heatedly. "You know what it means to transmit a disease like Jakob's to a helpless child. Surely, as a scientist and as a woman, you wouldn't want to take that risk."

"We might be lucky," Sarah said hopefully.

Adam shook his head. "Even if the disease were to skip our children's generation, it would almost certainly afflict our grandchildren. What could we say to those grandchildren? That we took a calculated risk? That you and I gambled, but that they lost?"

Sarah put her fingers to his lips. "Please stop, Adam." She looked pleadingly at him. "Let's not spend our last moments together arguing."

She moved closer, and he took her in his arms, but she was not reassured by that closeness. "There's nothing I can do or say to change your mind, is there?"

"Hush, Sarah," Adam whispered. "It's taken me a long time to accept this. We must both accept it. Don't make it more difficult for us."

Sarah stood, backed away and looked into Adam's face. "I think I've seen this coming ever since the day of Jakob's first seizure," she said bitterly. "I just wouldn't admit it to myself. Now I have to." She turned away from him. "I suppose you'll have to tell Father."

Adam nodded. "Under the circumstances, I can do no less."

"I'll wait for you outside," Sarah said. "Come and find me before you go. I'll need some time to find the courage to say good-bye." With that, she fled from the room.

Adam's eyes followed her, tears now beginning to cloud his vision. He had thought the most difficult task in his life would be saying the words he had just said to Sarah. Now he realized that an even more painful task lay ahead.

With great effort, Adam quieted his misgivings and approached Abel Krakowski's study. The two men had spoken together there once before on a much happier occasion. Today, Adam searched vainly for words in which to phrase his painful recitation. Abel made the task more difficult by embracing Adam as he entered the study.

"You look grim, my boy," he said. "I trust all is well at home."

Adam made an attempt to smile. "Better than I could have hoped," he answered.

"And is all well between you and my Sarah? She's been nervous and edgy of late."

"I suppose that's natural," Adam answered. "She's just completed a very difficult course of study. She had her thesis to write and then final exams."

Abel nodded agreeably. "I still think it's a great deal of trouble for a girl who's planning to get married and raise a family. However, Sarah's a brilliant girl. We're all proud of her, even poor Jakob." Adam looked distressed at the mention of Jakob's name, especially when Abel added, "Have you seen Jakob since you came back?"

"Not yet," Adam replied, "although I intend to before I leave."

Abel looked up, startled. "Aren't you staying for dinner?"

Adam blanched and shook his head. "I don't think that would be appropriate," he answered.

A look of puzzlement crossed Abel's face. "Why not?"

Adam turned away. "Mer Krakowski," he began.

"Abel," Krakowski corrected. "Surely, between future father and son, first names are appropriate."

"You don't understand," Adam protested. "We aren't, I can't…" He glanced desperately about the room. "May I sit down?"

"Of course," Abel said courteously. He gestured toward a chair, then sat facing Adam. "Tell me, Adam, have you and Sarah quarreled?"

Adam shook his head. "It's nothing so simple or easily mended."

"What is it, then?"

Adam cringed at the look of appeal in Abel's eyes. "I think perhaps you may already have guessed," he answered. Abel's eyes locked with Adam's own so that Adam could hardly speak the terrible words. "I must fulfill a very painful duty," he began haltingly. "I find myself unable to accept the honor you have done me in granting my request for your daughter's hand in marriage."

Abel's reaction showed that he had not guessed. "Unable to accept?"

"I've already spoken with Sarah," Adam said quietly. "She understands my reasons."

"And she is satisfied with those reasons?"

Adam nodded, his voice momentarily failing him.

Abel's voice was like a clap of thunder. "Well, I am not! You insult my daughter and my family's honor!"

"No insult is intended, sir. What has happened to Jakob confounds the wisdom of men. I've spent hours studying all that is currently known about neurological disease. I've discussed his case with professors far wiser than I. The best they can tell me is that Jakob has a hereditary form of degenerative epilepsy. They cannot give it a name, but they have seen it before. It is relentless and ultimately fatal."

"Ah," Abel exclaimed, "such is the judgment of doctors! But, after all, they are only men!"

"There is still much to be learned about the nervous system and the diseases that attack it," Adam said sadly. "It's an engrossing study, but…"

Abel nodded angrily. "Indeed! An engrossing study! That's what you call the sorrow that has overtaken my house?"

"I share that sorrow," Adam responded. "I love your daughter as I never thought it possible to love anyone. Yet, I cannot marry her. I'm not free to follow the dictates of my heart and deny the obligations of my name. That's why I've decided to leave Krakow, forever!"

"You're fortunate," Abel shouted. "For you it is ended. You can leave Krakow and forget. What about my Sarah?"

"I can never forget," Adam replied, looking into Abel's eyes. "Not as long as I live. Sarah knows that. I can only hope you will come to know it, too."

Abel's shoulders sagged. "So there is no resolution to this terrible thing." Sadly he shook his head. "What am I saying? What resolution can there be to Adonai's will?"

Adam came forward and took both Abel's hands in his own. "You wish for a solution no more passionately than I do, sir," he said hoarsely, scarcely able to hold back his tears.

Abel was equally moved. Tears of frustration and anger filled his eyes. "Adonai is all powerful and all knowing," he said brokenly. "Yet, there are times when His wisdom is incomprehensible. I'm an old man now; I don't care so much for myself. But my Sarah was so happy." The tears began to fall unchecked down his cheeks.

"I, too, was happy, sir," Adam said sadly.

Abel turned away from Adam, his hands covering his face. "This is the end of my family. As the ancient laws command, I free you from your promise."

"It is a freedom for which I never wished," Adam said quietly.

Abel raised his head and looked beseechingly at Adam. "How long will my son live, and how will he die?"

Adam hesitated, uncertain as to how he should answer. He must be truthful, yet he did not wish to inflict further pain. "I don't know exactly," he said haltingly. "He will grow steadily weaker. One day, he'll go to sleep and not wake up anymore. Before that happens, there'll be more frequent convulsions, then coma."

Abel nodded resignedly. "My younger son," he lamented, "is condemned to an early death. My elder son and my daughter are accursed by a mysterious disease that they dare not risk passing on to children." He walked to the window and looked out into the garden. Then, he turned once more to face Adam. "You have a duty to your own family which cannot be ignored."

"So my father reminded me," Adam responded.

"He is right, of course. Had our positions been reversed, I should have done exactly the same. I cannot hold it in my heart to blame you for what you have done, but I cannot accept it. This has all come upon me too suddenly. The doom that my entire family faces seems too overwhelming, too final." His voice broke. Without another word, he turned and left the room.

Adam stood alone, tortured with the memories of all he had enjoyed in the Krakowski home. Overcome with grief and loss, he wept unashamedly.

When, after several moments, he had regained a measure of composure, Adam walked out into the garden. Here, too, he was assailed by happy memories. As he walked toward the center of the garden, he saw Jakob seated in a wheelchair among his Euphorbia collection. Jakob looked up as his friend approached.

"You've c...come to s...sa ...say g...g...goodbye," he said haltingly, his speech now showing the obvious degeneration of cranial nerve function precipitated by the progression of his disease. It was an odd contrast with his clear perception of Adam's imminent departure.

Adam nodded. "Each time I visit a garden, I shall think of you here among the plants that you know and love so well."

Jakob glanced forlornly about the garden. He seemed lost. Hesitantly, he reached out toward Adam from his wheelchair. "I shall n...nev...er f...or...get..." He stopped, confused. It seemed to Adam that Jakob found it difficult not only to say the words but even to think of them.

Adam knelt beside his friend's chair and embraced him. For Jakob Krakowski, life held nothing but despair. Try as he might, Adam could think of no reassuring words to say.

The two young men remained silent for a few moments, gazing at the plants that surrounded them. Finally, Adam took Jakob's hand. "'Til we meet again, my friend," he said, unwilling to say a final good-bye.

Jakob smiled, his eyes brimming with tears. "Yes," he said, "may we m...m ...meet in hap...pi... ier ti...ti ..mes."

Adam squeezed Jakob's hand, nodded, and walked away. On an impulse, he turned back for a final wave of farewell. Jakob, gazing fixedly at his Euphorbia collection, did not see the gesture.

Sarah was waiting for Adam at the edge of the garden, out of sight of Jakob. She looked up as Adam came toward her, love and despair both mirrored in her eyes. Adam halted, gazing at Sarah with love. He opened his arms and she ran to him. They clung to each other in silence.

Sarah drew away first and gazed into Adam's eyes. "I suppose now that you will be leaving Krakow."

Adam nodded, lowering his gaze.

"When?"

"Soon," he answered simply. He reached out to her. "Sarah, dearest, what else can I do?"

She shook her head resignedly.

"That's just it," she said. "There doesn't seem to be anything that anyone can do." She looked piercingly at Adam. "I almost wish that Jakob had waited to get sick until after you and I were married. I wonder what you would have done then."

Adam stood in silence. There was little he could say in answer to her words. Finally, he looked at Sarah, and she could see the tears in his eyes.

"Do you wish me to go now?"

In lieu of an answer, she took his hand. Silently she guided him down a path that led away from the main garden. They came to a free-standing circular patio that her family had seldom used since Sarah's mother had died. It was partially enclosed and equipped with cushioned benches. A central round table completed its furnishings. The patio was shaded by tall trees and thick shrubs so that it could not be seen from the house. The air was heavily scented with roses, planted around the gazebo's periphery, their fragrance imparting a heady, intoxicating aroma to the atmosphere.

Sarah walked to the edge of the gazebo and leaned lightly on the rail. "When I was little, this was my favorite place," she said, savoring the poignant beauty of her surroundings. "Whenever I was sad or lonely, I would come here. My mother knew that, and she would always come and find me here. She'd console me and dry my tears. Somehow, she could always make everything right." Sarah looked at Adam, a subtle challenge in her eyes.

"Mothers are good at that," Adam said, avoiding that challenging glance.

"Even mother couldn't do anything about this," Sarah said bitterly. "She used to tell me about her uncle. He died young. And no one quite understood the cause. Now I know what it was. As far as Mother was aware, no one else in the family was ever ill like Uncle Saul." She turned away. "And yet, his illness has come between me and what I wanted most in the world. I don't feel any different from the way I always have, and yet, suddenly I'm an object instead of a person, an object of fear and horror."

Adam went to her and gently turned her to face him. "You're still a person to me, the most beautiful woman I've ever known." He kissed her tenderly.

Sarah moved in his arms, responding to his kiss and caressing the back of his neck. Adam was reminded of the way she had aroused him when they had first touched each other accidentally in the library. They had each reached simultaneously for the same book, and the contact had been like an electric shock, only much more pleasant. He felt that same desire for her now, stronger and more compelling, and more urgently to be resisted.

Sarah sank to her knees on the gazebo floor, drawing Adam down beside her, burying her face against his chest. "Hold me, Adam," she pleaded.

Adam held her closer, soothing and caressing her, trying vainly to reassure her even as he tried to find a way to say good-bye that would not wound her further.

She looked up at him. "When you go, my life will be over," she said, her voice hoarse. "I'll go on breathing and moving, but inside I'll be dead!"

Adam lifted her face and kissed her gently, unable to respond in words to the utter desolation she expressed.

Sarah clung to him desperately, her breath coming in ragged gasps. "Adam," she said tensely, "we're hidden here and we're alone. Can't we make love just this once?"

"Sarah," Adam answered, "we mustn't. You know that! "

Her eyes grew hard and defiant. "Why mustn't we? I've lost everything I hold dear. What is there left for me to lose? You say that you love me. Do you mean that?"

"You know I do," he said gently.

"Then show me! Can you go away and leave me forever without having truly known me?" Almost hysterically, she reached out to him, her fingers tearing open the buttons of his shirt and then stroking his naked chest. She kissed his cheek, his lips, and his throat, all the while clinging to him and trembling as he tried valiantly to restrain both her and himself.

At last, Adam could no longer struggle against both Sarah's desperate desire and his own burning passion. He had waited so long to find her, and when he had, she had fulfilled his every dream of grace and beauty. Then, almost as if Adonai regretted His generosity, all she meant to him had been snatched away before Adam could claim his beloved.

The present moment suddenly became paramount. The future and all that it might hold receded into the abstract. Adam surrendered to the demands of Sarah's compelling need and his own as they lay there in the shaded gazebo, warmed by summer's final glory and intoxicated by the scent of innumerable roses in full bloom.

Afterwards, when they lay still in each other's arms, Adam told Sarah of his feelings. He could not regret that they had shared these moments of love. In the years to come, the memory of their lovemaking would help to assuage, at least in part, his sense of bitter loss. He hoped it would do the same for Sarah.

Somewhere, he had heard it said or read that it was better to have loved and lost then never to have loved at all. That seemed a bitter irony to him at this moment, but perhaps on some future day, that sentiment might offer consolation.

An hour later, Adam and Sarah stood at the rear gate of the Krakowski property. Tears ran silently down Sarah's cheeks as Adam held her tightly, kissing her passionately and wishing the moment might never end.

Finally, Sarah broke away. "Now, my love, you must go."

"There's time yet," Adam answered, squeezing her hand. "And there's so much left to be said."

Sarah pressed her fingers to his lips. "The less said now, the easier it will be for both of us."

Adam glanced at her uneasily, his love and concern for her threatening to overwhelm him. "Will you be all right?"

"I'm sure I will," she answered with a small, brave smile.

Adam's eyes searched her face. "May I write to you?"

"What would be the point?"

"I'd know how you are, what's happening to you. At least, I would if you answered my letters."

"Oh, Adam, don't tempt me like this. Don't close the door on us and then half-open it again. That would be an exquisite form of torture."

"Sarah, I didn't mean it like that," Adam responded quickly. "I only meant, I care what happens to you."

After a long moment, Sarah nodded. "I know, Adam. I care about you, too. But if this must be good-bye, then so be it." She tried again to smile, but this time did not quite succeed.

Adam kissed her fingers tenderly, then turned and quickly walked away. Sarah watched him until he was out of sight, tears of frustration and regret wetting her face. She had sought to make Adam stay in the only way she could think of, yet when she had seen his resolve weaken, she had sent him away. That had been the most difficult decision of Sarah's life. Still, she consoled herself. Adam had left her with love in his eyes, mingled with tears of parting. Such a parting was much better than watching love slowly turn into hatred if the fearful potential of Jakob's illness were fulfilled in any of their offspring.

## CHAPTER FIFTEEN
## SWEET SORROW

The night before he was to leave for Warsaw, Adam packed and repacked the last of his possessions in the brown leather case which his cousins had given him as a going-away present. It was a handsome piece of luggage emblazoned with his initials, and it gave him a definite glow of pride. However, even the compulsive, almost frantic, activity of last-minute packing failed to relieve the tension that Adam felt.

Even now, he could barely restrain himself from returning to the Krakowski home and retracting his renunciation of Sarah. He loved her now more than ever. His body remembered hers with a yearning that was sheer torture. In his mind, he relived every detail of their last time together. Adam knew that if Sarah had not insisted that he leave, he would not have found the strength to part from her. He was grateful that his train was scheduled to leave early the next morning. There would be no opportunity for his resolve to be undermined further.

At last, he closed and locked the shiny metal fastenings of the new case and placed it near the door with his other bags. He undressed and went to bed, but he was unable to sleep. He got up, wrapped his dressing gown about him, and sat by his window.

He gazed unseeingly at the modest garden at the rear of the Polewski residence. The breeze bore a hint of rose fragrance that reminded Adam yet again of Sarah. Her words came back to him mockingly.

"I almost wish that Jakob had waited to get sick until after we were married. I wonder what you would have done then."

Adam still had no answer to that bitter query. He was shaken by the knowledge that his love and his vulnerability had betrayed him into committing the very act he should have avoided at all costs. Nevertheless, he had enjoyed every moment of their union. He had savored and gloried in the pleasure it brought him more than he had in any of the few such physical liaisons he had previously tasted. They had been empty, devoid of real feeling. With Sarah, he had joined emotionally as well as physically. He had experienced a fulfillment he had never previously anticipated, and without her, his future seemed bleak and empty. The thought of it made him want to weep, but it seemed he had shed all his tears on the day he had parted from Sarah. A knock at his door roused Adam from his painful reverie.

"Come in."

The door opened and Isaak poked his head around it. "All ready for tomorrow?"

Adam shrugged. "I suppose so."

Isaak stepped into the room and sat on the bed.

"Why so glum? I'd think you'd be enthusiastically planning for the future, yours and Sarah's."

Adam winced at the mention of Sarah's name.

"When do you expect to send for her?"

Adam shook his head bitterly.

"I don't," he answered, his voice was almost a whisper.

"You plan to come back to Krakow to practice?" Isaak asked, unintentionally rubbing more salt into his brother's psychological wounds. "I assumed you'd be joining Samuel Jedewreski."

Adam stood up so abruptly that he nearly knocked over his chair. "I probably will." he responded flatly.

Isaak rose from the bed, disconcerted.

"Has something gone wrong between you and Sarah?"

"Yes," Adam answered sharply. "Everything's gone wrong!" His shoulders began to shake with tearless sobs.

Isaak touched his brother's shoulder gently.

"Would it help to talk about it, or would you rather be alone?"

Adam shook his head dolefully and then reached out to clasp Isaak's hand.

"No, don't go. It's worse being alone. I just keep thinking about her." He seated himself dejectedly on the bed, his shoulders slumped, his hands clasped before him. "I waited a long time before I found someone I could love," he said wistfully. "We were supremely happy, ideally suited to one another. We shared the same beliefs, kindred ambitions. We even wanted the same number of children. You'd have thought nothing could possibly come between us."

"Yet something has."

Adam looked at Isaak and nodded.

"It's torn us apart," he answered sadly. "Her brother has degenerative epilepsy. Her great uncle apparently had it, too, though it was never discussed by her mother's family. "

Isaak looked stricken as the words registered. "You mean the disease is hereditary?"

Adam nodded and then went on to explain to Isaak the whole painful issue of his withdrawal of the request to marry Sarah and her father's reaction. Most painful of all was the recitation of Jakob's rapidly deteriorating condition, and what it meant for the Krakowski family.

Isaak glanced compassionately at Adam.

"How did Sarah take it when you told her all this?"

"I think she felt I had betrayed her."

"How do _you_ feel?" Isaak questioned.

"Like I've been betrayed, too. Not by Sarah, but by Adonai."

Isaak looked downward at his hands.

"I wish there were something I could say that would help."

"I wish there were something I could _do_," Adam answered.

Isaak looked anguished.

"I know how you feel, but you're the firstborn. Father would be beside himself if I were to consider marrying a girl from a family with a hereditary problem. But you," There was no need to finish the sentence.

"That's true, of course," Adam agreed, "but that's not what I meant. I wish that I, that we, the medical profession, knew more about such ailments. I wish we could somehow change the hereditary pattern to prevent the transmission of diseases such as this."

Isaak patted his arm reassuringly.

"Who knows? Perhaps one day you will do something to prevent them."

Adam looked at his brother mournfully, despite his appreciation of Isaak's efforts to cheer him.

"Even if I do, it will be too late for Sarah and me."

\* \* \*

Adam slept fitfully that night, tormented by memories of Sarah and by thoughts of all that might have been. Toward morning, he gave up trying to sleep. He bathed and dressed in a mood of depression that was only partly dispelled by Cousin Jada's perfectly-prepared breakfast. Adam, expressing his regret at their approaching separation, was surprised to find that Jada and Zaccahreus were not nearly so downcast as he.

"We're sorry to see you leave, Adam, but it's good that conditions have settled down to the point that you are able to go home," Zaccahreus said, clasping one sinewy arm around Adam's broad shoulders.

Jada, noting Adam's distraction, added lightly, "Who knows? We may come and visit you in Warsaw. I've never been there, and Zaccahreus has been promising to take me for years." She looked at Zaccahreus who winked at her.

"Perhaps in the spring, we'll come," Zaccahreus commented. "That might be the best time of all. By then, you'll be graduating."

"I'd love you to be there for my graduation," Adam responded eagerly.

Jada nodded. "We'll plan on it for then," she said. "That way it will seem almost like seeing our Jacob receive his degree." There were tears in her eyes as she spoke.

Isaak, touched by his cousin's feelings, tried to lighten the mood.

"That's a great idea," he said.

Adam reached out and embraced Jada tenderly. "I'll never forget all you've done for Isaak and me," he said warmly. "I shall look forward to your coming in the spring."

"Maybe," Zaccahreus said, "your girl can travel with us. With Isaak along, that will make us a foursome."

Isaak came to Adam's rescue. "There's plenty of time to make plans for spring," he said, picking up a pair of Adam's suitcases. "We'd better get started for the railway station or Adam is going to miss his train."

Adam picked up the remaining suitcase. His eyes swept the parlor which held so many joyful memories for him. This would always be his second home, a constant reminder of his student days in Krakow. Adam had come to love this city almost as much as Isaak did. Here he had fulfilled his dearest dream, the dream of becoming a doctor. Here, also, he had lost his most cherished possession, the hope of marrying Sarah. He must not dwell on that sorrow, he reminded himself sternly. He turned toward Cousin Jada.

"Are you sure you and Zaccahreus won't come with me to the station?"

Jada smiled and shook her head. "I'm not one for long good-byes, especially in a crowd. I'll only cry and embarrass you."

"I wouldn't be embarrassed." Adam said. "I'd be crying, myself."

"Jada's right," Zaccahreus said. "You and Isaak have last-minute things to say to each other. Your cousin and I will see you in the spring." He cuffed Adam's shoulder good-naturedly. "Off with the both of you now, and give our love to Elana and Ephraim."

September in Krakow was a magical month. The trees and shrubs wore their brightest foliage, the sky was iridescent in its clarity, and the Zakopane Mountains, still lush and green, seemed almost close enough to touch. Adam and Isaak had skied there last winter, and had climbed one of the nearer peaks in the spring. Adam remembered those moments of joyous comradeship as he gazed at the mountains that were visible from the platform of the railway station.

Isaak's voice reached him distantly.

"What are you thinking?"

Adam turned to face his brother, drawing his attention away from his reminiscences.

"I was just remembering. I wish you were coming with me."

"I wish I were, too," Isaak answered. "Mother and Father are going to be disappointed," he added as he handed to Adam a letter addressed to Ephraim. "I've tried to explain it all in here, though I'm sure I haven't done it very well. I'm counting on you to make them understand. Assure them I'll be home between terms."

"You'd better," Adam warned, "or you're going to have a lot of explaining to do."

The sound of a distant whistle drew their attention to the approaching train.

Isaak said, his voice husky with the effort to keep it from breaking, "It's not going to seem the same around here without you."

"Just don't get lost," Adam teased him. The two shook hands, then embraced awkwardly, unwilling to say good-bye.

Isaak's eyes were grave as he asked, "Are you going to be all right?"

Adam shrugged. "Sure!"

"If only my classes didn't start two weeks ahead of yours, I'd risk going home and then getting back in time."

"Don't be silly! You're just getting over pneumonia. What you need is rest, not excitement," Adam observed in his best professional tone. "Now, me, I need excitement."

"You need," Isaak froze as if he'd seen a ghost. He stared over Adam's shoulder.

Adam watched Isaak's face uneasily.

"What is it?"

"For a moment," Isaak responded, "I could have sworn I saw Sarah standing there on the platform."

Adam closed his eyes momentarily, then opened them and turned his head slowly. His eyes met those of a slender blonde woman standing opposite the two brothers on the platform. All the feelings he had sworn to stifle, the love, the longing, the frustration, welled up in him anew. His body started automatically to move toward her before his mind registered the fact that she was not truly Sarah.

Isaak's hand on his shoulder held him back. Slowly Adam turned and faced his brother. "It's unbelievable. She's so like Sarah."

Isaak nodded in assent. Meanwhile, the young woman was joined by a man slightly older than Adam. The two embraced, then turned and walked away along the platform, holding hands.

"Damned unlucky coincidence," Isaak said under his breath, picking up the two suitcases he had carried from the Polewski home. He nudged Adam toward the nearest passenger car. "Let's get you settled." He said it casually but there was nothing casual about the way he pushed Adam forward toward the lowered steps of the railway car. Adam paused at the bottom of the stairs.

"Am I always going to feel this way every time I see someone who reminds me of Sarah?"

Isaak's expression was one of sympathy.

"Adam, take my advice. Forget Sarah, for her sake as well as yours. Find another girl and marry her. The sooner the better."

"I love her, Isaak. And she doesn't even want me to write to her."

"Perhaps that's best."

"But that way, I won't know what's become of her."

Isaak put his hand on Adam's shoulder. "Sarah is a wise young woman. Her decision may seem harsh, but it's also the cleanest and kindest way to end an unendurable situation."

"I'll never love anyone else the way I love her."

"I know," Isaak responded. He spoke from his own memories of Mariska. "But you will love again, eventually." His words reflected his earnest hopes for himself as well as for Adam. Isaak turned and deftly handed up the bags one at a time to the train attendant. Having assured himself that Adam had his ticket and travel permit, he added, "I guess that's everything. Your transcripts and records, they've already been sent ahead?"

Adam nodded.

"Are you going to be all right?" Isaak asked again, a note of worry in his voice.

"Yes, of course." Adam grinned lopsidedly and punched Isaak on the arm. "Stop clucking like a mother hen." He jumped aboard the train as it started to move very slowly away.

"I'm going to miss you," Isaak called out, waving. Adam waved back as the train gathered speed. Isaak stood on the platform watching Adam's train shrink into the distance until it finally disappeared.

As Isaak walked back alone to the home of his cousins, he yearned for the school term to begin. Once he was involved in his studies, he would be too busy to feel homesick as he did now. Already, he missed Adam and the train had barely left. The weeks and months of the fall term stretched before Isaak bleakly. Yet, the sooner the term began, the sooner it would end. Then Isaak, too, would be boarding a train bound for home.

* * *

The entire Marjzendiak family, from Ephraim to Michael, met Adam's train, engulfing him with the enthusiasm of their reception. Amid the joyful embracing, Adam noticed that Ephraim was scrutinizing the faces of the other passengers getting off the train. Adam was heart-struck by Ephraim's questioning glance and his words of disappointment.

"Isn't Isaak with you?"

Adam reached into his pocket and handed Ephraim the letter from Isaak.

"Isaak has been ill lately, Father. The doctors at the University were against his making such a long trip at this time."

"It's not serious, is it?"

Adam shook his head.

"He's much better now. It's just that the next year of graduate study is going to be trying for him. Isaak and I discussed it at length before I left, and I agree that it's for the best. He was disappointed at not being able to see all of you now, but he's planning to come home at the fall term recess."

"You're sure he's all right?" Elana asked pointedly.

"Otherwise, I wouldn't have left him," Adam assured her. Elana in response to this assurance, felt comforted because of her confidence in her son's medical judgment.

Ephraim tucked Isaak's letter into his pocket.

Together he and Adam collected the accumulated treasures and memorabilia of four years of living and studying away from home. In addition to the three suitcases Adam had brought with him on the train, there were two large crates of books which had been shipped ahead and held at the station. Ephraim shook his head.

"Does the study of medicine really require so much paraphernalia?"

"I hadn't realized there was so much, and this isn't all."

Ephraim looked at him questioningly.

"It isn't?"

"Isaak is sending the rest of my books next week." Adam replied.

"In that case, its fortunate we moved to a larger house before you came home to stay." Ephraim's expression was one of ironic amusement.

Once they reached Plaz Marjzendiak and had Adam settled in the room set aside for him, Ephraim went to his study where, as soon as he could find a moment alone, he read Isaak's letter.

"Dear Father,

Needless to say, I hardly expected to contract pneumonia in mid-summer, and I am disappointed at having to forego the pleasure of seeing you as well as Mother, Leah, and Michael. By now, Michael has no doubt forgotten that he has two elder brothers.

Some day, I hope to make up to him for these years of enforced separation. Nonetheless, I am grateful to you for your selflessness in sending Adam and me to Krakow when you did. You gave us the opportunity to become our own men, to stand on our own feet. I hope in time that you can feel as proud of us as we are of you.

My love to all of you. Obviously, I'm still looking forward to my first view of Plaz Marjzendiak. Hopefully, I shall have that pleasure at the end of the fall term.

Until then, your devoted son,

Isaak"

After reading Isaak's letter, Ephraim felt reassured. He looked forward with excitement to the end of the fall term when he and his second son would have an opportunity to discuss in person Isaak's plans for the future.

# CHAPTER SIXTEEN
# MUSIC HATH CHARMS

On a mid-September morning in 1866, a messenger arrived at the Marzjendiak estate while Ephraim and Elana were having breakfast. The messenger carried an invitation to Elana to join Mira Pietrowska for luncheon at her home the following day. Elana showed Ephraim the invitation, written on elegant, scented notepaper.

She asked her husband, "Should I accept?"

"I see no reason to refuse," Ephraim answered reasonably.

"I never feel quite comfortable with Mira, despite her generosity to us. There always seems to be an ulterior side to her." Elana picked nervously at her hard-boiled egg as she searched for words to express her uneasiness. "She somehow manages always to put me at something of a disadvantage."

Ephraim raised his eyebrows in obvious surprise.

"It's only natural for her to invite you to lunch, dear. We're neighbors, with very close ties. You should feel free to do the same with her, and the Lord knows you've no cause to feel at a disadvantage with any other woman."

Fortified by her husband's confidence in her, Elana sent the messenger off with her acceptance. Later that day, she carefully chose an elegant, full-skirted, emerald-green silk chiffon dress and the accessories she would wear with it for the luncheon the following day. Eyeing herself in the mirror over her dressing table, she also decided to change her coiffure to complement the flowered and beribboned hat she had selected.

Promptly at 11:30 the following morning, Mira Pietrowska's coachman called for Elana. During the brief journey to the neighboring estate, Elana recalled the first time Mira had paid her a visit, bearing rose cuttings descended from the garden of Empress Josephine. Elana had subsequently made it a point to read about that famous garden and to view reproductions at the Warsaw Art Museum of Redoute's well-known paintings of the empress' prize roses. Elana smiled to think that at last her garden was indeed as beautiful as Josephine's if not as famous, just as Mira Pietrowska had predicted two years earlier.

As the carriage turned up the long Pietrowski driveway, Elana reflected on all that her neighbors had done for her family. Most recently, there was Ephraim's promotion at the bank and his appointment to the Bank Advisory Council. Earlier, of course, there had been the entailing of the land and the restoration of the Zielinski estate where the Marzjendiaks now lived. Most memorable of all was the family's dramatic rescue from their sacked and desecrated former home in the Stare Miasto. Indeed, there was much for which Elana had reason to be grateful to Mira and Franz Pietrowski.

As the carriage drew up before the house, Mira came to meet Elana. She welcomed her guest with warmth and enthusiasm, commenting on the glorious weather and the fact that it provided a perfect setting for their al fresco luncheon in Mira's gazebo.

"It sounds delightful," Elana agreed, her eyes appraising Mira's luxurious, high-waisted lavender afternoon dress. As beautiful as it was, Elana was pleased to note that her own outfit did not suffer by comparison.

As they walked through Mira's topiary garden, Elana asked, "Where are the girls?"

Mira smiled enigmatically. "Pola and Leah have planned a surprise for us. I arranged for their lunches to be served earlier."

This explanation aroused Elana's curiosity but she declined to comment.

Over lunch, Mira skillfully guided the conversation to a discussion of Leah's progress since commencing her studies with Madam Maria Boroska. "You must feel very proud of your daughter," she said. "Maria says she learns with remarkable quickness, and she doesn't forget easily. She's done particularly well with her music."

"Leah has always loved music," Elana responded. "When Adam gave her a recorder for her fifth Hanukah, it became like a talisman. Her playing seems to give her a great deal of satisfaction, and of course we are grateful to you and to Pola for the piano lessons."

"My pleasure," Mira said graciously, neglecting to correct Elana's obvious misconception.

Mira recalled memories of her own childhood, some of which she graphically related to Elana, injecting her stories with a humor and a wealth of detail which brought them vividly to life. Despite her earlier misgivings, Elana was drawn closer to her hostess by the candor and enthusiasm that Mira expressed.

"You and I met long after my father died," Mira continued. "He was a very prim and proper gentleman of the "old school" who felt that children should be seen rather than heard, and that women should keep to their proper place." Mira smiled grimly. "He wore a moustache, which he trimmed carefully every morning, and he would twirl it whenever he was agitated."

Mira made a wry face and reached up to twirl an imaginary moustache, mimicking her father's characteristic gesture and wringing from Elana a peal of laughter that paid tribute to Mira's talent as a mime.

"He named me Mira-Alexandra, and he would always call me that, no matter what the circumstances. He was an excellent provider for the family but dreadfully cold and never much aware of my feelings." She paused once more, as if wrestling with her own thoughts. When she continued, her voice took on a resolute tone. "I sympathize with Leah's love of music because I share it. I should like to assist her in developing her talent. "

Elana gazed thoughtfully at her hostess. "Why?"

Somewhat taken aback by the bluntness of the question, Mira replied, "So that she may achieve her full potential, as I never did." Mira leaned forward to emphasize her next point. "Leah possesses a marvelous gift. I don't want to see that wasted."

"Naturally, I'm very grateful for all your help," Elana responded. "However ..."

"However," Mira said, waving her hand deprecatingly, "enough of that for now. Let's enjoy our lunch and see what the girls have in store for us. We can talk more about my ideas later."

Lunch consisted of freshly baked bread, a salad of assorted raw vegetables garnished with an herbal mustard sauce, and a compote of fruit gathered from the Pietrowski's vast orchard. Mira's gazebo provided the perfect setting for this delightful repast.

Afterwards, the two women strolled back through the garden at a leisurely pace. Mira led the way up the veranda steps and into the music room. The furniture there had been rearranged to provide a stage-like setting, with the grand piano at its center. Mira gestured toward two Louis XV chairs placed side by side, and Elana seated herself expectantly as Mira moved gracefully to the bell pull to signal Pola that they had arrived.

Pola, wearing a demure dress of blue satin, decorated with lace-edged ruffles, entered the room. She curtsied to the audience of two and moved swiftly to the piano. Pola began her performance with a Chopin Etude, then proceeded to the composer's Fantasy Impromptu, followed by the Minute Waltz. Mira and Elana responded with enthusiastic applause as Pola completed her part of the program. Pola curtsied prettily and made a graceful exit.

Moments later, Leah entered. She wore a dress of cream-colored lace, trimmed with delicate pink silk rosebuds. A matching bandeau, made of the same flowers, held back her generous cascade of auburn curls. Elana recalled vividly the enthusiasm with which Leah had made this dress, and now she understood why Leah had referred to the garment as a "dress for a special occasion."

Leah had learned to curtsy from Pola. She executed the gesture with a charm that owed much to the gaucheness of youth. Leah then walked quickly to the piano and seated herself. For a moment she paused as though gathering her thoughts. As Elana and Mira watched, Leah's mood seemed to change. A wonderful composure settled over her and with it an air of self-possession which she normally lacked. Her hands hovered above the piano keys for a long moment. Then she began to play. Faithfully, Leah rendered the three Brahms Capriccios, which were her part of the program. Her execution was precise and polished, graced with a maturity that belied her youth and that enabled her to communicate, through the composer's notes, in a way that was not otherwise open to her.

Elana turned to Mira. "It's difficult to believe that this is Leah," she said wonderingly.

"I quite agree with you," Mira whispered. "If Brahms could be here to hear her, he would be pleased at her rendition." To herself, Mira added that if she had known where to find the famed composer, she might even have had the audacity to invite him to hear the recital in order to strengthen her position and facilitate achieving the goal she had set for herself.

When the performance ended, both women applauded. Elana rose from her chair and went to embrace Leah who responded with characteristic childish enthusiasm. Gone now was the poised, mature artist she had seemed during her recital a few moments earlier. Pola re-entered the room and she, too, generously applauded Leah's playing.

"That was lovely, dear," Elana said appreciatively. She turned to Pola. "You are a marvelous teacher."

The two girls glanced guiltily at one another and giggled. Mira joined them, taking Pola and Leah each by the hand. "Girls, you performed beautifully," she said approvingly.

At that moment, Maria Boroski entered the music room. "I agree. You both played <u>very</u> well."

"I wish you had taken my suggestion and joined us, Maria," Mira said, patting the teacher's shoulder.

"I listen better when I'm not distracted by watching," Maria answered.

Leah drew closer to her mother. "Mama," she whispered, "there's something you should know."

"What is it, dear?"

"Pola is my very dearest friend," Leah answered, "and she was my teacher at first, but for the past year, Madam Boroska has been giving me music lessons, just as she does Pola."

"Yes," Mira commented, "and it's too bad that she will soon be leaving us."

Leah looked at Mira in shocked surprise. "Madam Boroska is leaving?"

Mira nodded. "Yes, dear. I thought you knew." Mira turned to Pola. "Didn't you tell Leah?"

Pola blushed. "I was going to tell her after our recital, Mother," Pola answered. "I thought it might upset her if I said something about it before. I wanted today to be perfect."

"That's understandable, dear," Mira answered. She turned to Elana. "Despite the time and effort Maria has put into learning Russian, she is still prohibited from teaching in the schools. In Galicia, she'll have a much better chance to continue her career."

"Besides," Maria added, "I've taught the children all I can, both in academic subjects and in music. Now that things are getting back to normal, Erik has already entered secondary school. As for Pola and Leah, as you can tell, they are both ready for more advanced instruction."

As the small party walked out onto the veranda, Maria whispered a few words to Mira and then excused herself. Mira smiled and turned to the children. "There are treats waiting for you in the kitchen, girls."

Pola and Leah chorused as one. "Treats?"

"Your favorite, apricot ice and cookies."

As the two girls raced happily into the house, Elana called after Leah. "Don't be long, dear. We'll be leaving soon."

"Yes, Mama," Leah answered, and ran after her friend.

"That was truly a delightful surprise," Mira remarked. "Leah has come a long way in just two years, don't you think?"

"Indeed, yes," Elana answered. "She sounded almost professional."

Mira looked at her archly. "Hardly that. But she could be." Mira gestured toward a garden seat nearby and then seated herself beside Elana. "As I've told you, Leah has real talent."

"Pola does, too," Elana said warmly. "She plays quite expertly."

"Pola's technique is adequate for her age and the amount of instruction she's received," Mira said critically. "However, I've found a professional music teacher. He is the well-known Franco-Prussian pianist, Armand Krause. His rates aren't cheap, but if he's as good as I've been led to believe, he's worth the price." Mira moved closer to Elana. "I'm sure you'll be able to convince Ephraim of the value of having Leah continue her music lessons, especially when the services of so eminent a teacher are readily available."

Elana shook her head. "I'm not sure of that at all. Ephraim has enjoyed hearing Leah play on the rare occasions I've been able to bring him here to listen to her, but he feels that it's only a pastime, and not a very useful one at that. The last time I praised her playing, he said it was pretty but had no practical purpose."

"But you heard her," Mira protested. "You saw how transformed she was as she played. She was a different child, one moment awkward and unsure, then, at the piano, poised and serene, almost enraptured. Surely, you won't stand by and see all that taken from her."

Elana regarded Mira thoughtfully. "How expensive do you think the lessons will be?"

"With two pupils instead of one," Mira responded easily, "the rate for each will be less, of course. Not more than five zloty a week, I'm sure."

"That's a princely sum for music lessons," Elana said wistfully. "It's as much as an average laborer can earn in a week."

"But a pittance for the assistant manager of the bank," Mira answered. "And surely your daughter's happiness and self-fulfillment merit it."

"You really feel her potential is that great?"

"Beyond question," Mira replied sincerely. "I suspect, much as I regret to admit it, that your daughter is a much more promising pupil than mine. But why not first let Professor Krause interview her? He will tell us what we need to know."

Shortly thereafter, Mira arranged for Armand Krause to interview Leah. Krause was skeptical at the prospect of instructing so young and inexperienced a student, but he agreed to the meeting. Mira wanted to be present, but Professor Krause insisted on meeting with Leah alone.

During that interview, Mira waited impatiently in her garden, as tense as if her own professional future, rather than that of her young protégé, depended upon the outcome. Mira sought to vent her frustration at being excluded from the audition by overseeing the removal of several tenacious weeds that threatened some of her prize plants. The task took her and her head gardener the better part of an hour, but still the interview continued. Mira, her anxiety increasing with the passage of time, paced the spacious rear veranda of her home, hoping that she might overhear the conversation between Krause and Leah. Instead, what Mira heard was the lyrical melody of the Chopin Fantasy that Pola had played at the mini-concert for Mira and Elana. Today, it sounded even sweeter than on that previous occasion.

When Leah had finished playing, Mira heard the door of the music room open. Professor Krause and Leah emerged, both looking somewhat grim. Mira glanced from one to the other. "Well?"

Armand Krause looked at Mira, the faint outline of a smile playing at the corners of his long, mobile mouth. "She'll do," he said gruffly. "She'll do nicely."

Mira released a small sigh. "You will take her as a student, then?"

Krause looked surprised. "I believe I said that, Madam Pietrowska."

A smile of relief and gratitude spread over Leah's face.

* * *

When Elana mentioned the subject of Leah's taking advanced piano lessons to Ephraim, he rejected the idea flatly. "Leah plays the piano quite competently now, Elana. You said so yourself."

"She's only just begun to learn to play," Elana persisted. "There's so much more for her to learn. She loves music. The lessons will afford her many hours of pleasure and fulfillment. Every child needs that, and Leah especially. She's had a difficult time until recently. We both know that."

Ephraim paced back and forth in the room which served him as a study. He glanced at the deep blue drapes which Elana had made, the comfortable chairs from his own factory, upholstered to match them. He paused at the finely-grained desk with its hand-rubbed luster. He had learned that he thought more easily in these surroundings which Elana had decorated to suit his taste.

He hated to oppose his wife's request. Elana made few demands upon him. Furthermore, both of them were aware that Leah, as their only daughter, occupied a difficult position in the family constellation. Though Leah adored all three of her brothers, their lives were destined to move in directions quite apart from hers. Furthermore, since the Marzjendiaks had left the Stare Miasto, Leah's life had been a lonely one until she had made friends with Pola Pietrowska and found through her and her tutor a means of satisfying the hunger of her eager young mind.

Ephraim did not like to refuse his beloved daughter anything within reason. However, the more he thought of the idea of professional music lessons, the more misgivings he felt. Leah's learning piano from her friend was one thing, but professional music lessons, at a rate of five zloty per week, was quite another.

"Why are you suddenly so anxious to go along with Mira Pietrowska's wishes in this? Only the other day you were saying you felt ill-at-ease with her. Why should we send Leah to be taught by this German, anyway? We can hire a Jewish teacher for her who will instruct her in Hebrew music."

"And insult the Bank Commissioner and his wife? Would that be wise in your position?"

Ephraim smiled at Elana's sagacity. When she truly wanted something from him, she seemed to know exactly the proper strategy to employ. "No, it would not." He stroked his beard thoughtfully. "Very well. If it means so much to both of you, I'll talk with this Professor Krause and see what he has to say. But mind you, I don't want Leah getting any overblown ideas. In today's world, a girl cannot reasonably aspire to a career in music."

The following evening, Armand Krause came to Plaz Marzjendiak at Ephraim's invitation. Krause was a small man, only five feet six inches in height, but his slender frame made him appear taller.

Ephraim was impressed with the man's professional manner. "Tell me," he said like a banker asking a loan applicant for references, "what do you think of my daughter's abilities? Madam Pietrowska is swayed by her own enthusiasm, and my wife is influenced by her, but they are not professionals. I want your objective appraisal."

Krause gazed at Ephraim unflinchingly. "My objective opinion, Mer Marzjendiak, is that your daughter shows rare promise. She has perfect pitch and an impressive sense of rhythm. She also has great presence and poise beyond her years. If she is as committed as she is gifted, she can become a truly fine musician." Krause took his eyeglasses from the breast pocket of his coat and set them on the bridge of his nose. He eyed Ephraim speculatively. "However, I don't believe that this news brings you joy."

Ephraim smiled ruefully. "You're a perceptive man, Mer Krause. I want to see my daughter live a happy and fulfilling life, one that is not unlike that of other girls her age. She speaks often of this Marie Pleyel, whom she greatly admires. I will not encourage her to aspire to a goal that is beyond her achieving. The world in which we live is not a kind one. It's inclined to be especially unkind to those of Jewish origin."

Armand Krause nodded. "I quite agree with you, Mer Marzjendiak," he answered. "However, genius is not prejudiced in its distribution. It can endow Jew and Gentile equally. What becomes of that genius depends entirely upon how it is nurtured, channeled, trained, and encouraged. I am a teacher of music, and a very good one. I will teach your daughter everything I know. But, in truth, the matter is in her hands, and God's."

Ephraim considered Krause's comment for a long moment. Finally, he nodded. "Very well. If you feel she has that much promise, I'm willing to have you teach her. Be assured that I would not willingly deny my daughter anything for her own good. I want you, however, to keep me informed of her progress."

"Agreed," Krause replied. He gathered his coat and hat and took up his walking stick. Earlier in the interview, Ephraim had offered him refreshments which Krause had politely but firmly refused. Now, however, when Ephraim offered a second time, Krause accepted. They had come to an agreement between gentlemen and now, Krause felt, libations were in order.

After Armand Krause had departed, Ephraim thought long and hard about the agreement which he had entered into with the musician. He still had reservations regarding the ultimate outcome of this undertaking. Most of all, he was concerned that Leah should not be hurt.

*  *  *

On a brisk day in late September, Maria Boroska, valise and traveling case in hand, descended the stairs of the Pietrowski home. Dressed for travel, she was anticipating her journey with a mixture of pleasure and dread. Trains frightened her with their noise and their intimidating size. The distance between Warsaw and her destination in the suburbs of Krakow seemed formidable to a woman who had lived her entire life in one place. Maria resented the ill-fated revolution that had left her country the doormat of the Russian Empire fully as much as she resented the ugly Russian language with its coarse and awkward sentence structure. She was especially rankled by the arrogance of teachers imported from Russia to teach their ungainly native tongue to the Polish students.

Maria had spoken with Professor Krause earlier that morning, before he had begun the day's lesson with Pola and Leah. She liked the slim little man with the quiet ways. She sensed he had a force and vigor which his formal manners concealed. After all, he was a musical genius in his own right. He would do well by her girls, and he seemed the ideal person to bring out Leah's budding talent. If only Leah were not a Jewess, Maria thought, she might go far in music despite her gender. But then, who knew? By the time Leah matured, circumstances might have changed. Her father was affluent and well-situated, and Leah was gifted and determined. Her strong will showed in her chin and in the firm set of her mouth. Such a will might overcome great obstacles.

While Maria stood in the hall, waiting for the Pietrowski coach that would take her to the railway station, the object of her musings emerged from the music room.

Leah ran to Maria and threw her arms around her. "Madam, are you about to leave now?"

"Yes, my little one," Maria answered. "I'll soon be on my way."

"I shall miss you," Leah said sadly.

"And I, you, child," Maria responded, setting down her bags to return Leah's embrace. Pola joined them a moment later and she, too, embraced her departing teacher.

"I know it's best for you, Madam Boroska," Pola said seriously, "but Leah and I are especially sad to see you leave. Will you write to us?"

"Of course, and you will write to me and let me know how you're getting on."

Leah could barely restrain her tears. "You won't forget us, will you, Madam?"

"Never, child. Teachers have long memories, and both of you will live forever in mine. I shall remember your brother, too," Maria said to Pola. "He is always so charmingly full of mischief."

"It's too bad he's already left for school," Pola commented.

"He came to see me quite early and said good-bye. He brought me a box of home-made candies." In response to the sound of horseshoes and wheels on the pavement outside, Maria picked up her bags and moved toward the door. Leah and Pola followed her. Maria smiled at each of them in turn. "I expect great things of you, girls."

Mira Pietrowska was waiting on the veranda to see Maria off. A fondness had grown between the two women over the past two years. Mira hugged Maria warmly, then impulsively reached up and adjusted Maria's hat at a jauntier angle. "There," she said, "that's better." The two women looked eloquently into each other's eyes. "Be happy, Maria," Mira said. "God go with you."

"And may He stay always with you, Madam," Maria answered tearfully.

She turned and swept down the cement stairs of the veranda, trying vainly to hide her tears. Farewells were always awkward, she thought, but never more than when they were permanent.

# CHAPTER SEVENTEEN
# CHANCE ENCOUNTERS

By the winter of 1866, the revolution had been "officially" ended for more than two years. An eagerness for a return to normal pursuits and practices prevailed among the people of the former Congress Kingdom. The popular view was that the revolution had been the brainchild of misguided romantics, inspired by the dream of the poet Adam Mickiewicz as expressed in his patriotic epic, <u>Pan Tadeusz</u>. The real world, filled with frustration, tragedy, deceit, and death, had proved to be quite different from Mickiewicz's imaginary one.

The young Polish intelligentsia who filled the reopened schools and universities, eager to learn and advance under the new regime, rejected the concept of an unending struggle for national independence. Instead, they espoused a step-wise modernization of industry, agriculture, and business. Their long-term goal was to ensure that native Poles would one day quietly resume control of their country's wealth and national resources. This program of step-by-step, "organic" work toward a realistic objective became the prevailing doctrine in the renamed Vistula Provinces.

Adam Marzjendiak, recently returned to Warsaw, was caught up in the mood of the times. He looked forward to completing his academic courses at the end of the current term. After that, there remained only his clinical preceptorship and the passing of his oral examination for certification. At the Warsaw Akademy of Medicine, where that examination would take place, Adam's credits from Krakow had already been accepted.

Today, Adam was on his way to meet with his old friend, Samuel Jedewreski, to discuss the final arrangements for his preceptorship training. Samuel had opened a second office in the more elite downtown section of Warsaw more than a year ago. However, it was to his old office in the Jewish quarter of the Stare Miasto, the oldest part of Warsaw, that he had invited Adam for this early morning meeting.

Adam was seized by nostalgia as he came within sight of the ancient ghetto walls. Four years had passed since he and Isaak had left this place on an early fall morning just months before the revolution. Much had changed since then, but too many things had not. He glanced self-consciously at the six-pointed star on his coat. In Krakow, he had not been obliged to wear this badge proclaiming him a Jew. Since his return to Warsaw, Adam had found it difficult to adjust anew to this indignity. It reminded him that although his family had acquired property and a measure of affluence, they were still second-class subjects under the Russian Imperial regime.

Adam himself was now within months of earning his doctor's degree. Yet, under the strictly-enforced quotas for Jewish professionals, there was no certainty that he would be able to practice his profession except within the walls before which he now stood. While established practitioners such as Samuel had already gained a loyal following of patients, new doctors entering the field faced tremendous competition. The revolution and its aftermath of governmental reprisals and "relocation" of "undesirables" to Siberia had greatly reduced the population of Warsaw. Furthermore, the hardships of the conflict had winnowed out many of the older and weaker citizens. The hardier ones who had survived had learned to be both long-suffering and discriminating and, in many cases, were unlikely to seek the services of a physician. They had had their fill of tragedy, illness, and death as a result of the revolution.

Illness and death, Adam thought as he moved through the familiar streets of the Stare Miasto, were a physician's stock in trade. In his mind's eye he could picture Jakob Krakowski as he must be by now in the late stages of his illness. It was a haunting and depressing image that would remain with Adam for a long time to come.

Adam had not heard from Sarah since she had bid him a tearful farewell in her father's garden at Krakow. He wondered if all was well with her and if she had truly forgiven him for breaking their engagement. He remembered the pleasure he had experienced in their single hour of lovemaking and the resulting pangs of guilt. Even if Sarah had forgiven him, would he, Adam wondered, ever forgive himself for yielding to a temptation that he should have found the strength to resist?

As Adam entered Samuel Jedewreski's office, Samuel interrupted his earnest conversation with his nurse-receptionist and came forward to clasp Adam's hand. "It's good to see you, Adam. You'll find that not much has changed here."

"I was thinking that, myself," Adam answered, shaking the aging physician's hand. Then, as he moved toward the reception desk, Adam felt obliged to revise that assessment. One thing had changed. Samuel had a new nurse, one Adam had not seen before. She was much younger than her predecessor, though of similar coloring, with the same dark hair and ivory skin. There, the similarity ended. Her mouth was full and luscious, her amber eyes lit by a glorious iridescence. Adam noted these attributes as Samuel brought him forward and introduced him to the young woman.

The pretty nurse came to her feet and inclined her head toward Adam in one fluid, graceful movement, acknowledging the introduction. "Doctor Marzjendiak," she said softly. "I'm honored."

"Most of the time," Samuel commented, "you'll be working with Nurse Insbruk here in this office."

"I shall look forward to it," Adam replied, answering Meyhra's warm smile with one of his own.

Samuel led Adam to the inner office, giving him time to reacquaint himself with surroundings that had formerly been familiar to him. As a boy, Adam had, unlike other youth, enjoyed visiting the doctor's office and renewing his acquaintance with the man who was his hero and role model. The doctor had felt pleased and flattered by his young friend's admiration and interest and had opened to him a world of magic on the transparent stage of the ancient microscope that still sat at the corner of the desk.

Samuel gestured toward a chair opposite his desk. Adam seated himself, and Samuel settled into the somewhat worn chair behind the desk. "It's good to have you here, Adam. It's what I've looked forward to for a long time, you and I working together. It seems natural, somehow."

"I feel that, too," Adam responded, glancing contentedly about the office, as he recalled pleasant memories.

"I want you to feel at home," Samuel continued. "Think of this as your own office. Bring your books. There's plenty of room on the shelves. You can even bring your own microscope, if you like. I'm sure it's newer than this relic." He pointed toward the ancient instrument. "Rachel and I never had any children of our own," Samuel reminisced wistfully.

"Somehow, ever since you expressed a desire to become a doctor, I've felt as though I shared you with Ephraim in a sense. You've always seemed to be the son I never had."

"You've been my great hero," Adam said warmly. "Since I was a small boy I've wanted to grow up and be just like you, healing and helping people, easing their pain."

Samuel nodded. "It's a good life, rewarding and satisfying. But it can be frustrating, too. A doctor must accept the fact that there are some ills he cannot heal. "

"I learned that not long ago," Adam answered.

Jedewreski studied his young friend for a long moment. "You've known a very different life in Krakow, Adam. I could tell that from your letters." Jedewreski paused. "You've been away from Warsaw for a long time, and in more ways than simple distance."

"True," Adam answered. "I've felt the contrasts keenly since I came back. It's taken some getting used to."

Jedewreski looked at Adam thoughtfully. "Are you glad to be home?"

Adam paused to consider the question and how it was intended. "Yes," he said at last. "Home is still home, even when conditions aren't the best."

\* \* \*

Isaak Marzjendiak laid aside the letter he had just received from Adam. Since Adam's return to Warsaw, the two had corresponded continuously, almost as though they found more to say to each other at long distance than they had when they had shared the same domicile. Isaak smiled as he reread the closing paragraph of Adam's most recent letter.

> "I'm working with a young nurse in Samuel's office. She's very efficient and knowledgeable. She's also ravishingly beautiful. Her name is Meyhra and I can scarcely believe the way she makes me feel just by looking at me with those huge, gold-dusted, pale-brown eyes. I'm trying to work up the courage to ask her father if I can call on her, and dreading the possibility that he may say 'No'. Write soon. I'm looking forward to the end of the term and the chance to see you again.
>
> Love,
>
> Adam"

So it was true, Isaak thought. Time does sometimes heal life's wounds. Yet, after all the years since he had held Mariska's dead body in his arms, Isaak still felt the void her loss had left in his life. Would he, Isaak wondered, always be haunted by her memory?

If his personal life was in disarray, Isaak reflected, at least his academic pursuits were going well. Still, it was hardly a balanced ledger sheet. As grateful as Isaak felt for Adam's resilience in the face of heartbreak, Isaak felt a fleeting pang of envy that his brother had already found a prospective new love. The fact that he quickly banished such traitorous thoughts did not assuage Isaak's own loneliness.

He had resolved to submerge himself in his studies and thus bury the pain and the memories along with it. Admittedly, he was finding advanced political science fascinating. He relished exploring the intricate mechanisms by which social and political changes are brought about; the impact of ideas and ideals and the complex ramifications of seemingly insignificant events. Learning how public opinion can be measured, altered, and occasionally circumvented gave Isaak an understanding of and a healthy respect for power.

He wondered if somehow that power could be put to use righting the wrongs and easing the burdens of his fellow Polish subjects. He wondered also whether he would be able to play a significant role in reconciling the interests of Russian Poland's Jews with those of the Polish Christian majority. If he could make even a small contribution to that effort, perhaps the ache he felt whenever he thought of Mariska and the forces that had driven them apart might one day be eased.

At any rate, as the term progressed, Isaak felt that he was moving closer to his long-cherished goal. Within a year, he would begin his studies at the Akademy of Law and Ethics. He could hardly wait for that world to open for him. He hoped that the complexities of the law would distract him from the loneliness that was now his constant companion with Adam in Warsaw and the memory of Mariska's death sharper than ever.

Throughout his undergraduate years, Isaak's closest friend and frequent study partner had been Evyan Sukowski. Evyan, a year ahead of Isaak, had already begun law school and was looking forward to joining his father Petros in practice.

The elder Sukowski was a senior partner in a prestigious Krakow firm, and Evyan had introduced Isaak to him more than a year ago. Each had been favorably impressed with the other. On repeated occasions since that introduction, Petros had asked Evyan about Isaak's plans for the future. The seasoned lawyer saw in Isaak a promising candidate for his firm.

Isaak had frequently wondered what it must be like to practice law in a city where no quotas were imposed against the Jews and where his people were not obliged to wear a badge.

At the end of a November day in 1866, Isaak walked slowly across the campus of the University of Krakow. He was on his way to meet Evyan at the University Student Center. Today was the final day of mid-term examinations, and their meeting was to be a celebration for the two young men. They were planning to have dinner and wine at a new off-campus restaurant that had quickly gained a large following among the student body.

As Isaak crossed the quadrangle, relieved that the difficult and demanding battery of tests was finally over, the bell of St. Mary's church chimed three o'clock and that was followed by the familiar Heynal. Evyan's last exam would not be finished until five o'clock. Two hours to kill, Isaak thought. He wandered across the compound, feeling intensely homesick. He missed Adam terribly. Normally, with exams completed and the term half-finished, Isaak would by now be regaling Adam with his sentiments regarding the course subjects in general and the examinations in particular.

Lost in thought, Isaak at first failed to respond to the greeting of a dark-haired young male student who had paused beside him. The young man looked at Isaak and smiled. "You look like a lost sheep," he remarked agreeably.

Isaak returned the smile, but his expression was one of puzzlement. Slowly, memory asserted itself. "You," he exclaimed, "gave me and my brother directions on our first day in Krakow."

"I call that quite a memory. It's been more than four years."

Isaak's eyes lighted with mischief. "And you still think of me as a lost sheep?"

The young man grinned, acknowledging the pun. "What are you doing now?"

"I've just finished mid-terms," Isaak replied.

"I've just taken my last exam, too. By the way," the student said, extending his hand, "I'm Nicholas Koslowski. What's your name?"

Isaak took the extended hand and gave his own name.

"Where are you going now? Do you need more directions?"

Isaak savored the joke. "I've just got a couple of hours to kill."

"Really? Well, I'm on my way to Professor Tcharnowski's farewell reception," Nicholas offered. "The professor is head of the Botany Department. He's about to retire. There'll be lots of free food and drink. Why don't you come with me?" Nicholas was filled with enthusiasm as he contemplated the imminent feast he looked forward to enjoying.

Isaak grinned. "Sounds like fun."

Isaak fell in step beside Nicholas, meanwhile wondering why the name Tcharnowski seemed familiar to him. Certainly he had not taken any of the professor's classes. "You say he teaches botany?"

Nicholas chuckled. "He not only teaches it, he lives and breathes it. Plants are like people to him, with individual attributes and personalities." He paused thoughtfully. "You know, when I first took one of the professor's classes, I thought he was kind of crazy. Would you believe he even sings and plays music for some of his flowering plants?"

Isaak was taken aback. "You're joking."

"I swear on my honor," Nicholas answered solemnly. "He says music makes certain plants grow better, makes them fuller and bushier, even more resistant to disease. "

Isaak scoffed. "Is he serious?"

"Music is one of his hobbies," Nicholas said. "And guess what? He's proved his premise with controlled experiments showing that plants given the same fertilizer and volumes of water, one group with music and one without, grow at different rates. He demonstrated his theory for the senior class. It really worked."

"That's almost unbelievable."

"You would think so, but it seems to be true. After he retires, Professor Tcharnowski plans to continue his experiments on his farm near Przamysl. Eventually, he'll publish his findings in the major botanical journals. Who knows? He may even win an award."

Isaak looked with interest at Nicholas. "You really admire him, don't you?"

Nicholas smiled. "I started out thinking of him as eccentric, but now I know he's a uniquely brilliant man."

As Isaak and Nicholas walked toward the faculty center, Nicholas explained that he was seeking his Master's Degree in botany and that Professor Tcharnowski had formerly been his faculty advisor as well as his favorite instructor. He also recounted the tragic tale of a friend and fellow botany student whose peers had confidently expected him to follow in Tcharnowski's footsteps. That had been before the student had suddenly been taken ill. A mysterious wasting disease had cut short his aspirations to a career in teaching, and had ultimately ended his life. Nicholas did not mention his friend's given name nor his family name.

When the two young men arrived at the reception, Nicholas introduced Isaak to several of his fellow students. Isaak noted that all these aspiring botanists spoke colorfully of their special interests and that, without exception, they voiced admiration for the retiring professor. Isaak's curiosity was piqued. He was looking forward to meeting a man who inspired such admiration.

When at last the introduction took place and Isaak stood before Professor Andreus Tcharnowski, Isaak realized that Adam had already introduced them the preceding spring at a department picnic. That had also been the occasion of Isaak's first meeting with Sarah Krakowska.

"Marzjendiak," the professor echoed in response to Nicholas' introduction. "The name is familiar, and yet..." A puzzled frown crossed Tcharnowski's face.

Isaak smiled apologetically. "You're thinking of my brother, Adam. He attended medical school here. Adam and I are a great deal alike."

The professor gazed at Isaak with a look of speculation in his gray eyes that was slightly disconcerting. "I remember Adam well. Are you as dedicated to custom and tradition as he is?"

Isaak winced at the question, suspecting that the botany professor must be aware of the dilemma that had faced Adam and Sarah.

"I honor the traditions of my ancestors," Isaak answered truthfully, "and the sanctity of the family."

The professor's eyes seemed to bore into Isaak. "Even when those traditions interfere with your own cherished hopes and wishes?"

"Sometimes," Isaak answered, wishing he could end the conversation.

Nicholas glanced uncomfortably from Isaak to Professor Tcharnowski. He sensed a conflict in progress that he did not understand. "That sounds like a very weighty discussion for a party," he interjected. "Why don't you two postpone this philosophical debate for a more formal occasion?"

Professor Tcharnowski reddened. "You're quite right, of course, Nicholas," he admitted. "I suppose at my age, one does tend to get a bit too involved in certain issues." He turned to Isaak. "Forgive me if I put you on the defensive. You _are_ very like your brother, though I sense in you a vein of humor that I never encountered in Adam. I think you'll find that quality will stand you in good stead. Nothing eases the trials of life more than the ability to laugh."

"I know, sir," Isaak replied. "My people have learned to survive by being able to laugh, even when the only object for laughter is themselves."

The three of them were standing near one of the main tables. Nicholas, feeling compelled to create a diversion, picked up three glasses filled with champagne and proposed a toast.

"To laughter!"

Isaak responded, "To life!" He touched Nicholas's glass with his own and joined in the spirit of the toast.

"And to love, which gives purpose and meaning to them both," Tscharnowski said softly but earnestly. The three of them stood savoring the taste of the vintage, sharing the spirit of celebration.

At this moment, Isaak sincerely wished that Adam would indeed claim his Meyhra as his letter had stated he wished to do. Another glass of champagne, Isaak thought, and he might consider indulging such an impulse, himself, if only he could meet a woman capable of displacing Mariska's seemingly indelible image from his heart.

# CHAPTER EIGHTEEN
## LOOSE ENDS

As the afternoon progressed, the crowd at the reception in honor of Professor Andreus Tcharnowski seemed to expand. More and more members of the faculty and the student body came to pay their respects. Isaak stood by, amused as Nicholas once more filled his plate from the sumptuous refreshment tables.

Feeling himself an interested observer rather than a participant in the proceedings, Isaak watched the students as they flocked around the professor, shaking his hand and talking animatedly. Tcharnowski seemed to take a keen interest in each of them in turn. The man had a way of looking directly into the eyes of the person with whom he spoke, a mannerism that was both engaging and slightly disconcerting. When a break came in the throng, Isaak noticed a young woman approach the professor and engage in earnest conversation with him. She was small, slim, and enticingly shapely, with long blond hair that swung as she walked. Her face was turned away from Isaak as she and Tcharnowski withdrew a little distance from the main body of the gathering. Intrigued, Isaak seized Nicholas's arm and urged him to join the group forming an unofficial reception line around the guest of honor. As they moved closer, Isaak's keen hearing caught some of the conversation.

"I'm glad you came, my dear," Tcharnowski said. "It's very thoughtful."

Isaak strained to catch the young woman's answer. "You and Venetia have been like second parents to me."

"We're leaving Krakow soon," the professor stated. "Where will you go?"

She hesitated, and Isaak noted that her shoulders seemed to sag. "I haven't decided."

The professor's tone was intense. "You should go home!"

"I can't," she insisted. Most of the rest of what she said was masked by the din created by the other students, except for the last words. "I'll be all right. "

The professor's expression clearly showed that he doubted the validity of that statement. "I do wish you'd reconsider," he said. Then their tête-à-tête was interrupted as two other students approached.

"Good-bye, Professor," the young woman said, moving away. Her stride was easy and graceful, and there was something about her that was familiar to Isaak. He watched her move determinedly through the crowd toward the exit, and he felt compelled to follow her. Nicholas fell in behind him. The young woman glanced back momentarily at Professor Tcharnowski, a wistful expression on her face. It was at that moment that Isaak recognized Sarah.

Nicholas, noticing Isaak's reaction, turned his attention toward Sarah and, apparently recognizing her, he smiled and waved.

Isaak asked, "You know her?"

"Yes," Nicholas answered. "She's the sister of the friend I told you about. She's just been appointed to the faculty here."

Isaak broke in quickly. "Would you excuse me, Nicholas? I must speak with her."

"Sure," Nicholas answered, "but you'd better hurry. She seems intent on leaving the party."

Isaak moved rapidly to intercept Sarah and caught up with her at the door. When he introduced himself, she stared at him in sudden, painful recognition. "Yes," she said. "I remember you." She stood, tense and anxious, like an animal at bay.

Isaak smiled nervously. "How are you?"

"I'm fine," she answered without conviction.

He asked, "Do you have a moment?" When she nodded reluctantly, he led her to one of the small tables at the periphery of the hall. As they seated themselves, Sarah seemed to regain a measure of her composure. Hoping to put her still more at ease, Isaak commented, "I understand congratulations are in order."

Sarah's expression of surprise was genuine. "Congratulations?"

Isaak nodded. "I hear you've made the teaching faculty. I'm impressed."

Sarah smiled oddly. "I'm impressed by how quickly news travels on this campus."

"I thought you must have graduated by now," Isaak answered smoothly, "but it never occurred to me that you were teaching here."

Sarah gazed intently at him. "Don't you believe a woman can teach at a university?"

"Obviously, you can," Isaak responded. "In Warsaw, that would be nothing short of miraculous."

"This city has a long history of liberalism," Sarah said proudly. "Besides, I don't quite fit the standard stereotype for a Jewish woman."

Isaak gazed appreciatively at Sarah, openly admiring her fair, delicate beauty. "You're a unique and gifted woman," he said candidly.

"How very gallant of you."

They were both thoughtfully silent for a moment.

"You know," Isaak resumed, "I used to dream about studying at this university when I was a boy. And then, when Rabbi Meisels came to Warsaw, he spoke so warmly of Krakow, of how it was once an independent republic. He described it as the cradle of Polish liberty. "

"So it is," Sarah agreed.

Isaak's hazel eyes, as he spoke, were alight with enthusiasm. "He's chief rabbi of Warsaw now."

"He and my father are close friends," Sarah said. "They still write to each other often." The mention of her father unexpectedly brought Sarah close to tears. Isaak could not help but notice the abrupt change in her mood.

"Have I unknowingly said something to upset you?"

Sarah shook her head, unable to answer for the moment.

"It's obvious that the professor's leaving is a sad occasion for you," Isaak said to end the silence between them.

"It's sad for all of us who admire and love him," Sarah answered. "He and my brother Jakob were very close. The professor was his hero."

Isaak glanced at the crowd assembled in the huge faculty dining room. "He seems to fulfill that role for quite a number of students."

"He's one of the kindest people I've ever met, and his wife has been like a mother to me ever since my own mother died." Sarah paused as if searching for the right words. "Did Adam ever mention my brother to you?"

Isaak frowned. He felt thoroughly ill-at-ease.

"Yes, I believe he did."

"What did he say?"

"As I recall," Isaak said, anxious not to disclose too much, "just that he was your brother and that he was a brilliant scholar. He spoke mainly of you."

"I suppose you know," Sarah said tentatively, "why Adam and I didn't get married."

"I know he loves you very much," Isaak answered. "Leaving you behind was very painful for him."

"My brother, Jakob, was very ill," Sarah said slowly. She squared her shoulders as if she had suddenly come to a decision. "When Adam and I first met, Jakob was as normal and healthy as you are. He wanted to be a teacher, like Professor Tcharnowski." She looked away, unwilling to meet Isaak's eyes. "Yet, as much as I loved my brother, I was relieved when he died. Life had become an unending nightmare for him." The memory seemed to oppress her. "It happened about a month ago." She paused, her mood subdued. "I don't know what name the medical profession applies to the hereditary disease that killed Jakob, but once he became ill, there was no chance for Adam and me." She stopped abruptly, overcome by emotion.

Isaak felt increasingly uncomfortable. "You don't have to tell me this, you know."

Sarah's eyes filled with tears; she looked searchingly at Isaak. "Somehow I feel compelled to make you understand. Maybe it will help me to understand as well."

Taking Isaak's silence for assent, Sarah described to him the tragic course of Jakob's illness and the fact that her maternal great uncle had apparently suffered a similar fate.

"If I had any doubts about the inevitability of Adam and myself being forced to part," she concluded, "watching Jakob die put them to rest." She faltered for a moment, but then her voice steadied. "It wasn't Adam's fault. He had no choice, really. That last day, when he came to say good-bye, he was in torment, and I made it worse for him." She looked away.

"Goodbyes are never easy," Isaak said soothingly, trying to lift her spirits.

Her eyes met his, dull and lifeless, her whole attitude one of dejection. She turned and glanced at the students raiding the refreshment tables. Isaak, watching her, suggested that he bring coffee for both of them and, having extracted her promise not to leave while he was gone, he moved away.

Sarah's eyes lighted with recognition as a middle-aged woman came toward the table where she sat. The woman's face was gentle, her features soft and almost blurred. However, the eyes, a deep lavender blue, were vivid, sharply-defined and arresting. Her smile had a beatific quality about it as she drew near to Sarah.

Sarah reached out and clasped the older woman's hands. "I'm glad you're here," she said with more animation than she had yet shown. "I was afraid you weren't coming to the reception. I almost gave up and left. I knew I should see you when I came for my things, but ... "

Venetia Tcharnowski leaned toward her and the two women embraced. Then, as Venetia took the seat Sarah pulled out for her, she asked, "What changed your mind and made you stay?"

"One of the students wanted to talk with me," Sarah answered.

Venetia smiled knowingly. "Hoping to better his grade, I expect."

Sarah shook her head. "Nothing like that, Venetia. In fact, he's not one of my students."

Sarah's eyes met Isaak's as he started to return to the table. Taking her hint, he obtained a third cup of coffee and held all three of them aloft as he carefully threaded his way through the crowd. When he drew near, Sarah addressed him.

"This is Venetia, Mrs. Tcharnowski." To Venetia, she said, "And this is Isaak Marzjendiak."

The mention of that name had an astonishing impact on Venetia Tscharnowski. Her face, so gentle and expectant a moment earlier, suddenly took on a hostile expression as she asked, "Marzjendiak?"

"Isaak is Adam's brother," Sarah explained.

"Oh, I see," the professor's wife said crisply as Isaak set down the coffee and resumed his seat.

Sensing the tension between her old friend and Isaak, Sarah said to Venetia, "Isaak and I have had quite an enlightening discussion." She turned to Isaak and added, "It's good of you to want to talk with me under the circumstances."

"Look, Sarah, I'm Isaak, not Adam. There are no circumstances."

"I'm glad to hear you say that," Venetia Tcharnowski remarked. Her voice took on a warmer tone. "Perhaps you can help me talk some sense into this young woman."

Isaak's face mirrored his surprise. "About what?"

"Sarah has wanted to be a teacher all her life. Now, at last, she's been appointed to the junior faculty of the Biology Department here at the University."

Isaak responded enthusiastically, "I was just congratulating her on that noteworthy achievement."

"And did she tell you," Venetia asked plaintively, "that she plans to resign at the end of the term?"

Sarah glanced sharply at Venetia Tcharnowski. "Why should I tell him? It's my decision!"

Isaak was taken aback. "But you've only just been appointed."

"There are other universities," Sarah answered, her voice rising slightly. "With good recommendations, I can obtain another teaching appointment."

Isaak looked from one woman's face to the other, his confusion mounting. "You love Krakow, Sarah," he said gently. "It's evident in the way you speak about it. This city is your home. Your family is named for it. Why should you want to leave?"

Sarah's eyes were moist as she returned his inquiring stare. Her mood reflected an urgent desperation. "I need to get away from here. I need time."

Recalling Adam's emotional turmoil just before he had left Krakow, Isaak sensed that the key to Sarah's otherwise inexplicable decision lay in the need to put her feelings for Adam behind her. "My brother would be deeply distressed," he told her earnestly, "to think he had been instrumental in your giving up the opportunity of a lifetime."

Sarah cut him short. "Why should your brother have anything to do with this?"

"It just doesn't make sense," Isaak responded, perplexed.

Venetia Tcharnowski gazed piercingly at Isaak. "You seem a fairly sensitive, thoughtful young man," she said. "You resemble your brother, and yet the two of you are quite different."

Sarah turned to her friend, her eyes blazing. "Adam isn't devious and selfish the way you think, Venetia," she said earnestly. "I'm responsible for what's happened. It's not his fault!"

A terrible suspicion took root in Isaak's mind. "What <u>has</u> happened?"

Ignoring Sarah's efforts to silence her, Venetia Tcharnowski whispered fiercely, "Something that Sarah could hardly have accomplished on her own."

Isaak felt suddenly cold. Mrs. Tcharnowski's bitter words had just converted his suspicions to certainty. "Adam will have to be told," he said realizing that Adam would want to know that Sarah carried his child.

Sarah's head came up defiantly, as if she had read his thoughts. "Adam is not to know. Not ever!"

"But you won't tell your father or your brother Reuben," Mrs. Tcharnowski protested. "Andreus and I are leaving the day after tomorrow. Another teacher has already reserved the house. You can't stay there any longer."

Sarah shook her head sadly. "My father has suffered enough shame and sorrow already. I left home after Jakob's death because I can't bear to inflict any more upon him."

Isaak felt a deep sympathy and a growing admiration for Sarah. Despite the untenable situation in which she found herself, she did not rail against her fate, nor did she seem utterly vanquished.

Every chivalrous impulse within him was aroused to her defense. "Where will you go?"

"I haven't decided," Sarah answered. "There are dormitories for faculty members. I can stay in one of those until the term ends. But then I'll have to leave." She glanced downward, her face reddening. "This sort of secret can only be kept for so long."

"That, dear, is exactly what concerns me," Mrs. Tcharnowski said solicitously. "If you must leave, you should come with us. Oh, Sarah, you would love the farm. You could stay for as long as you like. You know that."

"Please forgive me if I'm stepping out of line," Isaak said, "but I should like to help if I can."

Sarah shook her head. "You can't."

"I'd like to be your friend," Isaak said gently.

"You owe no responsibility to me," Sarah insisted.

Her adamant attitude brought a note of exasperation to Isaak's voice, though he managed to keep his tone low. "Who's talking about responsibility? I spoke of friendship."

Sarah glanced nervously at Isaak. "You're very like Adam, you know," she said softly.

"But I'm Isaak," he said, "and I can't see you adrift like this and do nothing about it."

"I'll manage," Sarah said tightly.

Isaak reached across the table and placed his hand over hers. "Please let me help."

"I don't think you can," Sarah answered with a small, bitter smile.

Venetia Tcharnowski suggested, "Sarah, you might at least hear what he has to say."

Sarah glanced at the older woman and bit her lip, but remained silent.

"Before I came to Krakow," Isaak said, "my father gave me sufficient funds to choose whether I would live with relatives or on my own. When I decided to live with my cousins, as Adam did, I deposited the money in the bank. It's been there ever since, collecting interest. You're welcome to use it for yourself, and the child."

Sarah paled. "That's very generous of you, Isaak, and I appreciate your motives, but you must see that I couldn't take money from you."

"I don't need the money," Isaak replied.

"Perhaps not at present," Sarah answered, "but you may later, when you're ready to start the law practice Adam spoke of. Besides, I just couldn't, but thank you anyway."

Isaak searched his mind, seeking an alternative offer. "Then come and stay with me," he said.

Sarah looked startled. "With your relatives?"

"No. I'm getting my own apartment. It's time I was on my own. You can live there though instead, for as long as you like, as though it's yours. That will give you time to make some plans."

Sarah's eyes were full of gratitude as she said, "You really mean that, don't you?"

Isaak nodded. "I do, indeed."

Venetia Tcharnowski glanced from Sarah to Isaak, a contented smile on her face. She had been deeply concerned about Sarah's future from the moment her husband had decided to retire and leave Krakow. However, there was something about Isaak Marzjendiak that Venetia trusted instinctively. She felt that Sarah sensed it as well.

\* \* \*

Within the next two days, Isaak rented an apartment near the campus, explaining to Jada and Zaccahreus that he felt a need to be on his own despite his devotion to them. Jada protested until Isaak agreed to share meals with his cousins twice each week and to visit them often. Still, she could not understand the sudden restlessness that seemed to motivate Isaak's need for a separate dwelling.

"He's a man," Zaccahreus assured her. "That's reason enough!" He did not tell her what Isaak had shared with him in confidence since his meeting with Sarah, nor his own feelings on the subject of Sarah Krakowska. He had a sense of foreboding for his young cousin, but he understood quite well the complex loyalties that had fueled Isaak's decision. In a sense, Isaak's determination had its basis in the Leverite Obligation of a living brother to a dead one, although, of course Adam had not died. Zaccahreus only hoped that the woman was worth all the trouble she was causing.

Reluctantly, Sarah moved her few possessions to Isaak's apartment. She was uncertain of just how this arrangement was going to work. Despite the desperation of her situation, she was proud and independent by nature. She felt drawn to Isaak, but she was determined to be neither overly dependent upon him nor subservient. Moreover, her feelings for Adam were still alive and strong. Some day, perhaps, if her child lived and thrived, she would be tempted to take him to Adam and show him that his fears had been groundless. However, that scene of triumphal reunion, she realized, was for the present a fantasy that might never be fulfilled.

Attired in a sea-green traveling dress and cape, with a matching bonnet tied at her chin, Sarah surveyed her new home, suddenly overwhelmed with misgivings. Isaak had arranged to be excused from his last class of the day in order to be at home when Sarah arrived. He greeted her and led her to the room that would be her special private sanctuary. He took her bags and set them on the bed. Still, she stood silent and subdued, averting her eyes from his face.

"I hope you'll be happy here," he said at last, ill-at-ease with the prolonged and painful silence.

"It's a beautiful room," Sarah responded, glancing at the cheerful wallpaper and draperies and the delicate furniture. "It's very good of you to let me stay here."

"My pleasure," Isaak answered, anxious to put her at ease.

"I can hardly think that," Sarah protested gently.

"I'm serious, Sarah. I care about you." Isaak paused, searching for the right words. "Think of me as another brother. After all, that's what I would be, if things had gone as they should have."

"But they didn't, Isaak," Sarah said distinctly. "Somehow this is all wrong."

He moved closer to her and took her gently by the shoulders. "But you and I are going to make it all right. That's why you're here." He reached into his pocket, drew out a small satin box and handed it to Sarah. "As time goes on, you'll find that this will silence a number of questions that might otherwise be asked."

Hesitantly, she opened the box and withdrew the plain gold band.

"I guessed at the size," Isaak said nervously. "I hope it fits."

Sarah stood quite still, gazing at the ring.

"Well, put it on," Isaak urged.

She shook her head. "I can't," she began, but he silenced her, laying a finger against her lips.

"Trust me," Isaak said, smiling with more assurance than he felt.

Slowly, reluctantly, Sarah put the ring on the third finger of her right hand. Then, looking up at Isaak, she also smiled.

\* \* \*

In the next several weeks, it became apparent to Sarah that Isaak was totally sincere in his offer of help. He did, indeed, behave like another brother to her. He was kind and considerate, yet he stayed out of her way, determined to demonstrate that he expected nothing from her in return for his help.

As Isaak had expected, the landlord, the students and faculty all assumed that he and Sarah had become husband and wife. No questions were asked, no awkward situations arose. The routine of sharing a home, shopping, cleaning, doing the laundry, all interspersed with teaching for Sarah and studying for Isaak, soon fell into a pattern.

Winter swept over Krakow that year with the gentleness of a flight of doves. Isaak awakened on a morning at the beginning of December to find the earth blanketed in snow. It was a beautiful and affecting sight that reminded him of an earlier time in the plateaus above Warsaw. Mariska and he had made love in the cave behind the platform rock that overlooked the lumber mill. It had been a day very like this one, except that it had been the beginning of spring. They had been very young and innocent and had fallen deeply in love. And tragedy had resulted. Now Adam's first love had eventuated in an equally complicated situation, and tragedy could as easily ensue. Isaak was determined to prevent that outcome.

His feelings and motivations as he stood gazing at the snow were an impossibly tangled skein. A new and poignant period had begun in his life. He had come to discover, with the passage of time, that the concerns and misgivings he felt for Sarah had evolved into love. Or perhaps the idea of loving her had been in his mind all along, afraid to take root there because of Adam. Sarah was pregnant with Adam's child, and yet Adam was unaware of this. Was it possible that one day Isaak could fill the role in Sarah's life that Adam had abandoned? That thought tempted him; yet as a Jewish male, he was bound by the same obligation to reproduce and ensure the continuation of his family and his people that had impelled Adam to give up his love and his commitment to her.

Furthermore, even if he went to her, it was unlikely that she would accept him as her lover. Her heart was filled with Adam, and she was looking forward more and more to the birth of Adam's child. His name was frequently on her lips when she and Isaak were alone at dinner, reading together in the parlor, or on their way to their respective classes in the mornings. It was evident to Isaak that Sarah had accepted his proposal to think of him as a brother and a friend. Submerging his own feelings, Isaak accepted that role without complaint. Love, runs the ancient scripture, endureth all things and is patient.

\* \* \*

The holiday season settled like a benevolent mantle over Warsaw. The air was brisk and stimulating; the distant plateaus were laced with snow. The atmosphere was festive and expectant as Ephraim Marzjendiak walked through the streets of the Stare Miasto.

Since Samuel Jedewreski had opened an office in central Warsaw, Ephraim had no occasion to visit the older office in the ghetto. The newer one was near the bank and, therefore, more convenient for Ephraim. Recently, however, Adam had begun working part-time at the old office in order to fulfill the practical training requirements needed for his graduation. Considering the relationship that Samuel and Adam shared, it was a predictable arrangement. Ephraim, however, questioned the wisdom of Adam's electing to serve in the older location where practice, he reasoned, was more limited.

As Ephraim entered the office, he was greeted by an attractive and efficient young nurse who asked him if the doctor was expecting him.

"I have a standing appointment, whenever I can come in," Ephraim said grandly, a mischievous twinkle in his eye.

The nurse looked unconvinced. "Really? Your name, sir?"

"Marzjendiak," Ephraim answered smiling.

The nurse reacted with surprise. "Are you…?"

"Dr. Marzjendiak's father," Ephraim graciously supplied. As she gazed at him in something akin to awe, he asked, "Where are all the patients? Is it always this empty?"

The nurse shook her head. "Hardly. An hour ago it was like a flood. Your son is seeing the last of them now."

"Do the patients like him?"

The young woman considered for a moment. "They seem to trust him. They should. He's very good, although I'm scarcely the one to give an opinion."

"How long have you worked with Dr. Jedewreski?"

"About four years, now."

Ephraim looked at her kindly. "That's long enough," he said, "and you seem a level-headed young woman. "

Meyhra reddened slightly and looked away to cover her unaccustomed embarrassment before Adam's imposing father. She pressed a button that activated the bell in Samuel Jedewreski's office. Adam came out accompanied by the last of his patients to whom he was giving instructions on taking her medication. The patient thanked him and stopped at Meyhra's desk.

Adam was surprised to see his father. The two exchanged the usual amenities and then Adam led Ephraim into the office and closed the door.

"This is indeed a pleasant surprise," Adam remarked.

Ephraim glanced about the familiar office and nodded in satisfaction. "I use to wonder how you would fit into this setting," he said at last. "It suits you."

"That's high praise coming from you, Father."

Ephraim asked thoughtfully, "Is it all you hoped it would be?"

Adam shrugged. "Most of the time."

"Nothing pleases a man all the time," Ephraim responded.

"As a child," Adam said, "I used to think I knew everything about this place. The community, I mean." He smiled wryly. "How wrong I was!"

"The more we learn, the more we realize how little we truly know. It means you've grown up, Son." Ephraim embraced him warmly.

Turning away from philosophy, Ephraim addressed himself to the real reason he had come. "Speaking of growing up, what have you heard lately from your brother, Isaak?"

"I had a letter from him the other day," Adam responded.

"What did he say?"

Adam looked at his father somewhat somberly. "The major thing his letter said was that he won't be coming home this year. Something about increasing difficulties in his studies and a complicated report he'll have to write during recess."

"Did he give any other reasons?"

Adam shook his head. "Not really. He said there were other things he couldn't write in a letter. That he'd explain further when we saw each other in person next year."

Ephraim smiled sardonically. "At least he's consistent."

"Did he write to you, too?"

Ephraim nodded. "Almost the exact words." Ephraim stood as if to leave. "By the way," he added, "I was impressed by your nurse. She's quite attractive."

Adam smiled almost shyly. "I find her very impressive, too."

"Good!"

Adam looked up, somewhat surprised. "You approve?"

"She's a good Jewish girl, isn't she? She's strong and healthy and comes from a good family?"

Adam nodded affirmatively.

Ephraim winked. "So what's not to approve?"

"Nothing," Adam responded thoughtfully. "It's just that this has all happened so quickly. I loved Sarah deeply, and Meyhra is quite different from her in every way."

Ephraim smiled. "That's probably why she attracts you." He moved closer to Adam. "That plus the fact that after the rupture of your relationship with Sarah, you're doubly susceptible. Under the circumstances, I'd say you're very fortunate." He placed a hand on Adam's shoulder. "It's time you were thinking in terms of a wife and family. Nothing is more effective in erasing the pain of an old love than the prospect of a new one."

# CHAPTER NINETEEN
## LOVERS AND FRIENDS

On the fourth day of Hanukah, Meyhra invited Adam to dinner at her father's house in the Stare Miasto. He was delighted to accept. He had heard many intriguing stories about Meyhra's father, Teyvah, who owned a jewelry shop located on the site of the Marzjendiak family's former home. From this humble beginning, Teyvah Insbruk had already built a modest fortune. He had opened a second shop in the commercial center of Warsaw. Teyvah's only son, Eben, age twenty-four, had begun to establish a reputation as a shrewd and canny gemstone merchant, well-versed in the complexities of fine diamonds, rubies, emeralds, and opals.

Opals had only recently achieved a prominent place on the commercial scene. Prized for their fiery brilliance and warmth, they were growing steadily more popular as the opal mines of Australia and other exotic locales became better explored. The local markets were gradually beginning to reflect the wide variety of gem-quality opals, from milky white with multi-colored fire to almost midnight black with vivid colors in their slumberous depths.

Teyvah was particularly proud of his personal collection of opals. Meyhra had told Adam about it, and he was filled with curiosity as he walked the short distance from the medical office to the Insbruk home. Adam also recalled, as he knocked at the front door of the dwelling, that Meyhra's mother had been killed in the raid of 1863. He silently breathed a prayer of Thanksgiving to Adonai that his own mother had escaped a similar fate. Ephraim had briefly mentioned to Adam the fact that a Russian soldier had struck his mother on that occasion, but, wishing to spare his son pain, he had offered no further details regarding the incident, although Adam knew that baby Rachel's premature delivery and death had followed a few hours later. That entire day had been such a trying one, that its termination in tragedy did not seem incongruous.

Meyhra herself opened the front door of the Insbruk home, and both she and Adam shared a moment of wordless bliss as they basked in the mutual glow of each other's presence. They embraced tenderly, and then Meyhra stepped back to look searchingly at Adam.

"I was beginning to worry about you," she said. "It was good of you to let me go early, but it left you all the closing up."

"There wasn't that much to do," Adam replied. "You're just more efficient at it."

"The value of practice," Meyhra commented as she closed the door. "Running the office has become habitual for me."

"What would it take for you to consider making a habit of me?"

Meyhra's eyes lit with mischief. "The right question."

"And if I asked that question, would you say yes?"

"Why don't you ask and see?"

Adam seized her shoulders and drew her close. "I couldn't bear to hear you to say no."

She smiled archly. "Nothing ventured, nothing gained."

She freed herself from his clasp and ran into the kitchen, confident that he would follow her. When he did, she was just removing the bread from the oven.

"Here is where I feel most at home," she said happily, glancing about the kitchen. "Baking bread can cheer me out of my darkest mood."

Adam glanced at her thoughtfully. "When do you have dark moods?"

"When I look at this room and remember my mother," she answered.

Judging from the catch in her voice, Adam thought she was on the brink of tears, but after a moment she took herself in hand and glanced up at him reassuringly. "Tears don't help," she said. "I've asked you here to join in a celebration. What way is that to celebrate?"

"A wise philosopher, whose name escapes me at the moment, once said that tears and laughter are all one, two sides of the same coin," Adam observed.

"Well, I prefer the laughing side," Meyhra responded. "Father's not home yet. Why don't you help me by carving the meat?"

Taking fork and carving knife in hand, Adam did the honors, wondering aloud, "Is he often as late as this?"

"This family is not distinguished for its regular hours," she confessed. "With Eben and Father managing two shops and me working as a nurse in a busy medical office, I suppose that's to be expected." Even as she spoke, Meyhra heard a key turn in the front door.

Momentarily, Teyvah Insbruk stepped into the kitchen and embraced his daughter. Tall and muscular of build, Teyvah Insbruk exhibited a commanding presence that was not lost on Adam as Meyhra made the appropriate introductions.

When they were finished, Teyvah inquired if Eben was home yet, and Eben provided the answer by entering the kitchen door almost as if on cue. "There's always one last customer," he said lightly, by way of explanation for his tardiness. "I'll wash up and be right down." He disappeared up the stairs.

Before dinner came the ritual of lighting the fourth Hanukah candle and setting the menorah in the window. This and the prayer which the family recited struck Adam quite poignantly. He thought, I did these things with Sarah and her father and brothers. She, too, was the lady of her father's house.

The respective circumstances of the two families, however, were quite different. The furnishings here spoke not of habitual affluence but of sagacious frugality. The atmosphere was one of contentment and of love leavened with the careful husbandry that can transform limited resources into a stable fortune. Adam glanced comfortably about the table. He was enjoying the loving warmth shared by the family and the tranquil ambience of their modest home.

After dinner, Teyvah proudly showed Adam his famed opal collection. It was kept in a vault in Teyvah's study, camouflaged by a small but beautifully painted portrait of Teyvah's dead wife, Esther. The stones were carefully mounted, each in its own black case. There were twelve in all, each a different color, each differently cut, but all about the same size.

Adam gazed at them appreciatively. "They're magnificent!"

"They have a life of their own," Teyvah said proudly. "Their fire is due to their fluid content. They need the touch of human skin to maintain the moisture and the fire. From time to time, Meyhra bathes them in glycerin to keep them shining."

The changeful stones in Teyvah's case reminded Adam of Meyhra's unusual eyes, a mixture of amber, pale brown and hints of green, a combination sometimes described as hazel, with a propensity to change colors with the hue of her clothing. However, unlike most eyes so described, Meyhra's were predominantly a golden amber color; only greens and deep blues were reflected in them, but not other colors.

* * *

On the afternoon of the last day of the Hanukah celebration, Adam brought Meyhra to Plaz Marzjendiak. They came by hired coach, a luxury for which Adam was willing to pay so that he could show Meyhra the breathtaking panorama of the family estate as seen from the main access road.

"It's lovely," Meyhra said, her voice hushed with admiration. "I had no idea it would be so large."

"It was built by an aristocratic Polish family. The last owner died without an heir."

"Your father purchased it then?"

"Not immediately," Adam answered. "That came after the law barring Jewish ownership of property was rescinded."

"Your family must feel very proud," Meyhra marveled.

Adam nodded, smiling. "It does impart a sense of accomplishment," he said, "but it means much more than just the land." He turned to face Meyhra, his eyes alight with triumph. "It's the fulfillment of a long-held dream for my father."

"I'm impressed," Meyhra said admiringly. "It far exceeds my father's collection of opals."

Adam stopped the coach, reached out to take Meyhra's hand and drew her into his arms. "I didn't bring you here just to impress you," he said. "I brought you home to meet my family and to afford them the pleasure of meeting you." Their lips met in a gentle kiss.

When at last they broke that intimate contact, Meyhra said practically, "We'd better be on our way. Otherwise, we'll be late for dinner, which won't make things easy between your mother and me."

"Don't worry," Adam assured her. "Mother will love you. How can she help it? You'll love her, too. Trust me, I know."


As Ephraim and Adam waited on the terrace of Plaz Marzjendiak, sipping chilled drinks in anticipation of dinner, Leah laid the table and Meyhra helped Elana put the finishing touches to the evening meal. The two women shared a common bond of background and upbringing which went deeper than simple religious beliefs, and both were devoted to Adam. However, now that the family's firstborn son had finally brought home a young lady for his parents' approval, Elana found herself seized with doubts and misgivings that bore little relationship to Meyhra herself.

Adam had finally confided to his mother the brief, sad story of his love for Sarah and the reason for his ultimately giving her up. Elana had keenly felt her son's disappointment and disillusionment, but, unlike Adam, she found it difficult to put those sentiments behind her in the space of a few months. It had taken her almost a year to fully recover from Rachel's death. Now, as she watched Meyhra moving about the kitchen with self-assured grace, transferring the vegetables and potato latkes into serving dishes and garnishing the roast with green herbs, Elana experienced a strange sense of unreality.

The girl was real enough. She was much taller than Elana with broad shoulders, a long narrow waist and even longer legs that stemmed from narrow hips, making Meyhra's figure seem almost boyish in its athletic slimness. Elana wondered if so narrow a pelvis could really accommodate a full-term child. She wondered also if a woman who worked all day tending the sick beside her husband would be willing or able to devote sufficient time and energy to the raising of any children she did manage to produce.

Elana watched Meyhra critically, assessing her obvious assets and wondering uneasily if, like Sarah, there were undisclosed aspects to this prospective daughter-in-law, seemingly so perfect to fulfill the role to which she aspired. Admittedly, she was beautiful and intelligent. Her participation in the traditional Hanukkah ceremonies preceding the meal demonstrated that she was devoutly religious. Elana deliberately deferred some of the prayers she would normally have offered to Meyhra in order to test her and did not find her wanting. Furthermore, Elana had already ascertained that the Insbruk family was an old and well-established one in Warsaw. By every standard Elana could apply, Meyhra would make Adam an exemplary wife. Why, then, this gnawing doubt, this half-formed dread that plagued Elana even as she tried to welcome the girl that her eldest son had chosen? That question disturbed Elana all during dinner while Ephraim seemed totally satisfied with Adam's choice.

"I love her," Adam asserted to Ephraim while Meyhra lent Elana a hand in clearing away the remains of dinner. "I mean to make her my wife."

"I'm pleased," Ephraim responded approvingly, relieved that Adam appeared to have recovered from his earlier depression over Sarah. "It's time you were settled down and married."

"I agree," Adam said, pleased by his father's attitude and aware that Isaak also would be pleased to know that his elder brother was following his advice. "Now all I have to do is persuade my future father-in-law not to insist that I establish a flourishing practice before I can marry his daughter."

After dinner, when the members of the family exchanged gifts, Adam gave Meyhra a small, finely wrought charm suspended on a delicate gold chain. It was a replica of the mezuzahs that adorn the doorposts of devoutly Jewish homes.

As Adam fastened the charm about Meyhra's neck, he whispered in her ear: "This is the symbol of the home we shall one day share as husband and wife. Your father said yes."

Meyhra looked at Adam, then her eyes strayed across the room to Ephraim as he fastened his gift to Elana, a double strand of pearls, around her neck. Meyhra returned her attention to Adam. "Yes, I know," she said. "He told me." She smiled up at him. "Aren't you going to ask me?"

Adam looked pained. "You know how I feel," he stammered.

"But it's better to have you <u>tell</u> me."

Michael, amused at this interchange, and at last grown tired of being seen but not heard throughout most of dinner, chimed it, "Tell her, Adam."

Adam blushed despite himself. "Tell her what?"

"Whatever it is she wants to hear," Michael replied.

"I can see <u>you're</u> going to be popular with the girls," Adam observed.

Leah nodded her head sagely. "He already is," she said, noting Adam's embarrassment. She took Michael's hand and led him to a side table where the two younger children soon became engrossed in a dreidel game.

No longer distracted by his young brother's childish pranks, Adam turned his attention once more to Meyhra. "I love you," he whispered ardently. "It will be almost a year before I can begin to earn a living. Your father insists that we wait at least that long to marry." There was a wealth of longing in his voice as he added, "I wish it could be sooner."

"So do I," Meyhra answered with equally intense feeling.

Overhearing this exchange, Ephraim decided he would do all in his power to facilitate an early union between Adam and Meyhra. Ordinarily a great believer in letting the young learn by experience, Ephraim had come to know that experience can sometimes be an excessively hard taskmaster. In this instance, he felt a little help was in order and that the most efficacious way to assist Adam in forgetting his former ill-fated love affair was to ensure the prompt and joyous fulfillment of his new love.

* * *

In addition to his somewhat modest shop in the Stare Miasto, Teyvah Insbruk owned a second, more elegant establishment on Senatorska Street, not far from the head office of the Bank of Poland.

A few weeks after Meyhra's visit to Plaz Marzjendiak, on a singularly mild January day, Teyvah Insbruk stood in the main showroom of his newer jewelry store, proudly surveying its wares. He noted with satisfaction the crowd of prospective buyers eagerly examining the contents of the elegant showcases that displayed his stock of exquisite unmounted stones and the rare pieces of finely-crafted jewelry created by his staff of skilled artisans. He was pleasantly surprised to see Ephraim Marzjendiak, the eminent banker, enter his store. He recognized Ephraim immediately, having seen him pointed out outside the synagogue as one of the leaders of the Jewish business community in Warsaw.

Teyvah approached Ephraim swiftly, eager to make a good impression on the father of his future son-in-law. "An honor, Mer Marzjendiak," he said cordially. "How may I serve you?"

"I'm seeking a present for my wife," Ephraim answered. "Something rather special. It's for our wedding anniversary."

Teyvah Insbruk smiled in understanding. "What shall it be? A ring, or perhaps a broach?"

Ephraim's eyes fell on an unmounted brilliant-cut diamond residing in a place of honor near the rear of the main display case. "Something for a pendant," he said, admiring the diamond.

Teyvah's eyes followed his glance. "Ah, yes, a perfect stone. Four and a half karats. Not as large as some I've handled," he added proudly, "but beautifully cut. The table and the star facets are ideally balanced. The simplest of mountings is needed to properly display its beauty. You have rare taste, sir."

"Thank you," Ephraim said. "I believe, based on his choice of wife, that my son has inherited it."

Teyvah smiled appreciatively at this reference to his daughter's worth. "You are most gracious."

Ephraim gestured toward the rear precincts of the store. "May we continue our discussion privately?"

"Of course." Teyvah led the way to his private office, and seated Ephraim in a well-padded leather chair. "Allow me to offer you some refreshment," Teyvah said graciously as he poured Ephraim a demitasse sized glass of cordial and a second for himself. Only when they had toasted one another did they resume their business discussion.

"My eldest son has chosen a long and arduous course of study," Ephraim began candidly.

"Indeed," Teyvah said. "As a nurse, my daughter is well aware of that fact."

"I'm sure she is," Ephraim agreed. "Adam and Meyhra can look forward to a life of service and respect, perhaps even eventual monetary rewards. However, there will be very little affluence, luxury or convenience while they are still young." He paused meaningfully. "Unless, of course, they are fortunate enough to obtain some subsidy outside their own resources."

"True," Teyvah replied.

"Adam is twenty-seven," Ephraim continued. "That's late in life for a man to marry and begin raising his family."

Teyvah nodded. "I am willing to forego a few of the old ways in the interest of young love. After all, my daughter is twenty-four. Time does not stand still for her, either. Often, in the past, I've tried to persuade her to let me engage a matchmaker. But after her mother was killed, I hadn't the heart to continue to insist."

"As fathers," Ephraim suggested, "perhaps we can give the wheels of destiny a small shove forward."

Teyvah cleared his throat. "What sort of shove have you in mind?"

"I realize it is customary for the groom to post a 'bride price' much as Jacob did in laboring all those years, first for Leah and then for Rachel, before the ketubah can be drawn up. What sum would you consider equitable?"

Teyvah considered this proposal for a moment.

"Normally, I would expect the posting of approximately a thousand zloty to assure my daughter's future security. I suppose that seems steep, but then I feel my Meyhra is worth that sum, and I am prepared to make her a suitably handsome dowry."

"Beyond question, she is a young woman of outstanding merit," Ephraim agreed. He, too, considered for a moment. "How much is the pendant?"

"That stone would bring at least nine hundred zloty on the market," Teyvah answered. "However, for you, Mer Marzjendiak, let us say seven hundred."

Ephraim smiled. "I don't want you to lose money on the deal," he protested.

Teyvah was equally insistent. "You are my Meyhra's future father-in-law. Fair is fair! As I stated, seven hundred zloty."

Ephraim pondered the matter, then reached into the inner pocket of his jacket and withdrew a leather wallet. "Here are two thousand zloty to cover both amounts," he said, "the stone, the mounting, and the 'bride price.' I believe that is a fair offer."

Teyvah nodded agreeably. "Fair indeed, Mer Marzjendiak."

Ephraim acknowledged that courtesy with one of his own. "Call me Ephraim. By the way, Teyvah," Ephraim added, "I understand from Adam that you wish to acquire a new home. It's quite possible that I may be able to assist you."

This time Teyvah smiled broadly and nodded enthusiastically. "A wonderful idea. It's generous of you to offer."

*　*　*

April of 1867 was a bittersweet time for Sarah Krakowska. It was a month that reminded her of her first meeting with Adam, a meeting that had taken place two years earlier in the science laboratory of the University of Krakow. Within a few weeks, she would bear Adam's child. She hoped it would be a son, whole and perfect, and God willing, not flawed as Jakob had been with a hidden illness lurking in the shadows to make a travesty of all the promise that the young life might hold.

Recently, she had felt the child's movements grow steadily more vigorous. If she had not miscalculated, she might just be able to complete giving final examinations in her courses before the time of her delivery. Isaak had been most thoughtful, she reflected. No husband or lover could have been more considerate. And most thoughtful of all, though Sarah steadfastly refused to consider going through a wedding ceremony whose sole purpose was to make the baby's birth legitimate, Isaak had insisted that the birth certificate would list him as the father.

"You don't have to do that," Sarah had protested, almost angrily.

"I know that," Isaak had answered. "It's what I want to do."

Sarah had never come closer to loving him than in that moment. Her feelings had been in turmoil ever since. Now, she realized instinctively, was not the time for making life-long decisions. She would wait until after the child was born, and then she and Isaak would both be more certain of how they felt toward each other. Certainly, she felt very close to Isaak. He was a gentle and caring man and she would not be settling for "second best" if she were to accept his offer of marriage. Yet, she did not want a union based on guilt and motivated by necessity. If she married Isaak, she wanted it to be because it was what they both wished, a well thought out course of action for which there would be no cause for regrets and recriminations.

Moreover, in the back of Sarah's mind was always the painfully haunting memory of Jakob's final days. Until the day of her own death, she would hear the sounds of his agonized weeping and see the expression of pain and terror in his eyes. But even that memory was not as devastating as had been the days when Jakob's eyes and his mind had seemed a total blank just before he lapsed into terminal coma. Marriage would mean the possibility of more children, each of whom would be at risk, and then if they survived, there might be grandchildren. It was in those later weeks of her pregnancy that Sarah understood with dreadful clarity the awful apprehensions that had plagued Adam as his doctor's mind grasped the significance of Jakob's illness.

It was on an evening in the last week of April that Isaak came home from a visit to Jada and Zaccahreus Polewski to find the apartment empty. Sarah had had a seemingly endless stack of papers to correct and had apparently welcomed the prospect of a few hours to herself to complete the task. Her mood had been one of cheerful resignation and she seldom left the apartment lately after nightfall. Isaak could not help but feel concerned. He searched vainly for a note of explanation and was beginning to feel really worried when he heard a knock at the front door. When Isaak opened it, the landlord, Mer Alfred Krupinski, stood there gazing at him with a strange expression, half benevolent and half accusing.

"I wondered when you'd be home," Krupinski said.

"I've only been gone for about two hours," Isaak responded, wondering why the landlord made him feel somehow defensive.

"A lot can happen in that time," Krupinski said softly.

"What has happened?"

"I took your wife to the university infirmary."

Isaak's eyes widened in alarm. "Sarah's ill?"

"Hardly that. But in a few hours, I think you'll be a father, young man."

Isaak was halfway out the door. "I'd better get over there."

Krupinski's smile broadened. "Young parents are all alike," he said warmly, "always in a hurry. I'll take you there."

Hours later, after what seemed an eternity to Isaak, Sarah gave birth to a baby boy. It was nearly five weeks premature, small, wrinkled, and peculiarly quiescent. Yet it seemed to its surrogate father the most miraculous of beings.

Isaak's one mental reservation concerning the newborn child centered on Sarah's avowed intention to name him for his dead uncle, Jakob. Despite the time-honored Ashkenazi custom of giving the name of a revered deceased relative to a child so that the honored dead might "live anew," Isaak harbored a gnawing dread that in this case, to follow that tradition might be to unnecessarily tempt fate.

# PART THREE: FRUITION

It hath been told to thee, O man,
What is good and what the
Lord requireth of thee –
Only to do justly, to love mercy
And to walk humbly with thy God.

(Micah 6:8)

# CHAPTER TWENTY
## A TIME FOR TEARS

Sarah awoke refreshed that July morning, surprised to see the sun already high in the heavens. Normally, she would be up much earlier, preparing her and Isaak's breakfast and getting ready for class. Now it was summer. The regular session had ended, and with baby Jakob still so young, she had declined the invitation of the biology department chairman to teach in the summer term. Finding someone to care for her delicate premature baby for the last few weeks before final exams had been difficult enough. With the close of the regular school year, finding a replacement for summer would have been next to impossible. Fortunately, Professor Bayorski was a fatherly and understanding man. Under such difficult circumstances, he was unlikely to penalize the newest member of his staff for failing to fulfill his request.

Sarah sat up thoughtfully, relieved that she had no papers to correct, no lesson plans to finalize. During summer recess, she could truly get to know baby Jakob. She would come to understand him as the small but individual being he actually was. In her mind, she began planning for his future. She would start to teach him early, convinced that a very young child's mind was the most readily trained, the most pliable, the most easily accessible to instruction. Many educators had come to espouse this view, and to encourage young parents to commence teaching their children at an early age. Who, Sarah reasoned, was better suited to that task than a trained teacher?

Engaged in these musings, at first she failed to notice the prevailing silence, but then, abruptly, she felt the first stirrings of alarm. Her eyes strayed to the crib, just inside the nursery door. The room had originally been intended as a dressing room, but Sarah had transformed it into a baby's room so that the crib was close to her own bed, almost within reach. Jakob was naturally a quiet baby, but by now he was usually fretful for his feeding. She glanced at the antique clock on the dressing table, as her feet instinctively sought her slippers. As she moved toward the crib, she hastily wrapped her robe around her. She was nearly there when she was seized by an eerie apprehension.

She leaned quickly over the crib, seeking to assure herself that Jakob was sleeping peacefully. He lay on his back, pale and immobile. She bent down and picked him up, frightened by his stillness, and by the faintly blue color of his lips and eyelids. As she held him close, she realized that the baby was not breathing, and she could feel no heartbeat. Her mind rebelled. She refused to believe her own senses. Holding the baby tightly, she ran to Isaak's room, calling out his name urgently.

Isaak awoke and sat up, startled. "What's wrong, Sarah?"

"It's Jakob," she wailed. "I can't wake him."

Fully awake now, Isaak took the baby from her, carried him into the brightly-lighted kitchen, and tried to rouse him. Sarah lighted the stove to dissipate the morning chill, while Isaak gently slapped the baby's buttocks as he had seen the doctor do shortly after Jakob's birth. He laid the baby on the table, and the two of them worked over him for several minutes, both denying the undeniable fact that Jakob was dead. His skin was cool and was gradually assuming a waxen pallor. He had not moved or gasped or breathed since Sarah had first picked him up.

Finally, Isaak sank dejectedly into a chair.

"It's no use," he said, tears coming to his eyes.

Sarah shook her head. "No," she said brokenly. "No!" Then she screamed. It was a single anguished cry that blended grief and outrage, and expressed the wrenching torment of a soul suddenly bereft of hope.

* * *

Despite the brilliance of the early morning sunlight, Isaak Marjzendiak would always remember that July day in terms of somber hues. He stood, mute and grief-stricken beside Sarah Krakowska while the tiny, plain pine wood coffin of the infant Jakob was lowered into its grave. He watched as tears fell silently down Sarah's cheeks and trickled unheeded on the ruffled collar of her black mourning dress. Isaak, dry-eyed, felt a burning sensation in his throat and chest that rendered breathing painfully difficult.

Like a fragile spring flower, the baby had lived and died within a narrow span of time. A year from now, the marker on his grave would record a lifetime of scarcely three months. His prematurity, so the doctors at the university had said, had made the child an easy prey to a host of illnesses, not the least of which was the one he had probably received from his mother's ancestors. So immature a nervous system, the doctors had reasoned, must be extremely vulnerable to the destructive effects of the disease. Ultimately, however, little Jakob had died quietly in his sleep, his lungs filled with fluid that he was too weak to cough up and dislodge. The technical factors were immaterial. Sarah's baby was dead, and somehow the fragile link that had begun to bind Sarah and Isaak together was stretched and strained to the breaking point.

Isaak sensed this in the long silences that ensued between himself and Sarah, in place of the easy camaraderie and close communication they had formerly shared. Sarah grew restless and withdrawn. Her blue eyes took on a haunted expression, and she was never very far from breaking into tears. Isaak tried his best to comfort and console her, to bring a smile to her lips, no matter how briefly, and some measure of hope back into her heart, but it was all in vain. Sarah was mourning more than the loss of her son. She was lamenting the death of all her hopes for the future, the breaking of her last bond with Adam, and the final defeat of her brave but hopeless campaign against the lethal legacy of her mother's family. Amidst that devastating grief and loss, Isaak dared to hope Sarah would turn to him, that she would come to accept the love and dedication he was so willing to give her.

Instead, calling upon hidden reserves of strength, Sarah marshaled her inner forces and came to a private decision regarding the direction her life must follow in future.

Isaak was deeply saddened but not totally surprised when, four weeks later, just at the end of the "dark time" in the Jewish calendar, he came home to find Sarah's belongings packed and neatly stacked just inside the front door of their apartment. When Sarah emerged from the bedroom, she carried the black cloak and bonnet that she had worn since her period of mourning had begun. Their eyes met and Sarah's were tender and troubled as she said, "I waited to speak with you, Isaak, rather than leaving a cold, impersonal note. "

Isaak forced his voice to sound calm and steady as he said, "There's no reason for you to leave, Sarah. This is still your home. It will always be your home. Jakob's death hasn't changed that."

"It's changed me, Isaak," she answered. "A part of me is buried in that tiny coffin." She shook her head sadly. "I can never be quite the same again." She put down her traveling attire on the chair near her, but she did not move closer to him, so Isaak went to her.

"Of course you can't," he said soothingly. "Life changes all of us, and the reality of death changes us even more. We couldn't survive if we didn't learn to change and adapt."

"And surrender," she added, tears shining in her eyes. "Oh, Isaak, I wanted Jakob so much. I had such hopes for him. When he was born, I thought God had granted me a chance for all I had believed I couldn't have." She smiled bitterly. "What a fool I was! Life has nothing to offer such as I except bitterness and disappointment. "

Isaak took her gently in his arms. "Surely, you must know how I feel about you," he whispered.

Sarah nodded. "Yes, I know. That's the main reason I can't stay." She raised tear-filled eyes to his. "You offer me love, but you know I can't accept it. Love between us, Isaak, would be a hopeless parody. Every time we touched each other, Jakob's shadow would be there between us."

"Not for me," Isaak objected, holding her even closer. "I love you, Sarah. I haven't been able to feel that about anyone for years." His voice faltered momentarily. "Not since the first girl I loved died." He held her away from him and looked tenderly at her face as if memorizing each feature. "Sarah, you and I have each suffered losses. We're alike in a great many ways. We share the same tastes, the same background. Why can't we start afresh from now, from this moment, and go on together?"

Sarah reached up and embraced Isaak tenderly.

"Don't tempt me, my dear friend, my almost brother," she said softly. "Yes, it would be so easy to accept your offer, so comfortable to step from treasured friend to cherished lover. I do love you, Isaak. I admit that, but I can't let myself be governed by it." She backed away from him and shook her head. "Every time we made love together, we'd both be thinking of Jakob and wondering if the next child would be flawed like him."

"We needn't have children," Isaak began, but Sarah laid a finger on his lips to silence him.

"If I let myself," Sarah answered, "I could love you deeply, Isaak. When two people love each other, children are a natural result." She turned away. "We can't risk that. I can't! I can't go through a second, and perhaps a third time, what I've just endured." She faced him once more and took his face in her hands. "And I can't inflict that on you."

"I'm willing to take the chance," Isaak said levelly, meeting her eyes.

"I'm not," she replied sharply, "and I won't have you being a martyr, either."

"It's not martyrdom to be with the person you love, Sarah." Isaak reached out to her and drew her close. "Life is full of risks. Accepting those risks makes us stronger." He held her tenderly, willing her to understand his feelings, to accept his love, but he could detect the resistance in her body even as he held her.

Finally she drew gently but firmly away. "If it's any comfort, Isaak, leaving you will be the hardest thing I've ever done in my life."

Isaak looked steadily at her. "Not quite," he said.

Sarah thought for a moment, an ironic smile on her lips. "You're thinking of the day Adam and I said good-bye."

He nodded silently.

"Yes," she said. "This is very much harder. That Sarah was still a girl. I'm a woman now."

Isaak squared his shoulders and exerted a strong effort to keep his lower lip from trembling. "Don't go, Sarah. Not now, at least. In the eyes of the world, you and I are married. You stay here. I'll leave."

She looked at him in amazement, obviously appreciating the gallantry of that offer. "Why should you? It's your home far more than mine."

"Maintaining appearances is important, Sarah. There may be awkward questions as it is." He paused, glancing about the room, assailed by the memories it evoked. Here he had stood when Sarah had first arrived to accept his offer of providing a home for her and her unborn child. Even then, he had thought of the three of them as a family, but death had changed everything.

"I can move back in with my cousins," he went on. "They're always saying how they miss having me there." He looked at Sarah. "You can tell anyone who asks that I couldn't stand thinking about the baby every time I looked at the nursery." He grinned crookedly, trying to carry it off as nonchalantly as possible, but the tears stung his eyes in spite of his efforts. "Oh, Sarah," he said, "I do wish you'd give yourself more time to think about this, and about us."

Sarah shook her head in frustration. "I'll go mad if I think about us anymore. I can't afford to think in those terms. It's been a hard lesson, but I've learned it."

Isaak nodded, accepting defeat. He picked up Sarah's luggage and carried it back into her bedroom. Then he went to his own room and quickly and carefully packed his single bag. When he came back into the hall, Sarah stood at the door of her room, her eyes somber.

"This is all wrong," she said, almost angrily. "You can't go on making sacrifices for me like this. You've done more than enough. You've more than fulfilled the Levirate obligation."

Her reference to the duty of a surviving brother to assume responsibility for a dead brother's wife, and even to sire a child in his brother's name, stung Isaak.

"It's not Adam who's dead," he said, setting down his suitcase. "It's his son. Besides, my motives weren't based on obligation. I've tried to make you understand that."

"I do understand," Sarah answered. "It wasn't entirely obligation to the honor of the Marjzendiak name. You do care for me. I appreciate that." She clasped her hands nervously. "I'm grateful for all you've done, Isaak. I honor you for it but…"

"The rent is paid through the end of the fall term," Isaak said, feeling constrained to change the subject. "If you need anything."

Sarah reached out and gently put her hand over his mouth. "You've seen to all that, Isaak."

He nodded. "Yes," he said. "I guess I have." He turned toward the door, then glanced back. "Look, its true. I really couldn't stand to stay here and look at that empty nursery."

"I don't know how long I can either," she responded. "I do know that from this point onward, you and I must each get on with our own lives, and that will be easier to do separately. I pray that life bestows on you its highest blessings." She traced the outline of his strong chin with her fingertips. "God knows you deserve them, and you deserve a wife who can bring you joy and bear you healthy children."

Isaak spoke, seeking to forestall the finality of farewell. "Sarah," he began, but it had all been said. "Take care of yourself."

She smiled and kissed his lips. There was reverence in that kiss. There was affection and caring but no passion. If she felt passion, she was adroit in disguising it from him, although it was the one thing he would most have treasured from her. "You, too," she said, her eyes meeting his.

Sadly he turned away, not trusting himself to say anything more. Woodenly he picked up his suitcase, walked to the door, and let himself out.

The day had been warm, and a hint of that warmth still lingered in the twilight, but to Isaak it seemed that winter's chill already filled the air. He felt numb, but beneath the numbness lay a dull and steady ache that was destined, he was certain, to grow worse before the healing balm of time finally relieved it. He would always regret that Sarah had been unable to return his love, and he would never cease to remember and admire her courage and her strength.

In the lengthening shadows, he followed the familiar streets leading to the home of his cousins, Jada and Zaccahreus.

*  *  *

The end of summer passed for Isaak in a numb haze of remembered pain and loss. He missed Baby Jacob more than even he would have thought possible, and whenever the eyes of his mind envisioned Sarah, he felt a deep, crushing ache that persisted, seemingly for hours, undiminished.

He recalled with dismay how long it had taken before the pain of Mariska's death had begun to subside. In a sense, the coming of the uprising of 1863, with its year-long foreshadowing of tumult and reprisal that had forced Ephraim to send Adam and Isaak away to Krakow, had proved a double blessing. It had separated Isaak from the painfully familiar surroundings of home that would only serve to remind him of his loss, and it had supplied a source of terror and constant concern for the safety of his family that had forced the memory of Mariska into the unconscious background of his thoughts.

Now, he plunged with renewed vigor into the dizzying routine of study, of preparation for his comprehensive mid-year examinations. They would give him an indication of what the state legal licensing bar examination would be like. This ordeal constituted one of the most formidable academic trials on the European continent. Those privileged few who passed both the final Law Akademy comprehensive exams and the bar exams could view themselves as fortunate and vindicated. They were assured of finding employment, since candidates so credentialed were highly prized because of their rarity. Thanks to his friendship with Evyan Sukowski, Isaak was fairly certain of a position in the firm of

Sukowski, Sukowski and Petulaski, if he chose to accept it, once his legal curriculum was concluded.

If he passed the exams he faced now, and later passed the final comprehensive exams and the bar, it would mean he could have his choice of positions anywhere in Austria or Austrian Poland. Even if he returned to Warsaw, a possibility which at present did not attract him, his success in Krakow would still provide an entree to his chosen profession that might even override the impediment of his Jewish origin. However, Isaak was not thinking that far ahead just now. Instead, he was functioning almost automatically, engulfing information, analyzing and storing facts and precedents, correlating them with what he already knew, and filing them away for future reference. He tried deliberately not to think or to feel. He ate and slept with supreme detachment. He knew if he allowed his emotions access to his thought processes, he would be compelled to remember, and memory would undo him.

The school friends he had made during his years in Krakow found Isaak aloof in the days following his return to the home of his cousins. Not only that, but Jada and Zacharias also thought of him as inaccessible; they felt shut out and secretly hurt. They realized that something must have transpired that had wounded him deeply, and wisely, they avoided questioning him. To any who did ask, Isaak explained that he was preparing for his exams and that, just at present, he had time for nothing else. Because family and friends tend to be understanding, that explanation was accepted, though not without concern and some sense of rejection by him.

The result was that Isaak was left alone to pursue his academic objectives unhindered. Despite his attention to his studies, he still missed Baby Jacob, he still longed for Sarah, he still felt homesick for his family in Warsaw, and yet he wrapped himself deeper in the cocoon of self-imposed isolation. At one point, he wondered if he was punishing himself, but could find no cause for such a course of action, and so concluded that he was merely trying to avoid further hurt.

His efforts were unsuccessful. The hurt penetrated all the carefully erected layers of aloofness, of absorption in study, and retreat from access to his feelings. The sense of loneliness and loss spread through Isaak like a form of sepsis, poisoning his blood and blending day and night into an endless miasma of mental anguish that could be diminished by conscious effort, but not wholly vanquished.

The day of the comprehensive exams finally came. Isaak welcomed the ordeal with an acceptance that was almost masochistic. Here was an experience in which he could totally submerge himself. For the two days the test required, Isaak thought of nothing else. Except for the hours he slept, he was indeed entirely absorbed in taking and passing these exams, which would open the future to him. For that period of time, he was aware of little else.

When they were over, Cousin Jada prepared a meal of all Isaak's favorite foods, and set the table with the best china and crystal, filling the house with lighted candles and hanging streamers in a mood of celebration.

When Isaak entered the front door and saw the candles in their decorative holders and the festive streamers draped throughout the hall, the salon, and the dining room, tears came to his eyes, and he stood silently weeping.

"Oh but this is a time of celebration," Cousin Zaccahreus said with unshakable conviction. "It's no time for tears and lamentations."

Isaak allowed himself to be carried along by his cousin's mood of gaiety. He asked wryly, "How do you know I passed?"

"With all the studying and frowning you've done for the past several weeks," his cousin replied, "you can have done nothing else."

With that the two men embraced, Jada came into the hall and joined them, and Isaak, for the first time in many weeks, felt his sorrow somewhat eased. He knew he had done well on the tests. One always knows such things when one has achieved the level of academic advancement where he now was. He knew, and he could allow himself to feel joy and a sense of accomplishment. It was as though he was suddenly released from shackles and the burden of a ball and chain, so that he actually felt physically lighter. For the remainder of that day, and for several days thereafter, the thought of Sarah did not cross his mind, and later, when it did, it had lost much of its pain and bitterness.

That next summer passed for Isaak in a dim haze. There were numerous campus activities during the elective summer session, and he felt torn between wanting to shorten his obligatory curriculum and hasten graduation from the Law Akademy, and wanting almost desperately to see home and family. Illness had prevented his traveling to Warsaw with Adam during the previous summer break. Now, this summer, until very recently, he had been immersed in a cocoon that combined resolute study and emotional if not physical depression.

With the successful completion of his second year comprehensive examinations, he felt finally freed of the chains that had bound his spirit. Yes, he would always love Sarah Krakowska. She would occupy a special place in his heart even as Mariska would for as long as he lived. But one was no linger alive and the other had placed herself, for valid and laudable reasons, beyond his grasp. They met socially from time to time, and their meetings were invariably cordial and warmly friendly, but it was clear to Isaak that friendship was as much as he could expect from Sarah, and he must somehow content himself with that and endeavor to move on.

* * *

Thanks to the generosity of their respective fathers, Meyhra and Adam were able to set their wedding date in late August of 1867. Elana, resolved to be gracious despite her private reservations regarding Meyhra, conferred with her future daughter-in-law at length regarding plans for the wedding reception. Elana offered the Marjzendiak's ballroom, but Meyhra respectfully declined the offer, preferring that the reception take place, as custom dictated, in her own home.

However, as the guest list grew longer, the fact that the bride's house was too small to accommodate all the friends and relatives who wished to attend became apparent. Since the wedding would take place at the Great Synagogue, the simplest solution was to hold the reception in the courtyard outside the old building. This was, after all, the largest and most convenient location for the festivities following the ceremony, and the guests would not be obliged to travel the distance to the Marjzendiak estate.

Isaak had been taking his first year Law Akademy final oral examinations on the day of Adam's graduation from the Warsaw Akademy of Medicine. He had been unable to attend, and Adam had been deeply disappointed. The day that should have been the most rewarding of his life thus far had seemed to Adam incomplete without his brother's presence.

In early August, Adam wrote to Isaak stating that he was depending upon him to act as best man at his wedding. When Isaak's letter arrived confirming that he was on his way home, Adam was both relieved and delighted. The year that had passed since he had said good-bye to Isaak in Krakow seemed to him an incredibly long and eventful one. He felt that he and Isaak would have much to discuss when Isaak returned to Warsaw.

Fortunately, Samuel Jedewreski gave Adam the afternoon off so that he could meet Isaak's train without worrying about patients and professional commitments. The train arrived almost an hour late, and when Isaak stepped out on the platform, the two brothers ran to meet each other, embracing as fervently as if it had been much longer than a year since their last farewell. That event, they each recalled, had also occurred at a railway station.

"Welcome home, brother," Adam said joyfully. "It's been a long time."

"It's good to see you," Isaak answered with equal enthusiasm. He glanced about the remodeled station. "I see a lot has changed since I left."

"More than you know," Adam agreed.

As they walked together to the carriage, Isaak asked, "Tell me, what's Meyhra like? I know she's a nurse, but is she pretty? Is she anything like…"

He stopped short of mentioning Sarah's name. Sarah was still very much in his thoughts, but it was inconsiderate to remind Adam of his old love on the eve of his wedding. "I mean, is she blond or brunette?"

Depositing Isaak's case in the rear of the coach, Adam replied, "Meyhra is very beautiful. She's tall and dark-haired and her eyes defy description."

Isaak smiled, glad of the differences Adam had outlined and the fact that his prospective sister-in-law would not remind him of Sarah. "I'm anxious to meet her," he said as they mounted the driver's box.

As they drove away, Isaak commented, "I was sorry to miss your graduation, Adam. We'd both looked forward to it for so long." He paused, then added on a brighter note, "Cousin Jada was deeply impressed with Warsaw. She's spoken of her visit constantly since she and Zaccahreus came home."

"I'm glad they were able to come," Adam answered. "It was a real treat for them. Father showed them all over the city and the countryside."

"I can well imagine," Isaak responded, picturing in his mind Ephraim proudly showing his relatives the high points of his native city.

For the next few minutes, as Adam carefully negotiated the streets of downtown Warsaw, he acquainted Isaak with the new buildings and parks constructed in the younger man's absence. Finally, as Adam stopped to let the flow of foot and vehicle traffic pass at a busy intersection, he turned to Isaak and asked, "Have you seen or heard anything of Sarah recently?"

It was the one question Isaak had dreaded. Yet he had known it was inevitable. He considered for a moment. "A few months after you left Krakow," he said finally, "I met Sarah at a faculty reception. We talked at some length."

"How was she?"

"Fine," Isaak answered. "She had just been appointed to the junior faculty at the university. She seemed quite enthusiastic about teaching."

Adam seemed impressed. "I'm not surprised," he said. "Sarah is very gifted. She'll make a marvelous teacher. Have you seen or talked with her since?"

Isaak pondered his answer briefly, one hand playing idly with the appointments of the carriage. "I saw her often for a while," he answered at last, avoiding supplying further details. "I recently told her you were about to be married."

Adam kept his eyes on the road as he asked, "How did she react to that news?"

"She was pleased to know of your good fortune. It seemed to put her mind at ease."

Adam rearranged the reins in his hand. "Did she mention her brother Jakob?"

Isaak nodded uncomfortably. "She talked about him a great deal. Jakob's death has exerted a profound effect on Sarah."

"At least, Jakob's suffering is over," Adam remarked sadly.

Isaak nodded. "In a way, Jakob may be the luckiest member of that family."

"The Krakowskis are a doomed family through no fault of their own," Adam said. "It's so unjust! And there's still so little we doctors know about diseases like theirs."

Isaak sat in silence, remembering occasions when Sarah had talked with him about her brother Jakob and the tragic circumstances of his illness and death. Then there was that other Jakob whose death had been even more tragic.

"Adam," Isaak began hesitantly, "there's something I don't quite know how to say."

They were at the old barbican wall, just inside the gate that led to the Wola road. Adam seemed reluctant to respond. "What is it?"

Isaak searched for words to soften the blow but could find none that made the telling easier. Yet, considering the fact that Sarah had given him a letter for Adam, he felt he should at least mention baby Jakob in order to prepare his brother for what Sarah might have written. "After you left, there was a child."

Adam froze. "A child?"

Isaak nodded. "Sarah had a child."

"Oh my God! You're saying she bore _my_ child?"

"You were the only man she ever loved, or will ever love, I suspect." Isaak wondered if Adam could detect the pain he was feeling from the sound of his voice.

"Why didn't you write to me? I would have come back."

"You couldn't have changed anything, Adam," Isaak said tensely. "Sarah accepted your decision. She felt you did the right thing. She blamed herself for the baby."

"It wasn't her fault," Adam stated firmly. "I wanted her fully as much as she wanted me. But a child." His voice broke.

Isaak, struggling with his own painful thoughts, said, "He lived only very briefly. Sarah handled it all very well, actually. Far better than I did."

Adam, tears filling his eyes, was obliged to slow the carriage.

Isaak reached into his coat pocket and drew out an envelope. He handed it to Adam. "Sarah asked me to give you this. She said it was important."

Adam took the letter. "She didn't want me to write," he said wistfully, "but I should have kept in touch with her anyway."

"I doubt she'd have answered," Isaak said. "Certainly not at first."

Adam glanced at the letter and placed it in his coat pocket. He drove on in the direction of Wola.

As they approached Plaz Marjzendiak, Adam deliberately drove more slowly. He rounded a curve in the road, affording Isaak the full effect of a first view of the main gate. On each side stood a massive stone pillar. Above them, wrought-iron grillwork supported the tall bronze letters that spelled out the family name. Beyond that gateway lay the land with its expansive fields, manicured lawns, and beautifully arranged gardens that furnished a perfect setting for the main house. The surrounding plateaus and woodlands set off the estate much as an elegant mounting might showcase a brilliant gem.

Isaak was speechless for a long moment. "It's magnificent! Father must be very proud."

"He is," Adam responded. "It represents a much longer journey than just the distance between here and the Stare Miasto ghetto."

Isaak gazed in silence as they drove through the gates and up the road to the house. "Leah once wrote to me her impressions of the evening the family first carne here," he recalled. "It was as though the world had ended and then been created anew."

"For us, it has," Adam agreed.

When they reached the main house, Adam brought the carriage to a halt. Leah came bounding down the front stairs and threw her arms about Isaak, too full of emotion for words. Six-year-old Michael hastened down the stairs in his sister's wake, and then stood politely as Isaak and Leah embraced.

Isaak glanced down at Michael. "And here is the brother I haven't seen since he was a baby."

"I'm not a baby now, sir," Michael answered with grave dignity, extending his hand.

Isaak knelt and took the boy's small hand in his own. "Indeed, you're not, Michael," he said, "but even a grown man can give his brother an old-fashioned hug."

Michael grinned, put his arms about Isaak's neck, and hugged him enthusiastically.

Having heard the coach arrive, Elana stepped out onto the terrace and was greeted by the joyous reunion of her four children.

Isaak, sensing his mother's presence, looked up the stairs and saw the expression of love and delight in her eyes. Gently, he disengaged himself from Michael's embrace, got to his feet, and paused momentarily, savoring the picture Elana presented with her arms outstretched to him in welcome. She was about to descend the stairs. Instead, Isaak ran up to her and embraced her.

He had been away a long time and had often anticipated this moment of homecoming. However, the reality of seeing his family's estate for the first time, and most of all, being reunited with those whom he loved most far excelled anything he had imagined.

# CHAPTER TWENTY-ONE
## BEFORE GOD AND THIS COMPANY

On the eve of Adam's wedding, Elana, delighted to have Isaak at last home from Krakow, enjoyed the chance to talk with him in person and to see him in the flesh. She could hardly believe that her entire family was together under one roof for the first time since that night in late September of 1862, when they had shared a premature but solemn commemoration of Yom Kippur.

Isaak was the one member of the family to whom everything about the property was new and unfamiliar. Elana showed him the house and grounds, pointing out with pride the additions that she and Ephraim had made. For years, the house had stood empty, crumbling, and prey to vandalism. Mira Pietrowska had begun its renovation even before the Marjzendiak family had moved in. Ephraim had continued the process, little by little adding improvements to the house and revitalizing the farmlands. At present, the land yielded a respectable income and, in times of need, could feed the family for months. The graceful gardens surrounding the house, Elana explained, had been her personal project, and they were indeed majestically beautiful to behold.

Nonetheless, for Isaak, there was an element of unreality about the entire estate. The fact that the mills had come to belong to his family, following the easing of the ban on Jewish ownership of property, was one thing. After all, Mer Wishnieski had been desperate to sell them after the series of family tragedies he had suffered. The former Zielinski estate, with its palatial main house and acres of land was quite another matter. It was a showplace that now rivaled even the neighboring Pietrowski property. It seemed to Isaak impossible that his father's ownership of such a prize parcel of land could long escape the officious intervention of the Russian overlords, not to mention the envious notice of the upper and middle class Polish landowners.

That his father had successfully consolidated his position in the business community of Warsaw was a feat that Isaak could readily admire. What the younger man mistrusted was the permanence and security of that position. However, he was at home on holiday to participate in a family celebration. Therefore, he made an effort to cast aside his misgivings and to give himself up to the beauty and wonder that was Plaz Marjzendiak. For once, though Isaak had often pictured in his mind the splendid home his family had acquired, he had to admit that reality exceeded imagination, fulfillment outshone anticipation. This was a home of which any family could be proud, for at least as long as Tsar Alexander II's reforms of the laws governing ownership of land prevailed.

Standing beside Elana in her favorite place, the gazebo that overlooked the rose garden, Isaak felt a strong ambivalence. On the one hand, he was proud and delighted, on the other apprehensive. Gazing at the broad expanse of land spread out before him, Isaak remarked, "All this hardly seems possible, Mother."

"There was a time when it seemed unreal to me," Elana remarked. "That was before I started to plant the garden. Nothing establishes a sense of home more quickly than digging in your own soil." She smiled as she seated herself on one of the wrought iron benches. "Now I can't imagine living anywhere else."

Isaak kept his disturbing apprehensions regarding the political situation to himself. Glancing about the gazebo, he said, "This setting suits you. I can imagine a portrait of you painted just as you look now."

Elana smiled. "Your father has mentioned, more than once, having portraits painted of all of us. It's a tradition that seems to go with owning a place such as this."

"Rather a pretentious tradition," Isaak responded, "though in our case it might have a practical application."

Elana glanced at him, an expression half-amused and half-puzzled on her lovely face. "Practical?"

"Yes. Considering how long it takes even a major artist to paint such a portrait, a series of them, obviously posed in this setting, could serve as proof for future generations that their ancestors did indeed live here."

Elana gazed fondly at her son, more amused than ever. "You think they'll need such 'proof'?"

Isaak shrugged. "It could come to that one day," he said levelly. "Despite his reforms, I've heard it said that the tsar has no liking for the Jews of his empire. A show of leniency is expedient for the present. "

Elana nodded soberly. "One day, expediency might well dictate a change in the opposite direction."

"Unfortunately, yes," Isaak responded.

"Then all this would be taken from us." She turned to face her son fully. "Your father and I are aware of that possibility, Isaak. All of Central Poland is governed by the whim of one man in far-away St. Petersburg. Even assuming he lives up to his principles of reform, he, too, is only mortal."

Isaak moved closer to his mother. "So we live in the present, enjoying its blessings, while we dread the future?"

She reached up and took his hand. "While we look to our children to help us build for that future. It's the hope of all of us, not just the Jews but the Gentiles as well."

"Then you also think Poland will someday regain its independence?"

"I think the present system is too ponderous to last. It will fall by its own weight if nothing else. When it does, we must all be prepared."

Isaak smiled approvingly. "I'm glad to know you've given it some thought."

"Did you truly believe that your mother thought only of flowers and menus? You used to know me better than that."

Isaak knelt beside her.

"I've been away a long time. Perhaps too long. I used to know myself better in the Stare Miasto. Here I feel like a stranger."

Elana smoothed back her son's unruly hair, thinking that he was the only wavy-haired child in her family. "You'll get used to it, son. In time, it will feel like home."

Sitting here beside Isaak, listening as he explained his feelings to her as he had been accustomed to doing as a child, Elana perceived the basic differences in the philosophies of her husband and her second son. As their conversation continued, and Isaak spoke more openly of his intention to use the practice of law as an entree into politics, Elana feared that those differing philosophies might one day come into conflict. What, she wondered uneasily, would be the outcome of that inevitable confrontation? In the days ahead, whose view would prove correct, Ephraim's conservative stance or Isaak's more pragmatic but militant approach?

Ephraim came home early in honor of Isaak's homecoming and Adam's imminent wedding. Dinner was an occasion for joyous celebration, with special prayers of thanksgiving recited and extra portions of ritual wine poured. Ephraim, seated at the head of the table, looked at his family with pride and pleasure. He was deeply grateful that God had brought both his elder sons safely home and had blessed his own efforts to provide well for his family. Adam had found in Meyhra Insbruk the ideal marriage partner. If only Isaak would find an equally suitable wife, he thought, half his children would be well established.

However, Elana was remembering the afternoon Adam had first brought Meyhra to Plaz Marjzendiak. Elana had felt slightly put off by the younger woman's self-assured manner and particularly by her direct habit of speech. Meyhra obviously had an intimate knowledge of mid-wifery, human anatomy, and the manifestations of disease. As a helper in the office, she might be ideal for Adam, but as a wife, she did not quite conform to what Elana had been taught was the feminine ideal. Tonight would be Adam's last night at home with the family. Tomorrow he and Meyhra would embark on a brief holiday in Kazimierz -Dolny, a wedding gift from Ephraim, and then they would move into the modest but comfortable apartment Adam had rented in the ghetto section of the Stare Miasto, conveniently close to Samuel's old office.

Nothing remains the same, Elana reflected. She looked from Adam to Isaak, so alike and yet so different. "So much has changed for us in the last five years," she said, "since we were all together like this."

Ephraim raised his glass. "Let us drink to happy changes, then. By and large, life has been good to all of us. Let's hope that habit persists, and that we continue to enjoy the blessings of Adonai."

Isaak nodded and said, "Adonai grant that we continue to escape the notice of the tsar. May he remain blessedly occupied in St. Petersburg." He raised his glass, as had Ephraim, and drank the remainder of his wine.

"And may the underground politicians have the good sense to let sleeping dogs lie," Adam added.

"Which, of course, they won't," Isaak countered. "No politicians ever have the sense to let things alone. If they did, they'd have no justification for their existence, or their stipends."

Elana gazed steadily at Isaak, an expression of challenge in her eyes. "Why would anyone want the life of a politician?"

"Some things need changing, Mother," he answered. "In my view, it's better to be part of the process than its victim."

"Isaak has a point," Ephraim conceded. "Changes are an inevitable part of life. I personally believe in being prepared to meet them." He turned to Isaak. "Ask Adam to show you the family cemetery while you're here. There's more buried there than old bones. There's money held in the bank in each of your names, even Michael's, but…"

Michael looked up and grinned with satisfaction. "Good," he interjected.

Ephraim smiled at his youngest child, pleased that he understood the importance of his father's words. He then continued, "Banks are a necessity, but they are still the creatures of the state. Never rely entirely on anything the tsar controls."

"Our ancestors were wise," Elana commented. "They dressed their women in coins for ornaments. In the clothes they stood up in, many of them carried a sizeable fortune. I've often thought it's too bad that custom was abandoned."

Leah glanced at her mother's pearl necklace. "It wasn't abandoned entirely," she said with a knowing smile. "Gems are prettier than coins any day. And more valuable."

"Our Leah is growing up fast," Ephraim said. He looked proudly at his daughter. "Soon you'll be wanting precious stones of your own."

"Someday," Leah answered, "when I'm a little older and have occasion to wear them."

"The point is to have them, child." Ephraim responded with feeling. "Whether you wear them is a matter of choice. But to own them can mean the difference between having the price of survival and being stranded without means." He turned to Isaak. "That's why one grave out there has an unmarked headstone. It's rough and weathered to simulate great age. It marks the place of our secret storehouse. We must guard it well, and if we never have need of it, then we must guard it for those who follow us."

* * *

An hour before dusk, Adam followed the narrow path that led to the family cemetery. He came to a clearing and seated himself upon a broad, flat boulder. He was doubly grateful to his brother. Isaak had come home to play his proper role in Adam's wedding. Moreover, the distraction occasioned by Isaak's homecoming had allowed Adam a few moments of solitude before sunset. Adam withdrew from his pocket the envelope that Isaak had given him. Its flap was sealed with the crest of Krakow, surmounted by the six-pointed Star of David. Together, those two ancient symbols formed the seal of Sarah's family. Thoughtfully, Adam took out several folded sheets of paper, covered on both sides with Sarah's neat handwriting, and began to read.

> "My Dearest Adam,
>
> I can scarcely write this letter, and yet, in all honesty, I feel that I must. When we said good-bye a year ago, I felt bitter, abandoned, and devastated. I both loved and hated you, and moreover, I hated myself. In my mind, I knew you had made the only choice open to you, but my heart refused to accept that fact."
>
> As he read further, Adam came to understand the impact of that fateful decision from her point of view. Reluctantly, she explained her actions on their last day together, asking his forgiveness. She wrote that she had been driven by fear and desperation, and though Adam had known that from her words, the letter explored the depths of her feelings in a way he had not realized before. She generously thanked him for the gift of his love and for the one bright hour of passion they had shared. She did not regret that experience, and she wrote that he should not regret it either, as he had given her the most precious memories of her life. She felt that those

moments of intimacy would be her only glimpse of physical love, and she would always treasure them. Most poignantly of all, she left out any mention of baby Jakob, although Adam realized how much she must have wished to share with him the brief history of their child's life, and what he must have meant to her. Instead, in closing she wrote a final paragraph of farewell and blessing.

"I rejoice in the news that you are to be married. I pray you will be happy. Forget the past as I must also do. When you hold your first son in your arms, know that your Sarah blesses him from afar.

All my love always,

Sarah"

By the time he finished reading those words, Adam was torn by the conflicting emotions of grief for the loss of his first true love and a poignant respect for her courage, honesty, and innate dignity. Knowing the story of his brother's tragic love affair with Mariska Wishnieska, Adam understood Isaak's dilemma on learning of Sarah's pregnancy. He realized that Isaak had remained in Krakow during the winter recess of the preceding year in order to take care of Sarah and of Adam's unborn child. Even in the depths of his remorse, Adam blessed his brother's nobility of spirit. As close as they had grown in Krakow, only now did he fully understand and appreciate Isaak's deep capacity to love without the expectation of repayment.

In that hour of solitude, walking thoughtfully in the family cemetery, Adam came to terms with his internal conflicts. He resolved to begin his marriage to Meyhra with the example of Isaak and Sarah foremost in his mind. He had been blessed indeed to have known the love of such people as they, as well as the loving guidance of Ephraim and Elana. Most importantly, he had won Meyhra's love and devotion and he was determined to build with her a solid and mutually rewarding life.

Isaak vividly remembered Leah's letters to him over the past year. She had mentioned that Adam occasionally went to the family cemetery to pay his respects to Rachel, the infant sister he had never known. As Ephraim had advised him to have Adam show him the "grave" that held the treasure buried there years ago, when he was unable to find Adam in the house or the gardens, he sought him in the cemetery. As Isaak approached, Adam looked up from the contemplation of Rachel's headstone, and their eyes met. Adam thought of his friend Jakob, consigned to an early grave, and of that other Jakob, whose life, like Rachel's, had ended before it had scarcely begun.

Isaak stood beside Adam and joined his prayers with those of his brother for the future of the family.

Both brothers had made major sacrifices to protect that future, a future filled with uncertainties and peril but, nonetheless, illuminated by hope and faith.

\* \* \*

The following day, Adam and Meyhra were married in the Great Synagogue. Mira Pietrowska had generously donated the services of her dressmaker, Marie Doussoult. The dressmaker had transformed Meyhra's treasured length of ivory satin, a legacy from her mother, into a glorious montage of pleats and ruffles. Marie's skill was well-complemented by the bride's slim figure and elegant stature. As she stood beneath the wedding canopy beside her bridegroom, Meyhra was resplendently beautiful.

Rabbi Janowski had almost completed the Sheva Berakhot, the seven benedictions traditionally invoked to bless the groom and his bride. At the conclusion of this reading, ritual wine was poured first into a pair of goblets and then into one, symbolizing the mystical union of bride and groom in marriage.

The rabbi blessed the nuptial wine with the ritual words, "Blessed art Thou, Oh Lord, King of the Universe, who has created joy and gladness, bridegroom and bride, mirth and exultation, pleasure and delight, love, brotherhood, peace and fellowship. Blessed art Thou, Oh Lord, who makes the bridegroom to rejoice with the bride."

At the end of the blessing, the bride and groom each sipped wine from the single goblet. Meanwhile, the rabbi prayed: "May the groom, the bride, and all here present be honored, blessed, ennobled and made joyful by the union of this man and this woman in wedlock before the lord and this company." He turned his eyes to the bride and groom and addressed them specifically. "May you know," he intoned, "joy and honor, love, and the blessings of the Lord all the days of your life."

Isaak, acting as his brother's best man, wrapped within a napkin the second of the two crystal goblets used in the preceding ceremony and placed it at Adam's feet. Adam smashed it decisively. It was the traditional reminder of the destruction of the temple of Jerusalem and of the ultimate mortality of man.

Thrilled that the long period of waiting was at last ended, Adam kissed his bride and led her to the small room where custom provided them a few moments of seclusion in 'yichud,' the time of being 'alone together' as husband and wife.

The wedding reception that followed was held in the rear courtyard of the synagogue. The marks left by the fire of 1864 had faded. The library had long since been repaired, and a new school had been built adjacent to it.

Gathered in the courtyard were several generations of almost every family represented in the Jewish quarter of the Stare Miasto. The changes in the physical surroundings were also reflected in the people. Many of the younger wedding guests no longer lived within the Jewish quarter, and, among these, a growing number no longer attended synagogue. This was true even though the Jews had been given permission, during Wielopolski's administration, to build houses of worship outside the ancient ghetto. Such celebrations as this wedding afforded a rare opportunity for family members to visit in a setting that precluded conflicts over differences in belief or lifestyle.

Adam's closest friend during his early school days had been Lukas Kolvner, whose father had, at the time, run a small antique shop in the ghetto. The store had specialized in art objects from foreign lands. With time, its owner had prospered, its inventory had become more exotic, and the family had ultimately moved away in pursuit of wider opportunities.

As the reception progressed and the informal reception line was coming to an end, Adam found himself face-to-face with an older, leaner, but readily recognizable Lukas, who stood, wineglass in hand.

"A toast to the groom and to the fair and radiant bride," Lukas said, his handsome features alight with merriment.

Adam reached out to embrace his long-absent comrade. "Lukas! I can hardly believe my eyes. When did you come back?"

"That's a long story," Lukas replied. "More to the point, your bride is lovely. Congratulations! You're a lucky man, Adam."

Adam smiled triumphantly. "How well I know." He then introduced Lukas to Meyhra, who greeted her husband's friend graciously. Lukas could scarcely believe that the beautiful and statuesque Meyhra was both a nurse and the long-legged, awkward girl whose family had been his neighbors years earlier.

"But how are you doing now?" Adam's question turned the focus of the conversation upon Lukas, who briefly outlined his family's fortunes since leaving the ancient Polish city.

"You grow rich with your trading and selling," Adam said, half-teasingly. "I hope I can do half as well in my practice."

"You've done well already," Lukas responded, smiling once more at Meyhra.

Half-teasingly, Adam asked, "Are you such a wanderer that you don't have a wife yet, Lukas?"

"Oh no," Lukas answered. "Anna is in Zurich managing our store there, while I'm here, and Father's in Amsterdam."

Meyhra commented, "Is your family never together, Mer Kolvner?"

"Travel is both the blessing and the curse of the importing business," Lukas answered. "My fifteen-year-old brother Markos already dreams of traveling to distant ports in search of rare treasures."

Adam lifted his glass in a toast. "May you always prosper, my friend," he said. "By the way, where is Markos?"

Lukas's glance swept the courtyard. "He's here somewhere. He's probably filling his plate."

An hour later, after the wedding guests had appeased their collective appetite, the wedding couple arose from the head table to lead the dancing. The shtetl orchestra, composed of formally-trained and self-taught musicians, launched into a mixed program of traditional Jewish melodies and popular Polish songs. Adam and Meyhra bowed to each other, touched hands briefly, and then Adam led the men while Meyhra led the women. The two genders danced separately as was the custom. Only one dance did a man and woman dance together, and in that dance, they did not touch.

Young Markos Kolvner, making the most of his social opportunities, was becoming reacquainted with several former school friends. He had not seen them for the past several years during which his family had been away from Warsaw. He was also, as his brother anticipated, enjoying the sumptuous repast.

For most of the afternoon, Markos had been silently admiring a beautiful young girl from a distance, not realizing that she was Leah Marjzendiak. He and Leah had first met under somewhat embarrassing circumstances, painful for Markos to recall. At the time, Leah had been a somewhat awkward, self-conscious child. However, she had improved remarkably with the passage of time, and Markos, long over his childhood embarrassment and considering himself very much a man, at first failed to recognize her. She was dressed in a pink gown, frosted with ruffles and lace, and her rich auburn tresses hung down her back in thick, glossy curls.

Markos approached and stopped beside her, striving to calm his racing pulse. "Do you know the mitzvah tentzel?" He raised the napkin in his hand and offered it to her in the traditional gesture that preceded that form of dance, reserved for special occasions such as this.

Taken by surprise, Leah looked up at the handsome youth. "Yes," she answered. "We learned it in school." She referred to the shtetl school of the Stare Miasto. As Markos Kolvner led her to the area where other guests had begun the dance, Leah studied his face, intrigued by his gray eyes and abundant, straight, black hair. "Have we met before?"

"I don't think so," Markos answered. "I'm sure I'd remember someone as lovely as you are."

Leah smiled appreciatively. "That's very gracious of you," she acknowledged, adding, "I'm the groom's sister Leah."

Surprised, Markos stood still for a moment. Then, offering the napkin, he said, "Shall we dance before the music is over?"

Together, they moved through the complex patterns of the mitzvah tentzel, each holding the end of a festive napkin from the nuptial table. Markos moved with an almost professional grace, his back straight, and his posture flawless. He made a pleasing contrast to the other very young men at the reception, many of whom seemed clumsy and shy with girls and were unskilled in the social arts.

Leah's glance focused momentarily on Adam and Meyhra, then on the young man dancing with Elana. She recognized him as Lukas Kolvner, Adam's closest friend throughout his childhood and early adolescence. Leah looked from Lukas to the boy with whom she was dancing, noting the similarities of form, feature, and coloring. Markos had not mentioned his name, but obviously he and Lukas must be brothers. Suddenly, the occasion of her first meeting with both the Kolvner boys flashed into her mind. As the music ended, Leah could not refrain from laughing.

Her partner was understandably hurt. "What do you find so amusing?"

"You must be Lukas's brother."

Still puzzled, Markos responded, "That's right. I'm Markos Kolvner."

Leah's eyes sparkled. "The first time we met, you were playing a game of hide and seek with your brother and his friends. You hid from them behind a fence."

Remembrance dawned in Markos' gray eyes. "Of course. I had just climbed over that fence in order to elude my pursuers, and my trousers didn't escape without damage."

"I remember," Leah recalled, "the way you looked when you turned around and saw me."

"Well, I'm relieved to know that you're not laughing at me now," Markos said earnestly.

"If you remember, I didn't laugh at you then."

Markos smiled. "No, you were very sympathetic. Let us consider today a new beginning."

As Leah's eyes gazed wistfully into those of Markos Kolvner, the thought occurred to her that the future might hold more for them than simple friendship. Secretly, she admitted to herself that she hoped that would be true.

Isaak observed the festivities as though from the standpoint of a spectator, abstaining from joining in the dancing. Though he was pleased to witness his brother's happiness, he felt a gnawing dread. The music, the laughter, and the dancing seemed to him as unreal as had his first view of the family estate. How could these people indulge their revelry with such abandon? Where, he wondered, was the security, the permanence that such behavior seemed to reflect, when they were still governed by Russian Imperial whim?

Yet, he reflected philosophically, the ability to laugh, to sing and dance in the face of adversity and danger, these were among the techniques of human survival, as valuable in their way as the money and documents buried in the nameless grave next to Rachel's resting place.

# CHAPTER TWENTY-TWO
# THE RIGORS OF RECONSTRUCTION

A steady barrage of winter rain beat down upon Sigismund Square. The downpour flooded the streets and pelted the buildings with a force that reverberated harshly against the domed towers of the ancient tin roofed palace. Four stories below, Nicholas Milyutin, recently appointed Governor-General of Warsaw, sat in his spartan office. His assignment to this post had been carried out in an attempt to stabilize the hitherto ineffectual governing procedures of his predecessors. His dark mood matched the somberness of the weather as he read the dispatches he had just received from St. Petersburg. Those disheartening documents described a wave of growing student unrest, in the capitol city and throughout Mother Russia. Furthermore, they detailed the expanding illegal output of inflammatory propaganda from the underground press.

The last was a sore subject with the governor general. He knew at first hand the frustrations inherent in dealing with the clandestine journalists of dissent. They printed their inflammatory newspapers in basements and private apartments. Despite the best efforts of the militia and the secret police, these seditious newspapers continued to be blatantly distributed throughout the city. Their purveyors seemed to possess a charmed existence, and had managed up until now to disappear without leaving a trace. The pattern was the same all over the Vistula Provinces.

Milyutin was determined to crush those rabble-rousers. However, first he must find one of them, capture him, interrogate him, and then make an example of him, one that the stubborn Warsaw populace would not soon forget. Alexander Swietochowski, symbolic leader of the underground movement, and publisher of <u>Prawda</u>, was Milyutin's special target. The Russian was determined to one day watch that man swing at the end of a rope on a scaffold in the Citadel yard.

The memory of his predecessor's fate haunted Milyutin. Former Governor-General Gerstenzwieg, who had been appointed by the tsar to deal with the political crises of 1862, had taken a coward's way and committed suicide. If the current breed of Nationalist troublemakers expected a repetition of that weak capitulation from Milyutin, they were doomed to disappointment.

A knock at his door broke in upon Milyutin's thoughts. He looked up and called sharply, "Come!"

The militia garrison's commander-in-chief, Sergei Ratchikov, entered and saluted smartly. He prefaced his report with a brief catalog of his sources of information.

Milyutin was in no mood for pleasantries and preamble. "Yes, well, get to the point, man."

Commander Ratchikov responded crisply. "The point, sir, is this. While I didn't fully trust the reliability of this one informant, his news could be a useful clue to the new underground leadership in the ghetto."

Milyutin's interest was piqued. "Did you get names?"

"One in particular. Marjzendiak," the commander answered. "The suspect is a young physician. His father holds a seat on the Bank Advisory Council for the provinces. They're an important family among the Jews."

Milyutin savored this piece of information. Failing an opportunity to get his hands on Swietochowski, finding the latest leading Jewish dissident would serve his purposes almost equally well.

"Very good, Commander. Proceed, but remember, we need concrete facts, not the unsubstantiated word of a janitor. Bring me proof of the Jew's treason and we shall have our example."

Ratchikov nodded in agreement.

Milyutin continued, "We may even succeed in arousing the Christians to launch a new pogrom, for us to put down and restore order." He glanced significantly at Ratchikov. "Do well in this and there may well be a promotion for you. Soon!"

"Thank you, sir," the commander replied. He then clicked his heels, saluted smartly, and made his exit.

Left alone, Milyutin pondered the dispatches spread out on his desk. The fools, he thought. Russian Poland's economy has never been so prosperous. Thanks to their participation in Russian markets, Polish agriculture and manufacture are flourishing and expanding. And how do they thank us? They continue to complain and plot revolution. They're a stubborn lot, Milyutin concluded, Jew and Gentile alike. They'll never be truly assimilated into the Russian population. And yet, he recalled ironically, the tsar had appointed him, not only to quell the remnants of resistance following the uprising, and to implement Russification, but also to insure the peaceful integration of the Vistula Provinces into the Empire.

\* \* \*

On a clear but penetratingly cold morning in February of 1868, Adam Marjzendiak entered his office in the ghetto of the Stare Miasto. He had stopped on the way to attend two house-bound patients while Meyhra had gone on ahead to the office. Adam opened his door to find Meyhra seated at the reception desk in a state of near-shock. She looked up as he closed the door, her eyes shadowed with fear. She came to her feet, trembling visibly.

Adam moved quickly to her side, putting his arms protectively around her. "Meyhra, what's wrong?"

He was answered only by her rapid breathing as she pressed gratefully against him. Slowly, a shadow darkened the opposite wall.

"Doctor Marjzendiak?" The voice was softly menacing. Three men stood dressed in the dreaded gray and red uniforms of the militia; however, there was no mistaking which one was in charge, even if there had been no commander's insignia on the lapels of the man's jacket.

Adam felt a chill of apprehension as he turned. "Yes," he answered, instinctively stepping in front of Meyhra as if he would shield her from a blow. "How may I help you?"

"I can assure you, doctor," Commander Ratchikov retorted, "we are in the best of health. Your professional ministrations are not required."

"Then why," Adam asked, striving to keep his voice level, "are you here?"

The commander stood silently, his eyes boring into Adam, his hands clasped behind his back. Abruptly, he thrust them forward, revealing a folded newspaper. "We've come to return a piece of missing property to you."

Adam stared at the paper, his eyes betraying his mounting alarm.

"I see you recognize it," the commander said pointedly.

"I know what it is, of course," Adam answered cautiously, "but it's certainly not my property."

"Really?" The commander moved closer, so close that his pungent breath struck Adam full in the face. "Then why was it found in your office?"

Trying desperately to remain calm, Adam responded, "Commander, anyone of my patients may have brought that paper here, and then left it behind."

"As a loyal subject of the tsar, you should have destroyed it!"

Adam trembled. Sweat dampened his shirt. "How could I when I didn't know it was here?"

The Russian's voice hardly rose in volume, but its tone grew steadily colder as he said, "Doctor, you should be careful what documents find their way into your private office." He held the paper casually. "Your young janitor reported finding this on your desk yesterday." The commander nonchalantly gazed around the room, a slight smile spreading his thin lips. "I wonder what else we'll find of interest in your desk, Doctor."

With a curt nod, the Russian commander gestured his men into Adam's private office. He motioned to Adam. "After you, Doctor."

Adam turned and walked mechanically ahead of him. Terrified, Meyhra followed.

"The most likely answer to all this," Adam said nervously, "is that Vladimir Dubnowski made up that story to explain having a copy of Prawda in his possession. He's had some trouble lately with the local police."

Ratchikov stood watching while his two subordinates ransacked Adam's files, wreaked havoc with the drawers of his desk, and shoved several books to the floor in their search for incriminating evidence. All the while, the Russian officer stood beside Adam, enjoying his discomfiture.

Meyhra stood by the desk, her hands clenched at her sides, tears gathering in her eyes. No one spoke while the brief but violent search continued. When it was over, the room was in total disarray.

One of the militiamen came over to his commander and shook his head.

Ratchikov turned to Adam. "Dubnowski came to us quite voluntarily, obviously hoping to receive a reward. Loyal citizens are encouraged to cooperate with the government." He pushed Adam's back against the wall, openly frustrated that his men had found nothing incriminating.

"As for Jews, we have other means to ensure their obedience."

Neither Adam nor Meyhra had ever experienced the horrors of a pogrom but they had heard about them in detail from their respective parents and from the elders of the Jewish community. Each could envision one beginning in just this way.

As if in response to Adam's fearful thoughts, the commander suddenly gripped his throat and forced his head back against the wall. Adam gasped for breath and his knees started to buckle. The Russian commander's voice seemed to come from a great distance.

"Where is your safe, Jew?"

Meyhra stepped forward, attempting to draw the man's attention away from Adam. "I'll show you," she said as she moved toward the opposite wall.

She reached up to push aside the framed replica of a Da Vinci sketch of the human anatomy. Her fingers fumbled with the lock as she hurried to open the small safe door.

Ratchikov moved close behind her, his eyes lighting on her wedding ring. He had drawn his own conclusions when Adam had first entered, obviously concerned over Meyhra's distress. Now, the Russian seized Meyhra's hand and held it, assessing the value of the ring.

Meyhra looked up at him, too frightened to speak. The Russian gazed at her with a leering smile, then slowly released his grip.

Meyhra pulled open the safe, regretting that it held only a few zlotys and a small array of coins. Had there been more money hidden there, she thought, it might have proved sufficient to distract the commander from whatever his mission was in invading her husband's office and intimidating them both.

Ratchikov pushed Meyhra aside, stared at the meager sum, and then scoffed angrily. "You wish me to think that's all you have? You must take me for a fool!"

"No, commander," Meyhra answered hastily. "I deposited the rest of the money in the bank yesterday. We don't keep large amounts on hand."

The Russian nodded. "Of course." He glanced at Adam. "Your father being a banker, you would, no doubt, deviate from the usual pattern of your secretive race. However, don't imagine that your father's exalted position will save you from punishment."

Adam looked at Ratchikov, his voice hoarse with dread. "I've done nothing wrong." He coughed and cleared his throat. "The janitor is a liar! This denouncement is his revenge for my refusal to pay him extra money over and above the agreed-upon fee."

"Why is a Pole working for a Jew, anyway?" The question was asked almost in a whisper, but the implied threat was clear. It was not an uncommon practice for Russian magistrates to harass relatively affluent Jews by invoking and deliberately distorting the ancient eastern European law forbidding Jewish ownership of Christian slaves.

Meyhra quickly intervened. "The widow Dubnowski and her son maintain a cleaning service for several buildings in the Stare Miasto, including some here in the ghetto. They charge a standard fee, but lately, the son has tried to extort additional sums, unknown to his mother."

The commander silently regarded Meyhra and Adam in turn. "An enterprising young man," he remarked coldly.

He realized he had failed to secure the concrete proof his superior had demanded. Though intimidated, the Jewish doctor and his alluring wife had not betrayed themselves. A less prominent suspect could be arbitrarily arrested, held incommunicado, and repeatedly interrogated. Prisoners thus abused were often induced to "confess" the crimes of which they were accused. The present case held subtle ramifications, however. To move prematurely here could incite the indignation of the elder Marjzendiak's prominent banking affiliates at a time when Governor-General Milyutin was attempting to normalize conditions. On the other hand, if the young Jew could be provoked to violence, there would be no question of the validity of his arrest. Later, under the questioning Ratchikov would personally administer, the prisoner would willingly confess to almost anything.

Ratchikov's glance, as it fell on Meyhra, was deliberately salacious. He reached out, seizing her by the hair and forcing her to look up at him. "What would you be willing to do, I wonder, to persuade me not to arrest your husband?"

Meyhra's glance darted fearfully toward Adam.

Her eyes locked with his. She shook her head, silently warning him against any show of resistance.

The Russian commander smiled wickedly, beckoned his men to his side, and spoke softly to them. The two militiamen walked over to where Adam stood. Each took hold of one of his arms and they held him fast. Thus restrained, Adam watched miserably as the Russian commander, obviously enjoying himself, ran his strong, rough hands over Meyhra's neck and shoulders and slowly, tortuously down her back to her buttocks, kneading and caressing them sensuously, while all the while he watched Adam struggle futilely in the grip of his captors.

Soon, in compliance with the commander's whispered orders, one of his men would loosen his grip on the doctor. Awaiting this maneuver, Ratchikov fondled Meyhra's breasts and then crushed her against him. He forced her head back and kissed her lustily, thrusting his tongue into her mouth.

Ratchikov watched the expression of outrage on Adam's face, prepared to see the Jew's self-control crack. The Russian confidently expected to feel the impact of a blow that would galvanize his subordinates into punitive action. Meyhra remained motionless in his hands, refusing to react. He noted that she neither fought nor cried out. More disappointing still, her coward of a husband stood mutely impotent.

Disgusted and frustrated, the commander finally let the woman go, pushing her roughly aside as though he had grown tired of her. He walked back to where Adam stood as the two militiamen stepped away from the suspect. For a long moment, the commander and Adam stared at each other in a wordless duel of wills. Reluctantly, Adam lowered his eyes.

With a cruel smile, the Russian commander seized Adam's chin and forced his head back, compelling him to look directly at him. "For the moment, Doctor, we shall leave you to attend to your patients. However, you may be certain that we will keep you and your charming wife under constant observation, both here and at your home."

He released his grip on Adam and silently signaled his men. All three moved toward the door. There, the commander paused and added, "I suggest you be more observant in the future, Doctor. It may spare you further inconvenience."

When the militiamen had left, Adam was filled with self-loathing over having submitted without greater resistance to the indignities heaped upon his wife and himself. He slumped bitterly into the chair opposite his desk and leaned his head in his hands. "I failed you. I let him maul you like that, and I did nothing to prevent it."

Meyhra knelt beside him. "I thank Adonai you had the wisdom not to try. If you had, they might have killed you, and then raped me."

Adam looked up and searched Meyhra's face. "Are you all right?"

Meyhra nodded. "Are you?" She reached up and gently stroked Adam's cheek and smoothed the hair back from his forehead, examining his face with loving concern. A dark bruise marred his chin where the Russian officer had held it, and his throat was discolored where the man's powerful fingers had applied an almost strangling pressure. Impulsively, she hugged Adam and kissed him. As she did so, each could taste Ratchikov's saliva still in her mouth. So great had been her concern for her husband that she had ignored the hateful taste before. She turned away and retched. Adam gently wiped her mouth and then drew her close, trying to soothe her anguished shame and his own wretchedness.

The two of them clung together, each drawing strength from the other.

"We must thank Adonai we're both still alive and free," Adam said, his glance drifting dejectedly over the chaos that surrounded them.

Meyhra also looked about the office, her eyes deeply troubled. "That statement about continued observation. He meant it. They're not going to leave us alone."

"They'll have to," Adam said consolingly, "when they keep finding nothing."

Meyhra shook her head. "Then they'll invent something."

Adam reached up to stroke her cheek. "Darling! Darling, let it go."

"How? Pretend they never came?" An angry note crept into Meyhra's voice. "Why did they have to come here today of all days? I had planned such a perfect surprise for you. Now it's spoiled."

Adam took her face in his hands. "No it's not. What is it? Tell me. I never needed a pleasant surprise more." He kissed her tenderly, pressing her closer to him. He could feel her trembling in his arms, could taste the tears on her lips. "It's all right, Meyhra. It's over." He forced himself to smile, to forget for the moment the shame of the past several minutes. "Tell me the surprise, just the way you planned to."

Meyhra nodded then and smiled shyly. She scanned the room, searching for the antique music box that had once been her childhood treasure. The melody it played was a Jewish lullaby from the previous century.

Despite the disruptive search that the Russian militiamen had carried out, the antique music box, made in the shape of a miniature carousel, sat unharmed at the edge of Adam's desk.

Meyhra reached out and picked it up, then pushed the switch that set it in motion. As the lilting melody filled the room, Meyhra sang a few of the words in Yiddish, then broke off, weeping softly. "Oh Adam, what sort of world is this into which to bring a baby?"

Meyhra began once more to tremble, and Adam, keenly aware of her feelings, held her close and tried to comfort her despite his own misgivings. "It's still Adonai's world," he said.

* * *

For the next several weeks, Adam was plagued by nightmares. He would awaken shivering, covered with sweat, his mind still filled with images from his dream, images of Russian militiamen searching, disrupting, and destroying Jewish property, and attacking Jewish men and women. In one such dream, he saw Ephraim and Elana thus victimized and awoke screaming to find he had also awakened Meyhra. She questioned him, trying without success to learn the details of the dream that had so deeply affected him.

Even though they seldom discussed it, the frightening visit that the militia had paid to them continued to haunt them both. Without being told, Meyhra sensed that it was the memory of that event that must have awakened her husband. That dreadful memory was never far from the surface of her own mind.

She and Adam clung to each other, kissing and embracing, each seeking to reassure the other. Inevitably, they made love, passionately, recklessly, almost desperately. It was as though the shadow of danger sharpened their erotic appetites and intensified their need to express their love in physical terms. Such an intensely physical act as lovemaking, with its explosively satisfying culmination, symbolized for them an assertion of their existence that somehow made the ugly memory bearable and reduced it to terms that could be dealt with.

After they had made love, Adam fell into a peaceful sleep. Meyhra, watching him, relaxed though she did not sleep. She lay beside her husband, savoring the early stirring of life within her. Adonai had created that life. Her faith in Adonai assured her that He would know how to protect and nurture it, and that He would protect her and Adam, despite the perils that surrounded them. For centuries, their people had survived by relying on that belief and that faith.

*　*　*

Having sent Meyhra home early, Adam sat in his office completing the day's paperwork. It was late afternoon of a day in May. The weather was mild and pleasant, and Adam could see children playing outside his office window. Soon, he mused, he and Meyhra would have a child of their own. Perhaps before the passage of another year he would have saved enough zlotys to make the down payment on a new home, larger and more in keeping with his growing prosperity. Samuel had made him a full partner at the beginning of the year. The office in which he sat was now his own, and his practice was steadily expanding.

Abruptly, Adam heard an urgent knocking at his outer door. Momentarily, he sat frozen with apprehension. Patients seldom came this late except for emergencies. Could it perhaps signal another visit from Milyutin's militia? Worse still, was it a neighbor bringing him news of the militia's having invaded his home and perhaps assaulted Meyhra? Terrified by these apprehensions, Adam rose hurriedly from his desk and hastened to answer the frantic summons.

As he opened the door, he was surprised to find young Markos Kolvner standing on his doorstep. Though Markos' elder brother Lukas was a frequent visitor, both at the office and at Meyhra and Adam's modest home, Adam had not seen Markos since the day of his own marriage to Meyhra.

Such a look of earnest appeal shone in Markos' eyes that Adam feared some medical emergency had overtaken the Kolvner family, but Markos assured him that this was not the case. However, the young man glanced nervously about the waiting room, his movements betraying his agitation.

Adam took him into his office and seated him opposite the ancient desk, attempting to put him at ease.

Almost reluctantly, under Adam's urgings, Markos began to explain the reason for his coming.

"I've spoken with Lukas. It was he who suggested I talk with you as your father's firstborn."

Adam nodded, more mystified than ever. He encouraged his visitor to continue.

"I hoped you might be willing to act as my spokesman." The look of entreaty that accompanied the words engaged Adam's sympathy but did little to resolve his confusion.

"Your spokesman?"

"Yes," Markos said. "It's about your sister Leah."

That remark struck an odd note that caused Adam to ask somewhat sharply, "What about my sister?"

Markos looked up and met Adam's eyes. "I realize I'm still young," he said earnestly, "and I've yet to prove myself in commerce. However, my prospects are good and I plan soon to take my place in the family business."

As Adam continued to stare at him uncertainly, Markos tried to explain further. "Marriages have been arranged among our people for centuries."

Relieved to know the particulars at last, Adam tried not to sound either amused or condescending as he asked, "Are you saying, Markos, that you wish me to act as matchmaker between you and my sister?"

"I suppose that's one way to put it. Surely your father would listen to you in such a matter."

Adam was silent for a moment. Then he asked, "Don't you think this is a bit premature?"

"Leah is a very beautiful girl, and quite gifted. She will be much admired. I'd feel more comfortable knowing that an understanding had been reached between our families."

Adam patted the boy's shoulder reassuringly. "Markos, it will be three or four years before Ephraim will consider an offer of marriage for Leah. In the meantime, I'll tell him of your interest in her. When the time comes, I'll be only too happy to plead your cause. For now, I suggest that you work diligently toward establishing your place in the family business. Put some money aside toward the 'bride price.' And get your brother to bring you to our family home occasionally so that you and Leah can get better acquainted on an informal basis. That will lay the ground work for your later relationship. Leah will grow accustomed to your presence, and you will become more at ease with her." Adam shrugged. "After that, you'll have to let nature take its course and hope for the best."

# CHAPTER TWENTY-THREE
## CONTRADICTIONS AND CONSEQUENCES

Pierre Rebaumme awoke abruptly, shivering as much from fear as from the chill of the cold sweat that enveloped him. It was all happening again, the nightmare that he thought he had left behind when he had fled Paris. He could hear the Marquis de Marigny's angry words accusing him of cheating, could feel the man's slim, strong fingers clasped around his throat.

"I should have known better than to play cards with a Jew as though he were a gentleman."

Pierre had known that it was his accuser who had cheated at Faro and suspected that the other men at the table had known it, too. But he, Pierre, was the outsider. The other Parisian aristocrats had banded together behind the marquis, supporting his accusations. Even in France, the cradle of liberté and equalité, where all citizens were supposed to hold equal status, such events still occurred. Officially, the Jews of France were considered Frenchmen, equal before the law with other Frenchman of different persuasions and origins. Nonetheless, there were carefully guarded preserves that were not open to them.

Certain of the elite gentlemen's clubs of Paris were among the places that were still "beyond the Pale," despite the invitation Pierre had received with such enthusiastic anticipation.

The metallic clanging of the grandfather clock in the hall, striking the midnight hour, startled Pierre and at the same time reassured him. The nightmare had seemed so real, but Paris was far away, and so was his native Provence. He had crossed the border from France into Germany to escape the dreaded consequences of that false accusation, which could be years in prison if his adversary's lies should be upheld by the French courts. He had left suddenly, secretly, under cover of night, not pausing even to write a brief note of farewell to his Aunt Marie or his Cousin Philippe. His career in Paris, commenced so auspiciously with a handsome commission to paint the portrait of the daughter of the Duke De Cheynne, was ended before it had begun.

He had not dared even to return to his apartment in Paris. He had gone instead to his modest studio and then to the home of his mistress Marlene Ranier, who lived nearby and had posed for him often. She had packed for him the clothes he kept in her closet. Their parting had been passionate but necessarily brief.

In Germany, Pierre recalled, fellow Jews had treated him kindly but could offer little practical advice to a displaced painter whose major assets were the canvasses he had managed to bring away with him. Armed with these paintings and a small reserve of francs, Pierre Rebaumme had reached Warsaw, capital of the Russian Vistula Provinces. Here, at least, where the Russian influence was now indelibly imprinted on the social structure, Pierre's French extraction was a distinct advantage so long as he did not disclose his Jewish origins.

He had long since abandoned the practice of his faith, viewing it as a hypocritical capitulation to outmoded superstition. Many young western European Jews shared that view, to the outrage and shame of their elders. To assume the role of a secular and secret Jew was, in Pierre's case, an adjustment to economic necessity, a fact he seldom admitted even to himself. Instead, Pierre Rebaumme regarded himself as a fully emancipated Frenchman of Jewish background, unbound by the religious superstitions of his ancestors.

Pierre's thoughts inevitably led him back to a day in early spring of 1868 when he had sat with an elite assortment of patrons of the arts, the guest of Sophia Oslowska, wife of the mayor of the Warsaw suburb of Wola. The <u>Rendezvous</u> was one of the most fashionable new tea houses of Warsaw. It was modeled after the elegant Maisons du Manger that currently abounded in all the major French cities. Its atmosphere was distinctly western European and therefore a welcome haven for an expatriate Frenchman in obligatory exile. Moreover, Pierre's future had depended upon that gathering, for here he was to meet the legendary Madam Mira Pietrowska.

"Madam Pietrowska is one of the leading supporters of the arts here in Warsaw," Sophia Oslowska had told him. "If she takes an interest in you, your success is assured."

Pierre's first glimpse of Mira Pietrowska was a vision of bold, fierce, gypsy-like beauty, barely restrained by the confines of polite social protocol. The woman had exuded an elemental energy that was at once overwhelming and magnetically appealing. Her arrival in the foyer of <u>The Rendezvous</u> had sparked an electric impulse of excitement throughout the crowd gathered there. Her dark, perfectly-coiffed hair had been piled high on her head, cascading down one shoulder under a hat that was a frothy confection of blue-green watered silk and peacock feathers. Her matching gown, cut in the height of fashion, had displayed her voluptuous figure to perfection. Her contemporaries at the table had greeted her warmly, and Sophia Oslowska had introduced Rebaumme, extolling his talents in a manner intended to pique Mira's interest.

Mira had looked him over appraisingly, her dark, knowing eyes taking in every detail of his appearance. She took the empty seat next to Rebaumme.

"What brings you away from France, sir?"

"Curiosity," Rebaumme answered, in a voice he hoped expressed confidence and a bit of bravado. "That, and a sense of adventure."

Mira flashed one of her dazzling smiles. "And the knowledge that if things are not to your liking here, you can always return home."

"It's my intention," Rebaumme countered, "to make my home in Warsaw."

As lunch had progressed, Mira had plied the artist with questions, seeking to learn more about his background, his tastes, his interests, and his ambitions. Rebaumme, encouraged by her interest, had candidly discussed his techniques with certain stains and resins. As a result, Mira Pietrowska had invited him to her estate for an evening that included dinner and the opportunity to display some of his canvasses for her family and a small group of artistically knowledgeable friends.

Rebaumme's commission to paint the portraits of the Pietrowski family had grown out of that dinner engagement. Shortly thereafter, he had moved into the Pietrowski home where spacious quarters had been prepared for him and the solarium had been temporarily transformed into a studio for his convenience. Once convinced of his particular genius, Mira Pietrowska had become his wholehearted patron. Unfortunately, while the other guests at that dinner had voiced their enthusiasm for his work, none had made a solid offer.

Now, in early August, the artist was nearing the end of the Pietrowski commission. Franz's portrait hung in the hall at the head of the stairs, Mira's in the drawing room, and that of their son Erik in the library. Within two weeks at most, Pola's portrait would be completed, its protective glaze dry enough for framing. Unfortunately, as yet no further commissions had been offered. Pierre Rebaumme was growing desperate. The allowance provided by the interest from his deceased father's estate was hardly sufficient to support him indefinitely, and Pierre could not afford to draw upon the principal. That was his insurance, his safeguard against the vicissitudes of an uncertain future.

Lying awake in his bed, Pierre was tantalized by thoughts of Pola Pietrowska. Her classically aristocratic features, her smooth fine-textured skin, neither gypsy-dark like her mother's nor Nordic-pale like Erik's, her poise and graciousness, all these attributes haunted him. To many observers, the fifteen-year-old Pola was far less attractive than her ravishingly beautiful mother. However, to Rebaumme, she was the epitome of elegance, grace, and tranquility. These qualities he had successfully translated into her painted image. Furthermore, he was forced to admit to himself, he found her virginal, subtle young loveliness deeply compelling and disturbing. She embodied for him the lure of the shiksa, the forbidden fruit warned against by his Jewish upbringing. He was strongly tempted by her beauty, her graceful manners, and her unstudied, child-woman appeal. He acknowledged now, as he seldom dared to when she was present, the burning surge of desire that thoughts of her provoked.

Quietly and surely, she had found her way into his heart. Yet, he feared to yield to the temptation she represented. Once more, he mentally rebelled against the restrictions, stated and implied, so often experienced by the Jew living in a Gentile society.

\* \* \*

Mira Pietrowska stood in the solarium of her spacious home, her mind filled with plans for her soiree, scheduled at the end of August. Her daughter's painted likeness stood on the easel facing the east windows, and Mira was noting every detail of the portrait. Pola's familiar features were displayed to advantage against a garden setting of flowering shrubs and pillared porticoes and were set off by a demure, pastel-blue gown. Mira felt a glow of maternal pride. Her daughter might not be destined for enduring greatness in the world of music, but she had grown to be a handsome young lady who would hopefully one day make some fortunate young man a loving, decorative, and resourceful wife.

A faint footstep sounded behind her, and Mira turned in surprise to see her seventeen-year-old son Erik admiring the nearly-finished painting. The mother smiled as her son approached, savoring the handsome contrast of dark hair and fair skin that he presented.

Erik glanced at his mother. "He's good, isn't he?"

Mira nodded in agreement. "He's better than that. He's a real artist! When I look at this portrait, I see a young woman instead of the little girl I've always known."

Erik smiled knowingly. "He's painted much more than just the way she looks."

"Yes," Mira responded, "I think he's done that with each of us. It's the mark of the true artistic genius." She paused, studying her son's face. "He's painted qualities in your face that I hadn't noticed before either. You are very nearly a man now," she acknowledged thoughtfully. "Very soon, you'll have to decide where you want to go to complete your education."

Erik pondered that question for a long moment. "Where can a Pole go to learn his true identity? Our nation's youth mark time, compelled to study Russian subjects taught by Russians. That's hardly my idea of an education."

Mira drew closer to her son, an idea forming in her mind. "Our neighbor sent his two elder sons to Krakow. God knows there's little enough left to us here that's Polish."

Erik's eyes shone. "You wouldn't mind my going to Krakow? "

Mira smiled ruefully and shook her head. "It's not that far, and it would be far better than your staying here, marking time as you've said." Privately, she could envision Erik, at loose ends regarding his education, becoming involved in the underground movement. "I'll speak with Franz tonight about making the arrangements."

Erik embraced her warmly, then stood back studying her agelessly beautiful face. "Mother," he said seriously, "why not let me ask him?"

Mira looked approvingly at her handsome son. "Why not?"

At that moment, Pierre Rebaumme entered the solarium. Mira and Erik glanced in his direction and then all three turned their attention to the portrait in progress.

"What do you think, Madam?" The artist's voice was soft but compelling. "Is the work to your liking?"

"It's splendid," Mira replied truthfully. "Has my daughter expressed her opinion?"

"Not in words, Madam," Rebaumme answered, "but then I have found Mistress Pola to be a modest young lady, unlikely to comment upon a replica of her own beauty."

Mira gazed critically at the painting, an idea stirring in her inventive mind. "How soon will the portrait be finished?"

"Within a matter of days, Madam," Rebaumme replied.

"Good! Can you have it framed and hung within the next two weeks?"

"If Madam will tell me where she wants it displayed."

"There's a bare expanse of wall in the entrance hall that I've been saving just for this," Mira said, still gazing at the image of her daughter. Her eyes narrowed, and a smile of dawning inspiration lighted her face. "Hang it there, and meanwhile, I should like you to assemble as many of your works as you have framed. I've decided to display them at my party at the end of the month." She turned to face Rebaumme. "It will be a truly artistic evening. You'd like an opportunity to have your paintings viewed by some of the leading citizens of Warsaw, wouldn't you?"

Rebaumme nodded enthusiastically. "Indeed, yes, Madam."

"Then it's settled." Mira was obviously pleased with herself.

Pierre Rebaumme bowed respectfully. "Madam is most generous."

"And most astute," Erik said under his breath, well aware that his mother was not only ensuring a captive audience for Rebaumme's one-man show but also guaranteeing that her latest social entertainment would be the event of the coming season, the envy of every hostess of note in Warsaw.

* * *

Isaak Marjzendiak stood lost in thought on the steps of the library building of the Krakow Academy of Law and Ethics. The tiered lawns and paved walkways that graced the campus before him touched his awareness marginally, for his thoughts were in turmoil. The summer term had just ended with the last of his final exams, and Isaak felt certain he had scored well. In fact, this whole first year of graduate training had gone precisely as he had hoped. He had maintained an exceptionally high standing in his class. His ambitions seemed well on the way to being realized.

Upon completion of his course of study, a position awaited him with the prestigious Krakow-based law firm of Sukowski and Petulaski, where his best friend's father was a senior partner. Why, then, Isaak wondered, was he troubled and dissatisfied? Why, when he was not immersed in his studies, did he feel lonely and isolated no matter the size of the crowd that might surround him?

He knew the answer without asking. It sang in his blood, it burned in his brain. The answer even had a name. Sarah. With the university where she taught so close, it was inevitable that they should meet occasionally. Furthermore, they had remained friends. It was a friendship Isaak treasured. Yet, he was tortured by it because it fell so short of his desires. Every time he saw Sarah, Isaak's passion for her would be reignited, so that he found it difficult to look at her and not touch her, to be near her and smell her perfume and not clasp her in his arms, not kiss her.

With the exception of Mariska Wishnieska, the women he had known sexually had fulfilled a basic need in themselves and in Isaak but had not moved him in any deeply meaningful way. For Sarah, he felt a yearning that was akin to the cravings of a hungry peasant watching an ongoing array of savory dishes brought to a gentleman's table, close enough to smell but not to taste.

Evyan Sukowski, Isaak's closest friend, was away on holiday, relaxing at the home of his fiancé's family. Standing alone, textbook clutched in his right hand, Isaak was assailed by an overwhelming wave of homesickness. The more he thought of his family, the more the idea of a visit home appealed to him. He would write to his brother Adam, advising him of his intended visit and stating that he did not wish his parents to be told of it in advance. Elana's birthday was imminent and Isaak had decided to pleasantly surprise her.

Encouraged by his cousins, Isaak hastily packed a few necessities. Restless and filled with anticipation, Isaak boarded a late afternoon train in Krakow. Throughout the journey, he felt it moved far too slowly. Already, it was August 8th. Within a month, he reflected impatiently, he had to be back in Krakow for the commencement of the next term.

Mindful of Adam's joyous anticipation at the prospect of seeing Isaak again, Meyhra was in a buoyant mood on the morning of August 9, 1868. She was up quite early, dusting and cleaning in preparation for her brother-in-law's imminent arrival. She assumed Isaak would be staying at Plaz Marjzendiak, but Adam had stated that he wanted his brother to spend a few days and nights with Meyhra and himself during the planned three-week visit.

With so much work to be done at the office, Meyhra had had little time of late to devote to the duties of a housewife. As a result, she was quite sensitive about the appearance of the home that she and Adam shared. Part of this extreme sensitivity, she knew, was due to her awareness of Elana's silent disapproval of her career. Within Elana's traditional scale of values, Meyhra's place was in the home, exclusively.

However, soon, Meyhra consoled herself, the baby would be born. The ritual duty of a Jewish wife to her husband would be fulfilled, enabling Adam to ensure the survival of his family and to make his contribution to the unbroken continuity of the chosen people. Meyhra hoped the child she carried would be a son. Surely that would mollify her mother-in-law's misgivings, but that was in Adonai's hands. A baby, alive, whole, and perfect, would please Meyhra regardless of its gender, for Adam had more than once expressed concern that the baby might be born ill or damaged in some way. Inasmuch as no member of either family had ever harbored a birth defect, Meyhra was mystified by Adam's seeming preoccupation with that unlikely possibility.

She silently counted the weeks that remained of her pregnancy, thankful that the period of waiting was almost at an end. By early October, if all went well, she would hold her first child in her arms and put to rest both Adam's fears for the baby's health and Elana's uncertainties about Meyhra's adequacy as a wife and mother. Softly humming a lullaby, Meyhra laid aside her broom and started to descend the stairs to the first floor. She was careful to hold the handrail, Elana's warnings about the reckless way she "moved about like a carefree child" echoing in her ears.

Her own childhood seemed a very distant memory as she recalled the hardships her family had endured before her father had achieved the reputation of a prominent and respected jeweler. She thought of her mother, as she often did now that she was about to become a mother herself. They had always been close and Meyhra had admired her mother's untraditional independence.

Meyhra's desire to study nursing had grown out of her mother's teachings, nurtured by Dr. Samuel Jedewreski, a long-term family friend. That career choice had brought Adam into her life. She had found fulfillment in their love and marriage. Now, their union was about to be blessed by a child that both of them deeply desired.

With her mind filled with memories and hopes, Meyhra momentarily forgot the small threadbare place in the stair carpet that she had tried repeatedly to mend but had succeeded only in disguising. For Adam, with his sturdy men's shoes, the carpet posed little danger. Normally, Meyhra avoided the spot, stepping over that stair as she bounded up and down the staircase with a surefootedness that would do credit to a mountain goat. However, in the latter days of her pregnancy, she had grown heavier, slower, and less agile.

Suddenly, her heel struck and caught the worn place. A wave of self-disgust and anger welled up in her, quickly followed by fear. She tried to maintain her grasp on the handrail, reaching out with her other hand to clutch vainly at the wall. Then she felt the unwieldy weight she carried in her abdomen drag her off balance, pulling her forward and inevitably downward.

Panic seized her. She screamed, called out Adam's name, and fell, clasping her arms in front of her, instinctively seeking to protect the baby. A sharp pain assailed her ankle as it twisted and she rolled headlong down the remaining stairs. She came to rest on the carpeted floor, trying with professional objectivity to assess the extent of her injuries. Her legs were curled beneath her but seemed to be undamaged except for her right ankle. She tried cautiously to turn and straighten herself into a more natural position. As she did, a wave of nausea enveloped her and rapidly grew worse, accompanied by a heavy, dull ache in her abdomen and lower back. Tears stung her eyes. She gasped with the increasing pain, and then blackness fell, blotting out her every perception.

Only a few moments passed before Adam, roused by Meyhra's scream, found her huddled at the base of the stairs. An icy wave of dread swept through him.

"Meyhra," he called fearfully, hastening down the stairs. He knelt beside her and whispered, "Oh, no."

She lay frighteningly still. Her pulse was swift and bounding, its tempo irregular. Her face was pale and sheened with sweat. As he carefully examined her for fractures and other injuries, she moaned softly and opened her eyes, but they registered no recognition. Fitfully, she turned her head back and forth. Her words were muffled and distracted, but Adam understood one phrase clearly.

"My baby! My baby!"

\* \* \*

Meyhra opened her eyes, dazed and dazzled by an unbroken vista of white walls and whiter ceilings. A background of muffled voices accompanied her slow progress down this brilliant tunnel as she lay supine, helpless, and frightened. Instinctively, she knew she was in a hospital corridor, a patient occupying a passive role that ran counter to her normally assertive nature. She scanned the solicitous faces hovering above her, seeking one that she could recognize, but these were the faces of kind but unknown strangers. Where was Adam? What had happened to her?

Then she remembered the stairs, the fall, the feeling of dread and the mounting pain followed by darkness and emptiness. She felt no movement within her. All was quiet and still. Tears stung her eyes and coursed unchecked down her cheeks.

Drifting in and out of consciousness, Meyhra became aware of Adam's presence at her bedside. One look at his face confirmed her worst fears, and though he smiled at her comfortingly, his eyes betrayed the sorrow that he felt.

Turning away, she whispered brokenly, "I've failed you. Oh, Adam, I'm so sorry You wanted this baby so badly. You worried so much about it." She faced him then, all her weariness and disappointment painfully evident. "It was such a stupid accident!"

Silently, Adam concurred, and instantly hated himself for the traitorous impulse. He quickly suppressed that thought and the inner rage it triggered as he fought the temptation to tax Meyhra with her clumsiness. "I thank Adonai you weren't seriously hurt," he said instead, trying to console his grieving wife. "Later, when you're better, there'll be other children. Now you must get well and strong."

He held her tenderly in his arms until she fell asleep again, certain that he would never tell her of the few brief, tortured hours of baby Anna's life. After all, what purpose would it serve? To express his own feelings of desolation and loss regarding the baby's death would only wound Meyhra more.

Privately, Adam felt that Adonai had passed judgment on him for having yielded to Sarah's entreaties and then left her to bear his child alone. His ignorance of the outcome of his act did not excuse him in his own eyes, and he felt that Adonai had not excused him, either. He could not share his feelings of guilt and despair with Meyhra, however. For her, weakened and depressed as she now was, he must be strong and sure.

Yet he felt that by withholding from Meyhra the truth regarding his love affair with Sarah, and its tragic aftermath, he had betrayed both the women he had loved.

As he sat by Meyhra's bed, watching her sleep fitfully, Adam's thoughts chased each other around endlessly in his brain, giving him no peace. Worse still, he saw once more the hated face of the militia commander. He relived the shame of watching the man paw and fondle Meyhra while he, Adam, had stood paralyzed with rage and fear. Like so many times of conflict in life, there had been no easy course of action to follow in that situation, either. Bowing his head in his hands, Adam wept silently.

## CHAPTER TWENTY-FOUR
## AFTERMATH

Isaak stepped off the train at Warsaw, filled with joyous expectations. He was finally home. The buildings surrounding the station seemed cleaner and brighter than he remembered. The August sun was comfortably warm. He glanced about the platform to see if Adam had been able to get away from the office to meet him. However, mid afternoon was likely to be the busiest time of day in a doctor's practice, and Adam was nowhere to be found.

Isaak realized that a railway station is a dreary place to wait once the train and the crowds have left. Furthermore, most of the carriages available for hire would long since be engaged. Taking his traveling bag in hand, Isaak approached the one waiting public carriage and gave his destination to the driver. The man argued at first that the distance was too great and would restrict the number of fares he could transport during his work shift. Moreover, his glance, as he eyed the six-pointed star on Isaak's coat, was undisguisedly hostile. Only when Isaak offered to pay more than the standard fee did the driver nod grudgingly and reach out to take the money in advance.

Isaak shrugged resignedly, put his bag in the passenger compartment, and climbed inside the carriage. Despite the gleaming facade Warsaw had donned in its efforts at post-revolution refurbishment, underneath, little had changed. Jews were still outsiders, Isaak reflected, unwelcome at best, and ever obliged to pay more than others for goods and services, unless those benefits were obtained from fellow Jews.

Nevertheless, he sat back, determined to enjoy his ride. The scenery was pleasant despite the morose silence of the driver, and once they had passed the Barbizon wall, the scent of crops ripe for harvest filled the air. Isaak inevitably contrasted this journey with his first visit to Plaz Marjzendiak. On that occasion, Adam had driven Ephraim's carriage, and had taken the road that led to the main gate of the estate. Today, the hired driver, anxious to complete the fare as quickly as possible, followed a shorter route. This course led through fields of grain and expansive orchards that supplied the produce by which the Marjzendiaks were able to maintain the property.

At the main house, Isaak took his traveling case and stepped from the carriage, and the driver hastily departed. As Isaak walked toward the building, he heard carriage wheels screeching to a halt behind him. He turned, wondering why the sullen driver had come back. This carriage, however, was different. When Elana emerged, Isaak recognized the vehicle as Ephraim's own.

Isaak set down his case and moved quickly to greet his mother.

"Isaak." she said as he embraced her. "Oh, Isaak." She laid her head on his shoulder and sobbed softly.

At first, he mistook her tears for an expression of sudden joy at his unexpected homecoming. "I wanted to surprise you," he said, gently stroking her hair. "It seems I have."

Elana looked up at him and shook her head. "You've come home just in time to sit Shivah with us."

Now it was Isaak's turn to be surprised. "What?" He held her at arm's length and looked at her in painful bewilderment. "Which family member is dead?"

"Your infant niece," she answered sadly. "It happened early this morning. She lived only a few hours."

Isaak thought immediately of how this child's death must grieve his elder brother. "Poor Adam!"

"Poor Meyhra," Elana said bitterly. "All those months of waiting and hoping."

Isaak nodded, realizing from his experiences with Sarah the magnitude of a mother's sense of loss. He gathered Elana close once more, seeking to console her, to ease the sense of deprivation she shared vicariously with Meyhra. "What happened?"

"Come inside," Elana answered. "I'll explain."

Isaak had come home to an atmosphere charged with grief. The family's energies were focused upon funeral preparations. It was the last thing he had expected. Having set out seeking balm for his own frustrations, he felt strangely like an intruder. Regardless of Baby Anna's infant status, he could sense the impact of her death on every member of his family. Even seven-year-old Michael moved about the house in a mode of enforced quiet, speaking hardly at all.

Watching the visible signs of Adam's sorrow and disappointment made Isaak's own problems seem small by comparison. Furthermore, though Ephraim said little about his feelings, he seemed the most crushed of all by the loss of the expected child. Isaak knew instinctively that for Ephraim this new grief was equivalent to losing Rachel all over again.

Seeing his father from a new perspective made Ephraim seem to Isaak more vulnerable, and somehow more accessibly human than ever before. As the days of Shivah and then those of Sheloshim proceeded, Isaak perceived a growing closeness between his father and himself. The process begun long ago, when Isaak had confessed to Ephraim his deep love for Mariska and his utter desolation at her suicide, had come to fruition.

A few days after the death of their child, when Meyhra's physical recovery was sufficiently advanced, Adam brought her to Plaz Marjzendiak. He was reluctant, at least for the present, to have her staying alone at home while he was at work. He feared the impact upon her of the silent, empty nursery and the stairs that had been the scene of her fateful fall.

While her father and her elder brothers mourned, and Elana tended Meyhra with single-minded devotion, Leah demonstrated her growing sense of responsibility by the mature manner in which she took charge of Michael.

In the process of nursing and caring for her daughter-in-law, Elana was enabled to accept the death of her first grandchild. The two women came to a deeper understanding of each other during this period, becoming united in sadness as they had not been able to do in joy. Meyhra confided to Elana that she dreaded the thought of going home. Most intimidating of all for her was the prospect of facing the small room she had lovingly reserved to furnish as a nursery as soon as the baby was born. Despite the rapid healing of her young body, Meyhra's mind and spirit had not fully come to terms with the reality of her grief. She had never seen her dead child, nor had she attended the burial service. Now, there was only a void where there should have been a wellspring of activity, silence where a cacophony of baby noises had been happily anticipated.

As a result, Meyhra grew restless. She became irritated by activities that she normally enjoyed. Her attention span seemed to have constricted; books she had loved and reread with pleasure now failed to hold her interest. Normally communicative, she retreated into an uncharacteristic silence that distressed Adam, raising a wordless barrier between them.

Elana, remembering her own feelings after Rachel's death, was able to communicate with Meyhra and to understand her moods. What Elana could not do was to adequately explain to Adam his wife's intensely female reaction to her ordeal. Adam shared his wife's grief, but could not share her all-encompassing emptiness, her terrible guilt at having failed to fulfill her divinely designated role in life.

Frequently wakeful in the early morning hours, Meyhra would rise early, dress, and walk endlessly about the grounds of Plaz Marjzendiak. These long sojourns seemed the only activity that could calm her and tire her enough to afford her a few hours of restful sleep. Adam, lying wakeful and tormented beside her, wondered how soon she would turn to him for comfort, and if he would be able to give it to her when she did. When would she be ready, he mused, to return to their own home? Once they did so, how soon would their life together resume its normal pattern?

* * *

Late in August, Adam decided to put the question to the test. Meyhra made no objections when he broached the subject of returning home. Listlessly, she gathered together the personal effects he had brought to her in the hospital and packed them in the case Elana lent to her for the purpose.

Few words passed between husband and wife as Isaak drove them to their home in the Stare Miasto. Meyhra, Isaak noted, seemed fretful and distracted. Adam, after one or two abortive attempts to initiate conversation, withdrew into a shell of silence that even Isaak could not penetrate. As they drew closer to their destination, Isaak felt strangely apprehensive. What else, he thought uneasily, was likely to overtake his brother and sister-in-law?

Adam helped Meyhra alight from his father's carriage while Isaak took charge of their luggage. Though Adam had occasionally stopped briefly at home during the past several days, this was a difficult homecoming for Meyhra. Isaak, thinking he had best leave the two of them alone together for a while, was preparing his excuses for not staying as Adam opened the door and led his wife inside. Isaak, following at a short distance, was unprepared for Adam's shocked exclamation, and was even more agitated by Meyhra's hysterical screams. He ran the short distance to the front door. Then he, too, saw the total disarray that had provoked those outcries. Isaak made no sound as he beheld the senseless disorder to which his brother's home had been reduced. He was, quite literally, speechless.

Together, Isaak and Adam managed to restore some semblance of order to the chaos of personal belongings dumped from drawers and stripped from cupboards. More difficult to rectify was the apparent vandalism that had torn away wooden panels and peeled off whole sections of cloth and paper coverings from the walls.

When they were both too tired to do any more, they sat together in the living room.

Bewildered, Adam asked, "Why should this happen now of all times?"

Isaak shook his head. "There's no logical answer. There never is."

"I'm just glad Meyhra wasn't here," Adam said, grateful for the protective impulse that had led him to take his wife to stay with his family.

The two brothers spoke in hushed voices, trying not to waken Meyhra from the troubled sleep into which she had finally fallen. That had come only after a torrent of weeping over the despoilment of her cherished possessions.

"It's as if a hoard of looters had descended on the place, searching for treasure," Isaak commented, as much at a loss as Adam to account for what had taken place.

Adam looked up, his attention riveted by his brother's words. "Searching?" His eyes narrowed. "Searching! Of course." His voice took on a hard edge. "I should have known at once. Milyutin's militia."

Isaak's eyes widened in astonishment. "This was the work of the militia? I know they secretly instigate such raids, but…"

"I'm sure of it," Adam interrupted him. "I've seen them in action," he added with dreadful conviction. "They did something similar to my office, right in front of Meyhra and myself. And that wasn't all."

By the time Adam had finished his account, Isaak could feel his pulse pounding, the blood flushing his face. "I think I'll stay the night," he said, not wishing to leave Adam and Meyhra to face alone the aftermath of this devastating experience.

Isaak returned Ephraim's carriage, then stayed another two nights with Adam and Meyhra. His presence somehow made it easier for them to cope with this latest outrage, and to view the entire situation in practical terms. They could detect nothing of value having been taken. Nor did the militia return to place them under arrest. The wanton defacement of walls and panels was most likely either a desperate final measure of the search or else an expression of frustration that nothing incriminating had been found.

Furthermore, husband and wife could postpone facing their private estrangement while dealing with the physical emergency of repairing their damaged home. In that endeavor, Adam welcomed his brother's help, and Isaak was able to work off some of his tensions in the physical exertion of repairing or replacing panels, woodwork, and wall coverings. Doctor Jedewreski and some of Adam's neighbors joined the brothers in their efforts, glad to assist a fellow victim of the militia's ongoing campaign of intimidation, directed against the entire ghetto population.

Afterwards, over food and wine, the men exchanged tales of hardships each had witnessed or endured. This animated dialogue united them in a fellowship of mutual suffering.

"Unprovoked violence is their stock in trade," Levi Gebrach, the carpenter, asserted grimly.

"You can be sure this is only the beginning," Samuel Jedewreski interjected, betraying his distress over what had been done to his friend and protégé.

There was no mistaking the implications of that remark. The mood of apprehension rose higher in every man present as the threat of another pogrom filled their minds.

"I hope I'm wrong," Jedewreski added, answering their unspoken thoughts. "The good Lord knows I hope I'm wrong!"

Meanwhile, the women had gathered in Meyhra's kitchen to console her for her double loss. They had brought baked goods and casseroles, canned preserves and sweet meats.

These, added to the stores Elana had provided, would relieve Meyhra of meal planning chores for at least a week.

"You must rest and get strong," Avrah Gillel, the midwife, advised her. "The best way to forget is to have another child as soon as possible."

"Another child?" Meyhra's voice rose in disbelief. "How can you say that after all that's happened?"

"I say it <u>because</u> of what's happened," the older woman replied. "We need numbers to survive. Fortunately, Adonai has always made our women fertile. It's our duty to produce children, so our people can be preserved."

Meyhra stared desperately about her kitchen. This room and the nursery were the ones that had suffered the least damage, and yet the telltale signs of the militia's presence, even here, stifled and appalled her. The comments of her neighbors swirled about her like a roaring tide until she felt as though she was drowning in a sea of words. Her head seemed about to burst. It was Avrah who noticed her distress.

"Enough!" The midwife took her by the hand. "Come to bed, Meyhra. We'll take care of the cleaning up when the men are finished."

The other women nodded in agreement. None were brave enough to defy the pronouncements of the midwife.

"That's what neighbors are for," Avrah added as she led Meyhra upstairs.

* * *

When Isaak came back to Plaz Marjzendiak, the household was slowly returning to normal. Ephraim had dispiritedly resumed work a week after the funeral. Elana went through the motions of performing household chores. Michael mechanically pursued his studies. Leah, however, seemed the most profoundly disturbed. In contrast to her usual buoyant temperament, she seemed constantly close to tears.

When Isaak questioned her about this state of affairs, she took him to her mother's gazebo in the garden, where they could converse undisturbed.

In response to Isaak's queries, Leah reacted with unaccustomed defensiveness. Because they had always been close despite the disparity between their respective ages, Isaak was taken aback when Leah responded in anger.

"I don't know how to talk to you when you come at me like this."

"Like what? I'm worried about you. Don't you see that? You're like a totally different person."

"We're all different just now," Leah said, avoiding her brother's gaze.

He reached out and embraced her. "Not this different, tzatzkala."

It was his pet name for her, a carry-over from childhood, and its use under the present circumstances produced an unexpected reaction. Leah reluctantly burst into laughter. They both realized that it was the first time since Anna's death that she had laughed spontaneously. Impulsively, she reached up and hugged her brother.

"That's better," Isaak said, relieved. "That's my Leah."

"But now is not the time for laughter," Leah objected guiltily.

"On the contrary," Isaak countered, "now is just about the right time to start laughing again. You have your whole life before you, Leah. You can't spend it weeping about things you can't change."

"Poor Anna didn't get to have any life at all," Leah said. She turned away and sat dejectedly upon the seat that bordered the gazebo.

Allowing her a physical margin of personal separateness, Isaak said, "I know, and that's sad. We can never understand why such things happen, but life has to go on for those of us who are left." He paused as Leah turned to look up at him. "That's the way we keep faith with those who are gone."

She frowned. "How?"

"By living life to the fullest."

"You really believe that?"

Isaak nodded. "Yes, I do."

Leah considered that for a moment. "Then it's all right to go on with plans and lessons, even though it's still Sheloshim?"

"That's the whole purpose of Sheloshim, Leah. To prepare us to move back into the normal pattern of our lives."

"Can we still celebrate mother's birthday?"

"I think it's an absolute necessity," Isaak replied. "A time to weep, and a time to laugh; a time to mourn, and a time to dance," he quoted from Ecclesiastes. "Frankly, I think you've had your share of mourning."

A shy smile spread across Leah's face that belied the seriousness of her voice as she said, "Thank you, Isaak. You've taught me an important lesson."

\* \* \*

Ephraim's reaction to Isaak's account of the most recent outrage perpetrated by the militia paralleled that of his friend Samuel Jedewreski. The news seemed to confirm what he had already suspected.

"This latest rash of administrative abuses is an ominous sign." He paced the floor, restless and agitated. "They're not just targeting the artisans and laborers now. They've started to attack the professionals, the real and potential leaders among us. In the past, those were the ones they'd seek out." He paused thoughtfully. "They'd pretend to want reforms, to desire our opinions. What they really wanted was to spy upon us, to learn the sentiments and plans of our people. Apparently, now they no longer feel they need us even for that."

It was clear that Ephraim's focus was more than just concern for his son. He feared that the stage was being set for a full-scale assault on the Jewish community of Warsaw, and perhaps all such communities throughout Russian Poland.

Nicholas Milyutin received his unexpected visitor in the privacy of his office at the tin-roofed palace. The governor-general's curiosity was intensely aroused. He was formally acquainted with the lovely woman seated before him; however, he was at a loss as to the purpose of her present errand.

Mira Pietrowska prefaced her explanation of that purpose with her most beguiling smile. She produced an ornately decorated envelope and placed it on the desk.

"I wanted to deliver this invitation in person, Your Excellency," she said warmly. "Such things get passed through so many hands and can be so easily misdirected." She paused to permit him an opportunity to open the envelope and read the invitation's contents.

"Madam honors me," he said civilly but without commitment.

"I shall be honored if Your Excellency accepts," Mira responded. "I've come more than once before to deliver it, but your aides repeatedly insisted that you were far too busy to see me." It was a relatively safe half-truth. She had previously sent an invitation by messenger, and having received no response, had come in person for an answer on one prior occasion. This was her second attempt.

The governor-general had several aides, all of whom were constantly besieged by petitioners wanting some favor or other. Such numbers served to obscure the identities of individual supplicants, particularly unsuccessful ones.

"I am sorry, Madam, for your inconvenience."

"I realize Your Excellency is constantly engaged in affairs of state, but surely you must set aside some time for social endeavors."

"On rare occasions," Milyutin acknowledged.

"I can promise Your Excellency an entertaining evening and an opportunity to observe closely a representative cross-section of the major elements of Warsaw's social and economic environment."

"Madam Pietrowska, you are most generous, but…"

"Please, Excellency, at least consider the invitation," Mira persisted. "There's still quite some time to decide. Surely, a Sunday evening is a fitting occasion for rest and recreation."

"And observation," Milyutin added significantly. "Madam is most charmingly persuasive. I gather there are some particular elements whom you wish me to observe."

Mira smiled sweetly. "A man in your position, Excellency, can always profit from being personally aware of all his subject peoples. He should not be obliged to depend on the judgments and interpretations of others in assessing their value."

"A point well taken," Milyutin agreed. "Sunday, August 30th." He paused thoughtfully. "I shall look forward to Madam's soiree. It sounds interesting."

He took Mira's hand, brought it briefly to his lips, and then escorted her to the door.

As she rode home in her carriage, Mira pondered the preceding interview. All her social skills would be put to the test in blending the explosive human elements she was about to assemble into a harmonious social encounter. Yet, she felt equal to the challenge and, in fact, exhilarated by it. Moreover, if her plan was successful, and if Ephraim's suspicions were as well-founded as she surmised, he would be placed once more in her debt, not to mention Warsaw's Jewish population. She secretly hoped that the achievement of her objective in assuring Milyutin's presence would counter-balance any indignation Ephraim might feel at not having been informed in advance of Leah's performance at the Pietrowski party.

## CHAPTER TWENTY-FIVE
## AUGUST 30, 1868

The last Sunday of August dawned fair and clear. The breeze, even at that early hour, was pleasantly warm, contrasting sharply with the chill winds and morning fog of fall that would soon follow. Sudden climatic changes had long been characteristic of the area. However, for the present, summer was bidding Warsaw a glorious farewell.

Mira Pietrowska stood on her bedroom balcony, watching the golden sun rise above the east rim of the northern plateau. Pausing briefly before dressing to attend mass, and then proceeding to the interminable last-minute preparations for the party, she savored the glowing beauty of the morning.

The governor-general of Warsaw also awoke early that Sunday. To him, the day seemed filled with promise. He was meeting old friends from St. Petersburg at the Eastern Orthodox service that morning, and was planning to have breakfast with them afterwards.

Thanks to the invitation Mira Pietrowska had finally succeeded in extending, Milyutin had begun to seriously reconsider several of his plans, including the assault on the Stare Miasto ghetto, which was scheduled for early September. Madam Pietrowska's unique blend of compelling beauty and subtle diplomacy had intrigued him. She had also reminded him that he had heretofore held himself aloof from the social life of his subjects. He had sent operatives to watch them, agents to spy upon them in secret, and the militia to harass and, occasionally, to arrest them. However, he did not truly know them, and he certainly did not trust them. What, he wondered, did Madam Pietrowska really want him to see? Whatever it was, he was expectantly looking forward to it, and that curiosity was one of those small, indefinable factors on which human destiny can sometimes depend.

Later that morning, Isaak paced restlessly in his father's study. "I can readily see why it's important that you be there, Father," Isaak remarked, "but the Pietrowskis don't really know me that well. Most of their guests don't know me at all."

"I want you there, Son," Ephraim responded. "Adam and Meyhra obviously can't attend." Ephraim laid his hand on Isaak's shoulder. "Under the circumstances, perhaps that's just as well."

Isaak nodded, aware that among the Russian dignitaries on the Pietrowski guest list, and the guards who would inevitably accompany them, Adam would be hard put to keep his temper in check. The memory of the devastation of his home would be too fresh in his mind to allow the young physician to play the diplomat, no matter what the stakes.

"You've lived for years in Krakow. You've observed how government operates under Austrian rule," Ephraim continued. "Already you've learned much about the law. Furthermore, with your interest in a political career, you should find tonight very interesting."

Isaak regarded his father intently. "You're really serious about this, aren't you?"

"In these few weeks in Warsaw," Ephraim answered, "you've seen just how serious our situation has become. Disaster seems imminent. Tonight, you'll have an opportunity to observe the Russian administrators at close hand. Your insights could be valuable to us in planning future strategy to forestall this growing danger."

Isaak nodded in assent. "If you think I can be of help, Father, then of course I'll go."

Ephraim smiled. "I can almost guarantee you'll see and hear more at this party than you'd learn in a month of classes and lectures. Afterwards, we can talk about your observations." He then added on a more personal note, "By the way, I haven't yet told you how much having you at home during the time of our bereavement has meant to me. I think you realize it's more than just the death of a new baby. Who can know, except Adonai himself, what role that child might have played in salvaging the heritage of our people?"

Isaak clasped his father's hand in his own. "It's meant a great deal to me, too, Father. I've come to understand you in a way I never did before."

Ephraim nodded. "Perhaps, now that maturity has made you more objective, you'll also come to better understand the pitfalls of the life your people live here."

Late that afternoon, Leah sought her mother's company. She felt a need to calm both her excitement and her misgivings at the prospect of attending her first adult party. Madam Pietrowska had formally invited her in order to avoid any awkward objections that might possibly jeopardize Leah's attendance and, therefore, her performance. Fortunately, no such objections had been raised, but Leah felt guilty about keeping secret her part in the evening's entertainment. Burdened by that nagging guilt, she entered her mother's room.

Elana sat before her dressing table brushing her hair. She glanced up as Leah's image appeared in her mirror.

"Let me do that, Mother," Leah offered, taking the brush from Elana's hand. As she ran it gently but vigorously through her mother's hair, she added, "It's been quite a while."

Leah's thoughts went back to the first time she had been allowed to brush and braid the soft, luxuriant, red-gold tresses she so greatly admired. She had been a four-year-old child then, and had thought her mother a creature of mystical beauty whose bright hair reminded her of the angels of Jewish tradition.

Then she remembered the day the family had first come to Plaz Marjzendiak. She recalled vividly the raid on the Stare Miasto, the wreck of their former home, and the fire and smoke of buildings put to the torch, forming a terrifying backdrop to their flight from the main part of Warsaw. She thought also of the Russian who had assaulted her mother, and Rachel's birth and death. Tears came to her eyes.

Elana noted them and asked, "What is it, dear?"

"I was just remembering our first day here."

Elana studied her daughter's face. "You still think of Rachel, don't you?"

Leah nodded, moved that her mother's thoughts had so quickly paralleled her own. "I sometimes wonder how it would have been to have a sister." Her tone became wistful. "Of course, I love my brothers."

"I know," Elana said, "but it isn't the same, is it, dear?"

"No," Leah answered. "Their world is quite different from ours. They're encouraged to learn and to achieve. Sometimes the whole community makes sacrifices to help them win the careers of their choice."

Elana smiled ruefully. "Whereas, our paths are predetermined by our gender. We must invariably want to be wives and mothers because we're physically designed to play those roles."

Leah set down the brush and knelt before her mother. "I want that, too," she said vehemently, "but I want more. I want the right to choose what path my life will follow, what I shall do when my children have grown up and gone out to live their own lives. I want to create music that others can hear and enjoy, and remember."

Elana put her arms around Leah as though she sought to protect her from hidden danger. "What you desire, child, can be very demanding."

"No more so than being a doctor or a lawyer. It's just that boys are <u>expected </u>to make something of their lives, and when they do, everyone applauds their accomplishments. No one expects anything from us other than making homes and having babies." Her clenched fists gave mute testimony to the intensity of her feelings. "I think they should!"

Gazing earnestly at her daughter's determined young face, Elana warned, "I hope you aren't allowing Madam Pietrowska to fill your head with impossible dreams. I know she means well, but the world is neither kind nor fair, especially to us." She took Leah's face in her hands. "You bear the double burden of being not only a girl but a Jewish one. You can't afford to forget that, because no one else will."

Leah was silent for several seconds. Finally, she rose and resumed brushing her mother's hair. "In spite of that," she said, "or perhaps because of it, some day I will be a musician. I'll make you and Papa proud of me. I promise!"

She coiled the rich red gold hair gracefully about her mother's head, braiding a single strand of pearls through it to match the double strand that encircled Elana's throat. That single strand had once been concealed in the cover of the family prayer book. Only in that way had it survived the violent destruction of their former home. The pearls had a history that paralleled the family's own life story. They had once belonged to Ephraim's mother Adah.

Elana reached up nervously and clasped her daughter's hands. "You're so young, so vulnerable, and yet so determined. That can be a dangerous formula."

"It can also be a successful one," Leah responded with a confident smile. Somehow, putting her innermost thoughts into words had brought her a measure of composure. She bent and kissed Elana's cheek. "Happy birthday, Mama," she said eagerly. "You're going to be the loveliest lady at Madam's party. I hope I'll be half as pretty some day."

She found that she still could not bring herself to tell her mother about the surprise performance. However, now she felt she wanted to offer it as a special birthday gift, a pledge that she would one day keep her brave promise. As she turned and left the room, Leah refused to acknowledge the indefinable sense of foreboding that threatened to overshadow her joyful anticipation.

* * *

Mira stood with Franz to welcome their distinguished guests into the grand ballroom of the Pietrowski mansion. The reaction of those guests as they beheld the decor, and particularly the table and its centerpiece, ranged from astonished silence to freely expressed admiration. Instead of utilizing a single huge table for this occasion, Mira had obtained, from Ephraim Marjzendiak's furniture factory at Wola, a series of rectangular tables that she had assembled to form a quadrangle. In the center of the resulting open space a variety of potted plants blossomed in porcelain jardinières, set among a display of gracefully sculptured half-life-sized figures. Each of these portrayed a member of the ancient Greek Olympian Pantheon. It was truly an impressive array. Yet, for all its elegance, the arrangement was so skillful that when seated, the diners could clearly view one another at every table without obstruction.

The guest list read like a roster of the district's leading citizens. It included Minister of Commerce Josef Walenski and his wife Marina, Warsaw's Mayor, Francysk Oblitowski, and his wife Zara, Governor-General Milyutin, Viceroy Prince Viktor Cherkassi and his sister Alexandra, visiting from St. Petersburg, and Mayor Zygmunt Oslowski of Wola and his wife Sophia. Naturally, the leading members of the Bank Advisory Council had been invited. These included Josef Ludozski, Franz's former superior, Wilhelm Preyndich and his wife Myrna, and of course Ephraim Marjzendiak and his family.

Dr. Adam Marjzendiak and his wife Meyhra had sent their apologies. Having long been acquainted with the Marjzendiak family, Mira was well aware that the attendance of any of its members at a public gathering, within a month of the death of a family member, even an infant who had lived only a few hours, was a major concession on their part. Both she and Franz were mindful of the honor Ephraim thus paid to them, both as business associates and as friends.

In addition to the leading figures on the political, financial, and social scenes, Mira had invited the Eastern Orthodox Archbishop Mousourski, his wife Sandra, and leading members of his local clergy. For the sake of balance, and because of her own religious convictions, she had also invited Catholic Archbishop Felinski and two of his assistants, Father Fyodor and Father Erasmus.

Mira was undaunted by the potential pitfalls of assembling so varied a company. She felt confident that the menu she had planned, a cosmopolitan blend of Russian, French, and traditional Polish dishes, would be well received. She had personally supervised the preparation of each delicacy, as well as every detail of the impressive setting in which they would be served. However, the crowning touch was the array of paintings by Pierre Rebaumme, which ranged from portraits to landscapes, from seascapes to still life compositions. Rebaumme had carefully chosen the paintings in the exhibition to illustrate his wide range of techniques in color and texture. Even the frames of the paintings were unique. The panels were formed by a system of interlocking grooves that required no nails. The artist had designed them himself.

A festive mood charged the distinguished throng as they moved about the ballroom, laughing, talking, drinking, and admiring, to the accompaniment of an elegant gypsy string quartet. Following a social hour that allowed ample time and opportunity for pleasant interchange between those in attendance, Mira directed her staff to guide the guests to their allotted seats. Thanks to the care Mira had lavished on that unique seating plan, each guest enjoyed equal rank at the tables, with a member of the hosting family placed on each side of the quadrangle.

As the multi-course dinner progressed, Mira listened attentively to the conversations around her, alert for any sign of disharmony or confrontation. Having blended a diverse combination of guests, she was obliged to maintain an ambience of congeniality.

Before dinner, she had adroitly engineered a commission for Rebaumme from Mayor Oslowski without seeming to descend to the crassness of the marketplace. Ephraim had contributed to her success by mentioning the fact that he had long desired to have his wife's portrait painted. His words had reminded the Mayor that he, too, harbored the same cherished wish. Now in his late sixties, Oslowski realized that time was no longer his ally. He must seize opportunities as they offered, if he was to have those things he really wanted before his life ended.

His decision, enthusiastically expressed, influenced others at the party. Prince Cherkassi, during the soup course, contracted with the French artist to purchase a landscape. Milyutin, not to be outdone, selected a colorful still-life to add some sparkle to the drabness of his office walls. Thus, one of Mira's protégés was well launched while the evening was still young.

While she silently congratulated herself on the success of that campaign, to her right, Governor General Milyutin leaned closer to speak softly to her.

"I have noticed, Madam, that your roster of guests encompasses quite a variety, including several Jews," he noted. "Are they special friends of you and your husband?"

Mira smiled, pleased at the opportunity this remark afforded her. "Your Excellency," she explained candidly, assuming the point of view with which she felt certain her guest would agree, "one can hardly do business these days without dealing with Jews. In recent years, they've become the mainstay of the economy."

"Indeed," Milyutin responded, "they have gained considerable wealth and power, thanks to Wielopolski's reforms. It's a trend I intend to curb."

"Wielopolski's reforms?" Mira's delicate brows rose slightly. "Mer Marjzendiak was telling my husband, only the other day, how strong is the allegiance of his people to Tsar Alexander. His Imperial Majesty's liberal treatment has won their gratitude. It seems they look to him as their champion, feeling that local administrators can change with the tides of…" She seemed to be searching for the proper term. "Expediency?" Her expression was innocence itself.

Milyutin cleared his throat. "Which Mer Marjzendiak was that?"

"The Assistant Bank Commissioner," Mira answered, and pointed gracefully. "He's seated there next to Franz. They've worked together for years. During the uprising, he saved my husband's life."

Milyutin studied the face of the tall, elegant looking man sitting next to Franz Pietrowski, reviewing in his mind what he had learned from his own sources regarding Ephraim Marjzendiak's family. The senior Marjzendiak had risen high in the realm of finance and seemed to have become socially assimilated. Commander Ratchikov's investigation of the elder son had proved fruitless. Other probes of Jewish sentiment had also failed to confirm ties to the underground movement, which the Russians suspected to exist. The projected raid of the ghetto was the next measure on Milyutin's agenda. It would serve the dual purpose of catching the Jews unaware, and unearthing any hitherto unrevealed plots they had thus far managed to conceal.

It would also help to quell the restless agitation of the local peasants, many of whom had been unable to hold the land Tsar Alexander's liberal policies had granted to them. They would spearhead the attack, and thus would have an opportunity to plunder the "foreigners" whom they considered "obscenely wealthy" before the militia intervened to restore order.

Until now, Milyutin had been secretly pleased with the way he and his militia commander had devised that strategy. Now, it seemed, the more prosperous Jews were actually disposed to loyalty toward the Russian government. The tight-knit bonds of the Jewish social structure could be called upon to spread that disposition to the lower strata of the ghettos. By encouraging that attitude, peace and quiet could be cheaply maintained. The projected relocation of the Polish peasants could simply be accelerated, and Milyutin's administration would be credited with ensuring stability in these traditionally troubled provinces.

"Madam is well informed regarding the workings of the business community," Milyutin remarked. "I am honored to be your guest. So far, as you predicted, it has been an enlightening evening. Few hostesses of my acquaintance are either as innovative or as unorthodox as you are."

"I shall accept that as a compliment, Your Excellency," Mira said graciously. She was delighted when the governor-general subsequently mentioned an investment opportunity he wished to discuss with her husband at Franz's convenience.

When the time arrived for dessert, the room was darkened. The attendants marched in grand procession to the tables, bearing silver trays of spiced sweet cakes laced with liqueur and crowned by halos of blue flame. It made an impressive finale to an excellent meal.

"The flavor is a mixture of apricot and plum," Mira replied to Sophia Oslowski's inquiries.

"My dear," the Mayor's wife responded, "you've truly outdone yourself tonight."

"You're too kind, Sophia," Mira said, squeezing her friend's hand.

When all had finished dessert, Mira rose regally from the table and moved to the center of the enclosure. "I'd like all of you to join me in the main salon. Coffee will be served presently, but first I have a special surprise for you."

She led the way to the room she had indicated. It had been rearranged so that it could serve as a formal auditorium with chairs, chaises and sofas facing a dais that stretched across the entire wall at one end of the room. A twelve-member chamber orchestra had already assembled there. The guests quickly chose their seats and settled into them, awaiting the promised surprise.

The program began with a brisk rendition of the Eine Kleine Nachtmusik of Mozart. This performance was received with enthusiastic applause. The audience was in an expectant mood, waiting to learn what novel entertainment would follow.

Mira watched Ephraim glance nervously about the room. She knew he was looking for Leah, who had not joined the family in the salon. As the lights dimmed, a slight, female figure, attired in a full-skirted gown of dark blue-green satin taffeta, emerged from a side door.

Leah seated herself at the piano, not looking to the left or right. Her demeanor was aloof, her concentration absolute, as if she were aware of nothing outside the music she was about to bring to life. She seemed poised and completely self-possessed. Ephraim's gaze fixed upon her for a moment. Then his eyes sought those of his hostess. Mira's answering gaze was steadfast and unperturbed, candidly meeting his but offering neither explanation nor apology. Leah's performance must be allowed to speak for itself.

Leah sat quietly for a moment, establishing a rapport with the piano. Then she reached out, opened the keyboard cover, and gently touched the keys.

The selection she and Professor Krause had finally agreed upon after prolonged discussion was the Beethoven Concerto Number 2, Opus 19 in Bb Major. It was an ambitious undertaking for a twelve-year-old. Furthermore, the orchestral passages had required subtle modifications in order to fit the scope of the intimate chamber orchestra. Armand Krause himself had supplied some annotations to augment the interpretation of certain 'unmarked' passages, which Beethoven, in a manner similar to that of Mozart, had left deliberately to the creativity of the performer.

After a momentary hesitation, during which she successfully resisted the temptation to glance guiltily at Ephraim, Leah nodded to Professor Krause, who raised his baton. The rendition began majestically with a crescendo of chords in the piano's lower register. This was repeated by the strings and then by the winds, producing a stirring opening motif.

As the performance progressed, Leah, forgetting her moment of fear and her earlier misgivings, began to enjoy herself immensely. Everything else receded from her awareness, the room, the audience, the social gathering, leaving only the music. Following Professor Krause's advice, she relaxed and let the music possess her completely. A smile of satisfaction lighted her face, and her fingers moved over the keys, strong, sure, and inspired.

As Ephraim listened, his initial indignation turned to admiration. Soon, he found himself caught up in the presentation, in the music itself. He was familiar with the work, but it was not one of his favorites. Heretofore, he had found it somewhat pretentious. Tonight, as Leah played, he seemed to find new and hidden graces in the fluent musical phrases. Glancing surreptitiously at the audience, seeking to gauge their reaction to the performance, he felt a new and exhilarating pride in his daughter. The few pieces he had heard Leah play on Mira's music room piano had not prepared him for this mature rendition of a major concert piece with orchestral accompaniment.

At the conclusion of the work, Mira's guests rose to their feet and applauded with unrestrained enthusiasm. Ephraim joined them, tears of love and pride filling his eyes. A look of mutual pleasure passed between Elana and himself.

To Leah, that applause was an intoxicating sound. She curtsied as Mira had shown her, then walked to the edge of the stage and took Professor Krause by the hand. Leading him to center stage, she joined in the applause, smiling radiantly.

The guests began to move toward the little stage, anxious to express their approval individually. Ephraim was among them. Leah felt a small shiver of apprehension as she watched him approach.

"You might have told me in advance," Ephraim said softly as he embraced her.

"Oh, Papa," she said breathlessly, returning his embrace. "I was afraid I couldn't make you understand what this means to me. It's hard to put into words. I thought you might not let me go ahead with it."

Ephraim smiled. "Perhaps that's true," he conceded, "and that would have been a loss for us all." Then he let her go and the rest of the audience claimed her, showering her with praise, reaching out to touch her.

Milyutin bent from his great height to take her hand and personally express his approbation. "A musical delight," he said appreciatively.

Elana and Mira, close behind him, exchanged glances of triumph and vindication. That was high praise indeed from the taciturn governor-general.

Now the dancing began, and Isaak escorted his sister to the dance floor where he led her through the stately patterns of a minuet. Throughout the dance, Leah was breathless with anticipation of what he might say to her. Finally, she could restrain her curiosity no longer.

"Well?"

"Well," Isaak echoed, smiling playfully at her. "You're certainly one for keeping secrets."

"Oh, Isaak, don't tease," she begged. "What did you think of the performance?"

Isaak looked at Leah for a long moment. "I thought you were magnificent," he said simply. "What's more important, how did you feel about it?"

"Tonight," she replied, "I'm too happy to analyze anything. My head aches a little, my back feels as though it's in a vice, but my feet feel as though they're on clouds. I'm only sorry Adam and Meyhra aren't here."

"So am I," Isaak answered. "However, if you go on like this, one day soon they'll both hear you play." He forced a grin, adding, "And so, was it worth all the work and study?"

"Oh, yes," Leah enthused. "The work and study will go on. I've known that, from the first time I met Professor Krause. Oh, Isaak, you must meet him. He's truly wonderful!"

"I don't doubt that, if he could train you to perform as you have tonight."

Leah's next dancing partner was Markos Kolvner.

Since Adam's wedding, their friendship had blossomed. Her eyes sparkled as she watched him approach. Her heart leapt as he gallantly kissed her hands in tribute.

"I've been waiting to do that," he said. "You said you loved music. Now I understand just how much."

Leah's eyes shone with pleasure. "Do you understand, Markos? Do you, really?"

Markos nodded. "I think I do, and I must confess to a certain degree of jealousy."

Leah's facial expression mirrored her dismay. "Why?" she asked.

"I watched your face as the guests applauded," Markos answered. "It was quite a revelation."

"I'm not sure I know what you mean."

"You probably don't as yet," he continued, his eyes straying toward Armand Krause, who stood speaking earnestly with Ephraim and Elana. "I'm sure your teacher knows, though." He pointed to the piano across the room. "Whoever loves you will have to share you with that and with a host of other people vying to honor you for your talent."

Out of all he had said, Leah fixed her attention on one phrase. A joyous smile lighted her face. "Whoever loves me?"

Markos lowered his eyes. "I did mention that, didn't I?"

"Yes, you did."

Markos grinned sheepishly. "Come and dance with me, will you, before this waltz is over?"

"I shall be honored," Leah answered, dropping a regal curtsey, and then she was swept away on a wave of music, feeling joyously intoxicated, exhilarated, and delighted. After the waltz, she and Markos danced a schottische followed by a mazurka and then another waltz, while Ephraim watched them together and Leah felt him watching. She hoped he approved, but she was content for the moment to be dancing in the arms of someone she considered the handsomest, most gallant, most charming young man in Warsaw. At Jewish gatherings, men and women seldom danced together, the one exception to that custom being the Mitzvah tentzel at weddings and celebrations. But this event was a gentile one, and here the traditional rules did not apply.

Pola and Leah at last found a moment to talk. The older girl was selfless in her praise, and was truly happy for her friend.

"I knew you would play beautifully," she said generously.

"Madam should really have arranged for both of us to perform," Leah responded.

Pola shook her head. "My mother is a clever woman, Leah. She knew exactly how to make her party a complete success. I'm proud and happy for you." She took Leah's hand. "Now come and see," she added, flushed with excitement. "The fireworks are about to begin."

The women took their coffee on the veranda, and the men enjoyed after-dinner liqueur or brandy while the technicians prepared for the finale, the piece de resistance of the soiree.

The evening ended with an elaborate display of fireworks. Once she had adjusted to the explosive sounds and brilliant light effects, Leah, watching with Pola, enjoyed them thoroughly.

Ephraim, standing between Elana and Isaak, could not help but associate the brightly flashing lights and the staccato sounds with gunfire. There were nights he still dreamt of the massacre in Sigismund Square, and of the bloody uprising that had followed it just over a year later. He could vividly remember going to work through streets partly obstructed by barricades where guns barked, bombs exploded, and men and women fell dead who had taken no part in the conflict.

In the complex interplay of light and shadow, Ephraim watched his family's varied reactions to the pyrotechnic display, and prayed that they would never have cause to make such painfully unsettling associations.

# CHAPTER TWENTY-SIX
# PROBLEMS AND SOLUTIONS

On the first day of September, 1868, at the head office of the Bank of Poland, the fiscal year was drawing to its close. Ephraim Marjzendiak, the bank's assistant commissioner, had anticipated that the Pietrowski party on the preceding evening, the opening event of the fall social season, might extend late into the night. Even as Ephraim completed the tallies that reflected the closing status of the bank's major accounts, he remembered the evening with pleasure and a certain pride. The soiree, an unqualified success, had also served the quasi-political purpose Mira had envisioned, to demonstrate to the two leading Russian administrators a firsthand view of what the Warsaw social and economic structure was really like.

Heretofore, the tsar's surrogates had viewed many of their subject peoples, especially gypsies and Jews, as little more than savages. The official stereotypes classified the former group as lazy thieves and the latter as superstitious peddlers, often admittedly clever with figures, but intellectually limited and culturally sterile.

Within that context, Mira's hiring of gypsy violinists to serenade her guests prior to dinner, and arranging for Leah, a Jewish artist, to perform as the evening's central entertainment, had been a master stroke. The Russian cultural devotion to music and dance was as legendary as was its national adoration of all that was French. Mira had managed to capitalize upon both. She had simultaneously showcased Leah's exceptional musical talent and Rebaumme's paintings, and she had done both with elegance and style.

When Ephraim completed the presentation of his report to Franz Pietrowski, later that morning, the two friends sat engaged in earnest conversation.

"You should be very proud of your wife," Ephraim stated. "She truly earned her reputation last night. She deserves to be hailed as Warsaw's leading hostess."

"Even the mayor's wife agrees with you," Franz responded enthusiastically. "I must confess, I had misgivings about bringing together the Russian leaders and some of the people they govern. Mira and I sharply disagreed on this, but she insisted that the timing was right. All evening, I was dreading some unexpected confrontation. I could scarcely believe it when the party ended with nothing more explosive than the fireworks."

"They were indeed impressive," Ephraim said, making an effort to suppress his own sentiments regarding the concluding display. "One can only hope the long-term effects of the encounter will be as positive as the short-term ones seem to be."

"As for pride," Franz remarked, "you must feel a great deal of pride in Leah. She performed brilliantly. It's too bad that in another year or so, she'll have learned all that Armand Krause can teach her."

Ephraim frowned. "Too bad?"

"I only mean that there's no first-rate musical institution open to her in Warsaw. In fact, none of the really prestigious places readily accept female students."

Ephraim nodded thoughtfully. "That's precisely why I've begun to regret allowing her to study music in the first place. Any serious hopes she has of a musical career are doomed to failure, despite Professor Krause's enthusiasm. He actually compared her performance last night to Chopin's Paris debut."

"She was outstanding," Franz agreed. "If she were a boy, I'd say she just might become one of the few musical prodigies of her generation." Franz paused meaningfully. "As it is, well, frankly, I'm concerned for her future."

"Yes," Ephraim responded. "So am I."

"If there's anything I can do," Franz offered.

Ephraim shook his head decisively. "You and Mira have already done much for my daughter, but she is my child. The responsibility for her future is ultimately mine."

As he spoke those words, Ephraim recalled Leah's elation of the evening before, her beauty, her poise, and her surprisingly mature performance. Yet, the elegance of the party dress she had worn had not disguised the garish contrast between the yellow six-pointed star on its bodice and the deep blue-green hue of its taffeta fabric. Armand Krause might successfully ignore such details, but Ephraim could not afford that luxury. If, as Professor Krause seemed certain, Leah longed for a career in music, an option that was closed even to almost all Gentile women, how could anything but disappointment await her?

Yet, at the Pietrowski soiree, the cream of Warsaw society had paid her homage, not to mention the Russian viceroy and governor-general. Last night's audience had been a discriminating one. But then, a gracious guest does not deliberately insult his hostess.

Ephraim knew he was faced with one of two alternative courses of action. He must either dissuade Leah from her impossible dream, or he must try to find a way to make it possible.

* * *

Over after-dinner cigars and wine, Ephraim and Isaak finally had an opportunity to share their impressions of the Pietrowski dinner party and its possible ramifications. Tomorrow morning, Isaak would be taking the train back to Krakow. Recalling the long interval between the time his two elder sons had left for Krakow and the occasion when Adam had first returned to Warsaw, Ephraim privately wondered how long it would be before he would see his second son again.

How swiftly time passes, Ephraim reflected. How inexorably its passage can change our plans. Isaak, he knew, had already been tentatively offered a placement with one of Krakow's leading law firms. It was entirely possible that once the young law student had completed his training, he would elect to make his home in the more liberal Austrian sector of Poland. If he did, Ephraim could hardly blame him for that choice, although he would prefer to keep his family together.

"The viceroy voiced surprisingly liberal sentiments," Isaak said, bringing Ephraim's thoughts back to the conversation at hand. "If he can be believed, we may have been unduly pessimistic. However, I suspect his words were merely empty political window dressing."

"I think the governor-general is a more reliable gauge of how the wind is blowing," Ephraim responded. "He expressed an intent to curb the growing economic power of the Jewish merchants and businessmen. Madam Pietrowska's assurances of our loyalty to the tsar may not be enough to stay his hand."

"Especially if his treatment of Adam and Meyhra is any indication."

"Yet this man is looked upon in the Russian duma as a liberal. He's said to have sponsored the policy to free the serfs."

"I can hardly believe that, unless somehow, it served a private interest for him."

"Such men are often led by hidden motives," Ephraim noted. "Somehow, a way must be found to make our welfare seem to parallel the survival of his administration. That is our only hope."

"At least we've a powerful ally in your friend Pietrowski," Isaak conceded. "I can see why you like him. He's a man of ingenuity and vision."

"This family owes him and his wife a great debt of gratitude. We have them to thank for almost everything we own," Ephraim said earnestly.

"I'm not sure I like our being that beholden, even to apparent friends."

"There's an even balance on both sides of the ledger, Isaak. We're indebted but not servile. I've been a good friend to Franz, as well. We understand each other. That's a great deal to be said of men whose beliefs and backgrounds are as different as ours."

Isaak gazed admiringly at his father. "For a man who claims to deplore politics, you've quite the diplomat. I hope I can learn to be as good."

"You'll be better! You're engaged in the proper course of study. Just make certain you learn how to be as devious as those whom you oppose. It may not seem an admirable trait, but it can mean the difference between survival and destruction."

The two continued to reminisce, not only about social and political pressures within the Russian Polish provinces, but on other more personal matters as well. It became a restful exchange between father and son, a fitting culmination to the deepening understanding that had grown between the two men during Isaak's present stay in Warsaw.

Long after Isaak had gone to pack his portmanteau and get some sleep, Ephraim sat thinking about what had passed between them. His thoughts were in turmoil. He was deeply concerned regarding the imminence of the dangers facing Warsaw's Jews, many of whom, despite the liberal laws that Alexander II had allowed and Wielopolski had enforced, were still repressed, still held to a limited income and the lowest places in the socio-economic structure.

Despite the assurances of the Pietrowskis, Ephraim did not trust Governor-General Milyutin. Despite his own success in realizing his ambitions to own property in Poland, neither he nor any or his fellow Jews had yet achieved citizenship. His money, his position, his property could all be swept away by Imperial decree. Thus far, nothing meaningful had been achieved to reverse the precariousness of that situation.

\* \* \*

Early in September, large numbers of Polish peasants from the districts of Warsaw, Praga, and Wola were relocated to the farmlands in the Lithuanian sector around Vilna. Meanwhile, about one thousand Lithuanian peasants were transported to the flatlands of Byelo-Russia to assist with the harvesting of a record grain crop.

As Governor-General Nicholas Milyutin completed his reports to be dispatched to St. Petersburg, he privately congratulated himself on having solved the unrest in the Vistula Provinces in an imminently tranquil fashion. As for the Jews, he would continue to watch them closely. With the affluent members of that disturbing sect, he had no problem: the status quo was as dear to them as to the Russians. With the impoverished masses, however, Milyutin was prepared to employ stern measures at the first sign of trouble. Such disturbing signs were not apparent at present. He signed his final dispatch with a flourish and placed it within the courier pouch.

Commander Ratchikov chose that moment to knock at the governor-general's door, just as his superior sealed the pouch. Milyutin actually smiled at his subordinate. He was recalling Ratchikov's objections to the cancellation of the pogrom.

"The peasants will be loud in their disappointment, Excellency," the commander had said. "Despite statistics to the contrary, they expect to find much hidden wealth within the ghetto."

"That, Commander, is but one more reason why the peasants are not to be trusted," Milyutin had countered. "Besides, we will find a way to keep them occupied so that they will have no time to object. Is that not so, Commander?"

Ratchikov had, of necessity, agreed. Thus motivated, he had conducted the relocation process with admirable dispatch.

"Once again, Commander, your timing is excellent," Milyutin greeted Ratchikov. "The documents are ready."

"Very good, Excellency. They will leave within the hour."

Milyutin nodded and sat back, obviously pleased.

"All goes well, I take it, Commander." It was a statement rather than a question.

"Very well, Excellency," Ratchikov asserted. To say anything else would be an admission of incompetence.

"Good! Then you have my leave."

The commander saluted smartly, took the dispatch pouch, and quickly left the room.

* * *

On a mid-October afternoon, in the ghetto district of the Stare Miasto, Dr. Adam Marjzendiak was preparing to close his office for the day. Complaining of a headache, Meyhra had left much earlier. It was a noteworthy complaint since Meyhra never had headaches. However, in recent weeks, Meyhra had seemed to voice several unusual complaints. Things had not gone well lately between husband and wife. Their infrequent conversations had degenerated into either sudden, illogical arguments or frigid silences. Worse still, since the death of their child, they had not made love. They shared the same bed, hardly speaking, and not touching each other at all. The close physical proximity of the woman he loved, day and night, under these conditions of estrangement, was tormenting Adam beyond endurance. In an outburst of sudden rage, he picked up the chart in which he was writing and threw it angrily at the door.

He could hardly have been more surprised when the door to his inner office opened, and the chart was deftly caught by Lukas Kolvner.

"I must say, that's a unique way to greet an old friend," Lukas said good-naturedly.

Adam bit his lower lip. "It wasn't intended as a greeting. I wasn't expecting anyone, Lukas."

"Now that I'm here, you don't seem very pleased to see me." Lukas moved to the desk and carefully placed the chart on its surface.

Adam rose to his feet and took Lukas' hand in both his own. "I'm always pleased to see you, my friend. You know that. It's just..." Adam's voice trailed off and he shook his head.

Lukas took the chair opposite Adam's desk. He was silent for a moment, remembering the many occasions on which, as young boys, he and Adam had shared confidences. The closeness of male friendships in the social structure of Eastern Europe was legendary. It filled a unique need in the cultural constellation of human relationships that was lacking in most western countries. "Will it help to tell me about it?"

Adam could not meet his friend's eyes. "It's personal."

"I didn't think anything was too personal between lifelong friends." In order to fill the awkward silence that followed, Lukas added, "By the way, I heard what happened at your home. I regret I wasn't in Warsaw at the time."

Adam smiled bitterly. "I don't. You would have been as outraged as I was; maybe even more so. There's nothing you could have done about it. Fortunately, my brother was here. He helped us put things back together. The neighbors helped as well. You know how that sort of thing goes."

Lukas nodded. "Yes I do. We've had our share of unwelcome visitors. I suspect most of us have, at one time or another." He paused. "Is that what's still bothering you, or is it," His voice lowered as if he was reluctant to ask, "the baby's death?"

"It seems to have been one thing after another," Adam answered. "But that's not why you came, is it?"

"No," Lukas conceded. "I came to say good-bye."

"Where are you off to this time, and for how long?"

"Anna and I are moving to Zurich. The family has bought an import house there, and we're going to run it."

Adam stood to embrace his friend. "You're always off on another journey."

Lukas returned the embrace. "It's the way of the trade. One must go where there are treasures to be bought and sold, and a zloty to be made."

"It's too bad your friends can't go with you," Adam lamented, only half in jest.

"There are good things here, too, Adam, in spite of the Russians. Most especially, there's that beautiful wife of yours."

Adam turned away at those words. Tears filled his eyes and coursed slowly down his cheeks. "Forgive me," he said, embarrassed. "I don't normally break down like this."

"Perhaps," Lukas said, "that's the trouble."

Adam stared at his friend in open confusion. "I don't understand."

"I went to your house first, Adam. I thought you might be there by then. I spoke with Meyhra."

"She went home early," Adam said hesitantly. "She said she had a headache."

"I know," Lukas remarked. "Fortunately, she was less evasive than you are."

"What did she say?" Curiosity and concern marked Adam's voice.

"Enough to make me wonder what's happened between the two of you."

Adam turned away. "I'd rather not discuss it."

"I know," Lukas said. "You haven't been discussing it with Meyhra either. Silence isn't the best language between husband and wife."

"Some things defy discussion," Adam noted bitterly. "Meyhra and I have found it increasingly difficult to come close to each other lately." He paused, momentarily unable to continue. "We're together, and yet we're not." He buried his head in his hands, temporarily overcome by grief. Then, after a long, painful silence, he looked at Lukas.

"Yes," Lukas said warmly, "That can be a difficult thing between husband and wife. Don't imagine that I'm a total stranger to such difficulties. Anna and I also had our problems, but we've solved them, and they've brought us closer."

Encouraged by this admission from his dearest friend, Adam began to talk. Slowly, painfully, the tale of anguish, grief, and long-buried guilt came out then, including Adam's still remembered love for Sarah and his self-hatred over the end of their relationship. The parallels between the death of Baby Jakob and that of Baby Anna were also revealed. Finally, Lukas knew all the sad details that Meyhra longed in vain to understand, all the barriers that stood like Sheol's sentinels between Adam and Meyhra, preventing their enjoyment of yada, the special rites of physical intimacy between husband and wife.

"You must explain this to her, Adam," Lukas implored his friend earnestly. "The problems between you will never be resolved until you do."

"It's difficult to put it into words, Lukas," Adam said haltingly. "I've never been good at talking about how I feel. It's hard to maintain the image of strength expected of a man and yet confess a sense of helplessness, of vulnerability."

"I'd say you did extremely well at it just now."

"That was between you and me," Adam countered. "I could always talk with you. You're like another brother to me. But how can I say those things to Meyhra?"

"Tell her as you've told me, just as simply and just as honestly. Make her understand." Lukas winked and patted Adam's shoulder. "I'll tell you a secret I've learned from being an old, married man. Women love being idolized in public, but they hate it in private." He paused. "I'd better be going now, and you'd better get home. I'd say you have a major job of fence-mending ahead of you."

"I'd say you're right," Adam agreed. "Wish me luck. "

"I do," Lukas said, "but you won't need it. Your Meyhra is as sensible as she is beautiful. I told you the day you were married, you're a lucky man." He shook Adam's hand in a final gesture of farewell.

"Write to me," Adam said as Lukas turned to go. "I'm going to miss you."

"I'll be back," Lukas promised. "Warsaw is my first home. I've several ties here, including you."

Adam dreaded the next few hours. He anticipated that they would be among the most difficult of his life. If he had felt that relinquishing his claims upon Sarah had been an ordeal, that seemed now, in retrospect, relatively easy compared to the task of repairing communications with his wife. When the accident had first occurred, and the baby daughter to whom they had both looked forward had died, he had found it easy to console Meyhra. Later, however, as her tears were replaced by long periods of dry-eyed, tight-lipped silence, Adam had found himself at a loss. His own bitter frustration had tied his tongue. He had never been able to freely verbalize his feelings at the best of times. Now was surely not the best of times. He walked slowly homeward, pondering how he could verbally address the subject that was uppermost in his mind.

Throughout dinner, Meyhra was dutiful but distant. Her well-modulated low-pitched voice seldom broke the almost tangible silence. Finally, as she stood to clear the table, her slim, capable hands reached out to remove Adam's plate. He caught one of them in both his own and drew it to his lips. She moved instinctively to pull her hand away, but he held her fast, his eyes searching her face.

"That can wait, Meyhra," he said softly. "Sit down. We need to talk."

"We haven't for some time," she answered, her eyes avoiding his.

"I know. I regret that deeply," Adam admitted, "but talking is not one of my talents. I feel much more than I can ever say."

Meyhra resisted the impulse to respond in words. Instead, she gently caressed his hands with the fingers of her free hand, and her eyes tentatively sought his. Their glances locked, and Meyhra smiled as their lips joined tenderly and their breath blended in a kiss that communicated understanding and promised passion.

He gathered her closer, his arms encircling her protectively, and he whispered into her hair, "You've no idea how much I've longed to do that every night for weeks, but I dared not for fear you might not want me yet."

She drew back and looked at him. "But I did!"

His voice was muted by desire. "When?"

"Many times." She laid her head against his chest. "I feared I'd lost you. You've been so preoccupied, so distant."

Rather than chiding her for a similar aloofness, he took her face in his hands. He kissed her forehead, her eyelids, and her lips before he attempted to reply. "That can never happen. You'll never lose me as long as I'm alive. Somehow, we seem to have been at cross purposes, both wanting to break the silence, but neither daring to try."

"I thought there might be something, someone, in your life before we met. Someone you wish were here instead of me."

Adam struggled to hold back the tears those words tempted to fill his eyes.

"There was someone once, but there can never be anything between us again."

"I have no right to intrude on that," she said softly, engaging his eyes with hers. "Whom you knew in the past, and how you felt then is something separate and apart. But I want you now. All of you, your mind, your heart, and your body. I can't bear to share you with a memory."

"You don't have to," Adam answered. "I am yours. Please believe that."

"I want to," she said levelly, "but that's difficult to do when you won't talk to me. You always seem to be holding something back."

Adam nodded ruefully. "I seem to have been bottling things up inside for a long time now." He paused. "It's not that long ago," he went on, "and yet, in some ways, it seems an eternity. Her name was Sarah."

Meyhra considered that for a moment. "Do I remind you of her?"

"No," he answered gently. "You're quite different. I think that's one of the things I love most about you. That, and your wisdom, your innate stability. Even when I lose my temper, you won't maintain an argument. You won't raise your voice and yell back at me as I deserve."

"There's no sense in two of us saying angry, hurtful things. It only makes the problem worse," Meyhra responded. "I can never remember hearing my parents argue, even when I sensed they disagreed on something."

"But you have to talk things out eventually," Adam responded, remembering Lukas' words.

Meyhra put her fingers to his lips. "Talking and arguing aren't the same."

"No, of course not," he admitted.

Meyhra settled herself comfortably on the floor by Adam's chair. "Tell me about Sarah," she said, looking up at him candidly. There was a warm receptiveness in her eyes that strengthened his intent.

He talked to her then, as she requested, about Sarah and her family, about his poignant farewell to his first love, and of baby Jakob's brief life and tragic death. He spoke of Krakow and of his studies there, of the odyssey he had shared with Isaak in traveling from Warsaw to the Austrian-Polish border. He spoke of his wish to learn more about hereditary diseases and how they might be prevented or recognized early and treated. Once he started to speak, the floodgates of his dammed up feelings seemed to burst. He could not stop. When at last he fell silent, more than an hour had passed.

Finally, Meyhra got to her feet. She had listened patiently to all her husband had to say. Most of it she had understood, at least intellectually. More importantly, she could now perceive on an emotional level the reason for his dread of his child being born flawed, and his inability to express that dread to her until now. So much that had mystified her was suddenly clear, so clear that she was overwhelmed. She needed to be alone, to sort out her thoughts.

She glanced down at the remains of dinner still on the table. Slowly, she resumed the tasks of clearing it away.

"Meyhra," Adam said, his voice rendered sharp by concern, "have you nothing to say to me?"

"Yes." She raised her eyes and looked at him. "Some of it needs to be said with words, but more needs to be said with deeds. Why don't you go outside and let me finish here? I'll join you presently."

Adam was astonished. He felt he had laid bare his soul and his wife responded by immersing herself in housewifely chores. Shaking his head, he took his coat, went outside, and walked in the courtyard. Twilight had settled, and long shadows darkened the cobbled stones on which he paced. The trees in the narrow courtyard were already bare, and their outlines stretched nakedly skyward like skeletal spectres in the deepening gloom. Adam felt as naked as those trees. Yet he was not without hope. His wife had asked him for the truth, and he had been scrupulously if belatedly truthful.

It was not long before, true to her word, Meyhra joined him. She slipped her hand into the curve of his arm, and they walked in silence, watching the stars come to life in the night sky. This was a different silence, intimate and companionable, a friendly silence that enfolded them and bound them together.

Finally, she broke that silence. She spoke of her mother, and the sense of irretrievable loss she had felt at her mother's death. She recalled how her resolve to become a nurse had stemmed from that loss, and how easing the pain of others had ultimately laid to rest her own pain. She spoke of what the anticipation of Anna's birth had symbolized for her, her justification as a woman, and how losing Anna had reopened the old wound of loss. When the night wind grew damp as well as cold, Meyhra whispered, "Let's go inside," and she and Adam walked home, holding hands as they had often done in the early days of their courtship.

"My one regret," Meyhra remarked as they reached their front door, "is that we never talked this openly before. Each of us, locked in his own private grief and pain, failed to see what the other was feeling."

"We must never do that again," Adam said, squeezing her hand.

They went inside, took off their coats and locked the door. Meyhra smiled, intertwined her fingers through Adam's, and slowly led him upstairs. It was good to feel close to each other again. It reminded Adam of their wedding day and the moments they had spent alone together after the ceremony. He reached out to Meyhra and held her close to him, savoring the fragrance of her hair and the smoothness of her skin as he carefully unfastened her dress and undergarments and let them fall unheeded to the floor. She wrapped her arms about his shoulders and stroked the back of his neck as he bent to kiss her throat and breasts. She clung to him as he picked her up in his arms, cradling her and kissing her repeatedly.

When he laid her lithe, naked body on their bed, Meyhra reached up and caressed him. Then she stretched provocatively, invitingly, displaying her beautiful body for her husband's private delectation.

Adam had waited hungrily for this moment. He could scarcely restrain his desire any longer. He stripped away his own clothing and knelt beside the bed, his hands gently exploring Meyhra, touching and stroking her where he knew well what response his touch would provoke. Soon she was moaning softly. As he joined her in bed, she lay quivering beneath him. She reached for him and drew him to her. Her slender fingers encircled his manhood, gently stroking and massaging until she felt the fullness of his response to her touch. Then she guided him to the most secret recesses of her body and made him welcome.

\* \* \*

In the months following his return from Warsaw after the Pietrowski soiree, for his final year of study and the National Legal examination that he would have to pass in order to pursue a career in law practice, Isaak once more threw himself attentively into his work. He developed the habit of going to the library to study. Although he had most of the material he needed, and required only minimal use of the reference texts, the atmosphere there was quiet and conducive to the concentration he desired. He could be among people there, and yet be effectively alone and undisturbed. The silent presence of fellow-students was somehow soothing at this time, for he no longer sought to totally isolate himself, as he had done before, going off alone to study in the woods, or locking himself in the room he had once shared with Adam. The excursion home had done him good. As Ephraim had predicted, he had observed and learned much at the Pietrowski party, and he had profited psychologically from the change of pace.

It was during this period that Isaak began to notice that one student, a young woman in her late teen years, paralleled his habit of study, both in time and location. He found himself wondering at what hours she took her classes, and what courses she pursued. He stole a sidelong glance at her and thought with surprise that she could hardly be older than seventeen or eighteen.

She was tall for her age and gender, slim and well formed, with a long torso and longer legs, wide angular shoulders, small pointed breasts, a slender column of neck, and a head and face so delicately modeled that they might have inspired a sculptor. She was blonde, but not in the same fashion as either Sarah, whose curly hair was the color of wild honey, or Mariska, whose long, straight tresses had often reminded him of sunlight shining through a shadowed curtain of dense foliage. This nameless student had dark blond hair that coiled and curled in reckless abandon down her neck and across her shoulders, just barely blond and missing light brunette by a fraction, until the afternoon sunlight, slanting through the library windows, caught it and burnished it to a deep, rich golden hue.

Isaak grew accustomed to seeing her there at a nearby table, her head bent over a book that seemed to absorb her entire attention. He came to watch for her, to miss her if she came late, and to feel reassured if she was there when he arrived. They did not converse. They scarcely glanced at each other. Yet each was aware of the other's presence.

\* \* \*

In due course, Isaak took and passed his state exam, just as he had passed his senior comprehensive exams a month earlier. He decided to accept the position at the law firm in which his friend Evyan had already joined his father and uncle. For now, Isaak was content to remain in Krakow. He found himself making excuses for not returning home to live in Warsaw with the rest of his family. He was free to visit them, but for the present he admitted to himself, the focus of his life was Krakow, rather than Warsaw.

Thus it was that he wrote to Ephraim that he would be remaining for a time in Krakow after his graduation from the Law Akademy in order to gain professional experience before venturing into the difficult arena of law practice as a Jew under Russian rule. He knew his father would understand. After all, Ephraim had lived all his life under that yoke. What he might not understand was how it felt to be free of the limitations imposed in the Vistula Provinces, as Russian Poland was now called. Ephraim might yearn for the joys of freedom. Indeed, Isaak knew that he did deeply desire and treasure freedom, but it was from a distance, as a vision anticipated rather than familiar, a goal aspired to but not achieved. Isaak was relatively free here in Krakow, and having found a measure of freedom, he was reluctant to give it up entirely and live once more the limited oppressive life of those under the Russian yoke.

One of the earliest cases to which Isaak was assigned involved the controversy between a merchant, a native of Krakow, and a Russian ship owner with whom the merchant had entered into a business agreement. The Polish merchant, Jan Borowski, had purchased from a western European tradesman an assortment of textiles originally manufactured in southern Portugal and Spain. The tariffs on such goods, when transported overland from western to eastern Europe, were notoriously exorbitant. To avoid this curtailment of the profits, which he hoped to generate from the sale of the elegant fabrics, Borowski had entered into an agreement with a Ukranian ship owner named Fyodor Zuberov, a kind of joint venture from which both men stood to profit.

The ship owner had agreed to transport the goods from Barcelona, across the Mediterranean Sea and the Aegean Sea, through the Sea of Marmara (formerly the Dardanelle Strait) to the port of Istanbul on the Black Sea. At this point, the shipment was to be off-loaded from the larger transport vessel, the Sonya, to a smaller, faster vessel, the Sofya, which would carry the merchandise to the Bulgarian port of Varma where it would then be brought overland, on the final phase of its journey, through Sofea by train to Krakow. Fees in the Bulgarian port were much lower than those in European Mediterranean ports, so the Ukranian explained, thus justifying the use of two of his ships instead of one.

Borowski had been leery of this arrangement at first, but had capitulated when Zuberov had boasted that he could save two thirds of the port unloading fees in Istanbul by using his own men for the task, and then repeating the process at the Bulgarian sea port of Varma, which was now a cultural center. Dockworker unions had not yet come into being, and the arrangement, as outlined by Zuberov, was made to seem practical, economical and legitimate. In actuality, the plan had proved to be none of the above. All had gone well until the final transfer was to have been made from ship to train. There tragedy struck in the form of a storm. The ship had foundered and sunk in the harbor with the merchant's goods still on board, or so the ship owner claimed. The merchant contested that the loss must be made good. The Ukranian argued that the storm was an act of God, and that he had lost the ship in the process, and could not possibly compensate the merchant. He further stated that the loss had terminated the agreement between the two men. This controversy raged without redress until the merchant Borowski learned that the Ukranian Russian ship owner had marketed a shipment of exotic Oriental merchandise, including several lengths of cloth, on consignment through another merchant, and was building a pair of new ships from the profits.

Borowski claimed that the goods were his, that they had not been lost in the Bulgarian harbor, and that Zuberov was guilty of fraud. The Ukranian scoffed at these charges, saying that Borowski could not prove his case since the proof lay buried in the harbor of Varma. In truth, salvage of the wreckage would be so costly an undertaking that neither man could afford it, and so the matter seemed likely to remain unresolved. When Isaak found himself embroiled in this issue, he all but despaired of finding a solution. Witnesses who could provide reliable information regarding the loading of the cargo and the details of the ship's final hours were strangely not to be found. The crew of that last voyage of the Sofya were not regular employees of the Zuberov shipping firm, with the exception of the captain. The captain's statements paralleled Zuberov's contentions, but there were no other corroborating statements obtainable. The other crew members had signed on to other ships and gone their ways. None were currently to be found.

One late afternoon, over coffee at a local restaurant not far from the campus where both had been students, Isaak and Evyan discussed the relative merits of the cases each was handling.

"At least you know how to proceed," Isaak commented. "This question of silks and gauzes seems to have no answer, and meanwhile, the merchant gives me no peace, and the Russian scoffs and goes on about his business. I am certain he is hiding something, but there is simply no proof."

"What about the crew?"

"Those on the first vessel, the <u>Sonya</u>, are employed by Zuberov," Isaak answered. "They're not about to jeopardize their jobs by testifying against him. The second crew can't be found."

"There've been no inquiries from relatives? No hands were lost when the second ship went down?"

"None were reported."

"How very odd."

"I've thought that, too," Isaak commented. "Even in a storm, all hands don't normally abandon ship until it's obvious the ship cannot be saved. That's seldom the case when a vessel is in port. I can see it sinking with its cargo during a storm at sea, but in a harbor, it should have been protected. Certainly, something could have been salvaged. In this case, not even the ship's log was saved, although the captain survived."

He shoved the file of papers towards Evyan. "I'd like you to look these over, and tell me your opinion of the statements given by the captain and the harbor master."

"You think there's collusion?"

"I'm beginning to wonder," Isaak responded. Then, just at that moment, he was shocked to see the girl whom he had admired at the library approaching their table with Evyan's cousin, Olga Danuska.

"The world is often smaller than we think," Olga said brightly, bending to embrace her cousin. "I had no idea I'd see you here, Evyan."

"A delightful surprise," Evyan said, standing and returning the embrace. "You remember Isaak, of course."

Olga extended her hand. "Of course." She greeted Isaak warmly. "How are you?"

"Fine," he responded. "Do you care to join us?" Isaak got to his feet and pulled out chairs for the two girls. His eyes met those of the young blond girl, such a contrast in type to the dark-haired, dark-eyed Olga. A glance of joyous recognition passed between them, a foreshadowing that was not one of seduction but of simple pleasure.

"Thank you," Olga responded, and silenced the other girl's budding objection. She turned to Evyan. "I'd like you both to meet a friend of mine, Luvna Meyer. She's studying art and art history at the University."

As the two girls took their seats, Olga continued. "She's really quite good, though she's too shy to say so herself."

"I'm only just learning," Luvna said demurely, "and there's still a great deal to learn."

Realizing that any hope of discussing the case in hand further with Evyan was at an end for the present, Isaak turned his attention to Luvna. He questioned her about her interests, her ambitions, and her background, while Olga and Evyan discussed items of family interest.

Isaak was grateful to learn that Luvna's family was not too dissimilar from his own. He suspected that she was Jewish from the pendant she wore about her neck. It was in the shape of a mezuzah, the metal case containing a Scripture blessing that devout Jewish families affix to their doorposts. Now he came to know that her father was self-employed and owned an import business in Warsaw with a branch still located in Krakow.

The four young people ordered a light meal, and talked congenially together until early evening.

Isaak was fascinated by Luvna's precociously mature outlook. She wanted one day to paint canvases, but she also wanted to work actively with a museum or a gallery, collecting and preserving the work of other artists. Meanwhile, although her parents sent her funds from Warsaw, where they had moved upon leaving Krakow, Luvna worked at the University in order to earn pocket money and to gain a sense of self-dependence. She lived with a maiden aunt, her mother's sister Susana Halmuth, and enjoyed a very close, understanding relationship with this well-educated older woman who encouraged her ambitions and her talents. Luvna seemed unconscious of her beauty, oddly unselfconscious of her many favorable attributes, and wholly at ease conversing with a man who must seem to her much older than those with whom she attended classes. Isaak deduced that Luvna's attachment to her aunt was probably the reason she felt comfortable with people older than herself.

When they parted after dinner, Isaak regretted that the meeting must come to an end. He genuinely liked Luvna. In some ways, she reminded him of Leah, whose frequent letters over the past years had kept him apprised of her thoughts and feelings. His sister was growing up, filled with hopes, plans and ambitions very like Luvna's own. Given the world in which they both lived, Isaak wondered if either girl would ever be able to fulfill her ambitions.

\* \* \*

In the weeks that followed that meeting, Isaak's time was almost totally consumed with the Borowski case. Once again, he spoke with Captain Sandrofsky, captain of the smaller merchant vessel, the <u>Sofya</u>, to no avail. He also questioned the <u>Sonya's</u> captain, and was convinced that this man, a German named Hans Hetting, was candid in his statements to the effect that the cargo had been safely transferred from the <u>Sonya</u> to the smaller merchant ship, the <u>Sofya</u>, without incident. What Isaak did not quite credit was the necessity for making the transfer in the first place. Hetting explained that his large vessel did not usually enter the Turkish straits because of its size, but sailed between Mediterranean ports almost exclusively with an occasional voyage northward along the western-most European coastline to ports in Portugal and northern Spain. It was only by coincidence that he was currently in Krakow visiting his family.

There was still the unanswered question of what had happened aboard the Sofya between receiving the Sonya's cargo and sinking in the Black Sea. There seemed no way to get at the facts, and the time for filing the case, with its list of witnesses, was drawing to an end, when Isaak was visited by a small, wiry, swarthy young man who entered the office with an air of wanting to remain unobtrusive and unobserved. He wore what was probably his best suit, and his hair and short beard were neatly trimmed and combed. Yet, there was about him an almost oily appearance that seemed both foreign and somewhat suspect. He gave his name reluctantly as Augustus Rojas, and took the chair Isaak offered him with a distinct air of being ill at ease.

Isaak began the conference in the least threatening manner he could think of. "How may I help you?"

"As to that," Rojas responded, "it's I who can probably help you."

"Really?" Isaak gave the man his full attention. "In what way?"

"About eight months ago," ~the man replied, "I signed aboard a merchant schooner called the Sofya, under Captain Sandrofsky. I hear you've been searching for seamen who made that voyage. It was the Sofya's last foray."

"Considering the ship's fate," Isaak said, "you were very fortunate to escape."

Rojas smiled in a twisted, ironic way. "That was no great piece of luck. All of us got off her long before she went down."

"Still," Isaak said noncommittally, "it must have been a narrow escape with so little warning."

Rojas coughed and fidgeted in his chair, his eyes going to the windows suspiciously. They were leaded glass, tinted and opaque. The seaman smiled when he saw them. Then he began his tale. It was quickly told, and when he had finished the telling, it was obvious that his motives were those of revenge, because he had been slighted a goodly percentage of his agreed upon pay for the voyage across the Black Sea. Isaak questioned him closely, determined to learn if his desire for vengeance was so strong that he might have contrived his story of deceit and concealment solely to attain his own ends. Rojas responded by claiming that there were others who could confirm his statements. He named two other seamen currently in town, and gave the names of the ships on which they had sailed and where those ships were now moored. At least two of the men had relatives in Krakow, and as Rojas elaborated on his experience about the Sofya, it became clear that part of his reticence was due to fear of reprival and even of physical harm if his revelations became known.

When the man had left, Isaak felt his first sign of relief since taking the case. There might at last be some hope of prevailing. The seaman had finally signed the statement Isaak had taken down, and had departed promising to appear in court when summoned, but had refused to divulge his address. He said he was familiar with the court gazette and would therefore know when the case was called forward.

Isaak was less than optimistic that he would be able to ensure the man's appearance when needed. Moreover, he was none so certain that Rojas' story would be believed even if he were present to give it. He did wonder if one of the other two men might prove less nervous and less slippery. He thought that they might also present a facade that would seem more credible before a magistrate than Rojas, with his constant fidgeting and his preoccupation with who else might see him or overhear him. Isaak, therefore, decided to pursue the leads Rojas had given him.

In the course of that research, Isaak learned some important facts about the Sofya and her ill-fated last voyage. First of all, the ship had been quite old, had undergone frequent repairs in the two years preceding her loss, and had sustained three separate changes of her crew during that period. Captain Sandrofsky had been appointed her captain only hours before her final voyage. Finally, the elder of the two seamen Rojas had named, a Portuguese veteran of many voyages, readily volunteered upon questioning that the cargo the Sofya had carried was extremely heavy in view of the goods listed on the manifest. He further stated that the Captain had ordered all the crew off the vessel once she made port, and that he, Manuel Duarte, had seen the ship sink in an aureole of flame despite the storm that had raged that night.

"That ship was cursed," he avowed, "and she was scuttled more than likely."

Isaak was somewhat startled at that. "Why should the ship be scuttled?"

"To hide the cargo she carried. Explosives. If you ask me, most of them were off-loaded, and then the rest were torched. No one can convince me that ship was carrying dry goods. I was there."

Isaak asked, "How good is the market for explosives, now?"

"It's very profitable in certain quarters," the seaman answered. "Much more profitable than a bunch of silks and laces."

When Isaak was satisfied that he had learned all he could from the available former crew members of the Sofya, he set to work learning more about Fyodor Zuberov, himself. What he discovered formed a less than prepossessing picture. The man's early origins were unknown, but it was assumed by his contemporaries that his beginnings had been humble. However, he was not without ambition, and the ends had, for him, always seemed to justify the means. He was now a relatively wealthy man, having dabbled in a number of endeavors before launching into ship building. What had always remained a mystery was the source of much of his wealth. Even more of a mystery was the fate of both his former wives, each of whom had died under questionable circumstances. Yet Zuberov had never been called to account for their deaths.

The second and younger wife, a woman named Lyria Treskovna, had been a native of Krakow. With some well-directed inquiries, Isaak located the woman's brother, and after an in-depth talk with him, enlisted his aid.

\* \* \*

When the case came to trial, Isaak found himself facing one of his most illustrious opponents, an attorney who was originally from St. Petersburg. His name was Josef Gregor Yarabowsky. He was almost half a meter taller than Isaak, though Isaak was a relatively tall man, and the Russian had a physique that would have done credit to a wrestler. When Yarabowsky appeared before the magistrate in the robes of his calling, he made an impressive picture. His opening statements derided the case in hand as a travesty, a malicious attempt on the part of the merchant Borowski to discredit his client because of a misfortune that both had shared.

Isaak's opening comments were deliberately less impassioned. He stated, simply and clearly, that his intent was to prove that his client had been the victim of duplicity, and that his interests had never been of any importance to Fyodor Zuberov, despite the apparent joint venture into which the two men had entered.

Throughout the proceedings, Isaak maintained an almost stoic approach in contrast to the emotional semi-histrionic techniques of his opponent. Step by step, Isaak was able to undermine the credibility of several of Yarabowsky's witnesses, while confining his questioning of those prosecution's witnesses to the facts relating to the case, facts with which they were personally acquainted. Little by little, he was able to bring to light the fact that Zuberov had once, two years before, been accused of smuggling guns to Turkish insurgents. The charge had later been dropped for lack of evidence. Now, once again, Turkey was embroiled in an insurrection, and the <u>Sofya</u> had gone down in a port in Georgian waters, Georgia then being part of Russia. Yarabowsky scoffed at this news as totally unrelated until Lyria Treskovna's brother, Jaim, came to the stand. The Russian defendant and his attorney conferred seriously while this witness was being sworn in, and Fyodor Zuberov, who had heretofore worn an expression of amused disdain throughout the proceedings, now seemed genuinely concerned. His concern grew when Isaak put into evidence a bill of lading signed by Captain Sandrofsky for a consignment of "munitions and incendiary goods" that bore a date three days before his ship had gone down. The official listing of the ship's cargo had consisted of a large consignment of bolts of silks, brocades, laces, wools, and other textiles and these had been described in the contract Zuberov had signed with Borowski. They would have all but filled the cargo hold of the <u>Sonya</u>. It was impossible for them to have shared the <u>Sofya's</u> hold with the array of munitions that the vessel's captain had signed for.

When the magistrate handed down his ruling, the spectators in the court room, most of them Polish, applauded uproariously. Their countryman's cause had prevailed, and the Russian, Zuberov, had not only lost the case, but was remanded to prison with the threat that after his activities had been thoroughly investigated, his sentence might be severe indeed. The merchant's investment was ordered to be repaid from Zuberov's resources. Borowski could not thank Isaak enough.

When the two men parted, Isaak packed his briefcase and prepared to leave the building. Among the spectators who had applauded was Luvna Meyer. When she met Isaak in the huge hall outside the court room, her eyes shone with admiration and pride.

"I've never been to court before," she said in awe. "It's rather intimidating, but you were wonderful."

From a distant alcove, another spectator, who had watched and applauded Isaak's triumph, witnessed this exchange with interest. Sarah Krakowska was pleased to note that Luvna was young and beautiful. Perhaps, Sarah thought, Luvna might prove to possess those and other attributes in sufficient quantity to help Isaak at last to forget the past. Putting aside her original intent to congratulate Isaak personally, Sarah turned down a side corridor, found a rear stairway, and left the building, smiling quietly to herself. She had no wish to interrupt the tete-a-tete between the attorney and the young art student. Besides, she had cause to feel self-congratulatory; she had finally received her permanent appointment to the senior faculty of the University of Krakow. On some future occasion, she would talk with Isaak about that accomplishment when the two of them were alone. They had, after all, become good friends though not lovers.

# CHAPTER TWENTY-SEVEN
## 1869: GROWTH AND EVOLUTION

In 1869, only a few kilometers separated the ghetto of the Stare Miasto and Jyudmielkie Square, at the junction of the Old Town and the Stodmiesele (middle city). In terms of social and economic distance, however, that short span was almost immeasurable. In the month of June, Dr. and Mrs. Adam Marjzendiak moved into larger, more gracious living quarters on Gradski Street in the square. Located opposite a well-maintained park, the house was set amid homes recently constructed for members of the Polish industrial middle class.

For the young Jewish physician and his wife, it was a major advancement, made possible by Adam's expanding practice, and, to a lesser extent, by his recent appointment to the faculty of the Warsaw Akademy of Medicine. While the stipend paid by the teaching position was not overly generous, the appointment carried with it a measure of prestige of which Adam would not have dared to dream a year earlier.

Now, as he responded to the stimulus of interacting with young, eager, inquisitive minds, inspired by the same hopes and dreams that had led him into the study of medicine, Adam became aware that the practice of medicine fulfilled only a part of his goal. Teaching, he found, fulfilled a need of which he had previously been unaware. The laboratory courses especially enthralled him. Even as he assigned his students the research projects required for their doctoral degrees, the idea of undertaking research into the mechanisms of hereditary neurological disease, which had arisen during his time of medical training in Krakow, reasserted itself and now began to obsess him.

Adam communicated these sentiments to Meyhra, finding it easier in recent months to express his feelings more openly. He found that their marriage had been strengthened by the brief estrangement that had followed the death of their child. Adam felt especially grateful to his friend Lukas for providing the insight and perspective that he, himself, had been too close to his frustrations to perceive.

An exchange of letters between the recently settled Lukas and himself afforded Adam an opportunity to express his thanks. Shortly thereafter, Adam received a letter from Isaak. He knew instinctively that the letter's arrival meant Isaak would not be coming home that year before school reopened in September, and Adam felt saddened by that knowledge even before he opened the letter.

Isaak's letters were usually sincere but succinct. However, this one ran two full pages.

"Dear Adam,

I write this letter with a mixture of exultation and regret. The exultation stems from a chance encounter that has grown into what I hope will prove to be an abiding relationship. Her name is Luvna, and I can hardly imagine a more controversial young woman. She is very 'political,' fiercely Nationalistic, aggressively proud of her Jewish heritage, but shockingly irreverent of form and ceremony. She is much younger than I, eighteen to be exact. However, she is brilliant, well-read, outspoken, and unashamedly affectionate. She is also stunningly beautiful and graceful in the way a fawn is graceful. There is about her an untamed quality that has totally captivated my imagination. Is this love? I honestly don't know. What I do know is that I cannot bear to think of my life without her, and somehow I feel that must be what it means to truly love another human being. I have had this feeling before on two occasions, and neither ended happily. But now, I feel instinctively that Adonai is favorably disposed toward me.

So much for the good news. As for the regret, because of Luvna, and the fact that I cannot bear to be separated from her at present, I am staying through the summer term. Luvna will not graduate for two more years, so I have decided to remain in Krakow with the law firm I have joined until she can move to Warsaw with me.

I definitely plan to return home, but I feel the need to first acquire some professional experience in a setting less hostile to Jewish legal counselors than the Vistula Provinces.

Besides, I fear it will take me that long to face Father with the fact that the woman I love and make love to is not as yet my wife. Maybe by the time we arrive in Warsaw, that situation will have changed, or if not, I shall have become more thick-skinned about appearances and traditions.

Please try to understand my feelings in this matter and find it in your heart not to condemn Luvna and myself. Write often, take care of yourself, and try to make Father understand my prolonged absence without explaining it in too much detail. With Mother, explanations will probably be easier.

My love to you and Meyrha. Soon, hopefully, she will be ready to try again to have a child. I pray that this time, all goes well.

Your loving brother,

Isaak."

The atmosphere of Warsaw had changed subtly but definitely over the past few months. A spirit of liberalism had arisen that was reminiscent of the early days of Wielopolski's first term of office. Adam heard fewer complaints from his patients regarding Russian intervention in their homes and workplaces. Moreover, while quota restrictions still held Jewish and other minority students to a minimum, Adam had noticed that the grounds and corridors of the Akademy were no longer patrolled by militiamen. He had heard from Markos Kolvner that this was also true at the University of Warsaw, where Markos was currently a student.

Even the publishers of the underground press had grown more daring in recent weeks, and had taken to distributing their periodicals in public places. Admittedly, this was a token gesture, since no sensible citizen of Warsaw would risk being seen picking up a copy of Prawda, for example, or reading it openly in the streets. Nonetheless, such episodes as those that Adam and Meyrha had experienced had declined from the relatively commonplace to the exceptionally rare. Governor-General Milyutin, apparently recalling belatedly his reputation for liberalism, had begun to temper his policies of sternly legalistic administration with a leaven of superficial reform. Whether or not those subject to his rule trusted the sincerity of this change of stance, they were ready to take advantage of the opportunities the new strategy afforded them.

\* \* \*

On a warm afternoon at the end of July, Pierre Rebaumme, lately of Provence, and later still of Paris, stood in his studio on Lydenska Street, critically studying the newly-finished portrait of Elana Marjzendiak. Beside him stood Pola Pietrowski, admiring the work almost as much as she admired the artist himself.

Her enthusiasm was evident in her voice. "You've caught the expression in the eyes perfectly, Pierre. There's that wary, almost brooding look she has that her smile never quite erases."

Pierre turned to her affectionately. "So you've noticed that, too, my dear. You have quite an eye. I suspect, if you studied, you could paint one day."

Pola laughed. "Not with any success." She gazed up at him fondly. "I've no such ambitions, Pierre. I leave that to you."

Pierre glanced about the studio, noting with satisfaction the elegant appointments that embellished it. A single year had brought a tremendous change in his fortunes. The feelings of uncertainty and apprehension, that had plagued him when his commission from the Pietrowski family had come to an end, had been replaced by an aura of confidence, born of success and a new-found security. With the money paid him by Mayor Oslowski and Ephraim Marjzendiak, he had purchased this spacious house with its solarium, ideally suited to be used as a studio. Other smaller commissions had enabled him to acquire the French provincial furniture he favored. In these surroundings, he felt totally at home.

"I'm proud of you, Pierre," Pola said, interrupting his musings. "You've become the leading social artist of the day."

"Thanks to your mother's patronage," Pierre said soberly. "I'm truly very grateful to her."

Pola smiled, unable to resist teasing him gently. "What about me?"

He kissed her, tenderly yet passionately. "Gratitude hardly describes my feelings for you, as you well know."

Pola nodded contentedly, but then she shivered. "I wish I could somehow shut out this gnawing dread I feel every time I think of how father is going to react to the news of your background."

Pierre's arms encircled her protectively. "Why dread, my love? Your family is probably the most liberal in all Warsaw."

"It's not my family's sentiments I'm worried about," Pola responded. "But sooner or later, no matter how careful we are, someone outside the family may learn about your Jewish heritage and use it against us."

Pierre lifted her face to his. "Is this your way of telling me that you're afraid to marry me?"

Pola clung to him, shaking her head in denial. "No, Pierre, of course not. I love you dearly. Surely you must know that by now. "

"I hope I do."

"The Vistula Provinces are very different from France, Pierre. You've told me that countless times. Here, you could be fined and imprisoned just for refusing to wear the Star of David."

"Pola, it's been eight years since I attended a synagogue service. My father disowned me before he died. He could never accept the fact that I look upon the Laws of Moses as an ethical statement of logical human behavior. To me, it doesn't require supernatural sanctions or divine enforcement. I find no solace in the concept of a cold, judgmental deity. Why should I wear a symbol of something I don't believe? It's a stupid law that deserves to be broken!"

Pola put her hands over his lips, and he saw that she was trembling.

"Don't, Pierre," she whispered. "Please don't say such things. They tempt God's anger."

"You really believe that, don't you?"

She made the sign of the cross, and tears swam in her eyes, wetting her long, pale brown lashes. "Yes, Pierre, I do." She lifted her head proudly. "I know your beliefs differ from mine, and I respect that. But you must also respect my faith. We don't have to agree about religion. We're in accord on many other things."

"I've never ridiculed your faith, Pola. I never shall. I know how much it means to you. I simply can't share your convictions about a Supreme Being, or an afterlife. I believe our time is here and now, and we must make of it what we can."

She shook her head. "I wish I could somehow persuade you to admit at least the possibility of God."

"Perhaps, once we're married, you'll convince me of the error of my ways."

"Don't mock me, Pierre. I don't think you do anything wrong. You're a good man, and you have the potential to be a great one. I'm afraid, though, that you may never quite achieve that potential as long as you insist on denying to yourself who you are, and who God is."

Pierre pointed to the painting on his easel. "This is how I express my identity, Pola. This is my faith, and my immortality. It's the only religion in which I can really believe. If God is truly the origin of all the beauty and wonder that fills the world, then He will find a way to claim me through my art, which is, after all, only a reflection of His. But I can't find Him through temples, or rabbis, or prayer books written in other men's words." He reached out to her and drew her to him. "If you can accept me on those terms."

"I love you, Pierre. I can accept you on almost any terms. Just try to be understanding if I pray for you on my terms."

He laughed joyously. "Fair enough. While you're about it, pray that your father accedes to my request and sets the date for our wedding."

Her gaze was unwavering as she asked, "Will you tell him about your life in Provence, and your family? Or shall I?"

"I'll tell him. He's agreed to see me tomorrow afternoon. I'll tell him then."

Pola smiled triumphantly and clasped his hand. "I'll come with you."

Pierre shook his head. "No, my love. By now you must be running low on ways to account for the time you've managed to spend with me. The last thing we want is for your father to think the worst."

"My father would never think the worst where I'm concerned," Pola responded confidently.

"Yes, well, there are those who might. You'd best be going now." He kissed her fondly and then walked her to the door, where a framed miniature landscape leaned against the wall. He stooped and picked it up. "Don't forget this," he said, placing the small treasure in her hands. He bent and kissed the top of her head.

"Don't be surprised if I have business at the bank tomorrow afternoon." She raised a hand to silence his objections before he could voice them. "I want Father to know we stand together, and that I'm determined to be your wife, no matter what."

Pierre accompanied her to the carriage where her maid Paulette waited impatiently, filled with curious questions and ready to admonish her young lady for the length of time she had spent in the artist's studio, unchaperoned. Pola was ready for her, however. She took her place in the carriage and bade Pierre a decorous farewell, thanking him for his trouble.

"Give my best to Madam Pietrowska," Pierre said politely. "Be sure to express my gratitude for her continued patronage."

"Of course," Pola said, smiling. "The painting is delightful. She'll be so pleased." Then she turned to Paulette as the carriage drew slowly away. "The frame wasn't quite finished. I had to wait, but it was worth it. Just look at the workmanship."

"I didn't hear any hammering," Paulette objected.

"Of course not," was Pola's rejoinder. "I defy you to find nails in that wood. The parts are joined by interlocking grooves. It's a special construction he uses in all his frames. Mother adores it. The backs are perfectly smooth. They're even padded and can never damage her walls. It's a very time-consuming process, you see."

"I see," Paulette observed, "that the artist Rebaumme has more than one patroness in this family."

Pierre could just hear the sound of Pola's bell-like laughter as the carriage drove out of sight.

* * *

Pola waited in the office of Ephraim Marjzendiak while her father and the man she loved discussed her future. It was not an unusual situation, given the time and place, but for a young girl of Pola's independent habit of mind, it was an exquisite form of torture. She paced nervously from door to window and back, until Ephraim finally asked her to be seated. She complied reluctantly, but voiced her objections.

"I have every right to be there. It's quite wrong of Father to shut me out this way. After all, it's my fate that's being decided."

Ephraim smiled indulgently. "I hardly think you're on trial, Pola."

"It's Pierre who's on trial, and I should be with him." Ephraim knew to what the young girl alluded. He could scarcely believe that he had known Pierre Rebaumme for nearly a year and had not suspected his Jewishness until Pola had revealed it to him today.

"How long," he asked, "have you known about Pierre?"

Pola turned to face this man whom she had known since she was a child. In that time, his daughter had become her closest friend, despite the differences in their backgrounds. She considered her reply for a moment. "I've known since he began to paint my portrait."

Ephraim marveled at her answer. "That long?"

"He told me about his youth. He grew up in the Jewish community of Provence. His people were treated with equality. They had autonomy unlike anything you have here."

"Strange that such a liberal existence should breed such contempt for one's origins."

"Pierre isn't contemptuous of his origins," Pola defended him. "He simply feels that the ancient doctrines of his people are open to more than one interpretation."

Ephraim frowned. "Historically, when your church's clergy discovered Catholics daring to voice alternative interpretations of traditional doctrine, they burned them as heretics, along with many of our people who refused to espouse Christianity, or who returned to their old customs and beliefs after a period of conversion." His tone was bitter. "They called it the Inquisition!"

Pola blanched. That dark period in the history of her church had been treated with deliberate vagueness in the course of her education. Ephraim's words both frightened her and also aroused her curiosity. "One day, you must explain that to me in greater detail." She arose abruptly from her chair. "Just now, I feel I must go and learn what has been decided regarding my future."

She turned and left the room. Ephraim's glance followed her across the hall to the door of Franz Pietrowski's office. She paused momentarily to listen. He saw her open the door and go inside.

Quite some time elapsed before he returned his attention to the papers on his desk. Despite the bluntness of his remark about historic Catholic treatment of heretical opinion, he liked and respected the Pietrowski family. He could foresee nothing but tragedy if his friend and employer consented to a marriage between his daughter and the renegade artist, for so Ephraim had come to think of Pierre Rebaumme in the past few minutes. The man was no less talented, and yet Ephraim's opinion of him had undergone a radical revision. How much depth and integrity could a man possess, he wondered, who lacked all spiritual conviction and who could lightly renounce the lifetime of teaching that every Jewish male was obliged to undergo by his thirteenth birthday? Ephraim felt an inherent distrust of such a man. If Franz gave his consent to gratify his daughter's desires, and the marriage ended in disaster, would he blame Pierre alone, or would his assessment of the Jews as a whole deteriorate as well? Such a result went against logic, but was a not infrequent consequence of personal disappointment.

Ephraim was half-tempted to revoke the commission he had paid Rebaumme to paint the remaining members of his family, and to return the portraits of Elana and himself. But no, he decided, that would be unseemly; a petty reaction to his own resentment of the stand Pierre had chosen to take. Each man's conscience, after all, was his own. Besides, Ephraim had no wish to initiate a course of action that might exert a negative impact on Pola's future as Pierre's wife.

He shook his head as if to dislodge such disturbing thoughts, and went back to his work. Nonetheless, his eyes repeatedly wandered to the door of Franz's office, until he finally got up from the desk and closed his own door in an effort to put an end to the distraction which Pola's words and her situation had aroused.

"I couldn't stay away any longer," Pola announced, as if to excuse herself for intruding upon this interview between her father and her beloved.

Franz looked up at her fondly, willing to excuse his cherished daughter almost anything. "Do come in, Pola," he greeted her. "After all, this does concern you."

"Precisely my opinion," Pola agreed, taking the seat her father indicated. She was gratified that it placed her near Pierre; she glanced furtively at him in an effort to gain some clue to what had passed between the two men.

Pierre seemed calm as he responded to whatever Franz had said before she entered the room. "I feel I have been perfectly candid, Mer Pietrowski. Naturally, my concern for Pola's wellbeing is as great as yours."

"I wonder if you realize, Monsieur Rebaumme, in what jeopardy she will be placed if the truth about your antecedents should become generally known."

"My antecedents," Pierre said, "are less of an issue than my religious convictions. I'm certain there are many citizens of Warsaw whose ancestors once worshipped in synagogues rather then churches. They have chosen to forsake that path and have thus gained anonymity. I see no reason why I should not do the same. I have no family living in Poland. Indeed, what family I have left has tended to ignore my existence by mutual consent. I'm content to leave things at that."

Franz gazed thoughtfully at the young man before him. He could not resist a certain aversion for a man lacking in any religious allegiance. Yet, he was forced to admit, Pierre's lack of ardent dedication to Jewish principle and practice was convenient, in view of his intentions towards Pola. Under the circumstances, it seemed best to forget, as Pierre seemed quite ready to do, that he had been brought up to espouse Judaism. For some reason, the upbringing had not taken effect.

"You realize, of course," Franz asserted emphatically, "that the marriage must take place in church, and that any children must be reared as Catholics."

Pierre nodded. "I quite understand that." He reached out to take Pola's hand as he spoke, and glanced at her reassuringly.

"Furthermore," Franz added, "Pola, despite her precociousness in some respects, is still quite young. I couldn't consider allowing her to wed before her seventeenth birthday."

Pola opened her mouth to protest, but Pierre's slight shake of the head silenced her.

"That's nearly eight months from now," Pierre said blandly. "A wedding appropriate to Pola's station, and your own, will require that long to prepare. May we say that the wedding ceremony will be our mutual birthday present to Pola, whom we both love so deeply?"

Pola gazed from one to the other, hope, uncertainty, and joyous expectation, mirrored one after the other, in her face. She seemed virtually to hang upon her father's answer.

"Agreed."

Pola sprang from her chair. "Oh, thank you, Father!" She embraced her father and her fiancé in turn.

"Thank you, sir," Pierre said, taking Franz by the hand. "I promise you won't regret this."

"I hope you're right," Franz responded, although his eyes betrayed the fact that he doubted Pierre's authority to make such a promise.

## CHAPTER TWENTY-EIGHT
## FALL, 1869

In the Great Synagogue of the Stare Miasto, the Sabbath ceremony was drawing to a close. Rabbi Dob Barush Meisels, his voice weakened by advancing age and recent illness, was concluding the final reading of the evening.

"In the day of prosperity be joyful, but in the day of adversity, consider," he quoted from Ecclesiastes. "My message to you is that you consider carefully even in the days of prosperity. May God watch over His own and may His blessings continue to enrich us. Let all say amen."

"Amen," chorused the assembled worshipers, deeply moved by the Rabbi's words.

For the past three years, Meisels had addressed the devout orthodox Jews of Warsaw only very rarely. His health was failing; furthermore, the outspoken dissent that Meisels had earlier come to personify had declined sharply in popular appeal. The program of "organic work," established by the Polish Intelligencia following the failed rebellion of 1863, had led to unprecedented prosperity in the Vistula Provinces. As a consequence, the voice of Polish Nationalism, if not silenced, had softened to a whisper.

The recent boldness of the underground press was in fact a symptom of desperation because of its declining influence. The Russian administration had lately grown less fearful of the impact of clandestine publications on the collective consciousness of the people. Their own increasing affluence, as individuals and as a society, was proving to be an effective deterrent to the once popular passion for Polish sovereignty.

Along with the other citizens of the Vistula Provinces, the Jews had witnessed an improvement in their fortunes. Many of them no longer lived in the old ghettos, although by custom they traded there and attended Sabbath and religious services in the ancient synagogues. Despite their lack of citizenship, their influence on the economy was gradually expanding, and as it did, they were evolving more sophisticated ways to deal with the challenges of the changing times.

Meisels' brief but forceful homily this evening had addressed those new challenges to his people's faith. He had described them as snares to entrap the mind and draw attention away from the central theme of Jewish life. Although he ardently supported the spirit of the Hallakah, the Jewish Enlightenment, Meisels had vigorously attacked the mentality of the marketplace and the seduction of easily attainable possessions and property. Success, he had warned, could become a narcotic that dulled the awareness of men to their higher destiny. He had outlined the traditional readiness of the Jews to embark upon the "journey of deliverance," armed with the certainty of Adonai's favor and the consciousness of their mission as His Chosen People.

In conclusion, he had exhorted the people not to lose sight of that mission, not to be distracted from it, either by adversity or by newly-gained advantage. It had been a discourse of which the ancient prophets would have been proud. Many occupants of the women's balcony had been moved to tears, and even among the men, there were a number of moist eyes and lump-filled throats.

Ephraim Marjzendiak waited in the rabbi's antechamber after the service, anxious to speak privately with Meisels regarding a personal challenge that Ephraim was currently experiencing. The two men had long since ceased to disagree on politics. Indeed, their relationship had ripened into a wary but mutually respectful friendship in the years since Ephraim had worked diligently to effect the rabbi's release from prison.

Ephraim paced restlessly. He realized that he felt closer in spirit to Rabbi Janowski than to the former firebrand Meisels. Yet, he was more willing to discuss the issue that troubled him now with this learned and tough-minded man whom he had once considered an adversary.

Even as Meisels entered the room, Ephraim was remembering the September day in 1861 when he had stood in Sigismund Square, nervously observing the crowd while Meisels and his friend Archbishop Fijalkowski stirred them with their rhetoric. He vividly recalled his dread of this man's influence on Isaak and his fear that his son might be a part of that impassioned, ill-fated gathering.

"Ephraim," Meisels greeted him warmly. "This is indeed a surprise."

"I too, am surprised," Ephraim responded. "I find myself unexpectedly in need of advice."

Meisels removed his prayer shawl and folded it carefully away. His face remained blandly expressionless as he turned back toward Ephraim. "What sort of advice?"

"I have a friend," Ephraim began, "who faces a unique dilemma."

Meisels offered Ephraim a chair and then seated himself facing his visitor. "Human problems are seldom unique, Ephraim. They're just new to those of us who have not met them before. Who is this friend?"

Ephraim's glance met the rabbi's eyes somewhat reluctantly. "He's a Gentile businessman, whose daughter is determined to wed a Jewish tradesman."

"Then it's your friend who needs advice," Meisels observed.

Ephraim cleared his throat. "He has sought it, from me. He's given his consent, and yet..."

"He still has second thoughts." Meisels nodded. "Frankly, I'm surprised that he's even considered giving his blessing to such a marriage. I'm even more surprised to hear of a Jew who aspires to marry a Gentile here in the Provinces. Fortune seems to smile upon us at present. And yet, it is often at such times that hidden snares are most numerous." Meisels paused thoughtfully. "This young man is prepared to convert, to become a Christian?"

Ephraim shook his head. "I think not. I suspect he's merely willing to conform to whatever stipulations he must."

"I see," Meisels remarked wryly. "Neither a devout Jew nor an impassioned convert. Hopefully, he's at least passionate about the young woman."

"Her family seems convinced of that."

"Then why the second thoughts?"

Ephraim shrugged. "The uncertainty of what the future may hold for us all."

"Surely your friend doesn't expect you to be a prophet." Meisels seemed to reconsider that statement for a moment. "He may in fact expect just that. I suppose we all look to our friends to help us find solutions to our problems, especially if they've been helpful in past times of need."

"We've helped each other often," Ephraim recalled, "but I don't know how to help him now."

"I gather you don't approve of this marriage," Meisels concluded.

Ephraim frowned. "I just don't know what to make of Pierre Rebaumme." He instantly regretted the fact that his emotions had betrayed him into revealing the man's identity.

Meisels gazed curiously at Ephraim. "The artist? How is he involved?"

"He's the prospective bridegroom," Ephraim responded.

"But you said the girl had decided to marry a Jew."

"Rebaumme's family is Jewish. They're residents of France where there are no badges, no restrictions, no inequality, or so I'm told. "

"Ah," Meisels said, "now I begin to understand. With that background, he sees no difference between himself and this girl, while you see only the differences, and the dangers."

"Precisely."

Rabbi Meisels laid a hand on the table beside him and used it to push himself to his feet. Ephraim also stood and reached out to aid the older man, but Meisels gently shrugged off his hand.

"For as long as I can, I shall get about on my own. But thank you for the offer." He moved to the cupboard and retrieved his hat, his coat, and his muffler. "There is no easy solution to your friend's dilemma, Ephraim. None of us can read the future. Pierre Rebaumme, by his actions and his silence, has chosen to deny his heritage. It seems he made that choice long before he elected to take a shiksa bride. Perhaps the less restrictive ways of central Europe make such decisions easier. We fight hardest for the things that are threatened in our lives. The fear of losing them makes them seem that much more valuable."

"Rebaumme seems to value my friend's daughter," Ephraim noted, remembering just in time not to mention Pola's name, though if the wedding took place, soon all Warsaw would know.

"I dare say he does value her now," Meisels said. "There is still some uncertainty, still the possibility of losing her. Whether or not that feeling perseveres will depend on his moral strength, and the intensity of his commitment to her."

"Can a man who denies his faith and his people," Ephraim wondered aloud, "have moral strength or commitment?"

Meisels adjusted his muffler and put on his coat with Ephraim's help, this time not refusing the offer of assistance. "Each of us has his own overwhelming desire, his ruling obsession. Mine has been the freedom of this nation, and I shall not live to see it achieved. Perhaps this artist has found his obsession in a woman. He may be more fortunate than I in gaining his desire."

Meisels' words reminded Ephraim of the compelling passion that had swept through him in the moment when he had first seen Elana at the back door of her father's house in Grojec. He would have dared any odds, defied any obstacles to possess her. Indeed, he had defied her father, had even deceived him about his education in order to win her. But then he had made it right by accomplishing all that he had promised for her, and more. However, there was one important difference between Rebaumme's situation and his own. Elana and he shared the same traditions, the same beliefs. Between Pola and Rebaumme there existed no such bond to withstand the setbacks and hardships of life.

Ephraim looked at Meisels with evident concern. "And when he's wed her, what then?"

"Then," Meisels answered, "the rest is in Adonai's hands, as it is with us all."

Meisels turned and walked toward the door that led to the street behind the synagogue. Ephraim followed, aware that the conversation was at an end. Meisels opened the door and held it for him, and the two men walked together for a time in silence until Ephraim reached his carriage and Meisels turned down the short lane that led to his house.

Throughout the long drive home, Ephraim sat with Elana at his side, deep in silent thought. Elana did not ask the reason for his preoccupation. The two had been one long enough for such questions to be unnecessary.

In Franz's place, Ephraim knew he would not allow his daughter to marry a man of another faith, and certainly not a man who professed no faith at all. However, he reminded himself sternly, he was not in Franz's place.

*  *  *

On an afternoon early in December, Pola and Leah were in the older girl's sitting room, engaged in the type of lightly teasing dialogue typical of school girls.

"How," Leah asked, straight-faced, "can you be certain of his feelings for you? Is it the way he looks at you, or his smile? Can you tell from his touch when he takes your hand?"

Pola grinned. "It's all those things, and more. We love each other. We have for more than a year."

"But why," Leah persisted, "do you love him? What is it that is so special about him?"

Pola stood and paced the room for a moment, her face serious, a frown creasing her brow. "There're so many things, it's hard to put them into words. Pierre is different from anyone I've met. Oh yes, he's tall and handsome, and his eyes are like no others I've ever seen, but that's not why I want to be his wife."

Leah asked intently, "What is the reason?"

"It's his mind, and the way he expresses his thoughts. There's a directness about him, a singleness of purpose that I admire. Once he sets a goal for himself, nothing distracts him from it." She moved to the window and gazed out at the familiar setting of her family's garden. "And there's the way he sees things. I mean he really sees them, form and color in infinite variety, subtle shadings, and color values that other people never notice. Since I've known Pierre, I see things differently, too." She beckoned Leah to join her in the window seat, and pointed at the cypress tree that grew beside her window. "When I was small, I used to look out this window and think how ordinary that tree was, with its unrelieved green foliage and never any flowers. But then, Pierre made me see all the many shades of green it has, and how shapely it is."

Leah peered in wonder at the tree, as if seeing it for the first time. Then she laughed. "You're teasing me, aren't you?"

Pola shook her head. "Pierre says it has a dozen different values of green and blue, and now that he's pointed them out, I can see them, too." She turned to Leah, her eyes glowing with excitement. "Knowing him has made the world a brighter, more exciting place for me. I'm never bored with him, or tired. He can find beauty in the simplest things, and make them seem quite special." She hugged Leah fondly. "I've never felt this happy before. I never imagined it was possible."

Leah looked earnestly at her friend. "Can you really be totally happy, Pola, knowing the risks involved in this marriage?"

"Compared to what I feel, the risks don't matter." She paused, her enthusiasm momentarily dampened by Leah's serious words. "Oh, they matter to mother and father, and I know they exist. Pierre and I have talked about them, but he's more important to me than what other people think. And if it becomes too hard for us to live here in Warsaw, we'll have to look elsewhere."

"Would you really move away from your home and your family?"

"Leah, when I marry, my home will be with Pierre. Besides, the railroad runs between most of the major cities. If we did leave, I could always come back to visit."

Leah's eyes widened. "He means that much to you?"

"He means my whole life to me. Oh, Leah, you have so much to look forward to. When I think of myself before I met Pierre, I was a totally different person, a child. And now, because of him, I'm a woman. I know what I want, and I shall have it. It's like you, and your music. Just now, that's the most important thing in your life, isn't it?"

Leah nodded.

"Well, that's what Pierre is to me."

"I hope you'll always feel that way, Pola," Leah said with utmost sincerity. "I hope you'll never regret."

Pola put her hand over the younger girl's mouth. "Pierre has taught me that life is a matter of choices. We're free to make those choices and once they're made, it's pointless to look back. I won't regret loving him because we're each a part of the other now. When our children are born, they'll be part of both of us. I'll be too busy trying to teach them to survive in a world full of change and uncertainty to have time for regrets." She took Leah's face in her hands. "Now stop looking so glum and be happy for me. Some day, when you've found the man you're to love, then you'll understand how I feel."

Leah forced herself to smile, suppressing her inner doubts. She wished fervently for Pola's happiness, no matter what the odds against that outcome. At this point, she was not quite certain whether she cared if Pierre were happy or not. Leah, after all, had been reared as a devout daughter of Judaism. Pierre's cavalier renunciation of his own upbringing seemed to her either a callous betrayal of values she held dear, or else a demonstration of incredible shallowness of spirit. Either way, she felt repelled by him in spite of his undeniable talent.

Wisely, she kept her thoughts to herself as she dutifully resumed helping Pola compile her list of wedding guests, the task they had temporarily abandoned. As she neatly wrote names in Pola's ledger, her thoughts strayed to Markos Kolvner. She did not fully understand her friend's mood of seeming indifference to what Leah perceived as very real peril. However, she realized suddenly that her own life would seem colorless and hopelessly bitter if she were to be prevented from ever seeing Markos again. The image of his intent young face with its clear gray eyes, ivory skin, and finely chiseled features, was etched sharply in her mind. She found herself recalling the cadence of his voice, and the pressure of his hands as he had guided her in the final waltz at Madam Pietrowska's soiree.

His ambitious plans for expanding the family's import business both thrilled her and filled her with dread. She knew well the envy shown by the middle class Poles to those Jewish factory owners who had managed to prosper since the uprising. She could readily imagine an even more bitter resentment following in the wake of the innovations Markos hoped to accomplish. Nonetheless, Leah knew that she passionately hoped for the success of those plans, and that she would be delighted to share in the process of bringing them to fruition. Was that, she wondered, what Pola was feeling as the elder girl dreamed of and prepared for her wedding? Were the two of them so very different after all?

*  *  *

Scarcely a week later, Leah found the tranquility of her private world profoundly disturbed. In a sense, it was a joyous disturbance, one to which she had unconsciously been looking forward. Like a small pebble dropped gently into a pond, it began rather mundanely with a letter given to her by Professor Krause. The envelope had been addressed to him, and she was puzzled when he presented it to her with a ceremonious little bow.

"Welcome," he said, "to the world of seasoned musical artists. Here, ma petite, is what I feel represents the gateway to your future."

Such portentous words, such formality of manner, and yet it was entirely in character for her charmingly eccentric, brilliant piano teacher. The letter, she discovered, had been sent by the prestigious Berlin Konservatory of Musik, that legendary center of learning from which Professor Krause had graduated. The Dean of the Konservatory had written to Armand Krause, a "revered alumnus," to inquire whether he was currently instructing any gifted students whom he could honestly recommend to the Board for consideration for their international scholarship competition. The letter further stated that the three contestants who scored highest in the competition would be given the opportunity to study for three years at the Konservatory without charge; they would, in other words, each be awarded a scholarship.

When she read those words, Leah felt as if the floor had swayed beneath her feet. If she entered, and her application was accepted, it would mean the chance of a lifetime. For a week thereafter, she could barely contain herself. She slept fitfully, tossing for hours, her mind filled with thoughts of the famous Konservatory, and of the competition that could prove to be the key to gaining entrance to its hallowed halls. With her teacher, Leah debated the likelihood of her application being accepted. The fact that because she was a girl, she might therefore be considered ineligible, repeatedly recurred to plague her.

Armand Krause assured her that his letter of recommendation would counterbalance that drawback, and that his outstanding reputation as a musician and teacher would serve as surety for her candidacy. Still, Leah found herself torn between self-assured enthusiasm and profound self doubt.

Reluctant just yet to share either her secret hopes and plans or her apprehensions about them with her family, Leah contrived to discuss them at length with Markos Kolvner, who had become her special friend and confidant. The occasion was a walk in the Marjzendiak gardens during one of Markos's increasingly more frequent visits. In order to be near Leah, the young merchant had recently made a practice of bringing merchandise from his family's import shop for Elana's inspection. Often, if she favored an item, he would present it to her as a gift. On other occasions, when she refused to accept an outright present, he would grant her a large discount. Furthermore, he found ways to make himself useful by helping her in the garden or performing errands that insured he would have to return to the estate.

Today, despite the cold weather, the air was dry and brisk and the clear sky was filled with winter sunshine. Dressed warmly in cloak, muff, and bonnet, Leah walked with Markos along the well-swept paths, chatting and laughing like a playful child. She was three weeks away from her fourteenth birthday and had grown four inches in the preceding summer. The blue-green hue of her new ensemble complimented her auburn hair and her gold-flecked brown eyes. The chill breeze had brought a rosy glow to her cheeks, and her newly-increased stature imparted to her a regal grace that was not lost on her companion.

"But of course you must apply," Markos said decisively. "The worst they can do is to deny your application, and with Professor Krause's personal endorsement, there's no cause to assume they'll do that."

"Not until they see me," she said bleakly.

Markos turned to her, smiling. "When they see you, they'll fall in love with you just as I have."

"Oh Markos, they're all grown men, and seasoned musicians. They won't even see me as you do. Furthermore, once they know I'm a girl, I won't have a chance."

"Don't say that! Professor Krause accepted you as his pupil on the strength of your merit, not your gender."

"Professor Krause is a remarkable man," Leah answered. "If only there were more like him."

Markos was steadfast in his encouragement. "How do you know there aren't until you try to find out for certain?"

They walked on in silence for a while, enjoying the beauty of the scene around them. When they reached the gazebo of the rose garden, Markos gallantly swept the snow from the edges of the seat and the two sat down to talk further.

"My father thinks of my music as a pretty pastime," Leah said. "To him, it's something to occupy me until I get married. Although he enjoys my playing, he really doesn't take it seriously."

"But it's serious to you!"

"Of course it is," Leah acknowledged. "Sometimes I think it's the most important thing in my life."

"Then compete for the scholarship," Markos encouraged her. "Show him how wrong his idea is."

"That's what I want to do, Markos. That's what I think I should do. And yet, if I don't perform well…"

"You will," Markos interrupted. "I know you will. I have complete faith in you."

Markos took her by the shoulders and turned her so that she faced him squarely. "If you're really serious about a career in music, you're going to have to assert yourself. You're going to have to take advantage of your opportunities."

Leah looked deeply into Markos's eyes. "You really think I can succeed, Markos?"

"I'm certain of it."

Leah suddenly remembered Markos's words on the evening of Madam Pietrowski's soiree, when he had expressed a twinge of jealousy because of her dedication to music, triggered by the response of the distinguished audience to her performance on that occasion. Mischievously, she asked, "If I do succeed, Markos, will you mind terribly? Will you still love me?"

Markos laughed and held her closer. "How could I do otherwise? I'm bound to you for better or worse, Leah Marjzendiak. There'll never be another girl for me."

Thrilled by the promise of those words, Leah joyfully reached up and wrapped both her arms about Markos's neck. Gently, she drew his face down close to her own and pressed her mouth against his. Both were delighted. Their lips clung together and their arms twined around each other in a fond and increasingly intimate embrace until finally Leah broke away, blushing and embarrassed.

"We shouldn't," she whispered, hiding her face.

Markos took that face in both hands and tenderly lifted it. He gazed into her eyes and smiled lovingly. "There's nothing wrong in a kiss between two people who love each other," he said softly. "It's wonderful to learn that we do love each other. It's the first time you've let me know."

Leah returned his smile shyly. "It's the first time you've shown your faith in me."

Markos ran his fingers through Leah's wealth of auburn hair and drew her head to rest against his shoulder. "It won't be the last," he promised.

* * *

Buoyed up by the magnitude of Markos's belief in her talent, Leah decided to submit her application. Professor Krause was delighted, for he was as certain as Markos that his gifted pupil would acquit herself well. Only one obstacle remained, the application fee. Leah's parents were unfailingly generous with her; however, the fee amounted to thirty zloty, an exorbitant sum to be entrusted to so young a girl without a detailed explanation of her need for it.

Markos confirmed his statement of faith in Leah by offering to pay the fee himself. She was pleased and grateful; however, she felt awkward about accepting the money from him. Instead she elected to turn to Elana and to confide in her regarding the competition that she hoped would be the turning point in her life.

She chose a moment when her mother was engaged in preparing the evening meal. Although the family fortunes had improved dramatically over the years, Elana still did most of the cooking and planned all the menus herself. Leah admired her for this, considering it an evidence of her dedication to her family.

Leah stood for a few moments, quietly observing Elana from a remote corner of the pantry. When she saw her move to the stove to check the temperature of the oil she was slowly heating, Leah entered the room. An assortment of vegetables lay on the counter, ready to be chopped and cooked. Leah picked up a small knife from the drawer and began to prepare them. Intent upon her task, Elana was momentarily surprised. Then she smiled and moved to her daughter's side.

"I remember," she remarked, "when you used to plead with me to let you help in the kitchen, and then you could barely see over the counter top." She reached up and stroked Leah's hair. "Now, you're taller than I. Soon you'll be a woman, ready for marriage and the management of your own household."

Leah shook her head. "Not for a while yet, Mother."

"Markos seems very anxious to move in that direction," Elana observed. "He can scarcely take his eyes away from you. It's understandable. You've grown to be quite a beauty." As Leah looked up in response to that statement, Elana continued. "Do you feel equally drawn to him? If you don't, you should tell him now rather than letting him hope and plan in vain."

"I feel very close to Markos, Mother. I admire him very much. It's just that marriage and family still seem very far away. Besides," she added with a resolute stroke of her knife, "Markos and I are agreed that for now, I should concentrate on my music."

"My dear," Elana said earnestly, "we've spoken of this before. You have very little to hope for in that direction. You play beautifully and skillfully, but…"

"Opportunities in music are very rare for women," Leah finished the statement for her. "I know that, Mother, but I'll never forgive myself if I don't try. Don't you see? I have to make the effort. I'll never know if I might have succeeded unless I do."

Elana took hold of Leah's hands and lifted them from the counter top. "Professor Krause has trained you well, dear, and yet I'm sure even he must know the odds against any kind of career for you. In a sense, it was almost a cruelty. I sometimes regret persuading your father to let you study with him. I did it because of Madam Pietrowska's insistence, and because you seemed so sad, so lonely and restless at that time."

Leah disengaged her hands from her mother's grasp. "Mother, please don't regret that decision. Music is the joy of my life. No matter what the future holds, it always will be. And I shall always be thankful that you helped me to become acquainted with it." She dried her hands and withdrew the Professor's letter from her pocket. "Now I need your help again."

Elana extracted the carefully folded sheet from its envelope and read the words that had so fired Leah's imagination. "How can I help you in this, child?"

"Professor Krause has written a letter of recommendation for me, and I filled out the application. There remains only the fee that must go with it."

Elana listened while Leah explained the details of the competition as Armand Krause had outlined them to her. He had won that event many years ago, and his memories of the series of concerts, after each of which more contestants were eliminated, had filled Leah with a combination of excitement, hope, and dread. She trembled as she described them. Finally, she told her mother that the competition for their area would be held at Lodz.

"And now you want me to give you the money to compete for this scholarship, as your teacher did?"

"Yes, Mother, I do. I want that more than I've ever wanted anything."

"And if you fail?"

"Then at least I'll have tried!"

Elana silently considered that for several moments. Meanwhile, she took the vegetables Leah had chopped and cautiously placed them in the pan to cook. Then she turned back to face her daughter.

"Very well. We shall use this event as a test. I'll come with you, and you shall compete with many other talented young people. We shall see what the judges decide. Will that satisfy you?"

"Oh yes, Mother."

"And if you don't succeed there, will you finally give up this unlikely dream of yours and accept the world as it is?"

It was Leah's turn to think long and hard before she gave an answer. Finally, she nodded, determined that she would work hard to prepare for the test that lay before her. She was confident that, with Adonai's help, she would prevail upon the judges with her talent and her skill.

## CHAPTER TWENTY-NINE
## 1870: A NEW DECADE BEGINS

Since Adam had returned from Krakow, four years earlier, he and Leah had celebrated their birthdays together. Born in the month of January, though sixteen years apart, they had, by an undeclared mutual consent come to look upon the third week of that month as a cue for family celebration. It was a convenient period for merrymaking, as it was also the time of the semester break. The news that Isaak was coming home for a brief visit during a break in his law practice added to the family's festive mood.

For Leah, there was an additional cause for rejoicing. She had just received notification from Armand Krause that her application for the scholarship competition had been accepted. It was the most wonderful birthday present she could possibly have had. Although she deeply appreciated every token of affection that her family showered upon her, her highest joy derived from the knowledge of that acceptance and the tantalizing future which it seemed to promise.

It seemed to Leah that there had never been so glorious a birthday party. She had forced herself to sit still while Elana dressed her hair for the occasion. In the mirror, she saw a grown up young lady, partly familiar and partly a stranger. She exulted over her dress, a white confection of silk layered with lace and trimmed with pale blue ribbons woven through the edges of the lace ruffles. These were held in place with miniature ice blue rose buds. A matching blue bow fastened back the long, lustrous auburn curls.

Just before they went in to dinner, Ephraim had clasped around her throat a necklace from Teyva Insbruk's downtown shop, made of hand-worked silver and platinum, studded with pearls and garnished with small sapphires. It was a generous gift, a treasure to be cherished and passed on to one's progeny.

She threw her arms about her father's neck and whispered, "Oh thank you, Papa. It's beautiful."

"It's more than that, tzatzkala," Izaak commented. "It's worth a fortune. Quite a valuable present for a fourteen-year old."

"I'm almost a woman," Leah responded indignantly, drawing herself up to her newly-achieved full height.

"You look like a woman in that dress," Markos said admiringly. "A stunningly lovely one." He took her hands in his and brought them to his lips. Then, gallantly, he tucked one of her slender, graceful hands into the curve of his arm and led her to the table.

Adam followed with his mother, and Isaak escorted Meyhra. Ephraim was Mira's escort while Franz accompanied Pola. Although he had been invited, Erik Pietrowski, attending school in Krakow, had missed his train and, thus delayed, would not be able to attend the dinner party. Professor Krause arrived at the last moment, and hastily took his place on Elana's right as the family and their guests were seated. Ephraim gave the traditional blessing of breaking bread, and then the meal proceeded.

Leah, in a mood of exhilaration, was scarcely aware of the menu. She would later recall simply that everything seemed to delight her and that a warm glow filled the room. She recalled her statement to Isaak that she was almost a woman, and she glanced across the table at Markos, feeling his eyes upon her and enjoying every moment of his obvious admiration.

As Leah gazed about the table while the dessert course was being served, her eyes filled with tears. I'm happier than I've ever been, she thought. Then why am I crying? Instinctively, even as the thought occurred to her, she knew the answer. If she was this happy now, what could she look forward to in the future? Would her next birthday hold as much promise as did this one, or by then would her precious dream be lost to her?

As Elana brought in the large birthday cake, her eyes and Leah's met. The secret bargain the two of them had made lay like a shadow between them. Leah felt a momentary apprehension even as her family and friends wished her and Adam happiness. She knew with a sudden, painful conviction, that although her mother loved her dearly and did not doubt her talent, because of prevailing prejudice, she expected Leah to fail in the competition. That would provide an easy solution to the problem of Leah's musical ambitions. It was a singularly undermining thought; one that cast a pall over her heretofore unqualified enjoyment of the occasion.

Armand Krause, sensing the change in Leah's mood, and aware of the subtle nuances of the situation, pushed back his chair, came to his feet, and lifted his glass in a toast.

"To Leah," he said grandly. "May all her most cherished dreams come true. May her life be long, joyful, prosperous, and filled with success." He smiled, his eyes twinkling as everyone at the table joined in the toast, drinking, laughing, and applauding Leah. Her eyes, as she turned to him, reflected her gratitude and her love.

Ephraim then proposed a toast to Adam, wishing him success in his medical practice, his teaching career, and in the academic research on which he had recently embarked. There was a poignancy to the fact that he made no mention of the wish that was dearest to his own heart, that Adam and Meyhra would soon have a child to carry on the Marjzendiak name, to insure that the blood line of Ephraim's first-born son would be maintained.

\* \* \*

On March 17, 1870, after a prolonged and debilitating illness, Rabbi Meisels died. Warsaw's Jewish community deeply mourned his passing. The attendance for his memorial service filled the Great Synagogue and overflowed onto the steps and courtyard beyond. Meisels' son Isaak had come from Krakow for the service. His words of tribute to his father were a stirring reminder of all that the elder Meisels had contributed to the Jewish heritage, his writings, his sermons, his public service and political activities.

Rabbi Janowski conducted the service. He acknowledged receipt of numerous letters, many from outside the Vistula Provinces, expressing a sense of loss at Meisels' passing. A large number of the correspondents had not even been personally acquainted with the elder rabbi. However, his reputation as a champion of the Enlightenment and of the God-given rights of all men had endeared him to those who shared his sentiments. Janowski read excerpts from a few of the letters, and added commentary that expressed his own feelings for the man with whom he had not always agreed, but whom he could not help but admire.

Ephraim Marjzendiak, listening to his friend's words, knew them to be true. He, too, had not agreed with Meisels' methods, but Ephraim had revered the man and his motives. Even in his declining years, Meisels' wisdom, wit, and unfailingly optimistic faith in Adonai had been an inspiration to his people.

"Our beloved brother has set for us a glorious example in his death even as he did in his life," Janowski concluded. "He bore pain and suffering cheerfully and without complaint. With the death of Dob Baruch Meisels, an era of pride and passion has come to a close for our people."

*  *  *

On May 12, 1870, Pola Pietrowski's seventeenth birthday, Franz Pietrowski escorted his only daughter down the center aisle of St. John's Cathedral to the strains of the traditional wedding march, and gave her to her bridegroom. Despite Pola's undisguised joy and Mira's aura of triumphant self-satisfaction, Franz retained a small stubborn qualm of doubt about the advisability of this marriage. He liked his prospective son-in-law and wished him well, but his banker's soul would have been more at peace if Pierre were engaged in a more conventional line of work. Franz would also have preferred to have known Pierre much longer, and to have been acquainted with his family. Above all, despite Pierre's agreement to permit Pola to raise their children as Catholics, Franz would have liked Pierre to be a personally religious and God-fearing man.

The bank commissioner liked his world to be stable and predictable. He detested uncertainties and feared surprises. Order was the ruling tenet of his life. Yet he was giving his carefully reared and nurtured Pola in marriage to a man of foreign origin who earned his livelihood by painting pictures and relying upon capricious public whim to compensate him for his efforts. Franz knew well just how erratic human opinion can be. The career of Marquis Alexander Wielopolski had been a vivid example.

Wielopolski had first assumed power in 1860 amid widespread adulation. Both the tsar and a large segment of the Polish people had looked forward to his administration with happy anticipation. Yet within less than two years, the marquis had barely escaped two assassination attempts and had been forced to resign in disgrace in the face of revolution.

As Franz watched Pierre place the elegant wide gold wedding band on Pola's finger, he wondered uneasily just how long the artist's prosperity was destined to endure and, more important, how long his daughter's happiness would last.

The wedding reception following the ceremony was a gala event, which Warsaw's major dignitaries, economic and social leaders attended in great numbers. However, none of the groom's family was present. His cousin Philippe and his aunt Marie were his only remaining relatives. He had dutifully sent them a steady supply of funds throughout his stay in Russian Poland; he loved them both dearly, but the relationship between Pierre and his paternal aunt had characteristically been less than smooth. Marie Rebaumme De Mannier was adamantly Jewish. She had little patience with her intellectual renegade of a nephew, regardless of his charm and his undeniable talent. Furthermore, she resented Pierre's pervasive influence on young Philippe, whom she was determined to raise as a devout Jew. That was the only way to fulfill the promise she had made to her younger brother at the time of his death.

As he accepted the good wishes of the wedding guests, Pierre Rebaumme privately considered what his reaction might be if his orthodox Jewish aunt were to arrive on the scene, draped in her heavy white lace prayer veil, accompanied by cousin Philippe, wearing a yarmulke. In all honesty, he had to admit that he would be devastated. That was obviously why he had repeatedly postponed sending his aunt word of his marriage plans until after it was far too late for her to attend.

Gazing at his beautiful bride, with her honey-colored hair, vivid deep blue eyes, and delicate fair skin, Rebaumme felt fully justified, both in what he had done and what he had omitted. He knew there was nothing he would not do to demonstrate his love for Pola. He contemplated their future together with great enthusiasm and expectation.

*  *  *

On a warm day in late June, Leah Marjzendiak sat in the third row of wooden benches, temporarily set up to accommodate the contestants, at one end of the stage in the concert hall at Lodz. Her demeanor was calm and self-possessed as she surveyed the members of the audience. The first two rows contained the judges and other dignitaries of the competition. The remaining seats were filled by friends and relatives of the contestants and by local aficionados of classical music.

Lodz was a city with a long history of culture and elegance. Throughout the railway journey from Warsaw, Leah had sat with her mother, her teacher, and her beloved Markos, animatedly discussing all she had heard and read about their destination. By this means, she had sought to conceal as best she could her growing nervousness and anxiety. She was grateful that her mother had seen fit to gloss over the exact details of the scholarship in her discussions of the competition with Ephraim. Obviously, Elana had preferred to await the decision of the judges before addressing what should be done about the prize, if indeed there was a prize for Leah.

Except for thirteen-year-old Mischa Gregorvich, the Russian "boy wonder," Leah was the youngest of the applicants. Three scholarships were being offered to a field of thirty aspirant eastern European musicians, each of whom was well-trained and highly-recommended, and all, with the single exception of Leah Marjzendiak, were Gentile. Only eight of those thirty now remained in the competition, and Leah was grateful that she had survived the elimination process. At least, if nothing more, she could feel proud to have reached the final round.

Thus far, she had done well. She had performed at the peak of her capabilities. Every note had been produced with precision and clarity. However, she felt less certain of her interpretation. She feared her playing might have seemed mechanical because of her fears, her inexperience, and her youth.

Now, as the time for her last performance of the competition drew near, Leah could feel the palms of her hands moist with perspiration. She held them clasped primly together in her lap in an effort to control their trembling. Her eyes sought out her mother, her teacher, and her friend, hoping to catch the glance of at least one of them. Elana and Professor Krause were deeply engrossed in conversation, but Markos raised his eyes from the program in his hand just in time to engage her hopeful gaze. He smiled reassuringly and blew her a kiss. Leah responded by blushing, smiling shyly, and lowering her eyes.

Lately, she had found that Markos had only to smile at her or touch her ever-so-lightly and he could stir feelings in her for which she could find no name. She was half-frightened by those feelings and not a little disturbed, but she could not deny that she found the disturbance pleasurable. She risked a second glance to find that Markos was still looking fondly in her direction. She raised her hand in salutation, then was startled to hear her name announced by the moderator. It was her turn. This was the final test.

Leah rose to her feet, then stopped, willing herself to move sedately, forcing her features into a mask of calm self-possession. She smiled serenely, aware of Markos' admiring glance as she walked gracefully to the piano. She promised herself silently that she was going to enjoy these next few minutes. She would forget about the competition and remember only her love of music and her joy in playing it.

She took her place on the narrow piano stool, drew in a deep breath, and waited for a sign from the moderator. She stole a moment to look toward the row of seats where the judges sat waiting. Then, at the moderator's sign, she began to play. The strains of Mozart's piano Sonata in D Major filled the hall. The first movement, with its vigor and strength, contrasted sharply with the tender expressiveness of the second. Each provided an opportunity for the performer to showcase her varied capabilities. However, it was the final movement, with its exceptional counterpoint, that was the most difficult and most impressive segment of all. Armand Krause had chosen the work deliberately for Leah's last selection. He knew that Mozart's Germanic background would be especially pleasing to the judges from Berlin, and that Leah's virtuoso brilliance would highlight her performance of the composer's last piano sonata.

By the time the final notes of Mozart's work faded into silence, Leah felt an inexpressible joy sweep over her. She knew she had played superlatively, not only with technical brilliance but with the expressiveness that the composition demanded. She was happier than she had ever been in her short life. She heard the resounding applause filling the auditorium. She rose and curtsied, smiling graciously, exulting as the waves of approval seemed to engulf her. The feeling was as heady as the effects of her first taste of champagne at her birthday party given months earlier.

As she stood on the stage of the concert hall in Lodz, acknowledging the applause of the audience and the approval of the judges, she knew suddenly that her life had just turned in a new direction. The decision of the judges had yet to be announced, and all seven of her competitors had performed extremely well. Moreover, all of them were men, and Leah was objective enough to admit to herself that Gregorivich was by far the best of the lot. Still, that left two other scholarships to be awarded, and if the youthful Russian stood first, Leah firmly and honestly believed she held a clear edge for second place, regardless of either age or gender.

Armand Krause had warned her that the final decision must await the results of the other regional contests. Therefore, she was not surprised when the moderator, Henrich von Keller, announced from the podium that the names and standings of the winners would be published and their respective teachers notified within three weeks.

"Naturally," Herr von Keller concluded, "in every competition there are winners and there are those who do not win. However, all of you who have played here today can feel proud of your achievement. Each of you has something special to contribute to the world of music."

On the train back to Warsaw, Leah and Elana conversed earnestly, Elana cautioning Leah not to pin her hopes on winning one of the coveted prizes. Privately, Elana felt divided; if Leah was not among the winners, the child would be profoundly disappointed. She had worked diligently and well to prepare herself, and to Elana's untrained ear, her performance had seemed flawless. However, if Leah won, Elana feared that Ephraim might refuse even to hear of her going to study and reside alone in Berlin. They had no relatives living there as they had in Krakow, where Adam and Isaak had gone to study eight years earlier. Which, she wondered, would be worse for her daughter: not to win, or not to be able to accept her prize if she did win?

Elana's attention was temporarily distracted from this disturbing question by a youth in his late teens approaching from the opposite end of the railway car. He had the lanky coltishness adolescence often imparts to those who in maturity are destined to retain a slim and elegant grace. The youth's garments spoke of rural origins and had a distinctly foreign flavor. As he took his seat, Elana noticed that he wore a yarmulke and that his beard was just beginning to cast a dark shadow against his fair cheeks. What caught her attention about him most of all was the fact that nowhere on his clothing did he wear the tell-tale star-shaped badge. She smiled graciously and beckoned him to join her party.

Several details of his features and bearing titillated Elana's memory, and yet as the young man drew near, she realized that he was not, after all, the younger image of the man of whom he reminded her.

"Forgive me," Elana said, "but I couldn't help but notice that you, also, are Jewish."

"Yes, Madam," was the polite reply.

"But you're not wearing the Star of David," Elana said, her concern evident in her voice.

"But I am," the youth answered, lifting a star-shaped silver pendant from beneath his shirt.

Professor Krause, intrigued by the newcomer, entered the conversation. "I don't think you quite understand, young man," he said earnestly. "You must wear a yellow star sewn to your outer garment so that it's clearly visible."

The young man was plainly puzzled. Suddenly, he smiled.

"Would it help if I wore the silver star outside?" He adjusted the small pendant so that it shone metallically against the somber darkness of his shirt.

"Temporarily, yes," Krause said helpfully, "since it's obvious from your clothing and your accent that you're from another country. "

"I am French," the youth said simply, but he was obviously concerned by the suddenly serious mood of his new acquaintances.

As the party journeyed on toward Warsaw, the name and identity of the young man were revealed. He was a native of Provence whose widowed aunt had been his guardian. It was fortunate, he stated, that his people favored simple ceremonies and frugal rites, and that the Chabrah Kaddishah took charge of the details of preparing a body for burial.

The proceeds from the sale of his aunt's modest farm constituted the youth's only inheritance. Alone, he said, he could never have run the place. Far better to sell to a family of farmers than to let it go for taxes.

He had judiciously sewn the bulk of the money into his clothing, a tactic which made him seem less lean than he truly was. With the remainder, he had bought a railway ticket to Warsaw and financed his expense en route. As he candidly explained, he had but one living relative, whom he sought to join and reside with until he could find work and become self-supporting. That relative was Pierre Rebaumme.

Whenever he worked, Pierre Rebaumme required absolute quiet. He depended upon total concentration, total dedication of every fiber of his being to his art. Since their marriage, Pola had striven to maintain an atmosphere conducive to her husband's creative efforts. Today was no exception to that rule, even though within the confines of her own mind, Pola felt like screaming at the top of her voice.

Before her stood a young boy in picturesque attire, claiming to be her husband's only living relative. He was handsome, polite, and obviously well brought up. He possessed some of Pierre's most endearing features. They had the same coloring, and the pale, golden-brown eyes of the youth before her were almost identical to Pierre's. Young Philippe Rebaumme was quite a presentable young man. He was also undeniably Jewish, as proclaimed by his dress, his light trace of a beard and his haircut; even his manner of speech was definitive of his origin, though this was softened by the foreign quality of his accent.

Having the truth of her husband's origins known to her family and a few close friends was one thing; having it widely disseminated throughout the city was quite another. That could have far-reaching consequences that would exert a distinctly negative impact on them both. As she welcomed Philippe into her home, Pola recalled bitterly her words to Leah only a few months earlier. Truly, Pierre did mean more to her than what other people thought. Furthermore, she would willingly leave Warsaw rather than give him up. Nonetheless, she had never expected her love and loyalty to be so quickly and severely put to the test. With a smile that belied her feelings, she excused herself and went to call Pierre.

In his studio, the artist was applying the finishing touches to a portrait commissioned prior to his wedding. Because of the necessary interruption entailed by that happy event, he was now obliged to hurry to complete the work on schedule. The subject, he mused, was a young woman not much older than Pola but who was her direct opposite in every detail of appearance. The face in the portrait was gypsy-dark, crowned by a wealth of dark brown hair and highlighted by a set of finely-chiseled features, except for the voluptuous cherry-red mouth that smiled seductively from the canvas. Mayor Oslowski's twenty-year-old daughter Madjelin possessed a luscious beauty that glowed with exuberant warmth even in two dimensions. The painting seemed to possess a life of its own.

Pierre stood back to admire the finished work and became suddenly aware of Pola's presence. He faced her somewhat nervously, embarrassed at being found admiring his own handiwork and also overcome by a subtle guilt due to his basically male appreciation of the image of a beautiful woman who was not his wife.

Pola, however, failed to notice his discomfiture. She was far too engrossed in the problem presented by Philippe's unannounced arrival to feel any jealousy of either the painted image or the living model. In her mind's eye, she foresaw her world crashing slowly around her, her safe sheltered existence coming to an abrupt end. Privately, she wished there were some convenient secret place in which she might conceal her cousin-by-marriage indefinitely. All these months, she realized, she had blithely acknowledged the concept of Pierre's Jewishness, knowing well that it was a concept he himself rejected. Now, in the person of Cousin Philippe, she was forced to confront the fact of her husband's background, with all its painful ramifications. Notwithstanding her brave resolve, she shrank in fear from that confrontation.

Pierre's greeting of his cousin, the comradely embrace, the dialogue of reminiscences recounting their shared childhood experiences in France, all these played before Pola's eyes like the distorted images in a poorly-assembled kaleidoscope. Even after they had all retired to bed, with Philippe settled for the present in the guest bedroom, Pola could not shake off the aura of unreality that seemed to envelop her. On her wedding day, she had considered herself a woman, and since that day she had enjoyed the adult delights and perplexing frustrations of womanhood. However, with today's events she had matured in a wholly different frame of reference. Lying wakeful by Pierre's side, she realized that nothing about their lives would ever again be quite the same.

* * *

At the end of the second week of July, the Inter-Urban Post brought a letter to the home of Franz Pietrowski. It had traveled quite a distance to reach its destination. The letter's author and its intended recipient had never met. Their acquaintance had been purely by written correspondence. The missive began and ended with formal greetings and salutations. The bulk of its contents, however, was dedicated to facts, figures and similar detailed data, and was couched in quite scholarly terms. Yet, that letter was fated to change inexorably the destinies of many generations of the Marjzendiak family.

# PART FOUR: NEW DIRECTIONS

Now, if you listen to me and keep my Covenant,

You shall be my very own possession among all the nations;

For all the earth is mine, but you will be before me

A kingdom of priests and a holy nation.

(Exodus 19:5)

# CHAPTER THIRTY
## HOPE AND FULFILLMENT

Professor Armand Krause had been born in a suburb outside Paris, of a French mother and an Austrian father. Nonetheless, for many years, he had looked upon Berlin as his cultural home. There he had embarked upon the course of study that was to be the ruling influence of his life, music. There, also, he had met the one woman he had ever loved. When he opened the letter of notification from the Berlin Konservatory, which he had requested to be sent to his friend and sponsor, Mira Pietrowska, it was like receiving a greeting from his family. His parents and elder sister had died years ago. He had no other living relatives. However, the community of professors and students who comprised the Konservatory was like an extended family to him.

The news that the dean's letter conveyed filled him with joyful pride. His most gifted student had acquitted herself extremely well. She had even excelled Mischa Gregorivich, the prodigy of St. Petersburg. In his letter of recommendation, Krause had asked that the judges "overlook the obstacle of Leah's gender and consider her strictly on the basis of proficiency and skill." As a result of their compliance with that request, Leah had received the highest total score of any contestant that year. It was, Krause reflected, the vindication of his long-held convictions. He had, in a sense, staked his professional reputation on the Jewish girl's performance. In receiving the highest prize of the prestigious competition, she had exceeded even his expectations.

Now he must find a way to insure that she would be permitted to fulfill her ultimate potential. He was committed to the goal of seeing Leah pursue her musical career unhindered. To do that would require the cooperation of her parents. Her mother Elana, he knew, having discussed the matter with her at length during the journey to Lodz, would not present a problem. She had supplied the application fee, and had struck a hard bargain with Leah. Now that Leah had delivered on her side of that agreement, her mother, Krause felt certain, would do all in her power to make good on hers.

The father, however, was quite another matter. In many ways, Ephraim Marjzendiak was a confirmed traditionalist, bound not only by the doctrines of the orthodox Jewish faith, but also by the forms and customs of his social environment. Would he stand in his beloved daughter's way, or could he be made to see that the fulfillment of her destiny lay in music? Krause knew that he had a difficult task before him. However, he counted upon Elana to be his ally, to help him to achieve his objective for his exceptionally gifted student. Then, once that was accomplished, he could follow Leah's career with pride, but would be free to live his own life.

Already, without realizing it, he had taken a significant step in that direction. He had followed the lead provided by an old friend and colleague in Berlin, and had written to his former sweetheart, Hilda Boehm. The stated purpose of that letter was to extend his condolences on the death of her famous father, Helmut Boehm, owner of one of the largest and most successful antique houses in Germany. By that means, however, he also renewed their long-interrupted correspondence.

His mind and heart went back in time to the day when he and Hilda had last seen each other, more than eight years earlier. Krause had pleaded with his beloved to come east with him on tour, and to be married in St. Petersburg, but Hilda had demurred. She had been reluctant to leave home and family and the familiar sights and sounds she had always known. However, she had professed to love Armand Krause deeply, and had agreed to marry him upon his return to Berlin. Perhaps, if her father's health had not declined so abruptly, Krause might have succeeded in persuading her to fulfill that promise when his extensive concert tour was ended. As it had turned out, his efforts had been in vain. Hilda was her widowed father's only child, and when he fell ill, there had been no one else to care for him.

Reluctantly, Krause had left Germany, resigning himself to a life of continuous loneliness. He had not, like other youths he knew, joyously sown wild oats, becoming romantically attached to first one young woman and then another. Instead, he had followed an exceptionally sedate and sober lifestyle, devoting himself from an early age to the pursuit of his art. Hilda had been his only love, and circumstances beyond the control of either of them had obliged him to give her up.

Now, although he could not bring himself to rejoice at the death of Herr Boehm, he could not help but recall with some degree of bitterness the fact that the older man had inveighed against his daughter's choice of a prospective husband. He had described Krause as "an itinerant musician," stating that he preferred to marry his daughter to a stable businessman. That phrase stuck in Armand Krause's memory, rankling even after so many years. Well, at last it was Hilda's turn to decide her future, and Krause hoped he knew what her choice would be.

There was little wonder that Krause had silently applauded the brave stand taken by Pierre Rebaumme. The flamboyant artist had rebelliously followed his own convictions rather than those tradition and custom expected of him. Furthermore, he had somewhat recklessly married the girl his heart desired, ignoring the obstacles and the odds arrayed against him. Krause wished his fellow creative artist well, although he knew that with the arrival in Warsaw of Rebaumme's cousin, the odds against his and Pola's chances for lasting happiness had increased by orders of magnitude.

* * *

The meeting took place in the Marjzendiak salon to the accompaniment of strong tea brewed Russian style, and spiced cakes that owed their distinctive flavor to an ancient Hebrew recipe. Elana, Ephraim, Mira Pietrowska, and Professor Krause were all present. However, the person most concerned was conspicuously absent. Leah was waiting in the garden, with Markos Kolvner lending her what moral support he could.

"Surely," Markos said encouragingly, "your parents will be as proud of you as I am. What you've done is almost miraculous. How could they possibly say anything but 'yes'?"

Leah was grateful for his words, but her own hard core of realistic common sense contradicted their meaning. She paced the gazebo restlessly, feeling far less confident of the outcome of the confrontation in the salon than she had been on the stage in the competition at Lodz. There, she had stood on her own merit, but today everything depended on Ephraim. His decision would determine the course of her entire future.

When Pola had sought her support and encouragement, Leah had prayed that Franz would defy tradition and allow his daughter to marry the man whom she loved. Now, she prayed that her own father would abandon the prevailing prejudices of his time and concede that the judges of the highly respected Berlin Konservatory could adequately assess talent, regardless of in whom it might reside.

Madam Pietrowska had confided to Leah, shortly before the fateful soiree the preceding summer that she herself had once aspired to be a professional musician. Paternal prejudice had quashed that dream quite early, although Mira still retained the temperament, glamour and talent one might easily associate with a concert artist. Leah had heard her play the piano on several occasions, and had thought that, had Mira been permitted to continue her studies, she might have accomplished a great deal from an artistic point of view.

Leah did not think of herself as either glamorous or flamboyant. She saw herself as a determined and dedicated artist who would resist, with every fiber of her being, the concerted efforts of social pressure and misdirected ethical shortsightedness to deprive her of her dream. She loved and idolized her father. In a very real sense, the reverence she felt for him was second only to the devotion she had been taught to feel toward Adonai. Yet, on this one point, she was willing to do battle even with him. The question was how.

In practical terms, she had little in the way of private means. The few zloty she had saved from the personal allowance Ephraim had granted her over the past years would not even purchase her train fare to Berlin. In addition, although the scholarship would provide tuition and a room in one of the campus dormitories, the school's living quarters housed only male students. No real provisions had been allocated for the unlikely phenomenon of a female undergraduate, although three of the faculty members were women. Leah's agile mind was already pursuing the possibility of arranging living quarters with one of them even as her father was expressing his feelings on the subject of the results of the competition.

"Why," Ephraim asked in dismay, "was I not told the truth about the prize for which my daughter would be competing?"

It was the pivotal question all three of them had known he would ask. They looked at one another in mutual concern, but it was Elana who had a ready answer.

"Once the opportunity presented itself, it seemed cruel to deny her the chance. The truth is, it seemed only a chance, and a slim one at best."

"Are you saying that you allowed her to submit an application, and yet you expected her to fail?"

"Given the circumstances," Elana answered, "one could hardly expect she would succeed quite so well. Yet, I felt she was entitled to that one chance. She's worked hard on her musical studies. She came to me as her mother, having refused help from another source."

Ephraim's eyes went to Mira. "What source?"

"That's hardly important now," Elana replied. "What is important is that I made her understand that if she failed in this, there was to be no more said about a career in music." She paused meaningfully. "I share your feelings about such things."

"Do you know how I feel?" Ephraim's voice reflected hurt and disappointment. "I would have hoped you would after all these years. Yet no one has seen fit to tell me anything until now, when all has been decided."

Armand Krause stepped in to avert what he perceived as a budding family altercation. "The point is that she didn't fail. She has succeeded gloriously!"

"You've told her, of course." It was a statement rather than a question, and Ephraim's voice held a barely veiled note of disappointment.

Krause was momentarily astonished. "Of course!"

Mira's voice showed barely restrained exasperation as she said "You could scarcely expect him to do otherwise, Ephraim. The child has been a bundle of nerves for weeks, waiting for word of her standing. She has only performed in public on one prior occasion, and that was hardly comparable."

Krause glanced from Ephraim to Elana. "You must both be very proud of her."

"That goes without saying," Elana agreed, her eyes fixed upon her husband's face.

"And where is my part," he asked, "in all this? What role does the father play in this fait accompli? I should rightfully have been the one to tell Leah of her triumph. Now, I'm expected to send her to live alone in Berlin with my blessing."

"There was no intent to mislead you, Ephraim," Mira assured him. "You must realize that none of us dared hope for such an outcome."

"I suspect Leah did hope for it," Ephraim countered, "in spite of reason, logic, or reality. Leah is a child, and children dare to dream impossible dreams."

"And sometimes adults dream them also, and make them possible," Elana said soberly. "Surely, now that she has won, you don't intend to forbid her to go?"

"On such short notice, I have not had time to formulate any intentions. My wife and daughter have contrived, without my knowledge, to create this situation." He considered momentarily. "If we had family in Berlin, or even close friends."

"I may be able to help there," Krause interjected. "I'm leaving shortly for Berlin."

That revelation was met by a startled gasp from Mira. "You're leaving, Professor? When?"

"Quite soon," Krause replied. "I have taught Leah all I can, and just recently, a door has opened for me that I thought had closed permanently."

In that moment of surprise, it was Ephraim who truly understood what Krause was saying. "I take it you refer to a personal matter," he said. "Apparently, one of some delicacy?"

"Precisely!" Krause answered with a contented smile that spoke volumes.

"I wish you Adonai's blessing on your personal prospects, Mer Krause," Ephraim said earnestly. "You have trained my daughter well and have given her many hours of contentment. Whatever the future holds, I shall always thank you for that."

Krause sensed in those benevolent words an element of dismissal. "Do I understand that our part of this conversation is ended?"

Ephraim nodded. "You have brought me your announcement of Leah's outstanding achievement. I am grateful. Now there is much I must consider." He shook hands with Krause. "Thank you, Professor, and may Adonai's countenance always smile upon you and yours."

Krause took his leave, puzzled but powerless to do any more.

Ephraim then turned to Mira. "Was yours, Madam, the offer of help that Leah refused?"

"No, Ephraim, it was not," Elana answered.

Ephraim faced his wife. "I asked Madam Pietrowska."

"She doesn't know the answer you seek," Elana said. "Leah came to me rather than accept the money from the Kolvners. She felt that would be improper, especially in view of her feelings for Markos, and his for her. She felt it might bring shame to her own family. "

Ephraim smiled and nodded, evidently satisfied with his daughter's sense of propriety.

"We did nothing deliberately to deceive you, Ephraim," Elana continued. "I saw no reason to concern you about a matter that seemed more or less hopeless. I felt that Leah should get this thing out of her system, have it over and done with so that she would get on with the rest of her life, knowing she had tried her best. "

"She has tried and succeeded," Mira reaffirmed. "That's what we now have to deal with. We must find a way to help her address attainment rather than defeat." She glanced meaningfully at Ephraim. "I get the feeling that the two of you would be far happier if she had placed last."

"Of course not," Ephraim said decisively. "I'm proud of Leah. There's no question about that."

"Then you will allow her to accept the scholarship," Mira responded, unable to conceal her eagerness to gain a statement of commitment from Ephraim.

"If a way can reasonably be arranged for a 14-year-old girl to travel hundreds of kilometers to a strange town where she has neither family nor friends."

"You forget Professor Krause," Mira reminded him.

"Professor Krause is a bachelor," Elana objected.

"Perhaps," Ephraim said thoughtfully, "but that situation may shortly change."

* * *

In early August of 1870, Armand Krause prepared to leave Warsaw, having bid a fond farewell to the friends he had made over the years. His leave-taking of Leah Marjzendiak was especially poignant. On the day of her last lesson with him, she played, in addition to her assignment, his favorite composition, The Sonata Apasionata of Beethoven. Afterwards, the two strolled through the Pietrowski garden, visiting their respective favorite places and commenting on past events those sites recalled to mind.

Finally, Leah turned to her beloved teacher, barely able to restrain the tears burning within her eyes. "I can hardly believe this is good-bye and that I won't see you here anymore." Her glance swept the area wistfully. "The place will seem vacant without you."

Krause laughed mischievously. "Hardly vacant with Madam Mira presiding over it all. She has energy and personality enough for two. It's unfortunate that she was never permitted to realize her true ambition." He took Leah's hands in his own. "No matter what, you must never allow that to be your fate. As I said before, ma petite, when we first met, you have magic in these hands, and the world must feel that magic."

They seated themselves by the little man-made pond that was one of Mira's favorite places and Leah watched as Krause threw a pebble into its center. The waves rippled across its surface in a widening pattern.

"Life," he said, "is like the surface of that pond. Its pattern can be changed by the simplest events. A month ago, no one could have convinced me that I would ever go back to Berlin. That city holds so many memories for me, some of them delightfully sweet, others intensely painful. I left there filled with regret. Now, I return with joy."

"You're going to marry your Hilda at last," Leah said happily, remembering all that Krause had told her in just the past few weeks regarding his only love. Strange, she thought, that she had never before pictured him in the role of a romantic lover. Now, suddenly, that characterization seemed ideally suited to him. She imagined the two lovers as they must have been nearly a decade earlier, immersed in the joy of first love with eyes only for each other.

Krause's words recalled her to the present. "Yes, ma petite. We'll be wed almost immediately. You must come and visit us."

Leah smiled. "You know I will, Professor. My mother has promised to come with me. She wants to meet your Hilda. I'm sure she'll like her. If she does, my father has given his permission for me to accept your generous offer to stay with you both during my training period."

"Ah," Krause exulted, "the last obstacle is removed from your path. Now the rest is up to you."

"It is a dream come true," Leah responded. "I can hardly believe it. Everything has happened so quickly. It's as though from the day Madam first brought me here to meet Pola, some mysterious force has moved me in this direction. And now, thanks to you, my goal is in sight. How can I ever thank you?"

"You have only to be true to your gifts Leah and to the high principles your family have taught you. I know you will go far," Krause added. "I pray you will be happy."

Student and teacher embraced then.

"Au revoir," Krause said, moved almost to tears himself, "for a few weeks. In September, I shall see you again in Berlin."

Despite the optimistic reassurance implicit in that parting greeting, Leah could not restrain a qualm of apprehension. Could her dream truly be realized this easily, she wondered, or was there some hidden pitfall waiting just out of sight to ensnare and disappoint her?

* * *

Early September was a time of breathless excitement in the Marjzendiak household. Leah was enjoying the heady experience of being, just this once, the center of attention. For most of her life, at least as much of it as she could remember, either Adam or Isaak or, in his infancy, Michael, had occupied that role. Her own early childhood she could not readily recall, and little had been made of her thirteenth birthday, so unlike the Bar Mitzvahs of her older brothers. Of course, there had been the usual birthday party, shared with Adam. There had been choice gifts, and, to mark that particular occasion, the opening of an account in her name at the Bank of Poland with a sizable first deposit and a bank book presented to her by Ephraim. However, the custom of Bat Mitzvah had not become fashionable in eastern Europe at that time. The Jewish community at large took no special notice of the spiritual coming of age of its female members. No mention was made in the synagogue service, no calling up of the young girl on the sabbath following her natal day.

Having money of her own had been a thrill, but it was as nothing compared to the mood of exultation that currently possessed Leah. Her bedroom was the epitome of feminine chaos on the afternoon proceeding her and Elana's departure for Berlin. Wisely, Ephraim stayed out of that realm of hectic last-minute packing and repacking of items too precious to be left behind and yet difficult to fit readily within either of the two traveling cases Elana had recently purchased for her daughter.

A number of good-byes had already been said by then. Madam Pietrowska had given a special reception in Leah's honor, praising her achievement in the scholarship competition and predicting for her a bright future to rival that of Clara Schumann and Marie Pleyel.

At the end of that memorable evening, Pola had confided to Leah the special fears that plagued her, now that Philippe lived with Pierre and herself. Leah had done her best to be sympathetic and encouraging, but try as she might, she could not wholly absorb Pola's concerns. She was too distracted by the imminence of her own departure upon the adventure of her lifetime. Leah found herself feeling as though she had somehow moved beyond her friend. Even when Pola told Leah of her pregnancy, the younger girl, though she was glad for Pola, felt strangely isolated from her, as though a glacier had arisen between them.

Almost in desperation, Leah reached out and hugged Pola, astonished that no tears came to her eyes. "I shall miss you terribly," she said, striving to convince herself as well as Pola.

"I'll miss you," Pola responded earnestly. "You can't know what life has become since he came."

Leah looked at her, shocked at first. Then the meaning of the other girl's words dawned upon her. "You mean Philippe?"

"Who else? He glares at me with such disdain, almost as though he hates me, but Pierre doesn't seem to notice. They talk together for hours, and I feel like an invisible spectator, a stranger in my own home."

"Surely not," Leah hastened to reassure her. "Pierre loves you. You know that! It's just that Philippe is all that remains of his family. He feels responsible for him because of his youth, and the fact that he's a stranger here."

Pola nodded guiltily. "You're right, of course, but I'd grown so accustomed to having Pierre to myself. I don't like having to share him, and Philippe is so righteous, if you know what I mean. He tries his best to turn our home into a kosher household." She blushed suddenly and bit her lower lip. "It's not that I have anything against his faith, but neither Pierre nor I believe in it."

"It's all right," Leah said, understanding Pola's embarrassment "You don't have to explain to me, but why don't you ask Pierre to set him straight? He's a guest in your house. There are standards of courtesy."

"Phillipe thinks of me as a shiksa intruder in his family, hardly meriting courtesy."

"Then ask him to leave," Leah said indignantly.

"I can't, and I can't ask that of Pierre. Certainly not now, when the boy has nowhere else to go and no income."

"I wouldn't stand for his rudeness, if I were you," Leah insisted with the naive insensitivity of youth. "If you're wise, you'll make your own position clear before things grow worse."

"You really think they will get worse?"

"You have a child on the way to think of, Pola," Leah replied almost angrily. "You must fight for him as well as for yourself."

"I don't want to fight my husband."

"Of course not," Leah said matter-of-factly. "It's his cousin you have to confront. He seemed nice enough on first acquaintance, but obviously he's one of those young men who require a few plain words to open his eyes to the basic truths."

Pola smiled self-consciously. "You're growing up rather quickly, Leah. I'll take your words of wisdom to heart."

Much as she loved Pola, Leah felt strangely relieved when they said good-bye, promising to keep in touch by mail.

The hardest farewells, however, were the ones she exchanged with Ephraim and Markos. Ephraim waited until the last few minutes before the train left, almost as though he hoped Leah would change her mind and not go. Markos, however, had encouraged and supported her ambitions for the past two years. Even now, though the thought of her leaving pained him deeply, he looked forward eagerly to her success at the Konservatory, proudly predicting that she would please and astonish her instructors there just as she had Professor Krause.

On that last afternoon, he brought her a bouquet of fragrant red roses from his parents' garden and a small box of home-baked candies for her to take with her on her journey.

"When you taste them, think of me," he said fondly, "and remember that you are sweeter to me than all of them together."

Leah's cheeks flushed as she took the gifts from him. "I have something for you," she said, and handed him her cherished recorder. "Keep this safe for me until I come back. It will remind you of me."

"I don't need anything to make me think of you," he said. "I'll think of very little else while you're gone, but I'll take care of it for you all the same. Just promise you won't forget me amid all the glamour of Berlin."

She stood on tiptoe to kiss his lips. "I could never do that," she said, and in that moment, she truly meant it.

*  *  *

The Warsaw station reflected the changes that the entire Russian railway system had undergone over the past decade. It had expanded in size and grandeur, and so had the crowds that filled its waiting rooms and platforms.

Ephraim embraced and kissed Elana, then helped her mount the steps to the waiting train. All his love for her was plainly visible in his eyes as he let her go.

"Shalom, my love. Write often, and hurry back," he said, trying to keep his voice light.

"Shalom," she answered, gazing into his eyes. "Keep warm and dry. I shall worry about you with both your womenfolk away from home."

"I'll be worried about both of you, far away without me there to watch over you."

"We'll be fine "Elana said, "and I'll be back within a fortnight. I can depend on you to look after the farm, but the house and the rose garden are quite another matter."

"They'll survive," he assured her with a prolonged kiss, "but don't you stay away one day longer than necessary to see Leah settled."

When she had disappeared into the car, he turned at last to Leah. "Well, little one, this is the moment every father dreads. The day he says good-bye to his little girl, knowing that when he sees her again, she'll have changed irretrievably into a woman, one he may not fully recognize."

"I won't change that much in a year, Papa," she said gently. "Besides, no matter how much time passes, you and I will never be strangers, and I'll always come home." She stroked his beard as she had done as a small child. "It's as thick and silky as ever," she said, "and nearly as black." She hugged him hard, and he embraced her in return. "Thank you, Papa," she whispered, tears staining her cheeks. "I love you."

"I shall always love you," he responded, "no matter where you go or what you do or don't achieve."

He stood on the platform and waved to them until the train passed from view and only the ghost-like puffs of smoke from its engine remained, floating slowly upward, momentarily darkening the midday sky.

# CHAPTER THIRTY-ONE
## CONTRASTS AND COMPROMISES

Berlin in the early 1870s was a city of sharp contrasts and exciting changes. It was the home of German neo-impressionism, both in painting and in architecture, and the new and the old were everywhere juxtaposed, sometimes with bizarre results. Romanticism had become the dominant force in German music and theater. A wave of artistic nationalism, paralleling the prevailing political sentiment, inspired German composers and performers alike. French and Italian influences were being cast aside in favor of predominantly German themes and motifs. Beneath these conflicting cultural forces lay the conflicts between the social classes, between management and labor, between imperialistic values and those of the common man.

It was an invigorating time and place in which to find oneself. However, Elana Marjzendiak viewed these new surroundings as potentially fraught with peril for her teenage daughter, since Leah had never been away from home before. Leah, on the other hand, was mesmerized by all she saw, heard, and experienced in this sophisticated, cosmopolitan center of European culture. Elana, having noted her daughter's reaction, was relieved when she met Armand Krause's new bride. She found her to be a woman of poise, maturity, and a practical blend of earthy common sense and ready wit. Frau Hilda Krause would need all those gifts in order to effectively deal with the uninhibited exuberance of a fourteen-year-old.

Herr Krause and his charming frau welcomed their Polish visitors with undisguised pleasure. They showed them the sights of the city, and introduced them to the delights of the Berlin Opera, an experience that fascinated Leah profoundly. She found the style of conductor Carl Eckert electrifying, and she was thrilled by the sweep and power of Wagner's music. Die Meistersinger Von Nurmberg, which premiered that night, was her first experience of the composer's work. The anti-Semitic overtones of his underlying philosophy were too subtly expressed to be noticeable to her. Moreover, she was totally mystified because the opera did not receive generous critical acclaim. Stranger still was the fact that some of the audience were so boorish as to leave before the final curtain, having voiced their disapproval with hisses and cries of derision.

Elana decided not to attempt to explain either her own reactions to the performance or the basis for the mixed reception of the other members of the audience.

Before she was scheduled to leave Berlin, Elana insisted upon attending personally to Leah's registration, reviewing her curriculum, and meeting each of her instructors. The scholarship winners, gathered from each sector of Europe where the competitions had been held, were greeted at a formal reception held on the Sunday afternoon prior to the opening of the academic year. This was Leah's initial opportunity to meet most of her fellow students, only two of whom, Mischa Gregorivich from St. Petersburg, and Michiel Meihlbruch from Prague, she had ever seen before.

As had been expected, Leah was the only girl, and some of her peers were frankly critical that a girl had been permitted to compete for the chance to study in an institution of higher learning. Only the unparalleled fame of Clara Wieck Schumann, the ranking concert pianist of her day in central Europe, and the reputation of one of the school's leading alumni, Armand Krause, had opened the way for her, they said sneeringly. However, now neither of these esteemed musicians could be of further help to her. She would stand or fall on her own merit.

Elana advised Leah to ignore those remarks, and to concentrate on the positive aspects of her being present in this company. Leah was prepared to follow that advice, but it was clear to her that her years in Berlin were destined to be neither easy nor uniformly congenial. She was silently grateful that her mentor, Armand Krause, had recently been appointed to the faculty. Though he would not be one of her teachers, he had agreed to be her faculty adviser, and would thus continue to exert a guiding influence on her musical education.

On Elana's last night in Berlin, she and Leah dined with Professor Krause and Hilda. She was grateful that there were no other guests, although one of the young professors from the Konservatory who had missed the reception, dropped by briefly to meet Leah and to congratulate her on her achievement. His name was Heinrich Rheinsfeld. He was viewed as a musical prodigy in his own right. In addition to having been appointed a full professor despite his youth, he had recently composed an opera, the score of which he had brought to Armand Krause for his professional opinion.

Elana could not fail to notice the German musician's unusually striking good looks. She watched her daughter's reaction closely and listened throughout the meal to Leah's animated remarks that proclaimed how joyously she looked forward to her classes with Rheinsfeld and the other teachers she had met.

"Remember, Leah," Elana cautioned her, "that your main purpose here in Berlin is to study. There's much to see, much to distract you. However, you heard what some of your fellow students said at the reception. Even now, I'm certain some of them hope to see you fail. You must be sure to disappoint them."

"I won't fail, Mama," Leah reassured her. "I promise I'll make you and Papa proud of me."

"We're proud of you already, dear. Never forget that."

"As time goes by, you'll have more cause to be proud," Armand Krause stated firmly. "Leah has a bright future before her. "

"And before that," Hilda added soberly, "she has a great deal of work to do, and a world full of unthinking prejudice to overcome."

Frau Krause was thinking mainly of Leah's gender. Leah, however, was well aware that being female was not her only stumbling block. Already, she had perceived that, though Germany's Jews seemed integrated into the country's cultural fabric, there was still an aura of subtle rejection of them among the ruling classes of society. Even Frau Schumann had had to fight her famous father in court in order to marry her beloved Robert. In the course of the legal battle, Frederick Wieck had accused Robert of every conceivable offense from excessive alcohol abuse to having Jewish antecedents. It seemed to Leah impossible that a magistrate could ever have considered such charges seriously in a court of law. Nonetheless, the case had become a landmark in legal circles and had been whispered about socially ever since.

Leah reflected, as she thought about these matters, that she had come this far with the help and support of her family and friends. Now, as Krause had warned her in the Pietrowski garden, the rest was up to her. And as she was constantly aware, the one source of help and support on which she could unfailingly depend, no matter where she was and in what circumstances she found herself, was Adonai.

Leah's leave-taking of Elana was a model of fortitude. She embraced and kissed her mother without shedding a tear, an achievement that gave her no small measure of pride. She felt torn, however, wanting to ask her mother to stay and yet knowing that Ephraim was lonely without her. Leah had chosen this path for herself. Now she must pursue it. Much of the way she would have to tread alone, but at the end, if she was diligent, lay the rewards she sought. Those rewards had already crowned the efforts of her idols, Madam Marie Moke Pleyel in France, and Frau Clara Schumann, who was currently living here in Berlin. Some day, she hoped to be able to meet that famous lady in person.

* * *

While Elana was returning to Warsaw, and Leah was exploring the wonders of musical learning in Berlin, Pierre Rebaumme, responding to an authoritative knock on his studio door, found himself receiving an unexpected visitor. The man was of stocky build, an attribute that partly disguised his impressive height. He wore his dark hair, touched with gray at the temples, somewhat longer than the fashion of the day. A mixed gray beard and black moustache added a sinister grandeur to his bearing. His eyes were fierce, black, and slightly almond-shaped, reminiscent of Atilla or Genghis Kahn. The gray and red uniform of the militia, which he wore with a decided flourish, added a dimension of menace to the impression of power that he conveyed.

As Pierre beheld this intimidating apparition on his doorstep, the Russian announced himself.

"Deputy Marshall Vashily Deshenko." He stepped confidently forward, obviously intending to enter.

Resignedly, Pierre opened the door and stood aside.

Deshenko strode into the room as if he owned it, then closed the door resoundingly behind him. His sharp, dark eyes darted about the studio, recording every detail. Finally they rested on Pierre, assessing him coldly. "We have been expecting you, Monsieur."

Pierre was mystified. "Expecting me?"

"At the Office of Immigration."

"My permit has not yet expired," Pierre protested, his bewilderment increasing.

Deshenko smiled, but his saturnine face did not soften. "Under the circumstances, Monsieur, the permit is in need of some revision."

"I don't understand."

"I think you do!" Deshenko advanced further into the room, forcing Pierre to follow him. The tall Russian surveyed his surroundings with an air of satisfaction. "You've done quite well, I see." He turned to face Pierre. "Perhaps you've grown affluent so quickly because you've not paid the fee required of a Jewish businessman." He allowed the significance of those words to sink in as the silence lengthened, then added almost in a whisper, "I can only assume that your failure to report your true status, and to wear the required identification, is an attempt to defraud his Imperial Majesty, the tsar, of his just revenues."

Pierre shook his head. His mouth was too dry to speak on his own behalf. He felt as though he had entered a nightmare from which he must surely soon awaken.

"In all this time, some of your fellow Jewish cronies must certainly have made you aware of the law," the Russian was saying. Pierre's continued silence only seemed to anger the deputy. "What? No protests of ignorance or innocence? No pleas for clemency?" The Russian's left eyebrow lifted in mock surprise. "After all, you owe a considerable sum."

Pierre found his voice at last. "Am I under arrest?"

"That remains to be determined."

"As a French citizen," Pierre said levelly, "I have registered, and I am unaware of the necessity to wear any identification."

"Do you deny your Jewish origin?"

"I'm a Frenchman," Pierre replied. "It is my understanding that foreign citizens are required only to pay an annual immigration tax. Mine is paid and duly recorded."

"All Jews operating a business in the Vistula Provinces are required to pay a surtax," Deshenko explained patiently. "The law is quite explicit. It has nothing to do with nationality. Part of these monies are used to defray the cost of maintaining the synagogues that the tsar has generously allowed your people to build on Russian land."

"I attend no synagogue," Pierre said sharply.

"Nonetheless, you are a Jew!"

"How do you define a Jew?"

The Russian was obviously taken aback, but only momentarily. "A Jew is a Jew," he said, matter-of-factly. "It requires no definition. The fact that you look somewhat different from most of your kind does not excuse you from your obligation," Deshenko added. "You've enjoyed the tsar's free hospitality far too long. "

"Just what is it," Pierre asked, "that you people are taxing? Is it the Jewish religion, or do you seek to punish all those of Jewish ancestry?"

"It is my role to administer the law, not to analyze it," Deshenko answered. "Were I you, I should pay a prompt visit to the Office of Immigration, and get this matter settled before it grows any worse." Deshenko glanced meaningfully about the studio once more. "It would be a shame to have to confiscate such luxurious furnishings." With that, he inclined his head politely and moved towards the door.

Pierre followed instinctively, but Deshenko raised a hand to stop him.

"I'll let myself out," he said.

Pierre stood for a long moment after Deshenko had gone, still gripped by a sense of unreality. The surtax, compounded over the entire two-year period of his stay in Warsaw, would destroy him financially. With Pola pregnant with their first child, Deshenko's visit could not have come at a more inopportune time.

\* \* \*

Franz Pietrowski smiled reassuringly and offered his son-in-law a chair. "I'm glad you've come to me," he said earnestly. "Naturally, my concerns parallel your own."

Pierre Rebaumme gazed at his father-in-law with gratitude. He had approached this interview with mounting dread.

"As I see it," Franz continued, "your only hope of avoiding this cripplingly exorbitant surtax is to prove that you are not Jewish."

Pierre shook his head in frustration. "How can I prove a lie?"

Franz stared at Pierre for a long moment, his eyes intense, his expression deadly serious. "Have you not repeatedly denied any commitment to Judaism?"

"Yes, of course," Pierre replied, "but according to this deputy, that doesn't seem to matter. The tax is based on one's ancestry."

Franz raised a hand to stem the tide of Pierre's words. "Your ancestors are not subject to the surtax, Pierre. You are, but only as a Jew."

The color rose in Pierre's face. "What are you saying?"

"I'm suggesting a viable alternative to allowing yourself to be brought to the brink of bankruptcy by the Russian administration." Franz leaned closer. "If you were to embrace the Catholic faith, all such nonsense on the part of the governor-general would be immediately dropped."

Pierre shook his head. "So I'm compelled to become a Catholic, albeit in name only," he said, a note of self-loathing in his voice. Still, he was relieved to learn that accepting the designation of "Christian" would permanently remove the threat of the hated badges from his and Pola's descendants.

Franz rose to his feet, his voice harsh with the intensity of his feelings. "You must do what's necessary to insure your own and your family's economic survival." He moved from behind the desk and came to stand before Pierre, his hands resting on the younger man's shoulders. "I don't make this suggestion lightly. My faith is very important to me. But by now, you must see that the governor-general and his minions are infuriated by the way you've flaunted their precious regulations. You have successfully hidden your origins until now. To assuage their frustration, they're intent on ruining you, making an example of you. As Pola's father, I cannot stand by and see that happen." Franz began to pace the room nervously, as if driven to some form of physical activity. "Or course it's a travesty," Franz said, at last responding to Pierre's objections. "It shames me to suggest it." He stopped and faced Pierre squarely. "Yet, under the circumstances, what other course is open to you?"

Pierre lowered his gaze, remembering his precipitous flight from France. "Short of leaving Poland, I can see none."

From the moment he had first seen Pola Pietrowska, Pierre had been smitten by her child-woman allure. Very soon, fascination had ripened into love. With the deepening intensity of their mutual devotion to each other, Pierre had become very protective of her. Recalling Pola's distraught state of mind when she had first told him of her pregnancy, Pierre could easily imagine the effect an announcement that they must move away from Warsaw would provoke. The ancient Polish capital was the only world she knew. Her sheltered upbringing, fortified by the tenets of the Roman Catholic faith and the privileges her family had always been able to provide for her, had prepared her for nothing else.

Furthermore, since their marriage, Pierre had enjoyed unqualified success as a leading painter and portraitist. Indeed, throughout the Russian Polish sector, his canvasses were in great demand, thanks to the rich variety of subjects and techniques to which his talent gave him access. He knew well how to add vivacity and interest to a plain face, how to smooth and soften a line here, a wrinkle there without radically altering the subject's appearance. Furthermore, despite the usual lowly status artists were customarily accorded, Pierre Rebaumme was a familiar figure in the most fashionable drawing rooms of Warsaw.

Pierre was enough of a realist to admit to himself that this signal honor was due largely to the fact that Madam Rebaumme was the daughter of the Commissioner of the Bank of Poland. Still, the income he enjoyed enabled him to maintain his wife in the style to which she was accustomed. He harbored a secret sense of guilt that the increasingly widespread knowledge of his Jewish forebears had lately cast a shadow over the social life he and Pola had heretofore enjoyed. Sooner or later, that state of affairs was certain to put a strain on their relationship.

He could scarcely allow his stubborn pride to undermine all that he held dear at this point in his life. He was shortly to be a father, and after all, how much could he truly value his Jewish heritage? He had deliberately concealed it all this time and had thus literally painted himself into an untenably awkward corner. It seemed far wiser to accept the convenient alternative that his father-in-law offered than to cast fortune to the winds for the sake of intellectual independence. Pierre glanced up at Franz, who stood waiting for an answer.

The answer took the form of a question. "How soon can it be arranged?"

Franz nodded briefly, though his manner did not reflect the satisfaction Pierre had anticipated. "I'll see to the necessary arrangements," was all the bank commissioner said.

The silence that followed was heavy between the two men. Afterwards, Pierre could never feel quite certain whether he had responded as Franz had wished, or simply as he had expected.

* * *

St. John's Cathedral was all but empty on the October morning of Pierre Rebaumme's baptism. Under the sharp constraints of time and necessity, Pierre's course of instruction in the Catholic faith had been abbreviated, to say the least.

His sponsors were Mira and Franz Pietrowski, and of course Pola stood beside him, adding the reassurance of her physical presence as well as her moral support.

For an adult, the ceremony of baptism is fairly simple and brief. Furthermore, in the absence of a large assemblage of family members such as might grace an infant baptism, there were no guests to invite afterwards to the Rebaumme home to partake of a celebratory feast. Indeed, except for the lifting of the economic burden of the surtax, there seemed little to celebrate. No member of the small group present, with the possible exception of Father Josef Varshki, the officiating priest, held any illusions regarding the impact of this ceremony on Pierre Rebaumme's immortal soul. Pola suspected that he would rarely attend mass with her, and he would probably never receive the sacrament of communion. Nonetheless, the Vistula Provinces would number him among their Catholic subjects, and

Deputy Marshall Deshenko would be unlikely to call upon him in future. Pierre thanked his father-in-law for attending to the arrangements as he had promised.

For once, Mira could think of little to say. She embraced Pola, patted Pierre's shoulder, and turned away to wipe the unshed tears from her eyes. Never in her most outlandish dreams had she envisioned such a destiny for her only daughter. She had launched Pierre's career in Poland because she genuinely admired his talent. It seemed oddly incongruous that he had now become her son-in-law. Perhaps, she mused, this was her penance for harboring secret sexual fantasies regarding Ephraim Marjzendiak, fantasies she would never in reality have acted upon. Divine retribution, she thought, can sometimes be almost laughably ironic.

However, the practical side of Mira once more took control. She chided herself for such fancies. Pola looked radiantly happy. Even if Pierre was a reluctant Catholic, their immediate worries were laid to rest. What was more important, Pola's pregnancy was progressing well. She was the picture of health, and had no complaints except for an occasional concern over the oddities of her appetite and their impact on her figure.

Mira turned to Pierre. "Why don't you both come back with Franz and me for lunch? We'll make it a family party."

Pierre attempted to decline politely, but Pola seemed disappointed, and Mira insisted.

So there would be a celebration after all, and why not? Was not the rescue of a family fortune from ruin just cause for at least modest festivities?

The table was cleared and the family had adjourned to the drawing room by the time the door chimes rang. Pyotor Karchenski, who now served the Pietrowskis as both butler and chief coachman, answered them. The stockily-built servant was greeted by a distraught Phillipe Rebaumme.

"Is my cousin here?"

"I have no idea, sir," Pyotor answered, puzzled. "Who is your cousin?"

"Pierre Rebaumme, the artist."

Understanding dawned in Pyotor's face. "Yes, he is here."

"May I see him?" Phillipe's words were flawlessly polite, though his manner was one of intense agitation.

Pyotor admitted the young man and led him to the parlor. He then went to inform his employer.

"It's all right," Pierre said in an effort to reassure his father-in-law. "I'll see what he wants." Pierre, however, did not feel such assurance. What new emergency, he wondered, had brought his cousin to the Pietrowski home? Had he come by public coach? Surely he had not walked. But some powerful incentive compelled him to seek out his cousin. Unknown to Pierre, Phillipe had sought him first at the cathedral, and had there been directed to the home of Pierre's father-in-law by the priest.

Phillipe was pacing nervously as Pierre entered the room. The youth turned abruptly, his eyes bright with the intensity of his disgust. "You really went through with it, then?"

For a moment, Pierre was confused. "I don't understand."

"You call yourself a Christian now?"

Pierre's shoulders sagged. "I thought we had already discussed all this, Phillipe. You know my reasons."

"Yes," Phillipe responded angrily, "only too well."

"Sit down," Pierre directed, "and keep your voice low. This is not your home, nor mine."

Reluctantly, sullenly, Phillipe did as he was told.

"Circumstances," Pierre said calmly, taking a seat himself, "force hard choices upon us all. In France, this would not have been necessary."

"I'm beginning to regret I ever left France."

"You can always go back there," Pierre said. "I cannot. My life is here, and there are other lives involved with mine now. I have to do what's best for them."

Phillipe's voice was harsh as he said, "Why did you have to marry that shiksa?"

Pierre seized his cousin by the shoulders and shook him angrily. "Never say that to me again! Pola is my wife. We love each other. When you're a little older, perhaps you'll realize what that means." He turned away, regretting his moment of violence, yet unable to resist reacting to an insult to his beloved Pola.

"Is she worth denying your whole heritage?" Phillipe's eyes seemed to plead with his cousin. "Not just the faith. I know you don't believe in that. But there's everything else. Everything we are!"

Pierre nodded. "I've done what I had to do to survive. Surely you're not so young or so idealistic that you can't understand that. This is a different world, Phillipe. It has different rules."

"Markos Kolvner would never do what you've done," Phillipe lamented. "You've disgraced us both. You've brought shame to the memory of our family. If your father were alive, he'd recite the prayers for the dead for you."

"Perhaps he would," Pierre conceded. "Then again, being an adult, perhaps he'd be saddened but wise enough to know that sometimes, with life, one must make compromises."

Phillipe stood and faced his cousin, his eyes filled with tears. "I'll never forgive you for this," he said.

"Never? That's a very long time," Pierre remarked sadly, thinking that Phillipe himself had been the unwitting cause of the action Pierre had taken today.

"Never!" Phillipe moved toward the door.

Pierre followed him. "I'm sorry."

Phillipe paused and turned back. "I've packed my things," he said. "I'm going to move in with the Kolvners. You won't have to be reminded of what you've denied every time you come home and see me."

"You don't have to leave," Pierre said, seeking to dissuade him.

"I do," Phillipe insisted. "I'll feel out of place in a Catholic household."

"Nothing has changed at home," Pierre assured him.

"You've changed! You've sold your birthright for a few drops of baptismal water and the security you think they'll buy!"

"Then go," Pierre said bitterly. "Go to your friends. Revel together in your self-righteousness. Just pray that you never have to make any compromises."

Phillipe left Pierre standing alone in the center of the room, and departed without another word. A chasm seemed to have opened between the artist and his past. Nonetheless, there was Pola and the family they would found together. Encouraged by that prospect, Pierre went to rejoin his wife and his Christian in-laws.

* * *

Over the next several months, Leah and Pola exchanged many letters. They were filled with the poignant confidences that characterize the correspondence of the very young who are just embarking upon life's great adventure. Pola was due to deliver her first child within a month. Leah, meanwhile, was delighted to report the details of her progress at the Konservatory. She was named on the honors list and had distinguished herself in all her studies. Most wonderful of all, she had been permitted to meet Frau Schumann. The first lady of central European music had been impressed with Leah's performance at a Konservatory recital. She had subsequently consented to meet her in person, and had bestowed upon the aspiring young pianist her personal stamp of approval. Frau Schumann had declared Leah an outstanding exponent of Mozart and Beethoven. She had, furthermore, offered to instruct her privately throughout the summer recess at her modest but charming estate at Frankfurt-on-the-Oder. Naturally, Leah had said 'yes,' certain that her parents would understand that this was an opportunity not to be missed.

As for Pola's approaching confinement, Leah was nearly as excited about it as was the young mother herself. Both wondered if the child would be a boy or a girl; both considered possible names for either contingency, and both were secretly a little frightened at the prospect. Labor, birth, and the secrets that midwives have whispered to one another down through the ages had always been concealed from young ladies of polite society. These sheltered creatures were kept in decorous ignorance until love, marriage, and pregnancy compelled them to achieve a wider knowledge of the facts of life.

Pola's letter of April 25, 1871, announced the arrival of Paul Rebaumme, named for his deceased grandfather after the Ashkenazi custom, and recently baptized in St. John's Cathedral. Leah's letter, mailed in early May, spoke of her impatience for the school term to end. She wrote that she loved her work at the Konservatory. Nonetheless, in just the short span of time since their initial introduction, she and Frau Schumann had found that despite the differences in their respective ages, they shared many attributes and many interests in common. Frau Schumann was now aged fifty-one while Leah had celebrated her fifteenth birthday at the beginning of the year. Yet each was intensely ambitious, self-determined, and energetic. Moreover, both possessed daringly innovative minds. Leah was eager to set off with her distinguished new friend and mentor for a summer of delightful musical adventure in an enchantingly new and different location.

# CHAPTER THIRTY-TWO
## LOVE AND TRANSITION

On a June day in 1871, Elana sat in her favorite place, the gazebo overlooking her living collection of prize roses. From this vantage point, she enjoyed a panoramic view of the entire garden. Furthermore, with the glass screens she had caused to be set into the gazebo's framework and the decorative door she had installed, she could carry on her correspondence here, enjoying the summer's scenery without having her papers disrupted by its breezes.

The song of a bird in a nearby tree caused her to pause momentarily. How carefree he sounds, she thought. How different from our species, and yet who knows what concerns beset him as he prepares for his family?

Certainly, Elana was deeply concerned for her own family. She was in the process of replying to Leah's latest letter. Disappointment filled her at the prospect of not seeing her daughter for another year. Yet, the logic Leah had employed in explaining her request was unanswerable. Elana's words to her on their last night together in Berlin had been an admonition to study while in Germany, to resist distraction, and to make the most of her unparalleled opportunity. The offer extended by Frau Clara Schumann had indeed been a generous one. Moreover, Elana was pleased that in accepting it, Leah would thus be separated, for the duration of the summer, from the influence of Professor Heinrich Rheinsfeld. His name had recurred with disturbing frequency in Leah's recent correspondence.

Elana had experienced an unusual aversion to that young man upon their first meeting, despite his extensive learning and his obvious charm. Perhaps it was because of those qualities that she mistrusted him. In her mind, he symbolized a threat to her daughter's future, rendered all the more dangerous because of its subtlety and the attractiveness of the package in which it was contained. Leah had praised Rheinsfeld's extensive knowledge of musical theory and composition, which was the subject he taught. She had also paid tribute to his versatility and patience as a teacher, and to his skill as a concert artist. At no time had she dwelt upon his physical appeal nor his undeniable magnetism. As yet, Leah was still quite young, but Elana was realistic in her assessment of human feelings. The time was rapidly approaching when Leah would no longer be impervious to the type of assault upon her ripening maturity that Rheinsfeld represented. Most painful of all was the knowledge that in her own zeal to allow Leah every chance to achieve her ambitions as a musician, Elana herself had played a key role in exposing the child to temptations such as Rheinsfeld embodied.

Marshaling her thoughts, Elana wrote her reply, giving permission, with Ephraim's concurrence, for the child to accept Frau Schumann's invitation. She made it clear, however, that next summer, Leah must come home at the end of the regular school year. That done, Elana turned her attention to preparations to welcome home her second son Isaak, whose most recent letter to his parents she reread yet again. She was particularly moved by his closing paragraphs.

> "I approach this transition with mixed feelings, for it marks the end of a joyous period in my life. Krakow has become my second home, my place of refuge. Here I have found peace, knowledge, and a freedom I am loath to give up. Yet I find that as I grow older, I miss my family deeply. Furthermore, the people and places of my first home are poignantly

precious to me, not only as I remember them to be, but as I hope to be able to help transform them.

I fear that my ambitions may exceed my capabilities; nevertheless, I am compelled to test myself against the obstacles I know await me. Yet, do not be alarmed. In the course of my training, and especially in my practice of law, I have learned well the art of subterfuge and the subtle uses to which rhetoric can be put.

Most of all, I look forward to traveling the road that leads to Plaz Marjzendiak, and to being welcomed once more by those dearest to me, those with whom I share the ties of blood and belief, and thus the strongest feelings of belonging. For all these years I have been a man divided. Now I hope to be once more united in mind and heart.

Your loving son,

Isaak"

\* \* \*

Sarah Krakowska sat in the faculty dining room, cautiously sipping steaming hot tea as she corrected the final examinations of her senior biology class. She had nearly completed her task by the time Isaak Marjzendiak joined her. She looked up and smiled, genuinely pleased to see him, and exhilarated by the warmth and beauty of the mid-June day.

Though scarcely half over, already 1871 had been a landmark year for Sarah. She had been promoted to an associate professorship at the University of Krakow, thus fulfilling a lifelong ambition. She had won the respect of her students and fellow faculty members, and could look forward to a full professorship in the not-too-distant future. Moreover, with the help of a small circle of close friends, which included Isaak, Sarah had successfully revitalized her own sense of self-worth. A part of her still harbored a wistful love for Adam Marjzendiak, but that sentiment no longer dominated her life. She had accepted as fact the concept that romantic love was a blessing that would probably be absent from her future. That acceptance had brought with it not only resignation but peace.

Sarah had seen Luvna Meyer and Isaak together, reveling in the spontaneous joy of their mutual love. When Isaak had subsequently introduced the two women, Sarah knew, if she had ever harbored any doubts, that she had chosen wisely when she had sent him away after Baby Jakob's death. Renouncing the love Isaak had offered her had demanded a tremendous sacrifice of Sarah. However, to do otherwise would have been grossly unfair to him. She could think now of that sad series of events without being overwhelmed by loneliness and loss. She had indeed come a long way.

"Sit down and join, me," she said, beckoning Isaak to a chair beside her. "I'm glad you're here."

Isaak smiled wistfully. His mood was one of nostalgia as he glanced at the familiar surroundings. "It was here we had our first serious talk. Remember?"

Sarah nodded soberly. "As if I could ever forget." She paused momentarily. "I owe so much to you," she added. "I wouldn't even be teaching here now if..."

Isaak put a finger to his lips. "Shh," he said softly. "We promised never to speak of that again. It's a closed chapter. The present holds so much that's good, it seems ungrateful to cling to past sorrows."

Sarah's glance probed Isaak's face. "You really are happy now, aren't you?"

He grinned. "It's that obvious?"

"Love usually is," Sarah answered sagely. "I'm happy for you, Isaak. You and Luvna seem right for each other."

He looked thoughtful. "That's the way I feel, and yet, there's this gnawing fear that somehow..."

Sarah knew to what he referred, for he and Luvna had lived together as lovers for more than a year, a situation forbidden by Orthodox Jewish doctrine.

"Never mind what your family will say," Sarah assured him. "You and Luvna love each other. You belong together. When everything else is right between two people, marriage will come when the time is right. Meanwhile, who's to know?" She paused, then added playfully, "Some of my colleagues still wonder how you and I can be such friends after you moved out and left me. They're bursting to ask probing questions, but propriety holds them back." She grinned. "There's no reason why they should know, and I've no intention of enlightening them."

Isaak gazed at her affectionately. "Have you any idea what a rare woman you are?"

"I think perhaps I have," Sarah said mischievously. "After all, I'm unmarried, professionally successful, and well paid."

"I admire you, Sarah. Perhaps I envy you just a little."

"Nonsense," Sarah said emphatically. "You're only two years out of law school, and already you're a highly-respected trial attorney with Krakow's most prestigious law firm. You've done supremely well."

"It has been a good experience," Isaak agreed. "I love this city. I've enjoyed my life here. I hate to see it all coming to an end."

"Then it's settled. You really are moving back to Warsaw."

He nodded. "It's still home. Besides, Luvna's family lives there. She feels, now that she's graduating, that it's time to renew the family ties. As free-spirited as she sometimes seems, there's much in her that still clings to the traditional values."

"Which makes her the perfect partner for you."

"Nonetheless, there are times," Isaak said, frowning, "that I feel so much older than she."

Sarah moved closer, her voice dropping to a conspiratorial tone. "Shall I tell you a secret? For her, your most fascinating asset is your maturity."

The frown between Isaak's brows deepened. "How to you know that?"

"She told me, of course! Women do tell other women these things. She looks up to you, and she loves you very much. You're a fortunate man. I suggest you don't waste time brooding about nine years difference in your ages. Once you're settled in Warsaw, marry her without delay."

"That's your professional advice?"

"That's the advice of a friend who cares about your welfare." She reached up and brushed back the habitually unruly lock of hair that fell across his forehead. "I'm going to miss you."

"I'll miss you more than I can say," he responded, his tone serious and somewhat sad. "You will write?"

Sarah was momentarily silent. They were both remembering her refusal to accept correspondence from Adam when he had asked a similar question. How long ago their parting seemed to her now. For Adam and Sarah, the circumstances had been heartbreakingly impossible. Isaak and Sarah enjoyed quite a different relationship. They had side-stepped passion, despite the fact that each loved the other, and they had emerged from shared tragedy as staunch friends.

"Of course I'll write," she replied, smiling whimsically, "but only in answer to a letter from you."

He leaned closer and embraced her warmly. "That's a promise!"

One month later, Sarah saw Isaak off at the railway station. He had finally concluded all his work with the firm of Sukowski, Sukowski and Petulaski, and had said his farewells to his closest friend Evyan Sukowski. Both young men had felt a keen sense of loss, and Evyan had promised to pay Isaak a visit in the near future.

Three weeks earlier, Luvna had gone on ahead to Warsaw. She had wanted to visit with her family and put things right with them before Isaak arrived. It was a logical plan of action. There was much in the way of explanations and fence-mending that Luvna felt a need to carry out at this point in her life. Though she treasured the history and traditions of her people, she had not entered a synagogue for three years. Her father looked upon her as lost; her mother prayed constantly that her alienated daughter would one day see reason and return to the practice of her faith.

Isaak had deliberately exerted what subtle pressure he could to move Luvna in that direction. Meanwhile, he had never allowed his love for her to pry him away from his dedication to Orthodox Judaism, despite the lapse that their physical relationship represented. Yet, he could not deny his need of her, his dependence upon the intimacy they shared. In Luvna's absence, Isaak was restless and lonely. He missed his lover intensely.

Sarah had gently teased Isaak about his preoccupation as they sat at lunch in the restaurant near the station, awaiting the arrival of Isaak's train.

"The agony is almost over," she consoled him. "In a matter of hours, you'll see her again."

Isaak smiled. "Meanwhile, I haven't told you how I appreciate your help and your companionship these last few days."

"Frankly, I've enjoyed having you to myself again. It brings back fond memories."

Isaak reached across the table and took her hand in his. "Even now, after all this time, I often wish things could have been different for you and me."

She smiled wistfully and looked up at him, her glance clear and candid. "I'm grateful for the friendship we share, Isaak. Neither time nor distance can change it."

"But you deserve so much more!"

"I have a great deal as it is. Much more than I might have had." She paused meaningfully. "Don't feel sorry for me, Isaak. I've learned a very important lesson, to want the things I have."

When the train pulled away from the platform, and Isaak waved good-bye to Sarah, he was convinced that all would be well with her. He hoped it would be as well for Luvna and himself. The freedom of Krakow was behind them. Ahead lay the Vistula Provinces with their restrictions and confining regulations. There, they would encounter constant reminders that Russian Poland's Jews, though they might hold exalted positions and own valuable properties, were still outsiders.

* * *

On the rear veranda of the Marjzendiak home, Ephraim and Isaak sat close together, engaged in serious conversation. Isaak had just explained to his father the true status of his relationship with Luvna.

"Of course you must marry her as quickly as possible," Ephraim was saying. "This is an intolerable state of affairs. You have always been a devout man, Isaak. I can scarcely believe what you're saying now."

Isaak turned toward his father, his face mirroring the intensity of the inner conflict that he endured. "Many wonderful things in life can be ruined by being precipitous. I can't risk losing Luvna. She means too much to me. Just now, I don't think the time is right for us to marry."

"Why?" As Isaak stood and turned away, Ephraim rose and followed him. "Tell me that! For two years, the two of you have lived in defiance of Adonai's Law. In so doing, you've tainted the good name of the woman you claim to love." Ephraim laid his hands on Isaak's shoulders, turned him gently and gazed steadily at him, seeking an answer. "Why can you not marry her now?"

"You don't understand," Isaak said at last.

"Indeed, I don't. Every time I think I've come to know you, son, you find a new way to perplex me."

"Her parents want her to marry someone else," Isaak explained. "Someone nearer her own age. She's known him since childhood."

"That's all the more reason to hasten the wedding," Ephraim said reasonably. "Besides, if this other young man knows the facts, he must feel..."

"He doesn't," Isaak interrupted his father. "Luvna hasn't told them that part. She didn't dare for fear her parents might disown her. Her father is very strict. She's had nightmares about his saying the prayers for the dead and declaring that he no longer has a daughter if he were to learn about us."

"But surely she's introduced you to her family."

"Oh yes, we've met."

"They must have been favorably impressed by all you've accomplished so quickly in your career. They must realize..."

"I'm not the man of their choice. It's that simple. Luvna's choice doesn't seem to matter." Isaak began pacing restlessly once more. "When her parents moved to Warsaw, Luvna stayed in Krakow with her aunt. The family wanted her educated in the Krakow schools where there's no discrimination against Jews or women. She's a brilliant girl. She deserved that chance." He paused as if at a loss to explain what he wished particularly to convey. "But meanwhile, her father has chosen her husband. He's even decided where they're to live. He's disappointed and angry that his daughter questions the restrictions that our faith places on women. To him, she's a radical, a renegade." He sighed deeply. "Because she met me while she was at the university, he assumes that I've influenced her against her religious upbringing. In fact, I've tried to do just the reverse, but he doesn't believe that. "

"Perhaps Mer Meyer and I should have a talk," Ephraim offered.

Isaak shook his head. "Somehow, I don't think that would help. I appreciate the suggestion, Father, but this is something Luvna and I must work out for ourselves. Given time, I think I can win her father over."

Ephraim regarded his son probingly. "And meanwhile, you and Luvna plan to continue to live as you did in Krakow?"

"No, not exactly. Things are too different here. We'll see each other, of course. She's going to work in the office of the law firm I'm joining. We'll manage, somehow."

"You'll meet secretly to continue this clandestine liaison?"

"We'll do the best we can," Isaak answered stiffly. "We're not going to be driven apart by Levi Meyer's attempts to manage Luvna's life for her. She's not a child anymore."

Isaak turned and walked toward the house as though impatient to end the painful discussion.

"Son," Ephraim said, his voice carrying across the veranda, though he spoke softly. "What if history should repeat itself?"

Isaak stopped and turned warily to face his father. "In what way?"

"Mariska Wishnieska conceived your child and thus set in motion a tragic chain of events. What will you and Luvna do if she should become pregnant?"

Isaak answered resignedly, "We'll marry, of course, with or without her father's approval. However, for the sake of future peace, I'd prefer not to have to do that."

"Peace, purchased as you propose, can be an expensive commodity," Ephraim remarked. "I hope the price will not be more than you can pay."

"So do I." For one of the few times in his life, Isaak could not meet his father's eyes.

As he watched his son disappear into the house, Ephraim wondered if Isaak had not already paid too high a price in his quest for personal happiness. So far, each girl Isaak had loved – Mariska, Sarah, and now Luvna – had been beset by circumstances that complicated any hope of happiness for Isaak. Adam had told Ephraim about Sarah, since he had loved her first. He had felt a need to confess his own transgression, and to explain Isaak's role in salvaging the family's honor. Ephraim wondered if Isaak's newest relationship with the beautiful but controversial Luvna Meyer could lead to anything but further tragedy.

As the shadows began to lengthen, Ephraim's thoughts turned to his other children. Adam and Meyhra loved each other deeply, but since Meyhra had miscarried in the first year of their marriage, there had been no other children. Ephraim knew what a sorrow that was for both of them.

Michael, at age nine, was an undoubted genius whose intellect dazzled the tutors Ephraim hired to teach him. Already, he excelled most of the graduates from the local primary schools. Yet, within the Vistula Provinces, there was little room for Jewish students in the quotas of the intermediate schools, and the universities were currently closed to them.

Fortunately, fifteen-year-old Leah seemed close to attaining her most cherished goal, to complete her musical studies and attempt to implement a career. Yet, in order to even approach that goal, she had been obliged to leave Russian Poland.

Ephraim's greatest concern was that now that Isaak, his most politically motivated offspring, had returned to live in Warsaw, the young man's future showed less promise than it had as a valued member of a Krakow law firm. If Adam had found coming home to Warsaw a painful contrast to the freedom of his medical school days in Krakow, how much more disturbing would the new order of things in the Vistula Provinces seem to Isaak? Despite his joy at having his sons once more all together in Warsaw, Ephraim could not suppress a sense of foreboding.

Gradually, the reforms that had characterized the early years of Alexander II's reign were being reversed or seriously diluted by the dictates of 'expediency', and by the pernicious advice of the tsar's Slavophile ministers.

Ephraim surveyed the grounds of his estate but could feel no satisfaction in their contemplation. He wondered uneasily how soon the wave of change that was sweeping through the Russian Empire would come to encroach upon his right to hold this land, which was such a source of pride to him. He had dreamed of owning such an array of property for most of his life. Yet the history of his people reminded him how little there was, in terms of possessions, that had any real permanence.

Ephraim had tried to cultivate a habit of optimism after his release from prison following the 1830 rebellion, and particularly after he had met Elana and they had been instantly attracted to one another.

From the moment he had seen her at the back door of her father's home in Grojec, Ephraim had known that he would never rest until he possessed her. He would have done anything to achieve that goal. Indeed, he had gone to the length of lying to her father about his education in order to attain the father's consent. However, Ephraim had later made it right in a sense by applying himself diligently to a difficult course of study to prepare himself for the advancement to which he looked forward in the banking field. Ultimately, he had been able by this means to fulfill everything he had promised Mer Grojec, and had kept his promises to himself as well. From that time onward, he had viewed the future with confidence, certain that if he worked hard and adhered to his faith, Adonai would prosper him.

Certainly he had grown prosperous. The proof of his good fortune surrounded him. However, at this point in his life, when men normally look forward to a restful lessening of life's labors, the future seemed to hold much more of menace than of promise. Ephraim was forced to admit to himself that he contemplated the years ahead with mounting alarm.

* * *

Summer was drawing to a close, as was the brief but dramatic visit of Frau Schumann's distinguished guest and former rival, Franz Liszt. At age 60, Liszt seldom performed public concerts, and then only for charity. Time had banked his earlier bombastic fire, but had not curbed either his tutorial enthusiasm or his fondness for making the grand gesture. Having found Leah Marjzendiak ensconced as Clara's Schumann's pupil and summer house guest, Liszt had risen to the occasion and agreed to hear Leah play and to offer his opinion.

Leah, though in awe of the famous man, had performed with poise, grace, and skill. She had chosen a well-balanced program of Beethoven and Mozart, knowing she excelled in playing the works of these composers. Moreover, she had paid Liszt the tribute of ending her private recital with his own Hungarian Rhapsody No.2. Afterwards, she had modestly left the room so that the two professionals could feel free to discuss her renditions objectively. Had she been sufficiently ill-mannered to have listened unobserved, she would have heard herself praised. Liszt, though a flamboyant virtuoso, had stringent standards of musical performance. Praise from him was something to be treasured even in this somewhat mellower stage of his life.

"The girl has fire and brilliance," he remarked. "There is a quality that brings to mind Chopin. Not the wan wraith of his later years, but the young Chopin, as he was when I first heard him."

"I thought you would be impressed by her," Clara replied. "Yet that is not what I was seeking when I asked you to hear her." Clara paused as if searching for the right words. "Leah is a scholarship student at the Musik Schule in Berlin. Now, of course, it's called the Konservatory."

Liszt nodded. He was familiar with the history of the school's founding and evolution. "A rare circumstance in itself."

"She won first place in one of last year's regional competitions," Clara explained. "This summer, I've been tutoring her privately."

"Now you wish me to instruct her as well," Liszt interjected mischievously.

"I see you've not lost your sense of humor, Abbe."

"Human existence is an unending desert without humor," Liszt remarked thoughtfully. "Especially at our time in life."

"True," Clara agreed. "However, wise homilies do not answer my question."

"What was your question, mein frau?"

"Fire and brilliance notwithstanding, would you say she was nearly ready to face a critical and demanding public?"

Liszt gazed thoughtfully at his hostess. "She may well be," he answered. "She has the talent and the technique. Only time can say whether she has the endurance, and only that demanding public can say whether they will accept a Jewess as they accepted the dazzling daughter of Frederick Wieck." He took her hands and kissed them reverently. "These strong yet delicate hands confounded even me, and they're still as supple and beautiful as ever."

"You have not forgotten how to pay a compliment," Clara responded, gently drawing her hands away.

Liszt gazed at the river at the foot of the promontory on which the property stood. "This has been a rewarding visit. A nostalgic errand into the past, in a setting romantic enough to please the most temperamental of poets." Liszt paused. "Once I was determined to dislike you, Clara Schumann. I thought you an interloper in a realm reserved for men, but I was wrong. You have carved your own unique place in music. I wish your young protégé may do as well."

"I hope she will do even better," Clara Schumann responded, her eyes alight with humor and mischief to match that of her famous visitor. She, too, was filled with nostalgia as she thought of her young friend and pupil, poised on the threshold of womanhood, with her life and a potential career before her.

Liszt shared her mood, as his next words revealed. "If you had it all to do again, would you make any changes in your life?"

Clara shook her head. "No. It was all worth it. Having her here reminds me so much of myself years ago. She's just the age I was when I first became aware that I loved Robert. Little did either of us imagine how much we'd have to endure before that love could be realized. For me, a career in music was preordained by my father. All his life, he's gotten nearly everything he wanted."

"And a son-in-law he did not want. Do you and he ever speak of that now?"

Clara looked up at him. Even at 60, Liszt was still tall and erect, his mane of hair white but as thick as ever. His was a commanding presence, as had always been true of him.

"We seldom speak of our past differences now. We were reconciled years ago, and he adores his grandchildren. The very grandchildren he didn't want me to produce for fear they'd interfere with the future he had planned for me."

"We often seek to manage our children's lives, and seldom succeed. How many are there - eight?"

"Seven, now," Clara answered wistfully, lamenting still the death of her oldest child Marie in childbirth the preceding year. Moreover, 1870 had witnessed the hospitalization of her eldest son Ludwig for mental illness not unlike that of his father. "Still," she said, "I've been fortunate. I was a cherished daughter, then a beloved wife, a happy mother, and a successful musician."

"And I've no doubt the greatest successes are yet to come," Liszt said with obvious sincerity. He took her hand one last time. "I almost envy you, Clara Schumann. You have had the best life can offer, and occasionally the worst, and none of it has soured you or made you cynical and hard. At heart, you're still that young girl I remember, still eager to meet the future head-on, and yet willing to lend a hand to those who follow in your footsteps. I did you an injustice years ago. I, who have loved many women, could not appreciate or even admit to the genius in you. I recognize it truly only now that I'm an old man."

She assured him that there was still much in life to delight him, and that she had never looked upon him as a rival, or held any grudge toward him, though her father had. They parted in friendship, and Liszt gave Leah his blessing, predicting for her a glorious future if only she persevered in her studies, and followed her tutor's example of diligent practice and self-discipline.

# CHAPTER THIRTY-THREE
## COURTSHIP AND CONTROVERSY

Luvna Meyer sat at her desk in the reception area of the law firm of Wilshotski and Harnischk. The calmness of her demeanor belied the rapid beating of her pulse. Anger filled her, all but overwhelmed her, yet only the fiery light in her eyes betrayed her inner rage.

How could her father be so unfeeling as to come here to her place of employment and openly berate her for her rejection of Aaron Shaddeck? She had explained to him that she felt nothing more than friendship for that young man. Still, her father was determined to interfere, to compel her to join with Aaron in marriage, with no regard for her feelings. She felt all the more outraged because she had made every effort to establish a good relationship with her family, since her graduation from Krakow University. Moreover, she had dutifully moved back into the family home as her father had insisted, despite the restrictions this placed upon her personal freedom. How limited her life had become since returning to Warsaw. How seldom she and Isaak had truly been alone together in the past six months.

Luvna had, for some time, begun to feel cheated. She had in turn grown desperate to alleviate the present situation. Yet whenever she attempted to convey her sense of urgency to Isaak, he would caution her to be patient, and to wait until they could win her father's approval for their marriage.

Well, Luvna was tired of waiting, and patience was foreign to her nature. She was young, impulsive, and deeply in love. Small wonder that she was eager to find some means of bringing matters to a conclusion, so that she and Isaak could get on with their lives.

Except for Levi Meyer's visit, the day had gone well. Most of the partners had already left for the day before her father had arrived. Now, Mer Harnischk had just said good night to her. He had politely refrained from any mention of the verbal controversy he could not have failed to overhear from his private office.

Isaak was unaware of the conflict that had taken place in the outer office. As the newest member of the firm, his office was furthest from the reception area. He was completing his brief for the case he would plead next week, with no suspicion that his life was about to change irrevocably.

Luvna suddenly began to unpin and comb her hair. Afterwards, she pinched her cheeks briskly, and straightened her dress. She had come to a decision. Despite the garish yellow star on her bodice, she was pleased that she did not present the characteristic picture of a young Jewish girl in Russian Poland. The gilt-framed plate glass mirror opposite her desk confirmed this fact as she paused before it on her way to Isaak's office. She looked exactly what she was, an alluring young woman seeking the assuagement of her desires.

She knocked lightly, certain that he was alone.

"Come in," he answered, and looked up expectantly. He saw her framed in the open doorway. Her pale gold hair cascaded about her face like a halo of light. The outline of her slim yet voluptuous body, backlighted from the outer office, showed provocatively through the thin fabric of her pastel blue dress.

Levi Meyer had also objected to her choice of garments to wear at work, calling them goy and openly seductive. In truth, she was covered from neck to ankles, though the dress clung appealingly to her figure. Luvna sought to blot out the hated words from her memory. She gazed at Isaak.

Their eyes met, and Isaak arose from his chair, his pulse quickening. His glance lingered lovingly over every feature of her face, every well-remembered curve of her lissome body. They moved hungrily toward each other, and he could scarcely resist taking her then and there, but that would be too abrupt, too inconsiderate. He wanted to insure her pleasure as well as his own. He moved to the door and closed it, locking it with the thumb latch as an afterthought. Then he embraced her and kissed her. His arms clasped her to him, and his hands stroked and caressed her back and her buttocks. She pressed herself against him and her lips parted in a pleased smile as she felt the thrust of his manhood rising upward to meet her. Entwined in each other's arms, they sank to the floor, and the world seemed to shrink and fade away until only the two of them remained.

Later, as he held her close and whispered endearments against her silky hair, she clung to him, scarcely satisfied. These clandestine moments of intimacy no longer fulfilled her. Even in Krakow, they had never been free to openly admit the closeness of their relationship, and now they were reduced to these short, quick, stolen moments behind doors that might suddenly and unexpectedly be opened.

Luvna sat up abruptly, her unforgotten anger at her father still rankling, spoiling even her joy at making love to Isaak, turning the walls of the room into a prison. Under no circumstances could it be truly a love nest. It was too austere, too barren. The rows of scholarly law books, set on their neat shelves like silent sentinels, seemed to watch them malevolently. Luvna reacted with angry frustration to that fancied observation.

"We can't go on like this," she said, shaking her head. "Isaak, this can't continue." She got to her feet and hastily drew her clothes around her as if suddenly aware of her nakedness. Tears filled her eyes and spilled down her cheeks. "This room, these circumstances make me feel dirty."

Isaak's eyes followed her nervous movements as she paced the office. "I had no idea you felt that way." His voice sank almost to a whisper. "I thought you treasured our moments together. It seems I don't know you as well as I thought."

She turned in response to the disillusioned note in his voice. "Surely this secret, sordid existence doesn't appeal to you."

"Of course not, but it's only a temporary thing."

"Is it? Two years is a long 'temporary' thing!"

"It was different for us in Krakow."

"Only marginally. Orthodox doctrine doesn't change much with geography, or politics."

He stood and faced her squarely, obviously stung by the challenge in her words and manner. "What are you really saying, Luvna?"

She moved closer to him, put her arms around his waist and fitted her body to the contours of his, deliberately seeking to arouse him again. She was delighted when she felt him respond, and she dropped the garments she had wrapped around her body and opened herself to him. She was exquisitely aware of every separate movement that he made, savoring every moment of intimate physical union with him. She was intent on blotting out the hurt, the anger, and self-rejection that her father's words had precipitated. It was he who had made her feel cheap and soiled. With Isaak, she normally felt such joy, such exultation. She reached out now for that sense of elation; she reveled in the ecstasy of fulfillment and sought to prolong the slow release of tension that followed. Isaak held her close, covering her face and throat with kisses.

Only then did she remember the question he had asked earlier. What had she really been saying?

"I want us to feel free to be together like this whenever we want to," she said in belated reply, "not just when we can find an empty room and a spare moment. Let's elope to Praga if we must, but let's put an end to this shadow-life we've been living."

Praga. The name tasted bitter on Isaak's tongue as he repeated it. He and Mariska had tried that solution, only to learn that, for a Jew and a Gentile, there was no solution even there. However, Luvna and he were both Jewish. Perhaps a rabbi could be found who would risk marrying them without her father's blessing. Perhaps it was a course of action worthy of pursuit.

They were both still so engrossed in each other that neither heard the door of the outer office open and close. By now, both had donned their clothing but were once again locked in each other's arms, their lips joined in an impassioned kiss. It was only when the door to Isaak's office was forcibly thrust open and a shadow fell across the floor that first Luvna and then Isaak realized that they were no longer alone. Levi Meyer had waited and watched for his daughter to leave work, hoping to accompany her home and plead his cause further with her. Now he had returned to search for her, his concern mounting as he realized that only she and Isaak remained in the office building.

"In the Lord's name," Meyer roared. "I'll kill you both for this. My family will never live down this shame."

He seized Luvna by the shoulders and pulled her away from Isaak's embrace. Isaak reacted instinctively to protect the woman he loved. He picked up a metal lamp from the desk and ran toward Meyer to strike him.

Luvna, twisting furiously in her father's grasp, anticipated the impending blow and shouted, "No! No, Isaak, don't!"

Warned by her outcry, Meyer let her go and faced Isaak angrily.

Isaak stopped in his tracks, appalled at what he had almost done. He quickly set down the lamp. Luvna ran to him. In her haste, she stumbled and fell against the desk.

Her father glared at her. "You slut! You filthy whore! From this moment, I have no daughter!"

Luvna faced him defiantly, instinctively clasping Isaak's hand.

Meyer raised his arm as if to strike her. Then his face turned ashen, and the upraised arm fell to his side. He turned heavily, moved toward the door, but never reached it. Instead, he seemed to crumple from his great height, to shrink and cave in upon himself. He fell and lay unmoving on the thickly carpeted floor, his breathing a series of ragged, discordant moans that rapidly grew softer and swiftly sank into silence.

"Father? Father!" Luvna cried out, but still he did not move. Shocked, weeping, Luvna crawled to where Levi Meyer lay, turned his face upward so that his open, blindly-staring eyes were visible. She screamed hysterically and Isaak, realizing the extremity of what had happened, drew her to him and sought vainly to calm and comfort her.

\* \* \*

The winter season was in full swing. The lights along the Linden-Strausse were like a row of brightly gleaming gems forming a festive necklace whose glow the falling snow caught and reflected. The sleigh seemed to float along the street behind the bell-bedecked pony. The young girl's laughter rang out, merrier and more musical than the jingle of the bells.

"I've never been happier, Heinrich. I never knew life held such pleasures."

"You'll learn more about pleasure than you've ever imagined possible. Oh, Libschein, there's so much I long to teach you, so much of which you've been kept deliberately in ignorance. All that is about to change. You'll see."

The blonde man gazed soulfully at the lovely auburn-haired girl beside him. He admired her beauty and was tempted by her vivacious eagerness to experience all that life had to offer.

This ride along one of the most picturesque thoroughfares in Berlin was the culmination of a leisurely Sunday spent in sightseeing and merrymaking. As a crowning touch, Heinrich Rheinsfeld had treated her to an elegant dinner at Brachstein's, and Leah could scarcely express her gratification.

"What shall I see? What else is there to show me? Today's been so full, so perfect."

"I would show you life in all its glory," Rheinsfeld answered expansively. "I would like to show you love," he whispered, gazing fondly at her. "You know nothing of either. You're been wrapped like a delicate moth in a cocoon of your faith's creation. There's more to living than your rabbis preach in synagogue."

Something in his words faintly disturbed her. Yet she was having too much fun to heed the nagging misgivings at the back of her mind. This blonde giant, with his charm and elegance, his knowledge of music and concertizing, fascinated her. The world she had sampled today, a potpourri of museums, art galleries, coffee houses, shops, and restaurants aglow with crystal, translucent china, gleaming silver, and liveried attendants, all these things filled her with awe. They set her imagination reeling. Warsaw had held nothing to equal them, not even at Madam Pietrowska's most impressive soiree. Leah longed to be a part of this world, a realm that was the accustomed habitat for people such as Franz Liszt, Clara Schumann, and Heinrich Rheinsfeld. It was a world from which she had heretofore been banned by the yellow star that proclaimed her background.

Yet here was this handsome young German speaking to her of love, gazing at her with adoring eyes, as though she were a desirable woman instead of only a girl of sixteen. Perhaps the champagne she had drunk at dinner contributed to her exultant mood. Perhaps she was over-reading his words, misinterpreting his intentions. After all, today had been planned as a belated celebration of her birthday. She had felt lonely at having to spend a second birthday away from home, and when Professor Rheinsfeld had heard of it, he had undertaken to cheer her up.

"I don't want to think about anything else just now except this glorious day," Leah said with joyous abandon.

"You're right, of course. Why spoil a perfect occasion with references to Hebrew dogma and mythology?"

The smile faded from Leah's face. "Dogma and mythology? Whatever do you mean? Is that your opinion of my religion?"

"That's basically my opinion of any religion," Rheinsfeld answered candidly. "Such concepts comfort the weak, but the strong and resolute don't need them." He took her hand. "You and I, Libschein, we are strong. We are among the chosen few who make our own rules."

Leah gazed at him in fascinated horror, certain that she was too naive to tell how much of what he said was meant in jest.

He went on unabashed, totally unaware of her reaction. "Has anyone told you yet how beautiful you are?"

"My mother, Frau Schumann, and one other very dear friend," Leah answered hesitantly, thinking of Markos. How far away he seemed just now.

"In the eyes of an admiring public, I will show you your true self. In one more year, you will graduate. But even before that, I shall take you with me on tour. That's a promise!"

In the next few months, he repeated that promise to her on many occasions. At first, she laughed, but later she began to take him seriously. He was a man of the world. He knew well how to play upon the feelings of an inexperienced young girl. Furthermore, he did perceive her as beautiful, despite her Jewish background. In another setting, without that garish badge, he thought, he might be able to persuade her to disguise her origins.

It would be a novel experience for him to travel with her as his concert partner and mistress. She would think herself honored that he took notice of her, groomed her, tutored her privately at no charge, in exchange for the "pleasures of her company." He had no doubt there would be pleasures in abundance, and they would all be his, given time. He would make her forget this "friend" in Warsaw, and she would belong solely to him for as long as he wanted her. After that, well, she could always go back to Warsaw if she chose, but if she was wise, she would make the most of her career, and find some wealthy patron to protect her. Life was really quite simple, Rheinsfeld mused, reduced to its basic terms, without the emotional embellishments of either love or religion, neither of which he held in high regard.

\* \* \*

From the moment Elana read the last line of Leah's letter, posted from Berlin in early May, she knew she was facing a family crisis. It was the latest in a series. Such events tended to strike in threes, so she had once heard.

At the end of February, Luvna Meyer had quit her job, and had refused, from that time onward, to see or speak with Isaak. At first, Isaak had understood this reaction, or had thought he did. He had confided to Elana the events leading to Levi Meyer's death. He had seemed too ashamed to discuss them with Ephraim. However, as the weeks had passed, and

Luvna still refused to see him, Isaak had grown morose and withdrawn, burying himself in his work.

In early April, Meyhra had miscarried again, once more frustrating her own and Adam's urgent desire for a child. Thus, both Elana's elder sons were in a state of desperation. Moreover, her youngest son, Michael, was growing steadily more restless because the schools of Warsaw remained closed to him and all Jewish youths. And now, to further compound Elana's concerns, Leah proposed to go on tour with Professor Rheinsfeld at the end of the current school term.

Hilda Krause's letter disturbed Elana even more. The German woman expressed herself in terms that were precise and poignant. She had come to the conclusion that the young professor was up to no good where Leah was concerned, and Frau Schumann had left to take up a permanent teaching post at Frankfurt-Am-Main. She could, therefore, offer Hilda and Armand Krause no assistance in dissuading Leah from this rash course on which she was determined to embark.

Ephraim was engrossed in the accounts of the estate when Elana brought him both letters. He read them through solemnly, then looked meaningfully at his wife.

"This must be stopped."

That was all he said. What he did was to apply for a three-week leave of absence from the bank. Franz, when Ephraim had explained his reasons, was totally in agreement with his decision, and granted the leave without question, though it would entail considerable extra work for him.

The next morning, Ephraim left for Zurich. Ten days later, he arrived in Berlin, much to Leah's surprise. She was even more surprised when he told her she would not be returning to Berlin in the fall. She had instead been enrolled in the imminently prestigious Zurich Konservatory and Musik Holkschuler. She would live under the protection of Anna and Lukas Kolvner while she attended classes there.

"But Papa," she protested, "I don't want to leave Berlin. Not just now."

"Your father has chosen wisely," Armand Krause agreed. "You have learned much here in Berlin, but in Zurich, you will achieve even greater skill, greater polish. By this time next year, you will be ready to begin your musical career in earnest."

"But Heinrich would have taken me on tour with him," Leah said petulantly, withholding the fact that Rheinsfeld had spoken to her of love and the romantic adventures they would share while on tour. She was too naive to understand the true significance of those proposed adventures.

"Since when do you wish to take second place when you can be first?" Krause had chosen the most telling argument possible. He had appealed to her professional pride, her artistic vanity.

Reluctantly, even tearfully, she subsided. With Hilda's help, she packed her possessions and then said a poignant farewell to her former teacher and his wife, who had provided her with a home for the two years of her stay in Germany. Within the week, she was at home in Warsaw, feeling uprooted and dispossessed.

It was in that mood that Markos found her one afternoon in late June of 1872.

"I'm glad you're back," he said. "I've missed you." Shyly, he handed her the recorder he had given him to keep for her.

Leah gazed up at him, realizing that he was taller and older than when she had last seen him. The tiniest of lines had appeared at the corners of his eyes, and the creases beside his mouth were etched more sharply than she remembered. Furthermore, he had gained a certain poise she had not seen in him before. When she had left for Berlin, he had been a charming boy. Now, at twenty, he was a man.

"I've missed you, too," she said, aware only at that moment of just how much she meant it.

\* \* \*

Ultimately, it was Elana who insisted that Isaak, if he truly loved Luvna, must make a stand to win her.

"She's filled with guilt because of her father's death," he explained yet again. "The thought of me and what we've meant to each other brings it all back to her. How can I force her to see me, knowing that?"

"How can you refrain from ever seeing her again if you truly love her?"

Isaak paced the room restlessly. "I, too, feel guilty, Mother. I was actually prepared to kill him. If Luvna hadn't shouted at me, I would probably be in prison for murder right now."

"I doubt that, Son. I think you would have stopped yourself in time to prevent such a tragedy. However, Adonai has acted in His own way to furnish a solution to your and Luvna's problem. Yet, instead of accepting His will, you've only created more obstacles."

Isaak stared at his mother in surprise. She had stated the situation in terms he had not even considered. "Do you really think I can make Luvna see things the way that you do?"

Elana considered for a moment. "I've no doubt you can make her mother see them that way."

She did not add that she was well acquainted with Zelda Meyer, and that the mother of the girl Isaak loved had had her own problems with Levi Meyer.

\* \* \*

The Meyer home was modest in comparison with the Marjzendiak estate. The grounds were less expansive, and the house, though strongly built, was modeled on more conservative lines. It lacked the grandeur of the old Zielinski mansion that Ephraim had rescued from decay and, with the help of the Pietrowskis, had refurbished and restored. However, the wealth acquired over years of trading by Levi Meyer, and the taste of the wife he had selected for her blood lines rather than her beauty, were reflected in the decor and the furnishings that distinguished the house.

Zelda Meyer was proud of her home. Her position as its chatelaine and her devotion to her daughter Luvna comprised the very core of her existence. She had never known the love that is often shared by husband and wife. Levi had been a good provider, but never a considerate lover. Moreover, he had wanted a son to carry on his name, and he had not disguised from his wife his disappointment that she had borne him only a daughter.

Luvna had grown to be surprisingly beautiful and unexpectedly intelligent. Neither Levi nor Zelda was gifted with great physical appeal. However, Luvna had also inherited Levi's sharp wit and Zelda's innate taste. Thus, she had become the focus for the energies of both her parents. The result had been ultimate tragedy, in Levi's case. Failing to realize that a child is a person rather than a possession, he had driven Luvna to desperation, and had thereby precipitated his own demise.

As so often happens following such events, the woman of the house was left to pick up the pieces and restore order. Zelda was currently engaged in an attempt to do just that.

"You cannot remain forever in mourning, child. Your father's death was unfortunate, but his health had been recently fragile at best. You are far too young to retire from life."

Zelda Meyer spoke with an authority she seldom expressed. Heretofore, she had deferred to the dictates of her husband. Now, however, her husband was dead, and she had her child to consider, a child whose life had come to a standstill. Nine months had passed since Zelda had buried Levi, and still Luvna stayed in the house, moping as though the family still sat Shivah.

"You don't understand, Mama," the girl said tonelessly. "It's my fault. Everything that happened was my fault."

"Your father was a man of strong convictions. He felt he was always right, but none of us is always right, only Adonai can claim that distinction."

Luvna turned her pale face toward her mother. Her delicate coloring was muddied by prolonged weeping, and by the drabness of the black dress she wore.

"It seems I'm always wrong, even when I think I know what's right," she said bitterly.

Zelda looked closely at her daughter, seeking to gauge her reaction. "Do you really love this man, this Isaak?"

Luvna turned away from that direct gaze. She walked to the window and studied the windswept landscape. "I think I do," she answered listlessly. "I know he loves me."

"Even loving you, he won't wait forever."

"What do you think I should do, Mama?"

Zelda went to join her daughter at the window. "I think you should do what your mind and heart tell you."

She took Luvna's hand and led her to the couch near the large windows. "I'm going to tell you something, child, that I hope will help you to understand your father. Even more, I hope it will teach you a lesson about life. Try to hear me out without interrupting."

Luvna sat silently, listening as her mother recounted the story of her life.

Zelda had been an eager young girl looking forward to marriage in the Orthodox tradition. She had secretly hoped for a gentle lover as well as a husband to provide the good things of life for her and their children. Zelda related her disappointments, her continued physical frustrations, and the slights she had suffered because of her failure to produce a son. Yet she paid tribute to Levi's admirable traits. He had always been faithful to her, he had given her every sum of money he had earned, he had been generous with her relatives, and unfailingly dedicated to the service of Adonai. His donations had been a major factor in the building of the new synagogue. However, Zelda seriously doubted if Levi had ever truly known the meaning of happiness or pleasure.

"You are fortunate, child. You have a young man who loves you in every possible way. You have no idea what that means because you don't understand how bitter it is to lack love. Don't throw away such a precious gift."

Luvna gazed at her mother, her eyes haunted. "I still see Papa lying there, Mama, His sightless eyes still seem to be accusing me. I still hear his words. He called me a whore. He disowned me as his daughter!" She covered her face with her hands and wept bitterly.

Zelda raised Luvna's face and drew the girl into her arms.

"You must shut all that out and go on with your life. He lived his. Now it's your turn. You've punished yourself and your young man long enough."

* * *

When Leah came home at the semester break, it was to a household filled with frantic activities. Preparations were in progress for a wedding. True, it would not be an ostentatious affair. The bride's family was still in mourning. Nonetheless, a wedding is a wedding, and it was time Isaak was married. He was thirty-one years old. Besides, Adam's marriage had produced no children, and the family needed the reassurance of a child to carry on its traditions.

Leah entered into the spirit of the occasion, thinking that soon her own wedding day would come. She was content to think of her future with Markos at her side. They had already begun to make serious plans. In less than a year, Leah would complete her studies in Zurich. Heinrich Rheinsfeld was only a memory by now, a memory with the flavor of fantasy. She would often wonder what would have happened if her father had not come to Berlin last spring. Yet, in her heart, she knew he had been right to come.

When the invited company assembled in the grand new synagogue to attend the wedding of Luvna Meyer and Isaak Marjzendiak, it was indeed a memorable occasion. Many of the guests represented the high and mighty of Warsaw, both Gentile and Jewish. Isaak had begun to establish a reputation in legal circles, and the deceased father of the bride had been a well-known and respected merchant for many decades. In his place, his cousin Mordecai had come from Byello-Russia to accompany the bride and her mother to the synagogue, and to oversee the signing of the ketubah and the completion of the traditional ceremony.

Ephraim Marjzendiak looked on with a feeling of accomplishment and relief. For many years he had feared for the safety and happiness of his second son, the son that so reminded him of himself in his youth. He had distrusted his son's judgment when Isaak had first told him of Luvna and of their relationship in Krakow. However, seeing the expression of joy on Isaak's face served to put his fears to rest. After many frustrations and tragedies, Isaak had at last found love, a love he could openly proclaim, and hopefully with it, a measure of peace and contentment.

# CHAPTER THIRTY-FOUR
## WARSAW: 1873

The year 1873 began with a series of controversies, seemingly minor in themselves, but actually highly significant. The wave of industrialization that had already swept across western Europe was now accelerating in eastern Europe. A new class of entrepreneurs was gradually replacing the old landed aristocracy. Those larger estates that had not been subdivided functioned almost as independent agricultural units, each governed according to the personal ethics of its owner. Nonetheless, workers on those estates generally fared better than their counterparts in the urban-based factories. Air on the farm-estates was clean and clear; space was plentiful, and the hours were determined largely by the season and by the duration of daylight. Moreover, farm workers were now in short supply, so that their services were highly valued and comparatively well-compensated. This was an ironic state of affairs that had come about only since most of the former agricultural workmen had migrated to the cities in search of a better livelihood.

When the new industrial movement had first begun to spread eastward, Russian law had strictly forbidden the formation of trade unions. Fortunately, those laws were enforced with notorious irregularity in the provinces, and sometimes not at all. The Imperial presumption that structured associations among factory workers adversely affected production had led to this restriction. Surprisingly, such organizations, flourishing surreptitiously, had actually served to enhance the flow of work. Meetings occurred during lunch hours, since workers were not allowed to assemble otherwise, and the camaraderie that resulted accelerated the speed at which tasks were performed. The leaders among the workmen were quick to notice that lunch breaks were allowed to continue longer if the work quotas were met.

The factory owners, gratified by the high volume of production, showed themselves willing to grant some concessions to the laborers. This was on the basis of the work the men completed, and did not result from trade union posters or rhetoric. Higher pay and an occasional bonus were granted when deadlines were met or exceeded, and the resulting higher sales led to greater profits. Nonetheless, the working conditions improved only very slowly, hours were long, and injuries frequent. The ongoing hope behind the union efforts was that eventually, through collective bargaining, those who staffed the factories might one day gain a measure of control over conditions there. Unfortunately, thus far, the only place laborers had been able to effectively express their concerns had been on rare occasions in the polling places and in the law courts.

The opportunities for legal redress of industrial grievances usually involved accidents attributable to hazardous working conditions. Most of these were filed on behalf of the surviving relatives of accident victims. Occasionally, a horribly injured workman would be brought into court to illustrate, with terribly graphic realism, the lamentable conditions under which most factory employees were obliged to exist and to function. Even the most callous magistrate could occasionally be moved to pity by such tragic examples.

In recent months, the law firm of Wilshotski and Harnischk had found its calendar overrun with industrial grievance cases. Most of these had been assigned to the partnership's newest associate, Isaak Marjzendiak. In general, they were considered the lower echelon of trial duties, appropriate primarily to test the skills of an untried attorney. However, as conducted by young Marjzendiak, they were proving to be not only worthwhile legal undertakings, but also a source of growing prestige. Gratitude for these efforts was high among members of the working class. Furthermore, the wives of members of the upper class

...nded to seek diversion by attending public court hearings. Thus, Isaak found himself unexpectedly cast in the role of a local celebrity. More importantly, with the occasional winning of a substantial settlement, Isaak was able to bring into the firm's treasury a significant income.

While the senior partners of the firm were pleased with Isaak's trial record, they were mostly of a conservative turn of mind. They did not relish being perceived as a center of controversy. Yet, a plethora of controversial cases seemed to be finding their way to the doors of Wilshotsky and Harnischk in the late winter and early spring of 1873. The age-old struggle between the admirers of Peter the Great's policy of westernization and the Slavophiles who lauded the superiority of traditional Russian values had been resolved in favor of the latter.

Those leaders who looked upon foreign influences as a decadent and destructive element in Russian culture became the spokesmen of their time. Their views now determined Russian policy and served to facilitate the imposition of increasingly stringent measures against the non-Slavik members of the Empire's population. The Jews, the Ukrainians, and the Roman Catholics once again became special targets of the resulting bigotry. Obviously, the worst examples of this trend occurred in Russia itself, but in one form or another, it pervaded every province of Alexander's empire. In Russian Poland it was manifested as an intensified 'Russification' policy which even the most politically insensitive citizens could no longer ignore.

Arrests and reprisals directed against the forces of outspoken dissent again became commonplace occurrences. The innocent were detained and questioned almost as often as those who had truly engaged in the Nationalist effort. Once arrested, the accused might remain in prison for months before coming to trial. Judges presiding over such trials were bigoted and biased. Their rulings often supported the suppressive policies of the Slavophile influenced administration. As a result, a number of lawsuits were filed in an effort to fight the more offensive manifestations of this policy.

Isaak Marjzendiak soon found his practice weighted not only with industrial lawsuits but also with cases whose real basis was discrimination. Since the magistrates themselves were proponents of the prevailing Slavophilism, to win on the liberal side of such disputes required eloquence, skill, luck, and often a measure of duplicity.

It was late April of 1873. All the preceding night a continuous downpour of rain had drenched the countryside, imparting an atmosphere of unrelenting gloom. This dark aura matched perfectly with Isaak Marjzendiak's mood as he was driven by hired cab from the apartment on Lezno Street, that he and Luvna shared, to the rebuilt municipal building that housed the Supreme Court of Warsaw Province.

Despite the merits of his case, Isaak entertained little hope that his arguments would prevail before the Honorable Pyotor Dysnedovich, the Tsar's Chief Justice of Civil Judiciary Affairs in the Vistula provinces. The man's arbitrary narrowness of outlook was legendary. The controversy at issue was a simple one. Isaak's client, Maurice Jedewreski, a distant cousin of the eminent physician Samuel Jedewreski, owned a furniture mart whose items of merchandise were manufactured on the premises. Jedewreski managed the business personally; however, his senior cabinet maker was a Catholic Pole named Frederick Zobsienski.

The crux of the dispute lay not between Jedewreski and Zobsienski but between Jedewreski and the administrative authority of the Provisional Government, which had invoked an ancient Polish statute prohibiting Jews from keeping Christian slaves. Marjzendiak's contention, filed on behalf of his client, was that the statute in question was irrelevant to the matter at hand. Since Zobsienski was a well paid and voluntary worker, the interpretation of the employer-employee relationship as "slavery" was totally unjustified.

Throughout the early stages of the trial, Isaak had carried out a carefully calculated strategy. By skillfully allowing his opponent to summon and question a lengthy catalogue of witnesses who gave rather similar but inconclusive testimony, he had insured that the magistrate's patience would be tried to the utmost.

As the day wore on, the combination of poorly ventilated rooms in the building where the court session was held, the heavy judiciary robes required to be worn by the officers of the Court, and the repetitious interrogation of the Provisional Government's witnesses combined to exert an almost hypnotic affect on those present.

"You heard this argument taking place?"

The female witness in the box paused momentarily. Then she nodded. "Yes, I heard some of it."

Isaak stood to lodge an objection to the prosecuting counsel's inquiry.

"Argumentative," he commented. "And once again irrelevant. A partially-overheard conversation between the defendant and his employee by a customer does not constitute a valid basis for a charge of abuse. The witness has admitted she was not present in the rear of the shop. She has stated she heard only occasional words and snatches of what was said, that the voices were not raised, and that she is uncertain as to the cause of the discussion. It cannot even be validly entitled an argument."

The prosecuting counsel turned in exasperation to face his opponent. "Nonetheless, the witness's testimony serves to set the tone of the relationship and contributes to the foundation of the State's case."

"Objection denied," the magistrate ruled.

"No further questions," the prosecutor said with obvious satisfaction.

"I have several questions to put to the witness," Isaak stated.

"The hour grows late, Counselor Marjzendiak," Justice Dysnedovich commented. "I trust you do not intend to prolong this very simple matter."

Isaak bowed politely to the magistrate. "With all due respect, your Honor, and despite the lateness of the hour, I am obligated to defend my client's rights."

He approached the witness stand where stood the middle class housewife whose testimony he suspected to have been originally obtained under duress. The woman looked distinctly uncomfortable. Isaak employed his most disarming smile to put her at ease. "You have testified, Madam," he began, "that you entered the defendant's place of business shortly after midday to arrange for the construction of a set of kitchen cupboards."

The witness nodded, then remembered her previous instructions to answer aloud. "Yes, sir, I did."

"Did you have a particular style of cupboard in mind?"

"I knew in general what I wanted."

"But not the specific details?"

"Well, I left that to him. To the merchant. It's his business."

"Such matters as the selection of wood, the structural details, these were professional matters best left in the expert hands of a cabinet maker?"

The witness nodded enthusiastically, then added, "Yes."

Encouraged, Isaak continued. "Madam Leskovna, do you employ domestic servants in your household?"

"Objection," the prosecutor shouted. "Irrelevant."

"The witness's answer is material to the foundation of my client's defense. There is an obvious parallel between the relationship of chatelaine and domestic assistant and that of shopkeeper and industrial assistant." Isaak looked questioningly to the bench. "May I continue, your Honor?"

"Please continue, counselor," Justice Dysnedovich conceded, "But I hope you will bear in mind the time."

"Yes, your Honor," Isaak answered and turned back to the witness. "How many such subordinates are currently in your employ, Madam?"

"Two," answered the witness with a certain pride. She had once served in a domestic capacity and so rejoiced in her rise in station, thanks to an advantageous marriage. "They have both been with me for some years."

"A satisfactory relationship, would you say?"

"Quite."

"Madam, in your role as employer of these subordinates, do you ever have cause to discipline them, perhaps to impress upon them certain duties or instructions in which they may have temporarily lapsed?"

"Of course," the woman replied. "No servant is perfect, but they're both good girls, as willing as can be."

"You would hardly call your employment of these two ladies 'slavery,' nor your instructions to them abuse?"

She bristled at that. "I've never done a cruel act or uttered an abusive word to either one of them!"

"I'm sure you haven't," Isaak said. "Tell me, Madam, do you know what faith these ladies espouse who help in your household?"

Madam Traskovna regarded Isaak with a puzzled expression.

"No, I don't. I've never thought to ask."

Thanks to Isaak's forethought, both the domestics in question were waiting in the antechamber outside the main courtroom.

"With the Court's permission, I should like to afford Madam Leskovna the opportunity to repair that omission," he said and nodded to the Court Clerk. The two women were brought forward.

Justice Dysnedovich, desiring to show his control of the situation as well as to handle the matter with dispatch, addressed his own inquiries to the two intimidated women, much as Isaak had expected he would.

"State your names," the magistrate demanded imperiously.

"Jilna Vaslytowska, Sir," the younger woman answered.

"Maria Dizengold, your Honor," the elder, more educated of the two, responded.

"Where do you go to church?"

The two women exchanged fearful looks. With downcast eyes the younger one answered, "I don't, Sir. When I was little, my mother took me, but I haven't been to church since I grew up. Between keeping house for my family and keeping house for my mistress, where's the time for it?"

Maria was even more reticent than her colleague. She eyed the defense counsel furtively. "I go to synagogue after work, on the Sabbath."

The prosecutor came to his feet, incensed. "A renegade Christian and a Jew," he exclaimed.

"They're good workers," Madam Traskovna repeated.

"What Madam has just told us, your Honor, is that their religious practices or lack thereof have no bearing on their efficiency or the value of their work," Isaak said crisply. "I submit that is a common finding. With increasing industrialization, Christians, Jews, gypsies, and immigrants of a variety of origins have become both owners and laborers in our provinces. The law of 1560 forbidding Jews to keep Christian slaves applied to the then common practice of slavery. Our enlightened Tsar Alexander has freed the serfs and enfranchised the peasants, thus putting an end to slavery. I further submit that the charges raised in this action constitute an insult to his Imperial Majesty, and warrant dismissal on those grounds."

The prosecutor rose to his feet and opened his mouth to speak. The court room atmosphere, charged with the emotions of the assembled spectators, became a maelstrom of sound as those spectators noisily voiced their feelings. Discouraged, the prosecutor took his seat.

Justice Dysnedovich wielded his gavel repeatedly, calling for order. Finally, some measure of order and quiet was restored.

"Counselor, your point is well taken," he said, addressing himself to Isaak. On no account could even a hint of disparagement be permitted against the Tsar. "The charge is withdrawn," the magistrate ruled. "The defendant is dismissed and this hearing is hereby terminated."

The gavel sounded once more. The magistrate arose regally from his bench and descended the stairs. Only when he had left the chambers did the clamor of conversation resume.

"A clever ploy," the prosecutor remarked, "but it will not always prove successful."

"No strategy does," Isaak agreed congenially. He turned to address his client. "The charges against you are withdrawn, Maurice," he said, taking the other man's hand. "You may go now and try to make up for the income you've lost while answering these ridiculous charges."

His client was ecstatic. He drew Isaak's hand to his lips and kissed it as though the attorney were an emperor. "I can't tell you how grateful I am. I can scarcely believe it's over, and I'm free without paying a huge fine or losing my business."

Isaak inquired with genuine concern, "Have you had to close your doors during the trial?"

Jedewreski shook his head. "Fortunately, my eldest son is a good salesman. And Zobsienski has stayed at work in spite of everything," the merchant added gratefully.

"He was wise. He well may have wasted his time if he had come to watch this judicial circus," Isaak remarked. He glanced thoughtfully about the courtroom, then turned back to his client. "You deserved to win, although in this setting one does not always reap one's just desserts."

"It's all thanks to you, Counselor," Jedewreski responded.

"I'm glad you won," Isaak said with quiet sincerity. "It serves to restore somewhat my faith in justice."

"But it was you who won," Jedewreski exclaimed. "You were brilliant. Your fee." Jedewreski began, but Isaak interrupted him with a gesture of dismissal.

"Why," he said, "don't you send it to the office later?"

Jedewreski nodded gratefully. "I shall. And thanks once again. Shalom, Counselor." Jedewreski reached out and took Isaak's hand once more.

Isaak smiled warmly, at last allowing himself to enjoy his victory. "Shalom, Maurice."

The prosecutor, the deputies and other officers, even the majority of the spectators, had already departed. The defendant and his attorney were the last to leave the court, one transfixed with happiness and the glow of triumph over injustice, the other pleased but subdued.

Outside, the streets of downtown Warsaw had dried. The sky had cleared and was awash with hazy sunshine. The two men parted to go their separate ways, one to resume his life, the other to ponder how narrow is the margin between victory and defeat.

Isaak was not deceived by today's good fortune. He had invoked what amounted to a clever ploy, as the prosecutor had remarked. Next time, depending upon the circumstances, it might not work. In the meantime, as Adam would have said, Isaak was treating only a symptom, not the underlying cause of the problem. The cause, as the voices of political dissent were bravely proclaiming, resided hundreds of kilometers away in the Imperial palace at St. Petersburg. Frustrated by the unexpected outcome of some of his reforms and torn by personal and domestic conflicts, the Tsar Liberator had become, in seventeen short years, almost as oppressive and reactionary as his father Nicholas had been.

Isaak walked on in the late afternoon sunlight thinking about the conflicting forces at work in Russian Polish society. Occasionally, he would be invited to the secret meeting places of the growing underground political parties, although he seldom accepted such invitations. In the clandestine efforts of the labor unions and in the radical publications of militant groups such as the newly-formed "People's Will," Isaak saw the consequences of Slavophile philosophy at work. In defending the put upon, the disfranchised, the laborers crippled by the hazards of their work, Isaak had been welcomed into their midst. He had found himself in a no-mans land between the realm of the socially powerful and affluent such as the Pietrowkis and the Wilshotskis, and the shadow-world of the militants who sought newer, more effective methods to dislodge the hated foreign overlords from the east. Isaak walked a narrow and difficult path between those conflicting territories, belonging truly to neither.

To Luvna, he disclosed only a small part of what he saw and heard. With his law partners, he shared what they wanted to know, and for the rest, he kept his own counsel. Only with his father Ephraim was he at all candid. Father and son held long discussions regarding the real problems and forces at work in the society that surrounded them. Beneath the deceptively smooth surface of daily living and doing business, the tenacious spirit of Polish Nationalism was stronger and more determined than ever. However, it was doubtful that it would take the form of open revolution. Twice in the current century, that had been tried and had failed. What other alternatives, Isaak was prone to wonder, were open to those who met in secret as spring mellowed into summer, and summer ripened into fall?

* * *

Leah returned in triumph to her home in Warsaw, just as the leaves on the elm trees along the main drive of her father's estate were turning radiant shades of scarlet, orange, and gold. Markos Kolvner met her train and welcomed her literally with open arms.

"How good it is to see you again," he said, reluctant to release her from his embrace.

Leah stood gazing up at him as if her eyes could not be satisfied. A year had passed since they had last met, and in that time, Leah's world had changed. She was seventeen now and had gained a measure of recognition as a musician. She had been described in the Swiss press as embarking upon a career that promised to rival those of Marie Pleyel, now retired because of illness, and Clara Schumann, who was still actively concertizing and teaching.

However, in that moment of sweet reunion, Leah was a homesick young girl reveling in the arms of her beloved.

"All the time I was on tour, I was torn between wanting it never to end and wishing it were all over so I could come home and be with you like this." She hugged him without inhibition and laid her head gratefully on his shoulder.

"I treasured every letter," he whispered. "They brought you close each time I read them." He held her at arm's length and smiled. "Now that you're home, how will I ever be able to wait for the next six weeks to pass so we can be married?"

"On, but Markos, I have so much to do to be ready. It scarcely seems enough time."

Markos grinned ruefully. "I guess it depends on one's point of view."

As Markos and Leah rode in his family carriage toward Plaz Marjzendiak, Leah could not help but note in passing the changes that had taken place in her absence. Warsaw had expanded. Factories, shops, and modest houses now filled the area where open spaces had stretched before. Buildings encroached upon the wooded areas, and trees had been cleared to make room for further construction. As a consequence, Plaz Marjzendiak seemed much closer to the city.

Leah knew that her father had built another mill to produce lumber for the wave of urban building that had accelerated in recent years. He had proudly described the new mill in one of his letters to her in Zurich. Seeing the concrete representation of the events her father had described was nonetheless both a thrill and a shock to Leah, dramatizing, upon the occasion of her homecoming, the inevitable changes at work in the world she had known.

The Marjzendiaks celebrated Leah's homecoming with the festivities befitting such a joyous occasion. The Pietrowskis and the Kolvners attended as honored guests, and with the wedding of Leah and Markos imminent, the Kolvners were almost family. Ephraim offered a toast in Leah's honor.

"The Lord blesses us today with His bounty and fills our hearts with rejoicing. Our daughter has come home to us resplendent with honors, celebrated for her achievements." He smiled fondly at her. "Once I would not have believed it possible."

"Here in Russian Poland," Isaak said, responding to the toast, "it wouldn't have been."

"Thank God for the foresight of Professor Krause," Mira Pietrowska remarked.

Elana could not resist commenting, "And to Ephraim's initiative in enrolling Leah at Zurich where her career could be launched so promptly."

"I'm grateful to all of you," Leah said in acknowledgement. "To my family, to my teachers, and to my friends, present and absent. When you stand on a stage and listen to the applause, it's so easy to think you've earned it yourself, but you haven't. We can't do anything alone. It takes guidance, and encouragement," She glanced about the table at the faces of those dear to her and added, "and a great deal of love."

"Not to mention a generous supply of money."

All eyes turned toward Michael from whom the last remark had emanated.

"No one disputes the importance of money in transforming any dream into reality," Ephraim commented, amused at his youngest son's observation. "Neither a career, a family, nor even a nation can flourish without economic support."

Isaak smiled indulgently at his father. He was reminded, at the mention of a nation, of one of their recent discussions about the need for a Jewish homeland that could offer their people the stability of a political state. "Let's not get into that subject again, Father. After all, this is a celebration. No time for weighty subjects and sober discussions."

Leah glanced curiously at Isaak. "What weighty subjects?"

"Nations and notions," was Isaak's off-handed reply.

"You could hardly have chosen a more certain way to arouse Leah's curiosity," Markos remarked. "I've found that nothing excites her interest more than a half-answered question."

Leah grinned fondly at her fiancé, then nodded agreeably. "He's right, you know. Ever since I was a child, my favorite word has always been 'why?'"

"Why, indeed! A valid question deserves a valid answer," Ephraim said, obviously warming to his subject. "While you've been away, Leah, training and polishing your talents, we've been here witnessing the onrush of change around us."

"I saw how the city has altered in so seemingly short a time," Leah commented. "Parts of it were hardly recognizable. It's very impressive."

Ephraim nodded soberly. " Quite so. However, not all the changes here are positive ones, as your brothers, even Michael, can tell you."

"The political and intellectual climate," Isaak agreed, "has taken on an air of tangible stress and tension. Neighbor watches neighbor, friend glances uneasily at friend, as if expecting momentarily to be denounced to the Russians."

"We've always had that to some degree," Meyhra remarked, remembering the bitter experiences she and Adam had suffered at the hands of the militia.

Isaak nodded in agreement. "But now, I think you'll agree, things are growing slowly worse for every element of the population."

"The militants help to make it worse," Adam said bitterly.

"The militants," Ephraim interjected, "are a symptom, not a cause. Different people react differently to a crisis situation. Some confront it openly while others seek effective ways to go around it."

"The latter course," Pierre Rebaumme noted, "seems a safer one." Seated next to his Christian wife Pola, and wearing a small gold cross about his own neck, Pierre was a living example of his adherence to that philosophy.

"Some of us Jews," Ephraim responded, glancing pointedly at Pierre, "feel that the answer to what we are now facing is the establishment of a new nation. It's not a new idea, of course. It's as old as the Diaspora, the disbursement, itself. But now, the people, even many Gentiles among them, are really doing something about it." His voice rang with pride, making it obvious that he was among those involved.

Leah shivered with sudden apprehension. "In what way?"

Ephraim answered her briefly. He explained how the Swiss philanthropist Charles Netter had led a group of pioneers in founding an agricultural university, Mikveh Israel, near Jaffa. Its purpose was to serve as the foundation for a network of Jewish villages - the seeds of a new Hebrew nation to be built in Palestine on the ruins of the old one. "It's the only hope," he concluded, "that our people have of regaining their status as a nationality instead of a race of outcasts."

"It's a measure long overdue," Elana agreed.

"Father," Isaak said, "I know how much Netter's Mikveh Israel project means to you, but wouldn't the money you've contributed be better spent in trying to improve conditions here in the Vistula Provinces? After all, the Turkish Empire will never allow a new country to be carved out of its land."

"Not now, perhaps," Ephraim admitted, "but there's the future. A great many of us look toward that future when a Jew will have the choice of being a citizen in another land or in his own. It's been more than a thousand years since we've had that choice."

"If the Arab countries have their way," Isaak said sadly, "it will be a thousand more."

Michael, noting the somber mood that those words prompted, came to his feet. "I'd like to propose a toast to the newest addition to the household," he said cryptically.

Leah glanced at Adam and Meyhra. "A new baby?"

Meyhra shook her head wistfully. "Not yet, but we keep hoping. "

"Luvna?"

"No, dear," Elana intervened. "It's not a person, it's a thing, a surprise for you."

As dinner was over except for the coffee and dessert, Elana arose, took Leah's hand, and led her to the small study off the main salon. It had been transformed into a music room whose central feature was an imposing grand piano. The instrument had been built in Paris by the House of Pleyel. It was embellished by gleaming polished wood in a French provincial design, adorned with hand-painted roses.

Leah had never seen a more beautiful piano. She wondered what its tone might be, but would never have said to her father that one should never buy a piano for a pianist unless that pianist has tested it first. Instead, she seated herself on the stool and began to play.

The tone was pure magic. She chose Listz's concert Etude #3 in D Flat, a selection she had played for her final concert in Switzerland before her return home. As she played, she recalled the present that had first made her aware of the magic of music, the recorder that Adam had given her at Hanukah when she was nearly six years old. She relived the bittersweet events of her childhood in the Stare Miasto, and of the family's first night at Plaz Marjzendiak. She remembered her first meeting with Pola the day they had played a duet. She recalled fondly her music lessons with Maria and then the interview with Professor Krause that had set the stage for all she had lately achieved in music.

When she finished playing, the family sat silent for a moment and then they came forward to embrace her, one by one. The Pietrowskis and Kolvners followed suit.

Tears filled Leah's eyes. She had reveled in the applause of her public in the concert halls of Switzerland, but here, amid the silently expressed appreciation of those she loved most, her happiness was beyond description.

# CHAPTER THIRTY-FIVE
## WIDENING HORIZONS

As the day of Leah's wedding approached, the Marjzendiak household became a place of frantically joyous activity, all of it centered around the beautiful bride-to-be. Inevitably, twelve-year-old Michael, the family's youngest member, felt more and more isolated and ignored. He loved his sister dearly. They had been close friends throughout their childhood, and Leah had always protected and supported her younger sibling.

Since her return from Switzerland, however, Leah had had little time for the intimate talks and the tutoring sessions the two had shared whenever she had been at home before. Between fittings for her wedding dress, social events integral to the major ceremony, and visits from Markos, to which she looked forward as the high point of her days, Leah was totally consumed. Her attention was absorbed, to an unprecedented degree, in planning for her own future. This has been the case with prospective brides from time immemorial. Love, after all, especially among the young, tends to be an all-engrossing phenomenon; but, to a preadolescent boy, it can also seem an insoluble enigma.

In Michael's case, the sense of growing division from Leah, coupled with the family's concentration of all its efforts and energies on the wedding, created a void that left the boy puzzled and resentful. He observed the maelstrom of activity around him without feeling that he had any part in it. He moved about the house in unaccustomed silence. At meals, his often unintentionally humorous remarks were absent from the flow of conversation. Yet, from Michael's point of view, it seemed that almost no one noticed his withdrawal. He felt as though he had become practically invisible amid the festive preparations.

Being precocious, Michael had exhausted the range of subjects that the locally available tutors could teach him. Now, thanks to the rigidly-enforced quota system, his education was at a standstill, and because of his extreme youth, Ephraim was reluctant to send him to a school far away from home. Michael had argued repeatedly that he wished to attend school in Berlin, or failing that possibility, in Paris. Since French culture was greatly admired throughout the Russian Empire, Michael dared to hope that his father would accede to the latter request. Unfortunately, the family had no relatives or friends in Paris, and Professor Krause and his wife had moved from Berlin to Frankfurt-Am-Main, where Madam Clara Schumann now resided and taught.

Feeling that he had been thrown upon his own resources, Michael began to plan his own solution to the problem. Having learned the address and particulars of the intermediate level school attached to the University of Berlin, Michael applied to take the entrance examination, addressing the letter as if it had been written by Isaak on his behalf. Isaak, after all, was the one relative who seemed, at this point, to be still aware of Michael's existence. Since Isaak's return from Krakow, he and Michael had grown very close.

Whenever Isaak came to Plaz Marjzendiak to visit, he took Michael for long walks while Elana and Luvna became better acquainted. Occasionally, the brothers spoke "man-to-man" regarding Michael's future hopes and ambitions, and of his growing bitter resentment of the Russian administrative policy on education.

"When they first partitioned Poland," Michael remarked to Isaak, one afternoon in early October, "I've read that they rationed food to starve the people into submission. Now, it seems, they're intent on starving our minds instead of our bodies. For more than a year, I've been reviewing subjects I've already mastered. Mer Ezmanski has taught me all he knows. Now I'm just marking time and growing older."

"Michael," Isaak said gently, "you're only twelve years old."

"Within a year," Michael responded, "I'll be eligible for Bar Mitzvah. In the moral sense, I'll be a man, not that anyone has noticed."

"That's hardly true, Michael. We've just celebrated your birthday."

"I know, but even that was linked to a party in honor of Leah and Markos."

"Surely, you don't envy your sister the one most important event of her life."

Michael frowned. "She'll have many events in her life, Isaak. She'll have a career, but if I don't get on with my education, I'll have no life at all."

"Try to be patient with us, Michael," Isaak tried to reassure him. "Your time will come."

Unfortunately, Michael was not reassured. His spirits remained submerged in gloom until the morning when his daily journeys to the postal station at Wola were rewarded by an answer to his application. The gist of the reply was that his credentials had been accepted, and that he was eligible to sit for the entrance examination scheduled approximately one week prior to the wedding.

Now, he thought, he must act quickly and decisively. From a friend who lived nearby and with whom he sometimes spent the night, Michael borrowed a valise in which he packed three changes of clothing, a warm coat, a scarf and cap, extra boots, and the leather gloves his parents had given him for his twelfth birthday. From the account Ephraim had opened for him at the Bank of Poland, and in which he had faithfully deposited the entire sum of his allowance money since the age of seven, he withdrew all but a token sum. The major portion of the money went to purchase a railway ticket to Berlin. If he was frugal, the remainder would furnish his meals in transit and buy perhaps a week's lodging in the school dormitory.

Determined to make his own way in the world, Michael was confident that he could obtain a partial scholarship on the basis of his academic achievements. He intended to work at the school to earn the difference. Many young men had done that, and had gone on to build successful careers. Once his parents came to appreciate the seriousness of his resolve, they would begin to respect him as a person. Most of all, he counted upon Isaak's understanding and moral support.

On the night before he planned to leave Warsaw, Michael excused himself early from the dinner table, giving as his reason that he still had lessons to prepare for his tutoring session the following day. He used the time to write letters to his parents and to Leah. He intended to say his farewells to Isaak in person, and to leave the other letters with him.

Being young and single-minded, it did not occur to him that his carefully-thought-out plan of departure, devoid of sensitivity for the feelings of his family, would disrupt the household, cast a pall over his sister's wedding, and nearly break his mother's heart.

* * *

A tired and bedraggled Michael, chastened by the ordeal of carrying a heavy traveling case the full distance from Plaz Marjzendiak to Lesno Street, in the heart of old Warsaw, knocked on the door of Isaak's apartment. Disappointment awaited him there. Isaak had left early for his law office to prepare for the first day of a challenging trial. Luvna greeted her brother-in-law with a welcoming smile that hid her astonishment.

"Michael, do come in," she said. "I'm sorry Isaak forgot to tell me you were coming." She took his traveling case and led him into the kitchen. "Have you had breakfast?"

It was obvious from the expression on Michael's face that he had not, and that he was not only tired but famished. Keeping an eye on the time so as not to miss his train, he did justice to the meal Luvna prepared for him. He had yet to learn the devious ways of women, and the skill they can exert in coaxing secrets from a vulnerable male whose resistance is weakened by hunger.

"But how will you manage in a strange city, alone and without funds?"

"I have funds," Michael answered, proudly displaying his savings, "and I've already paid my train fare. I've arranged for everything."

"Except the fact that growing boys require a lot of food," Luvna observed.

She took the money from him, counting it solicitously. "You'll need much more than this; at least enough to last until your first paycheck." She paused thoughtfully. "Let me check my household money. I'm sure Isaak will agree with me that you need it more urgently with your train due in less than an hour." She pressed him to resume his seat. "Don't worry, Michael. With a hired coach, we'll reach the station in plenty of time, and then I've some errands to do. I'll just attend to them sooner than I had planned."

Still keeping the money clutched in her hand, and the railway ticket that accompanied it, Luvna left the kitchen, assuring her youthful visitor of her speedy return. Her words conveyed a co-conspiratorial air as she donned a traveling cloak and a hat, warm gloves, and a muff to keep out the October chill.

"When we reach the station," she said with a warm smile, "I'll turn the funds over to you with the ticket and the passes you'll need to cross the border into Germany."

Michael frowned at that. "Passes?"

"Of course. Had you forgotten Prussian Poland is a separate country, no longer part of Russian Poland? And then there's Germany itself. It's lucky for you Isaak has no plans to travel in the near future. You can use his passes since they don't name the bearer or his age."

They left the apartment and Luvna quickly found and hailed a passing public coach. Together they entered and took seats facing each other.

"Next time you plan a lengthy journey, remember things like border passes or you'll be stopped before you get very far, and maybe even detained and imprisoned."

Michael shivered at the thought her words evoked. The adult world held much of which he was totally unaware. The enormity of what he had undertaken began to intimidate him, and he felt his resolve weakening.

"I wanted to talk with Isaak before I left," he lamented. "Now there isn't time." He took out the letters he had written and handed them to Luvna. "Tell him I'll write to both of you from Berlin."

Luvna nodded sagely, continuing to engage Michael in earnest conversation about the imminent examination, the classes he planned to take, and the job opportunities that might be available to him. Never once did she suggest that his intricately woven plot was naive and impractical. She addressed him as if he were another adult, and therefore in every way her equal.

It was that fact that shattered him when he realized that the coach was nowhere near the station and the whistle of the approaching train was sounding distantly off to the left of where the carriage, slowing imperceptibly without his noticing it, had finally come to a complete halt.

"We're going to be late," Michael shouted. "He's taken the wrong way."

"No, Michael," Luvna said, shaking her head. "He's taken the right way."

"No! No!" Michael's voice rose higher, fueled by his frustration and mounting anger. "What have you done?"

"I've saved you from a horrible mistake, Michael, and from a very rude awakening. The world outside Warsaw is very different from what you imagine it to be. You won't believe me now, but one day you'll thank me for not letting you get on that train."

Michael opened the coach door. "You won't stop me," he said, but then he saw the pouch containing his money and ticket still in Luvna's hand. As he watched, she tucked it into her muff and sat calmly waiting for the storm of his fury to subside.

As the whistle sounded once more, announcing the train's departure from the station, Michael laid his head in his hands and wept bitterly.

Luvna placed her hand on his shoulder and said softly, "Don't you think you should go and see your brother now?" Without awaiting a reply, she signaled the coachman. They resumed their journey toward the offices of Wilshotski and Harnische, the destination she had originally given to the driver before they had mounted the steps of the coach.

A short time later, in response to Michael's bitter objections to Luvna's "treacherous" treatment of him, Isaak gave him a promise.

"Your mind will not be allowed to starve here in Warsaw. No matter what the Russians devise, we'll find a way around their academic road block. But for now, I'm going to send you home with Luvna, and put Mother's mind at ease. Trust me. I will help you complete your education. But remember one thing. A real man does not solve his problems by running away from them, nor stepping roughshod on the feelings of others on his way to achieving his own personal goals."

\* \* \*

October 29, 1873, dawned clear and sunny but with a crisp chill in the morning air, and a hint of snow from the northern plateau. In the Marjzendiak gardens, flowers were being gathered in preparation for the wedding reception. Gazing down from her bedroom window, Leah could not suppress a shiver of excitement. Her life was about to change forever, and she was torn between nostalgia and anticipation. Her gaze scanned the room which had been her special sanctuary for most of the past ten years of her life. Soon it would no longer be hers in quite the same way. Her personal belongings would be moved later today to the new home Markos had bought for them. Her brother Michael, she reflected, could hardly wait for time to pass. Leah, on the other hand, stood on the threshold of her future and glanced fondly back upon the treasured moments of childhood.

Looking at her reflection in the dressing room mirror, Leah remembered the day Ephraim had presented to her this first completed furniture ensemble from the factory at Wola. The occasion had been her tenth birthday, and she had felt delightfully grown up to own a real dressing table and a chaise lounge like the one in Elana's sitting room. Now, she was leaving those things behind, together with so many other childhood treasures.

At ten o'clock, Elana came to arrange her hair and to help with the intricate fastenings of her dress, the same one Elana had worn when she and Ephraim had been married so many years before. Although their coloring differed slightly, mother and daughter were nearly identical in size. The veil of hand-made lace with its accompanying pearl encrusted crown were Mira Pietrowska's contribution. Elana carefully draped the veil over Leah's auburn curls, centered the crown and then stood back to admire the finished product.

"There's never been a lovelier bride," Elana told her daughter, embracing her with a mixture of laughter and tears.

"Nor a happier one," Leah responded, as she removed the veil and laid it aside. Markos would place it once more upon her head following the Bedeken ritual in the antechamber at the synagogue, in commemoration of the ancient deception of Jacob by his uncle Laben in substituting Leah for Rachel at his first wedding. Now, Jewish bridegrooms beheld their brides unveiled first and then veiled them with their own hands.

Shortly thereafter, Ephraim knocked at Leah's door. He was dressed in his best attire to escort his daughter to the carriage, and later to the wedding ceremony, where she would be met by her bridegroom. Leah was pleased to reflect that the closeness she and Ephraim had shared throughout her childhood had survived her brief period of rebelliousness in Berlin, and had grown stronger with her attainment of young womanhood.

Around her neck, Ephraim fastened the collar of pearls that had been the one great treasure his family had managed to retain throughout all their changes of fortune and of residence. Elana had often thought of it as much too grand for most ordinary social occasions; she had preferred the single strand of pearls that had survived the fiery events at the Stare Miasto sewn inside a prayer book, while the ornate collar had resided in the vault at the Bank of Poland. But this was no ordinary occasion, and Elana and Ephraim had agreed that the elegant necklace should be their joint wedding gift to their only daughter.

"It suits you well, my child," Ephraim said as he turned her to face her reflection in the mirror.

"Oh, Papa," Leah said, at a loss for further words. Instead, she threw her arms about her father's neck and kissed him.

For the rest of her life, every detail of that day would stand out in Leah's memory; the countless brightly gleaming candles, the masses of vivid, fragrant flowers, the shining satin canopy, and the grandeur of the new synagogue. Every traditional word the Rabbi spoke, every response from Markos's lips and from her own seemed to seal their lives in permanent and perfect union.

After the ritual wine was poured and drained, Markos, so handsome in his ornate wedding apparel, so gentle and yet so strong, shattered the goblet that Lukas had placed beneath his heel, and then took her hand and led her to the private chamber where the bride and groom would spend their few moments of ritual seclusion alone together, the time known as Yichud.

Afterwards, the reception, the guests, and the dancing all seemed to blend into one gloriously dizzying whirl. Leah knew with an undefinable certainty that the exultation she now felt excelled anything she would ever experience on a concert stage.

The one sad note of the day was that Pola could not be there to share her happiness. The elder girl had given birth to her second child, a daughter this time, two days earlier. The delivery had been long and difficult. Despite her joy at having brought forth a second healthy child, Pola was totally exhausted. She barely got out of bed on the day Leah and Markos exchanged their vows and left on their wedding journey to Kazimierz-Dolny.

* * *

When they returned, a number of changes had occurred in the fortunes of the Kolvner family. Markos's father, Saul Kolvner, had suffered a stroke. For a week, he lay unconscious, his recovery uncertain. When he awoke, his memory was gone and his mind was a shadow of its former self. He would live and he would move, but he would never work again.

In Berlin, Lukas had enlarged the new import house, and had promoted Saul's assistant to manager of the Warsaw branch. Now, Markos must assume the management of the Zurich division.

Leah's reaction was a mixed one. In her year-and-a-half at the Zurich Konservatory and Musik Holkschuler, Zurich had become a second home to her, and the new appointment meant a major advancement in Markos's career. Nonetheless, she could not help but regret that her husband's new appointment meant she must leave behind her family, her friends, and everything she had heretofore thought of as home.

The next few weeks were filled with the turmoil of packing and the countless details inherent in the preparations for a total relocation. Nonetheless, Leah managed to find time to spend a few days with her girlhood friend, Pola, and to display her newly-perfected skill in baking in the bargain. On the last such visit, she took with her a basket containing jars of fruit preserves from Elana's well-stocked pantry that would serve to compliment the loaves of bread she had baked. She packed also a large kuchlen taken fresh from her own oven that very morning, cooled and generously frosted. The tasty kosher dessert bread was one of Pola's favorite delicacies.

Leah went to visit her friend in the fine coach that Markos had acquired from his father when the senior Kolvner had been forced to retire. This, too, would be taken with them to their new home in Zurich, and Leah tried to shut out of her mind the sorrow behind its acquisition. On this of all days, she was determined to be light-hearted. She would think only of the happy aspects attendant upon all the changes that were taking place in her life. Happiest of all was her new-found exultation as a wife.

Despite her joy at marrying Markos, throughout her wedding day she had felt a mixture of anticipation and dread as their first night together had drawn near. But Markos had proved to be a tender lover, supremely considerate of her feelings. She had not dared to question when and how he had learned to take possession of her with such gentle authority. She knew only that he had caressed and touched her in ways that calmed her fears and swept her to heights of bliss she had not known existed. She understood now much that Pola had tried to explain to her after her own marriage, much that Leah had found obscure and mysterious until now.

When Pola greeted her, the two friends embraced affectionately, each uncertain when they would see each other again. Leah admired the new baby, Victoirine Marie, and caressed two-year-old Paul, who seemed much too stoic and solemn for so young a child. The two young women spoke of pleasures shared, of secret girlhood confidences, and of their common love of music. They played duets, and Pola sang in her clear mezzo soprano voice to Leah's expert accompaniment. However, as the time grew near for the visit to end, Leah became increasingly aware of a sharp edge to Pola's manner and an element of conflict in her mood.

"And now, you're off to a grand new life," Pola remarked as they bade each other farewell in the garden outside Pola's house.

"I only wish Zurich were closer to Warsaw," Leah responded.

"I've always felt things happen for the best, Leah. Even your father-in-law's illness has led to better things for you and Markos, just as Mother's foiled ambition and my lack of real talent made her push you toward a career in music."

Leah stared at her friend in shocked surprise.

"Don't be amazed, dear. Surely you know that I both love and envy you. I always have. That's only natural. It never affected our friendship. And now, you will become world famous just like your idol Madame Schumann. That's why it's best that we'll be too far apart to encourage comparisons."

"You can't mean that," Leah whispered, taken aback.

"Of course I do. After all, I'm human. When I play for my guests, they will admire my pedestrian ability, blissfully unaware how amateur I really am. Besides, Warsaw is not the safest home for an internationally famous Jewish musician." She hugged and kissed Leah, then added, "Go now, and be happy. And write to me as often as you can."

With that, she turned and fled into the house.

* * *

The move to Zurich meant radical changes for Leah and her entire family. The house that Markos had purchased for Leah and himself now had to be sold. Isaac and Luvna were pleased to acquire it. The new bride and groom lived there for only a total of nine weeks.

In the last few days of that time, the Kolvners and the Marjzendiaks gathered to celebrate the birthdays of Adam and Leah, the promotion of Markos to vice president of the Kolvner House of Imports, and Isaak's advancement to the status of a senior partner of Wilshotski and Harnischk.

After dinner, the men remained at table over cigars and liqueur while the women adjourned to the salon for tea. It was then that Isaak broached the subject that had been in his mind since his sister's wedding.

He turned enthusiastically to Ephraim. "At last, we have a workable solution to Michael's problem."

Ephraim raised his eyebrows in evident surprise. "What solution is that?"

"What better guardians could there be than Leah and Markos? And you, yourself, went to Zurich to verify the merits of the Swiss educational system."

"That was mainly in music," Ephraim replied, remembering his concern after reading Leah's letter and the near-panic he had experienced. "It was, after all, an emergency."

Isaak nodded. "True, it was." He paused momentarily. "As I see it, so is this."

Ephraim considered Isaak's words carefully before he spoke again. "It would solve a great many problems, provided Markos doesn't object."

Isaak paused thoughtfully. "By the time the next school term begins, he and Leah will have been married for nearly a year. By that time, hopefully, a third person in the house will seem much less of a problem."

"Leah will be pleased," Ephraim agreed, "to have part of her family with her, and Michael will be free of the quota system that he hates. Once she's settled in her new home, Leah can make the necessary arrangements at her leisure. That way they'll both have something to look forward to, and Markos will have time to accept the idea."

"Knowing Michael," Isaak said, "he'll spend most of his time at school anyway."

"Your solution should put an end to the streak of rebellion he's been showing of late," Ephraim noted, obviously pleased with the idea.

By the evening's end, when the family took their leave of each other, Isaak felt relieved. He had found the means to put his father's mind at ease regarding Michael and to fulfill his promise to his younger brother.

When Leah and Markos left for Zurich, Leah assured her parents that she would come back to visit them often. After all, the railway system between Warsaw and the Swiss city was among the finest in Europe. Nonetheless, she could not shake off a feeling that the family was slowly starting to break apart. Adam had married and established his own family, and Isaak had done likewise. Now she was moving to another country, and soon Michael would follow. Elana and Ephraim would be left at Plaz Marjzendiak with only the house staff and farm workers. It was difficult for her to believe that her father was sixty-one and her beautiful mother fifty-four. Where had the time gone?

Spring and summer came and went and the year 1874 had run two thirds of its course when Michael left for Zurich. Because he would be away at school for his thirteenth birthday, Rabbi Schimmel had agreed, after much persuasion, to hold his Bar Mitzvah on the Sabbath preceding his departure. It was only three weeks prior to his birthday, and Michael had shown himself to be as advanced in his religious studies as he was in academic subjects . He had recited the prescribed passages of the Torah from memory and had spoken briefly afterwards regarding their meaning in terms of current events in the lives of the people.

Ephraim had been very proud of his youngest son. The boy had acquitted himself extremely well. He would, without question, be a brilliant scholar. He would also be 1,298 kilometers away from home.

Elana and Michael embraced and kissed each other good-bye. She gave him last-minute admonitions about keeping warm and dry, and then she went inside the house, discreetly leaving father and son to say their farewells undisturbed. Michael wanted to take leave of his parents at Plaz Marjzendiak rather than at the railway station in Warsaw. Ephraim would have preferred to spend as much time with his youngest son as possible, but, following Isaak's suggestion, he acceded to the boy's request.

The two of them lingered on the veranda until the last possible moment and then it was time for the carriage to leave. Ephraim filled some of the time with last minute instructions about travel passes and passports and which documents needed to be shown at which national frontiers on the journey from Russian Poland to Switzerland. Michael, now that the moment of parting had come, could think of very little to say. Instead, he gazed silently at his father as if trying to memorize every detail of his image to store away in his memory for the future. Finally, they shook hands, and Michael tried valiantly not to show the duality of his feelings. He wanted to go and study, to try his wings in a far off place. He wanted also to stay amid the known and familiar in the shelter of home and family.

"Don't hesitate to write if you need anything, son."

"I won't, Father. Don't worry. I'll be fine."

Ephraim looked fondly at his son. "Of course you will."

Michael picked up his new traveling case and stepped into the coach. Then, at the last moment, he ran down the stairs and hugged his father warmly, no longer holding back his tears.

Ephraim held his son close, not trusting himself to speak. When Michael turned at last and re-entered the coach, Ephraim slapped the lead horse's rump smartly, setting him off at a trot.

"Take care, son," he shouted, "and remember to write."

Michael waved from the passenger compartment, grinning and crying simultaneously. His great adventure had begun at last, but not without some regrets.

Ephraim watched the waving figure as the coach grew smaller and finally passed from sight. The last of his children had gone to make his way in the world. An era had ended, and as yet there was no new generation to follow the current one. This was the single major regret of Ephraim's life.

# CHAPTER THIRTY-SIX
## CHANGING PERSPECTIVES

Michael began his journey with sharply conflicting emotions. He had insisted on saying his goodbyes at home rather than prolonging them at the railway station and risking the embarrassment of giving way to tears. With his Bar Mitzvah already behind him, he was determined to prove himself a man. Nonetheless, by the time the train was an hour away from Warsaw, Michael was homesick and scared. For years he had dreamed of advancing his education, escaping from the injustice of the restrictive quota system. His pursuit of that dream had sparked his attempt to reach Berlin, and had brought him on this journey.

Now, as the train approached the border that divided the Vistula Provinces from the Austrian Polish sector, Michael recalled terrifying tales he had heard about the brutality of the Russian militia border guards. He knew his papers were in order. His father had seen to that, and like the careful banker that he was, he had left no detail unattended. Nonetheless, Michael could not suppress his growing feeling of vulnerability.

Glancing at his fellow passengers, Michael felt conspicuous. He was conservatively dressed; yet the yellow star on the jacket of his suit seemed larger and more obvious than ever. He was certain that some of the passengers were staring at it, while others, either more liberal or more sensitive, were trying deliberately to avoid seeing it. He huddled down further in his seat, and clasped his hands about his arms, trying awkwardly to cover the hated symbol of his people's ostracism. Finally, prompted as much by self-consciousness as by the increasing cold, he put on the greatcoat he had brought with him, and fastened it up to his neck. Still, he could not keep from shivering. The train, like all Russian trains, was poorly heated and even more poorly insulated, with the possible exception of those cars reserved exclusively for Russian dignitaries.

At Auschwitz, the first stop the train made near the border, Russian militiamen boarded every car. Some inspected the shipments of trade goods in transit, others were assigned to search passengers' luggage, while the officers collected and checked the travel permits each passenger carried. In the course of this inspection, several passengers were searched and questioned. As Michael watched in horrified fascination, two, a man and woman, were taken into custody, handcuffed, and forced to leave the train. Michael wondered if they, like himself, were Jewish. Their dress and appearance suggested that possibility. Yet they wore no star-shaped badge. Perhaps, Michael thought with a shudder, that had been the reason for their arrest.

Presently, the militia captain approached Michael. The Russian's eyes seemed suspicious as he remarked pointedly, "Traveling alone?"

Michael nodded.

The man seized him by the shoulder and pulled him roughly to his feet. "How old are you?"

Michael's mouth was so dry he could hardly answer. "Thirteen, sir." It was almost true; he would be within weeks.

The captain's glance swept the length of the car, then again focused on Michael. "You seem too young to be traveling alone. Are you sure you have no relatives on this train?"

"No, sir. None. I'm going to visit my sister in Zurich."

"Really?" The captain jerked at Michael's overcoat, pulling it open and stripping it away to reveal the yellow badge on his jacket. "Just as I thought. Another troublesome Jew." He held out his hand. "Where are your papers?"

Michael hastily produced them.

The officer glanced at them, then handed them back, still studying Michael as the boy returned his ticket and permits to his pocket. The Russian pointed to the journal Michael had dropped as he was pulled from his seat. "What's that?"

Michael's glance followed the pointing finger. He stooped to retrieve the small leather-bound book, most of whose pages were still blank. "It's like a diary," Michael answered hesitantly. "I've just started it."

The captain seized the book and quickly scanned its pages.

"What's this you've written here? 'For the first time, I'm leaving the Russian zone. It's good to be going.' Just what does that mean?"

The man's eyes bored into Michael with such intensity that the boy fought to keep tears out of his eyes and his voice. "I've never traveled so far away from home before. I've never seen any other country, and it's a year since I've seen my sister." He stammered before that merciless stare.

"You keep mentioning this convenient sister in Zurich."

"She does live in Zurich," Michael insisted. "Her name is Leah Kolvner. She teaches at the Musik Konservatory, and she plays concerts."

The Russian laughed scornfully. Scare one of these Jews, he thought to himself, and they'll say anything.

The captain looked Michael up and down coldly. "You might be traveling further than you planned." He paused. "What's to stop my arresting you here and now? You've concealed your Jewish origin under a coat. Surely you know that this badge must always be on your outermost garment. For that alone, I could send you to Siberia. I have the authority."

Michael blanched, terrified by the very mention of the name Siberia. He knew what the Russian had said about the badge was true, but he had not thought about the significance of what he had done in failing to transfer it to his coat. "I was cold, sir. I forgot."

"Of course. Those who break the law always have a convenient excuse." Then the Russian seemed to recall something the boy had said. He frowned. "This sister of yours, what did you say her name was?"

"Leah. Leah Kolvner."

A different light dawned in the Russian officer's eyes. "Leah Kolvner, the concert pianist?"

Michael nodded, wondering what ulterior motive lay behind the question.

A small smile played about the Russian officer's lips. "I've heard your sister play," he said with some surprise, then added with a certain pride, "I had the honor of guarding his Excellency, the Viceroy, when he visited Lublin last year. Leah Kolvner played the Tchaikovsky First piano Concerto there. She played it quite well, with much feeling. I did not realize she was a Jew." He handed the journal back, and as Michael clutched it nervously, the captain added, "I'd be careful what I wrote in that diary from now on, if I were you." The implied threat was unmistakable in his softly spoken words. Equally evident in the man's manner was the admiration of the traditional Russian for art and music, and for those who skillfully create and interpret them.

"I will, sir." Michael promised, relieved to see the captain turn away and move further down the aisle. With a sigh, Michael returned to his place, glad to have gotten past that brief but potentially deadly confrontation.

Nearly an hour elapsed before the militia detachment finally departed, and the train was allowed to resume its journey. However, the two missing passengers did not return, and their vacant seats were a silent reminder of the ever present power of Mother Russia over her subjects. When the train pulled away from the station, Michael was trembling. He drew out the oilcloth-wrapped package of home-baked cookies Elana had given him and began to chew them determinedly, more from gnawing fear than from hunger. He remembered the care with which his mother had prepared this delicacy for him. However, the fear he still felt rendered the cookies flat and tasteless. He wondered, when the train reached Austria, would that country's equivalent of the military police also inspect the train and its human cargo?

The fearful encounter through which he had just passed highlighted the fact that neither he nor any of his people were ever truly safe. Even his father, with his post at the bank and his estate, could be summarily dispossessed by an imperial whim at any moment.

Through the train windows, Michael could see the austere beauty of the foothills and mountains through which they were passing. He had never seen mountains so tall before. The sight made him feel smaller and more vulnerable than ever. Awed by the scenery around him, Michael felt intensely lonely. The other passengers all seemed wrapped in their own thoughts.

The train was scheduled to stop for almost an hour in Keshenev, just across the Austrian border, and there several passengers bought snacks at the small shops outside the station. Michael agonized throughout that time, dreading the appearance of another crew of uniformed officials. The Vistula Provinces had only just been left behind. Was freedom, Michael wondered, already an accomplished fact?

When the train left the Keshenev station, Michael glanced furtively about the car, wondering how many of his fellow passengers shared his heady sense of release.

An unexpectedly familiar voice asked him from the aisle, "Mind if I join you?"

Michael could scarcely believe his eyes. Hastily, he made room for his brother-in-law Markos Kolvner, inexpressibly pleased to see the face of a family member. As Markos took his seat, Michael could not restrain himself from asking, "What brought you here?"

"A mixture of pleasure and business," Markos replied, smiling. "I wrote to your father that I'd meet your train," he added, noting Michael's undisguised astonishment. "I guess he thought it would make a pleasant surprise for you."

"About now," Michael responded, "I could use a pleasant surprise. When we stopped at Auschwitz, I wasn't sure I'd get out of the Vistula Provinces. The captain of the border guard threatened to send me to Siberia."

Markos nodded in understanding. "The border guards like to boast of their authority. Lately, they've taken to boarding the trains at different stations, hoping to catch the unwary." He patted Michael's shoulder. "Anyway, that's all over now, and I've planned what I hope will be a delightful itinerary for us."

Pausing momentarily, he added, "By the way, Michael, perhaps it's time you learned the value of a little healthy arrogance. Jews are often accused of it, but a bit of exaggerated pride can be a powerful antidote against feelings of shame and guilt and fear."

Michael smiled ruefully, acknowledging the accuracy of his brother-in-law's analysis. Until Markos had joined him, he had been feeling all of those emotions. As the train sped westward amid the impressive Austrian Alps, Michael, though less jittery and depressed than he had been before, spoke very little. Markos, in an effort to draw him out, commented on the beauties of the countryside and the highlights of his business trip.

He ended by saying, "There's a friend I'd like you to meet; a self-made man in the truest sense. He was orphaned at age twelve. Since then he's been everything from a ship's cook's apprentice to an independent opal miner. He's bought and sold every kind of merchandise imaginable. Now, I hear, he's buying up newspapers from Minsk to Paris. You'll like him. I've known him since I was seventeen, and even to me, he seems larger than life."

\* \* \*

Markos introduced Michael to Hoffmeyer in the foyer of the Imperator Hotel in St. Moritz. The imposing Victorian structure was, as Michael quickly learned, yet another of Hoffmeyer's business ventures, and to all appearances, it was a vastly successful one. Albrecht Hoffmeyer stood a wiry six feet four, possessed a deep baritone voice, and a thick mane of chestnut hair. Beneath the hair lay a mind that could calculate a multi-columned set of figures or size up a character or a situation with equal ease. Hoffmeyer had amassed a formidable fortune before he had celebrated his thirtieth birthday. Now, at thirty-five, his many elegant estates throughout Europe, his extensive art collection, and his reputation as a raconteur were legendary. Meeting him, Michael could understand why Markos had spoken of him as larger than life.

Hoffmeyer characteristically capitalized on the thirst for new distractions that St. Moritz's growing influx of pleasure-seeking visitors displayed. Lately, he had initiated a local theater as the centerpiece for the entertainment program at his hotel. The result was a sold-out house, both in the auditorium and on the guest register.

During the weekend Michael and Markos spent in St. Moritz, Hoffmeyer and his aristocratic wife Lizavette showed them the high points of the elite Alpine city. Lizavette briefly explained the city's history to Michael. The resort had been built on the ruins of an ancient Roman military outpost and named for a martyred saint. It had subsequently flourished and was now a fashionable vacation spot for the privileged who could afford it.

When the time came to say farewell, the Hoffmeyers saw Markos and Michael off on a train headed west along the Swiss-Italian border. Markos was determined to make Michael forget the fearful beginning of his journey, and he thought he had found the ideal way.

Few natural spectacles have impressed the imagination of man like the first breathtaking view of the Matterhorn. The mountain rises solitary and aloof from its fellow Alpine neighbors, like a monarch enthroned among lesser courtiers. As the train drew into Zermatt station, the mountain's balanced symmetry seemed too perfect to represent the spontaneous product of haphazard natural forces.

Markos said nothing, allowing his young brother-in-law to revel in the majestic splendor of the elegant stony pyramid that dominated the landscape. Sympathizing with Michael's continued silent fascination, at last Markos said, "I can see you've fallen in love with the Matterhorn, Michael. It's a common infatuation that you share with countless generations of young men. Many have yearned to climb that peak."

Michael stared at him. "Why climb it?"

Markos nodded. "I suppose because it represents a challenge," Markos replied. "An Englishman named Whymper led the first successful climb to the summit in 1865." Almost as if he spoke to himself, Markos added more softly, "It's too bad the mission was marred by jealous rivalry between Whymper's party and another band of climbers. Had the two groups worked as one, instead of trying to outdo each other, tragedy might have been averted."

"What tragedy? What happened to them?"

Markos looked grimly at the mountain before them, and for a moment, Michael thought he might not answer. "Half the party fell to their deaths during the descent."

"Why does one have to climb it? Why not just enjoy it?"

"Unfortunately, many of us lack the wisdom to simply appreciate nature, without trying either to improve on it or tame it. Yet, for some of us, including me, this is more than just a mountain. It's a symbol of life's ultimate promise - the most cherished ambition, the most elusive achievement. To pursue that promise successfully is to conquer one's own limitations."

Michael frowned, puzzled. "I don't understand."

"I'm not referring to the physical conquest of rock and stone," Markos explained. "I'm speaking of the times when we meet what we think are insurmountable obstacles in life. Then it's good to remember that men have conquered even that." He gazed at the mountain with a look of rapture, and Michael, sharing his mood of exultation, knew that this was a sight and moment that he would never forget.

* * *

When Michael saw his first glimpse of Zurich, he could hardly wait to become familiar with the city that, for the next few years, would be his second home. He was nervous about the qualifying exam he must take to begin his school career. He was unfamiliar with the Swiss school system, and still felt naive about the world at large. He looked upon his years spent in Russian Poland as a prisoner might view his jail sentence. He felt unprepared for the very different world that now surrounded him. Nevertheless, with Markos' coaching and Leah's encouragement, he placed well on the test. He had successfully overcome his first academic hurdle.

That was at the end of October. School would not begin until January. The next two months passed swiftly and eventfully for Michael. Markos took him to his import house and showed him some of the wonders collected there. Leah accompanied him to the museums and libraries of Zurich, showing him the works of art the city possessed, and the wonders of library books and reference systems. The two also took Michael to a district meeting.

Like all the political districts of Switzerland, the one in which Zurich was located was called a canton, a term Michael had heretofore associated solely with the enforced conscription of the very young. Michael was greatly impressed by what he saw and heard at that gathering. The experience inspired him to initiate on his own a research project at the Library of Zurich. He wanted to know more about Switzerland's uniquely structured government and constitution. He studied the nation's history of hard-won neutrality, its custom of avoiding the international confrontations of its neighbors. He read that Swiss mercenaries had fought in the struggles for independence of many other peoples, but as a nation, Switzerland had remained steadfastly aloof. The result was a peaceful blending of many different ethnic groups into a unified country like no other on the entire European continent.

The year 1875 ushered in a new era for Michael. In the birthplace of Enrico Pestalozzi, founder of the personalized teaching system that emphasized the student's individuality, the boy's education progressed at a truly phenomenal rate. He was happy in a way he had not been since early childhood, before he became aware of the frustrations of senseless restrictions and quotas. His self-disciplined commitment to learning favorably impressed his teachers and won him a place on the Dean's list. Nonetheless, his sense of humor and his outgoing manner enabled him to get on well with most of his peers, including those whom he excelled in scholastic achievement.

Also in that year, Michael met a young Norwegian student named Jotyl Lermajcht. Jotyl had lost both his parents in a sledding accident, and had come to Zurich to make his home with a widowed aunt and her daughter. Michael and Jotyl were drawn to one another. Both had met with unexpected obstacles despite early economic advantages. In the course of the next three years, they became close friends. Those three years of study would be punctuated by brief visits home, always accompanied either by Markos or, less often, by Leah. All the family were aware that with each passing year, the border crossing checks were growing tighter and more painful for Russia's "alien" subjects.

Anna Kolvner, Leah's sister-in-law and Lukas' wife, visited the Kolvner home in Zurich on the occasion of Samuel's birth, and had cared for Leah for the first week of her convalescence. However, she had been pregnant herself when the time came for Frederick to make his appearance. Instead, Elana had come to Zurich and had spent a month taking care of her daughter, running Leah's household, getting acquainted with her grandchildren, and enjoying the company of her youngest son at this crucial stage in his intellectual and emotional development.

Michael had fond memories of that month. He and his mother had grown closer during that period than at any earlier time. Heretofore, Michael had not been sufficiently mature to appreciate Elana, not merely as a steadying influence in his life, but as an individual whose opinions, tastes and sensibilities mattered to him. Now, she no longer seemed one-half of an entity entitled "Mother and Father," and the lesser half at that. In the earlier years of their relationship, Ephraim had always seemed to his youngest child a strong, assertive, authority figure who was strangely aloof, almost God-like. In the last year before Michael had left for school, he had come to view his father much more realistically, and had learned to like as well as respect him.

Seeing his mother walk confidently into his sister's household, bringing with her harmony, tranquility and a luminous joy that calmed the two-year-old Samuel, catered to the concerns of Markos, and put Leah's mind at ease with a minimum of effort, made Michael see his mother in a new light. Light was precisely the right term for what Elana personified. It was, in fact, what she had seemed to radiate from the moment she had opened the back door of her father's cottage in Grojec to Ephraim's knock and had told him the way to the brewery where he hoped to find employment.

Throughout the months of revolution, hers had been the light that had helped Michael and Leah to flourish in what would otherwise have been a crushingly harsh and dismal environment. Her unfailing optimism, her steadfast faith in their ultimate well-being and survival, Michael realized, had also enabled Ephraim to face the every day dangers of the streets of Warsaw, even when they had become a battleground. For such a woman, a man would be willing to dare a great deal.

During Elana's Zurich visit, mother and son had really talked to one another. Michael had told Elana of his dream of becoming a writer, not in the vague terms of childhood fantasy as he once had done, but with the inspired zeal of a young creative artist aspiring to put his talents to the test. At first, he confided, he would become a journalist. Already he wrote for the school newspaper, and his articles had been favorably judged by teachers and students alike. One day, he asserted, he would write books that would convey an important message to his own people and to others, books that would inform and enlighten as well as entertain.

Elana expressed her confidence in her son's future. More importantly, she advised him in regard to the works of particular writers such as Conrad Meyer, Albert Bitzuis and Jean Jacques Rousseau. She felt he might wish to consult the writings of these outstanding Swiss-based authors for examples of style and content. Michael was surprised when Elana mentioned Jakob Burckhardt's prestigious historical text on the Italian Renaissance. Burckhardt taught at Zurich although Michael had not taken any of his courses. He would not enjoy that opportunity until he reached the educational level of the University. What he found most amazing was his mother's familiarity with the leading philosophical and literary authorities of the day. By the time she left, Elana had succeeded in fostering in Michael an even greater enthusiasm to achieve his goals.

When Michael had come home during his first winter recess, Luvna could not refrain from asking him if he had ever forgiven her for preventing his going to Berlin when he had planned to run away from home.

Michael smiled mischievously at her but nodded. "You're a devious woman, Luvna," he said, "but a wise one. All that has happened to me in Zurich might never have been if you hadn't intervened. For that, I owe you my thanks."

* * *

At the end of that four year period, there was the graduation ceremony, with the graduates gowned and marching proudly in procession to the campus quadrangle. It was one of the happiest memories of Michael's life. His parents, with Isaak and Luvna accompanying them, came to attend the commencement exercises. Adam and Meyhra were unable to get away now that Dr. Jedewreski had retired. Furthermore, during the early months of the year 1878, Meyhra had finally succeeded in carrying a child to term. This child was given the name Abrahm, commemorating, in a contracted form, the name of Abraham, the revered father of Judaism. Abraham had waited a long time to see the fulfillment of Adonai's prophecy. He and Sarah were both advanced in age, and indeed Sarah had laughed as she stood in the doorway of her husband's tent listening to the prophecy. How could parenthood possibly come to two such elderly people as they? But all things are possible to Yahweh, or as He is more commonly called, Adonai. In due course, Sarah brought forth Isaac, and so the Jewish nation came into being.

# CHAPTER THIRTY-SEVEN
# PLOT AND COUNTERPLOT

On a morning in early December of 1879, Jakob Gauduin, an out-of-work Ukrainian textile laborer, waited outside the Royal Opera House of St. Petersburg. The man was thin to the point of gauntness. He was shabbily dressed, and his coat was threadbare. The gusty winds that blew the remnants of last night's snow storm from the trees caused him to stamp his feet and rub his hands in an effort to fight off the numbing cold.

For six weeks, ever since he had lost his job at the local metal works factory, and his daughter Saundra had found work as a maid cleaning the toilets at the opera house, Gauduin had waited thus each morning. After all, it was his daughter's first employment, and she was only 15 years old. There were just the two of them now that Gauduin's wife Olympia had died of pneumonia the preceding winter. He felt a need to guard his child closely. Who could say what dangers awaited a young girl on the streets of Russia's capitol in the hours just after dawn?

Gauduin blew on his ungloved hands yet again. Surely, by now, the night shift must be ending. Where was Saundra? Thus preoccupied, he failed at first to notice the uniformed men who materialized in the morning mist on either side of him. He was too surprised, too frightened to have ready answers for their questions.

"Who are you? What are you doing loitering here on the Tsar's property?"

When the questions were answered by stunned silence, and then the man turned and tried to flee, he was promptly arrested. The militiamen made no allowance for the fact that they themselves struck terror in the hearts of most Russian citizens. Protesting loudly, Gauduin was dragged away. Ten minutes later, Saundra Gauduin came out of the servant's entrance at the rear of the theater and was dismayed to see no sign of her father.

Loitering is a minor crime at most, and once Gauduin had told his story to the Tsar's newly appointed Chief-of-Police, the official was inclined to let him go. Still, the chief mused, it did no harm for a peasant to cool his heels in prison over night. Tomorrow morning would be soon enough to sign the order for the man's release. Meanwhile, a brief stay in the Tsar's prison would teach him a valuable lesson - that imperial laws, even minor ones, are meant to be strictly obeyed.

That same evening, an event took place that would change the fate not only of Jakob Gauduin and his daughter but of many of the Tsar's subjects throughout the empire. A gala performance was scheduled at the Royal Opera House. It was the opening of the winter season. The Tsar and his entire family were scheduled to attend. A festive mood filled the city, due in part to the holiday season, and also to the easing of restrictions on public gatherings thanks to the empire's growing prosperity. The Tsar was going to celebrate with his people. He would make one of his rare public appearances. All thought of the grim pronouncements in the revolutionary underground press were momentarily forgotten by the Russian citizenry.

Andreivich Gorchakov, his secret police, and the militia under his command were among the few elements of the population who did not share the widespread jubilation. Their tasks, which included safeguarding the persons of the royal household, would be rendered more difficult on this occasion. They much preferred those times when Tsar Alexander was in a guarded and distrustful frame of mind. Gorchakov viewed this comradely regard of citizen-subjects as a weakness. Gorchakov, after all, was an offspring of the Russian aristocracy. He felt little kinship with "the masses", and still less trust of them. He took the underground press seriously, and nurtured a habit of always expecting the worst. It was not an ingratiating attribute in the social sense, but for a Chief-of-Police, it was a valuable trait.

There is a legend regarding a horseshoe nail. Its disappearance led to the loss of a battle and the shedding of much blood. On the night of that gala opening, a carriage wheel was the source of the mischief. It broke as the Tsar's coachman drove the royal family to the Opera House from their Winter Palace. As a result, the curtain was held. Obviously, the performance could not proceed in the absence of the guests of honor. All eyes were on the royal box. Everything waited upon the Tsar's arrival. Twenty minutes passed and still the royal family did not come. The occupants of the neighboring boxes grew restless, and moved into the halls outside the main auditorium. There they gathered to speculate on what could have delayed the Tsar and his family. It was recalled with mounting concern that threats had been voiced in the underground press against the Tsar. Furthermore, a revolutionary group know as "The People's Will," a major offshoot of the former "Land and Liberty" revolutionary group, had implemented two assassination attempts against the tsar's life earlier in that same year, one by a single assassin, Alexander Soloviev, in April, and one in November when, by a change in scheduling, the Imperial train had narrowly missed being destroyed by a charge of nitroglycerine. Could those prior events, they wondered, have a bearing on the failure of the imperial family to appear and take their seats?

As this issue was being debated, a thunderous roar filled the theater, smoke issued from the royal box, and flames could be seen mounting the velvet draperies that hung on either side. Those who had previously remained in their seats quickly rose and vacated them. The aisles were clogged as people struggled to reach the doors. Women fainted and men rushed to protect them from being trampled. Nonetheless, twenty people died of various causes, ranging from asphyxiation to heart failure. The theater was emptied; the performance was canceled. The streets outside the building became a scene of panic. Not one spectator could say with certainty exactly what had taken place, but rumors were rampant, most of them inaccurate.

A crudely made bomb had exploded in the royal box. Thanks to the broken wheel on the Tsar's carriage, it had exploded prematurely, destroying two of the seats and setting fire to drapes and upholstery. The box had been unoccupied, as had most of the adjacent boxes. Otherwise, there would have been disastrous consequences for the royal family and for several other members of the aristocracy.

Eight miles away, Tsar Alexander fumed at the humiliation to which he had been subjected. He was unaware at that time that his life had been spared because of the accident to his coach. His indignation fell on the poor coachman, who was soundly berated for his failure to maintain the vehicle in good order. No one could have been more surprised than that same coachman when later in the evening he was summoned and thanked by his royal master.

For Chief-of-Police Gorchakov, there was no such leniency. The manner in which his sovereign received him was anything but thankful.

"Gorchakov!" The Tsar all but spat the name. His voice was venomous.

Gorchakov nodded and closed the door behind him. "Majesty," he said, bowing formally.

Alexander got immediately to the point. "How dare you allow such a thing to happen? We might all have been killed."

"Surely, your Imperial Majesty is aware that a detachment of the militia had already entered the royal box in preparation for your arrival. They were once more, for the third time that day, inspecting the seats, the railing, everything that could possibly have been a repository for such a device. The final search was in progress at the very moment of the explosion. None of your party, Majesty, would have been allowed to occupy the box until that inspection was completed."

Alexander relented at these words. "I heard one of your men was killed."

"True, your Majesty. He died gladly in the service of his sovereign." In fact, Gorchakov could not make such a statement with certainty, but, in placating an irate tsar, anything was worth trying.

Alexander eyed the police chief narrowly. "Convey my condolences to his family."

"Of course, Majesty."

"And I want to know without delay the identity of the would-be assassins."

"Naturally, your Majesty. Inquiries are already in progress. "

"Inquiries?" Alexander's voice was instantly hoarse with rage. Thus goaded by his master's anger, Gorchakov recalled the Ukrainian laborer languishing since early morning in the royal prison. "An arrest has already been made, Majesty."

Alexander stared at the other man in disbelief. Then, realizing that the police chief meant this statement to be taken seriously, he smiled. "Good," he said with grudging admiration. "Very good! You moved quickly and decisively. I like that. Find out who the co-conspirators are. An example must be made. This dare not go unpunished."

"It won't, your Majesty. Martial law has been declared throughout St. Petersburg. By morning, couriers will carry the order throughout the empire. Within three days, all the provinces will be under stringent regulations. The perpetrators will not escape. You have my word."

"Serve me well in this," Alexander said, "and you will be rewarded. Your advancement will be assured."

Gorchakov bowed once more. Alexander extended his hand and the police chief kissed the royal ring of state. He then backed out of the room, grateful to be dismissed on a note of approval. He had arrived in terror of his royal master. Thank god he had remembered Jakob Gauduin. By sheer luck, he had decided not to release him until morning. Now, he knew, he must build an ironclad case against the man. He admitted to himself that he had little hope of finding the real conspirators. By now, they would be far away and well hidden, but that was of no consequence. His scapegoat was in his hands. With careful interrogation, the man could be tricked into unwittingly implicating others. Once they were hanged, no one would be the wiser, and Gorchakov's position would be secure.

* * *

The party that the Marjzendiaks gave in honor of Franz Pietrowski's promotion to President of the State Bank of Poland was restrained but nonetheless memorable. At the time it had been planned, it was to be a joyful and auspicious occasion, honoring the realization of the combined hopes and dreams of Franz and Mira. The fact that martial law had been instituted on that very day lent the proceedings a somewhat ominous overtone. If Franz, who had been singled out for special commendation by the Tsar, had not been the guest of honor, the event would in all probability have been ordered canceled by the Governor-General. As it was, the host and hostess and their guests tried to carry on as if all were normal. However, the party would now have to conclude quite early in order not to violate the curfew.

In the sitting room that had served Leah as a child, and which she still used on her visits home, some of the women had gathered in the interval before dinner was served.

"At least," Sonya Oslowska said to Mira with forced humor, "you'll be able to show off your wardrobe on the international scale it deserves."

Mira glanced about the candlelit room. "With things as they are, I should be looking forward to getting away from Warsaw. Instead, I'm dreading it. Oh, I know Franz will be honored in St. Petersburg, and that he's been asked to inspect all the branches of the Bank of Poland," she paused, then added, "but Tsar Alexander is no longer the rebellious, idealistic young liberal he once was. The Tsar Liberator." She sighed and shook her head.

"Have you heard the rumors on the streets this morning?" said Sonya Oslowska.

"With martial law declared without explanation," Mira responded, "rumors are all the people have."

Sonya leaned closer to her friend. "They're saying there's been an assassination attempt at the Royal Opera House in St. Petersburg. It failed, of course. But we will all be the worse for it."

Mira paled for a moment. Then she grew angry. "Those revolutionaries don't care what their actions inflict on the rest of the people. They've learned essentially nothing since 1863."

"They've apparently learned efficiency," Sonya said bitterly. "This last attempt was apparently rather too close to be ignored. The word has spread throughout the empire to quell the unrest at all cost. But most of the unrest is in Russia, itself. Why must the authorities persist in blaming the outlying provinces?"

"I assume," Mira answered, "it suits the private purposes of his Imperial Majesty's ministers."

"And directs attention away from the tsar's latest dalliance. This one, so it's rumored, is a very serious and long term affair. She's a princess, an orphaned one, and very beautiful."

"Yes," agreed Mira, "I've heard of her. They first met when she was twelve. Now she's grown up and usurped the gentle tsarina's place in his heart. How sad."

At that moment, the sound of a crystal bell echoed throughout the house. It could be heard clearly even in the rooms upstairs.

"Ah," Mira said, "it's time to go down to dinner, Sonya. I suggest we find our respective husbands and forget, for the moment, the problems of Mother Russia."

"Those are easy to forget," Sonya said. "The trials of our own land are another problem. When Vlad's current term as mayor is over, I've persuaded him not to stand for office again."

"That will be a loss for us all," Mira observed, "but undoubtedly a relief for you and Vladimir."

The gathering assembled at table, and dinner proceeded as planned. A festive atmosphere prevailed, albeit only superficially. The general conversation addressed social topics of the day; carefully avoided were frankly political and therefore inflammatory subjects that could reach unfriendly ears in the course of thoughtless repetition. The evening's festivities drew inevitably to a close. It had been a successful though less ornate social event than Mira Pietrowska's summer soirees.

Franz took his leave of Elana and Ephraim with a gravity that conflicted with the mood of the occasion.

"Next week, Ephraim, Mira and I will be in St. Petersburg. I don't know whether to be glad or sorry." The two men shook hands, then embraced briefly.

"You'll be sorely missed here in Warsaw," Ephraim responded. "But you've certainly earned the advancement, Franz. You deserve the Tsar's personal commendation. And when you come back, you'll have seen most of the major cities of Russian Poland. You'll have learned how they do business, their strengths and shortcomings. We'll have much to talk about."

Franz looked earnestly at Ephraim, seeking to reassure himself of the older man's understanding. "You know why I can't leave you solely in charge, old friend."

"With the current sentiments in St. Petersburg, that would be unthinkable. No matter what happens, somehow the Tsar or his ministers find a way to implicate the Jews. Just now, too much prominence for any of us would be a disadvantage for us all."

"Nonetheless, as always, I'm depending on you to oversee things."

"Of course," Ephraim acknowledged.

As the guests departed, Ephraim and Elana stood on the stairs of the wide veranda at the front of their home, gratified that the celebration had gone well but saddened also by the eminent departure, though only temporary, of the family's closest and most valued friends.

"I must say, I dread to see them leave," Elana said softly. She glanced at Ephraim, noting the widening wings of white at his temples and in his beard. "I feel so apprehensive, so vulnerable." A chill wind blew across the veranda, seeming to echo her words. She shivered.

Ephraim drew her closer, encircling her with his arms. "We are all vulnerable, my dear. Even Franz. So far, we've been blessed. We can only wait and see what the future holds."

"It's good that Michael will soon be going back to Zurich to enter the University. The contrast between Warsaw and Zurich, especially now, will be devastating for him. I'll be frightened every time he leaves the house."

"Michael's matured considerably these last four years, Elana. He knows he must be careful, for his sake and for all his family. Tomorrow, I'll have a talk with him. There's much that needs to be said, now that he's old enough to understand."

\* \* \*

Michael knelt beside a faded gravestone and ran his fingers over the roughened surface. Only the letters J and A, carved long ago by the stonecutter who had fashioned Rachel's headstone, remained legible. That had been done deliberately to make the grave seem older than the era of the Marjzendiak's possession of the property. The few Zielinski headstones that remained intact seemed its contemporary in age, and so Ephraim had intended.

"I often used to wonder what ancient ancestor lay buried here, with a marker so weathered the name was all but worn away. No one ever mentioned him, and I never dared to ask."

"This is our secret heritage," Ephraim said solemnly. "Over the years, I've come here, sometimes late at night, to add to it. There are coins here and gemstones wrapped well against the weather. And sealed with them in a thick, metal-lined, stone chest are documents and notes. At need, what's buried here may be the price of freedom, either for us or, if we're fortunate, for our descendants."

He glanced at Michael's serious young face. It was shadowed by the evergreen trees that had grown thick and tall over the burial yard in the years since Ephraim had first come here.

"Among the documents is the original deed to this property. Franz was wise as well as benevolent. He bought the property in his own name, then deeded it to me and my descendants in perpetuity, for services to him and his house. It's in the form of the old grant deeds of Kasimir the Great. It will stand before Russian and Polish law, long after the buildings here are decayed ruins. As long as the Marjzendiak family survives, this land will be its possession." He paused, then added thoughtfully, "As will the burning thirst for freedom and dignity that led me to acquire it."

"Why have you never told me this before?"

"You weren't ready to know before, son, but now you're almost a man. I just hope you won't be called upon too soon to assume the role of a man."

"I'm ready to take on that role, father."

Ephraim nodded gravely. "Yes, well don't be so anxious, Michael. A man's path can be a hard road to travel. As Jews, we have always carried a heavy burden. Tsar Alexander granted us land to hold the Polish rebels in check, to drive a wedge between the warring nationalities of his empire. For the same cause, he freed the Russian serfs, enfranchised the Polish peasants, and gave some of the rights of citizenship to the gypsies. They're too few, he thought, to make a difference, and too outcast to form strong ties with any other racial group. Our Tsar Liberator, it turns out, wasn't moved so much by altruistic motives, as by expediency."

Ephraim paused to watch the last crimson rays of sunlight fade slowly from the winter sky. "Now, I think," he went on, "Alexander regrets his generosity. One by one, he's taking back his token gestures. No one is safe - neither Jew nor Gentile."

"And yet, you stay."

"I stay because wherever I might go, even across the sea to America, it would take me decades to achieve what I've gained here. I'm getting older now. I would never live long enough to do all that again. For you, though, if it comes to that, things may be different." He turned to Michael. "That's why I've told you about this grave. It's meant to be a beginning, not an end. However, before you think of using what lies buried here, there's a task you must complete."

Michael nodded. "My education."

"Yes! Knowledge is the key to everything of value. Without it a man is only a slave, to his own passions and to other men. With it he can achieve wonders."

Michael smiled. "He can climb the Matterhorn."

Ephraim frowned, puzzled. "Matterhorn?"

"It's a mountain near the Swiss-Italian border, a mountain, and a symbol of everything worth doing. So says Markos. It's not the tallest mountain, but it's the hardest to climb."

"And therefore, the most tantalizing." Ephraim smiled knowingly. "For me, this land was the Matterhorn." He looked earnestly into Michael's face. The boy had grown six inches in the past four years. He was nearly as tall now as his father. "What does it mean for you?"

Michael considered the question for a moment. "For me," he said, "it's becoming a writer. A good one."

"No doubt you will," Ephraim remarked. "When you go back to Zurich, you will learn how to achieve your goal. You'll begin to climb your mountain." He glanced wistfully at the graves before them. "We are blessed, you know. In these troubled times, there are already three to ensure the survival of our name: Adam's son Abrahm, and Leah's sons Samuel and Frederich.. Though their names are Kolvner, they are still part of our heritage."

"One day, I hope to have a son, too."

"You will in time, Michael. I'll do all I can to help you reach your goals, as I've helped your brothers and sister, but even if I can't, you'll be safely away from here to pursue those goals on your own, if you have to."

They stood together, watching twilight descend across the length and breadth of the land that bore the name Marjzendiak. Both shared the same determination - that the land around them forever bear that name.

* * *

As martial law was implemented throughout the empire, fear gripped the people. Curfews were strictly enforced, and a rash of arrests ensued, many based on flimsy charges. The forces of law and order seized this opportunity to flex their political muscle, and their power was felt at every level of the social structure.

On the afternoon before he left for St. Petersburg, Franz Pietrowski summoned Ephraim Marjzendiak and Josef Zuczcheski, newly appointed as associate assistant manager, to his office to give them last minute instructions. It was a formality, but one that allowed Franz to watch the two men interact on their new footing.

"I'm depending on both of you to see that things run smoothly while I'm gone," he said, then glanced at Zuczcheski. "Ephraim has been here nearly as long as I have, Josef. If you have any questions, don't hesitate to consult him."

Zuczcheski stepped back a pace as if he had been reprimanded.

"Is that likely, sir? I mean, I have my own separate duties now. I think I know them well." Zuczcheski seemed to need to convince himself rather than his superior.

"Naturally," Franz agreed. "I relieved you of your share of the ledger deposit records so you could concentrate on investments. I think it's better that each of you have separate and distinct responsibilities. It's just that Ephraim has been involved in every aspect of banking. His experience can be invaluable to you, as your support will be to him."

Zuczcheski looked from Ephraim to Pietrowski, then lowered his gaze. The silence that followed seemed prolonged and marginally awkward. "Of course," he added belatedly, "you can rely on me."

For the next few minutes, Franz spelled out in detail exactly what he expected of the two men who would manage the bank in his absence. When he had finished, Zuczcheski excused himself, while Ephraim remained.

"I'm sure you realize," Franz said almost apologetically, "why all this is necessary."

Ephraim nodded. "Politics," he responded wryly, aware that his friend could not leave a Jew in sole charge of the Tsar's bank. "And rumor has it that things are about to get worse."

"In this case, reality is even worse than speculation." Franz paused to close the door that the departing Zuczcheski had left slightly ajar. "There's been another attempt to assassinate Tsar Alexander."

Ephraim shook his head. "Oh, no." A sigh escaped him. "I assume it didn't succeed."

"Apparently not."

"Whom have they accused?"

"I haven't heard," Franz answered.

"If they can, they'll blame us," Ephraim said sadly.

"There's no reason to assume they've found anything to implicate the Jews," Franz responded in an attempt to reassure his friend.

Ephraim shrugged. "When have they ever needed proof?"

"Don't jump to conclusions. This is almost certain to be the work of the underground revolutionaries."

"It's equally certain to be difficult to find them. They seem to strike and then disappear. It's hard to prove anything against them unless they decide to boast about it in their newspapers. If they'd achieved their goal, that might be a possibility. As it is, they failed, so why admit it?"

"You have a point," Franz conceded.

Ephraim considered for a moment. "I'm going to need your help, Franz. My son is scheduled to return to school in Zurich in three days. He'll need to leave tomorrow."

Franz was puzzled. "How can I help?"

"Before you leave, can you obtain a letter of safe conduct signed by the governor-general?"

"Yes," Franz answered thoughtfully. "I suppose so. You think a boy of Michael's age will need such a document?"

"I think we both know," Ephraim answered, "that in times such as these, no one is safe."

"Agreed," Franz said grimly. "You can depend on me."

That evening, the family gathered for dinner at Plaz Marjzendiak. Rabbi Janowski met with them and led them in prayer, giving all of them, and especially Michael, his blessing. Early the following morning, Ephraim drove Michael to the railway station. The December wind was raw and cold. The sky was leaden, and snow fell thick and soft, like a shower of feathers shaken from an overstuffed quilt.

Michael, sitting silently beside his father, could not help but compare this leave-taking with the time, four years earlier, when he had first left Warsaw. Then, he had been a boy yearning eagerly to be a man. Now, at seventeen, he felt torn between the desire to pursue his own path and a gnawing sense of guilt. He was leaving his family in a time of growing peril to return to the distant safety of Zurich. Michael and Ephraim had talked of many things during this visit, but there were still subjects left unaddressed between them - words of thanks, expressions of understanding, indications of Michael's concern for his father's safety and that of his family. Yet, in these final moments together, words were hard to find. The carriage drew to a halt, and Michael climbed out and reached up to remove his bags. Ephraim's hand closed over his, their eyes met, and Ephraim smiled reassuringly.

Together, father and son walked to the platform. Even at this early hour of the morning, the station was far from empty. It seemed there were many others eager to leave Warsaw without delay. There would be little chance to converse, but Michael realized that most of what needed to be said had already passed between them, much of it without words.

Michael turned to Ephraim as the train drew near the platform. He reached out to his father and clasped his hand. Ephraim embraced his son, then walked with him to the steps leading up to the railway car. There he paused and took a sealed, official-looking envelope from the inner pocket of his long black coat.

"Keep this safe," he cautioned Michael, handing him the letter of safe conduct. "As always, Franz has proved himself a reliable friend."

Michael nodded, taking the letter. "I only wish he were staying here. I'd feel happier then about going away."

"I find myself wishing that you didn't have to go away, son," Ephraim replied, "but wishes cannot change that which is." He urged Michael up the stairs to the train and handed his bags up to him. "Go now, son," he said, "and don't look back."

"I'll do my best, father. I'll make you proud of me." As the train pulled slowly away, Michael raised his hand and waved to his father.

Ephraim watched until the train disappeared in the distance.

He then retraced his steps along the platform and out through the station to his coach, parked in the yard. As he gathered the reins of his paired horses and prepared to mount the driver's box, three men clad in the red-trimmed gray uniforms of the militia surrounded him.

"You are Ephraim Marjzendiak." It was an accusation rather than a question.

"Yes, I am."

"You will come with us." The authoritative voice and manner of the speaker, as well as the insignia of rank on his uniform, identified him as the commanding officer.

Ephraim glanced at the man's saturnine face and shivered involuntarily, though not from the cold. "May I know why?"

"In due time. For now, all you need know is that you are under arrest, by order of his Excellency, the Governor-General of Warsaw." with those words, the commander signaled to his subordinates, who moved closer to Ephraim.

Ephraim patted his horses' heads, seeking, despite his own uncertainty, to reassure them. As he presented his wrists to the militiaman to be bound, he realized that until this moment he had dared to hope that even under martial law, his position on the bank council might somehow protect him. Certainly, he had never envisioned himself snatched abruptly from the normal framework of his life and led through the city's streets in irons, like a common criminal seized in an act of petty theft.

"I must get word to the bank," Ephraim protested. "Mer Zuczcheski will be expecting me."

"That's no longer your concern," the commander responded, brusquely. He led Ephraim to a carriage across the street from the railway station. As Ephraim climbed inside, hampered by the shackles that bound his hands in front of him, he noted that the pale winter sun was just emerging from behind its cloak of early morning clouds.

Soon, he knew, he would be imprisoned in the Citadel. How long would it be, he asked himself, before he saw the light of day again, if ever?

The last time Ephraim had gone to the Citadel of Warsaw, his mission had been to visit Rabbi Meisels, to assure the revered rabbi of the united support of Warsaw's Jewish community. Today he would have been grateful for a little support in his own plight. As he was being processed through the initial routine of imprisonment, he searched in vain for a familiar face, hopefully someone he had encountered in his capacity as assistant bank commissioner. He had hoped at least to send a message to Josef Zuczcheski, on whom Ephraim would have to rely to notify his family.

Unfortunately, Ephraim recognized no one among the prison personnel. It was only among the prisoners that he saw familiar faces, and seeing them, he grew more frightened. Among those he was joining behind bars were Dr. Samuel Jedewreski, who had retired from active medical practice. Also present was Mordecai Zendt, the eminent mathematician and teacher.

Ephraim stepped into the cell pointed out to him. A sense of hopelessness pervaded him as the barred door was slammed shut and the padlock fastened with a grating clank.

In whispered tones, he spoke with Samuel Jedewreski, locked in the cell adjacent to his own. It was thus he learned that the doctor was as ignorant of his own alleged crimes as was Ephraim. Apparently, none of the men here had been informed of the reason for their arrest.

At least, Ephraim thought with relief, Michael had escaped from Warsaw armed with a safe conduct letter signed by the Governor-General himself. In a matter of hours, the boy would be beyond the borders of the Vistula Provinces, safe in Austrian Poland on his way back to Zurich and the last phase of his academic career. Somehow, Ephraim must get word to Markos to keep Michael in Switzerland until matters returned to some sort of order at home, however long that might be.

When Ephraim had been imprisoned in his youth following the 1830 rebellion, he had at least known the reason for his incarceration. He had fought as a rebel soldier, been wounded, and captured on the field of battle. As he sat now in prison, he wondered whether, despite the fact that subsequently his life had been one of scrupulous conformity, the Governor-General had sought out his past and if that boyhood transgression had now come back to haunt him.

* * *

Franz Pietrowski departed later that morning from Warsaw's railway station. His wife Mira accompanied him. They left quietly, unobtrusively, with only their coachman to see them off. When Dennys Dubrowski, the Pietrowski coachman, turned his employer's carriage around in the railway yard, he noted with surprise a somewhat familiar coach and pair standing unattended. The hour was close to noon, and the horses seemed restless and cold. Dubrowski paused to see if the owner would shortly return, but no one came near. Being by nature sympathetic, especially to animals unable to fend for themselves, Dubrowski went nearer to investigate and then recognized the monogram etched on the front of the coach. Priding himself on being prudent and resourceful, Dubrowski inquired at the station office whether Mer Marjzendiak or any of his family had been recently seen at the station. It was thus he learned that a ticket to Zurich had been validated for Ephraim prior to the departure of the early morning train.

That had been four hours earlier. The horses were shivering now. Snow flecked their coats and formed a layer of fine powder on the surface of the coach. Obviously, the animals had neither been fed nor watered since morning. It seemed a most unusual mode of behavior for Mer Marjzendiak, who had always been noted for his kindness and care for his livestock.

Late that afternoon, Isaak brought what information he had gathered to Elana. Dubrowski had driven the family carriage to the bank, only to learn that Ephraim had not arrived at work that day. Since the law firm of Wilshotski, Harnischke and Marjzendiak was located near the bank, that had been the solicitous coachman's next stop. He could not leave his own employer's horses unattended any longer, so he had left Ephraim's coach and pair with the banker's son.

Isaak's concern and natural curiosity had led him to seek word at the infirmary, at the Governor-General's office, and finally at the Citadel where, he was told, Ephraim had been taken. Under the circumstances, it was surprising that the carriage and the horses had not been confiscated by the authorities. Obviously, the militia detachment that had arrested Ephraim had had other urgent business in hand or they would never have abandoned such rich spoils.

"But why was he arrested?" Elana could not keep the panic out of her voice.

Isaak took hold of her arm and gently helped her to a chair.

"It seems," he answered, "that certain sums of money have been reported missing at the bank. They wouldn't release any further details, not even who made the report. They would only say that father had been charged with bank fraud."

Elana gazed at her son in horror. Bank fraud under the Tsar's rule amounted to stealing not only from the bank's depositors but from the imperial government, indeed from the Tsar himself. If found guilty, Ephraim could be put to death for treason.

* * *

Michael was looking forward to his return to Zurich with greater anticipation than he had realized. The visit home after secondary school graduation had been gratifying at its outset, and traveling there in company with his parents had added immeasurably to his enjoyment of the journey. The idea, even the word homecoming calls to mind a particularly poignant type of nostalgia like no other feeling in the emotional spectrum. And Plaz Marjzendiak was a setting to rival the mansions and palaces of noblemen. There was little wonder that the young graduate had walked the paved pathways of his family estate for the first magical days of his sojourn there virtually entranced. But then the Vistula Provinces with their rigid restrictions and ominous ambience had begun insidiously to intrude.

He had overheard snatches of conversations between Elena and Ephraim, even between Ephraim and his estate manager Frederich Bodelair that told their own story of constant wariness, watchfulness and dread. Then too, there were the onerous rumors from Mother Russia spoken of in the streets by citizens at all levels of society. And Michael, now ready to enter University, could not fail to notice the mood of apprehension that his father had been unable to conceal when he had seen him off at the railroad station. The special travel permits and the letter of safe conduct that Franz Pietrowski had been called upon to obtain to ensure that Michael's return to Switzerland would be uninterrupted were themselves a painful sign of the times.

The train could not seem to move fast enough. When it had crossed the Polish border into Austria, Michael could feel his muscles relax. He laid his head against the back rest of his coach seat and breathed deeply and freely, savoring the feeling of release as might a prisoner just liberated at the end of his sentence. Yet his thoughts were with his family even as he exaulted over his own escape. He wished they were returning with him, and not just for a visit as they had done to see him graduate. He wished the whole family could relocate to Switzerland and never have to return to Warsaw at all.

# CHAPTER THIRTY-EIGHT
## TRUTH LAID BARE

Josef Zuczcheski sat in the anteroom outside the office of Governor-General Miklos Vishetsky. Having been summoned from the bank on short notice, Zuczcheski was ill at ease. In the two weeks since he had reported the missing funds, he had experienced a growing sense of guilt tempered with dread. Now, this preemptory demand for his immediate presence at the tin-roof palace, traditional office and residence of the leading military authority of Warsaw, had brought all his earlier fears sharply into focus. The longer he sat waiting, the more frightened he became. By the time Vishetsky called him in, Zuczcheski's throat was so dry he could scarcely swallow.

Once he was admitted to the Governor-General's presence, he stood for several seconds before Vishetsky's desk before the Russian finally glanced up at him.

"So, you've come."

"Your Excellency sent for me."

The Governor-General nodded. "Yes, I did." He seemed to study the Polish banker. "When you first came here, you came of your own free will. I did not send for you then."

"I," Zuczcheski stammered under the other man's continued scrutiny, "but did my duty, as I saw it, Excellency."

Vishetsky came abruptly to his feet. "You did what you thought would cover your own inadequacies."

Growing frightened, Zuczcheski protested, "I reported the problem as soon as I was aware of it."

"The problem, Mer Zuczcheski, as you so delicately put it, should have been obvious to you from its inception." The Russian seemed almost hostile toward his informant. It seemed from his manner as though, under the circumstances, a crime was more of an inconvenience than an advantage to the Governor-General's purposes. "Had your attention been on your duties, as it should have been, you would have known what was going on right under your very nose, weeks before you became aware of it, possibly even months before. Instead, you waited until the responsibility was safely shifted elsewhere, and then you dutifully came forward to report that you had found evidence of discrepancies."

"But I did find errors."

"Indeed, sir," Vishetsky interrupted him, "I don't doubt that. And who made those errors?"

Zuczcheski wiped his brow with his hand. "It's difficult to be certain, Excellency." Almost to himself, Zuczcheski added, "The woman has made some mistakes, which I've made her correct, and then there's the boy."

Vishetsky stared contemptuously at the other man. "Are you telling me, at this late date, that the old Jew is totally innocent?"

"I don't know who's at fault," Zuczcheski answered. "I've said that from the beginning."

Vishetsky advanced upon the banker until he stood mere inches away from him, towering over the older, smaller man with threat implicit in his every word and gesture. "You will stop saying it! Is that clear?" The Russian paused for greater emphasis. "Underlings are unimportant. Only three men could possibly be responsible for perpetrating a fraud of this magnitude against the Crown - you, Marjzendiak, or the bank president Pietrowski, whom his Imperial Majesty Tsar Alexander has only lately honored. Do you accuse him?"

Zuczcheski shook his head. "No, Excellency, of course not."

"And you have already vehemently pleaded your own innocence. That leaves only the Jew, and under the present conditions, he seems by far the most expendable." The Russian shoved the Pole backward, forcing him into the chair facing the desk. "I need hardly remind you that this is an offense punishable by death. Whether the money is recovered or not, this is a debt that will be paid in blood."

Zuczcheski cowered before the Governor-General, not daring to look at him.

"It's up to you whether it's Marjzendiak 's blood or your own."

Zuczcheski's shoulders sagged. "What am I to do, Excellency?"

"You will learn who wrote those false figures in the ledgers. It shouldn't be difficult. After all, they were originally your accounts, handled by your subordinates. You will then determine how that individual is allied with the Jew. The honor of the Crown is at stake here, and it will be upheld. When the case comes to trial next month, you will be prepared to testify, in detail and of your own certain knowledge, regarding this collusion to defraud the people and their monarch. Is that understood?"

"Yes, Excellency," Zuczcheski answered dejectedly. He felt as though he had already stepped on a trapdoor, as though a noose hung knotted about his own neck. "I understand."

*  *  *

Isaak stared out at the broad expanse of Plaz Marjzendiak from the multi-windowed solarium that bordered the rear veranda of his father's house. The scene was one of wintry, serene beauty on this January morning in 1880, but there was no serenity in Isaak. Every line of his lean muscular body held tension and a barely concealed anger. Impatiently, he turned to Elana.

"Everywhere I turn, I meet a stone wall. I'm no closer to a solution now than when Father was first arrested. Zuczcheski claims he can do nothing, yet he's the one with access to all the ledgers.

"Is there no way he can be made to let you examine those records?"

"Not unless the crown's magistrate intervenes, and without the express approval of the governor-general, that won't happen."

Elana's exasperation was evident in her gray-green eyes. "We can't expect any help from that quarter. Yet, the defense can't establish its case without access to the evidence against its client."

Isaak nodded bitterly. "The essence of Russian justice."

Elana came to her feet, as tense in her own way as was Isaak. "That's intolerable! We can't allow that to go unchallenged."

"I haven't," Isaak responded grimly. "I've filed a Writ of Demand against the Bank of Poland, insisting on the defense's right to review the records containing the incriminating entries."

Elana asked, "With what response?"

"So far, Zuczcheski's only answer has been that the bank can't function on a day to day basis without its ledgers. They'd have to close down. He said the books could be examined in court on the day of the trial and then returned immediately to the bank before closing."

Elana's eyes narrowed as she paced the room restlessly.

"To which ledgers is he referring?"

"The master ledgers," Isaak answered. "Why? Are there other ledgers?"

Elana paused thoughtfully. "Ephraim once told me that the records for each day's transactions are transcribed from the daily ledgers used by the clerk-tellers to the master ledgers at the close of the business day. The next morning, these are reviewed for confirmation." She glanced meaningfully at Isaak. "With Ephraim in prison, and Franz still away in Russia, that means Zuczcheski is overseeing the entire transcription personally."

"And he's the one who reported the funds missing in the first place." A current of understanding passed between mother and son. "I've written to Franz requesting his return to Warsaw as soon as possible," Isaak added in an effort to reassure Elana.

"He'll willingly speak on Ephraim's behalf," Elana stated with conviction, "provided he receives the message."

Isaak nodded. "Yes, assuming it's not intercepted before it can reach him. With everything in such turmoil, I distrust even the mails."

"I distrust Josef Zuczcheski," Elana commented. "There's an elusiveness about that man that disturbs me. I've never felt comfortable in his presence. I've often wondered why Franz hired him."

Isaak looked at her narrowly. "You think he's the thief? Because if that's true, we have little hope of proving it against him."

Elana shook her head. "I doubt Franz is that poor a judge of character. What I do suspect, though, is that Zuczcheski has grown so enamored of his newly-won power that he has no interest in relinquishing any part of it, no matter what becomes of Ephraim."

"Somehow, " Isaak remarked, "I must find a means of getting hold of those records before the case comes to trial."

They were both in agreement on that issue, but when Elana and Isaak parted, neither had settled upon the exact means to achieve their goal.

Isaak had previously expressed his concern that Elana was alone at the estate except for a few house servants and farm hands. With the Pietrowskis away in Russia, Isaak and Luvna had arranged to stay with her until Ephraim's release. Even now, faced with mounting obstacles, neither dared consider any other conclusion to the ordeal at hand.

That evening, as Elana sat before her dressing table mirror, brushing her hair, her mind replayed a scene she had lived four weeks earlier. It was the night of the party she and Ephraim had given in the Pietrowskis' honor, shortly before their departure for St. Petersburg. A small, dark-haired woman had brought papers from the bank. Elana had met the woman in the hall and had taken her to Ephraim's study to wait. Mer Zuczcheski had sent her to obtain Franz's signature on some documents that needed to be sent away first thing in the morning. In due course, the papers had been signed and the woman had departed, but not before Elana had formed the impression that there was something dimly familiar about her. When later Ephraim had told her the clerk's name, that had triggered no remembrance in Elana. Magda Laskowska was a name she had never heard before. Yet something about the unknown woman had haunted the outskirts of Elana's memory like a half-recalled melody.

The gypsy woman Magda Jardenska Laskowska had married a Polish tradesman when she was sixteen. Her darkly disturbing beauty had so attracted Fyodor Laskowski that he had not probed too deeply into her background. Magda had insisted on marriage before she would yield to his desires. His mother had warned him against the girl, but in vain. The marriage, held in St. Mary's Church in Warsaw, had been an elegant affair by middle class standards; however, eight months later it had been followed by Laskowski's untimely but natural death from a massive stroke. His young widow had assuaged her grief by attending school and "improving" herself. She had been an ideal daughter-in-law, so that Madame Mariell Laskowska, try as she might, could find nothing of which to complain. Until the day the old woman had died, Magda had indeed taken care of her as well as any true daughter might have.

In due course, the gypsy girl, using the identity acquired by her marriage, had completed her education and had progressed steadily from one job to another, each somewhat better compensated than the last. In the course of that evolution, late in the preceding year she had attained a position as clerk-teller at the head office of the Bank of Poland. By the time she came to that post, she had learned to dress conservatively, using her favorite vivid colors only as accents complimenting the darker more subdued shades she affected in her new way of life. Her clothes were made of the best fabrics she could afford. She wore little jewelry, kept her normally curly hair confined in a stylish French twist, and kept her makeup tastefully understated. To all appearances, she was a refined lady, apparently forced by reduced circumstances to earn her way in the world. Magda had indeed traveled a long road from her gypsy background to her present status. Even her own kin, had any still survived, would scarcely have recognized her.

However, Elana had grown up in a town whose population held a sizable gypsy element. Before she had reached the age of nine, Elana had spoken the Romany dialect as fluently as she did Yiddish, Polish, and classic Hebrew. Her father had been considered the most learned man in the town of Grojec, and unlike many of his colleagues, he had felt that a girl was as deserving of education as a boy. With four daughters and no sons, this was a less surprising attitude on his part than it might otherwise have seemed. He was a natural born teacher with only girls at home to teach. Despite his full-time job as estate agent to the wealthiest brewer in the district, he had needed the stimulus of his role as part-time school master.

Still less surprising had been Elana's affinity for the children of her family's gypsy neighbors. The Cossock raiders that had swept through the area had targeted not only the

Jews but the gypsies as well. Comrades in adversity, outcasts in mutual social and political disfavor, the surviving offspring of both groups had formed a common bond.

Elana, imitating her father's example, had taught her gypsy playmates Jewish dances and had learned some of theirs. She could play the castanets as well as any Romany child and had developed a real affection for their colorful costumes and free and easy ways. Dressed in the fringed shawls and ruffled skirts of her friends, with her vivid red-gold hair lying loose upon her shoulders, she could have passed for one of their own, even within the gypsy encampments.

Those childhood memories had enabled Elana to see through the many layers of training, fear, and carefully cultivated mannerisms to the real Magda. For all of the dark girl's ladylike ways, she was a gypsy. Elana was well aware of the fact that in Tsarist Russia and its provinces, gypsies were not hired to handle money, especially not in a bank.

Here then, if she could gain access to the gypsy girl, was Elana's key to the daily working ledgers of the Bank of Poland. With Franz and Mira both away, Josef Zuczcheski seemed bent on pursuing an unaccountably obstructionist course with regard to releasing the bank records on Ephraim's behalf. Magda Laskowska was the only available means of probing the secret of the bank fraud, and hopefully discovering the whereabouts of the missing funds.

* * *

Early the next morning, Elana drove to the bank. Though she stood briefly observing Magda Laskowska in her teller's cage, Elana was careful to avoid approaching her directly. Instead, she went to the cage of a young man whom she recognized instantly, Phillippe Rebaumme, the young cousin of Franz Pietrowski's son-in-law. She wondered briefly if the two cousins had made up their differences since Pierre had embraced the Catholic faith. She presented to Phillippe a withdrawal request that would enable her to pay household accounts over the next month.

Surprisingly, Phillippe stared at the request and blushed a brilliant red. Clearing his throat, he excused himself and disappeared into an office at the rear of the bank.

Elana instantly recognized that heavy oaken door. For years, it had led to Ephraim's office. Now, the voice that resounded from the open doorway was that of Josef Zuczcheski. Courtesy demanded that Zuczcheski should ask Elana to join him in the office and explain any difficulties behind closed doors. Instead, he said a few curt words to the young clerk-teller, ordered him out of the office, and slammed the door with hardly a glance in Elana's direction.

Phillippe could not conceal his embarrassment. He fidgeted and squirmed; sweat beaded his forehead. "I'm sorry, Madam Marjzendiak," he said haltingly, "but your husband's assets have been frozen. I can't release any money to you, although the ledgers show a sizable balance in all your accounts."

Elana stared at the youth as though he had addressed her in a foreign language. "That can't be true."

"I'm afraid it is, Madam. I've just spoken with the bank manager. It was he who confirmed it."

"Thank you," she said mechanically, maintaining her composure. She turned regally away, her head held high, and made her exit with all the grace and dignity of a queen. Inwardly, she was seething with anger. Once inside her carriage, she clenched her fists and pounded the cushioned seat beside her.

The driver, not looking back despite his natural curiosity, asked politely where madam desired next to be driven, and was told to return home immediately.

The following day, Elana surveyed herself in a full-length mirror in Leah's old room. Her normally pale red-gold hair was several shades darker. In fact, it was a rich auburn that rivaled Leah's in golden highlights and luxuriant curls. It hung about her shoulders, half concealing the brightly embroidered blouse dug out from a trunk in the attic. It, together with the tiered skirt she wore, had resided in that trunk since before Elana's marriage, in company with other youthful treasures. She had rarely looked at them for years, but now they would serve a needful purpose.

She clasped the bright gold necklace about her throat, hung the matching earrings in her earlobes, and draped the fringed embroidered shawl from Leah's French piano over the blouse. Even without castanets, she was the image of a vivacious Roma, still enjoying the peak of her charms. In her hands, she held a stack of valuable old coins extracted from the cache in the grave with the nameless marker. Most of the money there remained untouched. Elana was a frugal woman. She meant to make the bulk of what she had removed last as long as possible. Who could tell when Ephraim would come home? When he did, how would he earn his living in the aftermath of scandal and public humiliation? However, the coins in her hands were worth a fortune in themselves. With a last look at her altered image in the glass, Elana picked up a leather pouch from the table, dropped the coins into it, and drew its thongs tight. As she descended the wide, curving stairway, the name of a childhood friend rang in her mind. Feliciana Zareida. It was a proud and ancient gypsy name whose owner no longer lived. In Elana's present need, she thought it might serve her well.

The redhaired woman descended from the carriage several blocks away from the bank. She slipped out of the traveling cloak that had covered her from neck to heels and left it behind on the seat. Giving the driver last minute instructions, she turned and walked quickly away, the heels of her scarlet shoes playing a sharp staccato rhythm on the pavement.

If the situation she sought to remedy had been less grim, Elana might have felt ludicrous dressed in her gypsy finery borrowed from a bygone era. As it was, she merely hoped she would encounter no one who knew her well on the streets of Warsaw's Stare Miasto on her way to Senatorska Street

Once inside the bank, she stood for a moment surveying the tellers' cages. She saw Phillippe busy with a customer. She lowered her eyes and turned away. When she lifted them again, she was staring into the cold gray eyes of a blond giant of a man. They had not met, but she had heard Ephraim describe him once and the image had stuck in her mind. Albrecht Danishk was a hereditary aristocrat who viewed himself as on a level above his fellow employees. He had worked at the bank for less than a year, and already he was impatient for promotion.

With mounting uneasiness that she did not have to feign, Elana scanned the other cages, fearful that her quarry might for some reason not be there. Her luck held. There, at a corner cage, Magda Laskowska sat counting currency. No client stood before her. Relieved, Elana moved quickly to Magda's window and placed the heavy leather pouch that she had carried concealed beneath her shawl on the counter.

"I want to place these in the bank for safekeeping," she said softly in perfect Romany.

Magda looked up. Elana was a woman of medium height, but Magda was much smaller, and more diminutive still when she was seated. Obviously taken by surprise, the teller came to her feet. For a moment she said nothing but simply stared at the woman before her as though she beheld a phantom from her past.

"Can you help me, or should I ask elsewhere?"

Magda took the pouch and drew it towards her. "I'll help you," she said. As she removed the coins, a different sort of surprise shown on her face. The collection of coins amounted to an impressive sum. She looked at her client more closely, noting the coins in the earrings and necklace she wore, which were of a value almost as great as those she sought to deposit.

Elana gave the name she had decided to use, spelling it carefully so that Magda would remember it. When the transaction was completed, she spoke a term of comradeship traditional in the Romany dialect, a word that meant sister, friend, ally in adversity, fellow victim. She had not used it since her girlhood days in Grojec. She had last spoken it to the friend whose name she had borrowed, as she stood beside the child's deathbed. She vividly recalled her grief and rage at the senseless cruelty of the Cossack raider, who had ridden the little girl down and then gone on without a backward glance.

"I will see you again," Elana whispered to Magda as she turned to leave.

Near the side door that was closest to Magda's station, Elana paused and looked back. Josef Zuczcheski had moved to the woman's cage and was engaged in conversation with her. Magda was shaking her head as if in denial.

"Be sure to tell me if she comes back," Elana heard him say. Her hearing had always been sharp. "Little fox ears," her father had called her teasingly.

Well, she thought as she descended the stairs, she had aroused enough curiosity. Now she would wait and satisfy her own.

The lone occupant in the coach that followed unobtrusively as Magda Laskowska made her way homeward at the end of her shift was hardly recognizable as her flamboyant customer at the bank earlier that day. Elana's driver was skillful and devoted in his duties. No word passed between mistress and servant, and the coach did not seem to be pursuing the woman on foot. Yet by the end of the journey, Elana knew Magda's address and had already planned how she would make contact with her.

* * *

On the afternoon of a February day in 1880, Elana sat at a window table in Provenance, a fashionable coffeehouse in the elite section of the Stare Miasto, the "Old Town" part of Warsaw. She was in a nostalgic mood. As she glanced through the window, she could see parts of this section that had remained unchanged since she and Ephraim had first come to Warsaw from Grojec. They had been married only a few years at that time, and for Ephraim it had been a homecoming that he faced with mixed feelings. He looked forward to his promotion to the head office of the Bank of Poland. He had worked hard to achieve that goal and was anxious to avail himself of the opportunities it presented. However, with equal intensity, he dreaded seeing his father again, since their relationship had often been a stormy one.

Ephraim filled her thoughts as she waited to keep her appointment with Magda Laskowska. Since her seventeenth year, he had been the central focus of her life. From the day he had come to the back door of her father's cottage, seeking directions to the nearby brewery where he hoped to find a job, she had known their lives would be joined. As a young girl, she had never believed her friends' stories of love kindled at a first meeting and lasting throughout life. Well, now she knew how wrong she had been. After all these years, her feelings for her husband were as strong as ever. Otherwise, she would never have been here awaiting a relative stranger at this somewhat pretentious place.

This was, she anticipated, the last of these clandestine meetings, and today she had decided she would reveal her true identity to the woman who had become, for reasons of her own, Elana's ally and informant.

It had not been difficult to convince Magda that uncovering the identity of the thief served her own interests. As a gypsy, she knew at firsthand how ready most people were to believe gypsies were dishonest by nature. In fact, not long after Elana had sent the girl a note signed with the name she had assumed, the two had met and talked earnestly about that very issue.

In a surprisingly short time, Elana had gained the gypsy's confidence. She had soon revealed that although she was not truly a gypsy herself, she understood the Romany culture and the difficulties inherent in living as an alien in a land whose people did not readily accept outsiders of a particular background.

By their third meeting, Magda had revealed her own concerns about the position she now held. If her true identity were made public, she feared she might not only lose her job, but that she could be liable to criminal prosecution for concealing her Romany origin. She felt especially vulnerable working under the watchful eyes of Josef Zuczcheski. She had ample reason to both fear and dislike the man.

He had once employed her mother Sophia as a housekeeper. For three years, Magda had lived in his house, helping her mother dust and clean. Both had known that Zuczcheski's wife had a secret lover younger than herself, and Magda had seen her give that man a ring. Later, when Zuczcheski had taxed his wife with the fact that she no longer wore the ring that had been one of his most expensive gifts to her, she had accused Sophia of stealing the bauble.

The gypsy woman had been beaten to coerce her into confessing her crime. When she had staunchly insisted that she was innocent, she had been discharged. After that, Sophia and Magda had roamed the streets for quite a while before the mother managed to find other employment.

Elana had seen the bitter irony for Magda in the present situation. She had warned her not to be governed by her own wish to see Zuczcheski punished, but to seek instead for irrefutable proof of who had actually committed the crime, no matter who that person might be. Elana had also told Magda that she was Jewish and had a strong interest in proving Ephraim's innocence. She had been prepared to give the girl her name, but Magna had not questioned her further.

With patient determination, Magda had managed to gain access to almost all the daily ledgers, since the clerk-tellers did not use the same one every day. They were distributed at random and then turned in at the end of the work shift. They were used over a period of months until they were completely filled. Magda had found alterations in some of the entries, and already, today, she expected to have the information both she and Elana wanted so much to obtain.

As the time set for the meeting came and went, Elana grew restless and gradually concerned. She wondered if, despite her repeated warnings, Magda had grown careless, or the real thief had become suspicious of her. Several possible scenarios came into her mind, each of which she tried to dismiss. Nonetheless, an hour had passed and still she waited. She had nearly given up and decided to contact the girl later that night when she saw Magda cross the street and walk hurriedly toward the coffee house.

The gypsy woman seemed nervous and even a bit frightened, not that she lacked cause for such sentiments, but she seldom showed her feelings quite so clearly. Time and experience had taught her to be secretive in her own defense.

As Magda closed the front door behind her, Elana beckoned to her. Magda's gaze scanned the room before she moved forward. This was a more elegant setting than any Elana had chosen for them to meet before.

Magda asked as she joined Elana at the table, "Are you certain this is wise?"

"A public place," Elana replied, "frequented by many different kinds of people as a social setting is neutral ground." She observed Magda a moment longer, then added, "Do you think you were followed?"

Magda turned and glanced furtively toward the window. Then she shook her head. "I worked overtime. We were all very busy today. Several people are withdrawing their money. Another factory closed this morning. It's a bad sign."

"Such things tend to move in cycles," Elana remarked. "First prosperity, then decline."

"Mer Zuczcheski's temper seems to parallel the economic trends."

"Perhaps," Elana offered, "his own investments are in jeopardy."

Leaning closer, Magda said, "I think he may have more at risk than his money."

Elana raised her eyebrows. "From what you've told me, he seems rather a cautious man."

"He's a frightened man at present."

"Are his fears justified?"

"I think he realizes now that he'd have been wiser to have found the source of the deficit before bringing the theft to public notice." Magda paused meaningfully, then smiled. "Mer Pietrowski came back today."

Elana knew this, having seen her neighbors arrive the night before, but she pretended to be surprised. "How will that affect our plans?"

Magda shrugged. "Perhaps it won't. Mer Pietrowski has every reason to want the truth brought to light. His is the ultimate responsibility, and Mer Marjzendiak is his friend."

Magda hugged her shoulders, obviously pleased. " It's Mer Zuczcheski who had better watch himself. "

"I gather," Elana said, "he's no more popular with the other staff than he is with you. "

Magda's expression grew grim. "He's a cold, unfeeling man. No passion, no spirit. Everything measured in terms of goods and money. He cares for none of the other values. Perhaps that is why the thief enjoyed outwitting him. "

Elana's pulse quickened. She sensed in Magda a strong undercurrent of excitement, of nervous urgency that was unusual in the gypsy girl.

"You've learned something."

Magda nodded, apparently enjoying a new-found feeling of importance. She edged closer to Elana. "Yesterday, I saw him going over the ledgers other tellers had just been using. He likes to lord it over us. He's boasted that he'll soon be promoted to supervising clerk-teller now that Mer Zuczcheski has a new post. He thought that would disguise what he was doing, but I've watched him do it before. Suddenly, yesterday, it all clicked into place."

Elana followed her lead, hanging upon every word. "All?"

"Yes, don't you see?     He was practicing imitating the handwriting of the other tellers. He must have been doing it all along. That way, he would never be suspected, even if the sums were missed. And no one teller would seem to be taking out large amounts. It could all seem a series of incidental errors. Meanwhile, he grows rich at the depositors' collective expense."

Even as she asked the identity of the hateful person Magda described in such venomous terms, the revelation, when the gypsy made it, came as no real surprise to Elana.

"Danishk, of course. I should have known it would be he. Who else thinks he's above everything, even the law?" The gypsy girl added. "He'll get away with it, too."

Elana feigned surprise. "How can he?" She lowered her voice to a whisper. "If you found him out, can't a way be found to point out his guilt to his superiors?"

"It's not that simple," Magda answered, shaking her head. "He should never have been able to do it. The flaw was there in the banking procedures. To admit to what was done is an indictment of the whole banking policy. That would disgrace the Tsar. They'll go to any lengths to prevent that. I feel sorry for Mer Marjzendiak, but I'm not sure anything can be done to help him. The government needs its scapegoats."

Elana saw the truth of Magda's words and, behind them, the earthy gypsy wisdom of the woman herself. But Elana was Ephraim's wife. She had no intention of letting him be a sacrificial victim of the flawed, ponderous Russian banking system.

The two women ate a brief repast, washed down with spiced tea. When Magda rose to leave, she paused to ask Elana why she had wanted so desperately to know the information Magda had just supplied. She questioned why Elana had paid her in advance in old coins similar to the ones she had deposited at the bank.

"I had to know," Elana answered. "You see, I'm Ephraim Marjzendiak's wife."

Magda blanched, her eyes wide with shock. "But you look nothing like the woman I saw that night." Gradually, the truth dawned upon Magda. "You can't tell them how you know!" Her reaction had turned from surprise to terror.

Elana hastened to reassure her. "Of course I won't. Your secret is safe with me." She took the younger woman's hand in both her own. "You've been very helpful to me, Magda. Indeed, you've helped both of us. You may even have helped the Tsar himself." A smile came to her face. "The one person you haven't helped, of course, is Albrecht Danishk. He's far from safe, no matter how clever and superior he believes himself to be."

* * *

With the passage of time and the realization by gentiles that wealth was to be amassed in the practice of law and medicine, the professions had become restrictive. Quotas had been established in the schools, and it had grown increasingly difficult for aspiring young Jews to obtain an education, even in those skills where some of the teachers were Jewish.

Now, in the aftermath of yet another assassination attempt against the life of Tsar Alexander II, Ephraim's imminent trial crystallized the precarious position of the Jewish banker and brought his heretofore stable status into serious question in the minds of the public. The possible downfall of so time-honored an institution as the banking system understandably also jeopardized the faith of the common man in established socio-economic institutions.

# PART FIVE: ALL THAT GLITTERS

Yahweh is my strength and my song and He is my salvation.

He is my God and I will praise Him,

The God of my father, I will extol Him.

(Exodus 15:2)

# CHAPTER THIRTY-NINE
## RESOLUTION

Elana felt uncomfortable as she waited for Franz Pietrowski in his private study. Mira had not yet returned from an errand, and Franz had just come home from the bank. It was an awkward time of day to receive callers. Yet, Elana felt that the news she had to impart was too urgent to wait. Ephraim's future, his very life depended on Franz's ability to have the charges against him dismissed. In order to achieve that goal, Franz would need the facts Elana had learned from Magda Laskowska, and Elana must not betray Magda's trust.

Elana faced a dilemma with which she was still struggling when Franz entered his study. He came forward immediately and embraced her warmly.

"Forgive my tardiness, Elana. Thadeuz didn't tell me it was you." He held her at arm's length to look at her and added, "You're as lovely as ever."

Elana thanked him self-consciously for the compliment, then added, "You've only been away two months, and yet it seems a lifetime, so much has happened."

Franz nodded. "So I've heard." He led her to a chair, and seated himself opposite. "It's beyond belief," he said, shaking his head.

"And yet it's true, Franz. The danger to Ephraim is quite real. Otherwise, I wouldn't intrude like this."

"Nonsense, Elana. You and Ephraim are friends. You're welcome at any hour, and most of all in a time of need."

Elana's fear shook her voice as she said, "They're determined to make a scapegoat of Ephraim. Could it be because of the tsar's close brush with death?"

"There's more involved than that" Franz responded. "This latest was only the most recent in a series of attempts on Tsar Alexander's life." The event to which he referred had occurred at the Winter Palace, and though the Tsar had escaped personal injury, many others had been hurt. Some had died as a result of a bomb exploding beneath the royal dining room.

"I know," Elana responded. She was silent for a moment, considering Franz's comments, yet she could see no connection between the assassination attempts and the theft. Would the court attempt to link the case they were trying to build against Ephraim to the revolutionary group that had tried at least three times to murder the imperial ruler? Still, she must focus on what, for her, was the main topic to be addressed, the bank fraud. "If the true facts become common knowledge, it could undermine the Empire's whole economy."

Franz stared at her with a mixture of surprise and respect. "Elana, you always seem so quiet and self-contained that one tends to forget how knowledgeable you truly are."

"What I've learned over the years," Elana assured him, "is the most cursory sort of information. Ephraim has always been circumspect regarding bank matters. It's only since he's been in prison that I've come to understand certain details of the system." She checked herself abruptly, and then continued in a different vein. "How much do you really trust Josef Zuczcheski?"

Franz considered for a moment." I think he's basically honest, but totally uninspired. He's a plodder, but plodders are often useful to get the mundane work of the world done."

"That's true, of course, but such men, lacking imagination, may panic at a crucial time. In their panic, they can bring chaos and ruin down on others."

Franz leaned toward her. "Elana, what exactly are you trying to tell me?"

Elana rose to her feet, unable to sit calmly for a moment longer when she felt anything but calm. She turned to face Franz. "What if Mer Zuczcheski knows or suspects who the real thief is?"

"Surely he would confront him with his crime."

"Would he disclose that person's identity even at the risk of being held culpable himself? Would he risk censure for having failed to adequately exercise his own responsibility?"

Franz hesitated. "Considering the possible consequences."

"That's just my point," Elana said. "It's so much easier to report the crime to the authorities than to search it out himself. It asks so much less effort and risk to let someone else take the blame."

Franz went to her and took her hands in his. "You can be certain I won't let Ephraim take the blame when I know him to be innocent."

"Yet someone must take it, Franz. I've been made to see that."

Franz frowned. "Made to see it by whom?"

Elana looked away for a moment. "Franz, have you any idea how the money was stolen, or how much has been taken?"

He looked at her directly. "Have you?"

"Perhaps," she answered hesitantly, "I can imagine how such a thing could be done, assuming my ideas about the mechanics of banking are anywhere near accurate."

She chose her words carefully, knowing she could not afford to appear too knowledgeable in explaining the complex process by which she knew the funds had been purloined. She must seem to be an anxious wife, pinning her hopes on an imaginary scenario, based on sketchy facts. She needed to be perceived as surmising, from what little Ephraim might have mentioned to her in passing, how the theft had been committed. She could not dare presume to tell Franz how he should conduct the bank's affairs. Yet she had to arouse his suspicions to a point where he would have no recourse but to review all the ledgers for himself, leaving no part of the task to Zuczcheski. To that end, she pleaded; at one point she wept, and her tears were quite sincere.

Franz responded as she had hoped he would, arriving at the point toward which she wanted to maneuver him. What was more, he arrived there convinced that he had reached the decision on his own initiative.

"It will be a monumental task," Franz concluded, "but I owe Ephraim nothing less."

Both Franz and Elana were in agreement that Josef Zuczcheski's inexperience had led him to the ill-considered course he had chosen. Ideally, he should never have reported the theft to the Governor-General. Instead, without involving the Russian authorities, he should have pursued the solution of a basically Polish matter within Polish authority, researching the crime and the criminal himself, and attempting to recover the missing funds. Zuczcheski, like many others, had succumbed to the mood of overreaction that had followed the assassination attempts.

Now it was up to Franz. Elana would see to it that he identified the thief, but that was only the beginning. With the Russian authorities and courts involved, solving the larger problem would be a much more difficult task. Elana relied on Franz's ingenuity, but even for a man of his influence, it was going to be an extremely touchy task to extricate Ephraim from his present predicament without incurring serious damage to the Jewish banker's position and reputation.

By the time their interview ended, Mira returned and welcomed Elana with her characteristic exuberance. She pressed Elana to stay for dinner, and rather than be perceived as ungracious, Elana accepted the invitation, realizing ruefully that no one awaited her at home. Isaak was working late at the law office and Luvna was tending to her mother Zelda, who was quite ill.

By the end of the evening, Elana had learned all she could ever hope to know about St. Petersburg, Kiev, and Minsk. Even Vilno and Kovno, the latter the home of the newest branch of the Bank of Poland, were described in some detail. Mira sought to distract her with small talk, and Elana followed her lead, but only on the surface. Underneath, her mind was in turmoil.

*  *  *

With the trial scheduled to begin in less than a week, Elana was finally allowed to visit Ephraim. They spoke and reached out to touch each other through the bars of his cell door, while two militia guards stood by, watching and listening. A prisoner accused of a capital crime was permitted few privileges. It had required the combined effort of Isaak's law firm president, Arnholt Wilshotski, and Franz Pietrowski to obtain even this concession for them.

Now, as Ephraim held her as close as the unyielding bars of his cage would permit, Elana leaned her head against him and wept silently. She had planned to be bright and cheerful, but when Isaak had come to take her to the citadel, Elana had felt the pent-up pressures of the last several weeks ready to burst forth like a flood inside her. She had sat silently as they rode in the coach, striving to keep a tight rein on her feelings. On entering the prison, she had stoically followed the guards down the long corridors and stairways that led to the dark, depressing place of her husband's incarceration. Yet somehow, at the moment of reunion, her control gave way. She rushed to Ephraim and fell into his outstretched arms.

Isaak waited outside on this occasion. As counsel, he had access to his client that even stern Russian law did not attempt to deny him. However, until now, the sadistic citadel commander had seemed to take pleasure in keeping the other members of Ephraim's family from visiting him. Now, under orders from Governor-General Vishetsky, he had no alternative but to comply.

Nonetheless, Elana could not shake off a terrible sense of foreboding. She feared that this bittersweet reunion might prove to be the prelude to an execution rather than just the long-delayed coming together of a prisoner and his wife.

Ephraim stroked her hair gently, touching her as cautiously as he might handle a fragile porcelain figurine. "Elana, my dearest," was all he said for several seconds. Finally, he lifted her face to his and kissed her lips. Even in that cruelly public setting, she could feel his response to her nearness. The erotic tension that spread through him expressed itself to her in his touch, in the pressure of his body against the steel bars that divided them, in the burning heat of his lips upon her mouth. Responding to his kiss, she caressed him tenderly, seeking to relieve rather than arouse the needs in him that she could not yet fulfill.

"You remind me how good it is to be alive," he whispered. "Buried in this dungeon, one almost forgets. Is it light outside, or dark?"

"Still light, my love," she answered. "Soon you'll be able to see the light for yourself. Franz has returned," she added, "and he knows you're innocent."

"Everyone knows," Ephraim responded, "but few care. The tsar's honor demands a victim."

"It won't be you. Franz has sworn to that, and he has the ear of Tsar Alexander."

Ephraim was relieved to learn his friend was once again in Warsaw. He knew Franz would do all he could, but he held no illusions. Even Franz could not work miracles. The prison grapevine was an effective source of prevailing rumor, and word had spread that the Governor-General had given orders for a new gallows to be built. Ephraim had little doubt that he was intended to be that instrument's first victim.

Determined to maintained a brave facade, he held Elana close, smiled at her reassuringly, and said, "As always, my dear, you bring me words of love and hope."

\* \* \*

The partners of the law firm of Wilshotski, Harnishke, and Marjzendiak met with Franz Pietrowski at their offices on Archuletzki Street on the Friday afternoon before Ephraim's trial was scheduled to commence. All four men were grimly serious.

"Gentlemen," Franz said earnestly, "I've narrowed down the suspects to just three. All are relatively new employees. Each of them has been with us for only about a year."

Isaak looked at him sharply. "Then you've ruled out Zuczcheski?"

"Yes," Franz replied, "for a number of reasons, the most obvious being that it was he who reported the theft."

"That could be a clever ploy," Vladymir Harnishke remarked sourly.

"It could be in a very clever, confident, resourceful man," Franz said levelly. "Such a man could commit a major crime, report it to the authorities, and then withstand the strain of the ensuing upheaval raging around him as justice pursued its course." Franz paused and looked searchingly at each of the three attorneys. "Gentlemen, I can assure you that Josef Zuczcheski is not that man. Since the day I returned to Warsaw, Zuczcheski has deteriorated steadily. Today, he can scarcely perform his duties. However the current affair is resolved, he will undoubtedly be retired with a pension to live somewhere in quiet seclusion."

Wilshotski responded first. "You're saying that his mind has gone?"

"Let's say he has broken under the pressures of added responsibilities. The tree that cannot bend in a strong wind is often broken by a storm."

Isaak nodded. Franz had just handed them the blueprint of his solution to the problem. No matter who the thief proved to be, and Isaak already knew the criminal's identity from Elana, Josef Zuczcheski would be made to accept the burden of guilt, paid off, and turned out to pasture. What Isaak wondered was how Elana knew with such certainty that the Swiss-German teller, Albrecht Danischk, was the real culprit. To protect Magda, she had not dared to disclose everything she knew and how she knew it, even to him. "Which of your candidates," he asked, "do you most strongly suspect of unleashing this particular storm?"

"Two of the three," Franz answered. "What I don't know for certain is which of them is innocent."

That same afternoon, crouched in the shadow of the stairwell leading to the vault, Magda Laskowska could see without being seen. On three prior occasions, she had used this vantage point to watch Albrecht Danischk carry out his secret fraud. Today, however, it was not Danischk she observed altering sums and signatures. Instead, it was Philippe Rebaumme. Magda barely managed to suppress a cry of shock when he looked up toward the light for a moment and she saw his face. Cautiously, she crept away, keeping as silent as possible while her heart pounded. She was genuinely fond of Philippe, and she felt distressed to see him following Danischk's pernicious example. She realized he must have seen and understood exactly the same process that she had witnessed. Her reaction had been disgust and silent rage, but Philippe's had obviously been a desire to imitate and thereby derive profit.

Magda's disappointment was profound, so great that she tried at first to persuade herself that she had been mistaken, that she had misinterpreted what she had perceived. Yet she knew better. She knew with unerring certainty that there were not one but two thieves at work at the main office of the Bank of Poland. Because of their greed, a third innocent man was being compelled to suffer shame, ridicule, and imprisonment. He would probably undergo even worse punishment in future despite his friendship with Franz Pietrowski.

The gypsy woman wondered if Madam Marjzendiak had been able to do anything useful with the information Magda had given her. She had promised not to betray Magda. If she kept that promise, how could she convince even Mer Pietrowski of the validity of her accusations against Danischk? How could she prove the guilt of the suave, smooth, Swiss-German teller, whose intelligence and wit had thoroughly charmed many of his fellow workers? He had already managed to be placed in line for early promotion.

Magda had never liked Danischk. He was a bigot, and Magda had had her fill of bigots at a very early age. Her fellow gypsies shared her sentiments, as did the Jews. For several days, indeed since Mer Pietrowski's return to Warsaw, Magda had been engaged in a heated debate with herself over whether she dared risk going to him with what she knew. She had heard that he had called for all the master ledgers to be brought for his review. She wondered if he had already noticed the discrepancies, and if he had compared the newer entries with those recorded in the daily ledgers that the clerk-tellers had filled and were no longer using.

Throughout the remainder of the day, that internal debate continued. Magda could scarcely concentrate on her work. Twice she had to correct an entry. The second time it happened, she stared at the page before her, suddenly realizing that she had just found the means of easing her conscience. Instinctively, her glance strayed to where Philippe stood in his teller's cage serving a client, then moved to the other side of the lobby to Albrecht Danischk's work station. He had already closed his station and was totaling his ledger before turning it in at the end of his shift. Magda looked away toward the rear of the bank, wondering who might have instructed Danischk to close early. At that moment, she saw Franz Pietrowski enter his office. Making her decision, she silently closed her own ledger, drew the doors together at the front of her cage, and locked them.

She picked up her purse and keys together with her ledger and walked unhurriedly toward Josef Zuczcheski's office as each of her fellow clerk-tellers did at the close of every work day since Mer Marjzendiak's arrest. Half the tellers, including herself, had done this even when the staff had been divided between the two bank officers. Today was different. Turning to see where her other colleagues' attention was concentrated, Magda abruptly but smoothly altered her course. She entered the door adjacent to that of Zuczcheski's office, and closed it very softly behind her. Then she waited nervously for Mer Pietrowski to address her and bid her approach.

When she left Pietrowski's office by its rear door, nearly half an hour later, Magda felt relieved. The bank president had received her cordially. In fact, he had seemed almost to be expecting her. Even now, after the interview was over, she was still somewhat puzzled by his manner. Had he, she wondered, already known or strongly suspected most of what she had told him? Of course, Madam Marjzendiak had his ear, but even she had not known of Philippe's guilt. Mer Pietrowski had not mentioned Magda's gypsy lineage, so obviously Madam Marjzendiak had kept her confidence.

Magda also wondered how Elana Marjzendiak had so completely transformed herself that Magda had failed to recognize her in the gypsy woman who had come to her cage to deposit a pouch of valuable old coins. Not only her appearance, but her voice, her manner, even her movements had been thoroughly gypsy. Furthermore, her command of the Romany language had been facile and fluent.

But then, had not Magda herself performed a similar transformation in the opposite direction? Was not Mer Pietrowski's acceptance of her word as fact proof of her successful metamorphosis? He had thanked her with genuine enthusiasm, and when she had demonstrated how easily the changes in the ledgers could be made, he had complimented her for her powers of observation as well as her courage and integrity. Those were attributes usually considered lacking in the gypsy character. For the first time in many weeks, Magda Laskowska felt at peace. She knew she would sleep soundly that night.

*  *  *

On Monday morning, his Honor Michail Kirchlov, Chief Magistrate of the Tsar's high court in Warsaw, called the court session to order. The case before him was the matter of the Crown vs. Ephraim Marjzendiak. Vashily Dubrovsky represented the prosecution, while Arnholt Wilshotski, assisted by his partner Isaak Marjzendiak, represented the defense. Under the circumstances, Isaak would not have dared to undertake his father's defense alone. As was usual in widely publicized cases such as this one, the gallery was filled with the curious and the idle, who craved vicarious adventure. These people sought to satisfy their craving by witnessing the public ridicule and torment of the Tsar's legal victims. In recent months, such subjects had been numerous, and their fate had been uniformly unenviable. Today promised to be no less satisfying to the moral vultures in attendance. The fact that the accused was a wealthy and prominent Jew added interest to the proceedings.

An almost electric current of excitement blazed through the courtroom as Ephraim Marjzendiak was led to the prisoner's dock, and his hands were manacled to the rail in front of him. He stood erect despite the fact that his clothing was rumpled and his hair and beard untrimmed. The intent behind such treatment was intimidation and humiliation. Nonetheless, Ephraim faced the magistrate and the spectators with an air of serenity. In the context of the presumption of guilt that burdened any accused prisoner under the Russian legal system, his behavior was refreshing to behold. Most prisoners cowered in the dock, regardless of whether or not they had done what was charged against them.

Mer Dubrovsky rose from his place and read the lengthy calendar of charges leveled against Ephraim. The reading consumed ten full minutes. The spectators remained respectfully silent throughout this procedure. At its conclusion, they registered their approval in ad-libbed comments indicating their certainty of the prisoner's guilt.

"Hanging's too good for him," was repeated loudly several times, but Ephraim never turned to see who had spoken. His attention was riveted on his defense counsels, both of whom rose simultaneously to face the bench.

"Your Honor," Wilshotski began, "certain information has only just come into our hands that clearly proves the innocence of our client, and the guilt of the true criminal. We ask leave to approach the bench."

A storm of protest followed this announcement. Kirchlov pounded his gavel, seeking to restore order. He directed counsel for both sides to approach, and threatened to clear the court if any further disturbance ensued.

Mer Dubrovsky protested almost as vigorously as the crowd, though with greater restraint. He stated that he had not seen the evidence in question. He, therefore, resisted its admission before the prosecution could present its case. The defense countered with the fact that no less a personage than the President of the Bank of Poland had presented the evidence to Governor-General Vishetsky at the Tin Roof Palace, shortly after sunrise that very morning. The bank president had then brought a copy of the declaration to their law offices, immediately prior to the calling forth of the case. Wilshotski assumed, so he said, that the Governor-General had informed the prosecution in like manner. He went on to say that the thief had confessed his crime, and that the majority of the funds had been recovered.

Magistrate Kirchlov brought the court once more to order with repeated pounding of his gavel and threats of dire consequences to those who failed to maintain silence. He then accepted the documents offered by the defense counsel in support of his request for dismissal of his client. The Magistrate put on his spectacles and read through the papers briefly. As he proceeded, his lips compressed into a thin line. He glared balefully at the accused.

"Well, Mer Marjzendiak, it seems you are not a thief on your own merit after all. Instead, you are a trusting fool who should not be allowed to manage the funds of others." He struck his gavel down once more, and was about to pronounce on Ephraim a lesser sentence than the death penalty originally expected. However, before he could continue, Franz Pietrowski came to his feet and stepped forward.

"If it please the court, I, Franz Pietrowski, President of the Bank of Poland, and bearer of the Cross of St. Constantine, personally bestowed by his Imperial Majesty Tsar Alexander II, crave leave to speak on the prisoner's behalf."

That announcement gained the total silence Kirchlov had been seeking. Franz took his place before the bench, and both counsels stepped aside to make room for him.

"Your Honor's judgment on the bank officer who permitted this dreadful crime to take place is valid. However, it has been directed against the wrong man. The identity of both the thief and his superior, who is guilty by default, have been duly made known to Governor-General Vishetsky. I have here his written order for the disposition of this case." Franz glanced briefly at Dubrovsky, then handed the envelope, sealed with the Imperial crest, to Kirchlov.

The Magistrate adjusted his spectacles, read and then reread the document before him. His face grew red and then pale. Taking up the gavel, he struck it once more, then read the words that had relieved him of his authority in the matter before him.

"The perpetrators of the crime of fraud against his Imperial Majesty and his subjects in the Vistula Provinces are both foreign nationals. They are, therefore, not subject to capital punishment under Russian law. They will be banished for life from all Russian territories. Because these felons carried out their crimes thanks to the negligence of a superior, that superior will be ousted from his current position, and never allowed to serve the banking system again."

Here the Magistrate glanced for the first time at Ephraim since Franz's interruption. "You, prisoner at the dock, are discharged and released from the accusations against you." He paused momentarily. "However, as you have been suspected of a capital crime, you are deemed unfit to serve the Tsar in your former capacity."

Franz raised his hand in protest, but the Magistrate went on.

"You are demoted in rank to the post of clerk-teller, under the constant observation of the Bank President for a period of one year. If you perform satisfactorily, you may then be considered for promotion."

Kirchlov stood and struck the gavel one last time. "The case is dismissed. Court is adjourned." With that, he turned abruptly and left the courtroom without a backward glance or any acknowledgement of the consternation that followed his parting words.

The onlookers were deeply disappointed. They had anticipated a sacrificial victim to be hanged upon the Governor-General's newly built scaffold. Instead, the accused had been freed, even allowed to go back to work. Two other unnamed men had been banished, and the matter summarily terminated. Most of the drama had been played behind the scenes. Slowly the crowd broke up and withdrew, vainly voicing their frustration.

Guards unlocked Ephraim's shackles, leaving him massaging feeling back into his hands, while his family and friends closed ranks around him.

"Naturally," Franz whispered to Ephraim apologetically, "I never expected a directive limiting your duties at the bank. Vishetsky never addressed that."

"That's precisely why the Magistrate did," Wilshotski said bitterly. "It was the only area where his hands weren't tied."

"So," Isaak protested, "he has used what authority remained to him to cut my father's income in half at a time in his life when he has few working years left."

Ephraim intervened at this point. "Nonetheless," he said, "I have my life and my freedom. I'm not banished like Danischk and young Rebaumme, nor discharged from my job like Zuczcheski. He didn't even confiscate my property." He hugged Elana close and looked into her eyes. "We have much for which to thank Adonai. Tomorrow morning," he added with a sense of wonder, "I shall be back at my own desk."

Franz patted his shoulder. "Don't push it quite so quickly, Ephraim. Take a few days to get your bearings. I can manage until next week."

"I'll come day after tomorrow," Ephraim promised as he led Elana toward the exit. "I need to get back to work. I need the reassurance of familiar surroundings and routine duties."

"I need your stability, Ephraim," Franz said soberly. "I depend very heavily on you. I always have."

Ephraim nodded and took Franz's hand. "Only Adonai knows where I should be by now, but for you, my old friend." He paused, then added "Thank you for coming to tell me your news before the court convened. To think that there were really two thieves is utterly amazing."

\* \* \*

Two days later, Pierre Rebaumme stood with his cousin on the platform of Warsaw's railway station. "That's all I can spare for you at present, Philippe. For God's sake, use it wisely. It's too bad you were so free with the money you embezzled."

"I gave most of it back," Philippe responded petulantly. "And you've no cause to be so holier-than-thou. You're a "convenient Christian" on Sundays, and an agnostic the rest of the week. You've no loyalty to your upbringing."

Pierre seethed inwardly. "You're a disgrace to yours. It's lucky this is a public place, you little hypocrite, or I might be tempted to beat some sense into you. In France, perhaps you can manage to conduct yourself so as not to be a total embarrassment to your family name."

"At least I can show my face in France," Philippe retorted. "No one ever accused me of cheating at cards there."

"That was a lie, and you know it," Pierre said angrily. "If I'd become a Christian sooner, it would never have been an issue."

The train whistle sounded, and Pierre hurriedly handed Philippe the currency he had counted out. "You'd better get on board," he said. "You'll be in real trouble if the train leaves without you. Your grace period will expire before there's another."

"Don't worry, I'm going," Philippe responded, "but I'll be back." He turned and mounted the steps to the railway car.

"You'll be hanged if you do," Pierre shouted up at him.

"We'll see," was Philippe's unrepentant rejoinder.

The train slowly pulled away from the station, leaving behind a cloud of smoke. Pierre watched Philippe take his seat, but failed to notice, in the next car, the blond man staring coldly out the window at the retreating city.

Albrecht Danischk also planned to return to Warsaw at some time in the future. When he did, he intended to exact a terrible vengeance from those who had brought about his downfall.

# CHAPTER FORTY

## GROWTH AND CONFLICT: A BACKWARD GLANCE

When young Michael Marjzendiak had attempted his bold but impractical bid for independence, he had not been motivated solely by the impetuousness of youth. His dream to seek higher education in Berlin was based on a valid though idealized assessment of events taking place in Europe. The end of the Franco-Prussian War had been quickly followed by the forging, under Bismarck, of a United Federation of North German States. The Prussian leader had adroitly followed that achievement by uniting the other German states into one nation. By the late 1870's, Russia, no longer the leading power in Europe after the Crimean War, watched enviously as the strong United German Federation assumed the dominant political and economic role that had once been hers.

Berlin was the heart and core of the vigorous young new nation. The bold policies of Minister-President Bismarck, seen from a distance, had already electrified Michael's youthful imagination. He was tantalized by a compelling desire to experience at first hand the exciting atmosphere surrounding the charismatic leader. He wanted to record his observations and later to expand them into essays, articles, journals, perhaps even a book. That was Michael's ultimate goal. He wanted to be a writer. But a writer must have something to write about. He must have inspiration. Certainly, the energetic, decisive Herr Bismarck was a more inspiring subject than the readily influenced Tsar Alexander, who had moved erratically from enlightened reform to reactionary suppression at the advice of his changing ministers.

Michael was under no delusions regarding the motives behind Bismarck's accomplishments. Even at twelve, the boy had known from the lessons of history and philosophy that leadership is often linked to callousness and cruelty. Nonetheless, he could not deny the fascination generated by the German Minister-President's achievements nor the admiration he felt for a man who could govern and determine the fate of thousands of other men.

Michael loved the home he shared with his sister and brother-in-law; he was fond of his two young nephews, Samuel born in 1876 and Frederick born in 1878. Nonetheless, he found Zurich disappointingly unexciting, comparatively colorless. Certainly, with Switzerland's insistence on remaining aloof from the conflicts taking place among her neighbors, no world shaking events were in progress or likely to take place there. The self-sufficient nation steadfastly refused to be drawn into international disputes, no matter who the conflicting parties might be. Beginning in 1815 with the Congress of Vienna, the Swiss constitution had been successively crystalized into a model document of dynamic neutrality. That stance was not a dramatic one. It did not engender worshipful admiration. It would take some years for Michael to appreciate the foresight and diplomacy required to successfully maintain a position of political neutrality in a world repeatedly convulsed by conflicts and confrontations.

Zurich was not even the country's capitol although it had embarked on a course calculated to place it in a position of artistic leadership. It lay in a beautiful setting amid mountains capped by snow even in summer. The country's social and cultural milieu was an exhilarating blend of German, French, and Italian influences and the area around Zurich was graced by an array of quaint communities, museums, libraries and schools. Several times each year, its citizens donned their traditional attire to celebrate the various national festivals.

Except for the triumphs and crises of his school career, the mid and late 1870s passed uneventfully for Michael. He returned to Warsaw for most of his school vacations, thereby becoming increasingly aware of the growing restrictions at home as compared to the liberal atmosphere in Zurich. At the end of each school year he would be full of stories about his studies, his schoolmates, his sister's musical triumphs and his brother-in-law's expanding business success. In April, when he resumed classes at the start of the school year, he would regale his friends and fellow students with tales of the latest extremist measures employed by the Tsar's administrators to quell the undying Polish thirst for freedom. Greater prosperity in the marketplace, rather than curbing that tendency, as Alexander's advisors had predicted, had only served to whet the appetite of the citizens of the Vistula Provinces for further, more advantageous change.

Moreover, the social and intellectual unrest in Russian Poland mirrored a similar mood in the Russian homeland. There, dissatisfaction with Alexander II's rule, which had begun so auspiciously, had gradually but steadily grown to monumental proportions.

The crude but ingenious assassination attempts that had been made against the Tsar's life touched off violent repercussions. Part of Michael's naturally sympathetic nature lamented this state of affairs. He could not fail to recall the glowing terms in which Ephraim and Elana had once described the successive reforms implemented by the young Tsar Liberator at the inception of his reign. Michael's family owed their prosperity and especially their impressive estate to Alexander's initial liberal policies, despite his innate personal distrust of his Jewish subjects. Now, thanks to the Tsar's vacillation and his backsliding toward the reactionary practices of his father Nicholas, Alexander was a target for widespread hatred throughout his empire. The latest attack was by no means the first, although it had come the closest to achieving its objective. Sooner or later, Michael reasoned, one of those attempts on the tsar's life was likely to succeed. If and when it did, chaos would inevitably result. How would the aftermath of such a cataclysm affect his family and his friends in Warsaw?

Such speculations threatened to distract Michael as he participated in classes and socialized with his friends. They colored his conversations with Leah and Markos, and added a poignancy to his relationships with their children, especially with Samuel. The elder son was now three years old and was animated with a precocious curiosity not unlike Michael's own at the same age. Michael found that he could now fully appreciate the fortunate ramifications of Markos Kolvner's appointment as manager of the family enterprise in Switzerland. That event had insured that Markos's children would grow up free of foreign domination and the threat of war. The world was wide indeed. Michael's thoughts turned instinctively to the possibility that the rest of his family, Adam and Meyhra, Isaak and Luvna, even Ephraim and Elana, should explore ways of pursuing a life outside the confines of Russian Poland.

He had long since forgiven Luvna for deceiving and manipulating him. On his first visit home after starting school in Zurich, Michael and his sister-in-law had come to terms. Michael had admitted to her and to himself that his life in Switzerland, while not the same as he had envisioned it would be in Berlin, offered considerable rewards. It was well ordered and free of the turmoil and uncertainty that would have been his lot as a youth thrown solely on his own resources in a strange city.

However, he still dreamed of journeying to the great German capitol. For years, in his mind, he had endowed the place with all manner of heroic attributes, influenced by the works of certain German writers of the day, particularly Freytag and Romelin. He had studied the writings of these men in his academic courses. Later in his education, when the works of Nietzsche, who still taught at the Universitat Zurich, had come to his attention, Michael had begun to perceive the complex German state, with its dizzyingly complicated written constitution, in a somewhat more realistic light. He had subsequently revised certain of his opinions and had drawn fresh, innovative conclusions about the forces at work in Germany, which he wished to test by direct observation.

\* \* \*

The eminent professor of world history, Conrad Bruhn, was currently comparing the new German Republic, the Swiss Federation, and the United States of America, carefully pointing out both superficial similarities and underlying contrasts between the three. The American states had achieved a democratic form of government, impelled by the necessity of its diverse population to arrive at a workable set of compromises. Switzerland's three populations, fearful of partition in the rising tide of European nationalism, had evolved a strong central government to combat that divisive force. Bismarck's Germany, while united, was anything but democratic. Furthermore, its coming of age had been attended by an aura of self-glorification that was little different from the old feudal concept of the divine right of kings to rule and often to terrorize their less-privileged subjects.

It was during one of Bruhn's lessons in the fall of 1879 that the subject of Germany and its enigmatic leader came to be discussed in depth. At the end of the dissertation, Professor Bruhn concluded by saying, "I daresay Herr Bismarck couldn't care less whether his countryman look upon his victories as divinely preordained, but the idea of the Germans as a super race, entitled to prevail over their neighbors, is not only barbaric," he continued, facing his class squarely, "it's downright dangerous."

A young Swiss student named Eric Meilhart asked, "How is it dangerous?" He was frankly puzzled. "It seems a harmless enough fantasy to me, something to make the people feel good about themselves."

"And superior to a host of other groups of people," the professor replied. "That fantasy, as you call it, is a built-in time bomb, waiting to explode. It could conceivably embroil Europe in fresh wars of conquest. All men should feel they are as good as other men, but when they are taught to think of themselves as better, as a national entity, that means trouble for us all. Imagine, if you will, a whole race or nationality insisting on their divine rights - a nation of preordained 'kings' seeking subjects to rule."

"That does present a frighteningly explosive potential, Professor," Michael responded.

"I hadn't thought of it in quite that sense before," Meilhart agreed.

The German student Kurt Bauer rose instantly to his feet. His tone was sarcastic as he caught Michael's eye. "I fail to see the difference between Germans rejoicing that God has approved their victories over the French and the Austrians and the Jews claiming that they are God's chosen people."

Michael turned to face his fellow student. "The difference is in the purpose of the choice" he stated definitely. "And it had to be a mutual choice, the establishment of a Covenant."

"Your mythology," Bauer responded, "records that God awarded your people many victories in the past."

"And many defeats more recently. The point is that victory in battle was not the main object of that choice. Furthermore, it had to be a mutual covenant or it would have been of no value. God selected the Jews as a model to demonstrate His eternal laws."

"This is not a forum for theological debate," Professor Bruhn interjected. "If you gentlemen wish to discuss religion, please do so on your own time." He turned toward Michael, who like Bauer was still standing. "As for your observation, Marjzendiak, that the current European situation has a strong potential for conflict, that's quite true. The longer it takes to evolve, the more certain and the more terrible the conflict is likely to be."

"Meanwhile," Bauer commented, resuming his seat, "Switzerland will remain safely neutral, but won't be above turning a profit at everyone else's expense."

"The man or the country that learns to avoid being involved in the controversies of others has gone a long way on the road to wisdom."

The gong indicating the conclusion of the hour sounded just as Bruhn completed that valedictory statement. He therefore added, "Class is dismissed." He paused as the students rose to leave. "Herr Bauer, please remain for a moment." His dark eyes met the blue ones of the German student, who had turned in response to hearing his name. "I'd like a word with you if you please."

Bauer stared at Michael as if he expected to hear him asked to remain as well. Michael glanced challengingly at his erstwhile adversary, then moved toward the door in company with the other students.

When the room was empty except for Professor Bruhn and Kurt Bauer, the professor addressed his student with quiet intensity.

"In the future, Herr Bauer, I'll thank you to keep your philosophies regarding Prussian superiority out of this class."

Bauer was taken aback. "Well, Professor, I only said…"

"I heard what you said, sir. I've heard it from many sources. I've read it in the commentaries of your countrymen. In my view, no man and no nation is more or less deserving than another. Some are more fortunate than others, some more technically proficient. That does not make them supermen, nor gods."

"You've been too much influenced by your colleague Nietzsche, Professor," Bauer said chidingly.

"Yes, well, you might do well to study Nietzsche's works more closely. He's one of your countrymen who doesn't suffer from delusions of superhuman grandeur. You should get to know him, perhaps take one of his courses."

Bauer shrugged, dismissing the suggestion. Instead, he turned the conversation to the point that had annoyed him most. "I noticed you didn't reprimand that sanctimonious Jew with his 'model for God's law' talk."

"If you remember, Herr Bauer, it was you who introduced the Jewish question into the discussion."

Bauer's blue eyes flashed with resentment. "If you had grown up in Frankfurt, in the shadow of Rothchild's Bank, as I did, and had heard them boasting about their preordained place in the divine scheme of things, all the while they dominated the workings of the economy, you'd hate them as I do."

Professor Bruhn stared at Bauer with a mixture of surprise and revulsion. "Hate, Herr Bauer? Hate is a strong word."

"And a factual one. Many of us feel as I do. And in the new united Germany that Bismarck has formed, things are going to change. You'll see. All Europe will see. We're going to be the major power here, and very soon. And the Christian Socialists, led by Adolf Stoker, will put an end to the Jewish economic domination of our country. Perhaps in time, that example will have its effect on the rest of Europe."

"I assume, Herr Bauer, that you refer to an evolutionary process of reform rather than to violence. Certainly, I hope that is your intent."

The student grinned defiantly. "I refer to whatever process is necessary to achieve our goals, Professor. After all, it is our country!"

* * *

Michael found himself replaying his confrontation with Kurt Bauer in his mind, recalling the undisguised animosity behind the German student's words. He wondered what had suddenly sparked Bauer's open hostility. After all, Michael was not the only Jewish member of the student body, nor the only one enrolled in classes that included Bauer. He had heard, of course, of Adolph Stoecker, the clergyman-turned-politician who had founded, in the early 1870s, the fiercely anti-Semitic Christian Socialist Movement, which Bismarck and his ministers tolerated in order to achieve their wider objectives. What Michael could not perceive at a distance was how extensively Stoker's narrow, disruptive, pseudo-Christian doctrine had permeated German life and thought. He could see the superficial results in Bauer's adversarial manner, but he could not yet gauge their far reaching consequences.

* * *

Michael Marjzendiak had looked forward to his years at the University, both as the culmination of his education and as his introduction to the adult world. On neither account was he to be disappointed. However, the introduction was destined to be a stormy one.

From the day Kurt Bauer learned of Michael's origins, he began to plan his strategy to encompass Michael's downfall. His determination to achieve that end was sharpened by his perception that Michael could so easily be misperceived as deriving from some other stock. Bauer could openly hate a Jew who was obviously Jewish, but Michael's unusual appearance made it clear to him that he could actually be surrounded by countless people whose origins were unknown to him. For this reason, he looked upon Michael as more pernicious than most of his kind.

Now Bauer concentrated his attention upon Michael with unceasing scrutiny. He studied his habits, noted his special interests, his friends and favorite companions, his usual places of study, the areas of the campus he regularly frequented, even what hobbies and diversions he pursued. The object of all this effort was at first unaware that he was being so closely observed, although he sensed the fact of Bauer's animosity. In the weeks following Professor Nietzsche's guest lecture, Bauer was often heard to refer to Michael as, "that pernicious secret Jew."

To those who reported this epithet to him, Jotyl Lermajcht among them, Michael protested that he had never once attempted to conceal either his background or his religion. What he failed to realize was that to Kurt Bauer they were one and the same.

Jotyl Lermajcht sat in the campus square on an afternoon in early August of 1879. For nearly an hour, he had read his Comparative World Literature assignment devotedly, but now he found his attention wandering. The beauties of the sunny day distracted him. His eyes strayed to the foothills and more distant mountains that were clearly visible from his vantage point. So engrossed did he become in the contemplation of his surroundings that he failed to note the almost stealthy approach of a fellow student. Only when he spoke did Jotyl recognize the identity of his unexpected companion.

"They're almost as beautiful as the mountains of Bavaria," Kurt Bauer remarked.

"I've never visited Bavaria," Jotyl responded, "but to me they're reminiscent of parts of Norway."

Bauer sat beside him on the bench "I've wanted to find you alone," he said. "I wanted to ask how you happened to become so friendly with that Jew, Marjzendiak."

Jotyl studied Bauer for a moment. "You don't like him, do you?"

The bitterness in Bauer's voice was unmistakable. "I don't like any Jew!"

"Really? How many have you known well?"

"My father's had dealings with several of them. They're an arrogant lot, grasping, greedy, and unfailingly self-important. They're not to be trusted, either. Not with your money, your property, nor other men's women."

Jotyl raised his eyebrows. "Our experiences with them have obviously been quite different."

Bauer stared at Jotyl. "How many have you known well?"

"Five or six, though none so well as Michael Marjzendiak."

Bauer scoffed. "Hardly an extensive catalogue. Yet you think you know this one Jew well? Perhaps I can introduce you to a side of him you've not yet met."

Jotyl laughed openly. "I doubt there's any side of him that you know better than I do, Herr Bauer. We've known each other since secondary school. Over the years, we've become quite well acquainted."

Bauer shook his head. "It's almost unthinkable that someone like you should willingly choose friendship with such as him." The German student's eyes traveled briefly over Jotyl's thick blond hair, pale skin, and gray-blue eyes - classic Nordic physiognomy. "No doubt a flaw somewhere in your upbringing."

Jotyl got quickly to his feet and closed the book he had been studying. For a moment, he was tempted to strike the German student in the face and wipe the smug smile from his lips. But, that was probably exactly what Bauer wanted. The result would be demerits for Jotyl, and the possible risk of expulsion if he were the one to strike the first blow. The Norwegian student's glance raked the surrounding campus, wondering if this meeting had been prearranged and if some of Bauer's friends were watching.

Jotyl nodded formally in Bauer's direction, and said, "Nonetheless, I reserve the right to choose my own friends." He turned abruptly and walked away.

As he watched Jotyl's retreating figure, Bauer whispered under his breath, "That's a choice you may live to regret."

Jotyl did not hear the whispered threat, but he felt a sense of menace in the cold, almost mechanical manner of the young man with whom he had briefly spoken. For a moment, he considered mentioning the encounter to Michael, but then he decided that it was better to keep such matters to himself and not distress his friend. After all, despite his self-professed dislike of Jews, what could Bauer really do to Michael? Switzerland was a free and neutral country and Bauer would find relatively few allies among the student body who shared his biased views. Besides, Michael had always excelled in his physical education classes. He was surely a match for the wiry Bauer, even allowing for the fact that if the issue came to blows, Bauer would probably fight dirty. Every student knew a few dirty tricks of his own, and quickly added to that store by watching the conflicts of others.

As he walked across the campus, Jotyl himself dismissed the German student's bitter words as the idle venting of his spleen. Jotyl attributed the outburst to some fancied slight dealt Bauer by the offspring of one of his father's business associates. The young Norwegian reflected that sending Bauer to Zurich for his university degree had probably been the German family's way of broadening their son's perspective of life in the world at large. Hopefully, in this international milieu, Bauer would gain a new point of view regarding not only Jews but other nationalities as well.

* * *

In the first week of October, shortly after the beginning of the fall term, rumors ran like wildfire through the student body of the Universitat Zurich. The unthinkable had happened. The text of a term final examination had been stolen, copied, and then returned so that the theft had gone unsuspected until after the test had been given. It had only been during the term recess, when most of the students were away from the campus, that the tell-tale copy had been discovered. The thief had been clever enough not to copy the questions and their answers in his own handwriting. Instead, he had used the printing press on which the student newspaper was printed. It had been a clever ploy, since the student newspaper press was often run at odd hours of the day and night in order to meet the periodical's publication schedule.

The printed copy had been found hidden in the basement of one of the student dormitories. Since the subject was philosophy, knowing the questions in advance was actually more valuable than having the model answers. There were no hard and fast correct answers to most of the test questions. They furnished at best a study guide that would have enabled the thief to know in advance on which concepts he should concentrate his efforts in order to write an exemplary final exam. The majority of the class had obtained passing grades in the course. And no one instructor had made up all the test questions. A total of eight professors rotated as course moderators, and each contributed two questions at the conclusion of the term.

Only two of the twenty-seven students enrolled in the course had received essentially perfect scores on the final test. They were Michael Marjzendiak and Werner Gundt, and both lived in the dormitory in which the incriminating copy had been concealed, but of the two, only Michael served on the student newspaper. Werner was far more interested in sports and other extracurricular activities. He had shown little interest in philosophy at the beginning of the term, and had only seemed to settle down and study after doing poorly on the mid-term test. Had he not improved markedly towards the end, he could not have passed the course, and would have risked being dismissed. For that reason, he should have seemed the more likely culprit.

Michael, on the other hand, had excelled in nearly all his courses, including philosophy, from the beginning of the term, and had been in no danger of failing that or any other course. At first, the Dean had seen no reason to question Michael since his performance had been an expected one. However, after an unsigned letter, protesting the inequitable way in which the investigation was being handled was received in the Dean's office, Michael and three other students, who had done extremely well on the test in question, were called in and interrogated.

Finally, after every effort to identify the thief had been exhausted, it was announced at a student assembly that the theft had been perpetrated by an unknown party, and no accusations would be made. It was also announced that all future examinations in the Department of Philosophy would be oral, administered individually to each student by a panel of professors. That news was received with some dismay by the student body, and afterwards a chorus of objections was raised because oral examinations were notoriously more difficult than written ones. The students tended to feel themselves at the mercy of the idiosyncrasies of the individual professors, and questions could be asked of one student that might not be posed to another.

Over the next few weeks, a small minority of the students withdrew from courses in the Philosophy Department, including Kurt Bauer. Subsequently, more anonymous notes of protest reached the Dean's office, openly accusing Michael of the theft and the Dean's office of covering up the facts, since Michael was on the Dean's List and was looked upon as an outstanding student.

"Who else," read one such note, "had access to the printing press where the copy was made? Furthermore," the note went on, because the key to the faculty office had proved, on testing, to also unlock the press room, "who else could have taken and returned the master copy without being detected?"

In a dilemma over how to combat this campaign of sedition, Dean Schtandych finally sent for Michael.

"Surely, sir, you don't believe this of me," Michael responded when he was shown the notes.

"What I believe is immaterial," the Dean said. "If these protests continue, it could undermine the morale of the entire student body."

"The entire student body doesn't believe it, either," Michael commented. "They can't, given my overall scholastic record. I'm beginning to think I know who started these rumors."

"If that's true, you must tell me his name."

Michael shook his head. "That won't solve the problem, sir, but there is a way that will."

"I'd be grateful for any suggestion."

"If I submit to an oral exam by the Philosophy faculty, and let my grade be determined by that, the rumors and letters will stop."

Dean Schtandych considered that proposal for a moment. "You may well be right," he said, "but that's rather a risk, isn't it?"

"Not as much of a risk as letting this campaign of accusation and innuendo go unchecked. If I don't take a stand now, I won't have a moment's peace for the rest of my stay here."

"Very well," the Dean responded. "I shall schedule the examination for next week. Is that agreeable to you?"

"Quite," Michael replied. "The sooner this is over, the better."

Privately, Michael resented the necessity for this move. He would far rather have challenged Kurt Bauer to a fight in the quadrangle behind the student center. He felt certain Bauer had actually committed the theft and left the evidence to implicate Michael, but he had no concrete proof, no facts to substantiate his gut impression. On the other hand, Michael was proud of his memory, and felt certain of the outcome of the oral exam. On several occasions, he had demonstrated his ability to repeat whole passages from a variety of textbooks, and to apply the information they contained to solving practical problems. It was simply that he regretted the fact that Bauer had placed him in the position of having to disprove a lie, of being made to seem guilty unless and until he could demonstrate his innocence by showing beyond any doubt that he had nothing to gain from stealing the test.

Jotyl's reaction, on learning of the scheduled oral examination, was one of even greater resentment than Michael's own, and Jotyl expressed his outrage far more vehemently.

"He deserves to be horse whipped, not pandered to and placated," Jotyl fumed. "If it were I…"

Michael shook his head. "You had nothing to do with it, Jotyl. What Bauer feels toward me is a categorical hatred. I simply never expected to meet with that here in Zurich."

The night before the exam, Michael tossed and turned, troubled by dreams. He awoke tired, but confident of his knowledge. He presented himself to the panel of professors whose assessment of him would determine the course of his future university career.

The questions were asked in sequence, one by each of the three men. They increased in complexity as the afternoon wore on. By three o'clock, Michael could hardly stand before them, but he held his head high even when his eyes threatened to close, and his voice was steady, reflecting confidence and certainty. Friedrich Nietzsche was among the three, and he asked the last question. He called upon Michael to explain the concept of the Uberhistorisch Man.

Michael's answer required five minutes to complete, but when he had finished, the other professors applauded, and Nietzsche nodded his approval.

"You just may be the one student among your peers who has truly understood what he read. The world, after all, is an accomplished fact that we need not so much to explain as accept, and accommodate. Its intricacies and puzzles can only be mastered by mastering ourselves."

Michael left the room barely able to believe the long ordeal was over. He had come through it successfully, retaining his high score in the class, and satisfied that he had vindicated himself with regard to the theft.

As he had predicted, the letters of protest to the Dean stopped abruptly after the results of his re-examination were made public. Subsequently, Gundt and the other three students who had previously been questioned also submitted to oral examinations, and all four passed. Officially the mystery was never solved, though Michael and Jotyl felt certain they knew the identity of the thief. Both agreed that they would accomplish nothing, however, by voicing their convictions without proof. Thus, Bauer was never brought to retribution for the harm he had done. Nonetheless, the next term, and indeed the next school year, passed relatively uneventfully.

At the end of 1879, Michael was scheduled to graduate. He returned from a visit home to begin his final year at the university, filled with hopes and plans for a bright and exciting future.

\* \* \*

Michael could never afterwards be totally certain exactly how the altercation had come about. He and Jotyl had been seated at the front of the Commons, deeply engaged in earnest discussion regarding the world history essays they had just received back from Professor Bruhn. Jotyl was less than thrilled about his grade. However, since history was not one of his favorite subjects, he was not surprised nor profoundly disappointed. He had been given a passing grade; that was what mattered.

Michael, on the other hand, was ecstatic. The usually stolid and taciturn professor had been generous with praise for Michael's work, both regarding style and content, and had accorded the essay an almost perfect score – 99 percent, an A plus. Only one other student in the class, a young woman named Susan Sampter, an English History major, had been similarly rewarded.

As other students poured out onto the Commons, Michael continued trying to explain to his friend the professor's critique of Jotyl's work. To Jotyl, history was like a dead subject; nothing the teacher could say or do could seem to make it come alive for him as it did for Michael and Miss Sampter. Yet Jotyl could become entranced by a mathematical problem or a theory in physics. And his grades in those subjects were uniformly excellent. In rhetoric also, he excelled.

For Kurt Bauer, however, the subject of world history was a painful, frustrating topic. He saw it all as a political tapestry of constant struggle between ethnic elements and between warring social classes. His essay had so portrayed the period under discussion, and it was further colored by the author's personal bias and racial prejudice. The work lacked objectivity as a result, and therefore failed to fulfill the assignment of discussing the events at hand as a journalist of the day might approach them. Michael, aspiring to just that role, had been in his element and so had done well in fulfilling the assignment.

Bauer had gotten a glimpse of Michael's paper but had been too far away to clearly note the grade. Now, coming face to face with Michael Marjzendiak with whom he had differed on so many points, he abruptly snatched the document from its place at the top of Michael's stack of books, his eyes scanning the paper to ascertain what score his rival had achieved. His jaw went slack when he read it; his face grew flushed, and his pupils dilated.

"I don't believe it!" he exclaimed. "You Hebrew toady! What service did he demand from you to get a mark like that?"

The innuendo was gross, and obvious. An intentional insult issued to provoke Michael's rage. It almost succeeded, and would have if Jotyl had not responded first.

"You Kraut bastard!" Jotyl shouted. "What a filthy thing to say!"

Kurt Bauer struck Jotyl in the face, knocking him to the ground. Michael rushed to his friend's defense, grasped Bauer's right arm before he could attack again, and twisted it painfully behind him, forcing him to his knees. In the German youth's ear, he hissed one word.

"Apologize!" When only silence followed, he added, "Do it or I'll break your arm."

Bauer fumbled frantically in his pocket with his left hand, seeking the knife he always kept there in case of an emergency, intending to slash the boy's face. Another student, Howard Fawkes, guessing Bauer's malicious intent, seized his left arm and drew it forth, revealing the knife clutched in his hand.

"You'd better watch this one," he warned Michael. "He's tricky. You could end up with this blade buried in your gut." Fawkes offered the knife to Michael, but he had his hands full so Jotyl took the weapon instead, getting to his feet at the same time. Howard Fawkes shook his head disgustedly, then turned and walked away.

Meanwhile, Bauer struggled and sputtered in an effort to free himself, determined to make no apology until Jotyl held the knife at his throat.

"I'm sure you heard the man," he said. "You owe him an apology."

"An apology? To a Jew? Never!" Bauer spat the words out as venomously as he could, despite the pain he was feeling, and the fear borne of uncertainty as to Jotyl's intentions.

Plagued by conscience, Michael finally released his hold, and simultaneously persuaded Jotyl to take the knife away from the German boy's throat, but Jotyl refused to return it to him.

"Didn't your parents ever teach you not to play with sharp objects?" he teased. "This is far too dangerous a toy." He folded the knife and deposited it in his own pocket.

"Give it back! It's my property!" Bauer protested.

"Which you had every intention of using on my friend," Jotyl countered. "One more word, and the whole incident will be reported to the dean. Is that what you want? Because if so, I'll be glad to oblige."

Kurt Bauer glared from one to the other of the two friends in humiliated silence. There was no response he could make. A report of concealing a lethal weapon, made against a student could mean automatic termination, utter disgrace.

"Very well," Michael remarked. "This little scene will remain a secret. I doubt that Fawkes will reveal it. He's a fellow German, like you. But he obviously didn't approve of it either. If there's a repetition of this sort of thing, he'll be a valuable witness."

Bauer got to his feet, spat on the ground to show his contempt, and stalked away.

"Well, there's a fine kettle of fish," said Jotyl.

Michael shook his head gravely. "We've not seen the last of this," he said. "Bauer won't give up."

"No," Jotyl agreed, "and he won't fight fairly, either. We'd better watch each other's backs from now on."

That incident left a foul taste in Michael Marjzendiak's mouth that would cast a pall over the remainder of his time at the University. He could never let his guard down while on campus. At the home of his sister and brother-in-law, he could scarcely relax because he feared to reveal just how deeply he perceived the bitterness to be between himself and the German student. Even in his letters home, he did not fully explore or divulge his true feelings, but they had surely begun to color his views of what the German culture must be like if it could produce such an individual as Kurt Bauer.

\* \* \*

The glory of a winter sunrise was a miracle Ephraim had missed for many weeks. Even after having returned to something akin to his normal routine of life, there were still moments when the brightness of day seemed to overwhelm him. His eyes ached from the sunlight, yet he welcomed its glare. Even in winter, he could feel and savor its warmth. It offered a sharp contrast to the dankness of the Citadel's lower levels, where he had experienced a constant penetrating chill.

On his first morning back at work, he had deliberately driven toward the ancient Citadel. He had approached just closely enough to see the top of the new gallows that stood in the walled yard outside the prison. That starkly skeletal structure had come close to being the scene of his last moments of life. Even as he drove away toward the Bank of Poland's head office, he could not suppress a shudder, nor could he erase from his mind the memory of that gallows and all it symbolized.

It was fitting that he should remember it, for the significance of what had befallen him, and how narrowly he had escaped an even worse fate, would serve him well in the coming days and years. Josef Zuczcheski had returned to his family estate, unpunished and essentially uncensured, thanks to his exalted family connections. Albrecht Danischk had escaped the normal consequences of his crime because he was a foreign national and enjoyed the protection afforded by his government's standing in international affairs. Philippe Rebaumme had also escaped, his crime unpublished because his cousin was Franz Pietrowski's son-in-law. He had been quietly banished, and had been compelled to return what funds still remained in his possession, or at least as much as he had admitted to still having on hand.

The punishment of each of these men had been uncharacteristically light in view of their guilt and the customary penalty it merited under Imperial Russian law. Ephraim, on the other hand, had been exonerated of any criminal culpability, but he was a Jew. He had been publicly insulted and called unfit to serve the Tsar in his former post. For one year his income had been limited by legal decree, and even Franz would be watched to ensure that nothing was done to lighten the sentence . Although Ephraim was free, the presumption of guilt, the stain of shame that accompanied suspicion, still remained to haunt him.

In his heart, Ephraim knew that none of this would be true if he could lay claim to any other nationality, or if, like Pierre Rebaumme, he worshipped in a church instead of a synagogue. He was a citizen of no country on earth, not even the one in which he lived and worked. For as long as the Jews were men and women without flag or homeland, for whom no government spoke on their behalf, what he had suffered, and far worse, would continue unchanged. That change would not come about as a matter of course. The Jews themselves would have to do something positive to achieve it.

It was the increasing awareness of that fact that had given impetus to a renewed determination among European Jewry to pursue the establishment of an independent Jewish state. Preferably, that state would be located in Palestine, where the old homeland had been. In any event, it would be a nation with a legally constituted government, a constitution, and the recognition of other world governments. The realization of that goal was becoming for Ephraim more than an intellectual ideal, a distant dream to which he contributed surplus funds. It was becoming, without his being consciously aware of it, a growing obsession.

At the station once occupied by Albrecht Danischk, Ephraim worked in silence, striving to suppress the bitter memories, the rebellious thoughts that repeatedly intruded into his mind. He found it difficult to concentrate on the sums before him. The customers who stopped intermittently at his work station, to ask questions or to conduct cash transactions, considered him efficient but preoccupied.

To Franz Pietrowski, however, the change in Ephraim's manner was painful to observe. He had known Ephraim for more than forty years, had watched him evolve from a young, brash, somewhat rebellious clerk-teller into a mature, capable, self-possessed banker. Franz had watched Ephraim win the sometimes grudging respect and confidence of all who knew and dealt with him.

To see him now, tight lipped, withdrawn, communicating only the bare essentials necessary to perform his assigned duties, filled Franz with concern. He waited expectantly for Ephraim to knock on his door and accept the solace of friendship that he had to offer. Ephraim, however, came to the bank, did his daily assigned work, and then left without exchanging more than a polite greeting with his superior and friend of many years.

At the end of a day in mid February, when Ephraim had been free for about a month, Franz sent for him. Ephraim came, bringing his ledger, and stood before the desk across which so many confidences, so many shared experiences and reminiscences, had been discussed over the years. He stood wrapped in a dignified silence that encased him like an unbreachable armor.

"Sit down, Ephraim," Franz said warmly. "It's time we talked about what's troubling you."

Ephraim seated himself, his jaw tight, his eyes unreadable. "Talking won't mend what's troubling me, Franz. I think you know that."

"I know that not talking about it isn't helping," Franz responded soberly.

Ephraim sat for a moment, lost in thought. Then he looked earnestly into Franz' eyes. "There's nothing you can do, old friend," he said at last. "There's nothing they'll allow you to do to help me. They've made it into law."

"Laws can be gotten around, Ephraim. We both know that."

"Not when they're imposed as a sentence," Ephraim responded bitterly. "Not when the Governor-General's agents are sent to check on the bank's records every week, as though he fears the theft will be repeated. It doesn't matter that I was proven innocent. They're still determined to make me guilty."

Franz came to his feet and walked around the desk to stand beside his friend. "They can't do that."

Ephraim shook his head. "You've no idea how terribly one can be tempted. The expectations of others can exert their own strange compulsions. Why bother to remain guiltless, one wonders, when innocence merits a sterner sentence for one than guilt does for another?"

"It will last no more than a year," Franz protested.

"A year can seem like a lifetime!"

"Perhaps, in a few months," Franz offered in an attempt to ameliorate his friend's anger and bitterness, "when something more important occurs to claim the administration's attention, I can get them to drop the sentence altogether."

"You've already done more than anyone could have asked, Franz. Forgive me if I've seemed ungrateful. I haven't meant to. It's just that," Ephraim's voice shook with rage. "It's all so unjust!"

Franz touched his shoulder gently. "I have private funds that are not recorded here at the Bank, Ephraim. If there's anything you need, anything at all, don't be too proud to let me help." He paused thoughtfully. "I learned, when I came back from Russia, that your assets had been frozen while you were in prison. That's not usual, at least until sentence has been passed, but Elana confirmed that it was true. She said there were repairs and maintenance work that you had scheduled, which she had to forego."

Ephraim grinned sheepishly. "Odd that you should mention that," he said. "With every storm, this past month, I've gone from room to room checking for leaks."

"Have you found any?"

"Not so far, but the winter isn't over yet, and the spring rains are soon to begin."

"We'll get through them, Ephraim," Franz assured him, "the winter storms, the spring rains, just as we've gotten through everything else that life has thrown at us, by working together. Just remember that you're not alone."

The two men's eyes met, and Ephraim's face slowly took on an expression of wry humor.

"The one good thing to come out of all that's happened is that my youngest son, determined to prove that he's now a man, has taken a job. In spite of all my admonitions, his brother-in-law finally told him about the charges against me, and why Elana couldn't send him any more allowance money. He responded by going out on his own to earn the allowance."

"Like father, like son" was Franz' rejoinder. "I seem to remember a young clerk very much like that. You can be proud of Michael, Ephraim. He's every bit as independent and strong-willed as the rest of that brood of yours. I guess he really has grown up. The time has gone by so quickly."

Ephraim agreed. "Don't I know it? He's even had his first major fight."

Franz smiled, remembering his own similar encounters in adolescence and early manhood. "Did he win?"

Ephraim nodded. "From what he writes he did, though that may not be the end of it."

Ephraim did not elaborate on his own apprehensions regarding the conflict that his youngest son had described between himself and a bigoted young German student. The Frankfurt-born youth had tried unsuccessfully to turn the entire Swiss-German segment of the student body against Michael, simply because he was a Jew. The legendary rise to prominence of the Rothschild family in that city had produced, among the latest generation of German youth, a particularly virulent backlash of anti-Semitic feeling. The ultimate consequences of that surge of violent sentiment still lay hidden in the uncertain future. For Ephraim, the immediate concern was for his youngest son's academic career, and for his physical safety, miles away from home and family. According to the calendar, Michael was very nearly a man. Nonetheless, Ephraim wondered if, as a father, he had succeeded in preparing Michael to face the world outside Russian Poland. That world, which Michael had craved to explore, contained pitfalls as deadly as those he had sought to escape at home.

The two friends talked on together about a wide range of subjects, while the routine of winding down the bank's functions proceeded at the periphery of their awareness, not requiring close personal supervision after so many years.

Nothing definitive had been resolved by their talking. Yet, somehow the layer of ice that had seemed to bind Ephraim's heart and mind had melted. The sharp, painful bitterness had lessened, and he and Franz had moved easily back into the accustomed closeness of the old days before the coming of Albrecht Danischk.

On his part, Ephraim's letters to his youngest son concealed much that he was experiencing, much that he felt but dared not voice, even to Elana. His heart was filled with bitterness and resentment, not directed towards any one person in particular, but instead against the spectrum of circumstances that he felt were tightening about him, his family and his people.

Before she left that day, Magda Laskowska brought her own ledger and those of her fellow tellers for Franz' nightly review. Her manner was properly respectful and polite. She said nothing outside the usual order of things. Only her gaze lingered on Franz Pietrowski a little longer than necessary. Then she turned and withdrew, closing the door softly behind her.

Franz glanced at the ledgers piled on his desk. "My work, it seems, is just beginning. Now I review all the day's records personally, and each teller keeps the same ledger day after day until it's filled."

"I've noticed," Ephraim commented. "A better system than the old way, but not without flaws. We must find a better method, one that weak men like Philippe and wicked men like Danischk can't distort to serve their own purposes." Unconsciously, he was once more thinking of himself as Franz' second in command.

Franz nodded in agreement, but his attention was divided. "Did you notice that young woman who brought in the ledgers?"

"Magda Laskowska? Yes, of course," Ephraim replied. "She's worked here for more than a year; more like a year and a half, or almost two years."

"We both have cause to be grateful to her," Franz remarked. "It was she who brought the details of Danischk's stealing to my attention. Amazingly enough, Elana first made me suspect how it might have been done. Then that girl Magda confirmed it. She had actually seen him changing the figures, forging the initials of other tellers. Being fairly new, and a woman besides, she was afraid that she might be blamed. She also saw Rebaumme copy Danischk's methods, like a child imitating a school hero. If it hadn't been so deadly, it would have been laughable; and it took two women to see through it all."

"It does give one food for thought," Ephraim reflected aloud, his train of thought merging in the old manner with that of Franz. What Franz had said reminded him of one more blessing Elana had brought to him. She had helped to set him free.

Outside the bank, Magda Laskowska was met by a tall, dark-haired young man who spoke earnestly with her, then took her arm and escorted her home. It was not their first such meeting at the end of her day's work. Shortly after she had started work at the bank, the same young man had come to her work station to withdraw funds from his account. Later, he had made a practice of coming only to her to handle his monetary transactions. They had chatted briefly on those occasions, until finally, he had rallied the courage to ask her out for dinner, and she had accepted with mixed feelings, flattered but wary.

Nonetheless, Magda had come to look forward to seeing him whenever he came home between school terms to spend time with his family. This past winter, he had remained at home because a severe cold had persisted and had later turned into pneumonia. She had worried and fretted until he was well enough to come to see her again.

It had been during his illness, when she had heard it said at the bank that the son of the institution's president was quite ill, that she had begun to suspect who he really was. By that time, it was too late. They had already become close friends. The attraction had grown steadily stronger, and had inevitably evolved into something far deeper than friendship.

"I've only one more term," the young man said. "Then I'll graduate from law school. We'll tell my father at that time."

Magda shivered, and not just from the cold. The revelation of which he spoke was one she dreaded making. After all, his father was her superior, Franz Pietrowski. Erik had just done her the honor of asking her to marry him, but he was four years her junior. Furthermore, the subject of her background had never yet been discussed between them. It was well-known by now that Franz Pietrowski's daughter was married to a converted Jew, successful artist though he might be. How, Magda wondered, would the bank president react to the prospect of his only son marrying an older woman who was also a gypsy?

She would, she knew, have to face that prospect before she could forge an answer to Erik's proposal. She might, without apology, pursue a career that was normally forbidden to descendants of her lineage. That was a matter of business, of kopeks and zloty, of survival. However, her relationship with Erik was in quite a different realm.

Within that context, she could be neither secretive nor clever. Contrary to the popular stereotype, gypsies have their own inflexible code of ethics. Magda, while availing herself of the opportunities her previous marriage to a Polish businessman had afforded her, was inherently proud of her identity and her heritage. And in matters of personal behavior, she was basically an honorable human being.

That walk home was the longest she had ever taken. The night that followed that unexpectedly eventful day was the most prolonged, most sleepless one she could recall. She spent it wrestling with soul-searching questions and difficult decisions. They were questions no one else but she could answer, decisions she alone would have to make.

# CHAPTER FORTY-ONE
## CONSPIRACY

Decisions, like comparisons, can be odious. Both involve the considerations of opposite alternatives, opposite entities. Both demand that one set of issues or values be preferred above another, and both entail the surrender of something that may have been previously prized in order to embrace an opposing choice that is currently desired.

Ephraim was divided by the bitterness and pain of his experiences of the past several months. For most of his life, he had desired to own an estate and a parcel of property such as was now his and whose boundary was marked by his surname in bold bronze letters. Yet now, each day, after work, when he approached that imposing estate, he was filled with ambivalence. This was home and yet, somehow, it no longer felt like home. He lived there with his wife of many years, he oversaw the management of the place and he derived revenue from most of the crops that were grown on this land. Yet there were times when he felt himself to be a stranger in a strange country.

He loved this acreage; he took pride in the house and in the gardens that Elana had so devotedly designed and planted, had cultivated and grown to their present grandeur. Adonai had blessed him beyond even his wildest dreams. Surely he should feel grateful for those blessings. But in truth he was like a man who, once rescued from adversity, continues to look behind him, watching for the next calamity to overtake him.

*  *  *

In. St. Petersburg, Tsar Alexander II was afflicted with a similar form of ambivalence. He had become disillusioned with his erstwhile violent program of reforms that seemed to breed more unrest and more vigorous controversy rather than the tranquility for which he had hoped. In frustration, he had turned instead to his personal life. His wife Maria Alexandrovna had aged and withered, her once delicate and yet formidable beauty had become a frail and faded wraith of its former allure. In 1880, Maria was gravely ill; in truth, she was dying, although it is uncertain whether her true ailment was tuberculosis, malignancy, or the ravages of a broken heart.

Alexander visited her almost daily, drank tea with her in the mornings and conversed with her amiably, often solicitously inquiring about her health. Yet the open secret of his second family with the orphaned princess Katerina Dolgorukaya was like a festering wound in her heart. She avoided speaking of it, and yet the situation must have been one of intolerable humiliation and grief for the ailing Tsarina. And though he loved Katarina, whom he affectionately called Katya, and was proud of the children she had borne him, a son and two daughters, the double life he was living was a source of shame and guilt for him that could not be denied. It had divided his family, turned his son Alexander against him, and divided the loyalties of the Imperial Court into factions. The royal household was in grave disarray and Alexander was at a loss as to how to repair that volatile rift.

In February of that historic year, 1880, a number of seemingly unrelated events were moving towards a culmination that would merge them into a driving force destined to change the course of Russian history and the fate of the Eastern European Jews.

Stefan Khalturin, a moderately adroit carpenter gifted with an engaging personality, and motivated by ties to the People's Will, the militant successor of the revolutionary organization formerly known as Land and Liberty, sought and secured a position on the staff of Tsar Alexander's Winter Palace. This young man, physically attractive, well spoken and intelligent, managed to persuade his superiors to provide him a room on the premises so that he would be readily available at whatever time his services might be required by the wishes of the Tsar and his family. That proved to be a major miscalculation on their part that would later cost several members of the palace guard and staff their lives.

Into his room Stefan Khalturin brought each day packets of dynamite in small quantities, which he cleverly concealed in his bedding. By February 5th, Khalturin had smuggled into the palace a sufficient amount of the dangerous explosive to construct a very effective mine that he secreted in the Winter Palace basement two floors beneath the royal dining room wherein, every evening, the royal family gathered for dinner.

On this particular occasion, Tsar Alexander's primary guest was Prince Alexander of Hesse, the Tsarina's beloved brother. As fate would have it, the prince's arrival was somewhat delayed, his train having been held back by a blizzard. Dinner, which was to have commenced at six o'clock, the time that Khalturin's associates in the People's Will had instructed him to set the mine to explode, was delayed. Alexander II, his sons, Vladimir and Sasha, as the younger Alexander was often called, and his guest were all spared. They suffered neither injury nor death. They had been approaching the targeted room but had not yet reached it. However, the royal guardsmen, whose quarters were located on the level below the dining room and above the basement, were present at the time of the explosion, and some of the serving staff and kitchen personnel were also working in the area.

Sixty-seven people were either killed or terribly injured by the blast, an outcome that outraged and deeply saddened Tsar Alexander, and further undermined the health of the Tsarina Maria Alexadrovna, whose grief at this event was inconsolable. It was rumored in St. Petersburg that the course of her physical decline took a decidedly downward turn as a result of this latest assassination attempt upon her husband's life.

Had the plot succeeded, she would have lost her husband, her two surviving sons (the eldest, Nicholas, had already died of tuberculosis of the bone) and her brother at one blow.

As for the People's Will, their leadership embodied in the infamous E.C, or Executive Committee, was devastated by the "failure" of the Winter Palace explosion. More than sixty people had been killed or seriously injured, and yet the intended target of the attack survived unhurt. He and his sons attended the funeral service for the explosion's victims. He conducted conferences and meetings with his ministers, he still lived with his mistress Katya and her children, bringing them into the Winter Palace on secret visits in defiance of his marriage vows. And despite his orders to the contrary, his Tsarina had soon learned of the terrible explosion and was overcome by grief and fear.

Stefan Khalturin, in particular, moved under a cloud of depression and defeat. He had been so certain of success. The newspaper reports recorded the severe damage that had taken place in the "Yellow Dining Room", as the royal dinner area was called. His plans and calculations were proven accurate, his construction of the explosive device had been efficient, and yet, because of circumstances that none could have predicted, he had failed. The fifth attempt on the life of Tsar Alexander II had miscarried.

* * *

On February 9, 1880, the Tsar called another meeting at the Winter Palace. On the preceding day, Alexander had met with his ministers and with his oldest living son Sasha, in order to formulate a strategy in response to the recent catastrophe. All had spoken; the heir apparent had expressed his repressive, reactionary views, but no constructive steps had been achieved. On this date, four days after the Winter Palace explosion, the Tsar announced his decision. It took his hearers by surprise. He was resolved to create a Supreme Administrative Commission to carry out the war on sedition. This body would exercise extraordinary powers; its chairman would govern all the highest state institutions, including the Gendarme Corps. Even the Third Department, the supreme investigative branch of the Russian Police Force would be answerable to him.

The thirty-six year old Tsarevitch confidently expected that he would be named to this post, that his father, shaken by the events of the preceding few days, was about to abdicate his powers in all but the name, to his son. The ministers half-expected the same, but all were doomed to disappointment. The man slated to be Chief Commissioner of Russia was not Sasha Romanov but General Count Mikhail Loris-Melikov, the brilliant Armenian general of the Balkan War. The Tsar chose this man for very specific reasons. He was outside the intrigues and in-fighting that characterized the inter-relationships of the various court factions, he was outside the retrograde party that favored a return to the strict autocratic philosophies of the Tsar's father Nicholas I and had embraced his son Sasha. Loris-Melikov was equally unaligned with the liberal bureaucracy that favored a placating conciliatory approach to the youthful nihilists of the revolutionary groups including the People's Will. Loris-Melikov thus fulfilled the Tsar's criteria. He was a logical minded militarist with a deep respect for law, both in form and in spirit. He was courageous, far-sighted and yet diplomatic, knowing when to present a pleasing façade to those who might wish to thwart or oppose his programs. Yet, he could act positively and swiftly when such action was necessary.

His courage was put to the test almost immediately by a petty bourgeois Jew from Minsk who, acting on his own, attempted to assassinate the newly-appointed Chief Commissioner late in February by shooting at him as he arrived home from a meeting with the Commission officers. The bullet tore the Count's coat and his uniform, but did the Commissioner no bodily damage. Louis-Melikov reacted by falling immediately to the ground as if wounded, then promptly rose up, seized the gunman, disarmed him and knocked him down. The Cossacks who were employed as the Count's guards, inspired by his bold example, seized the would-be assassin, Ippolit Mlodetsky, and conducted him to prison.

In accord with recently-enacted military law, the man was hauled off to prison; the crime investigation was completed that night, the trial took place the following morning, February 21st, and the execution by hanging took place in Semenousky Square, St. Petersburg, immediately thereafter.

The eminent writer Fyodor Dostoyevsky, who in his youth had revolutionary sentiments, witnessed the execution. He himself had once been sentenced to die in that same square but had been granted a last minute reprieve. For Mlodetsky, no such leniency was forthcoming.

Nonetheless, by appealing to the Russian people for support for his Commission and it's program of reason and law, Loris-Melikov, trading on the popularity he had unexpectedly gained for his bravery under personal attack, won over large segments of the population. By meeting frequently with the Grand Duke Sasha, the Count was also able to allay the young man's suspicions regarding the detailed report he was preparing at Tsar Alexander's request. Using Loris-Melikov as his agent, the Tsar was able to close down the infamous Third

Department, have it's files transferred to the Ministry of the Interior and form a Special Police Department. As ominous as that action may have seemed at first view, it led at the time to a more liberal imperial stance. Many former victims of the secret police were freed from exile and others were released from surveillance.

In order to balance these liberalizing maneuvers, Alexander commanded Loris-Melikov to appoint Sasha's former tutor, the rigidly aristocratic Konstantin Petrovitch Pobedonostsev to the post of chief procurator of the Holy Synod. Thus he sought to strengthen the Orthodox Catholic Church and simultaneously distract Pobedonostsev from interfering in the revived program of reforms upon which he and his chief commissioner were now embarked. Evidentiary symbols of this program included the firing of the Minister of Education County Dmitri Tolstoy, a rabid enemy of reform, whose downfall even the People's Will hailed in their leaflets. The cooperation of the Commission with the Russian press instead of attacking was another such symbol, as was the adoption of a less repressive approach to the youth and students even when they exhibited rebellious behavior one day and repented and tried to make amends the next.

On the surface at least, the aging Tsar's regime seemed to be prospering. There was peace and quiet throughout his realm. Even in the Vistula Provinces, there was a lessening of tensions and a relaxation of restrictions that was felt and savored in every segment of society, including the region's Jewish communities. And when Franz Pietrowski petitioned the court to be allowed to reinstate Ephraim Marjzendiak in his former post as Chief Cashier at the head office of the Bank of Poland six months before the court ruling had stipulated, the petition was granted much in the same spirit that a prisoner was granted early release from his sentence on the basis of good behavior. The reprieve stipulated, however, that the Jewish banker's stipend could not be restored to its former level until the full year had passed. The appointed authorities were still playing the old game of giving with one hand and taking back with the other, and the Tsar and his Chief Commissioner were too far away and too engrossed in matters of state to intervene.

Meanwhile, the downward spiral that the Tsarina's life was pursuing accelerated despite the calming trends on the Russian socio-political landscape. By April, she seldom left her bed. She set her affairs in order, dictated her will and wrote her final letters, including one to her husband, not at her desk but from her bed or while reclining on a couch in her boudoir. Her ladies-in-waiting helped her with these tasks, surprised at her forbearance and her all-forgiving attitude toward her husband. They knew that, under the circumstances, with the woman whom the Court mocked as "the odalisque" living nearby and paying regular visits to her lover at the Winter Palace, they could not have maintained such an accepting attitude in her place.

When she died during the early morning hours of May 22, 1880, Alexander was at Tsarskoye-Selo with Katya and their children. Having been assured the night before by his wife's physician that she would live through the night and probably through several more, he was shattered when he received word from the Winter Palace that she had been found dead in her bed by her chamber lady early the next morning. He returned to St. Petersburg forthwith and implemented a forty-day period of mourning in her memory. He did, however, allow the festivities attendant upon the unveiling of the Pushkin Monument in Moscow to proceed as planned. Fyodor Dostoyevsky's speech on that occasion remains to this day one of the greatest legends in Russian Literature and literary history, for in that speech, delivered with love and without rancor, the writer sought to reconcile the warring factions that divided Russian society, the Slavophiles and the Westernizers, the retrogrades and the liberals, the staid older citizens and the volatile, rebellious youth. One of the most famous quotes from that speech is the following excerpt:

"We must be Russian and be proud of it, the Slavophiles say. But to become a true Russian, you must be the brother of all men. For the destiny of the Russian is indubitably European, universal as is the Westernizer's dream. Oh, the nations of Europe, they do not even know how dear they are to us!"

This appeal to unite in love and humility before God all of Russia was destined to elevate Dostoyevsky to a pinnacle of prominence as a prophet to the Russian people. Yet, it is doubtful that this was his intent. He did not take advantage of the situation for his personal aggrandizement. Instead, he continued to live in a humble apartment, obscure and unprepossessing, and, probably unknown to him, located next door to an enclave of the People's Will.

* * *

No sooner had the memorial service for the deceased Tsarina Maria Alexandrovna concluded than her widower, Alexander II announced his intent to wed her successor Ekaterina Mikhailovna Dolgorukova, and he began making plans for the ceremony that would take place in secret at Tsarskoye Selo. The bride's name would be changed to her Serene Highness Princess Ekaterina Mikhailovna Yuryevskava, and she and her offspring would enjoy no rights of succession. It was to be a morganatic marriage.

The ceremony took place on July 6, 1880. The bride received her new title and her altered name, and though she had no rights to succession, she would, thereafter, be a witness and a participant in many of Alexander's meetings with his ministers. Her favor would become sought after by those desiring influence with the Tsar, and her reputation as the "odalisque" would continue to be derided, a point of discord among Alexander's family and his courtiers.

Equally outraged were the Russian youth and the liberal intelligentsia. The marriage was supposed to be kept secret, but such secrets as Alexander II was attempting to keep rarely remain secret for long. An awkward amorous entanglement may, for a time, be concealed if one is clever at dissembling and careful of appearances. But after the wedding, bride and groom became inseparable. Katya went everywhere with the Tsar; she moved into the apartments lately occupied by the dead empress-Tsarina, she rode with him in the royal train, and after yet another assassination attempt which failed because the dynamiter overslept, Katya and their children rode with him in his coach, determined that not even death would separate them.

They were united in another sense when at the end of that fateful month of August, Loris-Melikov brought to his sovereign the outline of the constitution that would, if enacted, forever after limit autocracy. This document was calculated to satisfy at last the Russian people's hunger for some form of constitutional self-government patterned, at least in part, on the governments of many of the Western European nations. The outline, and the program that it proposed, though modest by European standards, was a total departure from Russian autocratic tradition and would for the first time in that country's history foster the principal of popular representation whereby officials elected by the people's vote would participate in the formulation and enactment of new laws.

Alexander had long dreamed of this goal. Now he had at his side the man who was capable of bringing that dream into the realm of reality. And with his beloved young and vibrant new wife beside him as well, he was finding the energy and enthusiasm to once more pursue his youthful ambitions to bring a new era to his homeland.

In preparation for the outrage of the court and the retrograde politicians that he envisioned would follow the publication of his greatest reform, Alexander bestowed upon Count Loris-Melikov the ruler's highest honor, the Order of St. Andrew, on August 30, 1880, and Katya was witness to the historic event. In the days to come, when Alexander grew uncertain, fearful, ready to vacillate and retreat from his high purpose, she would be Loris-Melikov's ally, the force that would buttress her husband's resolve. Now, she felt, the long conflict was about to end. The nihilists, the young revolutionaries who had in the early Spring of 1880 demanded a constitution as the price of relenting in their lethal attacks against the person of the Tsar, would have their demands fulfilled. Their raison d'etre would cease to exist. What they had sought by revolution would be achieved by the Tsar's own good will. Peace would ensue for Russia.

It was a beautiful dream. Unfortunately reality seldom follows the course of such dreams. The very factions that the reform agenda was conceived to reconcile, the retrograde nationalists and The People's Will, were both opposed to the reform's enactment. The retrogrades feared the end of the aristocracy while the revolutionists feared that the populace, elated with their constitutional gains, would turn irrevocably away from sympathy with the revolution. Time was growing short for both factions.

Perhaps the most persuasive argument in favor of the ardent enthusiasm of the Serene Princess for the proposed reform was the series of mysterious letters that she had begun to receive as early as May of that eventful year of 1880. The letters were unsigned, they were delivered, first to Tsarskoye Selo and later to the Winter Palace, by an unknown messenger or messengers. They purported to emanate from a secret association loyal to the Tsar yet privy to the inner workings of the E.C. of the People's Will. This group, according to the letters, styled itself the Secret Anti-Socialist League and its members held meetings dressed in black robes and hoods. Each missive warned of further attempts planned against the Tsar's life. Near the end of that year, the letters grew more specific. They presented details of the latest plot and implored the Princess to dissuade the Tsar from continuing his almost ritualistic custom of reviewing the changing of the guards at the Mikhailovsky Menage and their parade every Sunday at noon. The route that the Tsar's coach followed was always along one of two streets on these Sunday excursions, either Malaya Sandeskaya Street, or along the Catherine Canal. On weekdays, the Tsar's routes were frequently changed, his destinations often undisclosed. There was a measure of safety in this unpredictability. But the Sunday routes were inflexible, and herein lay the monarch's chief vulnerability.

Then, after the first of the year, 1881, the ominous and terrifying letters, each of which Katya fearfully showed or read to her imperial spouse, ceased altogether. No further warnings came by unknown routes. The source of these threatening yet reliable documents has never been disclosed. The identity of the author of the letters was never revealed, although Count Loris-Melikov's Secret Police Division was entrusted with the task of seeking out him and his secret associates. Their efforts came to naught. And as difficult as it is to believe, the specific warnings in the final letter, that proved to contain the true details of the sixth assassination plot by the members of the People's Will, went unheeded, both by the Tsar and by the Chief Minister of the Court, Count Alexander Adelberg.

As the Tsar and his chief commissioner worked tirelessly on their groundbreaking project, an obscure, unpretentious agent of the People's Will was diligently working, unsuspected, in the offices of the new Special Police Department of St. Petersburg. His name was Nikolai Klenochnikov, and he was gifted with a photographic memory. This situation enabled him, under the guise of fulfilling the demands of his job, to ferret out valuable information regarding the activities of the special police and the intelligence that they gathered about the People's Will, the most active and most militant of the revolutionist associations. This man had formerly served as a file clerk in the Third Department where, over the course of a year, he was awarded the Order of St. Slanislov. Now, as a trusted employee of the Special Police branch, he learned the identity of Alexander Zharkov, the agent whom Loris-Melikov had chosen to infiltrate the ranks of the People's Will. Had that agent survived to carry out his assignment, the fate of Alexander II might have been quite different. As events fell out, Zharkov was stabbed to death by another Alexander – Alexander Presnyakov, a member of the Executive Committee. It was also thanks to Klenochnikov that the list of the terrorist group members compiled by the cowardly and traitorous Grigory Goldenberg, following his capture, offered as the price of his survival, was stolen and destroyed.

Nonetheless, the efficient work of the Special Police resulted in the apprehension and trial of "The Sixteen" in the late fall of 1880. All but five of those terrorists received lighter sentences; the five were condemned to be hanged. By this time, the bombings seemed to have stopped. Alexander had his new young wife, and the populace, initially appalled by the quickness of the marriage, was in a forgiving mood towards all parties. They applauded when the Tsar pardoned three of the five. If only he had pardoned them all, perhaps the People's Will might have hesitated in the prosecution of their murderous plans. As it turned out, the two October executions hardened their resolve.

It was at the end of the following month that the historically decisive meeting took place that sealed the Tsar's fate. The gathering commenced in an unpretentious apartment complex rented by a young Jewish woman who had been trained in both midwifery and sewing. She was blonde, small and fine-featured, but not really beautiful, nor even pretty. Her most appealing feature was her smile. Her name has been variously recorded as Gessia or Gesya Gelfman and also as Hessia Helfman. Despite unverified rumors to the contrary, she was the one conspirator of Jewish origin directly related to the final assassination plot. Yet, although after her hurried exit from her home city of Mozur in the province of Minsk, a journey she had undertaken to avoid an arranged marriage to her father's aging best friend, she had become actively engaged in one revolutionary organization after another, actual physical violence and brutality repelled her. She became fascinated by the dynamic energy and enthusiasm of the young revolutionary activists she had met in Kiev while training as a midwife and supporting herself with her talent as a seamstress. She was not deeply religious and had not attended a synagogue since she had left home at age 17. Resentful toward her father for arranging her marriage without consulting her, she was nonetheless quite fond of her mother. By joining the revolutionists, first in Kiev, where she had been arrested for possessing and distributing illegal literature, and later in St. Petersburg, to which she had returned after escaping from a Katorga establishment in Siberia, she had found a haven, a home to substitute for the home she had abruptly abandoned because of her father's betrayal.

Among these young Russians, who followed their own rules, she became exposed to the revolutionary concepts of sedition, terrorism, and free love. By late 1880, when the strategy-planning meeting took place, Gesya was twenty-eight years old and was living with Nikolai Sabin. Apart from his lineage, little is known about this young man beyond the fact that he was handsome, intelligent, volatile, and was a member of the Executive Committee of the People's Will.

Sabin possessed an unusual skill; he could simulate at will almost any handwriting style that he encountered, so that, if he chose to write a letter to the friend or companion of one of his acquaintances, the recipient would have sworn in court that the letter had been written by the other party. The E.C. had used this skill of his in the past to carry on its correspondence with the popular press, and Sabin was included in every phase of the planning of that fateful sixth assassination attempt.

Although he agreed in principle with the necessity of limiting the power of the imperial autocracy, the concept of violent disruption of the social order and the idea of violent physical assault and murder clashed with his personal, landowner-class instilled principles.

While the other members of the E.C. gathered that day in his lover's apartment enthusiastically called for Alexander II's blood, Nikolai Sabin dared to mention the growing rumors of constitutional reform, the goal they had all sought, the objective to which they had formerly devoted so much rhetoric in their meetings and in their clandestine literature.

"What if the rumors are true?" Sabin asked. "What if the recent editorials in the popular press are accurate? According to them," he went on, "the Tsar is preparing to unveil his most momentous reform yet. What amounts to a constitution supported by popular vote."

Andrei Zhelyebov, the head of the E.C., with the physique of a gladiator and the heart of a lion, turned toward the slim, slight young man who had challenged him.

"You actually believe those rumors?" he asked. "Does anyone here truly credit the idea that a Romanov bully would willingly consent to the limitation of his autocratic power?"

"Isn't that what we've worked for?" Sabin responded. "Isn't that what we've demanded in exchange for calling off the attacks against him? What if he's finally giving in? What if he really is working toward true constitutional reform with this Armenian Chief Commissioner he's appointed?"

Zhelyebov smiled benignly at the naïveté of his younger colleague.

"All the more reason to double our efforts," he said. "Just now, the sympathies of the people are with us. The two executions have just occurred. Even the aristocrats are appalled by them. They are asking why mercy was not shown to all five main prisoners instead of only to three. If we wait, if we back down in our campaign, the popular opinion will wane. If we allow the autocrats to present some anemic program of watered-down liberal government reform, our revolution will lose its momentum."

He turned to face them each in turn.

"No, I say! We must not falter. We must not wait. Above all, we must not give Alexander II the initiative. We are the moving force, the motivating spirit of the Russian people. In order to retain that spirit, we must fight Alexander with every weapon we can mount. We must strike, and we must kill!"

"Agreed!" said Nikolai Rysakov, rising to his feet for emphasis. "We dare not allow the Tsar to win over the people's good will. If anything, we should hurry to attack and destroy him before he can seduce the masses with these rumors of far-reaching reforms. And if they're not mere rumors, if they are true, then so much the worse for us. If Alexander succeeds in implementing any program that even resembles constitutional reform, then our cause is lost."

"We must not rely on a single weapon, either. Several of us must strike at once." This was a sentiment expressed by Sofia Perovskaya, the daughter of the former governor of St. Petersburg, the granddaughter of the governor of the Crimea. Her friends called her Samechka. Zhelyebov was her lover, and even he feared her fierce resolve and iron will. She was petite and despite her large forehead, she was strikingly attractive with her bright blue eyes and light brown, almost blond hair. Because of her small stature, she rose to her feet to continue her comments.

"The Tsar Liberator has become what all autocrats become with the passage of time, no matter how benign they may seem at first. The Jailor. The Oppressor. The task before us is above personal enmity and individual grievance. This man, this regime, this family has become a stumbling block in the way of progress. In order for our nation to advance, that stumbling block must be removed! Alexander must die!"

Hessia's eyes strayed to the face of her lover. Instead of looking insistent, as did their co-conspirators, Nickolai looked troubled. His face was a study in warring emotions. Only that day, he had sent yet another letter to the Serene Princess, warning her of imminent danger. It had been couched in flowery terms, laden with fanciful descriptions of the ritualistic ceremonies of the secret society of which he had represented himself as the head, the Great Leaguer. More to the point, however, the letter, like its predecessors, outlined details of the People's Will organization, its structure and composition, its offices and the number of its members. And yet again, the "Great Leaguer" had warned the young wife of the dangers inherent in the Tsar's predictably inflexible habit of reviewing the changing of the guards at the Mikhailovsky Menage, witnessing the parade that followed, and then returning to the Winter Palace by one of two fixed routes.

Now, as he sat among the conspirators listening as they forged their deadly plan of attack, he felt a demoralizing sense of guilt and fear that he dared not share with any other living soul. Not even his lover. His one consolation was that, should that most recent epistle, or any of the others that he had begun sending last May, ever be discovered by the members of the E.C. or by the Special Police Division within Loris-Melikov's Ministry of the Interior or the administrative commission that was its driving force, the exuberant calligraphy that he had scrupulously persisted in using in that correspondence could not be traced to him.

* * *

The cheese shop on Malaya Sandeskaya Street, situated in a basement apartment that had been rented by Alexander Baranimikov shortly after the fateful November meeting of the E.C., opened for business just in time to take advantage of the holiday season of late 1880. The roles of the shopkeeper and his wife were enacted by a florid-faced nobleman named Semyov Bogdonovitch and the pretty brunette Anna Yakinova, both devoted members of the People's Will. They assumed the name of Kolozev. Business flourished and the digging of the tunnel under the street commenced in January of the following year, 1881. The intent was to mine that tunnel in preparation for the passage of Tsar Alexander's coach on his return trip from the Mikhailovsky Menage. And since they could never be absolutely certain which of the two routes the Tsar would travel on any given Sunday, there had to be an alternative plan to cover the Catherine Canal route. Bombs that could be hand-carried and forcefully thrown were required in order to secure that contingent route, and the bombs would have to be constructed, transported to an agreed upon location, and picked up by those members of the group selected to play the pivotal roles of the bomb throwers.

Whichever street the Imperial carriage pursued, the plotters covering that route on the fateful day were doomed to die with the ruler. Whoever remained in the cheese shop to detonate the underground explosive would almost certainly be blown to oblivion by the mine and buried in the rubble. One man would perform the deadly chore; the cheese merchant and his wife would not conduct business after noon on that Sunday. Instead, as on every Sunday, they would close the shop, and then they would leave. The bomb bearers who would disperse along the Catherine Canal would either be killed by their lethal missiles or else captured or shot by the Tsar's Cossack guards or the police escort. The men chosen for those assignments considered themselves heroes, patriots, servants of the Russian people. They felt honored to participate in the assassination of the targeted monarch. They were willing to resign their own lives in order to change the course of their nation's history. And change it they would if their brutal plan achieved success.

The letters to Princess Ekaterina Yuryevskaya ceased abruptly after the Christmas holiday. The last one actually warned her of the details of the bomb plot although neither that last letter nor the preceding one divulged the actual names of the conspirators. The princess, terrified for the safety of her husband, prevailed upon Count Loris-Melikov to send agents of the Special Police Division to inspect the shops along Malaya Sandeskaya Street. In late January, two special agents visited the cheese shop and invaded the living quarters at its rear. One actually pounded on the false wall behind which the tunnel was still in the process of being dug, and questioned the contents of two large barrels containing the dirt that had been removed to excavate the tunnel under the street. Miraculously, after checking through the packages of cheese at the top of each barrel, this expert investigator accepted Yakimova's explanation that the receptacles were used only to store cheese delivered to the shop periodically. The men left the premises, satisfied that the place was what it seemed to be, the innocent small business of a local tradesman. It strains belief that the hollow echo from the false wall was not perceived by these policemen. It seems incredible that they could actually have stood on the site where the conspirators were playing out their desperate subterranean drama and have suspected nothing. This failure served to undermine the credibility of the "Great Leaguer's'" letters, although every word they contained regarding the plot was true.

At about that same time, in the apartment that was next door to that of Fyodor Dostoyevsky, N.M. Kalathevich, the contact agent of the E.C.'s so called Guardian Angel, the mole in the Special Police Department, Nikolai Kletochnikov, was arrested. This was a major coup for the Special Police, and it led very shortly to the arrest of the mole himself. Because Kalathevich put up something of a fight, it is likely that the famous novelist next door heard the struggle and became alarmed.

That night, Dostoyevsky was stricken by a major hemorrhage that, three days later, claimed his life. According to his wife's letters, the novelist was aware of his impending death. He sent for his children, he read to them from the Bible, and he received the last rites of the Orthodox Church. As he composed himself for the end, it is likely that his thoughts went back in time to the day of his own arrest, and the occasion of the sentence of execution passed upon him. His life had been spared by a last-minute reprieve. But for the officers of the E.C. who now, one by one, fell into the hands of the authorities, there were not likely to be any such timely reprieves.

Hearing such next door neighbors as Alexandra Korlev, who had rented the apartment the year before, followed by Alexander Barranikov, who had subleased it in turn to his co-conspirator Kalathevich, it seems at least possible that Fyodor Dostoyevsky may have heard snatches of heated conversations through the thin walls of the modest building. Had he paid close attention to these exchanges, he might have learned some details of the assassination plot. But the author of The Devils, a novelization of the motives, methods and ultimate objective of the revolutionaries, was now an ailing, elderly man. He had no desire to involve himself in the machinations of the nihilists, as many called the revolutionaries. He sought peace, and claimed that his one role model was Christ. Dostoyevsky had planned to write a sequel to his novel The Brothers Karamazov in which the youngest brother, Alyosha, the monk, would leave the monastery and become a revolutionary, a terrorist. An outline of that planned sequel was found among his papers, but he never began work upon it. Probably, he felt reluctant to tarnish the image of his most admirable and beloved character, the one who most closely paralleled his role model.

\* \* \*

On a day late in February, 1881, the four young bomb-throwers – Nikolai Rysakov, a nineteen-year-old student; Ignati Grinevitsky, aged 24 and also a student; Ivan Emelyanov and Gimiofei Mikhailov met with their supervisor Nikolai Kibalchich, the E.C.'s demolition expert, to receive their instructions. By this date also, the tunnel below the cheese shop was completed, the mine was ready to put in place and the mechanism to explode the device would then have to be detonated. The target date was Sunday, March 1. By this time, Barranikov, Kalathevich and Kletochnikov were in prison. Andrei Zhelyebov was now the head of the E.C. and he and his lover Sofia Perovskaya were in charge of the assassination plot. Final arrangements were made regarding where the bombs were to be constructed, where they would be brought so that the four young men could retrieve them, and where each man was to post himself along the Catherine Canal route.

On February 27th, while visiting his friend Mikhail Trigani at his apartment, Zhelyebov, together with Trigani, was arrested. The two were imprisoned in the Fortress of Peter and Paul where they would be questioned. The People's Will had been dealt a crucial blow. Most of their major leadership was now in Special Police custody. The next day, the Tsar rejoiced when Loris-Melikov brought him the news. He shared that sense of triumph with his wife, and both felt relieved. At last Alexander began to feel safe.

And Loris-Melikov had also brought him another cause to rejoice, the final draft of the long-worked upon reform provision that was to bring the preamble to constitutional government in Russia into being. The sixty-one year old Alexander thought of this as the happiest day of his life since his coronation and his signing of the Emancipation Act freeing the serfs. Even his marriage, which finally placed a stamp of moral approval upon his long-running liaison with Katya, had not infused him with the sense of triumph and achievement that this day of February 28, 1881 brought to him.

Meanwhile, in a secret apartment overlooking Voznesensky Bridge in St. Petersburg, the remaining members of the Executive Committee convened what each knew might be their last meeting, their last day on earth. The bombs had yet to be prepared for the four young men. The mine had still to be placed in the tunnel. With all the original leadership figures in custody, it was the women of the E.C. who fueled the aggressive spirit of the People's Will, women such as the classically beautiful Vera Figner, the tempestuous Alexandra Mikhailova, the delicately built but iron-willed Alexandra Korba, and the fiercely energetic and passionately revolutionary Sofia Perovskaya, who led the meeting and who, with her lover in prison, was now the leader of the assassination plot. Like a general on the eve of battle, the diminutive Perovskaya gathered her troops around her with her single-minded determination. She infused into the demoralized men who remained to her the relentless, selfless courage of the fully-committed revolutionary to whom personal considerations are meaningless, and to whom the goal of nationwide revolt was everything.

"We may not survive tomorrow," she told them, "but that does not matter. What matters is that Alexander II must not survive tomorrow! Whatever it takes to achieve that result, we shall do. Tomorrow is the day on which we take our country back from our oppressors. We shall act tomorrow. No matter what, we act!"

She shook her fist in the air for emphasis, and every person present followed her example, every one of them echoed her sentiment.

"Tomorrow we act! We strike at tyranny!"

"We shall strike the tyrant dead!" said Perovskaya. That was the conclusion of her stirring speech, and afterwards she wasted no time. There was much work to be done.

"Each of you knows your assignment," she affirmed. "Get to work!"

Within the hour, all members not directly involved in the mechanics of the assassination attempt had left the premises. Nikolai Kibalchich and three assistants worked on making the bombs, while Vera Figner prepared casings for the bombs by cutting up tins that had contained kerosene.

By morning the bombs were ready. Perovskaya, who had been persuaded by Figner to rest on a couch while the actual work was in progress, took two of the bombs to the rendezvous apartment. Kibalchich later took the other two to the same destination. Rysakov, Grinevitsky, Emelyanov and Mikhailov would retrieve them from there. Perovskaya met them at the apartment to give these men their final instructions and to tell them the secret signal she would use to alert them to what they should do if the Tsar, instead of returning to the Winter Palace by way of Malaya Sandeskaya Street, chose the Catherine Canal route. This latter itinerary would make him an easier target because of the sharp turn at the end of the canal that would force the coachmen to slow the carriage horses to a pace that was barely a trot. In that contingency, the woman would take out a handkerchief from her bag, flourish it and then daintily blow her nose. The bomb throwers would then be obliged to abandon their stations on the mined street and hasten to four other pre-arranged posts along the canal. Perovskaya would thus be the lookout in charge of surveillance, the "spotter" who would notify the troops of the Tsar's final choice of passage.

Whichever way Alexander traveled, unless fate went terribly against the conspirators, the Tsar was doomed.

# CHAPTER FORTY-TWO
## ASSASSINATON

On the morning of March 1, 1881, the sky over St. Petersburg was clear, the weather almost spring-like. The Tsar viewed this as a favorable sign that God was smiling upon him, and that his latest efforts at reform, Loris-Melikov's constitutional amendment, would be successful.

After a morning service in the small church of the Winter Palace, Tsar Alexander and Princess Ekaterina had coffee together in the green dining room, a smaller and less formal location than the yellow dining room that had now been repaired following the tragic explosion there in the preceding year. In his study, the Tsar signed Loris-Melikov's proposal draft into law and the two men embraced and congratulated each other.

Alexander was well aware that he had taken a step that would place him in direct opposition to the retrograde conventionalists who surrounded his eldest surviving son and legal heir, Sasha. He knew that the majority of the Romanov family would be loud in their criticism of this, his most radical reform to date. They would blame his young wife, with her liberal sentiments, for her influence in bringing this upheaval to pass. And Alexander also knew that while his first wife, Empress Maria Alexandrovna, with her rigid and somewhat bigoted views still lived, he would not have signed nor even promulgated such a document.

Young Katya with her all-encompassing love for him, had restored his youthful zeal and enthusiasm for change and growth. She was a powerful advocate for the Westernizing elements of Russian society, and she firmly believed that her husband was embarked upon the proper path to defeat the revolutionaries. But on this fateful morning, as he was bidding her a temporary farewell prior to his customary Sunday excursion, the Serene Princess was suddenly seized with an anxiety panic that left her anything but serene. She clung to him with tears in her eyes and pleading entreaties on her lips.

According to some sources, the only means by which he was able to calm and quiet her was to make ardent love to her there and then, almost immediately prior to his departure. Did the princess, one is inclined to wonder, suddenly lose her courage and serenity because she remembered the Great Leaguer's warning letters advising her to dissuade the Tsar from his Sunday mid-day ritual? Did she have a pervading premonition she could not shake off that this would be the day? Is it possible that the fierce energy of Sofia Perovskaya, that so fueled and agitated the rebellious spirits of her subordinates, was powerful enough to reach even the private chambers of the Winter Palace? None of this can be known with certainty. But history records the fact that the wife of Alexander's brother, the Grand Duke Mikhail Nikolayovich, who was to accompany him on the journey to the Menage, was similarly affected and almost hysterically begged him not to join his brother on that occasion.

Neither wife prevailed. Both brothers went on the fateful journey, as did Sasha, the Tsar's heir. During this period, the heir made every effort to please and placate his father, so fearful was he of being superseded by the son of the Serene Princess. Thus the fate of the entire Romanov regime was riding that day on the fortunes and efficiency of the agents of the People's Will. Their success or failure would forever alter the course of Russian history, and thereby would powerfully influence European and even American history as well.

The Tsar, as was often the case on these Sunday expeditions, wore the uniform of the Sapper's Battalion, the Life Guards of which were among the guards who would participate in the parade. His guardsmen greeted him affectionately and paraded smartly before him, gaining his approval and adding to his high spirits. On this morning, he had reached the Menage via the Pevchesky Bridge over the Catherine Canal at about the same time that the bogus merchant and his wife were leaving their cheese shop on Malaya Sandeskaya Street. The dynamiter, Mikhail Fralenko replaced them there. Calmly, he set up the detonation device and then proceeded to enjoy his lunch while watching from the window of the shop. Mounted police were patrolling the street, obviously in anticipation of the Tsar's arrival. But then they left, which meant a reprieve for Fralenko. The Tsar was returning home by the same route by which he had left it, the Catherine Canal.

The four bomb throwers stationed on the street near the shop also watched the Police depart. They followed behind them at a safe distance, their eyes searching for Sofia Perovskaya. She was waiting for them on Mikhailovskaya Street, and when she saw them, she drew out her lace handkerchief and gave them the agreed upon signal. Then, walking casually so as not to attract police attention, she reached the Kuzansky Bridge and stopped, gazing toward the center of the canal, observing the actions of her troops. Three of the four reached the canal, but one, Gimiofei Mikhailov, never reached the scene. As an occasional soldier will sometimes do, he had deserted his post and had gone home, overcome with fear. Now, only three bomb throwers remained. Perhaps the odds were changing in Alexander's favor?

As was his custom on Sundays when he traveled by way of the Catherine Canal, on his return trip he would stop to visit his cousin the Grand Duchess Ekaterina Mikhailovna who lived at the Mikhailovsky Palace. These two relatives held very different points of view, and this Ekaterina strongly disapproved of Alexander's second wife, who had the same first and second name. Despite all of her cousin's entreaties, nothing would persuade her to accept and embrace the Serene Princess. She welcomed his visits; she ever served him and his brother tea, but her opinions of his marriage and his reforms were inflexible.

While Alexander sipped his cousin's tea and endured her insulting slurs against his beloved wife and her illicit offspring, his assassins awaited him on his planned route of return to the Winter Palace. It was growing late. Katya would be worried about him, and his efforts at persuasion had proved futile once again.

"I will never, never accept that slut, and don't you dare attempt to have her crowned empress! The whole family will turn against you."

That was her parting remark. The venom of it stung Alexander even as he rose and kissed her hand in farewell. His brother, the Grand Duke Mikhail Nicholayvich elected to remain with the Grand Duchess a while longer. Perhaps he hoped he might prove more persuasive in reconciling the opposing family factions than Alexander had. He was noted for his effective diplomacy, and now, with what his older brother had shared with him during the parade, some details of the new reform, he needed those skills more than ever.

Alexander took his leave of both relatives, returned to his coach, and commenced his return journey to his home, his wife and his children. Three obstacles stood between him and his destination; obstacles in the form of bombs. Nikolai Rysakov was the first to approach the carriage. It was to have been Gimiofei Mikhailov, but he had panicked and bolted, so Rysakov took his place. Though young, fair, slender almost to the point of frailty, his aim was true but his knowledge of physics was faulty. He threw the handkerchief-wrapped bomb under the Tsar's coach from the front, sending it between the horses' hooves and hoping it would explode beneath the Tsar's seat, shattering his body and dispersing its parts in all directions. He took no thought for the fate of the innocent horses. But the bomb, pursuing an arc-like trajectory, exploded behind the carriage, damaging its rear panel, killing a Cossack guard and a teen-age sausage vendor, but leaving the Tsar unharmed. The smoke and the noise were incredibly intense for the first few seconds, and many of the guards and a few onlookers were thrown to the ground as well as the bomb thrower himself. But the explosion had totally missed its target.

Had Alexander heeded the pleas of his coachman Frol and his Chief-of-Police Adrian Dvorzhitsky to either return to the only slightly damaged coach or to get into one of the accompanying police sleighs and quickly leave the scene, he would almost certainly have escaped the assassination plot. But some perverse instinct drove him to play the role of the invincible autocrat who knows no fear and is above common sense safety measures. He took time to walk toward the would-be assassin Rysakov who was already in custody. He insisted on being shown the hole in the street left by the bomb. Even flanked by Cossack guards and a police escort on foot, he could not be adequately protected.

Ignati Grinevitsky waited by the fence as the Tsar and his entourage approached the first explosion site. He seemed to be as shocked and immobilized as the other people on the street by the explosion. In retrospect, it is obvious that all civilians should have been evacuated from that area of the Catherine Canal before the Tsar drew near to the bomb site. Rysakov had been heard to shout to someone in the crowd that had gathered as he sought to elude capture. To the police mind, and therefore to Dvorzhitsky, the threat of a second assassin lurking nearby must inevitably have suggested itself. Hence, the surrounding guards and police staff.

Yet no one walked in front of Alexander in that danger-laden street. No one compelled the loitering young man to move away. Instead, they watched in horror, taken by surprise as he suddenly turned, raised both arms and threw his lethal missile at the feet of Alexander II.

Twenty people were instantaneously thrown to the ground, all wounded to varying degrees, but the Tsar was the one most seriously injured. The bomb had shattered both his legs; blood in copious quantities was flowing from his body.

"Help me," he pleaded weakly, and as his aids, the Cossacks and the police belatedly encircled him, many injured themselves though not fatally, Sofia Perovskaya, watching from the far side of the Kuzansky Bridge opposite the canal, exulted in her victory. She had won the day. The Tsar would not recover from his wounds. He would die a few hours later in his wife's arms.

In her mind, she envisioned the imminent uprising of the Russian people, the unstoppable revolutionary wave that she and her colleagues had worked and fought to set in motion. In that oncoming human tidal wave, her lover, she hoped, would be freed to rejoin her. It was a dream fulfilled, or so she must have assumed at that moment. Little did she imagine that thirty-seven years would pass before that disruptive dream actually came true.

Responding to the Tsar's plea for help, those members of his entourage who were physically able moved quickly to his aid. They covered him with coats and lifting him from the dirty, wet, snow-littered street, they carried him to Colonel Dvorzhitsky's sleigh. The military hospital was located nearby, and Dvorzhitsky wanted to take him there where he could receive immediate treatment for his injuries. Had that plan been followed, the monarch, though gravely wounded, might have survived. His remaining years would undoubtedly have been spent confined to a wheelchair. However, he would have been able to implement his final, boldest reform, and he could have seen his four "love children" by Katya grow to adulthood.

"I'm cold," the Tsar whispered. "I'm so cold. Take me to the Winter Palace without delay." He said no more. He had neither breath nor strength for more. Over Colonel Dvorzhitsky's objections, the dying Tsar was brought through the streets of St. Petersburg, bleeding profusely, his wounds unattended, and he was taken to the Saltyka Entrance of the Winter Palace. The doors of that entrance were far too narrow; they had to be removed so that the makeshift litter could be brought inside the building and carried up the broad marble steps to the study where, years earlier, the Tzar had signed the Emancipation Act and had subsequently liberalized laws allowing non-citizens such as Jews to own property for the first time in the empire's history.

This afternoon, a different kind of history would be made. As the Romanov clan gathered in deference to the dying Tsar, the young princess, soon to be a widow, entered and fell upon her husband's torn and bleeding body. Father Bezkenov, the Tsar's spiritual advisor, gave him communion and administered the last rites of the Orthodox Catholic Church. When the Tsar drew his last shuddering breath, the princess screamed and fainted. Grief stricken she surely was. But now, she must have realized, the long awaited constitutional resolution would die unborn, unratified and unpublished. Count Loris-Melikov, her friend and confidante, would be forced out of office. And what of her own position? She was not a widowed empress, she was merely a morganatic wife, deprived of status by her husband's death.

Across the room, Alexander's heir, the Tsarevich Alexander III, and his diminutive wife Maria Federovna, the former Princess Dagmar of Denmark, stood staring down upon the now lifeless body of Alexander II. The Tsarevna's face reflected sorrow and grief. But the gaze of Alexander III was grave, regal and pitiless. His eyes were reminiscent of those of his grandfather, the iron-fisted Barracks Master of Eastern Europe, Nicholas I. One glance from these granite-hard eyes was enough to strike terror in the heart of Ekaterina Yuryevskaya. There is little wonder that she fainted. All her future hopes and dreams had been shattered and decimated by the same bomb that had claimed her husband's life. She was carried unconscious back to her own rooms, the rooms that Empress Maria Alexandrovna had once occupied. The Tsarevich had bitterly resented her being installed there, displacing his mother's memory and defying the sensibilities of his family.

When Katya awoke in her own bed, she shivered and shed fresh tears. She had her four children brought to her. She sought to console them as best she could, but there was no one to console her. What fate awaited her now? What terrible vengeance would the new Tsar exact from her for having stolen away his father's love from his mother in her declining years?

For the present, the grieving widow need not have worried. Alexander III, upon ascending to his father's throne, faced daunting issues much more relevant to the survival of his own autocratic regime than his sentiments regarding his dead father's second marriage. Regicide had just been committed within the realm. Every effort must be brought to bear to find the perpetrators of this atrocity and to mete out to them swift and merciless justice. Furthermore, the heir felt strongly the obligation to provide for his father a funeral service befitting his station. The former Tsar's favorite painter, Konstantin Markovksy was brought in to paint the final portrait that would memorialize Alexander II as he lay in state prior to that service. The artist had been the senior Alexander's friend as well as his portraitist, and the man wept as he worked on the project, the last service he could render for his friend and patron.

* * *

Within a matter of hours, the other two bomb throwers, Ivan Emelyanov and Gimiofei Mikhailov, were taken into custody. Grinevitsky, who had thrown the fatal bomb, had lived for only eight hours and had died from his injuries in silence without betraying his comrades. Sofia Perovskaya, who had been recognized as she stood observing the assassination, and who was afterwards driven to desperation by the indifference of the populace to the fact of regicide, the failure of the revolution to follow, and the realization that her love Andrei Zhelyebov would not be released from prison, walked the streets of St. Petersburg in despair. In that state of mind, it was inevitable that she would be caught either by the Special Police or by the City Commission's agents.

Two days after Alexander's death, Gesya Gelfman's apartment was raided. She and Nikolai Sabin were both there as it was early morning. The woman answered the door and was immediately seized. Her lover was in the bedroom. When the arresting officer ordered him to come out, Sabin drew his firearm from a bureau drawer, but he did not attempt to escape. Instead, he turned the weapon on himself and committed suicide before he could be arrested. The motivations that lead an individual to so desperate an act as this are complex and are usually known only to the person involved, but the conspirator who had written the letters composed by the Great Leaguer of the Secret Anti-Socialist League dared not be compelled to testify in court before his co-conspirators. Nor could he expose his family to being associated with the revolutionaries. Instead, he chose to take his secrets with him to the grave.

Of the members of the People's Will who had gathered on that fateful day in Gesya Gelfman's apartment to plan the strategy of the final assault upon the Tsar's life, only four eluded capture and reached safe haven in other countries. The women leaders were all captured including Vera Figner and Alexandra Korba. Neither of these two women was destined to be hanged. Indeed, Figner survived in her imprisonment to see the dawn of the Bolshevik revolution. She later regained her freedom, wrote memorably of her experiences and exploits, and lived until 1943. But Sofia Perovskaya, her lover, the imposing Zhelyebov, the demolition expert Kibalchich and the three surviving bomb throwers were all hanged, publicly and inexpertly, following a public and notorious trial. With one exception, all remained resolute and refused to divulge details or names of other revolutionary associates. The single exception was Nikolai Rysakov, the youngest of the group, who, intimidated by his captors, broke down in prison, confessed his role in the plot, pleaded for clemency, and exposed as many of his comrades as he could. He thereby earned the scorn and rejection of his fellow imprisoned conspirators, and his defection did not earn him any mercy.

All those who were directly involved in the bomb plot were hanged except for Figner and Gelfman. Why Figner was spared is not known with certainty. She became something of a museum display for the administration to point to as an example of imperial justice. Gelfman was found in the course of the group trial to be pregnant. Russian law afforded protection to pregnant women, and the local and foreign press mounted a campaign on her behalf that caused her death sentence to be deferred until after her delivery and later commuted to life imprisonment.

The child she delivered was a girl, and Gesya named her Gretle. The mother suffered unspeakable torture during this confinement. The guards inflicted their fury upon her for her role in the assassination, a role that had been exaggerated out of all reasonable proportion. At best, she could justly be accused only of having given aid and comfort to the plotters. She had played no direct role in the carrying out of the actual assault.

Following her delivery, and despite her suffering, her strong constitution enabled her to nurse and care for her baby. However, within a few days of the birth, the guards, in defiance of Russian laws governing maternal rights, took the baby from its mother during the night. Obviously, they took the point of view that the law did not apply to a Jewish mother who had participated in a conspiracy against the chief of state. They left the newborn at a foundling home outside the prison walls where the offspring of other female prisoners had found their way in the past. Usually, these babies were marked with identification tags and receipts were filled out to prove their delivery to the facility. This formality was waived in the case of Gretle Gelfman Sabin.

Many sources have assumed that the child died and was buried anonymously. But Gesya's mother, with whom her daughter had kept in contact, learned of her grandchild's fate. She went to the foundling home, asked to see the latest arrival, and, left momentarily alone with the baby, wrapped her in a blanket, took the child and disappeared. Gesya had already died the day before of peritonitis. No record remains of the grandmother's ultimate fate, nor that of the child. This silence on the part of history may have been of the grandmother's making. It certainly would have worked to her advantage and that of her grandchild.

\* \* \*

What does remain is the bloody record of the pogroms that spread throughout the entire Russian empire shortly after Alexander II's death. The involvement of Gesya Gelfman in the plot was expanded out of all proportion to its real extent. The Peoples' Will was represented, by the new Tsar's ministers and in the Russian press, as the cover for a Jewish conspiracy to overthrow the crown. In every major city of the empire, Jews were hunted, attacked, imprisoned, robbed, and often killed. In many instances, even those who escaped such physical abuse found their property forcefully seized and confiscated. The Peoples' Will essentially ceased to exist! Certainly it would never again enjoy the prominence and the vigor that it once had possessed. A few of the members escaped to Zurich and Berlin carrying with them the memory of the success of their mission despite its heavy price. The seeds of rebellion had been dispursed for the present but they had not been eradicated.

Violent reprisals indiscriminately directed against minorities whose members could be proven or were even believed to have cooperated with the assassins became the order of the day. Thanks to the involvement of Gesya Gelfman, the Jews were not only included in this group, they were officially indicted as authors of a secret conspiracy against the Russian nation. Perhaps the worst atrocities of the time occurred in Odessa where the dreaded pogroms recommenced in 1881 and progressed throughout the Russian Empire.

An Odessa physician named Leon Pinsker who had witnessed the pogrom ten years earlier in his native city was still unprepared for the unmitigated brutality which characterized the current riotous anti-Semitic demonstrations closely following Alexander's assassination. That experience inspired him as it did many Russian Jews to actively pursue the cause of establishing a new Jewish homeland in Palestine. Moises Leib Lilienblum, a former seminary teacher, began publicly to espouse the cause of "Zionism"[6] arguing that

Jews should no longer be content to be aliens in a foreign land but should and indeed must return to their own land. In this he revived and reinforced the philosophies of his namesake Moses Hess who in 1862 had written Rome and Jerusalem in which he argued strongly and urgently for a Jewish commonwealth in Palestine. His work had attracted few readers upon its initial publication, but now growing numbers of Jews, many of them dispossessed and despoiled by violence, became attracted to his doctrines.

Ephraim Marjzendiak too had become caught up in the new wave of enthusiasm for the re-establishment of a Jewish homeland in order to assure Jews throughout the Diaspora a safe haven to which retreat would be possible in the event of civil upheaval in the various countries of their residence. Only by the elevation of the Jews once more to the status of a true nationality, reasoned the leaders of the 'New Israel' movement as it was coming to be known, could Jews wherever they were located be protected from the unfair treatment that had so traditionally been their lot. Once a recognized government existed to plead their cause in a forum of other recognized governments, so it was felt by these men, the safety and security of Jews everywhere could be better protected and assured. Logistical and if necessary military pressures could conceivably then be brought to bear on their behalf. As things now stood, no matter how efficient, how prosperous or how patriotic Jews might be, dwelling as foreigners in a land not truly theirs, their position would remain forever precarious as it had been in Spain and England from which they had been summarily expelled as a people.

It seemed that Russia might now be embarked upon a similar course. Mass deportations of Russian Jews were taking place at an alarmingly frequent rate as Jewish families outside the Pale were forced by the imposition of the 'May laws', the temporary laws passed in May of 1881, to abandon confiscated homes and businesses in rural Russia and to accept displacement to the cities. The term temporary laws distinguished these measures as policies signed by Alexander III without having been passed by the Russian legislative body, a prerogative enjoyed by the Tsar in addressing emergency situations. Unfortunately, the temporary laws in this case became permanent and were essentially never reversed until the time of the Russian Revolution of 1918.

In this way, the liberal measures which had been passed by Alexander II were set aside without ever having been officially repealed and the rights of Jews to ownership of property beyond the Pale were effectively rescinded. Thus the rural Jewish communities were abolished. These issues had in the months since their enactment inspired more than one heated discussion at the Marjzendiak dinner table. Tonight, August 5, 1881, was no exception.

"I've read those essays, father!" said Isaak. "In theory they're unarguably logical and sound. But how long ago were they written? Palestine is an occupied land now. Realistically what government of modern Europe is going to sponsor and defend a Jewish recolonization there over the objections of the Turkish empire and the Arab landowners and tradesmen whose caravan routes run directly across what was once Israel and Judea?"

"Isaak," remonstrated Ephraim, "you state the circumstances as they are, not as they should be and will be. Have you not been saying for years that the Jews should unite with the Poles to re-establish the Polish nation? How is that so different from Jews all over
_____
[6] *The term 'Zionism' was not actually applied to the movement to resettle Palestine until 1886 when it was coined by an Austrian journalist.

Europe uniting to re-establish a Jewish nation? There are many non-Jewish statesmen and writers who agree with that concept. Jean Henri Dunont and A. S. Petavel of Switzerland, for example."

"Such men agree in principle perhaps," admitted Isaak. "Theories are cheap when you don't have to do anything to back them up except print tracts and plant trees." This last remark was especially odious to Ephraim who had contributed to the cause of Palestinian re-colonization and had personally helped to finance the establishment of Mikveh Israel near Jaffa, a school of agronomy founded by Charles Netter in 1870. This institution served to provide technical staff, equipment, and funds to assist in the settling of colonists and the cultivation of farmlands in the newly established Jewish villages such as Vikhron Yavkov and Rishon Le-Zion.

True, this constituted a tenuous and precarious beginning, a far cry from the establishment of the new Jewish nation. But for the first time in nearly two thousand years a new people had taken root in the land, had planted, ploughed and cultivated it, had made the yishuv, the Jewish community in Palestine, a tangible reality, a viable nucleus on which more ambitious efforts could be built. Elana looked up in alarm as Ephraim got to his feet and stared down the table at his second son. The flow of conversation that had hitherto provided a background to the exchange between father and son abruptly ceased as Ephraim's deep voice was raised.

"That's all you can see in what has been accomplished outside Safed, Hebron and Jerusalem? The planting of a few trees?"

"Trees, crops, even villages scattered like seeds over a barren landscape. Surely you don't call that the founding of a nation, the building of a new Israel!" was Isaak's rejoinder.

"Thus has begun every nation on earth, son," said Ephraim, keeping a firm grip on his rising temper. "Every county in Europe, in the East beyond Russia, even in the New World far to the West where many of our people have settled; they all began with a dream and a handful of men striving to turn that dream into reality. Always it is the farmers who come first and furnish the food supply. Then the herdsmen, the craftsmen, the artisans, the builders of cities, the founders of industries, the men of finance and commerce that make a nation wealthy and strong and independent. But it has to start somewhere. There must always be the few before there are many. Thus did Israel of old begin with the survivors of a migration from Egypt and their descendants following a self-trained army whose greatest weapon was their faith in Adonai. Surely," said Ephraim in conclusion, "you don't find fault with that model." Isaak shook his head, his eyes lowered before his father's piercing gaze.

"The model was appropriate to the time," he answered after a brief pause. "and of course I recognize the courage and self-sacrifice of those colonists. But think how much effort and money has been invested to accomplish such meager results. A few villages struggling to survive in a hostile environment, subject to the laws and whims of foreign rulers. How much better could it have been spent in easing the burdens of our fellow Jews right here in Warsaw or in helping to dislodge the Russian despots who prey on our country like a horde of predatory insects devouring everything in their path? If Alexander II degenerated into a willing tool of that sadist Pobedonostsev[7], his son Alexander III, whom that monster tutored as a child has become his alter ego."

---

[7] Constantin Pobedonostsev who from 1880 to 1905 served as chief procurator of the Holy Synod, lay director of the Eastern Orthodox Church, arch anti-Jewish nationalist and author of the 'Judicial

Ephraim nodded sadly in agreement.

"We have seen the results of his handiwork!" exclaimed Michael rising to his feet even as his father resumed his seat at the head of the table. "The 'May Laws' have forced thousands of Jews into the cities seeking work that the Polish labourers guard as jealously for themselves as a wild stallion protecting his harem. Of course this incites conflict and further riots. And the new Minister of the Interior, Count Nikolai Ignatiev, working in collusion with Chief of Police Von Phleve, fills the Russian press almost daily with anti-Jewish editorials branding us as vicious, dishonest and persistently revolutionary. No wonder the attacks continue. Secret Russian agents appear mysteriously in a town or city and almost immediately the Polish citizens are incited to riot against their Jewish neighbors. Then come the curfews, the punitive taxes, the seizures of goods and real estate and the deportations. I'm frankly amazed that the local authorities haven't confiscated this property!"

Elana turned pale at these words, glancing from her husband to her youngest son.

"Could they do that?" she asked in horror.

"In theory, yes," said Leah who was visiting with her parents from her home in Zurich. "In actuality this land is under the jurisdiction of Wola rather than Warsaw and the mayor of Wola is an old friend of father's. He's been in office for years and the people adore him. I think we are safe as long as he lives."

"That's probably true," agreed Ephraim, beaming proudly at his beautiful and accomplished daughter. She had over the past few years matured into a poised lovely woman just past the first bloom of youth but still retaining the sleek, gently curving figure of a young girl rather than a matron with two sons. She sat now at the family dinner table flanked by those two young sons, Frederick and Samuel, directly across from her husband Markos Kolvner who was now a respected and highly prosperous merchant in international trade.

The Kolvners were Swiss citizens now. Markos, alarmed by the events that had for years been building toward a violent climax in Russia, had taken that step to assure the safety of his family whenever any of them had to travel outside 'neutral' Switzerland. And with Leah so devoted to her parents and brothers, the trips to Warsaw were frequent indeed. This gave Markos ample occasion to visit with Adam. Despite the difference in their ages, Adam was now one of his closest friends and had professionally advised him to take his father Saul Kolvner back to Zurich on a 'visit' that had become permanent as the wave of Slavophilism burgeoned, giving rise to increasing anti-Jewish sentiment.

"So our family and our home are safe," said Isaak bitterly, "but only as long as Mayor Oslowski survives. Who knows what the next mayor will be in terms of political sensibilities?" He glanced from Elana to Ephraim.

"That would be to read the future," Elana remarked, "and only Adonai can do that. Let's rejoice that Leah and her family have come to visit us, and let's hope their visit will not be marred by any untoward events." She paused momentarily, then added, "Adonai be praised for his graciousness to us thus far."

---

Constitution' in late 1881.

"And we do indeed thank Him," commented Adam, "for bringing Leah home to us in triumph from her latest concert tour! Since none of us was able to attend any of the concerts, perhaps she will honor us by recapitulating her performance after dinner."

* * *

On a late afternoon near the end of March, 1882, Ephraim Marjzendiak came home from work to find the row of trees along his driveway aflame, a path of living torches. They lighted the way to the house, which stood ablaze against the twilight sky. Fear propelled Ephraim forward. The horses of Franz Pietrowski's carriage, which the bank president had lent to him while his own was being repaired, could not seem to travel fast enough. The last few kilometers between the row of burning trees and the wide veranda of the house seemed to take an eternity to traverse.

Ephraim's breathing almost stopped as he thought with horror of what might already be Elana's fate. He vividly recalled that day years before when he had returned to the ghetto of the Stare Miasto to find it a raging inferno. His house had been reduced to a wreckage in which his pregnant wife and his two younger children hid in terror. What, he wondered fearfully, was he about to find now? Ephraim's mind replayed every prayer and sacred invocation he could think of during those last seconds of terrified flight. As soon as he reached the house, he opened the door and rushed inside, forgetting caution and his own safety in his haste, calling out Elana's name as he ran up the smoke-filled stairs.

## CHAPTER FORTY-THREE
## INFERNO

Elana Marjzendiak had always slept lightly. As a girl, she discovered that she required less sleep than did her younger sisters, and that fact enabled her to retire late and awaken early, feeling refreshed. As a young mother, she found that she could sense the state of her children's well being even when she was in what seemed a deep level of sleep, and that she could awaken instantly if one of them cried or coughed. In recent weeks, however, Elana slept poorly, and often not at all.

She knew why. Ephraim, since his release from prison, was restless in the night, getting up to pace the rooms and corridors of his home, unable to remain quiet in bed while his mind raged in turmoil. At a time in his life when he expected to be satisfied with his accomplishments, to have achieved security and a level of respect commensurate with his capabilities, his career had suffered a severe setback, through no fault of his own. The guilty actions of others exerted this devastating effect upon him and his family. Added to these personal burdens were Ephraim's concerns for his people, who were suffering even more acutely than he as the pogroms continued to expand in volume and fury.

Elana shared both his concerns and his insomnia, so that the normal workings of her internal rhythm were disrupted. On that fateful day, when Polish peasants attacked the Marjzendiak estate, prompted by similar events throughout Russia, and by the blind eye turned to them by local authorities, Elana was attempting to bring her household accounts up to date. Despite her best efforts, fatigue, accumulated over several weeks, overwhelmed her. Her head sank on her arms, and she slept at last, peacefully and deeply. She did not hear the muffled footsteps outside the house, nor did she hear the faint crackling of the burning torches thrown through the few open windows of the upper floor of the house, one in the master bedroom, adjacent to her sitting room.

On any other occasion, she would have been instantly alerted, but the crisis did not erupt when she was prepared to deal with it. Instead, it caught her unaware. When the bedroom drapes and curtains caught fire, flames spread to the carpet. The heat smoldered in the solid wood furniture, which did not easily burn but which blackened as a result of its protective coating of varnish. The bed clothes burst into flames, as did the tiered skirt of Elana's dressing table; in other upstairs rooms, similar events were occurring, as well as in a few of the ground floor rooms.

When a window in the salon on the ground floor was shattered, the sound was reflected in Elana's dream. Abruptly, the pleasant fantasy world in which she tarried shattered also. She came awake with a start, fearful and coughing. Her breath came in labored gasps; the air seemed fetid, hot, and terribly oppressive. She stumbled to her feet, almost falling as she clung first to the desk, next to the file-drawer cabinet, and then to the chaise lounge. She was surprised to find herself not only groggy, presumably from sleep, but also weak and light-headed. In those first moments of wakefulness, she did not realize that she was for several minutes inhaling smoke.

Through a sheer effort of will, she reached the half-closed door to the master bedroom and found it warm to her touch. Mystified and frightened, she cautiously pushed it open further. A draught of hot, smoke-laden air struck her in the face. She gasped and coughed, striving to see through the gray haze and the spreading tongues of orange flame that blocked her passage to the outer door. Not for the first time since the family had lived at Plaz

Marjzendiak, Elana silently cursed the architect hired by the Zielenski family decades ago. He designed the house so that the only exit from her sitting room, and from Ephraim's dressing room, was through the main bedroom. The smaller rooms had no separate access to the upstairs hall. Now that short-sighted design trapped her.

She sought vainly for a path to the door through the obstacle course of burning carpet and hangings, and smoldering furniture just catching fire. Because of the cloak of grey-black smoke, she could see none. Terror gripped her. She screamed aloud, the harsh sound torn painfully from her parched throat. It was a cry of anguished despair, but in those crucial final seconds before flame filled the entire room, that cry reverberated through the upstairs hall.

Ephraim heard it and quickened his pace. He now knew where his wife was, and he ran in that direction, intent on finding her and taking her to safety. As he reached the master bedroom, the door creaked open, sagging on hinges half melted by the intense heat.

"Elana," Ephraim called hoarsely, as the acrid smoke assaulted his throat.

"Ephraim, be careful," Elana warned, glancing upward as a shimmer of light, reflected from the crystal prisms of the overhead chandelier, caught her attention. At that moment, the light fixture swayed dangerously and fell from the ceiling with a splintering crash. Ephraim dodged around it, his eyes scanning the scene of devastation for a way to reach Elana. She stood transfixed in the sitting room doorway. Desperately, he dashed through smoke and flame, swept her up in his arms, and turned back toward the door. Even in that few seconds, the fire had spread, breaking all boundaries, billowing upward and out in a solid wall of flame across his path.

He glanced at Elana's face and saw terror in her eyes. His own observations confirmed her fears. There was no way out through the bedroom. Even as he stood considering what alternative route there might possibly be, the bed collapsed. Its canopy exploded in a shower of sparks. One spark caught a trailing lock of Elana's hair and set her dress afire. Ephraim backed into the sitting room, set Elana on her feet, and closed the door. Hastily, he beat out the flames on her dress and hair with his hands and dashed water on her from the carafe, which was set on a side table. Her shoulder was reddened and beginning to blister, but the flames had not reached her face. He clasped her to him in an effort to calm her shuddering while he sought some means of escape.

A bolt of lightning blazed briefly through the sitting room windows, followed by a deafening clap of thunder. The fire had not reached this room, but it would in a matter of minutes, possibly seconds.

"We can't stay here," he whispered to Elana, not yet daring to put into words the desperate plan forming in his mind. He drew her to the window, then reached up and, with a mighty yank, pulled the draperies down, dragging their rod and fastenings with them. He quickly stripped the fastenings away, and then repeated the process at the second window.

As a youth, in prison after the 1830 rebellion, Ephraim was befriended by a sailor who was incarcerated for smuggling contraband goods. The man taught him many things, among then the various knots used on board ships to secure the sails. That knowledge served Ephraim well in the current crisis. He tied the draperies into a wide rope, grateful for the exaggerated height of the floor-to-ceiling windows. The drapes, thus joined, made a length of fabric as long as the distance from the second floor of the house to the ground level. Ephraim looped one end of the makeshift rope and tied it securely around Elana's waist. She looked up at him, and the fear faded from her face. She read reassurance and hope in his eyes, and she put her arms around his neck and kissed him.

Ephraim pushed open on tall window panel and then its neighbor.

"We must hurry," Ephraim said softly. He tied the other end of the drape rope to one of the vertical ornate metal poles that garnished the window framing. He then lifted Elana over the sill, and began gently to maneuver her down the wall. "Hang on wherever you can, dearest. I'll lower you as carefully as possible."

Cautiously but quickly, he lowered her to the ground. Lightning flashed twice more, followed by the inevitable thunder. By the time Elana reached the veranda below, rain was streaming down in a torrential cloudburst.

As Ephraim climbed out and started to descend the drapery rope, flames burst through the sitting room door with a deadly hissing sound like nothing else he had ever heard before. Not daring to glance upward, he climbed down as fast as he could, slipping on the now-wet drapes, and clinging to the rain-slicked stones that formed the side of the house.

When he reached the ground, he could scarcely believe that he and Elana had escaped safely from the burning trap that was their home. Their eyes were red and swollen from the heat and irritation they had endured. Their hair was singed, parts of their skin were blistered, and their throats were raw. Both were coughing painfully, and they shivered, soaked to the skin by the rain, but they were alive.

Ephraim glanced around them, momentarily disoriented. The rain extinguished the fire along the driveway. Further away, puffs of smoke arose from several parts of the fields and gardens. Above their heads, a section of the roof gave way over the upper floor of the house, and rain poured in. It would soak the interior furnishings, but it just might also extinguish the flames before the entire building was consumed.

Through the shattered salon windows, rain fell in a slanting sheet while the flames sputtered and danced, and slowly died in a final spurt of dense black smoke. If only the walls held, and the storm continued in its current fury, their home might yet be salvaged, but the magnitude of the necessary repairs would be enormous.

Now he must get Elana to shelter. The Pietrowski coach still stood near the front veranda. The horses were facing away from the side of the house where the bulk of the flames raged. They neighed shrilly, and shook their long narrow heads, causing a shower of raindrops to spiral in all directions. They were well disciplined creatures, trained to stand and await a coachman's signals. Their eyes were protected by blinders so that they could see only ahead of them. They stood now before the closed carriage, and Ephraim and Elana ran to that vehicle like sailors running to a life raft.

Ephraim gently lifted Elana into the carriage, stripped off her garments, and wrapped the lap robe closely around her. He climbed down, closed the doors to keep out the rain and cold, and mounted the driver's box. As he turned the horses in a tight circle, he could not but compare the present with the past. Once before he drove a coach owned by Mira and Franz Pietrowski away from the ruins of his home, with Elana in the carriage, and flames raging behind them. On that occasion, Mira was with them, and Leah and Michael were huddled at the women's feet, all of them frightened of snipers' bullets, and of being stopped by the militia.

A kaleidoscopic array of memories flooded through Ephraim's mind as he drove down the path of his home and turned at the gate along the road that led to the Pietrowski estate. Elana's paroxysms of coughing spurred him faster. They were a warning to him that she had not escaped unscathed. He had no idea how long she had been trapped by the flames, breathing smoke and the toxic fumes of burning cloth and wood.

He drove the horses at as brisk a pace as he dared on the slippery road that joined the two estates. He could see the lights of the Pietrowski mansion growing larger and brighter as he approached the building, and as he drew nearer still, he could hear the alarm bell on the estate sounding sonorously, summoning help from the volunteer fire crews of nearby Wola.

Mira was at the front door when Ephraim carried Elana inside. Without a moment's question or hesitation, she led him up the wide front stairs to Pola's former bedroom, and flung back the blankets and sheets.

"I'll see to her," she promised. "Go to Franz' closet across the hall, Ephraim. Get those wet clothes off and put on a robe." She paused only to draw a breath while she pulled the bed clothes up over Elana's still form. "I'll have Louise bring you both a hot drink. Then you'd better get into bed here with Elana, and keep warm. Franz has summoned the fire crews."

"I heard the bells," Ephraim responded, "but I don't know how much good they'll be able to do."

"We saw the fire from the parlor window," Mira said as she jerked nervously at the bell pull that would summon the maid. "Franz was about to come over to your house when we saw you racing up the drive. The other carriage is still outside."

"I saw it," Ephraim said, "but I didn't stop to think why it was there."

Even as he spoke, Franz opened the door, took in the situation at a glance, and came to stand by Ephraim.

"Thank God, you're safe," he said. "The volunteers should be at your place by now. I'm going over there to see what can be done." He clasped Ephraim's shoulder. "You know we'll stand by you in this."

"The Governor-General," Ephraim began, but Franz cut him off.

"Damn the Governor-General! What I do with my private money is my own affair. Now get those wet clothes off. I'll have a hot bath run for you, and a glass of mulled wine brought." He moved toward the door. "I'll be back soon, and don't worry. Everything will be all right."

"It will," Ephraim said gratefully, "with friends like you two."

\* \* \*

As time passed, Ephraim would have even greater cause to treasure the help of his friends, Mira and Franz Pietrowski. Without them, he and Elana would have no roof over their heads. The roof and upper floors of Plaz Marjzendiak were a ruin of water-soaked furnishings, blackened walls, and collapsed timbers. Fortunately, the lower floor escaped with only limited damage. The salon held blackened furniture and the wallpaper was smoke-stained, but the dining room, kitchen, Ephraim's study, the library with its walls lined by row upon row of books, and the other downstairs areas escaped essentially unscathed.

The fields had yielded their harvest long before the attack, and for some reason, the grain houses were not vandalized.

On the morning following the fire, Ephraim surveyed the damage, accompanied by Franz and Mira. When they found the storage silos unharmed, Ephraim expressed his surprise.

"No doubt," Franz speculated, "they planned to come back, and once the property was left deserted after the fire, steal the grain at their leisure."

Ephraim wondered aloud, "Did they really expect we'd just give up and leave?"

"Many have," Mira commented, "throughout the provinces. The devastation has been quite widespread, and in many areas, no helping hand has been offered. Rebuilding must be a very daunting prospect to your people under such circumstances."

"Especially if you have to start from scratch," was Ephraim's response. "At least we still have half a house left. The gardens are no longer a show place, but resurrecting them may lift Elana's spirits, once she's fully recovered. The grounds will still yield crops, and meanwhile, there'll be food to eat."

"What puzzles me," Mira said, "is where your workmen were when all this was happening."

"They were probably attacked and chased away," Franz said, still shocked by the extent of the damage. "What never ceases to amaze me is that people do these things with no thought for the lives that may be lost."

"Jewish lives," Ephraim said, bitterly, "are of no consequence to those people. Otherwise, this sort of thing would never be done. What's worse, they know that no matter what dreadful acts they commit, the authorities won't prosecute them nor even pursue them."

\* \* \*

In the weeks and months that followed, the Marjzendiak estate was the scene of fierce activity. Repair work proceeded rapidly on the main house. Work on some of the smaller buildings that contained temporary quarters occupied by workmen staying on the property during the growing season was also undertaken, but at a somewhat slower pace. The permanent homes of the foreman and the estate agent were totally destroyed and would have to be rebuilt. For the present, they lived in rooms on the first floor of the main house. Their presence provided the atmosphere of people still living on the damaged estate, and probably served to keep scavengers and vandals at bay. Furthermore, Franz paid men he could trust to patrol the grounds when the work crews left at night in order to discourage a repeat attack.

By late spring, Ephraim was able to bring Elana home. She had more or less recovered from her ordeal, however, there was at times a wheezing note to her breathing, and her voice had a hoarseness to it that never completely subsided. Dr. Jedewreski, though currently retired, examined and cared for Elana at Ephraim's request, and he was pleased at her progress. Nonetheless, he said her lungs would probably never be quite the same.

The final details of the monumental repair work were yet to be completed, but the house was once more inhabitable. Both Elana and Ephraim felt better about being once more in their own home. With secretly armed men on guard and with a trio of trained dogs that Franz brought from Germany as added protection, they felt fairly safe. They also felt it was safer for Mira and Franz not to have to be constantly on guard whenever there was a knock at their front door or the sound of horses' hooves in their driveway. On such occasions, with Elana and Ephraim staying with them, they had their guests absent themselves temporarily and retire upstairs until the identity of the caller was known.

The pogroms that began in 1881 were destined to continue well into 1882, springing up again sporadically even when the authorities were finally ordered by the new Tsar Alexander III to intervene. This young ruler held no brief for his Jewish subjects, but he was tired of strife and destruction in his provinces. In their lawless raids, the marauding bands of peasants and unemployed workmen took to attacking the property and persons of citizens other than Jews. Complaints were lodged by several families of means and status. Anarchy threatened to overwhelm the Empire, and Alexander III soon realized that he could gain neither the respect nor the support of fellow heads of state with chaos raging unchecked throughout large areas within his realm.

While law and order were gradually reestablished, the lives of the citizens slowly returned to almost normal. A rash of literature was published that condemned the lawless era that immediately followed Alexander II's death. Although the administration did not dare bring to light the program of new reforms that the Tsar Liberator signed into law on the morning preceding his death, some concessions began to be made regarding representation of the people at large in the governing bodies or the sjeim and dumas throughout the Russian Empire.

The effect of these political events on private citizens was felt as a loosening of restrictions on public gatherings, and fewer militia seen on the streets, in the public parks and buildings. A diminished aura of fear of continued reprisals against citizens whose names paralleled those who were known or suspected to have worked with the Peoples Will was also noted.

In the late summer of 1882, Ephraim's life and his estate showed few signs of the ordeal they endured. He could stand once more on his rear veranda and see his fields green and productive, and his gardens bright with colorful flowers.

Nonetheless, Ephraim's mood in those seemingly peaceful days was not one of contentment. Instead, he felt an undercurrent of dread. He knew why. Peace and prosperity were fragile entities. He knew them previously, after times of turmoil and struggle. They were fleeting at best. Even his hold on the land on which he stood was ephemeral. It could be taken from him by legal decree, just as his position and his income, lately restored, had been taken away.

He owed much to Franz and Mira. They took great risks on his behalf. And he would be eternally grateful. Nonetheless, it should not have been necessary. The old bitterness lay buried near the surface of his thoughts. Even the tranquil beauty of his revitalized lands and his restored and repainted home could not completely assuage the anger and the pain he still felt whenever he recalled that night when he came home to find his house in flames, and nearly lost his wife and his own life as a result.

* * *

On a late summer day in 1882, after Michael returned to Zurich to complete his university career, Ephraim and Isaak stood within the gazebo that somehow escaped the attention of the malicious marauders who so devastated the Marjzendiak estate. Isaak, like Michael, could sense the changes in Ephraim's manner and the alterations in his attitude towad life that these so visibly reflected. Though many years younger than his father, Isaak endured a huge spectrum of emotional upheavals and traumas that gave him insight into what Ephraim was now going through. He moved closer to his father, engaging his attention without actually touching him.

He asked, "What are you seeing when you look out over all this now?"

Ephraim seemed to come back to the present as if from a long distance, either in time or space. He shook his head as if to clear it.

"I see a battlefield," he said, his voice hushed. "I see my brother lying dead in a pool of his own blood, surrounded by murdered comrades."

Isaak swallowed and looked briefly away.

"Not the answer you expected, is it?" Ephraim said, smiling bitterly. "Not the sentiments I would wish to feel, either." He paused, gathering his thoughts. "I always believed that if I ever owned a place like this, it would be the answer to all my prayers, the realization of every hope and dream I ever entertained."

"And somehow it isn't." Isaak remarked, feeling a profound sympathy for his father. He understood the sense of frustration the older man was feeling. He learned that life has a way of turning even one's triumphs into failures simply be turning upside down the circumstantial landscape in which they are achieved. They had never spoken of Joshua's death before, and Ephraim mentioned his part in the 1830 rebellion only obliquely, in passing. Yet Isaak knew to what he referred.

"He saved my life," Ephraim said, his voice laden with remembered grief. "He took the saber thrust meant for me. I seized the Russian infantryman who killed him by the throat and squeezed and twisted until I felt his neck snap. He fell motionless to the ground, paralyzed and helpless. He died quickly. I saw the light of sentiousness fade from his eyes. But that didn't bring my brother back. Nothing I could do would ever reverse that tragedy. Nothing I've done since that day has undone the devastation of my brother's death."

"And you still miss him," said Isaak. "You still grieve for him."

Ephraim nodded.

"I wasn't even allowed to bury him," Ephraim responded. "I sat Shivah for him in prison as best I could. But it was a Russian prison, and when I came home more than a year later, my father would scarcely speak to me. He seemed to sense somehow that I was responsible for Joshua's death. Joshua was his favorite. He was the son my father loved."

"Surely he loved you both," Isaak said softly, "just in different ways, like you love each of us."

Ephraim shook his head grimly. "He never forgave me," he said sadly. "I tried to make it up to him by giving him grandsons, but I never truly felt that he forgave me."

Ephraim took a seat in the gazebo, suddenly feeling older than his years could account for. When Isaak joined him, their eyes met.

Ephraim asked, "Do you still think of Mariska?"

Isaak was taken aback by the question.

"There's a part of me that never stops thinking of her," he said after a moment's hesitation. "There are times I wonder what our child would have been like."

"Does Luvna know?"

The silence was so prolonged that Ephraim half expected that there would be no reply, but there was.

"We've never talked about it, not in detail. She knows that I fell in love in my early twenties and that it ended. Badly. Sarah she knew about only as a friend. I try to live in the present, to enjoy the things I have and not lament what's gone beyond recall."

"That's all any of us can do, son."

"Then enjoy all this now, while you can," Isaak said. "You can't forget what's past, and you can't predict what's to come. We never can. Those things are known only to Adonai. He that gives, He that takes away."

Ephraim came to his feet and stared out across the garden and the buildings in the distance, a few of which were still under repair.

"It's summer," he said thoughtfully. "The tree in full foliage doesn't dread the nakedness it will undergo in winter. In winter, I doubt that it looks forward to the spring to come."

"But it does come," Isaak opined. "If we endure and are patient, it does come."

After Isaak went home to join his family Ephraim walked to the veranda of his house. He walked the grounds for what seemed ages, but was in fact less than an hour. Elana joined him there and sat quietly beside him. He reached out to her and drew her to him, their thoughts silently intertwined.

"It's somehow all more precious now," she whispered against his chest, both of them remembering how close they had come to losing everything.

"Yes," he answered, but after a momentary pause, he added softly, "but no less vulnerable, even as we are."

# CHAPTER FORTY-FOUR
## THE TIDES OF TURMOIL

The most anticipated social event of the entire school year at Universitat Zurich was the Summer Festival. It was more than a dinner dance, more than a party, for it combined the elements of an informal early afternoon picnic with an evening soiree that lasted until midnight. Merchants set up colorfully decorated booths. Singers and dancers entertained at the picnic. It was an all day affair. It represented the hopes and aspirations of every student for the remainder of the year. Occurring as it did so soon after the beginning of classes in April, and lasting for most of an entire day, the festival was always planned by the students as well as the administrative faculty, and characteristically took place at a location some distance from campus, although it began at the school compound around midday.

Students who had not previously formed social ties either in the previous year or, if they were freshmen, at the start of the current year, habitually hastened to find a partner for the occasion much as modern students look forward to finding a date for the class prom.

Jotyl, who had an "understanding" with the daughter of his aunt Eleanor's next door neighbor, had no concerns regarding the festival beyond the need to arrange transportation to and from the dance in the evening. And while he and Batavnia Merrivan were not officially engaged, both hoped that their very amiable relationship would endure the test of time and would evolve into the traditional long-term bonding of marriage and family.

Michael's situation was quite different. Whereas no discriminatory policies prevailed either in the academic or local social conventions, Jewish students at the University were few in number. Men students outnumbered women five to one, and Michael, though a popular figure among the student body, had forged no close ties with any of the young ladies in his underclass years.

Now, as a senior classman, he was perplexed to find himself without a partner for this major social event. True, he was friends with three of his female classmates. One of them, Alexia Wahlstrom, he had tutored in Physics, and she had thanked him effusively when, because of his help she had passed the final exam in her junior year. But this was north central Europe in the 1880's. Well brought up young ladies did not go out unchaperoned with young men of only brief acquaintance even to the campus events in the evening. The Festival soiree was the one exception to this rule and parental and faculty chaperones oversaw the proceedings at the picnic and also at the dinner dance once the couples arrived there. The young men might call for their partners and transport them to the event, but afterward they must return the girls home, take the rented carriages and horses back to their stables and be inside the dormitories by curfew at 2:00am. Considering the distances usually involved, this constituted a very tight schedule and failure to conform to the curfew carried a heavy penalty, two weeks suspension from classes and all campus activities. For all these reasons, Michael had simply avoided attending the Festival in previous years.

This year, however, would be his final opportunity. In the last year of University the male students were encouraged to live on campus. The senior men's dormitory was a huge building that contained more than sufficient rooms to accommodate every student. In the third and fourth year, many on-campus social and academic events made living off campus impractical. Thus Michael now lived in the dormitory but spent many weekends with Leah and Markos Kolvner. With Leah and Markos urging him to participate more fully in campus social life as well as the academic pursuits in which he customarily excelled, Michael at last summoned the courage to discuss his dilemma with his close friend Jotyl. The two young men had grown closer than ever after Jotyl's bout with pneumonia during the previous year. For a time it had seemed he might not recover. Both he and Michael had tried to accept that sad state of affairs and Jotyl had insisted that Michael not postpone his visit to his home any longer. The two friends had parted on that occasion on a very sorrowful note, fearing that their farewells might be permanent. Michael had silently wept as his train departed from the railroad station in Zurich. And Leah and Markos, realizing the cause of his obvious depression, had attempted to cheer him up as they saw him off on his homeward journey. Yet nothing had really lightened his spirits; not even the sight of his beloved family had totally assuaged his mood of depression. He had been at home for nearly three weeks before Aunt Eleanor's letter arrived announcing that Jotyl was on the road to recovery. Jotyl's own correspondence had reached Michael two weeks after that, near the end of February. Only then had he truly began to enjoy his vacation and had reveled in the family gatherings, the outings, even the visit to the local opera house that Elana had planned for his benefit.

Now that the term of their senior year had begun, Michael and Jotyl were inseparable. It was during one of their visits to their favorite study setting on campus, a clearing on a height overlooking a lake, that Michael broached the subject of the upcoming festival.

"Is it really necessary," he questioned, "to bring a girl even to take part in the campus picnic?"

Jotyl smiled and winked at his friend. "Who do you think brings the food?" When Michael looked at him blankly, Jotyl added, "The girls, of course! The student center provides some items but most of the picnic staples are brought by the women students and by the off-campus guests of the men. Usually, they're not willing to share, so over the years, everyone has learned to make certain he finds a girl, for that day at least."

"And I gather for most, its not a problem."

"Well," Jotyl hesitated momentarily, "its not if you ask in time."

"The festival is in two weeks," Michael said, a note of alarm in his voice.

"Right," Jotyl agreed. "It's a week from next Saturday." Michael bit his lower lip. "Surely you've asked someone by now," Jotyl said, aghast when his friend shook his head in denial. "What about that girl you tutored last year? What was her name?"

"Alexia," Michael answered.

"That's the one! She was all over you when she made it through without a hitch. I was sure you two had become close friends."

"We are," Michael said. "Good friends. But not on those terms. She already has a partner for the festival. Guy Thorn."

"They went together last year, "Jotyl remarked. "He also took her to the Junior dance at the end of the school year in January." He stopped then, becoming painfully aware of the look of chagrin on Michael's face.

"We talked last week," Michael confessed. "She's hoping he'll ask her to marry him. For her sake, I hope he does."

"Alexia's pretty and smart. And her family has means and status. He'll be foolish to let her get away," said Jotyl.

"You're taking Batavnia again, aren't you?" Michael asked, already knowing the answer.

Jotyl nodded with a wink. "Who else?" he answered. "And I must say, it's causing some problems."

"What kind of problems? Batavnia's been your girl almost as long as you've been here."

"Yes, well, you know that, she knows it and my aunt knows it, but…"

"But?" Michael inquired, his curiosity aroused.

"But my cousin Sophie doesn't quite understand that I can't take both her and Batavnia at the same time."

"Of course she does! It would be too awkward." He paused, gazing at Jotyl. "Wouldn't it?"

"Awkward! Incongruous! Embarrassing! You name it," was Jotyl's response.

"Who took Sophie in the past?"

"That's just it. She didn't get a chance to go before. But now, she's a junior. Her grades are impressive. But her social life is a zero."

"I know exactly what you mean," Michael responded." Your cousin and I would make a good team. I'll bet she's even on the honor list."

"She is," Jotyl said enthusiastically. "She, and that British girl in World Literature." It was then that the answer to both of their problems occurred to him. "Of course!' he exclaimed. "You're right. You and Sophie will make a good team." Michael's earlier remark had been intended in the figurative sense, not the factual one. Now as he considered the possibility of dating young Sophie Promultz he was overwhelmed with doubts and misgivings.

"Your cousin and I?" Michael asked. "Are you certain your aunt would approve?"

"You and I are friends, have been all these years. She's never raised any objections."

"You're her nephew, her dead brother's son. But you are not her daughter."

"So?" Jotyl asked, genuinely puzzled by Michael's reticence. He could perceive no basis for it until his friend finally put it into words.

"She won't mind if her daughter goes out with a Jew?"

"How can you ask that?" Jotyl said, his face and voice both betraying the depth to which he was hurt by that remark.

"I don't mean to offend, Jotyl. You know how close I feel to you. But we come from different worlds. In Warsaw, I couldn't dare to hope to go out socially with a gentile girl, especially one of 'means and status' like Sophie, or Alexia for that matter. Were it not for her feelings for Guy, she might have said 'yes' out of gratitude. But your cousin," His eyes fell. The Promultz family, after all, were related to Swiss royalty.

"Look at me, Michael," Jotyl said sharply. "You are at the top of all your classes. Nearly everyone on campus looks up to you."

"I can think of one who doesn't." Michael interjected.

"Well, you can't win them all. No one's perfect, and no one pleases everybody. But I'm sure Cousin Sophie would be honored if you were to ask her to be your companion at the festival."

"You mean that?" Michael asked.

Without bothering to answer that query, Jotyl added "And so would I."

* * *

The morning of the Festival dawned clear and cool, awash with bright sunshine shadowed by gray-white clouds. A fresh breeze stirred the leaves and branches of every tree, and wafted the fragrance of the many rosebushes that adorned the commons to every corner of the Universitat Compound. The merchant booths offered countless wares to tempt almost every taste and budget. Some of the booths promised sumptuous desserts, fruit juices and exotic beverages. The merchants themselves had donned their bright, picturesque regional costumes since this year, the Universitat Festival coincided with an Italian saint's feast day in the Catholic Church. That morning, Michael walked to the local synagogue and attended the morning Sabbath service. He felt an element of guilt because the festivities he planned to attend would commence before sundown. It was one of the few concessions he had made to Gentile customs as a student in a secular institution of learning.

By noon, the picnic crowd was already assembled. A band of underclassmen musicians provided the musical entertainment from a hastily constructed stage. Later in the afternoon the stage would serve as a platform for abbreviated performances of dramatic excerpts ranging from Chaucer and Shakespeare to Homer and Goethe. The local dance academy would also present a varied program of short works, some dramatic, some unabashedly comedic. Then the students themselves, as invariably occurred, would indulge in a round of folk dances and group songs, many of which were representative of their respective national cultures.

By four o'clock, a massive array of balloons were released, filling the air with color, and some of the balloons were deliberately popped. This was a signal for the students to disperse and prepare for the evening festivities to follow. Attire abruptly changed from the rustic and casual to the dramatic and formal. Boutonnières and corsages were exchanged and duly fastened into place. Then a caravan of colorful horse-drawn carriages, rented from the two nearby stables, left the campus on their way to the brilliantly lighted, streamer-decorated Kretakke pavilion twelve kilometers distant, where the day of revelry would culminate in a multi-course gourmet dinner and the dance to which every participant looked forward with joyous anticipation.

For some, life choices would be made on this night, bonds would be forged, promises made, and heartfelt words whispered. For others, the occasion was an opportunity for self-indulgence, light-hearted fun and delightful escapism.

Then, as is always true on such occasions, the merriment would end, the revelers would depart, and reality would claim center stage once more as classes resumed on the following Monday. Sunday was a transition, a bridge between the day of youthful abandon and that of duties and obligations. For many, it was indeed a day of rest, a chance to catch up on lost sleep or to complete assigned projects left unfinished until the last minute. For the devout Christians in the student body, it was a day to rise early, despite a late preceding night, and hurry to attend worship services in one of the many denominational chapels off campus.

For Michael and Jotyl especially, the ending of the soiree was a time of revelation and the discovery of not one unpleasant surprise, but two. One occurrence took everyone by surprise. Amid the feasting and dancing, few of the revelers had glanced out the windows; none had paid much attention to the distant roar of thunder, and the curtains draping the windows had masked the rare flashes of lightning snaking across the indigo night sky. Only when they left the pavilion did they realize that, while they had dined, danced and drunk libations indoors, nature had been holding a late night party of her own, a summer storm. Some of the students, Michael, Jotyl and their respective partners Sophie and Batavnia among them, huddled briefly on the terrace, hoping the downpour would diminish to a drizzle as summer storms in the region often did. When their hopes were rewarded a few minutes later, each couple dashed to their carriage and scrambled inside, mindful of the time constraints to which they were subject.

Michael and Jotyl had rented a larger carriage than most, so that they might make the journey to the soiree together. A few other parties had done likewise, some for company, others for economy. That decision was soon to have unexpected consequences.

Neither young man had once that day given a thought to Kurt Bauer. Both had seen him briefly at the picnic, but he had seemed engrossed in entertaining his beautiful blonde partner and enjoying the proceedings. He had not even glanced in their direction. Or so they had thought.

Before they had traveled one quarter of the distance back to the main part of Zurich where both Batavnia and Sophie lived (neither girl had rooms on campus since there was only one women's dormitory, and competition for quarters there was fierce), all four became aware that something was amiss with their carriage. The two horses seemed to be straining with increasing effort against a less and less movable load. Finally, Michael, who was driving, stopped the carriage, turned up his collar, tied his scarf around his head and got down to take a close look at the wheels. What he saw brought the image of Kurt Bauer sharply to his mind.

"Damn!" he exclaimed in exasperation. "I might have known. The day seemed to be going far too well. Of course it couldn't last."

"What is it? What's gone wrong?" This was a chorus from the other three occupants.

Jotyl, imitating Michael's example, got down to crouch beside him and both examined the axle that joined the rear wheels together and supported most of the weight of the vehicle. The thick metal rod had broken near the left wheel, but it had not done so spontaneously. Instead, it had been filed halfway through so that with each turn of the wheel, the two segments of the rod had twisted apart. Twelve kilometers in each direction was too great a distance for that situation to persist without disaster, and to add to the problem, the pavement was now wet with rain and dangerously slippery.

Only a sliver of the rod now held the wheel in place. Had it snapped completely apart, the carriage would have crashed and death or serious injury to all the passengers might have been the result.

"The man is an imbecile!" Jotyl fumed.

"But we can't prove it," Michael remarked. The two friends exchanged glances. It was true; they knew Bauer was the culprit. Neither of them had any other enemy on campus, and neither of the two girls had a serious rival. The women students, few in number, tended to bond together, their kindred interests stronger than any differences between them. Most had beaux off campus.

Time was passing, however. The curfew was drawing nearer, and every carriage that passed was a lost opportunity to enlist help. The rain was falling heavily again, and all the vehicles moved with caution and at a snail's pace. Behind them, Jotyl recognized the carriage of a classmate who was also a friend, Herman Herring. Herman lived off campus with his family on a street that bordered the University. Batavnia and her mother lived nearby. Careful to avoid the deeper puddles, Jotyl hastened to intercept the approaching carriage and hail his friend. Herman stopped his horse, pulled on his hat, and climbed down to greet Jotyl.

"What happened?" he asked as he drew closer.

"Our carriage broke down" Jotyl explained without going into details. "I need you to do me a favor."

"Of course," Herman responded, "What can I do to help?"

"It's almost one o'clock," said Jotyl. "The carriage is stuck. We have a broken axle. Can you take the girls home for us?"

Herman nodded, but moved forward even as he spoke. "Of course," he answered. "That won't be a problem. But maybe I can also help you repair the axle. Let me take a look at it." With that, he crouched and took hold of the broken ends. He saw what Michael and Jotyl had seen, and he drew the same conclusion they had reached. "Somebody doesn't like one of you," he said sharply. "That was a despicable thing to do, and on Festival Day of all days."

"And what a way for the day to end, with a storm," said Michael.

"You'll all be soaked before you get back to campus. And if I take the ladies home, how will you two get back? Herman was trying to think of a practical solution to the problem that they faced. Like a true friend, he was making it his problem as well. And fitting four people into a standard size carriage meant to comfortably accommodate two was going to be a tight squeeze at best.

"We have two horses," Michael said. "If each of us takes one of the horses…"

"They have no saddles," Herman objected. "Besides, they're not used to carrying riders. They might buck."

Michael looked crestfallen as the truth of Herman's statement occurred to him.

"Look," said Herman, "I have a better idea. You two get back in the carriage and try to stay dry. First, though, we'll tether your horses to my carriage. We'll fasten them up in tandem. With three, I'll make better time." Michael and Jotyl nodded in agreement. "I'll take the ladies home, then come back for you. I don't have to meet a curfew since I don't live in one of the dorms."

"Would you really do that?" Michael asked, humbled by the generous offer.

"Of course," Herman answered, "That's what we're here for. To help each other out in the bad times. I'd say this situation qualifies as one of those."

Quickly, they unfastened the horses and re-aligned them in accord with Herman's suggestion. Michael and Jotyl thanked him again and saw him off, both bidding good night to their respective partners. Then they were left alone to wait in the broken carriage which sat tilted to one side, its left wheel askew due to the axle which had broken completely in the course of moving the horses.

Within a few minutes, they heard a carriage approaching from the direction Herring's coach had taken. Jotyl started to get out, but Michael stopped him.

"He can't be returning this soon. It will take longer than this, even with three horses," Michael said. "And all the other carriages have been going the other way, back into the center of the city."

"What do you think it means?" Jotyl asked.

"I don't know," Michael answered. "But somehow, I don't like it."

He grasped Jotyl's arm and yanked him out of the carriage. They darted to the side of the road and disappeared behind a broad cluster of shrubs. They had barely reached this makeshift hiding place when the approaching carriage stopped beside their own and the lone passenger emerged, glancing quickly in all directions. It was definitely not Herman Herring's carriage. The man was not Herring either. The rain was lessening and the emerging moon, shedding some of its veil of clouds, shone clearly on his face for a few brief moments. It was the face of Kurt Bauer. A smile of triumph spread across his face as he beheld the wrecked carriage. He came nearer to glance inside but did not seem surprised to find the vehicle empty. Chuckling softly to himself, he reentered his own carriage and turned it cautiously on the slippery road. Then he headed back the way he had come, increasing his pace as he went. It was already one o'clock in the morning. He had barely an hour to return his own carriage and reach his dormitory before curfew.

Unfortunately, Bauer, Jotyl and Michael shared the same building, the senior men's dormitory, and it had only two entrances, both of which would be locked promptly at two o'clock.

* * *

At one forty-five that morning, two muddied, wet and very bedraggled young men knocked on the door of the house of the Dean of the Universitat Zurich. The windows were dark and the dwelling was silent, but as the knocking continued, lights went on in the upper story and footsteps could soon be heard approaching the front door. When the door opened, they were met by a half-awake but exasperated professor whose face was only vaguely familiar to them, as they had seen him mainly on their first day at the institution four years earlier, and then later only on rare occasions as he passed them in the corridors or the grounds. His name was Erick Schtandyck, he was fifty-seven years old though he appeared to be somewhat younger with sandy hair just beginning to show strands of gray at his temples and sideburns. Normally, he was clean shaven but at this hour, a shadow of beard darkened his cheeks and chin. The dean had attended the soiree out of a sense of obligation, but he and his wife had departed early. Michael's only other occasion to know the dean personally had been at the time of the stolen philosophy exam and Michael's own unique solution to the problem. Now, having been asleep for scarcely two hours, the dean's temper, on being abruptly awakened, was sanguine.

"What in the name of all that is holy are you doing here at this hour?" He glanced at the hall clock and scowled. "It's almost curfew. Shouldn't you be in your dorms? I warn you, coming to me won't gain you either time or clemency."

For answer, Michael presented the short segment of the broken axle from the carriage while Jotyl voiced the answer to the dean's question.

"We're locked out, sir. We didn't know where else to go."

"Nonsense," the older man snorted. "You have nearly a quarter of an hour until the doors will be locked. If you hurry, you'll just make it. And what's this you've brought me?" He took hold of the length of metal and glanced at it.

"Both doors are already locked, sir. We tried them fifteen minutes ago. Someone locked them early." This came from Jotyl.

"We suspect that someone sabotaged our carriage to make us late, or else unable to get back on campus at all." This was Michael's response.

The dean looked from one youth to the other, and then at the damaged axle rod he had taken from Michael.

"Come inside," he ordered them. "We need to talk, and it's too dark and damp to do it here on the doorstep."

The conversation was brief and to the point. Dean Schtandyck rushed upstairs, hastily dressed, then came down and donned his heavy coat. He snatched an umbrella from the holder by the door, handed his two guests each an umbrella, and quickly led them to the Senior Men's Dormitory.

As they approached from the east side of the building heading for the rear door, another darkly clad figure approached from the west. They met at the door, and Dean Schtandyck called out, "Stop! Who's there?"

Obediently, the man stopped and held up a ring of keys. He had recognized the dean's voice. "Just locking up, sir. I was instructed to lock these doors last."

"Then you haven't locked this dormitory as yet?" the dean wanted to know.

"Not yet, sir. I was just coming to do that now."

"Try the door," he directed.

The younger man complied and found the door to be locked.

"That's strange," the custodian remarked. "Who would have locked it? These dorms were my assignment. The junior and senior dormitories, including the one for women. I don't understand."

"Were any of the other dormitories on your watch locked before you got there?" the dean persisted in his questioning.

"None, sir. This is the only one."

"Unlock this door," said the dean, "then go and check the front door." When the custodian had gone to carry out those instructions, the dean turned to the students beside him.

"You two go inside. Lock the door behind you, go to your rooms and get some sleep. I'll sort this out in the morning." The man's voice sounded grim.

\* \* \*

When morning came, Michael was relieved when he realized it was Sunday. There would be no classes today. He awoke exhausted in mind and body. He had enjoyed the day and the evening, but the events that followed had ruined his earlier enjoyment. In retrospedct, he almost regretted having gone to the Festival at all, despite the fact that Sophie Promultz had been a charming and gracious companion, and they and Jotyl and Batavnia had frolicked together as carefree as children throughout the event.

There was still the matter of Kurt Bauer to be resolved. The dean of the Universitat had solemnly stated that he would sort that matter out this morning. As he bathed and dressed, Michael was tense; his hands were shaking. He was waiting to be summoned to the dean's home since all the offices on campus were closed on Sunday. When Jotyl knocked on his door, he jumped.

"Who is it?" he asked, instead of the usual "Come in."

"It's me, Jotyl," he was answered.

Michael opened the door and greeted his friend warmly.

"You're up early, too," Jotyl remarked. "Most of the guys are still sleeping. And they were all in bed before we got in."

"I woke up as soon as it was light," Michael responded. "I couldn't stay in bed any longer. I guess I'm still chilled after last night's rain. You and I got soaked to the skin."

"Right," Jotyl agreed ruefully.

"You need to be careful about things like that," Michael warned, concern in his voice. "You can't risk another bout with pneumonia."

"I'll be okay," Jotyl said. "I feel fine. I put an extra blanket on the bed and turned up the heat in my room." He paused uneasily. "I guess we'll be hearing from the dean sometime today."

"So I assume," Michael said. He moved to the window and looked out across the campus. He had thought that, like most summer storms, the one last night would be followed by clear blue skies and bright sunshine. Instead, the sky was overcast, its color steel gray, opaque looking, hiding the sun from view.

"I'm going over to my Aunt Eleanor's," Jotyl said. "Want to come along?"

Michael hesitated for a moment, then smiled and nodded thoughtfully. "Sure," he said. "I guess if the powers that be want to find us, they will."

And so the friends donned warm coats, scarves and caps and left the campus. No one had told them to remain available, and they had done nothing to make them feel guilty.

By noon, all the students in their dormitory had gone out to enjoy their Sunday, leaving all the rooms in the building empty. For the next two hours, members of the grounds staff meticulously searched the premises, seeking a file that might have been used to cut through a steel axle rod. The incriminating tool was found hidden in a drawer beneath an assortment of socks and underwear in the quarters of Kurt Bauer. When he returned to his room, Bauer, feeling safe and self-confident, never bothered to check the contents of his dresser drawers.

Nothing was said or done regarding the matter of the wrecked carriage until the daily routine of the campus commenced on the following Monday. The stable owner was notified of the location of his missing property by the dean himself. As for Kurt Bauer, he was handed a note during his first class that morning that Dean Schtandyck wished to speak with him in the dean's office at 11:00 o'clock that morning.

Only when he arrived to keep that appointment and saw the metal file lying in plain sight on the dean's desk did Bauer's façade of self-assurance begin to crack. He could not keep his shock and guilt from showing in his face.

"I see you recognize that implement, Herr Bauer," was the dean's opening remark.

"It's a file, sir," was all Bauer could think to say.

"Indeed it is," said the dean. "Do you know its history?"

"It's history, sir? I wouldn't associate a history with so common a tool as this," was Bauer's response.

"Don't be flippant with me, Herr Bauer! You have a great deal of explaining to do." He picked up the file from the desk. "This common tool was found among your personal effects yesterday."

Bauer opened his mouth to protest but the dean silenced him with a gesture of his hand.

"Don't bother to protest a breach of your privacy, young man. Every room in your dormitory was thoroughly searched, even those of the victims of your very dangerous, wicked practical joke." The dean reached beneath the desk and extracted the entire axle, in two parts, one short and one longer, and the bent left wheel to which the short portion had been attached.

"I'm certain," he continued grimly, "these items are equally familiar to you, are they not?"

Bauer shook his head, but could voice no audible words of denial. Finally, he glared defiantly at the dean. "Just what is it you're accusing me of?" he asked.

"A foul and malicious act that could have caused serious injury to four of your fellow students," he was answered. "Two of those students were ladies. In order to carry out your contemptible scheme, you destroyed a merchant's property, put four lives in jeopardy, and set a black mark against the most esteemed social event of the school year." The dean grew angrier with every word he spoke.

"My father…" Bauer stammered, but Schtandyck cut him off.

"Oh yes, young man, your father will be notified. He'll have to pay for the carriage you effectively destroyed. As for your punishment, a special session of the Board will shortly be convened to make that decision. You will be notified of the result. Until then, you are confined to your rooms." The older man paused for breath.

"My classes…" Bauer began, but the expression on the dean's face stopped him in mid-sentence.

"You'll be lucky if you're not suspended from classes altogether. Now go. I won't hear another word from you. There is no excuse for what you've done. Yet you're not a stupid man, On the contrary, you're quite brilliant. It's that fact that so offends and frightens me. Yes, frightens me! Your kind is a danger to other people. In a position of power, you could be a real menace."

Bauer stared silently at the dean before him, totally at a loss for words. His eyes fell, and he turned and left the office.

On Tuesday morning, the Dean sent for Kurt Bauer once more, and the student knew better than to say anything to further inflame the older man's feelings against him.

"It's the decision of the Board of Directors of this institution that you be suspended from classes for a period of two weeks."

"Good," said Bauer in reply. "I shall go home and spend the time with my family."

"That might be a wise choice on your part," said the dean. "However, before you do, you will be given a schedule of assignments to complete. On your return, you will submit those assignments to your various instructors. If you complete them appropriately, your absence will not endanger your grades. Otherwise, well, that remains to be seen."

A strained silence prevailed between them for several moments.

"You should be grateful for the leniency you have been shown," the dean remarked coldly. "Fortunately for you, my other suggested penalties were overruled." He sat at his desk and proceeded to sign a stack of papers that lay there. Then he looked up at Bauer. "You are dismissed," he said. He did not look up again when the door closed loudly behind the departing student.

* * *

Kurt Bauer was furious to realize that not only had his scheme to discredit Michael and Jotyl failed, but he had become the victim of his own foul play. As punishment for Bauer's skullduggery in sabotaging the carriage Michael had hired, the German student was given two weeks suspension. Coming so close in time to graduation, such a penalty could result in a failing grade in one or more of his last scheduled final exams. To think that this smug young Jew could have lost him his class standing and possibly even interfered with his graduating on time was more than Bauer could bear. His Teutonic pride overwhelmed him. No matter what, Michael Marjzendiak was going to pay and pay dearly for crossing Bauer and shaming him as well.

All during his two weeks of suspension, Bauer brooded over the outcome of his malicious prank. Though he worked conscientiously on his assignments and completed them in time, his pride had been dealt a major blow. He had been humiliated and degraded. The sting of that shame gave him no peace. It spoiled the time he was able, despite the compulsory assignments, to spend with his family. On the train back to Zurich, he was overwhelmed with rage.

Despite the fact that he knew his free time would have been better spent in study, Bauer stubbornly took to stalking Michael and his friend Jotyl. Within three days, he knew their every favorite haunt, from the just off-campus coffee house where they met with class friends, to the grassy ledge above the quiet lake where they sometimes studied together. Carefully he planned what his next move would be.

It was during the last week of the term that Michael and Jotyl decided to schedule study sessions independently since some of their courses differed. The last final exam for each of the two young men was scheduled to occur on a Wednesday afternoon. Jotyl's was a written test, but Michael's examination was oral, administered by the two full professors of chemistry. It was Michael's least favorite subject, one he never expected to have to use again. Nonetheless, he had lavished upon it many hours of study as it was part of the arts and science general curriculum and he needed a high grade to maintain his class standing and his place on the Dean's honor roll.

The two friends had planned to meet at their special place above the lake at the close of the examinations. As fate would have it, Michael completed his test first, arduous though it was, and so he was the first to arrive. The ledge was reached by traversing a series of grassy terraced step-like plateaus, each generously landscaped with lush evergreens. This meant that the path was largely in shadow, and therefore care was required to safely travel it at this late hour of the afternoon. It was already four o'clock.

Some of the older trees were surrounded by large and medium sized smooth stones. Most of these had been brought up over a period of years from the lake bed below to decorate the terraces. Along the margin of the ledge lay a parapet formed from the same stones. This formation served a duel purpose, ornamentation and safety. Somewhere in the dim, half-forgotten past of the campus was a legend, partially based on fact, of a young student exulting over his final grades who had run headlong up the path shouting for joy and had fallen to his death from the high ledge. His body had been drawn out of the lake days later, much to the consternation of the faculty and the student body alike. There had been recriminations and anger on the part of the student's family, and rumor had it that money had changed hands, though formal charges had never been filed.

Remembering that tragedy, Michael instinctively slowed his steps, his senses alert for some sign of his friend, whose test he had assumed would require less time since it was given in Classic European Literature, a less demanding course discipline than Michael's had been.

Soon it would be graduation day, and then would come the time of departure. Michael was in a nostalgic mood, pensive, introspective, yet intuitively alert to the glorious panorama around him. He was aware of the various shades of grass and foliage, and brief snatches of blue sky etched with fleecy clouds filtered through the trees. Glancing upward, his eyes caught a furtive movement, half-concealed by the branches of a tree. A bird trilled, but no bird native to this environment was of the magnitude of whatever was moving above him.

Startled, he stepped backwards as the object moved forward. That instinct saved his life. A large stone struck the earth less than thirty centimeters in front of him. Immediately thereafter, Kurt Bauer dropped to the ground, his features contorted with rage, his stance combative, his movements aggressive, his fists flailing out in an effort to take Michael by surprise and knock him senseless.

The rock, landing harmlessly but conspicuously, undermined the element of surprise, which would have given the German youth the advantage. Forewarned, Michael dropped to a crouch and struck his opponent forcefully in the midsection, knocking the air from his lungs and causing him to bend forward in pain laced with sudden nausea. This left him vulnerable to a second volley of punches, these landing on his throat and chin. Bauer fell forward, winded but still cocky. Pausing only momentarily to catch his breath, the German student leapt to his feet and launched a barrage of blows against his taller but leaner adversary.

Michael stumbled, still moving away from the rock. He stumbled, but did not fall as Bauer had hoped he would. Instead he straightened up, advancing, fists raised to protect his head and face, body pivoted to protect the more vulnerable parts of his torso. The stockier Bauer pummeled Michael wherever he could strike him, seeking to wear him down, striving to maneuver him toward the stone parapet at the edge of the area where they fought.

Still puzzled by the suddenness and viciousness of the attack, and slightly disoriented from the blows to the head that he could not totally forestall, Michael was fighting a defensive battle. Yet he knew somehow he must win it. His survival depended upon it. Every instinct he possessed warned him that this adversary was out for blood. Kurt Bauer meant to kill him. Within that context, the unsubtle efforts to force Michael toward the edge of the clearing could have but one objective, to maneuver him into falling over the parapet into the rock-strewn lake below.

At this realization, anger filled Michael Marjzendiak, not the unreasoning rage of hatred that motivated the German youth, but the calculated righteous anger of the oppressed directed against the oppressor. This conflict had no reasonable justification. It had no right to take place. Yet here it was, marring the pastoral beauty and customary tranquility of the most picturesque area on the campus. And while Michael sought for a strategy to end it decisively, his crafty opponent prepared to implement what he had plotted as his final assault. Despite his greater weight, Bauer could not overcome Michael's determined defense. Trickery and deceit were the means he now chose. To that end, he drew back his right hand as if to strike another blow, dropped his left hand into his trouser pocket and drew forth a knife equipped with a snap blade. The metal glinted in the fading sunlight as Bauer unleashed that razor sharp blade and poised to strike.

Michael, unarmed, knew a moment of naked fear. How could he defend himself now? What strategy would save him in this extremity? Without pausing to think or plan, he threw himself to the ground and rolled his full weight against his opponent's legs, forcing him off balance. As Michael had hoped, the knife fell from Bauer's grasp; it struck the rock parapet and ricocheted several feet away, landing in the thick, concealing grass.

But another pair of eyes, aided by spectacles, noticed the weapon's trajectory. Professor Arden Sloane, English by birth but now a Swiss citizen, was one of the chemistry teachers who had administered Michael's oral exam. He had been impressed with Michael's responses and had wanted to discuss one of them with the student in greater detail. Michael had rushed away after the test, eager to meet his friend, unaware that he was being followed by not one, but two different men, one young with evil intent, and one middle-aged, but of benign motivation.

Now all three had met. As Kurt Bauer crouched in the grass, his eyes searching for his weapon, Michael jumped to his feet and stood, breathing heavily, warily awaiting his enemy's next move. Professor Sloane's deftly sweeping gesture in scooping up the knife took both of the younger men by surprise. Both realized at once the political significance of the situation. The odds had abruptly changed from life versus death to graduation versus disgrace, and neither knew what nor how much the soft-spoken, strict disciplinarian professor had seen.

Guilt was the origin of Bauer's first words.

"Professor," he said, in mock joviality, "how long have you been here?"

"Longer than you'd like," he was answered. "Both of you, come with me!" Sloane turned without a backward glance, knowing both students would follow.

A third, Jotyl, arrived at just that moment, having run all the way from his classroom, acutely aware of being late to meet his friend. Now, looking at Michael's face and seeing the blood and the darkening bruises, he asked breathlessly, "What happened?"

"Be glad you're not involved," Michael responded, which did nothing to calm Jotyl's concerns. He fell silently into step beside his friend, willing to lend moral support regardless of the circumstances.

On the walk back to the professor's office, Sloane offered Michael his handkerchief and told him to "clean himself up." To Bauer, he had said nothing, since leaving the scene of the fight.

When finally Sloane, in the privacy of his office, addressed a question to the German student, Bauer was reticent to reply, and when he did, there was a surliness in his manner that was not lost on the older man.

"Did you really intend to drop that rock on Marjzendiak?" Sloane asked incredulously, hardly able to grasp the idea that the young man had actually been bent on murder.

"What difference would it make?" the student answered.

Sloane was aghast. "It would have killed him! Don't you realize that?"

"So there'd be one less Jew to plague the world!" Bauer all but shouted, "One less scheming, conniving Jew to steal what's rightfully ours. Don't you get it, Professor? Are you so muddled by all this academic grandeur that you don't see what they're up to?"

He might have said more, added more fuel to the fire, but Sloane silenced him with a harshly administered slap across the mouth.

"Silence, you ill-bred imbecile! Not another word from you! Get out of my sight! I'd pack my bags if I were you. I'll see you out of here tomorrow if it's the last thing I ever do!"

Gazing balefully at the professor's face, Bauer did not for a moment doubt that the man was filled with scorn for him. He had gone much too far. Pride and rage had betrayed him into exposing the hateful ugliness of his soul. They had also possibly deprived him of the prize he had most strongly coveted. Had he bridled his temper and curbed his tongue, Bauer surely would have graduated near the top of his class. His and Michael's grades were so close that it would be difficult to rank one above the other. Sloane could not prevent his graduating, but he could block his participation in the graduation exercises, the baccalaureate ceremony, and the triumphal procession across the green that was a time-honored tradition of this institution. The boy's father was already en route to attend these ceremonies. Now Bauer would be sent away in disgrace, his degree held for a time as a penalty, and subsequently mailed to him at some future date with no ceremony to mark its bestowing.

Of course, he blamed these dire consequences that he so richly deserved on Michael Marjzendiak. Of course, gazing later at his own image in the mirror, he failed to comprehend the fact that his own worst enemy was himself. Instead of feeling a belated sense of remorse, all he could think of was how he still might find a way to gain revenge.

He did not pack his belongings. That, he felt, could wait. He did realize Professor Sloane had far-reaching authority at the university. However, he did not truly believe that the older man would make good on his threat, especially against a student whom he knew to be gifted. In the heat of anger, Sloane had spoken, but given time to reflect, he might be persuaded to relent.

*  *  *

Kurt Bauer met his father's train in a distinctly subdued frame of mind. The elder Bauer, who was named Heinrich, was by contrast jubilant. This was his first visit to Switzerland. His son's enrollment had been accomplished by mail, and all subsequent correspondence had followed that same route and had been commonplace and favorable. The two week suspension had been left to Kurt himself to explain, and he had done so with duplicity and subterfuge so that his family had no idea of what he had done to merit the punishment. His son's demeanor was, therefore, mystifying in the extreme. He looked questioningly at the young Kurt wondering if he was feeling ill. The stiffness of his son's manner and the stilted nature of his speech bespoke some undisclosed malady that caused the father to hesitate in questioning him. As they entered Kurt's room, the father tried to initiate a conversation.

"Your exams have gone well?" he asked.

"Very well, yes," was the reply, though stated with no enthusiasm, no expression of rejoicing.

"You're relieved to have them behind you," the father said, and then noted with surprise that all young Bauer's favorite pictures, placards and memorabilia had been taken down from the walls and piled in a corner of the room. His luggage, not yet packed, stood ready by the door. "Isn't all this a bit premature?"

Young Bauer stood before his father, unable to meet the older man's gaze. "I've started to get ready to leave," he said soberly. Just that; nothing more. The elder Bauer stared curiously at his only son.

"Just what is it that you're not telling me, son?" the father finally asked.

"What sort of question is that?" Kurt countered, striving to put on an air of bravado.

"A direct one," his father responded. "One to which I require a direct answer! What have you done that you must slink away from campus five days prior to graduation?"

Silence was the only answer he received. It did not satisfy him. It only gave rise to ugly suspicions, following one upon another like a cavalcade of demons. He knew his only son was possessed of a volatile temper, and that he had once before initiated a physical confrontation with a young Jewish student. That had been in his sophomore year. The father had thought that conflict had been put behind him and his son. The penalty assignments young Kurt had been compelled to fulfill earlier this year had marred his visit with his family and had never been fully or satisfactorily explained.

But, this most recent episode must be beyond belief if the young man was to be barred from any share in the graduation ceremonies of his senior class. Aggravated almost beyond bearing, the father seized his son by the arm and forced him down upon the bed, towering above him. His face distorted with anger, the older man demanded "You will tell me!" For a moment longer, the son remained defiant. Then abruptly, his angry resolve crumbled.

"All right," he said in a whisper that was almost a hiss. "If you must know, I tried to kill that arrogant Jewish bastard! I can't imagine why, but his chemistry professor followed him across the Commons after his final. He must have seen the whole thing. It's Sloane who's threatened to have me sent down before I can graduate. He's a stiff-necked pompous ass who…"

He got no further. He was unable to say anything more, because at that point, he felt his father's hands clasped around his throat and over his mouth.

The older man held the boy in a vice-like grip and shook him hard, causing his teeth to rattle within his head.

"You," he shouted heatedly, "are a disgrace to your entire family! To think that my son was only prevented from committing murder by the last minute intervention of another. And had your evil plan succeeded, how did you intend to dispose of the body?"

Young Bauer glanced up at his father, his breathing labored, his face bruised by the old man's fingers and flushed to a beefy red hue punctuated with purple streaks.

"I hadn't thought that far. I hoped while we were fighting, he might fall over the cliff."

"And if he didn't obligingly fall, you would have thrown him over? Is that it?"

"I don't know." young Bauer answered miserably. At this point his thoughts were in utter confusion. All he could remember of the incident was the unreasoning rage and the abject humiliation.

The father recovered from his own emotional storm well in advance of his son.

"Where can one find this man Sloane?" he asked mildly, swallowing his own rage as best he could. His pulse was pounding in his ears, and his own breathing seemed on the point of choking him. He glared at his son, his soul filled with shame and revulsion. What, he wondered, had he done that God should curse him with such an offspring? His was a proud and noble family. Some of his ancestors had fought under the standard of Charlemagne. One of his relatives had served with Bismarck. Never had there been a hint of dishonor upon their name. He had come to this ancient city to share in his son's triumph, not to taste the bitter ashes of disgrace.

Nevertheless, he directed his steps to the chemistry professor's office on that hazy gray morning, prepared to consume quantities of humble pie if that was what required to salvage his family's pride, and his son's successful completion of his collegiate career.

When Arden Sloane heard the man's name, he extended his hand in greeting.

"I've half expected you," he said, "Please sit down, Herr Bauer."

Instead of acceding to the professor's request, the anguished father got painfully to his knees, his head bowed, his vision blurred by tears.

"Professor Sloane," he said, "you see before you a father bowed by shame. I must plead with you on my son's behalf, but more than for him, I plead for the honor of my family. There has never until now been any stain on the name of Bauer. He says you are committed to having him expelled from the university without his credentials. Has he not earned them?"

Sloane leaned forward and lifted the kneeling man to his feet.

"If you mean did he pass his exams, the answer is that he did. But to merit graduation from this institution is more than a matter of letters and numbers, Herr Bauer. It involves integrity, honestly."

The senior Bauer nodded in agreement. "You are right, Professor. I cannot argue with your logic. My son is guilty of a shameful act and a still more heinous intention."

"He sought to take another student's life, and for no better reason than the matter of his origins and his faith." The professor's tone reflected his outrage. "Do you now ask me to ignore the ignominy of that intent?"

The father shook his head. "Such things cannot by ignored, neither by man nor by God. But, if God is as I believe him to be, He is capable of forgiveness."

Professor Sloane was a Catholic. At those words, he made the sign of the cross.

"Lord knows we're all in need of forgiveness!" he said, "And so, you would have me forgive your son for what he did?"

"I pray that you can find it in your heart to do so," the father replied.

"Herr Bauer, I'm not the one he wronged!" Sloane stated emphatically.

"Who is the other student?" Bauer asked.

"His name is Michael Marjzendiak. Your son has mounted a campaign of harassment, slander and physical attack against that boy. This latest incident is an accumulation of more than two years of torment. With the best of Christian intent, I find it hard to forgive. But if Michael can forgive it, if his Jewish beliefs do not bar him from that resolution of this impasse, then I will withdraw my mandate for expulsion."

"Where is this Michael to be found?" the father wondered. "Are there classes still in session?"

"Test results are normally posted. However, in chemistry and literature, some of us ask that the students return for a final class to retrieve their essays and projects. Michael will be in my classroom at 11 o'clock this morning. If you can wait here, I'll send him to you after I've finished with him."

"Will he talk with me, do you think?" the father wondered.

"We can only learn that by giving him the opportunity," Sloane replied. Privately, he doubted whether he himself would be willing to face such an interview in Michael's place.

After a long wait, Herr Bauer saw a sandy-haired young man walking slowly towards him along the corridor outside Professor Sloane's office. Surely, this fair-haired, almost Nordic-looking youth could not be the hated Jew that had so aroused his son's ire. This young man's appearance paralleled that of most of Herr Bauer's family. Turned loose in a room filled with Bauer's relatives, this boy would be difficult to categorize as different. Without the distinguishing yarmulke, it would be impossible to identify him as a Jew.

Michael paused momentarily in the doorway, as if uncertain whether or not to enter.

"You are Herr Bauer?"

"I am Kurt's father," the older man said. "And you are Michael?" When Michael nodded in assent, Herr Bauer added, "I didn't think you'd come."

"Professor Sloane told me I should."

"Did he also tell you why I asked to see you?"

Michael gazed into the old man's eyes, mystified. "He said you wanted to ask forgiveness for your son, but is that what he wants? Forgiveness? From me?"

"Just now," said the father, "I'm not sure if he realizes the enormity of what he's done. He's brought a stain of shame upon his family such as we have never known. We have fought in battle, yes, shed blood in time of war. That is a debt of honor. But never before have we sought to shed innocent blood simply because it flowed in the veins of one who is different from ourselves, one who speaks another language, espouses another faith."

He stared hard at Michael, who returned that stare with calm directness.

"You don't seem that different," the old man continued. "What was it that sparked such enmity between you and my son?"

Michael smiled bitterly. "I believe it was the banking success of the Rothschild family," Michael answered. "At least, that's what he cited the first time we disagreed in class."

"And later?" Herr Bauer inquired. "What caused your later disagreements?"

"Religion, politics, racial supremacy," Michael answered. "I think we must have argued at one time or another over nearly every controversial subject except the same girl."

"At least you don't share the same taste in women," the father observed, striving to inject a note of humor into the grim conversation.

"That's just as well," was Michael's rejoinder. "I should hate to have come to blows with your son over a girl." Michael hesitated, as if reluctant to continue. "Did he mention to you that he wanted to kill me?"

"Regrettably, he did." The father answered. "It's for that reason I asked to meet with you. I share the shame and guilt he has brought down upon the family. If you can't forgive him, at least try to forgive us!"

"I scarcely know you, Herr Bauer," Michael responded. "We have no quarrel of which I am aware."

Herr Bauer gazed for a long moment at Michael, as if trying to take his measure.

"Did your professor tell you he intends to bar Kurt from graduation?" he asked. Michael's eyes widened in surprise.

"The grades have been published," Michael stated. "Kurt scored well in all his courses. Nothing can bar him from graduation!"

"That may be true. But if he is sent away from here in disgrace, all those years he worked toward completing his course of study will be wasted." The senior Bauer shook his head. "Perhaps you look upon that as a fitting revenge. No one could blame you for harboring those sentiments."

"That decision isn't mine to make," said Michael. "That's up to Professor Sloane and the university faculty and board."

"Not entirely," said Herr Bauer. "Herr Sloane is basing his decision on whether you are willing to forgive your adversary or not. If you are, he will drop the charges against my son."

"And if I'm not?" Michael asked.

"Then my son and I will leave Zurich tonight. Forever. And the stain of disgrace will be his everlasting legacy."

This was a heavy burden to place on one so young. Michael felt this weight as if it were a palpable, physical load. Such matters belonged to Adonai. Yet, if Michael had died beneath the dropped stone, or in the lake, would Ephraim have forgiven his murderer? Possibly, he would not have, at least not immediately. The Swiss courts would also have had a say in the penalty exacted from young Kurt Bauer.

None of these issues were relevant, as Michael realized. He was alive. Since he was long past his Bar Mitzvah, in the spiritual context of his faith, he was a man. Therefore, the decision was rightfully his. Professor Sloane had known that when he rested his future actions against young Bauer on Michael's choice.

On one side of the ledger was the law of "an eye for an eye." On the other was the fact that when Adonai's chosen people turned against Him and broke His laws, He chastised them but He did not desert them. Every year, they were given a day on which to atone for their transgressions, and those still alive at Rosh Hashanah had their names inscribed anew in the Book of Life.

As for Kurt Bauer, what did he believe? Did he think God held him responsible not only for his actions, good or bad, but for his intentions as well? If Michael forgave the boy for his family's sake, would the proud young Kraut consider that forgiveness a boon or a burden; a sign of weakness in Michael, or a testament of strength?

The person most concerned appeared to be the boy's father, the man who stood before him now, his head lowered, his pride demeaned, his family honor tarnished in his own eyes, by his own kin. Surely that was punishment enough for an older man who seemed not to share his son's prejudices or arrogance.

After several moments of deliberation, Michael looked at Herr Bauer.

"I shall ask Professor Sloane not to pursue his resolve to bar Kurt from the graduation on my account," he said solemnly. "Whether or not I forgive him is a matter private to me. I feel it should remain private."

With that, he turned and retraced his steps, the sound of his heels against the hard wood floor echoing gradually into silence. Herr Bauer sank to his knees, tears streaming down his face. In his heart, he thanked God for Michael's generosity.

When he returned to his son, who was in his room waiting to know his fate, the father found him at last packing his belongings. He froze in mid-gesture when the door opened. For a long moment, he did not turn to see who stood there. Herr Bauer gazed at his only child, his mind in turmoil, prey to conflicting emotions to which he could scarcely accord a name. Anger and pain there surely were. Also, there was disappointment and disgust. He would never again be able to fully respect this young man who was his own flesh and blood, and yet seemed somehow foreign to him. But there was also pride in the boy's scholastic achievements. Michael had admitted that Kurt had scored well. Overriding all those other feelings was relief. His son would graduate.

"The young man whose life you sought to take has seen fit not to seek vengeance against you," he stated. Young Kurt looked at last at his father.

He asked, "How do you know that?" He was obviously shocked.

"He told me!" was the reply.

"You spoke with him?" the young man asked. "You begged him on my behalf? How could you do anything so disgraceful?" Anger and shame shook his voice.

"What you did, was that not disgraceful?" the father questioned. "To seek forgiveness for the commission of a crime can hardly equal the shamefulness of the criminal act. I've assured your graduation, you ungrateful whelp! Don't you dare show your temper to me!"

Young Bauer sat down on the bed beside his luggage. His face was a study in dejection and wounded pride.

"Did anyone see you talking with Marjzendiak?" he asked. "Was there anyone close enough to hear what was said?"

"We spoke alone," he was assured. "Do you think I would permit our shame to be made public? You've done enough of that as it is. I shouldn't contribute further to it."

Their eyes met, and the young man's eyes looked away first.

"Pack your things," the father said, "As soon as graduation is over, we're leaving. The sooner we're away from here, the better!"

* * *

Graduation Day dawned clear, crisp and cold. The graduating students were grateful for the warmth of the long, black gold-lined gowns. All thoughts of conflict and controversy were banished from their collective consciousness. In most instances, the eyes of the proud parents were on them. Who among them would dare not to be on his best behavior? Though it immensely rankled him to know that he owed his participation in these solemn rites to Michael Marjzendiak, whom he hated no less today than he had for the past four years, even young Kurt Bauer was willing for once to ignore those sentiments. He reveled in being present, dressed in his cap and gown; he felt pleased to know that his father was watching with his pride intact. Perhaps, from a higher vantage point, even his deceased mother was watching as well. For every young man and woman gathered on that campus, it was a grand day to be alive.

Ephraim Marjzendiak was in attendance. Elana, though she had wished to make the journey, was now in too fragile a state of health to venture so far away from home. Leah stood in her stead with Markos and both her sons at her side.

When Michael stepped forward in response to hearing his name called by the dean, Ephraim was tempted to applaud, but restrained the impulse. Instead, he breathed a sign of relief. Today, his youngest surviving child was completing his formal studies. Despite conscriptions, pogroms, ethnic bias and prejudicial restrictions, Ephraim had managed to fulfill his paternal obligations to each of his four children. Three had already achieved their long-sought goals. He and Elana had agreed before he left Wola that Michael's graduation gift would be a journey to Berlin. How it would be arranged had been uncertain until now.

But that had been Michael's dream, first secretly and then by open admission. Luvna had blocked him when he had been eleven, but now he was an adult. Now, at long last, he would see the German capital first hand. Leah and Markos were planning to go there to visit Lukas and Anna, Markos' brother and sister-in-law. The timing seemed perfect, an arrangement made in heaven.

Adam and Meyhra had sent Michael a beautiful hand-tooled suitcase while Issak and Luvna's present was a soft leather wallet filled with Deutschmarks. Neither brother had been able to get away to attend the ceremonies in person. Both had written letters filled with apologies, self-recrimination and guilt because the pressures of work prevented them from attending this milestone in their youngest sibling's life. Elana's letter, by contrast, was filled with her joy at Michael's achievement and with heartfelt maternal advice. She obviously regretted her absence from the graduation ceremonies, but the tone of her letter was primarily positive and celebratory, with no mention of frail health and no flavor of complaint or self pity.

It read in part:

> "On this momentous day, my dear son, you stand as if on a mountain top, gazing toward the future on the shoulders of Adonai, armored like the Joshua of old. Know that I am with you in spirit, Michael. I share your joy, I revel in your triumph; I am confident of your ultimate success in life, just as you have succeeded in your academic career. No mother ever loved nor admired a son more than I do you at this moment."

Ephraim was thankful to Adonai for ensuring that none of the lingering prejudice that still hung over him since the bank fraud incident, and the anti-Jewish sentiments following Alexander II's assassination had blocked his traveling from Russian Poland to Switzerland for this glorious occasion.

Michael was not valedictorian nor salutatorian, but he had achieved high honors; magna cum laude. He suspected that Kurt Bauer might have obtained a similar honor, but, thanks to Professor Sloane's intervention, that accolade had not been awarded to the German youth. Sloane had promised Michael that he would honor the Jewish student's request and not block young Bauer's graduation, but he had said nothing about additional commendations. Kurt Bauer graduated on that day, but that was all. When the final list of exceptionally honored students in the graduating class was read, Kurt Bauer's name was not among them, while Michael Marjzendiak's was.

When all the rituals, commendations and ceremonies had concluded, the graduates stood apart with their families, feeling nostalgic regarding the four years just ended, yet eager for the next chapter in their lives to begin. Michael, exulting in the realization that his graduation present was the journey to the German capital of which he had so long dreamed, felt as though he almost had climbed the Matterhorn, and his mother's reference to standing on a mountain top seemed poignantly prophetic.

He was going to accompany Leah and Markos to Berlin, taking with him a generous allowance from his parents. Markos' mother Elsa would stay with Samuel and Frederick, and his assistant Albert Menzell would oversee the business in his employer's absence. The family would be gone for a month; that was not nearly long enough for Michael to see all that he wished to observe in Germany. Nonetheless, he would have the chance to visit at least some of the sights of which he had read. A sense of adventure, almost of unreality, took hold of him. It had taken eight years, but finally, Michael's dream was about to be realized.

# CHAPTER FORTY-FIVE
## A DREAM REALIZED

Berlin in 1882 was the center of a rapidly expanding industrial economy. It was still a city of excitement and of sharp contrasts, but now there were wide divisions between its social classes and vigorous conflicts between the ideologies and goals of those classes. Its elitists were inherently a military aristocracy. Its bourgeoisie was an ever-enlarging kaleidoscope of industrial entrepreneurs of varied origins, financiers, educators, professionals, and the more successful of its artisans and artists. Largest of all was the working class, and herein lay the major source of its ongoing conflicts. While priding itself on its accelerated economic growth, its substantial artistic pre-eminence, and its academic achievements, Berlin, and indeed all of Germany, was caught in the grip of depression.

It was a peculiar depression by modern standards. While prices declined, the rate of unemployment was stable since other countries were still able to purchase German exports. Buying power was thus increased so that the average wage earner found himself able to afford an ever-growing array of goods and services. Rather than stemming the tide of social struggle, this paradoxical prosperity only whetted the appetite of the working class for more freedom and greater power. That sentiment found its means for expression in the Social Democratic Workers' Party. This group had grown rapidly in recent years, keeping pace with Germany's industrial expansion, and agitating for reforms that would more equitably distribute the rewards reaped by the productivity of the working class.

At the same time, Berlin, thanks to the phenomenal expansion of the city's industries and exportable products, was being favorably compared with other cities such as Paris and London in financial prestige and even in cultural achievements. To many Europeans, even those of non-Germanic extraction, Berlin had become the leading metropolitan center of Western Europe, the hub of the cross currents that were then on the rise within the general continental environment.

It was a well-known fact that Jewish industrialists, Jewish financiers, teachers, lawyers, physicians and other intellectuals had made a major contribution to the progress, not only of Berlin, but of the entire German-Prussian empire. It was a well-known fact that was often politely ignored. The military, the diplomatic and civil services were closed to Jews, as were opportunities to own property in certain elite areas of the capital city and other major German cities. In Berlin, the southern and western residential districts remained the strongholds of the propertied class, and immigrants from eastern Europe were absorbed almost exclusively into the northern and eastern sectors.

It was within these areas that even the wealthiest and most influential of Berlin's Jews lived, and it was they, rather than their less affluent brethren, who tended to downplay their Jewishness. De-emphasizing the differences between themselves and their Gentile fellow Germans had become a politic strategy employed to keep anti-Jewish sentiment at low ebb. Here, at least, as well as in France, Jews had full citizenship, if not full access to all avenues of endeavor, and Germany, under the skillful leadership of Bismarck, was the youngest, most aggressive, fastest growing nation in Europe.

When Michael Marjzendiak finally fulfilled his dream of coming to Berlin, he found himself as overwhelmed by all he found as his elder brothers had been years earlier when they had come to Krakow and had experienced at first hand the heady atmosphere of freedom that characterized that ancient Polish city. The aura that permeated Berlin in the early 1880's was an intoxicating blend of brash materialism, religious dogmatism, affluence, and arrogance. The very arrogance of which some observers accused the Berlin Jews was in reality a leading attribute of Berlin's entire native population.

The people who filled Berlin's streets, who paused to enjoy lunch in its colorful cafes, browsed in its shops, and wandered through its museums and art galleries, carried themselves proudly, whatever their class identity. Their mode of dress was serviceably elegant though not ostentatious. Their conversation was marked by constant references to German achievements such as the newest methods of tempering steel, the latest advances in textile manufacture, the most recent refinements in upgrading engines for tractors, trains, and other machinery. They boasted of their art, their literature, even of their political confrontations.

Wagner's music continued to be an unfailing source of pride to the German spirit. His elevation of German myths and legends to a level of near divinity had inspired many of the nation's youth to think of their homeland as a new Olympus where supermen, borrowed from Nietzsche's philosophies and taken out of context, ruled supreme. Michael, who had heard Nietzsche lecture and had admired his work, found this philosophical distortion ironically amusing. Yet, he was aware of a deadly potential beneath the facade of self-glorification, which that distortion fostered.

True to his promise, Albrecht Hoffmeyer welcomed Michael to Berlin upon his arrival there with his sister and brother-in-law. Hoffmeyer made a point of showing the new arrivals "the sights" in the busy, bustling German capital. He also made good on another promise he had made eight years earlier. He offered Michael a place on the staff of his newspaper, aptly named The Berlin Observer. Michael responded to this opportunity as a rose responds to sunlight; he practically blossomed. He made the most of every assignment he was given and his natural gift for words seemed to predict for him a bright future.

In his work as a journalist for the Observer, Michael soon frequented the highest levels of the political and social scenes. He overheard Bismarck's advisors conversing over beer, and occasionally sipped a glass of champagne at an elite social gathering.

Thanks to his fair hair and gray eyes that belied his Jewish background, he was eventually assigned to attend an address by Adolf Stoecker, Court Chaplain and chief spokesman and founder of the Christian Socialist Party. This rapidly growing church-sponsored political organization was intended to oppose and subvert the Social Democrats.

Michael had heard rumors about this group long before coming to Berlin. Much of what he had heard had seemed grossly exaggerated. Now at last he would learn the truth about their beliefs from their most revered and outspoken orator.

As he took his seat in the impressive Werthmein Auditorium, duly appreciative of its grandiose architecture and artistic embellishments, Michael noted with interest the wide range of spectators whom the Court Chaplain had attracted. Most numerous were members of the heterogenous middle class. That was no surprise. They were the largest contributors to the membership of the Christian Socialist Party. The elitists constituted an elegant, but numerically token audience. However, the large number of artisans and workmen, most of whom arrived just before the speech was scheduled to begin, was somewhat unexpected. As the backbone of the rival Social Democratic Workers' Party, members of this group seldom fraternized with their state church-supported opposition. The evening took on at this point an element of intrigue.

Just as the lights were about to be dimmed, Michael was joined by his long-time school friend Joytl Lermacht, a Norwegian orphan, whose aunt, living in Zurich, had given him a home and insured his education. The two young men had known each other throughout Michael's academic career in Zurich. They had graduated from University in the same class, and had unexpectedly traveled to Berlin on the same train. Joytl had found work on a rival newspaper that was entitled <u>Germania</u>, and was sponsored by both the Catholic and Lutheran churches. However, this had exerted no impact on their friendship.

"This is a pleasant surprise," Michael remarked. Joytl and he embraced warmly.

Joytl asked, "Are you covering 'old fire and brimstone' as well?"

Michael nodded.

Joytl smiled ruefully. "I've heard him before - in Church. I understand this performance is a bigger draw than the opera tonight."

A twinkle of mischief sparkled in Michael's eyes. "Really? Perhaps I should stop bemoaning my sad lot and settle back to enjoy the show."

"He's quite a forceful speaker," Joytl admitted grudgingly. "He's also the main reason I've stopped attending Sunday services since I've come here."

Michael glanced sideways at his friend, genuinely intrigued. Before Michael could question him further, the speaker was introduced with a brief resume summarizing Stoecker's rise to power in the Empire through his achievements in the Lutheran Church.

A hush fell over the audience as Stoecker appeared on stage and made his way to the podium. He was tall, neither slim nor portly, with an erect stance and courtliness of manner that commanded attention. As was his custom, he wore his chaplain's robe and cap even though tonight he was not speaking from his pulpit. He raised his right hand as if in greeting to his audience.

From the third row, where Michael sat with Joytl, he could see the man's iron-gray eyes alight with an almost fanatic energy. He was obviously pleased with the size of the crowd. The huge hall was filled to the last row. This was a testament to the extent of Stoecker's influence, for the event had not been publicized as a political rally for the Christian Socialists, but rather as a public address to the citizens of Berlin by their Court Chaplain.

A smile of satisfaction illuminated Adolf Stoecker's face as he began his address. "People of Berlin, it is my honor and my delight to speak to you tonight on a subject of grave importance to us all - the future of our great nation. Currently, that future is threatened by the acquisitiveness of those among us who do not share either our grand dream for the Empire nor our Teutonic background."

Stoecker paused for the spate of expected applause called forth by that reference to national pride in the record of German achievements. He enumerated a few of those achievements in the interval of silence that followed, pausing once again to allow his hearers an opportunity to express their pleasure at this self-congratulatory litany. It was one of the Chaplain's most successful strategies in bringing an audience around to his personal point of view.

"We have indeed come far along the road of sociopolitical evolution from a collection of city-states and provinces to our present status as a respected imperial power. We are the equal of any European nation that now exists, and we have within ourselves the potential to outclass them all."

This time, he was interrupted by a torrent of applause. He was playing upon the most vulnerable and least attractive emotions of these people with all the skill of a virtuoso playing upon a musical instrument. Even the working men and women, swayed by Stoecker's appeal to their pride of origin, joined in the adulation.

"We are a strong, resilient people, intelligent, technically proficient, endowed with the physical and mental stamina that has placed us on the forefront of the progress of western civilization. With these attributes, there is no worthwhile goal we cannot achieve. But we are not without impediments on that path to future achievement. Our society is not free of drawbacks and problems.

One of our greatest intellectual leaders, an expert in the teachings of history and politics, Heinrich Von Treitschke, has clearly defined for us the nature of the problem."

The speaker paused dramatically, much as a stage detective about to reveal the name of a sought-after criminal might pause before providing the solution to the crime. His fierce glance swept the hall, challenging his hearers to disagree with what he was on the point of revealing to them.

"You know the identity of the adversary within our midst. You see him every day, dressed in his dismal garments, with his unshorn hair and untrimmed beard. The Jew walks among us, proudly proclaiming his difference from us, calling himself 'the Chosen of God'. Him we can easily recognize. Yet, there are others of his kind who are more subtle, and, therefore, much more dangerous. These are the Jews who try to imitate us, who dress and speak as we do. Do not be deceived by this. They are as pernicious, as destructive as their more obvious brethren. They appropriate our goods and steal our accomplishments, calling them theirs. It is their speculation that has brought us into depression. It is their ill-gotten goods that are now being offered to us as the means of our salvation. They propose to loan to the nation the financial means to reverse the results of their own destructive actions."

Here once more, Stoecker paused for dramatic effect and let the adulation of the crowd reward his oratorial efforts.

"We must not yield to this temptation. Instead, we must find other means, yes, even foreign means and foreign money, to be paid back at fair rates. Such transactions have at least the merit of being carried on among equals.

We are in the midst of a war as fierce as any we have yet fought. It is a deceptive war, waged with covert weapons. It is described by its adherents as a social revolution, led by liberal men to achieve liberal aims. Do not believe these misguided spokesmen. I have emphasized again and again the need for healthy social reforms built on a Christian foundation. I look toward a culture that is Germanic and Christian. I hunger for a society that is free of Jewish subversion and Jewish supremacy."

Once more, as if on cue, those among the spectators who were constituents of the Christian Socialist Party clamored effusively in response to Stoecker's diatribes.

"I call upon you to join me in this fight. I pray that all Germans will see the truth of my words and the necessity of pursuing my objectives, for they are mandatory if Germany is to achieve her rightful place in the pantheon of nations, if Germans are to gain their divinely appointed role in the affairs of men."

This time, the speaker's words were met by a mixed expression of feeling. Many cheered and stamped, but still others booed and several of the working class members of the audience rose to their feet and moved toward the exits, insulted by Stoecker's reference to the liberals as misguided tools of Jewish deceit.

Stoecker remained silent until order had once more been established. He then continued.

"The enemy is clever. He is eloquent and deceptive. Some of our German brothers are misled by this eloquence, this disguise of false intellectualism. Thus did Lucifer mislead the fallen angels into Hell. Do not follow that terrible example. Do not let Germany be misdirected down that path to national ruin."

With mounting passion, Adolf Stoecker worked his remaining audience up to a fevered pitch of feeling. By the end of his speech, he had them hanging upon his every word. His major goal, to defeat the vote for the German government to accept the loan offered by a consortium of bankers, German, French, and British, many of them Jewish, in order to diffuse the depression that still gripped Germany, was only part of the reason for his presentation. He hoped, by this means, also to gain new constituents to the Christian Socialist Party. In the interest of achieving that goal, he targeted the financial consortium, describing it as an international Jewish conspiracy.

"To accept the devil's gold is to accept the devil's mode," he concluded. "Germany is a Christian country, a Christian people. So we must remain."

Following a few more closing flourishes, Stoecker left the stage to the accompaniment of wild cheers and applause that recalled him twice more before he made a final departure. For several minutes afterwards, people thronged the aisles, discussing portions of his presentation and expressing their own views and interpretations.

As he left the auditorium, Michael turned to Joytl. "Did those sound like the sentiments of a religious man to you?"

Joytl shook his head. "That's what I meant when I said he had turned me against attending Sunday services. But he is eloquent, persuasive, and powerful. For his purposes, that's an unbeatable combination. People listen to him."

"But do they really believe such ridiculous rhetoric?"

Joytl's eyes swept the crowd of departing adherents to Stoecker's philosophy. "He seems to be saying what many of them want to hear. Logic and reason don't have much to do with their incentives."

Michael grinned sardonically. "You're becoming a cynic, my friend. Yet, the size of the crowd confirms what you say. It's just appalling that anyone could take all that nonsense seriously."

"You'd be surprised," Joytl said levelly.

"I can see such ideas taking root in a setting of real poverty and oppression," Michael admitted grudgingly, remembering conditions at home in Warsaw. "But look around you. Despite all the talk of depression and national debt, these people are comfortable and well fed. Most of them have money in the bank, though probably less than they otherwise might have."

"And so they want more," Joytl responded. "This man gives them a scapegoat from whom to wrest it. Those who seem to have more and are somehow different from themselves. Such as your in-laws, the Kolvners. He's preaching a philosophy of hatred against those who are different. Because of it, he's a truly dangerous man, a 'respectable revolutionary' with the support of the State Church behind him."

Michael felt a chill of alarm at his friend's words. The philosophies of Adolf Stoecker embodied a concept of envy and distrust of all things non-German. Furthermore, he had specifically attacked the Jewish bankers and financiers whom he accused of first despoiling and then attempting to dominate the German economy.

After the exchange of a few more words, and the promise to meet again the next evening at the opera house where Leah was scheduled to play a concert, Michael and Joytl bade each other good night and went their separate ways. Joytl proceeded to an apartment in the southern part of town, while Michael returned to the home of Lukas and Anna Kolvner, with whom he was staying while in Berlin. As he went, Michael's thoughts were in turmoil. Letters from Ephraim and Elana had told him, as dispassionately and calmly as possible, that the pogroms continued on a recurrent basis throughout the Russian empire. And here, in Berlin, supposedly the center of western European progress, men such as Adolf Stoecker spoke freely and openly of a prevailing policy of hatred and intolerance against the Jewish segment of the population.

Michael had long perceived intellectually the basis for his father's often-voiced opinion that the Jewish people would never truly be free or safe until they had a government of their own to speak on their behalf. Now, in Berlin, the city that had been for so long the goal of his hopes and dreams, he found himself understanding that need on a deeply visceral level.

* * *

In the Kolvner home, there was a spirit of camaraderie and celebration that Michael was loath to dispel with talk of what he had seen and heard that evening. Leah and Markos, who had traveled to Berlin with Michael, were flushed with excited anticipation. The social visit to Lukas and Anna was being combined with a carefully planned career move for Leah.

Leah Kolvner had not appeared professionally in Berlin until now, despite her earlier training at the Berlin Konservatory. Now, she felt, she was returning in triumph to the place where she had come so perilously close to being seduced away from all she treasured by the lure of false promises and a false love. She found she could scarcely remember the name of Heinrich Rheinsfeld. The memory of his face eluded her completely. How young, how totally naive she had been then, she mused. How wise her father had been to take her away to Zurich where her musical training had truly blossomed and where she had found fulfillment in that ever neutral land. For all these years she had stayed away from Berlin, half afraid to return to the scene of her girlhood successes and her adolescent follies.

Now all that had changed. She was a matron and the mother of two fine sons. She was also a highly respected musician who was favorably compared in the European press to the renowned Clara Schumann, who still played concerts in Germany and elsewhere on the continent, and to the late, great Marie Moke Pleyel, who had been the idol of Leah's childhood. Madam Schumann had shown her favor, had taken an interest in her talent, and had predicted for her a bright future. Tomorrow night, having accepted Leah's personal invitation and traveled from her home in Baden-Baden for the occasion, the great lady would be in the audience.

Germany's leading newspapers headlined the Berlin debut of the widely acclaimed Warsaw-born pianist L. M. Kolvner, for so Leah insisted upon being billed. There were still those who denied the full measure of merit to an artist of the feminine gender. By using her name in that novel and noncommittal form, she unintentionally added to her image an aura of mystery. And, like her mentor and friend, Madam Schumann, she characteristically concertized dressed in black, despite the fact that with her fair coloring and rich auburn hair, blues and greens were her favorite and most flattering colors.

The black gown she wore for this occasion was resplendent with glittering jet beads and Alencon lace inserts, and had full length loose fitting lace sleeves that allowed ample freedom for her arms as her gifted fingers flashed across the keyboard. Those in the audience seated close enough to the stage to see her face were struck by her finely chiseled beauty as well as by her razor-sharp technique and clear, lyrical style.

Berlin audiences could be viciously critical and had been known to defeat more than one young artist, driving some from the stage in abject shame. They could also be effusively generous to those who satisfied their demanding standards.

In deference to her audience, Leah had chosen an all-German repertoire composed by Mozart, Mendelssohn, and, of course, Beethoven. Given the prevailing sentiments within the city, it proved to be a felicitous choice, and she executed each selection brilliantly, concluding the program with Beethoven's Sonata Apassionata. Berlin audiences traditionally preferred a lengthy program, and Leah was somewhat surprised to find that like the concert-goers of Italy, those in the German capital were provided copies of the musical scores of the program selections so that they could follow every note as the artist performed them.

In this setting, with the chauvinistic atmosphere that now prevailed in Berlin, this custom of providing the full score of the concert program to all attending the performance created an excessively judgmental and intimidating situation for the artist, especially an artist making his or her debut there. Nonetheless, Leah Kolvner emerged triumphant, having won over an audience among whom there were many prepared to be hostile. One newspaper, <u>Germania</u>, had highlighted not only her foreign birth but her Jewish origin. The journalist had been careful to emphasize that her appearance did not fit the standard Jewish stereotype.

On the evening following Adolf Stoecker's latest tirade against what he described as the non-German forces at work within the country, and his singling out of Jews who did not look or dress like the popular prototype called to mind by the term "Jew", Leah's concert could not have been more precariously timed. Her success was rendered that much more satisfying by the circumstances in which she was forced to perform, and when, at the concert's conclusion, Madam Schumann rose regally in her box and loudly applauded Leah's work, the audience followed her example and gave the artist a standing ovation.

Backstage, after the concert was over, and Leah had played not one, but two encores, the two female virtuosi renewed their friendship and relived highlights of their earlier association. They had kept in touch by letter, but Madam Schumann's career and her teaching commitments had fully occupied her time in Germany while Leah's family obligations had meant that her concert engagements centered mostly in the Scandinavian countries, with only rare appearances in Rome and Paris. She had visited her home in Warsaw and had performed there to a warm reception, but she no longer felt at home in that setting. She had yet to concertize in England, and though she had appeared briefly in

Frankfort and Baden-Baden on her one visit to her mentor since graduating from the Konservatory in Zurich, this was indeed her first major concert in the "New Germany" of Bismarck.

When the two women emerged from the stage door, they were met by an assortment of youthful militants, all members of the Christian Socialists who carried miniature German flags and banners displaying inflammatory slogans such as "Germany for the Germans!" and "Jewess, go back to Jerusalem!" They had not been present there earlier when Leah had arrived, when she had felt assailed by doubts, stage fright, and premonitions of failure or audience hostility. Now, thrilled by her own excellent performance and by the unstinting welcome of its reception, she was totally unprepared for this anti-climatic confrontation.

Jeers and obscene shouts emanated from the throats of the young men gathered in the street. Leah feared that they might even be armed and that they might intend to attack her, angered by her success on stage where they obviously would have preferred her to have disgraced herself and thereby her people.

Two factors saved the situation. One was Madam Schumann herself. She stepped forward in her usual regal manner, drew herself up to her full height, and addressed the troublemakers in flawless German.

"You know me," she said. "I am one of you. I am as German as anyone could be. I am also a musician. Music has no national boundaries, no race, no religious denominations. Music is the language of the universe, the word of God translated into terms men can hear and understand - provided they have understanding." She paused only momentarily. "You, there," she called out to the youth who stood at the head of the group. "If you lead these youngsters, show yourself men of understanding. Show yourself true Germans, true Christians. Disperse and let us pass."

The second factor was the timely arrival of the hired coach Lukas Kolvner had arranged for to bring his sister-in-law home from the opera house. The horses trotted smartly up to the stage door with the large gray coach in tow, forcing the ruffians to give ground.

Taking advantage of their momentary disarray, Madam Schumann seized Leah's arm and skillfully guided her into the coach, closing the door sharply behind them.

"Go quickly," she shouted to the coachman, as the young men outside raised a cry of protest.

Alarmed, the driver jerked on the reins and prodded the horses forward. In the narrow back street, there were those who tried to reach into the carriage windows, but their efforts were in vain. Within seconds, their quarry had fled, leaving behind loud cries of frustrated fury.

Leah would never know for certain if they would really have physically attacked her or merely verbally assailed her with their epithets and slogans, but the experience had unnerved and terrified her. It was a unique event in her career, one she hoped never to have repeated. She could not thank Madam Schumann enough for her intervention.

*  *  *

As the two friends had planned, Michael, unaware of his sister's unsettling experience following the concert, and Jotyl, who had not been assigned to write the newspaper's review since arts and culture was not his department, adjourned to a nearby tavern to reminisce and enjoy a beer before heading to their respective homes.

Both agreed that Leah's concert had been an unqualified success, and a far more enjoyable experience than the Stoecker lecture the night before.

"Viewed strictly as entertainment," Jotyl remarked, "the fire-breathing dragon put on quite a show last night. But it certainly didn't qualify as either art or culture."

"How did you describe it?" Michael asked. "I didn't get a chance to read today's edition of <u>Germania</u>."

Jotyl glanced carefully about the dimly lit tavern before formulating a reply. "Well, one has to be careful not to offend the powers that be," he answered. "Nonetheless, I think discerning readers, adept at ferreting out what's there between the lines, will be able to get a good idea of what the presentation was really all about."

Michael looked closely at his friend, his mood thoughtful. "Have you been able to determine as yet what the basic philosophy of <u>Germania</u> really is?"

Their eyes met and Jotyl smiled a crooked smile and nodded.

"Unfortunately," he said, "I think I have."

"And?"

"Let's just say that my newspaper and I have some major conflicts of policy. That said, it is a good job. The pay is phenomenal, especially considering that this is a time of depression."

"Will you stay?" Michael wanted to know.

"On the job or in Berlin?" Jotyl asked.

"Both," Michael responded.

"I came to Germany," Jotyl said, "to learn first hand what Bismarck's new creation is truly all about." He shrugged. "I'm learning fast. It was never my intention to make this place my home. But despite Adolph Stoecker and his pack of wolves, the people here are a diverse lot, an intriguing study. I may give it a year, just to gain the necessary experience to further my career as a journalist." He took a sip of his beer. "But my future, I think, is back in Zurich."

"Your future," Michael interjected, "has blue eyes and light brown hair."

"Right," Jotyl agreed. "And I would never subject her to the hidden agendas and two-faced posturing that's going on here. One day, like your friend Hoffmeyer, I'd like to start my own newspaper."

"That's the spirit!" Michael exclaimed, then lowered his voice. "Learn what you can from the bullies and the hypocrites and then find a way to use it against them, to unmask them so that the rest of the world can plainly see what they really are."

"Is that your plan, too?" Jotyl asked.

"In a way, yes." Michael answered enthusiastically. "Being a journalist for me is a means to an end. One day in the not too distant future, I hope to be an author."

"You've mentioned that before," said Jotyl. "What is it that you truly intend to write? Essays, novels, exposes?"

"Perhaps all of that," Michael said, his eyes alight with the passion of his most cherished ambition. "I see chaos wherever I look. Here in Berlin, at home in Warsaw, and even in Zurich where people like Kurt Bauer try to transplant their poisonous sentiments even to a peaceful, neutral nation. I want to combat that chaos. I want to rip it out, root and branch."

Jotyl gazed at Michael with undisguised admiration. "I've no doubt you will," he said. "Just be careful where and how you express those feelings."

Both young men glanced about, assessing whether or not they were attracting any unwelcome attention. The hour was growing late; the tavern was beginning to empty. No one seemed to be watching them and the tables nearby had already been cleared so that no late revelers sat close enough to hear what they said.

"Madame Schumann is still quite a force on the musical scene," Jotyl remarked, deliberately changing the subject. "I loved the way she led the standing ovation. And your sister is a consummate pianist. She's probably one of the best of her time. It's amazing what she's accomplished."

"Especially since she's a woman," said Michael.

"Gender shouldn't matter when it comes to art," Jotyl remarked. "Of course, it usually does. But talent, genius, those are a realm apart. One can't choose but pay tribute to real ability, no matter where it resides. It must have been quite something, growing up in the same house with her."

Michael smiled and nodded.

"Yes," he said, "I guess it was. It sort of creeps up on you. It's there, and you're obliquely aware of it, and yet somehow, you're not. Until something happens that forces it on your attention."

"What was it that happened in her case?"

"She won a continent-wide competition to study at the music conservatory here in Berlin."

"Here? In Berlin? I thought she studied in Zurich." Jotyl could scarcely believe that he and Michael had been friends for close to nine years and he, Jotyl, had never known that fact before.

"Zurich came later," Michael explained. "For two years, she studied in Berlin."

"So tonight was like coming home," said Jotyl.

"Well, yes and no," Michael remarked. "She looked forward to playing here tonight because she and Madame Schumann are friends, sort of a mentor and protégé relationship. But with the Christian Socialists in the ascendancy in Germany, I know she's had second thoughts."

"And who could blame her?" said Jotyl. "But at least it all turned out well."

Within the hour, Michael, arriving at the home of Lukas and Anna Kolvner, after bidding his friend good-night, learned to his horror that all had indeed not turned out well.

\* \* \*

In the safety of the Kolvner residence, soothed by her sister-in-law Anna, Leah regained a measure of her usual composure, but she would not forget what had happened to her here in Berlin, where she had once felt admired and welcomed.

Meanwhile, in the salon, Lukas, Markos, and Michael conversed over mugs of mulled wine.

"Even in the midst of depression, I would never have expected such a thing," Markos said in tones of shock and outrage.

"That's because you don't live here," his brother told him. "If you did, you'd know to expect anything. Berlin is a tinderbox just waiting for a match to be lit."

"He's right," Michael interjected. "Until last night, I thought the rumors I'd heard at school were just that. Overblown rumors. Last night I learned differently. These people dress well and speak in cultured voices, but their sentiments are like a volcano, poised to erupt at any moment, on the most unexpected provocation." He turned to Lukas. "I find myself truly afraid for you and Anna, living here among them, raising your children on this precipice of smoldering anger and hate." He shook his head. "To think that once I dreamed of living here myself. Now I know I was better off where I was."

Even as he spoke those words, Michael had grave doubts that anywhere on the European continent was a good place to be. The Tsar-Liberator, with his peculiar blend of covert reactionism, coupled with a deep-seated desire for social reform, was dead, the victim of assassins. In his place, his son, Alexander III, reigned in growing chaos over Russia and all the Russian-held lands, including those where his family still lived. This new tsar lacked his father's vision and his charisma. Only time would tell how his rule would affect the lives and fortunes of his subjects, but thus far, the signs and portents of his rule were not encouraging in the least.

Even in Zurich, Michael had tasted the bitter fruits of prejudice in the person of a German-born student who resented the power and wealth of the Rothchilds and their fellow German-Jewish financiers and bankers. Throughout Europe, the rugged winds of industrial revolution and irreversible change raged. The youth of that continent's many nations faced a tumultuous future.

# CHAPTER FORTY-SIX

## DRAWING ROOM DIPLOMACY

On the morning following Leah's concert in Berlin, the artist and her international merchant husband Markos Kolvner decided to cut short their visit to Germany. Despite the audience's favorable reaction to the concert, and the glowing reviews of the major periodicals published that morning, Leah could not forget the ugly demonstration outside the opera house, nor the uglier sentiments that had provoked that event. Determined to avoid a repetition of the experience, she and Markos hired a public carriage to take them to a small suburban station outside Berlin rather than leave from the main railway terminal within the city.

It was thanks to that decision that Madam Clara Schumann was able to dissuade her former student and current colleague from her course of retreat. The formidable lady arrived at the house of Lukas and Anna Kolvner, to which she had delivered Leah the preceding night, early on the following morning to pay a call on Leah and to extend to her an invitation to stay with Clara as her guest. Madam Schumann had planned a reception for Leah, partly because of the unpleasant encounter that had sparked Leah's abrupt departure. Another part of her reason was sheer perversity. She thought to embarrass the more blatantly bigoted elements of the capitol city's population by inviting them to socially pay homage to the talented Jewess and daring them to refuse to attend. Because of her complex motivations, Clara was surprised and disappointed to find that she had missed her friend by minutes.

She asked sharply of the maid who answered the door, "Where has she gone?"

"She's left the country," was the reply.

At that point, Anna Kolvner came to the door and intervened, just as Madam Schumann asked, "She left just like that?"

"Madam Kolvner is taking the mid-morning train back to Zurich."

To Anna's credit, she did not allow herself to be bowled over by the somewhat authoritarian approach of the famous lady. Instead, she asked her to come inside and led her to the drawing room. There, behind closed doors, she added, "I'm sure you can understand her reasons, Madam Schumann. You were there last night. "

Clara Schumann did indeed understand, but she herself was a fighter. Therefore she brushed aside such sentiments and got directly to the point. "Which morning train is she taking, and from where?"

Anna was equally direct. "The nine thirty express from Betschwald. "

"The suburban station. Ah, yes," the famous lady responded. "I see." And indeed she did. In her mind, she was already planning the route she would direct her coachman to take in order to intercept her friend before she could reach that destination. She immediately made her apologies for her abrupt arrival and even more sudden departure, and then left as dramatically as she had arrived. She was determined to forestall Leah's leaving the country for a variety of reasons, and Clara Schumann characteristically achieved what she was determined to achieve. She had proved that conclusively when she defeated her father in court and won the unprecedented right to marry whomever she chose despite parental objections. She had even retained the right to claim her mother's legacy inherited from Clara's grandfather and thus hers, independent of either her spouse or her father.

The energy and singleness of purpose that had sustained her then served her again now. When her coachman had skillfully forced Leah's hired carriage to the side of the road, Clara stepped down from her coach, vigorous, erect, and brisk of step despite her age of sixty-three years. She pounded sharply on the carriage door, obviously intent to persevere until the door was opened.

"Madam Schumann," Leah exclaimed in surprise. "Whatever are you doing here?"

"That was precisely the question I planned to ask you." Unaccountably, Leah blushed, at a loss for words.

"My wife," Markos interjected, "has decided that she's finished with Germany."

"If you'll let me come inside," Clara said pleasantly, "perhaps I can persuade you both to reconsider that decision."

Leah made room for her on the seat and Clara, availing herself of the opportunity thus granted, employed the next quarter of an hour in putting forth the argument she had prepared so carefully. At length, she succeeded in convincing Leah that the hasty retreat she had planned would be both awkward and unseemly, not to mention cowardly. Furthermore, with the loan initiative due to be decided shortly by the voters of Germany, the withdrawal from the scene of her latest professional triumph by the only Jewish female concert pianist in Europe would contribute only negatively to her people's image and their prestige. It was, in short, a step she simply could not take.

The fact that the reception took place two nights later was a tribute to Clara Schumann's tenacity, her organizational prowess, and her far-reaching influence. The fact that Leah was able to steel herself to attend the affair given in her honor was a testament to her self-possession under stress. Markos was genuinely concerned.

"I can agree with Madam Schumann's asking you to be her guest if she wishes," he said reasonably. "I despise anyone's trying to dictate to me whom I can choose as a friend based on his own prejudice; but forcing you down the city's collective social throat is quite a different matter. Frankly, I'm worried. I don't want you put on display like that in this hostile environment, without even a stage and an orchestra pit between you and them."

Clara Schumann overhead that remark and decided she agreed with the sentiment behind it. On no account did she wish to place Leah in jeopardy. As much as she trusted in the validity of her influence and the security of her place in the hearts of her countrymen, she was nonetheless unwilling to take chances with someone else's safety.

"But my dear Madam Schumann," the chief of police protested when she called upon him at his office, "that's a most unusual request, almost unheard of."

"Under the circumstances I've related to you," Clara Schumann responded, "I think it's a most reasonable request. Furthermore, I think the last thing you, as chief of police of Berlin, can afford to do is to ignore the possibility of public unrest erupting at a social gathering here in your city. I feel certain neither the Emperor nor Marshal Bismarck would approve."

"I'm sure you're correct, Madam," the chief agreed reluctantly. "They'd probably view it as a dereliction of duty on my part."

"That fiasco that ensued after the concert the other night should also have been foreseen, and prevented," she added briskly, and then stood looking up at him, an air of challenge infusing her petitely built, yet imposing person.

"Very well, Madam. You can rest assured, there'll be no repetition of that kind of nonsense." The man capitulated as gracefully as possible. Returning to his desk, he took paper and pen. "What time does your reception begin?"

"At seven o'clock," Clara Schumann answered, providing him with the address of the house wherein she was currently lodged. "However, there may be some early arrivals. I should judge you'll want your people in place some time before that. And of course," she added, "you'll do me the honor of gracing the event with your presence? Then no one will dare to step out of line."

"I'm flattered, Madam. How can I refuse such a gracious invitation?"

"I was relying on the hope that you wouldn't refuse," Clara Schumann replied.

After discussing further with him precisely what precautions he intended to take to safeguard her premises and her guests, she rose to leave.

"To be utterly safe, Madam, I feel I should leave some men stationed at your home for some time after the party as well."

Clara nodded in agreement. "Yes, of course," was all she committed to words, but they both understood the police chief's meaning.

Early on the morning following the reception, Clara fully intended that she and her guests would leave Berlin, and indeed leave the country, the Kolvners to return to Switzerland while she had planned a vacation in Vienna. She would remain there for some weeks, allowing the inevitable tensions that would follow to be dispelled.

No social event of the season was more memorable, better attended, or more extensively reported in the press than Madam Clara Josephine Schumann's soiree honoring the pianist L.M. Kolvner. Leah still clung to that noncommittal professional name although by now all Europe knew she was a woman, and music lovers admired her no less because of her gender. Numbered among the guests were several local and visiting foreign dignitaries who knew and respected Madam Schumann, as much for her courage and charisma as for her artistic accomplishments. The evening was an unqualified success, and the policemen stationed outside were kept busy and free of boredom. As their chief had anticipated, would-be gate crashers were plentiful, and one or two young ruffians equipped respectively with sticks of dynamite, stink bombs, and, in one case, a slender vial of acid, were arrested and taken to jail. Fortunately, the chief of police felt no undue compulsion to reveal the results of his subordinates' efforts to Madam Schumann. She would never learn just how right her instincts had been in seeking his intervention. She had quite likely saved both Leah's career and her looks by the exercise of forethought and healthy suspicion, prompted by Markos Kolvner's fearful concern.

The social editor of <u>The Berlin Observer</u>, a striking and gifted woman with the unusual name of Rayna Jheungwhold, was in attendance at the soiree. She had earlier reported one of Leah's concerts in Stockholm in salutary but freshly perceptive terms. Her approach had been from what she hoped coincided with the artist's point of view, giving her readers new insights into the world of music and the rigors of concertizing. Rayna was twenty-nine, widowed, extremely well educated, literate, articulate, and inclined to describe herself as a liberal. She loathed the ostentatious posturing and rhetoric that characterized Adolf Stoecker's Christian Socialist Party. And with one exception, the Jewish merchants, scholars, and businessmen of her acquaintance bore no resemblance to the ugly stereotype that Stoecker strove constantly to keep before the German public's collective imagination. The one exception was a man whom his Jewish co-religionists also disliked. Therefore, she knew living examples of that stereotype did indeed exist, but she was equally certain that they were exceedingly rare and provided no real justification for Stoecker's attacks. What he said and did was based on political expediency and personal bias, and these were attributes that enraged the opposing liberal Social Democratic Worker's Party and their sympathizers.

As Rayna gazed about Madam Schumann's salon, her eyes sought out and instinctively identified the "political" guests present. These included the dyed-in-the-wool conservatives who nonetheless shunned Stoecker's cliches, the upper middle class liberals who tended to be all talk and little action, the intellectuals of the upper and lower middle class, many of whom actively opposed the concept of Christian Socialism though for vastly different reasons, and the bored sophisticates who liked to think of themselves as above such "petty" considerations as politics, but who readily became involved if their private interests were threatened. Rayna realized, as her glance swept over her fellow guests, that she knew most of them either personally or professionally; she knew their politics and the motivations behind it.

Turning to her escort for the evening, she smiled knowingly and asked, "Why do you think your sister's friend was so anxious to arrange this party? I must say she's done a superlative job of it in virtually no time at all."

Michael Marjzendiak took a moment to observe the scene before answering. "Madam Schumann is not only a great friend but a devoted fan of Leah's. It all goes back to my sister's student days. Did you know she attended the Berlin Konservatory for two years before going on to Zurich and graduation?"

"As a matter of fact, I did," Rayna replied. "Her winning of one of the competitive scholarships here is legendary."

"Really?" Michael smiled at that reference to his sister's early achievements. "Do you suppose the young hoodlums who demonstrated outside the building during and after her concert knew that?"

Rayna shrugged eloquently. "I don't believe their type would care, or if they did know, it would be a matter for resentment, a Jewess taking up a place in the class and keeping out a German."

"But…" Michael began, his temper and his color simultaneously rising.

"Never mind," Rayna interrupted the utterance that might have followed, "that there's an international competition, and never mind that there are never enough German applicants to fill all the places each year. Those are facts. The bullies and upstarts you've described don't deal in facts. Their fuel is emotion, and the least laudable emotions at that."

Michael was silent for a moment. "You really do understand, don't you?"

"I should," Rayna responded. "These are my people. I'm not always proud to admit that, but it's true."

To turn her mind from an unpleasant line of thought, Michael asked, "Would you like to meet my sister in person?"

"I already have, in Stockholm. I interviewed her when she was just beginning to concertize and I was just starting out to make a name for myself as a journalist. We were two women trying to make good in fields that are traditionally dominated by men. Your sister and I have much in common." Rayna added, "I'd like very much to talk with her again."

Michael guided her through the throng of guests to where Leah stood beside Madam Schumann, looking radiant and poised in a dress of dark green satin taffeta that perfectly complemented her faintly ruddy coloring and luxuriant auburn hair. Madam Schumann wore black as usual, an elegant black dress of watered silk overlaid with Alencon lace. The two women were very different in origin and appearance as well as in age - yet they were quite alike, both strong, ambitious, assertive, and determined, yet both deceptively feminine and distinguished by an air of vulnerability that was only partly valid.

Rayna was a sharp contrast to both of them. She was tall and leggy, with shoulder-length hair that was half-way between ash-blond and pale brunette, changing colors with the lighting around her. Her eyes were blue-green set in a pale cameo complexion. She was the absolute embodiment of the svelte sophisticate, yet she had just told Michael in capsule comments that at heart she was still the young, eager journalist striving, now that she had made a name for herself, even as Leah had done in music, to hold her own in a man's world.

"I don't know if you remember Frau Jheungwhold, Leah, but you've met before in Stockholm" Michael said by way of introduction.

Leah looked up at her brother in fond recognition, and then her eyes met those of Rayna and she smiled. "Yes," she said, "I remember. Your article was most complimentary."

"I meant every word," Rayna said, "and this time, you were even better. I willingly took part in the standing ovation." Her attention then moved to her hostess, and she thanked Clara Schumann for her invitation, giving Michael and Leah an opportunity to exchange a few more words. Privately, she wondered what Leah would say if she knew the sentiments Michael unknowingly inspired in Rayna. She was older than he by seven years and several months, and she was distinctly gentile, but Michael's ripe young male magnetism and lack of experience with women struck in Rayna a responsive chord. He reminded her in many ways of the husband she had loved deeply and had lost to a tragic accident.

She glanced at him beside her, and felt a lump rise in her throat. The forbidden fruit was always the most desirable. After a few more complimentary remarks exchanged with Leah Kolvner, Rayna and Michael moved away, deeply engaged in mutual impressions of the event and those participating.

* * *

Eight days after Madam Schumann's soiree, the initiative to accept or reject the consortium loan came to a vote and passed by a respectable margin. Michael, who had risen to a place of note on <u>The Berlin Observer's</u> staff, was assigned to write the editorial comments. He could scarcely contain his enthusiasm. Adolf Stoecker had received one of his first major defeats.

Writing under the byline of Michael Marjak, a pseudonym he had adopted at Herr Hoffmeyer's suggestion, he outlined briefly the arguments that had been put forward in support of the consortium proposal, contrasting them with the Christian Socialist arguments against the issue. Employing a spare, crisp, semi-satirical style, he concluded with a summary of the economic necessities which had inevitably led to the measure's passage. He wisely made no overt mention of the loss of prestige for Stoecker. He simply stated the facts as objectively as possible and left the reader to draw his own conclusions.

His employer, Albrecht Hoffmeyer, applauded Michael's journalistic excellence and admired his objectivity. He also congratulated himself on his knowledge of people. Michael had the makings of an outstanding writer. He would go far if his potential was fulfilled and allowed to flourish. Hoffmeyer wondered if it would be given the opportunity, considering the forces currently at work in European society in general, and Germany in particular, forces like Stoecker and his constituents. They were not likely to accept defeat gracefully. There would be more speeches and further demonstrations, and ultimately there would be incidents and outrages involving prominent Jews who had helped build the consortium. The ungrateful would inevitably rise to bite the hand that had fed them.

Michael had little suspicion that the invitation Rayna extended to him at week's end to join her for a skiing holiday had been inspired, as much by his employer's concerns for him and his desire to get Michael out of Berlin for a while as by Rayna's undisguised pleasure in his company. Thus far, they were platonic friends who enjoyed being together. The difference in their religious ideologies seldom arose even as a topic of conversation, since Rayna was more of an agnostic than a Christian, and she respected on principle the Jewish philosophy if not its dogma and rituals.

She waited agreeably until after temple service before calling for Michael at the Kolvner home. Lukas was faintly disapproving of Michael's friendship with her, mostly on the grounds that she seemed too outspoken and aggressive for a woman. Michael should have called for her, not the reverse, in Lukas' opinion. On a practical level, Michael reminded him, that would have risked their missing the train and having to wait until morning. Michael, eagerly looking forward to a holiday away from the tensions and turmoil prevalent in Berlin, once the loan issue had been decided, had no wish to wait.

* * *

The Bavarian Alps are equally as breathtaking as the Swiss Alps, though Germany's loftiest mountain, the Zugspitze, towering 2,964 meters, has seldom been compared to the Matterhorn. From time immemorial, young people have been drawn to the mountains, lakes, and forests of Bavaria, especially during the winter sport season, when snow creates a glittering, enchanted carpet throughout the area. Now, once more, the romantic beauty of the Bavarian mountains wove its intoxicating spell.

Rayna and Michael took the train to Garmisch-Partenkirchen, nestled at the base of the rugged Wetterstein mountain range that included the Zugspitze. They talked and lunched on cheese sandwiches and pickles as the train pursued its picturesque course through the Bavarian countryside. As time passed, Michael found himself wondering how he could possibly have failed to notice before the shining golden-amber hue of Rayna's thick, wavy hair, the musical lilt of her frequent laughter, and the sheer infectious energy of her vivacious nature. Her smooth, delicately pink-highlighted skin shone like fine porcelain, and her blue-green eyes reminded him of the lakes he had seen shimmering among the hills above Zurich. Most impressive of all to Michael was Rayna's exuberant personality, and the subtle challenge that seemed to underlie her jovial yet provocative manner. She seemed a new and different person outside the confines of their mutual working atmosphere, and this new Rayna was undeniably fascinating.

On their first morning, they hiked together through the foothills of the Alpine range, carrying with them a picnic lunch that somehow took on a magical aura in this fairy-tale setting. Rayna, filled with excited anticipation, urged Michael to join her on one of the lesser slopes until he grew more accustomed to the unique qualities of the Bavarian snow. Later, they would dare the heights together.

That evening, they dined at the lodge and talked far into the night over glasses of ale, each disclosing a little more of his private thoughts and cherished ambitions, two close friends, growing indefinably closer.

The pair set off at dawn the following morning, eager to begin their adventure. They carried their skis strapped to their backs, together with the other necessary equipment, and small packs of food as well. Rayna had predicted that they would probably be away until mid afternoon. The climb to the top of the run would take nearly an hour, and there were many sights she wanted to point out to Michael on the way.

As a very young girl, she had come here with her parents on several occasions. This area had long been one of her favorite sites. Now she looked forward to an opportunity to share its wonders with her new-found friend.

The sun climbed higher even as Rayna and Michael climbed the foothills surrounding the Zurmetz Pass and moved upward along the craggy terrain of the lesser Wetterstein peaks. As they rounded a curve and came to a break in the solid wall of snow and stone, Rayna exclaimed with delight and pointed ahead. Michael's gaze followed her pointing finger, and a gasp of unexpected pleasure escaped him as he beheld the summit of the Zugspitze, crowned by an aureole of vari-colored lights.

The snow on the mountain's highest slopes acted as a prism, breaking the light into its components, while the gentle haze of moisture above reflected the colors in a circular sweep that danced and pulsed as if with a life of its own. Only at this time of day could the phenomenon be seen.

Rayna's smile as she gazed at the sight was one of rapture. "Isn't it magnificent?"

Michael could only nod in agreement, his eyes fixed on the mountain's towering shape. Slowly, he turned to look at Rayna's upturned face, rendered even more beautiful by the play of light reflected there. Hers was the golden allure of the Lorelei and the Rhinemaidens of legend. He hungered to reach out and touch her, to clasp her to him. Did he, he wondered, dare to yield to that impulse? How would she react? He hesitated to spoil the wonder of the moment and the quiet pleasure of their friendship by being too precipitous.

As if she had read his mind, Rayna leaned back against the vertical face of the mountain where they stood, her head tilted back, her eyes and her smiling lips inviting his kiss. Overwhelmed, he bent and pressed his mouth to hers, his hands reaching out to stroke her hair, somehow like his mother's in this light, and yet also quite different. The contact sent an unexpected jolt of feeling through his body. Their lips clung together and Michael felt his pulse quicken; his breathing almost stopped. A wave of glorious giddiness possessed him. He folded his arms tightly around Rayna's supple waist and held her close to him while their impassioned kiss crescendoed in a dizzying spiral of sweet voluptuous oblivion.

When he let her go, their eyes met and locked, each seeing the other for the first time in a totally new light. Michael had met and been attracted to other girls, but never in quite this way. Rayna had known other young men, and one, her husband, she had known intimately, but none had struck so deep a responsive chord in her as did this young man about whom she still knew so little and hungered to know so much. Half alarmed by the depth of feeling kissing him had aroused, she stepped away from the mountain wall.

Michael instinctively reached out to protect her from falling.

"Let's hurry," she said quickly. "We'll miss the best of the snow. In an hour, the slopes will be crowded."

Reluctantly, Michael followed her further up the mountain, staying as close to her as possible, wanting to touch her and yet holding back, still awed by the impact of what had just passed between them, and eagerly anticipating its repetition.

They climbed together for the better part of an hour, and then Rayna showed him the full expanse of the valley below. The hotel lodge was only a tiny rectangular shadow at this distance. The peaks of the towering Wettersteins were arrayed around and above them like sentinels posted along the barricade of an ancient castle, silent, remote, and breathtaking.

Michael had seen the Swiss Alps from a respectable distance, passing among them by train. Today, he stood amidst the natural wonders of the Bavarian Alps, close enough to reach out and touch them. Beside him was an even more intriguing natural wonder, one he had touched and marveled at the touching, and knew with unarguable certainty he would touch again, but how intimately he could not dare guess.

The afternoon passed quickly and exquisitely. Rayna was an expert skier. Her skill and confidence inspired a kindred confidence in Michael. Earlier, at school in Zurich, skiing had been at best a lukewarm pastime for him. Now, with Rayna beside him, prodding, teasing, challenging him to dare greater heights and faster speeds, he felt a reckless exhilaration, a zest for the sport that had heretofore eluded him.

When at last they returned to the plateau where she had first shown him the glories of the morning sunlight on the Zugspitze summit, Rayna and Michael opened their packs and shared a luncheon of simple fare made wondrous by their togetherness. She was tempted to seduce and then yield to him then and there, but the place was too open, too accessible. Besides, he was so young, so inexperienced that she felt treacherous for having such thoughts about him. She was of two minds. She strongly suspected he would follow where she led, just as he had on the mountain slopes, and she could lead him to undreamed of pleasures that would bind them together, possibly for a lifetime. But would that be a betrayal of the trust he had placed in her by giving freely of his friendship?

# CHAPTER FORTY-SEVEN
## STREET POLITICS

In the aftermath of the consortium loan vote, feelings still ran high on both sides of the question. The workers were relieved to know that their jobs and their incomes were safe, while their employers were delighted that their businesses had a good chance of remaining operational and solvent. However, for those who were neither employers nor employed, opinion was divided. The intelligentsia and the upper classes favored the measure, and had assured its passage with their votes. It was easier for the rich to have the money come from other sources rather than submit to being taxed, while the upper middle class professionals, professors and scholars believed that the loan, with its low interest funding, was a healthy move toward ending the depression.

Nonetheless, there were those, and they were many - the ultraconservatives, the ultrareligious, and most especially the idealistic youth and the militant students, who resented seeing their country beholden to the "Jewish foreigners." This attitude prevailed despite the fact that the vast majority of those who had introduced the initiative were native-born Germans, many of them gentiles. The others, though of Jewish ethnicity, included several who had not seen the inside of a synagogue for years. The cost of assimilation, of social and business acceptance, in the new German Republic was the surrender of a certain degree of identity, a cost that had been paid by quite a few Jews, people who still saw themselves as Jews, though a-religious ones. The heterogenicity of this group, and the price they were willing to pay for freedom of action, of expression, of economic opportunity, was but poorly understood by their gentile compatriots.

To those who resented "The Jews" as a concept more than either as a religious group or as a people, such fine distinctions were irrelevant. To the young Christian Socialists who roamed the streets in gangs, seeking opportunities to affirm their beliefs with actions, those gradations were nonexistent.

On the Monday following the vote, when all the tallies had been completed and the election results were finalized, not only had the consortium loan been approved, but several new legislators had been placed in power, most of whom had argued in favor of its passage. On the preceding Sunday, Adolf Stoecker had given a stirring sermon from his pulpit, decrying the gullibility of the German electorate and predicting tragedy for Germany as the inevitable result of that election.

Early on Wednesday morning, at a time when enterprising tradesmen went to their shops to prepare for a new business day, several Jewish businessmen were met by a spectacle of devastation. Perhaps the worst such scene filled the site of Kolvner Imports, Inc. The entire establishment had been wrecked. Precious porcelain and crystal pieces of enormous value and rarity had been reduced to unrecognizable shattered shards. Wood screens, panels, and fine furniture were now piles of splinters. Even the glass display shelves were broken and crushed, and the doors and windows had been systematically smashed.

Only the metal safe, welded to the floor and fabricated of steel that was tempered by a new process that resisted extreme temperatures, remained unbreached. Within its spacious confines was the money that had not been deposited in the bank before the close of the business day on Friday. A few choice pieces considered too priceless to remain out from under lock and key, and those items marked "sold" that had not been taken by their buyers also resided there, but that was all that remained intact. Certainly, there was not enough supply left to meet even one day's demand.

Lukas Kolvner was speechless. He stood in the midst of the ruin of his business and wept bitter tears of frustration, anger, and disbelief. Why, he wondered, had this been done, and by whom? Then slowly, the answer dawned upon him, and he wept even more bitterly. If enough local Jewish businessmen could be ruined in this manner, it was possible that the loan could still be blocked, or so the initiative's opponents must have reasoned. He wondered, in that moment, who among his friends had suffered similar acts of vandalism and wanton destruction.

When his first assistant Eli Holtzman arrived a quarter of an hour later, he found his employer trying vainly to sweep away some of the massive array of broken glass and porcelain fragments. It was too great a task for any one man to accomplish. Holtzman stood awe-stricken, halted between the extremity of his amazement and the compulsion to offer his help.

"Herr Kolvner," he said, "what on earth has happened?"

"As you can see, Eli, for the present, I'm out of business, and you my friend, along with the rest of my staff, are out of a job." He thought but did not say how ironic it seemed that, while he and his associates had sought to safeguard the jobs of German workers, it was he and his own work force that had been brutally dispossessed.

The temptation to give up was almost overwhelming, but Lukas Kolvner resisted that urge. Instead, he persevered in his efforts to bring some order out of the chaos that surrounded him, and Holtzman hastily joined in those efforts. By the time the first prospective customers began arriving, at least most of the rubble left by the vandals had been cleared away and assembled in a rear storeroom for later disposal. The sale of two or three choice remaining treasures from the safe made it worthwhile that Lukas had come into the store. He could repair his shop with the proceeds from those sales, but it would require months to restock his inventory. He wondered if it would even be worth bothering to make the attempt.

The Christian Socialists, he knew, would still be active, and the young ruffians who had done the damage would still roam the streets of Berlin. In several cities, suburbs, and villages throughout the country, there would still be those who believed Jews shed the blood of Christian children in their religious ceremonies; there would still be parents who cautioned their children against any contact with the "heathen" who had "murdered Christ."

Suddenly, although he was only thirty-nine, Lukas Kolvner felt very old, very tired and depressed. His family had worked for many generations to build up their multi-national business. They had struggled to become an integral part of the countries in which they had prospered, to play an active role in the social and political life of their varied places of residence. Yet, there was always the resentment, even envy, underlying the facade of acceptance, of "hail-fellow, well met," that formed the surface of their dealings with those among whom they lived and traded. Most often the slights were subtle, sometimes even unconscious, on the part of those who dealt them out. Occasionally, there would be barbed words spoken in sudden anger, and unwritten rules that barred Jewish membership in certain groups or Jewish attendance at certain functions. However, as Lukas and all his contemporaries knew, since the days of the Inquisition, and the forceful expulsion of the majority of English Jews, acts of outright violence against his people had been only sporadic throughout central Europe.

Now, it seemed, thanks to Adolf Stoecker, a new and different kind of Inquisitional terror reigned, and it, too, had the stamp of religious approval. It was, in fact, a kind of pogrom, although none would openly apply that term that was so widely known in the lands under Russian dominion. Germany, after all, was an enlightened nation, inhabited by people who considered themselves far advanced beyond the Slavic and Mongolian nationalities to the east.

How bitterly Lukas Kolvner viewed that pretention to advancement as he surveyed his ruined shop. He mused that, with the exception of the gypsies, every other nationality that dwelt within Germany's borders had the protection of a government on which to rely in times of peril - everyone but his. For him and his coreligionists, and those with whom he shared a distant ancestry, there was no authority to speak, no attache, no consul, no ambassador. In a world where the spirit of nationalism was growing inevitably stronger, he was a man without a country, and he had never felt that lack more keenly than he did now.

* * *

When Rayna and Michael returned to Berlin, still reveling in the glow of their shared holiday, they were unprepared for the emotional letdown that awaited them, both jointly and separately. The young vandals who had sacked hundreds of Jewish places of business had not spared the work places of several of their gentile sympathizers. The offices of <u>The Berlin Observer</u> had not escaped unscathed, though the presence of the night staff had aborted the attack and curtailed the extent of the damage. Most of the presses were still functional, and the latest edition would still reach its readership, but the premises were a scene of chaos reminiscent of the literary accounts of Armageddon.

Herr Hoffmeyer called the members of his staff together as soon as they had arrived for work. The inner sanctum of his office, located at the center of the building, was one of the few areas where order still prevailed. All of the newspaper employees gathered there gratefully, relieved to escape from the rampant disarray outside.

"Now, my friends," Hoffmeyer greeted them, "you see firsthand the face of Reaction. It's an ugly picture, to be sure, but what we have experienced here is but a microcosm of events elsewhere. In a day's time, with diligence and energy, we can have our office almost back to normal, and without missing a single edition." He paused dramatically, then glanced grimly at each face in turn. "I've learned that other enterprises have not fared so well. What I want from you are details of those disastrous events, but that's not all. I want a composite picture that vividly portrays not just the impact on the obvious victims, but the far-reaching effects of atrocious acts like this on our entire society. I want you ladies and gentlemen," and he glanced meaningfully at Rayna, "to gaze into the crystal ball and tell your readers what this situation says about their future."

He dismissed them to their several tasks after a few more words, but Michael he took aside and spoke to him in private.

"You'll probably be the most anxious to describe your perceptions of what's happened, but I think in your case that would be unwise."

Michael, unaware of his brother-in-law's tragedy, wanted to know why. Hoffmeyer found it difficult to explain without divulging what he had heard from Eli Holtzman, whom

Lukas had sent to the newspaper office looking for Michael to warn him. The two had missed each other by minutes.

"I want you to stay here today, Michael, and work with me on an editorial I plan to write. Despite your unobtrusive looks, I'd prefer you not be on the streets today." He raised a hand to silence Michael's protest. "Trust me. I have my reasons, and they're valid ones. I haven't steered you astray before."

Michael shook his head. "No, sir, but I'd like to know what's happening out there. I'd like to see for myself."

"You'll know," Hoffmeyer responded. "You'll find out soon enough." And to himself he added, "And then you may not want to know."

Later in the day, when members of the writing staff returned from their assignments, Michael did indeed learn more than he cared to know about events in the streets of Berlin. Not only had shops and offices been vandalized, but private homes as well. Furthermore, there had been a few instances of physical abuse directed mainly against Hasidic Jews whose dress and unshorn hair set them visibly apart from all other citizens of the city. As new information was gathered, Michael's concern for his in-laws mounted, despite Hoffmeyer's repeated assurances that he felt certain they had not been harmed.

At last, Michael asked Hoffmeyer directly, "Have you heard from them?"

Hoffmeyer faced his protege resignedly. "Herr Kolvner sent his assistant early this morning to inquire about you," he replied. "He was very worried for your safety."

"Why should he be? I look as German as you do."

"Yet you are known to be a relative of the gifted and renowned Frau Leah Kolvner, and even she, only about a week ago, was accosted almost immediately after her performance had earned a standing ovation from the audience."

Michael was forced to concede the truth of that, but his anxiety regarding the Kolvners was greater than ever. "What had Lukas seen or heard that made him so fearful for me?"

Hoffmeyer paused momentarily, reluctant to explain the details of what had been done to Lukas Kolvner's shop. Finally, he concluded that full disclosure was the best course of action. Michael would learn the details eventually, anyway. "He had seen the total ruin of his import business. Vandals broke in last night and smashed everything that wasn't locked away where they couldn't find it."

Michael looked at him with slowly dawning horror. "Oh, no," he said. "It's no wonder he was afraid." Then a new and more terrifying thought struck him. "What about Anna and the boys?"

"As far as I know," Hoffmeyer answered, "their home was not attacked. Herr Kolvner was mainly concerned that you not go out to investigate any of the vandalism." He chuckled to himself. "I think he's acquainted with your temper. By the way, have you reviewed the drafts of the items your colleagues have written about the day's events?"

Michael nodded grimly. "It's as you said - an ugly picture, though not a surprising one given the ecclesiastical provocations. The people involved have been led to think they're fighting a holy war, and war has no rules."

"Only one," Hoffmeyer cautioned him. "To win! Victors seldom care how their victories are achieved."

It was a sobering thought. Michael realized that the Christian Socialists had viewed the vote as a defeat for their cause, just as he had done. Instead of accepting this particular defeat with grace, they had reacted with violence, determined to intimidate, to terrorize those who opposed them. With the approval of the Chancelor of the State church, they could get away with their blatant terrorism and still cloak their actions under the mantle of the word 'Christian.'

Despite the fact that many of his friends and colleagues, including Herr Hoffmeyer and Rayna Jhungwold, considered themselves Christians, that term had, in the past several hours, assumed for Michael a particularly sinister meaning. The editorial that Herr Hoffmeyer included in the next edition of the Berlin Observer conveyed that sentiment in graphic terms. The byline was Hoffmeyer's, but much of the phraseology, and even more of the spirit of the piece, was Michael's.

\* \* \*

That night, after a brief conversation with Lukas who had come to speak with him at the newspaper office, Michael accepted Herr Hoffmeyer's invitation to spend the evening with his employer and his wife. Rayna, also, was invited, and though nothing specific was said regarding the weekend she and Michael had spent together, there was between the two of them a poignant wistfulness that was bittersweet.

"Despite my best efforts," Rayna said, as coffee was being poured, "I'll never convince you now that Germany is a beautiful country. Tonight, I find it hard to believe it myself." She shivered involuntarily. "I found no beauty in Berlin today, and Berlin is the heart and soul of the German Republic."

"Life is one grand paradox," Herr Hoffmeyer said philosophically. "We speak of the 'Republic,' yet it's governed by an emperor. We behold beauty and ugliness, freshness and decay, side by side. Such juxtaposition is commonplace. The objective is not to accept it as commonplace. When we cease to be outraged by that which is outrageous, then we descend to the level of beasts, and even lower than beasts."

Rayna smiled ruefully. "I'm afraid we're already there. Tomorrow, all will be business as usual. We shall all benefit from the consortium loan, and likely forget that those who made it possible have paid for it in double coinage. No matter what words we speak or write, we cannot change the bitterness of that injustice, nor can we ever repay that aspect of the debt."

"Some of us might try," Hoffmeyer said thoughtfully, glancing at Rayna.

Michael looked at her, too, long and searchingly. He reached out to take her hand, seeking to console her for the sadness he knew she felt. Tears swam in her eyes.

"I've never before felt ashamed of who I am," she commented bitterly. "When our several principalities became one nation, I was only a child but I was as proud as anyone. Yet tonight, I'm embarrassed for my country, and especially for my city."

"I, too, am German, Rayna, though I was born in Lucerne," Hoffmeyer responded. "Tonight is not a good time to remember my origins. If my father had lived to see this day, he would have wept."

Frau Hoffmeyer, who had listened silently to this exchange, now voiced her sentiments on the events that had occupied the attention of her husband and their guests all evening.

"What has taken place is lamentable, I know," she said. "Nonetheless, shared national origin does not make the innocent culpable along with the guilty. We cannot blame ourselves for what a party of fanatics has done, and I'm certain the Jews won't feel estranged from all Germans because of it."

"It's difficult to say, my dear," Hoffmeyer responded, "how it feels to be a victim, when one is safe and secure. It's possible that one may feel estranged from all humanity after being subjected to certain forms of brutality. The dog that bites the hand of the man who has fed it may possibly turn that man against all other dogs for life. Who could blame the man?"

After that, Hoffmeyer sat silently for a few moments. Then he rose from the table. "Rayna, my dear, will you stay the night and keep Lisavette company?"

"Of course," she answered, "and thank you. I'd just as soon not go home alone tonight."

"Very good," he said, then turned to Michael. "I think it best I take you home, Michael, and that's just as well because I have some business to discuss with Herr Kolvner." He went to his wife, who stood to receive his embrace. "I may be late, my love, but don't worry," he said reassuringly. "My discussion with Herr Kolvner may take some time."

As things turned out, their discussion occupied several hours, and Albrecht Hoffmeyer returned home just before dawn. He was physically tired, but felt somewhat relieved of the mental burden that had oppressed him earlier. He had tried to find a way tc combat the effects at least, if not the cause, of the wave of destruction that had filled the preceding day. That knowledge helped to restore his peace of mind as well as his pride in his identity. He spent the few hours left to him for sleep in a guest bedroom so as not to disturb his wife. He scarcely admitted to himself, as he was dosing off, that he would rather not discuss with her the solution he had decided upon just yet.

Lizavette Hoffmeyer did not share her husband's feelings on the subjects of political justice and shared social guilt. Despite their enduring mutual love and similar backgrounds, their life experiences had been quite different. She had lived a sheltered life of plenty, while he had been orphaned at the age of twelve, and had learned early on to fend for himself. He knew life from both sides - as a young adventurer making his way against odds, and later as a seasoned, successful entrepreneur with sufficient capital to convert his dreams into realities.

Last night, driven by a kind of generic guilt, he had offered to risk a large portion of his capital to restore much of what had been destroyed in Berlin. His resources, though extensive, were not without limit. Events beyond the capital city he could not address, but within the confines of Berlin, he could do much to alleviate the damage.

He had been genuinely surprised when his initial offer had been gently but firmly refused. But then Lukas Kolvner had admitted to his guest and to himself that he could not truly speak for his colleagues, who had suffered crushing losses comparable to his own. He knew the measure of his own bitterness, the depth of his personal outrage, but he could not gauge theirs nor say how they would respond to Hoffmeyer's offer of help out of their present plight. He could only bring the offer before them, and allow them the chance to choose for themselves.

Albrecht Hoffmeyer felt confident that the collective choice of the Jewish merchants and businessmen would be a practical one, that they would set emotion aside and opt to survive commercially. He, therefore, slept peacefully that Thursday morning, and waited for word from Lukas Kolvner, unaware that the wait would entail nearly three weeks.

During that period, Michael received a letter from his father that contained distressing news on several levels. It read in part:

"The enforcement of the hated 'May laws' has exerted a particularly pernicious effect in the Russian-Polish provinces. They have erected a political ghetto that in many ways is much more limiting than the physical walls of the old ghetto. One cannot pass outside these legal walls raised by the new Tsar and his ministers. The old reforms of Alexander II, now largely reversed, are more appreciated in their absence than when they were in force."

The letter went on to express in greater detail the freedoms that both Gentiles and Jews had lost. Michael read that section with impatience although he understood intellectually the significance of his father's concerns. Nonetheless, he searched eagerly for word of the family, and soon found it on the letter's second page.

"Your mother's health, never strong since the fire at Plaz Marjzendiak, has now declined alarmingly. She seldom complains, but her energies are easily exhausted, and the sounds of her breathing, especially at night, are increasingly alarming."

Toward the end of the letter, Ephraim added that Elana greatly longed for the sight of her two younger children, and that her only real lament was that the demands of their respective work and personal commitments had taken them far away from home. Ephraim went on to remind Michael that, although the two older boys had fled Warsaw to escape conscription and had only returned years later, they were both now settled at home with their families. Luvna, was even now expecting a child. But no sooner had Adam and Isaak returned than Leah had pleaded to be allowed to study her beloved music abroad. She had scarcely come back from Zurich to be married when her husband had been called to take over the family business in Switzerland. Now Michael worked in Berlin, and his mother, knowing instinctively that she might have little time left to her, hoped ardently for the reunion of her family while she could still enjoy the experience.

His father's letter, long and detailed, left Michael feeling both concerned and guilty, although that had obviously not been Ephraim's intent in writing to him. Ephraim had always been an avid letter writer. Had he chosen to compose a journal, it could, no doubt, have served to chronicle the major events of his time. Correspondence was his medium of self-expression, in a sense, his hobby.

Beneath the facade of conveying the news at home to his son, Ephraim had unconsciously betrayed his growing fear that he would soon lose his wife, and his dread of what life would be like without her.

Michael grasped that dread and shared it. Elana was his model of the ideal woman, the first love of his life, the standard by which he judged all other women. He could not imagine a world in which she did not live and move. He could not picture the home in which he had grown up without her guiding presence.

Warsaw, with all its restrictions, was, nonetheless, the site of that home. Berlin, the goal for which he had longed for so many years was, after all, no better, no less violent, no less ranged against those who shared his heritage, than was his native city. In some ways,

Michael thought uneasily, it was even worse. It had promised so much from a distance, but at close range its glories had proven ephemeral and tawdry.

True, he had made friends here whom he valued highly; he had learned the journalistic skills that he hoped to use in the future as a writer of books and essays, but the cultural advancement, the freedom from mindless reaction and repression that he had sought were nowhere to be found. Only later would he come to appreciate the fact that these very disappointments had given him the insight that would be the driving force behind his literary career.

\* \* \*

The letter Lukas Kolvner had been awaiting arrived from Amsterdam at the end of October. Once he had read it, he felt a sense of relief that even he had not anticipated. His friends in the north had not failed him. The powerful association of Jewish merchants in that city had voted unanimously to extend both economic and material assistance to their beleaguered German brethren. Once again, the sensitive collective social consciousness of the dispersed Jewish people had come to the rescue of one segment of their far-flung community.

When Lukas met with Albrecht Hoffmeyer, it was to tell him that his offer had been welcomed and deeply appreciated by the Berlin Jews, but that they had managed to secure financial help from another source. Herr Hoffmeyer's advice and influence in achieving the restoration of their respective businesses was, of course, gratefully accepted.

"We feel honored," Lukas said, "that a man of your stature is concerned for our welfare. That is why we are glad not to have to call upon you for money. There are those among your people who would resent such a gesture, and they might find ways to attack you and yours. This way, you are free to encourage trade with us without any direct connection. That, after all, may be even more of an advantage."

Hoffmeyer nodded with a wry smile. "I have never been more graciously refused in my life," he said.

"It is not a refusal," Lukas protested, "merely acceptance of a different kind of help."

"Herr Kolvner, you have missed your calling. You should've entered the diplomatic service."

"Believe me, Herr Hoffmeyer, the merchants of this world were the original diplomats, long before government evolved to a degree that would permit mutual negotiations." Lukas paused momentarily. "Now I have decided to take this opportunity to move my place of business to a new location. Something unpretentious. No large display window, simply a small glassed in niche near the front door, with one choice piece, nothing more, to indicate the treasures within."

"Quite discreet," Hoffmeyer responded, "and considering recent developments, very wise. I have several holdings throughout the city. I've no doubt there is something to be found among them that will be to your liking."

"No doubt," Lukas agreed, and shortly thereafter, the two men parted amiably, Albrecht Hoffmeyer gratified to be of some assistance, and Lukas Kolvner with his pride intact.

\* \* \*

In the months and years of his life spent in Berlin, Michael could remember most vividly his time spent with his friend Jotyl Lermajcht who, like himself, had chosen his career in journalism, and, like Albert Hoffmeyer, aspired to own and publish his own newspaper. Michael made it a point to introduce the two men, and Jotyl profited from that introduction, from all he learned from the larger-than-life editor-journalist and entrepreneur. Hoffmeyer, with his wife, Lizavette, made his home wherever he found himself at any given time, and possessed the capital to purchase and to make that home a splendid one. If only, Jotyl thought, he could emulate Hoffmeyer's example, he would be able to formulate an effective strategy for success. Hoffmeyer's house in Berlin was a mansion that could have served an emperor as his palace, but was set upon a somewhat smaller tract of land. Here, he had entertained royalty, and he boasted jovially of the heads of state who had paid him visits there and at his other estates. But he was also a pragmatist, a practical man who understood the harsh and often brutal world in which he lived, although he did not always agree with what transpired within that world.

Both Michael and Jotyl learned much from this man, from his circle of acquaintances, and from Berlin itself and the country which it dominated.

Reyna Jheungwhold showed Michael the social scene, introduced him to her friends and to some of the people she did not consider friends, and it was thus he learned that Kurt Bauer, his schooldays nemesis in Zurich, had not settled in Frankfurt on the family estate on his return to his native country, but had instead relocated to the German capital.

Michael was surprised that Reyna even knew Bauer, but he gradually came to understand how that could be. After all, a journalist must maintain many contacts, congenial or otherwise. One can never predict who may become a valuable source of information. And Bauer's transition to Berlin was predictable, given his father's outrage at his son's disgraceful behavior towards Michael, and given the fact that Adolf Stoecker, young Bauer's idol, held his office as head of the state church and chaplain to Kaiser Wilhelm I in that city.

Under these circumstances, it was inevitable that the two former classmates should meet, that the meeting should be stormy, and that the entire episode would come to a controversial conclusion. Adolf Stoecker was the catalyst that would lead to the confrontation.

For more than two years following the Consortium Loan Vote, Stoecker consistently agitated against its implementation and dismissed its benefits. His inflammatory rhetoric had precipitated the violent demonstration that had culminated in the destruction of two thirds of the Jewish-owned business in the capital city.

Albrecht Danishk, the clever thief who had caused Ephraim to be temporarily imprisoned and almost sent to his death, had also played a major role in that catastrophic event. He had planned the strategy of the attack although he had stayed in the background. He considered himself a step above the rabble that roamed the streets and carried out the mechanics of such brutal actions. He liked to keep his hands clean. He was content to let others do the dirty work and take the risks which that work entailed.

Since his graduation, Kurt Bauer had achieved a certain level of affluence and stature in the field of investments. By that means, he had come to Stoecker's attention and had become one of the chaplain's confidantes, enabling him to play an active role in the policies and procedures of the Christian Socialists. Though financially well-situated, Bauer, unlike

Hoffmeyer, avoided the luxury of an expensive showy domicile. Instead he favored simple, Spartan surroundings and enjoyed watching his carefully invested capital grow.

Reyna, and therefore Michael as well, learned of this connection after the fact, but only Michael knew from his father's correspondence of Danishk's ugly history and the evil of which he was capable. Danishk and Bauer, united in the same cause, could prove to be a deadly combination, and with Adolf Stoecker as their mutual mentor, they constituted the triumvirate from hell.

By asking cautious questions and through judicious probing, Reyna learned that Danishk had also planned the demonstration outside the opera house on the night of Leah's Berlin concert, and that Bauer had been apprehended and briefly detained outside Madame Clara Schumann's Berlin residence on the occasion of her reception in Leah's honor three nights later. Bauer it was who had formulated the diabolical scheme of secreting a vial of acid on his person to be used against Leah Kolvner. He had learned of Leah's Jewish origin; he had further learned that she was Michael Marjzendiak's sister. The same sister who lived in Zurich and had provided for Michael a home in his earlier school career and an ongoing refuge when, in the last two years of his university career, he had taken a room on campus.

Studying Leah's pictures in the local newspaper, Bauer was forced to admit that the famed musician was attractive, even beautiful, if a Jewess could be accorded that accolade. Well, Bauer decided, he would destroy that beauty, corrode it with concentrated acid, and effectively end her musical career. That was to have been his ultimate revenge against Michael Marjzendiak.

The scheme had failed. Thanks to Madame Schumann's foresight and ingenuity, Bauer and his fellow would-be party crashers had been halted before they could make an entrance, and had been taken into custody. Only Albrecht Danishk's intervention had effected their prompt release. Kurt Bauer had long brooded over the failure of his efforts against Leah Kolvner, and at first, not having encountered Michael in person in Berlin, he had not associated the Berlin Observer's political journalist, Michael Marjak, with Michael Marjzendiak. The altered name, shorter and more readily pronounced than Michael's family name, had been the result of Hoffmeyer's suggestion. It provided a much easier byline to fit into a newspaper column.

It was only after Jotyl, Michael, Reyna and Bauer had attended a fundraising reception given by the Philanthropist's Committee of the State Church of Berlin that the young German rabble rouser realized his oversight. Now, he thought, it all makes sense. The pieces fitted neatly into place. His adversary, Michael, had somehow insinuated himself into the good graces of the well-known financier Albrecht Hoffmeyer and had secured a place on the staff of Berlin's leading newspaper. No doubt his famous sister had planned her concert in Berlin to be able to visit with him. Possibly it had been at Michael's suggestion that she had timed her appearance to precede, by only a few days, the occasion of the Consortium Loan Vote. Her cultural triumph in Germany's capital city on that occasion had certainly cast the Jewish presence in Germany in a favorable light, and her obvious association with Madam Clara Schumann had contributed to that positive image.

Kurt Bauer, with the aid and encouragement of his ally and colleague Albrecht Danishk, determined that he would find a way to overturn the outcome of that vote. He would somehow nullify its effects so that the Jewish Coalition would not be successful in maintaining their stranglehold on the German economy. If the devastation of their places of business had not achieved that goal, then he and his Christian Socialist compatriots would initiate a new and more effective strategy. And he would also manage to bring about the downfall of Michael Marjak in a way that he could not escape and would never forget.

By waiting for almost fourteen months after the looting, breaking and burning orgy that had wreaked such havoc on the German Jewish businessmen, the Christian Socialists allowed their prey to regroup, to clear away the rubble and rebuild their markets, their fine stores and offices. The passage of time, as it so often does, would create in them a false sense of security, would undermine their watchfulness and allay their concerns. There is, after all, a time honored belief that lightning does not strike twice in the same place. That belief is actually erroneous, as any good meteorologist can testify. If the same conditions persist that attracted the first strike, a second such deadly strike is well within the boundaries of probability.

The first strike had taken the form of a sinlge unified cataclysm of wanton, all-encompassing destruction. It had been planned so that all the victims who had been targeted would find themselves under attack at once and that would ensure that none would be able to help any of the others.

In the fall of 1883, the new campaign assumed a different format. There began a series of explosions across the Jewish commercial sector of Berlin. While a number of these occurred at night after business hours were over, an even greater number occurred during the daylight hours when business was in progress, when buildings were occupied and when the destruction of valuable but inanimate property would serve a counterpart to the infliction of injury and even death upon merchants, their personnel and clientele. Since many of those who traded with the Jewish merchants and bankers were Gentile as well as Jewish, this deployment of agents and resources would not only terrorize Berlin's Jews, but would also terrify their Gentile customers and sympathizers. The goal was two-fold; to cripple the Jewish economic community and to discourage the non-Jewish population from consorting with and supporting them.

Adolf Stoecker not only favored this wave of attacks, he preached about them from his pulpit. He prophesized their spread from one German city to another, predicting that, by this methodology, the Jewish scourge would soon be eradicated from the German nation. He called the period in which these events took place a time of war, and he urged the other German citizens to join in that war on the side of Christian decency.

Fortunately, by this time, the positive effects of the Consortium Loan had demonstrated the results predicted by its proponents. The depression had subsided and the German economy was advancing. From a political standpoint, there was no logical justification for the assaults. They were more than a nuisance; they were counterproductive to the Empire's long-term objectives. Because of his perception of the conflict between what the country was trying to accomplish and what the Christian Socialist-backed incendiaries were doing, Reich Chancellor Bismarck sent for the Court Chaplain in late September and met with him behind closed doors.

"These raids must stop," said the Chancellor, with quiet but determined emphasis. "Whatever it is your constituents think they are doing, they are tearing Germany apart. This is the Germany we have all fought and worked and sweated to build from a confederation of petty principalities into a great nation. I will not allow your religious views and those of your supporters to undo that work. If you control them, and I believe you do, call off your hounds. Otherwise, I will see you defrocked and dismissed from your post in disgrace!"

Stoecker knew that Bismarck, as the second most powerful man in Germany after the Kaiser, could fulfill what he said. When Stoecker opened his mouth to protest his innocence of actual involvement in the campaign of destruction, Bismarck raised his hand for silence.

"Your audience is at an end, Chaplain," he said. "We have nothing further to discuss. I know you to be a most effective speaker. Employ that talent to terminate these lamentable atrocities if you hope to retain the power and position you still enjoy!"

With those words, Chancellor of the Reich Bismarck rose from his chair, signaled to the two trusted retainers who had accompanied him to this private meeting, and left the room.

Stoecker sat where he was, his face impassive, but his mind and his heart were racing. He had been instructed in no uncertain terms to put an end to the upheaval. He was in no doubt as to why. German Gentile citizens of moderate sentiments had protested against what was going on. From the laborers to the intelligentsia there had risen a backlash against the militant extremism that had permeated the Christian Socialist party. Germany was presently at peace with her neighbors. Her trading position was a favorable one. The majority of her citizens wanted to maintain that situation. And Gentiles had been injured and/or killed by some of the explosions. His subordinates in the plan had gone too far. The most extreme among them would have to be muzzled and restrained. If they resisted, well, they were expendable.

* * *

October Twenty-second was the date Bauer chose for his personal mission of revenge. It was a Wednesday, and in the early morning hours, the typesetting and assembly staff of the Berlin Observer were busily and noisily engaged in preparing their early edition for distribution. The main door to the building was locked; at this hour, no other personnel would be likely to enter or leave the newspaper office. The trucks that would transport the finished copies of the periodical to the various newsstands and Stadbahn terminals throughout the central part of the city had not yet arrived.

Yes, the main door was locked, but locks have never yet deterred a determined and resourceful burglar from breaking and entering to achieve his ends. Kurt Bauer lacked neither determination nor resources, and he was on a mission of personal vengeance. Against the background noise of the presses, the cautious breaking of a basement window was not audible on that fateful morning. The masked black-clad intruder slipped agilely through the window, and melted into the shadows. His goal was the editorial office where he felt certain Michael worked.

When he reached that location he was obliged to retreat and conceal himself in the men's lavatory while the cleaning crew swept and tidied the one area that the evening staff were not occupying. He had to wait for more than half an hour. At one point, he hid in a stall and stood crouching on the water closet until one of the night crew had concluded his necessary visit and departed.

The janitors had left the editorial office door unlocked and slightly ajar, a dereliction of discipline on their part. It worked to Kurt Bauer's advantage. Awaiting his opportunity, he slipped into the massive office space, quietly closed the door and locked it from the inside. Now he was at liberty to reconnoiter at leisure. The various desks, set into partially enclosed cubicles, were arranged about the periphery of the rectilinear space, with the managing editor's desk at its center.

That, Bauer concluded, must be Hoffmeyer's desk, but which one of the cubicles belonged to Michael Marjak? How would he be able to make that determination? Making use of the dim lighting in the room, he began to search the drawers of the peripherally placed desks. Periodically, he would pause in his search, listening for sounds that would warn him of approaching staff members.

As a boy in his native Frankfurt-on-Main, he had once worked as a student observer on a local newspaper, before leaving to attend Universitat in Zurich. That experience reminded him that morning editors often arrive at disconcertingly early hours. For that matter, specialty reporters have been known to end their late-night assignments well after midnight, and to return to their assigned desks to compile their reports before going home for a few hours of much-needed rest. Some of those reports might be needed to highlight the early edition; others would be placed on the morning editor's desk to await the afternoon printing.

As Bauer was busy ransacking the sixth of the fourteen desks, he heard a key inserted into the lock. He tensed as it was turned, making a grating sound, and then the door was opened. A tall, lean but well-built man stood in the entryway, his identity concealed by the shadows resulting from the marginal degree of illumination. Kurt Bauer froze momentarily, then folded his svelte, athletic body into a jackknife posture and crawled beneath the desk. He waited there, consciously restraining his breathing and striving to slow his pulse lest the newcomer be warned in the darkness by a random unexpected sound.

The figure moved from the door to the central desk. He opened a portfolio, withdrew a sheaf of papers and deposited them in a wire basket. The man then turned away, moved toward the door, and stopped abruptly in his tracks. He stood as if pondering a question in his mind, then altered course and headed toward the very desk beneath which Kurt Bauer crouched uncomfortably.

The intruder held his breath. The second man, obviously a staff member, stopped at the desk, reached across it, and turned on the desk lamp. He then began rifling through papers on the desk's surface, searching among them as though he was seeking an item that had been misplaced. The search seemed to go on interminably. Bauer could scarcely endure to remain in his constricted crouch for another moment. He was seized by a sudden cramp and was compelled to move one leg to relieve it. His foot struck the wheeled base of the chair, causing it to move a few centimeters backward away from the desk.

The searching staff member gasped in astonishment, came swiftly around to the front of the desk and collided with Bauer as he was extricating himself from his awkward hiding place.

Both men fell to the floor, bruised, winded and taken by surprise. Bauer's domino-like mask was knocked aside by the impact. The light from the desk lamp fell full across his face. In that moment of mutual recognition, Michael Marjzendiak and Kurt Bauer exclaimed in mutual shocked dismay. Bauer leapt to his feet. Michael dove after him, his hands reaching to gain a hold on his fleeing adversary.

Bauer had the element of surprise on his side. He reached the door and gained the corridor before any of the night staff noticed the disturbance. Michael dashed after him, intent on catching and detaining him. His mind reeled at what Bauer's intention might be in invading the news office and hiding beneath his desk.

Bauer's footsteps echoed on the basement stairs as he charged down them, two at a time. Michael's feet pounded close behind him. The German youth's immediate goal was the broken window that had been his point of entry. Almost out of breath, he reached that goal, threw himself through the opening, fell to the ground outside, rolled and rose to his feet with lightning-like speed. His body bent instinctively forward and he took off at a run toward the nearest S-Bahn station.

Michael, reaching through the window, caught at his enemy's collar and almost held him. Only Bauer's forward momentum broke his hold. Undaunted, Michael jumped through the pane-less window and followed in swift pursuit. As he gained the street, two of the young journalist's colleagues appeared from around opposite corners of the building.

"Look for a bomb in the Editorial office!" Michael shouted without missing a step or slowing his pace. His colleagues, mindful of recent events, ran for the rear entrance, shouting warnings to their fellow workers inside.

From the direction in which Bauer fled, Michael could guess his destination. The early-morning urban trains began their schedule at this time. He himself had arrived on one of them, frustrated that he had left behind an important legal document, a contract he had been asked to review and give his opinion by his friend Lukas Kolvner, Marcos' brother.

The arches of the S-Bahn station loomed in front of him as he pursued Kurt Bauer's fleeing figure toward the shadows of the station's entrance. Michael quickened his pace, keenly aware that once inside, the S-Bahn station's unique architecture would afford his quarry a broad array of possible hiding places from which to launch an assault. He had not forgotten Kurt Bauer's propensity for surprise attack and concealed weapons. The memory of what the man had tried to do to Leah rose in his mind. The hideous though imaginary picture of how her beautiful face might look now if Bauer had succeeded in his evil plan filled Michael's heart with rage.

Just before Kurt Bauer reached the station entrance, Michael caught up with him. Driven by outrage born of years of torment at this man's hands, he grasped the German by the throat and slammed him hard against a steel girder. The blow produced a telling effect.

The scalp, due in part to the perpetual need of the hair to have access to a generous blood supply, is permeated by a vast network of small and medium sized vascular channels. This anatomic structure is what causes scalp wounds to bleed out of all proportion to their magnitude. When Bauer's head struck the metal girder, a torrent of blood cascaded down his neck and the side of his face, temporarily blinding his left eye. The impact created a small crack in the back of his skull. A shower of stars bedazzled his unimpeded right eye, and a wave of dizziness overcame him. Michael, momentarily blinded by fury and haunted by the suspicious fear that, despite the apparent seriousness of the damage he had sustained, Bauer might feign defeat only to draw forth a knife to stab him, struck the wounded man another blow, this time to the chin. That was accompanied by a blow to the solar plexus.

Whatever Kurt Bauer had consumed at dinner had not fully digested. The remaining contents of his stomach spewed forth in a sour-smelling surge of particles and fluid that fouled his own clothing and spattered on the garments Michael wore as well. Kurt Bauer slumped to the pavement, his consciousness fading as he fell.

Michael was moved to kneel and lend him aid, a wave of guilt sweeping through him at the thought that he had caused this degree of injury to another human being. But then, he saw the tell-tale flash of light reflected from the razor-sharp blade of the knife as it fell from the fallen man's outstretched hand. Repulsed, he backed away. Unspeakable thoughts chased each other through his brain. He shook his head as if to clear those wicked thoughts away. He could not trust himself to stay near this foe who had dogged his college years and had threatened his sister's safety. But he would notify the local authorities of Bauer's plight and ensure that help was sent to him. Otherwise, he might bleed to death where he lay, and Michael, righteous indignation notwithstanding, did not want Bauer's blood on his hands.

* * *

That late October experience in 1883 Berlin left a lasting impression on Michael Marjzendiak. He found that he could not shake off an ongoing sense of foreboding; a foreshadowing that bordered on despair.. When he later learned that an as yet unprimed bomb had been hidden in the slender case that Bauer had left behind in his haste to escape, Michael's depression was absolute. Every day, he moved about the newspaper office and the Kolvner's Berlin home in a miasma of nervous apprehension. He expected to hear momentarily of another explosion, another catastrophe. He felt certain that Bauer had not worked alone in implementing the avalanche of tragic destruction that had recently plagued Berlin and its suburbs. He knew the Christian Socialist party had been at least covertly involved. The sudden change in tactics of Adolf Stoecker's biased sermons only served to further arouse his suspicions. Where, he wondered, would the next blow fall?

Lukas and Anna Kolvner tried their best to lighten his somber mood. The Rosh Shoshanna celebration, a time of universal rejoicing within the Jewish faith, with prayers of gratitude and thanksgivings to Adonai for another year of life, became to Michael a time of uneasy quietude, like the lull before a storm. Ten days later, on Yom Kippur, he could scarcely force himself to concentrate on the ritual prayers of atonement. He kept seeing Bauer's face as he had last beheld him, half covered by blood, vomit staining his clothing and a knife in his hand. The year 1883 had almost ended before any change was perceptible in Michael's unremitting depression, and that constituted not an improvement but a worsening of the situation.

The letter Ephraim had written to his youngest child was deliberately non-committal. That in itself was unusual and therefore covertly ominous. He wrote of the rigorous winter that had descended upon Warsaw. He mentioned the increased workload that Adam and Meyhra were being forced to endure as a result. He even touched lightly on the fact that his close friend Franz Pietrowski had lately been "under the weather." When he came at last to the subject of Elana, he mentioned how heavy a burden the preceding winter had placed upon her, and he added that he engaged in constant prayer that the current winter would not pose as severe a threat to her health as had its predecessor.

Then he turned his attention to the proceedings of the Banking Advisory Council, to the many political faux pas of the current tsar's administration, and to the dark atmosphere that the wave of pogroms throughout the Empire had imposed on Russia's Jewish subjects.

Finally, he inquired as to when Michael might be coming home for a visit. Significantly, he added:

> "Your mother has missed you profoundly, throughout all your years of absence, first in Switzerland, from which you would, at times, come home, and more recently in Germany, which seems to hold you in its thrall like the legendary Lorelei. Having missed your graduation from the university, she longs for the opportunity to look upon you once again and enfold you in a mother's loving embrace.

Please try to fulfill her desires as soon as possible, despite your busy schedule and engrossing work. Both of us miss your presence and pray for your success and safety.

Love to you always,

Ephraim.

Michael reread that letter, endeavoring to interpret the hidden meanings behind the words. They included a subtle reproach, but it was gentle and loving. Yet Michael felt certain that there was more than unfocused concern beneath his father's recurrent mention of the weather. His mother had scarcely recovered from her illness the year before. Now, Mer Pietrowski, despite his strong constitution, had been recently ill, and his mother's lungs, as Adam had explained, were abnormally vulnerable now.

Near the end of December, Michael wrote his father and mother a lengthy joint letter in which he recounted the less frightening events of his stay in Berlin. He obliquely mentioned that he had once more encountered his old nemesis Kurt Bauer, but he did not elaborate on that meeting nor its outcome. He simply stated that he missed home, despite its drawbacks and limitations, more than he had imagined would be possible, and he promised that he would soon come home to Warsaw to stay.

On the evening before he was scheduled to leave Berlin, Michael dined with Rayna Jheungwhold. They chose a modest dinner house whose food and wine were of excellent quality, and whose owner was a personal friend of Rayna's. His warm greeting, together with the quiet ambience of his establishment, provided an oasis of sanity and peace in which to say their good-byes. They sat savoring the wine and the music of the Bavarian violin trio. They recalled their holiday in the sun-lit Alps, and the love and friendship that had blossomed between them. Each knew that, in the world in which they both lived, that love was hopeless, and that made it all the more precious. Michael was keenly aware that his family would never accept Rayna. In turn, she could not escape the fact that her circle of friends and colleagues would reject Michael just as thoroughly. They had only this one night left to share. Both wished the evening could go on forever, but nothing in human experience, good or bad, ever does that.

The restaurant owner, as aware of that fact as his special guests, came to Rayna as the restaurant was closing and discreetly handed her a key. He whispered to her that he had thought perhaps she and her friend might wish to end their tete-a-tete in private, and he had two apartments upstairs which he occasionally rented. As the other diners were leaving, Rayna led Michael up the stairs at the rear of the building. In the early hours of morning, after they had made love, Michael said impulsively, "I'll remember this occasion forever."

Rayna smiled sadly. "I know you will, my friend," she said, "and so shall I, but you must remember everything that has happened to you here, even the things you'd rather forget."

"Who could forget?" Michael's tone was bitter for the first time that evening.

"You'll remember with your heart," Rayna said seriously, "but I want you to remember with your mind. When you get away from here, look back upon this period in your life with the objectivity of distance and the detachment of a journalist. Tell the world, just as

Albrecht said, what events such as you have seen here have to say about the future. That will be a service. That will keep it all from having been in vain."

Michael nodded and gazed at her with undisguised admiration and wonder. "You're quite a woman," he said simply.

"Try to remember that, too," she said, "when you're far away, and tonight is a distant memory. Know that while there are people like our chief clergyman, Stoecker, there are others, like Albrecht and me, who don't agree with him and what he stands for, and what he wants to make of our country."

"I know," Michael said in response, "and I will remember."

When Rayna was asleep, Michael let himself out and took a hansom cab home. He felt a sense of loss with the realization that he and Rayna would probably never see each other again. Still, he felt gratitude and the bittersweet knowledge that a very special chapter in his life had closed.

Joytl and Batavnia Lermacht, recently wed and just returned from their wedding trip to Vienna, met with Michael for breakfast the following morning. His train was scheduled to leave in the early evening, so choosing to share breakfast allowed them a comfortable margin of time to spend together.

After the amenities had been dealt with, Michael said, "I can scarcely believe that you're still here in Berlin. I thought you'd be living in Zurich again by now, but instead, I'm leaving, and you're staying!"

"Yes," Jotyl agreed, "but not for long. I promised my mother-in-law I'd bring her daughter home safe and sound within six months."

"Do you think you'll be able to tear yourself away that soon?"

"From Berlin?" Jotyl grinned. "No problem. I think we've both seen enough of Chancellor Bismarck's "blood and iron" world to last a lifetime. Once I tie up some last minute loose ends, Tavnia and I will be on our way."

"Good," Michael remarked. "I'll be worried about the two of you until I know you're safely out of the clutches of the Christian Socialists."

"Speaking of that motley crew, I can barely believe I missed all of the excitement. Did that lunatic Bauer <u>really</u> leave a bomb under your desk?"

Michael nodded.

"He really did! The good news is it wasn't set to explode. Apparently I surprised the would-be saboteur before he got that far."

"You were very brave to pursue him!" Batavnia remarked. "He might have killed you."

"That, I think, was the idea." Michael shook his head in disbelief at the memory of his narrow escape. "I knocked him unconscious just as he was drawing his knife to stab me."

"I'm not surprised," said Jotyl. "As I recall, that was one of his standard tricks. It's just too bad you couldn't have had him arrested."

"What good would that have done? His comrade Danishk would have just bailed him out in a matter of hours. Just as he did before. No, I think it was a far more fitting ending to our story that he had to depend on me to see that medical attention reached him in time. His pride will never recover from that."

The three friends ate and talked and laughed together until late in the morning, reminiscing about their school day memories, the carefree escapades, the studies, the exuberant joy and near-calamities, especially Jotyl's long and frightening illness. They tried to pretend that this rendezvous was not a final farewell, but somehow they all knew better. Their lives were turning along different paths. With the Lermachts and Markos and Leah Kolvner living in the same city, it was possible that Michael might one day visit Zurich again, but they would be different people by then, older, wiser. The magic aura of youth and school, of student pranks and post-adolescent perils would be gone forever. They would look back upon this time through the distorting lens of experience and maturity, and inevitably it would have lost much of its luster. Besides, Jotyl was now an "old married man"; he and Batavnia were a couple, while Michael was alone, still a bachelor with no prospects as yet of finding a wife.

* * *

On the train that was taking him home from Berlin, Michael thought of the several wrenching leave-takings that had formed the prelude to his departure. Each had been poignant in its own way, but most difficult of all had been the farewell to Lukas and his family at the railway station. Lukas's emphasis, Michael recalled, had been the perception of what had befallen him and his friends in terms of the past, the history of his people.

Thanks to his own inclinations and the prompting of people such as Albrecht Hoffmeyer and Rayna Jheungwhold, Michael viewed those same events in terms of the future, the impact of Adolf Stoecker and his kind on the thoughts and actions, not only of his contemporaries, but on generations to come. That viewpoint appalled him far more than anything he had already seen or heard. He felt a deep sense of dread for the future of his world.

# PART SIX: THREADS IN A TAPESTRY

May Yahweh bless you and keep you;

May Yahweh let His face shine upon you and be gracious to you!

May Yahweh look kindly on you and give you His peace!

(Numbers 6:28)

# CHAPTER FORTY-EIGHT
## THE SHAPE OF THINGS TO COME

Michael's homecoming was an unexpectedly eventful one. Long afterwards, he would recall that occasion as a time of conflicting positive and negative impressions. After sensing the ominous overtones of his father's letter, Michael was delighted to find his mother up and about, although she had grown visibly more frail. She had lost weight, and her beautiful face, though still youthful, had assumed a grayish pallor that was disturbing. If one looked at her with a clinical eye, as her eldest son Adam often did, one would notice that her lips and nail beds had a faintly bluish cast that betrayed diminished lung function. Her step was still brisk, her movements graceful, but she grew tired easily, and she had developed the habit of retiring after mid day for an afternoon nap.

Another change in the household that Michael noticed at once was the presence of his Aunt Judyth, Elana's youngest surviving sister, whom Michael could scarcely recall having met before. She had visited Elana and Ephraim only rarely, having lived at some distance from Warsaw in the rural town of Zetbec on the Russian-Polish border. Travel was limited for Jews in that sector of the Tsar's empire. The laws of the Pale of Settlement were closely enforced although the bold in heart could find ways to elude them. Aunt Judyth lacked her eldest sister's initiative, her love of challenge, and her flair for adventure. Where Elana had delighted in acquainting herself with the lore and language of her family's gypsy neighbors, Judyth had hung back, declining Elana's frequent invitations tc join her on her visits to the gypsy camp.

As a child, Judyth had grown to love the cobbler's son Aram Mylinski, and after Elana had married and left the family home, Judyth had wed her childhood sweetheart. She had followed him loyally from town to town while he vainly sought to make his fortune. Never more than marginally successful, Aram had died three weeks before, and Aunt Judyth had been forced to sell all their possessions in order to pay his debts. Childless despite three pregnancies that had failed to produce even one live birth, and bereft of all she had held dear, Judyth had written to Elana, on whom she had always depended as a young girl. Elana, ever generous, had enthusiastically invited her widowed sister to come and live with Ephraim and herself, at least until Judyth could decide upon her future.

Their middle sister Miriam had followed Elana's example; she, too, had been fun-loving and adventurous. She had loved the color and the drama of the Gypsy settlement, and had learned to play their music on the violin, though she had never aspired to a professional musical career. Instead, she had married an ambitious and somewhat arrogant itinerant merchant. For the first few years, they had lived a life not unlike that of the gypsies themselves. However, now Hiram Hollbeck was a wealthy man; he and Miriam owned a home in Amsterdam and a flourishing import business that rivaled that of the Kolvner family.

The Hollbecks had visited the Marjzendiaks on several occasions in the early years, but Hiram and Ephraim, thought outwardly respectful of one another, had never been on truly friendly terms. Hiram, inclined to be boastful of his good fortune, had belittled Ephraim, who at that time still occupied a lowly position at the Bank of Grojec. Furthermore, Hiram's attitude toward matters of religion was less than devout, though he never interfered with Miriam in that regard. Understandably, as time passed, the visits had grown rare, though Miriam alone was scheduled soon to arrive for a reunion with her two surviving sisters. Esther, the fourth and youngest of the Grojec girls, had died late in her teens. She had nursed her father in his final illness and had ultimately contracted the "lung fever" that had caused his death. Both lay buried in the Jewish cemetery at Grojec.

Aunt Judyth, though shorter and slightly more plump than Elana, had much of Elana's coloring and her former dynamic energy. She loved to work for hours in the garden, and at the moment of Michael's arrival at Plaz Marjzendiak, she had just entered the house with a basket of flowers in her arms, prepared to arrange them in all the downstairs rooms. She had never before had access to a garden as fabulous as her sister's, and Michael, in later years, would tend to think of his Aunt Judyth as "Judyth of the Flowers".

Another unexpected change was in Ephraim himself. Though he worked as hard as ever, and was still slim and erect of bearing, the years had begun to take their toll. His brown-black hair was now liberally mixed with gray, and wings of white had spread throughout his beard. The furrows in his forehead were deeper, and in the past two years, he had been obliged to wear glasses in order to read. Also, he no longer drove his carriage to work as he had once delighted in doing. Instead, he had hired a driver who also did other chores about the estate. The custom Franz Pietrowski effected as a privilege of his rank, Ephraim accepted grudgingly as a necessary consequence of his gradually diminishing vision.

On his first day back at home, Michael wandered about the estate, noting changes here and there as he went. The house no longer bore the scars of the fire, but the repairs had subtly changed its character. The renovations had added modern touches that were subtly out of sync with the original architectural concept. Even the storage buildings had been changed; living quarters had been added to house a permanent staff, part of whose function was to safeguard the property from vandals and intruders.

Ephraim had grown first cautious and then progressively distrustful as a result of the upheavals of recent years. There was a heavy padlock on the front gate; a gatehouse had been added to accommodate a gatekeeper and his family, and the entire property was enclosed behind a high iron and concrete wall. Previously, only the main house had boasted a partial fence, and that had been more for show than safety. To Michael, that new wall symbolized more than an effort to protect his family's property. It was tangible evidence of Ephraim's growing sense of isolation and alienation from those around him, of his unvoiced desire to escape from his environment, both physical and circumstantial. Ephraim had indeed escaped the ghetto long ago. Now, as a result of the fear and anger arising in reaction to what he had suffered, he had built a self-imposed ghetto of his own. Michael was disturbed by that perception, but he could not dismiss it. He knew his father too well to delude himself that his impression was born of his writer's imagination. Elana's illness had curtailed his parents' social life, and its cause, the fire and the pogrom that had incited that devastating event, had erased Ephraim's former optimistic trust in the future. Ephraim now sought to lock the world outside, except for that part of it in which he was obliged to work and move.

On the Sunday following his arrival, Michael's family attended a wedding. As compared to the nuptial ceremonies of Pola Pietrowska and Pierre Rebaumme, it was a modest one. The bride was a widow, and Erik Pietrowski was a man of temperate tastes and moderate means, who did not like to trade either on his father's reputation or his generosity. Furthermore, though Franz had voiced no overt objections to his only son's choice of wife, neither had he shown unqualified enthusiasm. After all, Magda was older than Erik and her previous marriage had produced no children. What if her marriage to Erik proved equally barren?

Magda continued to work at the bank. She had even been promoted as a reward for her role in bringing to justice the real culprits in the matter of the theft. Franz was compelled to admire her courage, both in that instance and later when, as a result of Erik's repeated proposals of marriage, she had come to Franz and asked to speak with him in private. Franz had been mystified by her request, but had graciously granted her an audience.

When she came to his office, he asked, "What can I do for you?"

Not accepting the chair he offered, but wishing to face him standing on her feet, Magda had gotten immediately to the point of her visit.

"I am uncertain whether or not your son has mentioned his intentions to you," she began formally though not without trepidation, "but he has asked me to become his wife." Before Franz could say anything to interrupt her, Magda raised her hand and plunged bravely ahead with her dissertation. "I love him very much, and I have reason to believe he loves me. But such matters are seldom that simple. Much depends on the feelings of his family. That can make all the difference between a happy, successful marriage and the converse."

"You're quite right, my dear," Franz said without making any further commitment.

"You, sir," Magda went on, "have been most kind to me, and I am appreciative of that kindness. It is partly that which moves me to tell you something now that I had resolved never to reveal to anyone."

Franz was intrigued and puzzled by this somewhat ominous preamble, but said nothing, determined to allow her to continue uninterrupted.

Magda did not mention that she had already divulged her secret to Madam Marjzendiak. She told her story simply and succinctly.

Franz listened intently as Magda revealed her background and the series of circumstances that had led her to her present career. He was impressed by her inherent honesty, especially in view of the commonly held belief regarding gypsies. She said she could not continue to deceive the man who was the father of her husband-to-be, regardless of the consequences. After hearing her out, Franz vowed that her secret was safe with him and that he would not stand in the way of his son's wishes or try to dissuade him from his intentions. However, Franz could not shake off a gnawing fear for his son's future and that of the offspring that might possibly someday bless the marriage.

* * *

The bride was radiant despite her somewhat muted nuptial finery. As a widow, she could not wear bridal white nor a long train. Instead, her gown was of champagne-colored satin, garnished with lace, the creation of Mira Pietrowska's latest dressmaker. Magda had insisted on playing an active role in determining the style of the dress rather than meekly accepting the French woman's directions. The result was a superlative model of the couturier's art. It had a paneled, low-necked bodice topped with a thick lace insert stretching from upper bosom to neck, beset with tiny tasselettes of fine fringe at its border that were held in place by gilded beads. This was the only concession to Magda's gypsy heritage. The skirt was moderately full with a minimum of supporting petticoats, and its rear panel swept the church carpet barely a few inches beyond the length of the other panels as the bride passed down the aisle to meet her bridegroom.

She walked unescorted except for Pola, who was her Matron of Honor, Pola's diminutive daughter Victoirine, who scattered white rose petals in her path, and Pola's elder son Paul, who solemnly carried the wedding ring wired to a satin pillow.

Michael felt vaguely uncomfortable attending a wedding, even a modest one, in a Roman Catholic cathedral. He recalled vividly the impressions his brother Isaak had once confided to him regarding Isaak's sole excursion into a Russian Orthodox church to attend his beloved Mariska's funeral. Today was a joyous occasion, and yet it seemed to Michael strangely out of rhythm. He could not shake off the feeling that the participants seemed peculiarly wooden and unreal. Perhaps it was the length of the nuptial mass, or it may have been the words spoken in Latin, a language the church had chosen because it was a dead language and therefore unchanging.

The reception that followed was impressive and well attended, hosted by the senior Pietrowskis, and executed with impeccable taste. No less would be expected of Mira Pietrowska, whatever her sentiments might be, and in this instance, she carefully kept those sentiments to herself. In her youth, she had heard herself described as "dusky as a gypsy" by certain upper class Polish ladies. The description had been inaccurate; though her hair was extremely dark, her skin was a delicate ivory. Those same ladies had 'cut her dead' because her father owned a factory but not an estate. Having learned that Magda truly was a gypsy, Mira could imagine what her girlhood had been like. Her sympathies were with this determined young woman who loved her son and had the courage to pursue the fulfillment of that love. Magda Laskowska was one of the few subjects on which Mira and Franz did not wholeheartedly agree.

Pola had befriended Magda out of loyalty to her brother, whom she idolized. She was mystified by her husband Pierre's standoffish attitude toward his proposed sister-in-law. After all, Magda's background was only slightly more scorned than his own. Like Pierre, Magda had risen above the stereotypic confines imposed by her origins; she had achieved recognition in a field from which she would ordinarily have been barred. But then Pola's liberal instincts had been shaped by her friendship with Leah, otherwise she would never have married Pierre in the first place.

Both Pola and now Erik had married for love rather than advancement or expediency. She for one was happy with the long term results of her marriage. She hoped the same would hold true for her brother. In the great hall of her parents' estate, Pola Rebaumme looked proudly at her beloved husband and her children, and thanked God for the daring that had led her to brave her father's objections and insist on marrying the partner of her choice. She was pleased that Erik had done likewise. Fortunately, she could not see into the distant future.

* * *

For Michael Marjzendiak, Magda and Erik's wedding day would always stand out in his memory, not because of the ceremony or the reception, but because of the events that followed. By now, winter was in full sway. The high holidays were already passed and the later holiday season, that included both Hannukah and Christmas, with its exhausting round of activities, was approaching. In addition, the family, delighted to have Michael once more at home, planned a belated birthday celebration for him. Aunt Judyth, assuming many of the responsibilities that would normally have been Elana's, rose gladly to the occasion. By a happy coincidence, Aunt Miriam arrived at about the same time, making Elana's joy almost complete.

Only Leah was still absent from the family circle. There were new restrictions imposed by Tsar Alexander III against travelers from Switzerland entering the peripheral provinces. After all, the remnants of the Peoples' Will had set up their headquarters in exile in Switzerland. The intervention of the revered Franz Pietrowski had been required to break down that particular barrier, inasmuch as Leah had taken Swiss citizenship in order to facilitate her musical career. Now, the earliest she would be permitted to come home in this year of 1883 was late December. Throughout the waning days of that year, Elana reveled in the reunion of the rest of her family, and silently counted the days until December 20th when Leah would arrive at last

That year's winter was one of the harshest in recent memory. Heavy storms pounded the countryside day and night, while the winds blew bitterly throughout the area of Warsaw and its suburbs. The schools closed early for their winter recess, and a wave of respiratory infections kept the clinics and hospitals inordinately busy. Adam and Meyhra found themselves working around the clock on more than one occasion, and Meyhra soon fell into the habit of leaving their young son Abrahm at Plaz Marjzendiak, overnight or for days at a time, as the circumstances demanded.

Elana delighted in those times, although she deplored the situation that made them necessary. She loved having her grandson with her even though his inexhaustible energy occasionally tired her. Ephraim also grew quite close to the child during this period, seeing in him the image of Adam at that stage in his development, and reliving with this youngest of his grandsons his own earlier days as a proud father with his firstborn son.

Abrahm was five years old now. He would soon be at the age to begin preparing for his bar mitzvah, and Ephraim took hold of this opportunity to assume a major role in that preparation. Ephraim could not know it then, but that decision was to prove life-saving for both himself and, years later, for Abrahm as well.

Meanwhile, Isaak chose this time to regretfully sever his association with the law firm of Wilshotski, Harnishke and Marjzendiak.

"I've decided to stand for public office," he told his senior partner, Vladymir Harnishke. "Given the present political situation, I think it's only fair that I resign. I wouldn't want the firm or its partners to suffer from their association with me."

"Nonsense, Isaak," Harnishke replied. "You've brought only credit to this firm since you first joined us."

"But times have changed," Isaak persisted. "The Tsar Liberator is long dead, and most of his reforms with him. Surely you see the irony of the fact that the most important reforms he ever initiated were signed into law on the morning of his death. Those misdirected revolutionaries, by assassinating him, overturned the very benefits they'd agitated so long to achieve. Alexander III naturally repealed much of what his father had signed, and things have gone from bad to worse ever since."

"And you think you can reverse that trend by giving up your law practice and moving against the tide of anti-Jewish feeling that this latest Tsar approves?"

"I don't know," Isaak admitted, "but I'll never know if I don't try."

"What office do you plan to seek?"

"The Mayor of Wola is resigning. He's old and his health is failing. That will be a start. The people of Wola are a liberal lot, mostly industrialists and their workmen. I plan to appeal to them, to their sense of equity and justice."

"I wish you well, Isaak," Harnishke stated. "Naturally, I'm disappointed to lose such a valuable colleague, but I'm willing to help your campaign in any way I can."

"Your help," Isaak said, "and your goodwill will be deeply appreciated."

The two men shook hands, and then Isaak turned and left his friend's office with mixed emotions. He felt a keen sense of loss, of bereavement at taking his leave. A major chapter in his life was closing, and he had no foreknowledge of what the future held in store for him. Yet he saw the growing chaos around him, and knew that this was not a time to acquiesce, to meekly accept the tearing down of everything positive that had been achieved during the preceding generation. He strongly believed that one man, at the right time and place, could make a difference. Now he must learn if indeed he was that man.

"I hope you're not too disappointed by my decision," Isaak said later that afternoon to Luvna. It was nearly sundown, and the Sabbath was about to begin.

She embraced him impulsively. "I'm not disappointed at all. It's time we got some new challenge into our lives. Lately, things have been too static, too tame. I knew it couldn't last."

Isaak stared at her in wonder. "Tame?"

Luvna laughed. "Not in the world around us, but privately, yes. A full-time practice with a respected, conservative law firm."

"Where I have always taken the controversial cases."

"And won most of them, to the applause of nearly every intelligent citizen of Warsaw."

"What would you have had me do?"

Luvna lit the Sabbath candles, blew out the taper, and gazed at her husband through lowered lashes. "Something like what you're doing now."

"You're not worried about our future? There's no certainty that I'll win, and if I lose, there's no guarantee that I'll get another position as secure as the one I've just given up."

Luvna moved closer and put her hands in his. "I took the chance of marrying you, Isaak, against my father's wishes, even despite his dying curse. I'm hardly likely to be frightened by the uncertainties of an election,"

Isaak took her in his arms and kissed her. "There's more to it than uncertainty, love. There's real risk. The pogroms could start again at any time."

Luvna nodded knowingly. "They could in any case. Nothing is certain; no one is safe. If you can help to change that, why not try?"

"I love you," Isaak said simply, his hands caressing her swollen belly, feeling the movement of the life growing within her. "I always will."

While they repeated the traditional words their people had spoken for generations to welcome the Sabbath, the sun set, the sky darkened, and night fell.

In another Marjzendiak household, Adam and Meyhra clashed over the excessive demands of his work coupled with the additional hours he was spending on his neurological research.

"One can only do so much," Meyhra said angrily, pacing the floor in his study. "With this epidemic, we're both stretched to the breaking point. You can't continue working around the clock indefinitely."

"But I'm so close," Adam protested. "I know it!"

"Good," Meyhra responded encouragingly, "but give it a rest for now. Give yourself some rest." Her voice broke then. "You'll die if you don't, and what will Abrahm and I do without you?"

"You don't understand," Adam argued.

"I do understand, Adam. I do, believe me. I know you've never completely gotten over Sarah, and Jakob, and baby Jakob. I know you never will unless you can somehow find a breakthrough that will open the secret of the malady that killed both Jakobs." She knelt beside him and took his face in her hands. "But Adam, dearest Adam, you won't find that breakthrough by pushing yourself beyond endurance. You'll simply defeat every dream you hold dear."

"It's you I love, Meyhra," Adam assured her.

"I know that. I'm not jealous of your research. It's an integral part of you. I realize it's something that you _must_ do. I ask only that you pursue it realistically, with some chance of success rather than the certainty of self-destruction." She paused thoughtfully, then added, "Once we're out of this nightmare epidemic, I'll help you all I can. I promise!"

Adam said lovingly, "I can always count on you."

"Of course you can," Meyhra agreed, burying her face against his chest so that he would not see the tears in her eyes. Lightly, her hand brushed the little carousel music box on the desk beside him. It began to play the Hebrew lullaby she recalled from her childhood. The keepsake held so many memories for Meyhra, some joyous, others bittersweet. She held her husband soothingly, and let her mind drift back over the years they had shared, the perils, the traumas, the professional collaboration that had built Adam's medical practice step by step, as well as the tragedy of their lost first child, the revelation of his first love, and the dark secret that had torn her from him. That secret would haunt Adam for as long as it remained a secret, even from the medical profession. Only its solution, and its potential cure, if that were possible, would set him free. And as long as he was held bound by that specter from the past, so was she.

* * *

'Freedom," Ephraim was saying earnestly, "is always the ultimate goal. Freedom of choice, freedom of speech, freedom to think and act according to our own conscience. Freedom to travel from one place to another without fear of being accosted or imprisoned." Ephraim paused and looked directly at Abrahm. "These are freedoms we do not have, but on the other side of the world, in that country I've told you about, the constitution guarantees all its citizens just that. I'm not sure I believe all I've read and heard, but if it's true, living in such a place would be like reentering the Promised Land."

Abrahm nodded enthusiastically. "It would be, wouldn't it, grandfather?" He pondered his own question for a moment. "If it is true, grandfather, why don't we go there?"

Elana, Miriam, and Judyth, seated with Ephraim, Michael, and Abrahm at the dinner table, smiled indulgently at the child.

"Abrahm, dear," Elana commented, "life is never that simple. The country of which your grandfather speaks is thousands of kilometers away. Its citizens have laws that restrict the entrance of foreigners into their land."

"But grandfather says that many people from this part of the world have already gone there, and made homes for themselves."

"That's true, dear," Elana responded, "but I'm certain that it wasn't easy for them."

"Nothing that's worth doing is ever easy," Ephraim said, "but that doesn't mean it should not be done."

"Are you telling Abrahm he should run away instead of standing his ground and fighting back?" It was Miriam who asked the question, no doubt echoing Hiram's sentiments.

"When to fight back against impossible odds," Ephraim answered, "invites extinction, then it is wise to retreat, to seek an alternative course." He glanced briefly at Miriam. "There's no shame in such a strategy. It is the logical thing to do." He seemed to dare her to contradict him.

"What," Judyth wondered, "of the efforts to rebuild a Jewish homeland in Palestine? I understood you favored that effort."

"I favor any effort that holds out the hope of a better life for our people." Ephraim's eyes swept the faces of the members of his family gathered around him. "What I don't approve is the hopeless rebellion we have seen tearing this country apart intermittently for more than 50 years." He turned toward Miriam once more. "You've been lucky, my dear, to have escaped to a civilized country. In Holland, human beings are treated as such. There are no compulsory badges, no invisible wall of hate, no smoldering hostility waiting just below the surface to erupt." He added the last words as he turned his attention to his youngest son, whose account of recent events in Berlin had led to the present discussion.

"I daresay," Michael interjected, "that situation exists to some extent in every country of the world. Some are just worse than others."

"That's rather a grim outlook," Judyth commented. "What of this new Promised Land, if your view is really valid?"

"I don't believe in a new Promised Land," Michael replied. "I did once, but I've learned better. At close range, the most attractive system, which seemed perfect from a distance, loses much of its charm. I don't know which is worse, trying to fight back, accepting what's dealt out, or taking off for parts unknown and hoping to better one's lot in a foreign land whose rules and hidden pitfalls you don't even know."

"Travel has made you cynical, Michael," Miriam remarked archly. "Later on, you must tell me of your experiences in much greater detail."

"They'd bore you," Michael said almost harshly. "I'm sure you've seen much more of life than I have in all your travels, Aunt Miriam. I've only seen a small part of Austrian

Poland, and lived briefly in Switzerland and Germany, while you've visited nearly every major city in Europe." He smiled blandly. "Why don't you bring me up to date instead?"

"I suspect we could have some interesting discussions," Miriam acknowledged. She turned to Ephraim. "Your youngest has matured remarkably, Ephraim." To Michael she addressed her next question. "What do you hope to do in life now that you're home?"

"I shall write," Michael responded. "Meanwhile, if it's possible, I hope to find work on a local newspaper."

"That," Ephraim asserted, "will probably be difficult, son. The current Tsar is squeezing the Vistula Provinces very tightly. Jobs for Jews are very limited just now. However, I could use your help here at home, if that's not too demeaning for you. This place has grown despite the problems that surround it. I can hardly handle my obligations on the Banking Council, my duties at the bank, the running of the mills and factories, and managing the estate all at the same time."

"I'll help, of course, father. You don't have to ask," Michael offered graciously.

Ephraim nodded, extremely pleased. "Thank you, son," he said gratefully, not realizing that the very pressures of which he sought to be relieved were the force that was helping to hold him together in the face of Elana's waning strength.

* * *

That night, a new storm ravaged the city, blowing out windows, uprooting trees and shrubs, and scattering debris throughout the streets of Warsaw and its suburbs. Elana's health declined abruptly after that. She took to her bed with yet another severe cold that soon attacked her already weakened lungs in the form of pneumonia.

Adam did not trust himself to undertake his mother's care alone. He was too emotionally involved. He called in his younger associate, Aaron Hubermeier, to assist him, and Meyhra temporarily moved into Plaz Marjzendiak to act as Elana's private nurse.

Meanwhile, Leah finally arrived from Switzerland. She was appalled when she realized the seriousness of her mother's state of health. She silently cursed anew the restrictive policies of Tsar Alexander III that had kept her away from home for so long when her mother had obviously needed her.

The battle for Elana's life consumed several weeks. These turned gradually into months, and that ongoing confrontation wore down the physical and emotional reserves of her family. It was a process of attrition that took a heavy toll on each of them, but most of all on Ephraim, who looked upon Elana as the mainspring of his life. Winter faded into spring, and for a time Elana improved; she rallied with the change of seasons. The time came when she could sit in her garden, draped in a heavy wool shawl, enjoying the glorious spring sunshine and savoring the fragrance of her beloved roses.

When it seemed she would recover, Miriam returned at last to Amsterdam. However, Leah was distrustful of this latest reversal of what she instinctively recognized as an ongoing downward trend. She wrote to Markos and explained that she would need to remain in Warsaw for at least another month, possibly two months.

Events in Warsaw were not improving. The fear of a new pogrom hung over Tsar Alexander III's far-flung territories as the international political scene grew progressively more stormy. The Tsar's ministers were ever watchful for a scapegoat on whom to blame the Empire's troubles, and in the spring of 1884, those troubles were multiplying geometrically. The Three Emperor's League, that was intended to unite the rulers of Prussia, Austria, and Russia, was proving ineffectual. Meanwhile, the Polish political parties, that sought to revive the spirit of nationalism in the Provinces, were constantly hounded and suppressed. The fact that the most active of these groups, the Polish People's Party, contained a few young idealistic Jews, including a teenaged girl named Rosa Luxemburg, gave the Tsar's advisors the excuse they needed.

In towns and cities throughout the wide sphere of Russian domination, government agents mysteriously appeared, inciting the local laborers to anger against the Jewish migrant workers, men who had been forced off their farmlands by the odious "May Laws," and made to move to urban areas where jobs were dangerously scarce. Almost overnight, violence erupted.

The Marjzendiak family felt no less threatened than their more impoverished co-religionists. Even concrete and iron fences are not impregnable against forceful assault. While Elana fought her brave battle for recovery, Ephraim and his sons and daughter watched events in the surrounding area, and wondered fearfully what would happen next.

# CHAPTER FORTY-NINE
## AGAINST ALL ODDS

"We'll never give up!" It was a shout of angry defiance hurled by what seemed the most unlikely of rebels. She was short, slim, and vulnerable looking, with fine dark hair and pale skin. She was young, only 13, but already she had attained some degree of respect and a lower echelon level of leadership among the student dissidents who followed the ideals of the Polish Peoples' Party. Fortunately, in the turmoil that had surrounded her at the time of the raid by the militiamen, none of those dreaded minions of the Governor-General had paid her much attention. Had they noticed her among the spectators hanging upon the idealistic words of Boleslaw Limanowski, she might have been arrested along with the senior party leaders and the other spectators. At the last moment, some anonymous well wisher had shoved her bodily under a table, and there she had remained, trembling with terror until the vandals and the Russian militia had gone.

Now, an hour later, she stood on the roof of one of the shorter structures in the oldest section of the Stare Miasto, gazing wrathfully at the wreckage and rubble below. Broken masonry and shattered glass filled the streets, along with piles of personal belongings that had been seized and dragged out of private apartments in nearby buildings.

In the past, this sector had been traditionally a part of the old ghetto, but the gates had long since been removed. Most of the more prosperous inmates had availed themselves of Alexander II's reforms and moved to more affluent quarters. Others had taken their places. Refugees of vastly mixed extractions had become interspersed with the remaining Jews, most of whom stayed out of habit or because they owned shops and other businesses in the neighborhood, and wanted to live nearby. Now, thanks to this latest outbreak of looting and wrecking, that incentive had been effectively removed.

As she stared at the desolation below her, Rosa Luxenburg was distracted. The acrid smell of smoke assailed her nostrils. The morbid magnetism of flames, leaping skyward from scattered buildings that had been not only pillaged but torched, caught her attention. Repulsed, she looked away and silently vowed vengeance. If it took her entire lifetime, she would find a way to overturn the power of the Tsar who was the ultimate author of this atrocity. One man, she thought bitterly, should not wield that much influence over the lives of millions of people at a distance of thousands of kilometers. His hatreds and prejudices should not be able to inspire a kindred hatred in others, nor empower them to act on that hatred with such impunity as had been shown today.

Peasants and local bullies, led by the Tsar's secret agents, had devastated the area around her. Their goal had been ostensibly to eradicate the rebel leadership of the Proletariat and of the People's Party, both of whom had headquarters in the Stare Miasto. In that process, they had wrecked the homes and properties of nearly every Jewish and Lithuanian family still living in the "Old City", the Stare Miasto, the first built sector of Warsaw.

Rosa did not live here, though she had come here often, just as she had done today, after school. Her home was in one of the more affluent parts of the city. Her parents did not wholly approve of her political views, and cared even less for her affiliation with the student branches of these political groups. Only her sister Anna sympathized with her sentiments, and even she did not share in Rosa's activities. Today, Rosa felt terribly alone, and somehow, because she had hidden from the militia, and had thus escaped possible arrest, she felt ashamed. She should have been with her colleagues in jail by now, she thought, and probably facing transportation to Siberia. It did not dawn upon her that so heavy a penalty was not likely to be inflicted even by the Governor-General on so young a rebel and a female one as well. She realized that she was fruitlessly brooding over the tangible after-effects of violence, giving way to impotent rage instead of doing something constructive. Further shamed, she attempted to get a firmer grip on her emotions. Abruptly, she wiped away her tears, glanced cautiously about her, and proceeded to climb down from her vantage point and slip away unobserved.

Half an hour later, she was pounding insistently on the door of an attractive home in the "New City" sector. When the door was opened, Rosa was met by a familiar face, that of Luvna Marjzendiak. Rosa was well acquainted with Isaak and his wife since the days before she had entered the Second Girls' High School of Warsaw. She had hidden in the upper balcony of one of the court rooms to watch Isaak plead a case. She had admired him from that moment, and had managed to make friends with him and his wife Luvna in order to gratify her hero worship at close hand.

Luvna was dressed to go out, and her surprise at seeing young Rosa was evident, but she greeted her guest graciously.

"Rosa," she said warmly, and then, taking in the significance of the girl's disheveled appearance, added, "come inside quickly." She glanced up and down the street with apprehension evident in her every movement.

Rosa complied, her gait hampered by the hip injury she had suffered two years earlier. With a trace of bitterness in her voice, she asked, "They haven't come here yet?"

"By 'they,' I take it you mean the militia."

"I do," the girl responded.

"No," Luvna said, and bade Rosa follow her into the salon. Rosa took the chair her hostess offered her.

"Wait here," Luvna said, "I'll bring you something to eat and drink. You look as though you need it."

"I don't want to eat and drink," Rosa said defiantly, pounding her small fists into the chair arm, "I want to fight them, any way I can."

"We all do," Luvna responded. "Don't you think Isaak and I want that, too?"

"But are you really willing to do anything productive, to take any risks?" Rosa looked about her and noticed for the first time the stacked crates and the fact that her hostess's cherished collectibles were all missing from the tops of tables and from the corner cabinet shelves. "You're moving, aren't you? You're running away, looking out for your personal safety now that you've a baby on the way."

Luvna could not mistake the bitter scorn in the young girl's voice. The sound grated on her nerves, and made it difficult for her to maintain her attitude of gracious forbearance, despite Rosa's youth. She rounded on the girl, tempted to address her in the same rude tone; then she relented. The disparity between their respective ages and stations made verbal counter-attack ludicrous. Instead, Luvna laid aside her cloak and bonnet, and took a seat on the sofa facing Rosa's chair.

"I think," Luvna said soberly, "there are a few things you need to understand, my dear. There are many ways to fight a common enemy, whether that enemy is a person, a group, or an idea. And sometimes, ideas are the hardest enemies of all to fight."

"The important thing," Rosa said, "is never to stop fighting. I've made a solemn vow about that."

"So has Isaak," Luvna responded. "He fights in a special way. He works within the system that the tyrants have established, using it against them wherever he finds a way." Before she could continue, Rosa interrupted.

"We need to throw out their system entirely."

Luvna shook her head. "That's a monumental undertaking, and furthermore, it may not be possible. However, Isaak has decided to stand for public office. That's why we're moving. We're going to Wola to live so that we'll be residents of the city for the required number of months before the election."

"Elections," Rosa said derisively, "are useless. The people really have no choice, no say in who governs them, nor by what rules."

"That's just the point," Luvna countered. "If one of the people can accede to a high enough office, then some real progress can be made. The rules just might be changed."

"As long as a Romanov rules in St. Petersburg," Rosa said bitterly, "nothing will ever really change."

Luvna stared at the girl before her, sympathetic but disturbed by the intensity and the cynicism Rosa expressed. Despite the grim realities Luvna knew only too well, the hard core of anger she sensed in this adolescent girl filled her with foreboding. Children in Warsaw were robbed of their childhood at an early age, and forced to become miniature adults. This was true regardless of gender or extraction, though it was probably most true of Jewish children, especially since the violence that had erupted following the assassination of Alexander II. What, Luvna wondered, would become of this girl in the months and years that lay ahead? Would she follow the path of political agitation on which she seemed already to have embarked, or would personal desires and needs sway her in a more conventional direction?

"Wola isn't that far," Luvna found herself saying. "If you'd like, you can always come and visit us there. I'll leave you our new address."

"It might be awkward," Rosa said hesitantly. "I wouldn't want to spoil your husband's chances for election."

"How could a young girl like you do that?"

"I'm a revolutionary," Rosa answered proudly. "We're not widely accepted. Several of my friends were just arrested."

Luvna tensed at that news. "Is your family safe?"

"Oh, yes," Rosa replied. "They're safe. They don't believe in taking chances, or getting involved."

"Rosa, dear," Luvna said earnestly, "they took a chance when they moved to Warsaw. It was far safer in Zamose, where you were born. "

"My father," Rosa responded, "said that opportunities were greater in the capitol city. Now that I've grown up," she added sagely, "I think I know what he meant."

Luvna strove to keep any patronizing tone out of her voice as she said, "The dangers are also greater here. I'm not sorry to be moving outside the city, even if it's only a few kilometers away. Still, it is a risk. If Isaak isn't successful, it's unlikely that he'd be able to open a private law practice on his own at present."

"Because of being Jewish?"

"Mostly that, yes. With the new quota system, we don't know as yet if one more Jewish attorney in so small a city will exceed the nine percent limit. "

"Some day," Rosa said thoughtfully, "things like class and religion will cease to exist. Then, there'll truly be equality."

Luvna never went on her intended errand that day. Isaak, accompanied by Samuel Jedewreski, the man who had once been Adam's teacher and later his partner, came back with a hired van. They set about moving the personal belongings out of the house in which Luvna and Isaak had lived since the year following their marriage. Neither Luvna nor Isaak had taken time to accumulate more than a few prized objects. Their possessions were easily contained in a few boxes and crates and each had only one large suitcase that held their entire store of clothes and accessories. Very few pieces of furniture were their own. The rest had been sold to neighbors and friends who would call for them later, and had been left a key.

Scarcely had they finished packing the van and driven away when the vandals and looters arrived in the area. Several middle class Jews lived there. Some had businesses there as well, and these were the special targets of the assault. The house that the Marjzendiaks had just left was located quite near a block of such shops, and it, like them, was left a pile of rubble. The furniture they had taken with them was all that survived intact. That which they had sold was totally destroyed. The same scene was repeated in a dozen other neighborhoods, though many Jewish homes escaped unscathed, including that of the Luxenburg family. By nightfall, the sky above Warsaw was smudged with smoke and the black residue of charred wood. The air was charged with outrage and laden with the sounds of weeping.

For the present, Luvna and Isaak had narrowly escaped tragedy. A large number of their neighbors had not been so fortunate. Later, when the couple learned what had happened, both were appalled, and what was worse, they feared that the terror was far from over.

The pogroms of 1884 spread to involve nearly every segment of the Russian Empire. Nevertheless, although the Russian economy prospered, her prestige among the powers of Europe declined. She had lost a war with Austria and more recently, another with Japan. Alexander III did not command the respect that his father had, and using the Jews as scapegoats did not solve the nation's problems nor salve her damaged national reputation. True to Peter the Great's predictions, Russia was falling behind the countries of western Europe. Her unwieldy system of government hung about her limbs like a ball and chain, slowing any attempts at progress. Her youth were resentful of the restrictions under which they lived. Her workers were bitter, and her middle class frustrated, while her aristocracy continued to live in an elegant, unreal world, and time, leaving them behind, moved inexorably forward toward the twentieth century.

* * *

The advancing age and ill health of Mayor Vladamir Zygmunt Oslowski, a beloved figure on the local political scene, created a dilemma among the people of Wola. He was a liberal in the truest sense, and as such, was hardly popular with the Russian administration. Yet he had remained in office for nearly 18 years. His secret was simple. He fulfilled and satisfied the needs of the people whom he governed. Wola, an industrial suburb of troubled, turbulent Warsaw, was a peaceful oasis in the midst of storm. This was true despite the city's mixed ethnicity, its increasing number of factories, and its expanding middle and working classes. The nationalistic political parties that flourished in Warsaw had gained no real foothold in nearby Wola. In practical terms, that city was no cause for administrative concern, and so the Governor-General and his staff had ceased to concern themselves regarding it. Wola was an area that could be and was conveniently ignored. The militia had other valid concerns to attend to.

When Mayor Oslowski announced that he would not seek reelection, the citizens of Wola found themselves in a quandary. They were far less political minded than most of their neighbors. In the recent past, as the city had grown in population, paralleling the advance of the Industrial Revolution, the mayor and the City Council had worked harmoniously together. Of course, there were the Russian-appointed council members, but they were native Poles, after all, a carry-over from the days of the Congress Kingdom. Like Oslowski, they had grown older in office, but they had been young when appointed, so that now they were middle aged but still fit and willing to serve.

When the time came for the announcement of prospective candidates for the mayor's office, Isaak Marjzendiak presented his credentials carefully, wording the obligatory statement of candidacy to emphasize the positive and downplay any negative aspects.

Isaak had never attempted to conceal either his origins or his beliefs. But neither did he intend to base his campaign on Jewish interests. Instead, he stressed his commitment to the needs of the working class and the crucial necessity for harmonious interaction between labor and management. He knew that the landowners and several of the industrialist employers might fear or resent this upstart Jewish lawyer, so for them he detailed that he was Polish born and bred, had grown up in Warsaw, and had only left the area for a few years to seek an education, which could not be obtained locally in the face of the quota system that had existed at that time, and indeed still did.

As a matter of fact, the current quotas were even more stringent, and not only did they apply to institutions of higher learning, the number of Jewish physicians, lawyers , university professors, and other professionals who might work within a given community were set by law. Jewish members of the bar in Russian cities had been reduced since late 1881 from twenty-seven percent to nine percent. If his candidacy was unsuccessful, Isaak would find it extremely difficult to establish an independent law practice, even in liberal Wola. As a result, he threw himself whole-heartedly into his campaign for mayor.

The man whom the Russian administration hastily brought forward to oppose him was a Russian-Rumanian self-educated peasant named Boris Youskevitch. He was a foreman, recently promoted, in one of the local factories, a man of the people who was expected to speak the language and gain the confidence of the working population. Pitted against the polished, well-educated Jewish lawyer, saddled with his 'outsider's' image and his non Christian beliefs, the Russians thought their hand-picked candidate would succeed without difficulty. After all, the Poles were known to distrust Jews. Pogroms were easily instigated throughout the Provinces. It was felt in the exalted circles of the administration that no one would dare vote for a Jew in these times.

Boris Youskevitch wore his candidacy like a mantle of unruffled assurance. He had lived in the vistula Provinces for many years, and had learned to speak the Polish and Lithuanian languages fluently. In times of stress, he still lapsed into his native Russian, but then with the Russification that had followed the Rebellion of 1863-64, Polish had become a forbidden language. It was no longer taught in the schools. No contracts or legal documents could be written in Polish. Books, plays, even newspapers in the Polish language were banned. For a time, Alexander II had relented in this regard, but his son Alexander III had revived the old restrictions, so that even public debates involving more than 20 people, must be carried on in Russian.

The laborers particularly resented the enforcement of that regulation. It meant that even when a large group of them gathered for entertainment in a tavern or public house, they could not speak openly in their native language. Certainly, no political rally could be conducted in Polish, and no debate between candidates could proceed except in the official Russian language.

Thinking himself in a position of advantage over his Jewish opponent, Youskevitch challenged Isaak to a public debate before a meeting of the Lumbermen and Cabinet Makers Union, the largest of the legal labor unions in Wola. Legalizing certain of the labor unions had been one reform granted by the Tsar Liberator that Alexander III had not rescinded.

Apprised of the protocol that the debate must follow, Isaak had willingly accepted the challenge. He viewed it as the best way to put his platform before the people, since he knew that in addition to the labor union members, many other citizens would be in attendance. Indeed, Isaak welcomed the opportunity to publicly confront the Russian foreman.

The meeting took place in the early evening on a Friday night, which meant Isaak had to forego the Sabbath services in order to attend. The time had been chosen deliberately by Youskevitch in the hope that Isaak would be obliged to refuse, and to attempt to reschedule the encounter, a move that the Russian intended to refuse. In this, the Russian was fated to be disappointed. Perceiving the foreman's real motive, Isaak elected to adapt to the necessities of the moment. He had decided to go all out in this effort, and he held nothing back.

Youskevitch spoke first, presenting his plans for the city of Wola and its citizens in rather grandiose terms, and proclaiming his endorsement by certain influential members of the City Council. These men, the Russian appointees, were present in the audience. They had given Youskevitch their endorsement because they had no choice. They had agreed to be present for the debate because the Governor-General had sent them each an invitation that was in reality an official ultimatum.

"I speak for the common people of Wola," Youskevitch began expansively. "I am one of you, a laborer who works with his hands. I understand your needs, and I will work for your interests."

At this point, several men who had been previously paid to applaud, earned their stipends by cheering, clapping, and stamping their feet to signal their approval.

"The aristocracy have their own interests, and they will be served by electing a so-called intellectual to office. We don't need the intellectuals with their vaunted education, their money, their influence, and their arrogance. We might as well elect old Pietrowski himself as the son of his toady on the Banking Council. Remember the way that Jew got off at the last minute, and the whole damn scandal was hushed up? If any of us had been involved, you can bet we'd never have got off so easy."

Youskevitch glanced tauntingly at Isaak, but Isaak refused to be goaded into an emotional outburst. He sat calmly silent, only the tightening of his jaw muscles betraying his agitation.

When at last it was Isaak's turn to speak, he rose from his place on the dais and crossed to the podium. For a moment, he looked at the sea of expectant faces before him, some encouraging, some hostile, and others merely curious. His friend and advisor, Samuel Jedewreski, was among them. Toward the back, he saw a face which looked vaguely familiar, and yet he could not place it.

"I appreciate the opportunity to speak with you this evening," he began, his voice carefully neutral. "As some of you already know, I was born only a few kilometers from where we are now. I grew up in Warsaw, and as a youth I was a laborer, just as many of you are. The lumber mill that still stands at the junction of the Wrepz and Vistula Rivers was my place of employment."

"Did you work for your father?" It was Youskevitch who asked the question.

"No, sir, I did not," Isaak replied. "At that time, the mill was owned by the Wishnieski family. It was later bought by Madam Pietrowska who then sold it to my father. That was at the time when Jews were only just beginning to be able to own property. Now, although all of us have lost many rights we once enjoyed, every man who can afford it can still buy his own plot of land. I for one want to maintain that right for us all." He cleared his throat and glanced meaningfully at Youskevitch. "I have no secret agenda, no private interests to be served. But I do know what it means to work with my hands, to live under the threat of danger from factory equipment. In those days, I even helped to design safety measures for the men working with the large power saws that cut the trees into lumber."

"I can testify to that," a man said from the back of the room. "My father was your foreman, Joseph Skilrjet." There then was the answer to Isaak's unasked question.

Isaak lifted his hand in greeting. "How is Joseph?"

"He's as well as a crippled old man can be," Friedreich Skildrjet answered tersely. He was making it clear that he was not in collusion with Isaak. In fact, until that evening, the two men had never met. Friedreich had been raised by his mother. She and Joseph had lived apart for many years and had only been reunited in the latter part of their lives.

"Many of you also know," Isaak continued, "that I left Warsaw to attend school. When I finished my training, I came home to practice law. Many of you who are here tonight have been my clients. Those of you whom I have represented know me and my record. "

"Here, here!" It was a few isolated voices at first, but then the chant built to a louder timbre, a more unified sound. The men who were its' source constituted a majority of those present.

Isaak raised his hand for silence. "My background is law, and labor. I believe those are fit credentials for a man who seeks to govern and help guide a town of industrialists and laborers. However, only you can decide if I'm right. But I feel I should also tell you that to me 'the law' means law and order. Change is inevitable. It's part of nature. We can play a role in shaping that change, and by so doing, we can benefit from it. But civilization and anarchy cannot co-exist. Progress is a building process, not a tearing down. It's my hope that all of you, that all of Wola and I can work together to attain some degree of progress for ourselves, for our city, and in some small way, for our country."

It was not truly a speech, although that is what it had started out to be. Instead, it became a simple statement of what he felt, what he had felt as a young man longing to better his station in life. Those same sentiments had inspired him as an eager law student with ideals of justice and rectitude. The same longings had filled him as a son wanting to see his father achieve his dream of owning land in a place where no Jew had ever owned property before. He had seen the impossible made possible, and standing there on that dais, Isaak Marjzendiak began to believe that he could see that miracle happen again.

The applause that greeted him was long, loud, and gratifying. Conversely, the envious hatred in his opponent's eyes was naked and absolute. Isaak shuddered involuntarily. The thought came unbidden to his mind that someone had walked on his grave.

\* \* \*

Three months later, during a family dinner at Plaz Marjzendiak, as Isaak waited tensely for news of the outcome of the election, his family attempted to reassure him.

"Given the choice of you or Youskevitch, there can be little doubt which one they'll vote for," Michael asserted with more confidence than he truly felt.

"You're a native born Pole," Ephraim added, "not some imported rabble-rouser brought in by foreign dignitaries."

"But won't the people be afraid to vote for someone Jewish in these times?" Leah, of all the family, was the least optimistic about her brother's chances of success. The obstacles placed in the way of her coming to visit her mother had depressed her, and events since her return had only added to her feeling of gloom.

"They'll be even more reluctant," Adam said "to vote for a Russian. This is the local workers' one chance to express their true feelings. They know you've been their friend, pleaded their cause in court time after time. They're sure to come through."

"I wish I shared your certainty," Isaak responded, trying not to allow himself to make too great an emotional commitment to winning against the odds he faced. "Then, too, there are the landowners. They make up a small but significant minority. And they're against me."

"Even if you do win, Isaak," Elana wondered, "how can we be certain the votes will be tallied honestly? The Russian Magistrate is the final authority in case of a dispute."

"Only if it gets to that point," Adam assured his mother. "If there's a clear majority, there'll be nothing to dispute."

"It'll also be the first time in memory that a Jew has ever won a public office in this area," Adam said. "In Krakow, of course, things are different. But here..." There was no need to finish the statement. They all knew only too well the bleak history of this part of Poland since the partitions had begun in the previous century.

"If you had seen the enthusiasm of the men at some of the rallies," Luvna said cheerfully, seeking to dispel the mood of gloom she could sense around her, "you'd be much more hopeful. I went to two of them," she added, but Isaak interrupted.

"Over my protests. A political rally is no place for a woman, especially a pregnant woman!"

"Well, I can assure you," Luvna asserted, "having watched the proceedings personally, that Isaak has a strong base of popular support. Those men virtually hated Youskevitch. Among themselves, they called him names like 'Russian pig' and 'Tsarist spy.' Remember, this election is a very local issue. It will attract little attention from the authorities."

"At least at first," Isaak said levelly. "Of course, if I should manage to be elected, then they might start paying attention. Very pointed attention. These are still the vistula Provinces. It's been more than twenty years since we've had the autonomy of the Congress Kingdom."

"I never thought I'd see the time," Ephraim stated, "when I'd think of those as the good old days. When we were living through them, I prayed for them to end. Lately, I've wished we could go back in time to the early days of the Tsar Liberator. Then there was at least hope, and a breath of fresh air. Wielopolski seemed to promise so much. It hardly seems possible that he delivered so little, and ended by precipitating the very rebellion he had promised the Tsar he'd prevent."

"Promises can be hard to keep," Isaak observed dryly. "Political promises are the hardest of all to fulfill. Let's hope, if I get the chance, I'll be luckier than Marquis Wielopolski."

Samuel Jedewreski, at age 70, was a vigorous man with a purpose. He no longer practiced medicine. He had left that field of action to younger men with stronger nerves and steadier hands. But when Isaak, the younger brother of his friend and former partner Adam Marjzendiak, had decided to enter politics, Jedewreski had offered to assist his campaign. It was precisely the kind of challenge that the retired physician welcomed. Now he had important news to convey, news of the utmost urgency. He could hardly wait for the hired coach to reach the Marjzendiak estate. The gatekeeper seemed shod with lead. His hands on the lock moved like frozen molasses. Jedewreski almost wanted to drive the horses the last few meters himself.

Judyth Mylinska answered the knock at the door, and was startled at the abrupt manner of the elderly man standing there. She and Jedewreski had not met until that moment.

"Let me in," he all but shouted. "I have brought important news!"

Ephraim and Isaak rose from the table as one when the elderly physician entered the dining room

"Come in, Samuel," Ephraim said warmly. "Shalom, my friend. What is this important news?"

Samuel took Ephraim's hand in both his own, momentarily too overcome to speak. Then he turned to Isaak.

"My boy," he said, "today you have made history. Wola is a small city, but to become its mayor is a giant step for one of us, and never more than now."

Isaak was astonished. He had hoped, he had worked and dreamed, and prayed, but he had never quite fully believed he would succeed, especially this first time. "But the landowners," he said in wonderment. "They didn't trust me!"

"The landowners," Jedewreski said, "are a strange lot, clannish and narrow minded, but they hate foreigners."

Ephraim smiled knowingly and nodded his head in silent agreement.

The entire family surrounded Isaak, all of them eager to embrace him at once. He had won against seemingly insurmountable odds, and they were jubilant. Yet there was a flavor of ambivalence in their rejoicing. When, each of them wondered, would the next blow fall?

## CHAPTER FIFTY
## TIGHTROPE

Isaak Marjzendiak, Mayor of Wola, sat in his new office, reading and re-reading the note that had been delivered anonymously to his secretary. It was signed with initials only. "L.W.," and was couched in terms that were intriguing, to say the least.

"Honorable Mayor:

It is necessary and urgent that we become more closely acquainted. It would be advantageous to all parties if we could meet on neutral ground and privately."

So the letter ran in part, and ended with a promise that the letter's author would again contact the Mayor for details of the meeting.

Isaak turned the letter over in his hands, troubled by conflicting emotions - curiosity and concern. L.W. must stand for Ludwik Warynski, he reasoned. Small wonder that Warynski did not wish to come openly to the City Hall of Wola. Though no magistrate had issued a warrant officially ordering Warynski's apprehension, almost certainly, he would be arrested if he were recognized in a public building by a member of the militia. Only the fact that he had been absent from Warsaw during the recent assault on the Stare Miasto had saved him from meeting that fate already.

Warynski made many such trips throughout Austrian and Russian Poland, speaking and working on behalf of Proletariat, the party he had founded. He obviously considered himself a patriot and a revolutionary. Yet it was well known that he did not espouse the nationalistic goals of Boleslaw Limanowski's rival Polish Peoples' Party. Limanowski, flamboyant, brilliant, and charismatic, had deliberately tailored his party's program to appeal to all levels of Polish society. By contrast, class struggle was Warynski's ruling principle, and the Polish working man was his prime objective. Naturally, he wanted the economic and personal support of the affluent. He needed their largesse, but the working class' were the backbone of his program, and he identified with their needs. The differences between these two men were reflected accurately in the respective parties that each led. Both these groups had policies widely divergent from that of the outlawed and now exiled Peoples' Will, whose base of operation, formerly in St. Petersburg, had relocated to Zurich.

Nonetheless, only a few years ago, the three revolutionary organizations had worked in cooperation with one another. On one occasion, before the assassination of Alexander II, one of Warynski's lieutenants had even signed a pact with the Peoples' Will while his superior was away from Warsaw. Now, that pact was a source of embarrassment and concern for Warynski. It was also one of the major reasons that he worked underground, constantly in hiding from the militia, obliged to seek clandestine meetings and to avoid large public gatherings as much as possible.

And now, Isaak reflected ironically, Warynski wanted to see him. Politics often forges strange alliances, but this was one alliance he could ill afford to enter into. After all, he had only just won the election. In the early days of his law practice, he had occasionally attended rallies given by certain underground political groups. Good luck and caution had enabled him to avoid being tarred with their brush. Now, caution was more crucial than ever. This, he knew, was only the beginning. In his mind, he could picture the inevitable procession of favor-seekers who would soon appear, figuratively or actually, on his doorstep. If he yielded to one, the others would swarm like a hive of bees around him. The various warring factions, struggling for power in the rugged netherworld of the political underground, would come to him for support, for a favored position over their rivals, for privileges, even for money since his father was a banker.

As mayor of an important industrial city, Isaak would be under constant scrutiny by the Russian administration. As a Jew holding public office, he would be mistrusted, misconstrued, and publicly maligned. He owed it to his people and to his family, as well as to all those who had believed in him and voted for him, to carry out the duties of his office in as exemplary a fashion as possible. One major motive for his candidacy, one he had not discussed with anyone outside Plaz Marjzendiak, had been to safeguard his family estate. This had seemed a necessary precaution once the friendly, aging, former mayor had retired. Another motivation had been the fact that, with the diminishing quotas for Jews in the practice of law, he could foresee that soon he would have no available means of earning a living. For all these reasons, he might meet with the notorious political leader, if circumstances permitted, but he would make no commitment to either Warynski or to Proletariat.

After lengthy and secret negotiations, the meeting took place in the basement room of Old Salzburq, a picturesque restaurant on the outskirts of Wola. Samuel Jedewreski accompanied Isaak. Ludwik Warynski came alone and in disguise. The noted political activist had allowed his beard and sideburns to grow long. He wore a hat not unlike those of members of the ultra Orthodox Hasidic Jewish group, and a long dark frock coat. The restaurant's basement area was furnished to resemble a beer garden. If the three men were observed enjoying beer and cheese at their obscure corner table there, they could easily be mistaken for three Jewish friends animatedly arguing a point of Talmudic principle. The setting was just right, since a group of non-citizens might choose such an out-of-the-way place to conduct their private debate.

After the usual opening pleasantries, the talk moved swiftly to the critical issues.

"According to your correspondence," Isaak began, speaking softly, "we have some urgent matters to discuss. I'm afraid you have the advantage of me, Mer Warynski. I don't know what those matters are."

Warynski gazed pointedly at the new mayor. "Are you quite sure of that?"

"That's a strange question," Jedewreski interjected.

Isaak kept his temper by a stern effort of will. "How could I know your desires in advance, sir?"

"Considering your history," Warynski replied, "I would have thought we had a great deal in common."

"Apart from the fact that we were both born and raised in Poland," Isaak responded, "what other factors have you in mind?"

"You disappoint me, Mayor Marjzendiak. I represent the dispossessed, the uncompensated, the traditionally abused. In other words, the laborer. Since you were once of that group, I hoped you would understand. Then, too, there's the collective history of your people - again, by tradition, dispossessed and abused." He grinned conspiratorially. "Wola is a city of industry, a fertile field for exploration."

Isaak sat very straight, his voice now scarcely above a whisper. "Exploration or exploitation? Surely you don't wish me to believe that you expect me openly to approve your political activities in my city? That would be to presume me a fool, and fools make poor allies!"

Warynski nodded approvingly. "Well said, my honorable mayor. The Governor-General could hardly fault that response."

"Was my active support of your policies truly what you had in mind," Isaak inquired, "when you arranged this meeting?"

"Surely not," Jedewreski remarked. "Not in these times."

Warynski paused only momentarily, taking a generous sip of his beer. "Actually, I envisioned a quiet talk between gentlemen of similar motives and desires."

"My desires," Isaak responded, "are a private matter. My motives are to fulfill the duties of the office to which the people of Wola have elected me. I've no intention of betraying them. To bring down the wrath of the Russian administration on their collective heads would be the worst possible betrayal."

"A pity you see things in that light," Warynski said blandly. "I'd hoped you and I could be friends."

"Mer Warynski, this conversation is not about friendship. It's about political expediency, about class struggle, and rebellion. You and your colleagues have some rather notorious associates. If you or they were to become conspicuously active in my city, it would mean disaster for Wola. I'm not about to lend my approval to such a scenario."

"And if the intellectual Mer Limanowski were to approach you, once he's released from prison, would your response be the same?"

Isaak pondered that question only for a moment. "Assuming he'll be released, which is doubtful at present, yes, my answer to him would be exactly the same. Wola is a prosperous, growing industrial community. Its labor force takes pride in their work. Its revenues have burgeoned along with the growth of the entire Empire's economy. The people here have gained from being part of that economy. I don't intend to jeopardize that." He paused for emphasis. "I'm not proposing to transform the city into a police colony, and I cannot regulate things of which I'm unaware. But to openly cooperate with an illegal organization would be suicide, both for Wola and for me."

"I see," Warynski responded, finishing his beer. "Your attitude is not unexpected. In some ways, it's quite commendable. I pride myself on being adept at communication, Mayor Marjzendiak. I think we understand each other very well. I'll try not to place you or your city in jeopardy."

Isaak gazed at Warynski, his eyes seeming to probe the other man's mind. "Is that a promise, Mer Warynski?"

Warynski extended his hand, but Isaak did not take it. "A promise, Mayor Marjzendiak. I'm known to be a man of my word."

With that, he stood and bowed formally. Isaak and Jedewreski rose also. Without further exchange of words, the three men left the restaurant. Warynski vanished abruptly into the shadows as soon as he was outside. Isaak and Samuel Jedewreski tarried a few moments to exchange opinions regarding the encounter just concluded.

"He's more of an intellectual than he likes to admit," Jedewreski observed. "He prides himself on this facade of being one with the common man, but he's as educated as you and I. Do you believe he's honest in what he said?"

Isaak nodded. "He's basically honest, but he can still be a very dangerous man. However, as long as there's is no warrant issued for his arrest, I can't deny him access to the city's streets unless, of course, he openly violates the law."

"So, if he's safe to pursue his own goals anyway, why set up this elaborate charade to ask your permission for something you obviously can't permit?"

Isaak smiled wryly. "He wanted my assurance that he won't be persecuted as long as he stays virtually underground."

Jedewreski shook his head. "I'm not sure I understand."

"He also wanted to be sure I won't play favorites with any of his rivals. In both respects, he got his wish, but we've not seen the last of Mer Warynski. Quite the contrary, I think we've just seen the battle lines drawn."

That meeting was to prove an important milestone in Isaak's political career. In some ways, it set the tone of his term as mayor. He must not be perceived as subversively permissive by the administrative hierarchy. At the same time, he must not seem proRussian or oppressive to the common people. It would be a difficult tightrope to walk. Tonight he had taken the first step along that perilous pathway.

The later months of 1884 saw a decline in anti-Jewish incidents. Alexander III had not reversed his anti-Semitic policies. However, for the present, his attention had been directed elsewhere. There were economic and civil problems at home. St. Petersburg seemed every day to be more like an armed camp. It was surprising how effectively the People's Will managed to pursue its goals at long distance. Assassination attempts and disruptive incidents continued to occur despite the most stringent precautions. In Kiev, the Governor-General was murdered.

This event was followed by mass arrests and hangings. However; no Jews were identified among those who were apprehended, so that the local authorities were given no excuse to pursue and persecute the Kiev Jews. The quotas were not relaxed, nor were petty torments abolished, but for the present, Jewish lives and property were granted an unofficial respite from unprovoked violence. It seemed as though some member of the Tsar's Advisory Council had finally grasped the principle of cause and effect, and perceived that unprovoked attacks can provide the provocation for forceful resistance and bitter revolt, with costly results for the Empire.

Late in the fall of 1884, Luvna gave birth to her first child, a son named Johann. It seemed that in this time of uncertainty, the Marjzendiak family was bringing forth only sons. First Adam, then Leah, and now Isaak had all produced a new generation of male offspring, almost as though some natural wisdom within their biological mechanisms was creating an army of potential soldiers for the family's defense. To Luvna, the birth of her son ended a long period of private but painful self-recrimination. At last she could feel that she was no longer being punished for causing her father's death. When she had finally decided to follow the dictates of her heart and marry Isaak, her mother and all her in-laws had rejoiced that she had put that tragic episode behind her.

The human mind and spirit, however, are not that easy to persuade. Only when Johann was born, whole and perfect, did Luvna herself believe that Adonai had forgiven her willful, prolonged and passionate transgression of His law. Only then did the terrible image of her father, berating her as a whore in the very moments following her physical union with the man she loved, finally recede from her memory.

In the days that followed Johann's birth, the time-honored rituals attendant upon the birth of a male child were enacted. The Chair of Elijah in the synagogue at Wola was once more utilized by the rabbi to perform the rite of circumcision. Afterwards, the family celebrated with food and drink in the modest but attractive, newly-built house that Isaak and Luvna now called home.

To Isaak, this event, occurring within months of his election as mayor, constituted the closure of a circle that had begun more than 20 years earlier. He recalled his restless youthful ambitions, his angry impatience with the restrictions that were the consequence of his heritage, his frustrated love of Mariska Wishnieski, with its tragic outcome. All these seemed to have come to resolution in this climatic period of his life. He was 43 years old. As he held his infant son in his arms and beheld the serenely beautiful face of his wife, he knew a sense of fulfillment and of peace that had not been his before. All that the Lord had denied and delayed in his life had now been balanced with a fullness that brought to mind the words of David's Twenty-Third psalm. Indeed, his cup ranneth over.

With the end of 1884, winter came once more to the northern sector of the vistula Provinces. With it came a recurrence of the epidemic of pulmonic infections that had brought so much suffering to the area's population the year before. Elana, scarcely fully recovered from the siege of pneumonia that had so depleted her physical resources on that prior occasion, now fell victim to an even more serious episode of the same complaint. From this illness, despite all that her eldest son and his colleagues tried to do for her, she could not seem to improve.

Early in January of 1885, the family members gathered to be with her in the closing days of her life. Even Leah was much more readily able to obtain an entrance permit to the Vistula Provinces than had been the case a year earlier. Part of the reason may have been that she was concluding a tour of cities in France when word came by telegram that she was urgently needed at home. Visitors' permits were easier to obtain from starting points in France, the country still greatly admired by Russia.

Elana's sister Miriam also returned to Warsaw in order to be with Elana one final time. Though Ephraim's letter to her did not specifically state that Elana was dying, the words that he did not write were more eloquent than those he did. Reading between the lines, Miriam fully expected the worst when she arrived at Plaz Marjzendiak.

Instead, she found Elana awake and sitting up in bed, her shoulders covered by a heavy shawl and a book in her hands. The room was oppressively warm and humid thanks to several towel-wrapped steaming kettles placed strategically on tables around the bed. The windows were closed, though sunlight streamed cheerfully through the light, crisp curtains.

"Dear sister," Elana exclaimed and reached out to embrace her younger sister.

Miriam knelt beside the bed and took Elana in her arms, noticing with alarm how thin and frail she appeared, and how much she seemed to have aged in this past year-and-a-half. Her hair was still bright red-gold, though the edges were touched with gray. Her skin was still fine-textured and translucent like expensive china, but it was stretched tightly over the bony framework of her face. Her features looked pinched and worn, her mouth drooped at the corners, and there was a bluish cast to her lips that seemed to deepen even as Miriam gazed at her face.

Miriam began nervously rearranging the pillows on her sister's bed, smoothing the sheets, trying to make Elana more comfortable.

Finally, Elana said firmly but gently, "Stop fussing, dear, and sit down. You're making me nervous. It's too warm in here to move about so much. But I need the steam to breathe." A prolonged fit of coughing cut short further conversation and afterwards, Elana was too weak to do anything other than lie back and rest. Miriam sat beside her, holding her hand until she slept, tears and memories flooding the younger sister's eyes and mind respectively.

During this time, Mira Pietrowska, alerted by her husband to the serious nature of her neighbor's illness, set aside an hour in the late morning of a relatively mild January day to pay an unannounced visit to Elana. An ominous sense of dread came over her when she learned that the object of her visitation was still in bed. Judyth admitted her, once she realized who it was who had come to call, and announced Elana's guest with a show of respect which she felt was appropriate to Mira's station.

"Dear," she said, "you have a distinguished visitor."

"Not at all," Mira interjected. "I'm Elana's next door neighbor. We're old friends."

Elana moved to sit up to greet her neighbor.

"Do come in, Mira," she said in welcome. "How thoughtful of you to visit me. I wish I were better able to receive you."

"I wish I had known sooner how ill you still were. I had thought you were much better by now."

"For a while, I was," Elana acknowledged. "The spring and summer are my best seasons. When winter returns, my health seems to take a turn for the worse. This winter has been the most destructive for me. I seem to have no strength left, and breathing grows daily more difficult, more painful."

This recitation deeply distressed Mira, to whom illness had always been a formidable and frightening adversary. Elana's pallor and the drawn appearance of her face caused Mira to cringe inwardly all the while she kept an encouraging smile upon her face.

"My dear, I brought you some thick soups and puddings to bolster your energy. I hope they tempt your appetite. You've grown truly thin just since I saw you last."

"I'm often not very hungry," Elana responded. "But Judyth is a good cook. She tries her best. I'm just not a very cooperative patient."

"One never blames the patient, my dear," Mira said soothingly, "just as those teachers of which I've read never blame the pupil if he fails to learn. The teacher just needs to try harder."

"As you must know, Mira, my lungs have never been the same since the fire."

"Yes," Mira admitted. "I've often suspected as much, though no one else has put it into words."

"The doctors are doing everything possible," Elana stated. "Yet, smoke and fire-damaged lungs can only respond so much." Elana looked levelly at her guest. "We've all had to accept the fact that I'm dying."

Mira rose from her chair at the bedside and knelt to put her arms around Elana.

"You must not surrender so easily, Elana. In a sense, we are all dying, slowly. The point is to keep death at bay as long as we can, by every means at our disposal. One must not give up hope!"

"Except," Elana cautioned, "when hope is an exercise in futility that saps the energies of those we love, and when it hinders our own preparation for the inevitable."

Mira shook her head vehemently. Her eyes swam with tears.

"No!" she said. "No! You mustn't talk that way, or even think that way. Hope is always worthwhile. It's what God gives us to live by."

Elana took Mira's face in her hands, trying to console her.

"Faith, Mira. Faith is what we live by. Job retained his faith, even in the face of what he believed to be impending death."

"But Job lived," said Mira. "And so will you."

"Only for as long as Adonai wills it," Elana responded.

For several moments, Mira sat silent, aware that she dared not pursue this line of thought any further.

"Is there anything I can do, anything you want or need that I can get for you?" She desperately wanted to feel needed, and Elana sensed that clearly.

"If you could, perhaps, continue to keep an eye on my garden, as you did when we first came here, that would give me peace. Judyth is wonderful at the basics, but you are an expert with roses."

Mira's face lighted at these words.

"Oh, but of course," she agreed readily. "It would be a pleasure to see that the rose garden and all your exotic plants are well maintained. I won't send the gardeners. I'll come myself. I promise."

Elana was growing more tired by the minute, but she felt relieved to know that she had made Mira feel more at ease, and at the same time had helped to lighten the burden of her sister Judyth.

"Thank you, Mira," she said breathlessly. "I truly appreciate that. Now, I think I'd better try to rest a bit."

"Of course," Mira agreed. "I'll just stay here until you fall asleep. And if you think of anything else I can do, don't hesitate to send for me. You know how close Franz and I feel to you and Ephraim."

Elana nodded contentedly.

"Yes," she said, "I know." And on that note, she lay back upon the pillows of her bed and slept.

* * *

When Leah reached home, she went straight to her mother's room. Ephraim was with Elana, and Leah was overwhelmed by the surge of emotion that shook her as she saw once more these two beloved people who had shaped and guided her life from infancy. She recalled with nostalgia the first memories of her father; she had twisted her tiny fingers through his thick dark beard and he had let her hold him thus, her prisoner, while she stroked his face with her other hand, exploring this imposing phenomenon that responded to the name of "Papa". She remembered, too, how she had loved to brush her mother's hair, and how mature and honored she had felt when she was first allowed to do so.

Close physical contact with those she loved had always been important to Leah. The need to touch them both was strong in her now. She went to Ephraim and put her arms around his neck.

"I'm glad you're home," he said softly, and she felt rather than heard his relief at the knowledge that the authorities had not kept her away too long to see her mother again.

Elana was asleep as Leah sat down by her bed and brushed a stray lock of hair away from her face.

"You're tired, Papa," Leah said. "You go and rest for a while, and let me sit with Mama."

Ephraim shook his head dejectedly. "I may not have much time left to spend with her," he said. "I can hardly believe what Adam and Samuel say is true." He referred, of course, to the doctors' pronouncement that Elana, who had successfully endured the previous similar sieges of infection and congestion of her weakened lungs was, on this occasion, unlikely to recover.

"I know," Leah responded, "but you must still rest. It won't do Mama any good for you to get sick as well." She patted his hand affectionately. "Go and rest. I'll come and get you in a little while. I'd like to be alone with her now."

Reluctantly, Ephraim left the room, his gait and manner reflecting his weariness and his resignation to the inevitable. Leah sat watching her mother's face in repose. She had admired that face throughout every stage of her life. To her, it seemed little changed. In sleep, it was agelessly beautiful, free of anxiety, and relieved of the discomfort Elana experienced now with almost every waking breath.

"I love you, Mama," Leah whispered, as she held her mother's hand. "We've always been able to talk with each other. Even now, I feel as though you can hear me even in your sleep, and I'm sure you're thinking as I am. What will become of Papa without you?"

Leah woke with a start, shocked to find she had dozed. Elana's hand was still clasped in hers, but now Elana's eyes were open, and she was gazing lovingly into Leah's face.

"I knew you'd come in time. I just knew." Elana paused for breath. "I'm glad you're here," she added, unconsciously echoing Ephraim's words. "Your father will need you now. Adam and Isaak are wonderful men. Even Michael's grown up now, but Ephraim will need a woman near him when I'm gone, at least at first." She paused and had to cough and wipe her mouth before she could go on. "Judyth means well, but somehow, she and Ephraim don't seem to really talk to each other. She's a bit afraid of him, and he doesn't understand her."

"It will be all right, Mama," Leah reassured her, but Elana shook her head.

"I don't think it will, dear. Judyth is alone in the world, but she's proud. She'd never beg him to let her stay on, once I'm no longer here, and he won't ask her to, even though he needs her." Elana paused to catch her breath, then looked at Leah sadly. "Once you go back to Zurich, and you must take care of your own family, this house won't run itself."

"If Aunt Judyth were to stay," Leah said thoughtfully, "that would solve both their problems, and put your mind at ease."

Elana nodded, stifling a cough. "It would," she admitted. "That issue decided, and knowing that Michael is settled like the rest of you are, is really all I ask of God before I..." Coughing stopped any further words, and Leah noted that her mother's skin had taken on a grayish hue.

"Don't worry about it, Mama," Leah said soothingly. "I'm here. I'll do all I can to help."

Elana smiled and lay back, obviously exhausted by the effort that so much talking had cost her. Soon, she was again asleep.

Michael entered the room a short time later, but Leah silenced him, trying to assure that her mother would rest.

Michael beckoned her outside into the corridor. When she had closed the door, he asked, "How is she?"

Leah shook her head, tears swimming in her eyes. "She's even worse than I feared before I came, and she's growing rapidly weaker. Oh, Michael," she whispered, "we're losing her. It doesn't seem possible, and yet it's true."

Michael embraced his sister in an effort to comfort her. Because he was the youngest, Leah had always seemed to him a second mother, but Elana had been the anchor of the entire family, the heart and soul of the household. Her beauty and strength had seemed ageless and indestructible. And now all that was slipping away.

Leah started suddenly as memory flooded through her. "I promised to call Papa."

"He's asleep," Michael said.

"He won't want to sleep with mother growing worse," Leah responded. "Would you stay with her while I call him?"

"Of course," Michael agreed, taking up his post beside his mother's bed. He sat there, gazing at Elana's face, still so beautiful in repose, so mysteriously ageless. He also knew that when she awoke, every breath would be an effort that would leave her tired and spent.

"If only there were something I could do," he whispered, "to make this easier for you." He didn't expect a response. He had said it so softly that he was certain she could not have heard him. Yet her eyes opened, and she smiled.

"There is," she said, "Pray for me, my son, my last born living child. And later, afterwards, when you think of it, visit me sometimes, and bring me flowers." She paused to breathe, and the fine puckered lines appeared between her brows. "I know that's not usually our custom, but the flowers are so lovely in our garden, and I do so enjoy them when they're in bloom." She reached up and clasped his hand in hers. "That will be our secret, a language that only we will share. And when you find that special one who claims your heart, be sure to bring me flowers then, when you and she are one. That will make my heart laugh and sing for joy."

That was the special concern that filled her with fear as she came closer to the end. Of all her children, he, her youngest, was still alone. He, of all her children, had not yet found his place in life. She fell asleep again still holding his hand.

When Ephraim returned, Michael stood and moved aside, surrendering his place to his father, watching as the older man resumed his vigil at the bedside of his life-long love. A few whispered words passed between husband and wife, but her strength was waning rapidly and talking took a heavy toll on the energy that still remained to her. She knew that those she loved had gathered near her. She sought to acknowledge each with a glance, a tired but affectionate smile. But much of her effort was confined to simply drawing the next breath. Her lungs, scarred and damaged by the smoke from the fire that had almost destroyed her home, would not be able to fulfill their allotted task much longer.

Elana awoke fitfully several times that day, but she was too weak to say anything more. Toward nightfall, she lapsed into coma, and the family members took up an all-night vigil in her room, their heads bowed, their lips moving in barely audible prayer.

Early in the morning, just after dawn, she rallied briefly. She opened her eyes once more and recognized those around her. She smiled, trying to sit up, and whispered a final endearment to Ephraim, who sat with his arms around her. "I'll never truly leave you, my dearest one," she said, so softly that he had to strain to make out the words. "Never. I'll always be with you."

Ephraim nodded. They smiled at each other, and then he gently laid her back on the pillows of her bed. By the time the sun was high in the heavens, Elana Marjzendiak was dead.

Ephraim tore his clothing and wept bitterly. His sons and daughter tried vainly to console him, but for such a loss, there is no real consolation. He and Elana had been husband and wife, life-long lovers, intimate friends, and soul mates. No one could truly know the depth of Ephraim's grief except himself.

Elana had meant something distinctive for each separate member of her family, and for each of them, her death was meaningful and painful in a different way. Of her children, Adam and Isaak had known her longest, and they had loved and revered her in that special way that sons reserve for a loving, caring mother. She was to both of them the ultimate symbol of womanhood, the model against which they compared all other women, even their wives.

Leah shared with her the knowledge and experience of a wife and mother. To her, Elana had been teacher, friend, and role model. She would miss her mother for as long as she lived.

To Michael, who had known only one brief bittersweet taste of love, Elana was still the most important woman in his life. He, like Ephraim, felt totally bereft by her death. Perhaps that was a blessing in disguise, since that bond would probably bring them to depend more on each other, once the first wave of grief had subsided.

Ephraim sat by Elana's coffin for the day it remained in the house, with candles at its head and foot. Black cloths covered the mirrors in the house and the portraits on the walls. The men of the family did not cut their hair nor trim their beards. No one in the house wore leather shoes, and, in accord with tradition, the family members occupied low stools or sat on the floor. It was in this time that expressions of grief were encouraged in order to facilitate relinquishment of that grief in the time to follow.

Leah assumed a major role in the family preparations for Elana's funeral. Since according to Jewish tradition, the service and the interment must take place as soon as possible, and since Ephraim could scarcely focus on this necessary activity while so overwhelmed by his loss, it fell to Leah, with some help from Adam, Michael and Meyhra, to organize the details of the service. The engaging of the Hevrah Kadishah to prepare the body; the arrangement with the rabbi to officiate; the notification of relatives and friends; the seating order of all the attendees in the spacious family synagogue; the decision of who would speak the tributes for Elana and in what order, all of these issues fell heavily upon Leah's shoulders. She was grateful to be able to render this final service for her mother; yet the fact that such service was needed filled her heart with anguish. Tears frequently blurred her vision as she sat at Elana's desk in her redecorated sitting room, refurbished since the fire, the after effect of which had ultimately claimed her life.

Ephraim, Adam, Isaak and Michael would all address the mourner's gathered to bid a final farewell to Elana Marjzendiak. Franz and Mira Pietrowski, their son and daughter and their respective spouses, Magda and Pierre, would all be in attendance. Several of Ephraim's colleagues on the Banking Advisory Council were also scheduled to be present. When at last the final details were in place, Leah went to bed, her head pounding, wondering how she would face the saddest day of her life thus far.

The funeral ceremony for Elana Marjzendiak was dignified and simple despite the large number of people who were in attendance. Out of respect for Ephraim and his family, and what each of them in their own individual way had contributed to the community among both the Jews and the Gentiles, every segment of society from Warsaw and Wola was represented. Those whom Ephraim had helped with financial crises, those whom Elana had consoled, nursed and/or fed in times of illness, during the rebellion of 1863, during the pogroms, the episodes of harsh weather, sporadic crop failures and economic depression all came to pay their respects. Laborers whom Isaak had represented in the courts, families who owed to Adam the recovery and survival of fathers, mothers, sons and daughters now gathered to make evident their gratitude and their support in return.

The Banking Advisory Council on which Ephraim now served all attended, walking in procession behind Franz and Mira Petrowski. As they followed Elana's coffin into the synagogue that had been built on the old Zielinski estate, now Plaz Marjzendiak. Fortunately, that structure, begun as a family place of worship, had over the years been expanded more than once, and since the fire that had so ravaged the main house, the synagogue had almost tripled in magnitude. Still, it could not comfortably contain all the well wishers who wanted to bid farewell to Elana, and for those who remained outside, chairs and benches had been provided.

Since Rabbi Meisel's death, one rabbi had served briefly in his place. In this year of 1885, a rabbinical counsel shared those duties. The representative whom they had sent on this occasion to officiate was a middle-aged, scholarly gentleman of moderate height and slender build with a carefully trimmed moustache and mahogany-brown beard. His name was Hiram Wecheler and he was originally from Kiev. When the Governor-General there had been assassinated, Rabbi Wecheler, like many of his co-religionists, had elected to relocate, and several had followed him to Warsaw. The feared and expected pogrom had not descended upon the Kiev Jews, but the rabbi and his family and the members of his congregation had never been able to return home.

And so, on this clear, cold January morning, Rabbi Wecheler led the prayers and blessings for Elana Marjzendiak's solemn service. All three of her sons participated in the readings from the sacred scroll, while Ephraim spoke briefly but sincerely of his beloved spouse's exemplary life as wife and mother, of her long struggle with pulmonary disability, and of her uncomplaining fortitude and patience in the face of declining health.

For this sorrowful occasion, Leah had prepared a reading from her personal journal that she had recorded on her long railroad journey from Paris, and then had committed to memory after having read it to her dying mother shortly before Elana's demise. The reading took the form of a poem in blank verse, and although Leah, an accomplished musician, did not think of herself as a poet, when her reading was concluded, there was not a dry eye in the building, nor was a sound uttererd for several moments after she had resumed her seat. These were her words in tribute to her mother's life.

"A Mother.

A mother must play many roles in her life.

Some are expected, some strain belief.

First she must stand by her bridegroom's side,

Walk in ritual circles, and drink ritual wine.

She must follow as he bids her, live by his rules,

But never forget she both follows and guides.

She must help him to build his hopes and his dreams;

She must share in his laughter, weep with his tears,

Bolster his courage and quiet his fears.

But then comes the challenge she faces alone,

The challenge that only a woman can know.

For she bears the danger, the pain and the strain

From which come the offspring that carry his name.

She is the fountain to nourish and nurse

The seed with which Adonai blesses the earth.

She is the cradle, she is the light

To bless and to lead in the darkness of night.

She is the teacher, the molder of clay,

She is the pattern that points out the way.

She is the anchor that secures the ship,

She is the sextant that safeguards its trip.

She is the bridge that traverses the tide,

She is the road and the map and the guide.

She is the lighthouse, the port in the storm,

She is the fireside, cozy and warm.

She sets us out on the journey of life,

She sees us through all our travail and strife.

She, our beginning, our fond bon voyage,

She is our advocate, and our defense.

She is the friend who will never relent.

She is the ally on whom we rely,

She is the helping hand always close by.

She is our strength when we fear we will fail.

She is the listener to all our sad tales.

She watches patiently, though far we roam.

She is our welcome when at last we come home."

* * *

In the days of Shiva, the initial week-long period of mourning stipulated by Jewish tradition, Ephraim, following the first outburst of demonstrative grief, grew silent and withdrawn. It fell to Leah, together with Aunt Judyth, to attend to the smooth running of the household. Michael, who had not yet settled on a career in Warsaw, took over the running of the estate and the mills.

Once Elana was buried in her coffin in the family cemetery, it was as though all light had gone out of Ephraim's life. Though neighbors and friends, including Mira and Franz Pietrowski, brought food and words of encouragement, Ephraim could not eat. He spoke little and seemed to require almost no sleep. Leah grew fearful that he would fall ill and might soon follow Elana in death. He spent an inordinate amount of time beside her grave. So much so that Leah came to regret the close proximity of the burial ground to the house. With Elana gone, Ephraim was adrift, overwhelmed by a loneliness more profound and tangible than even he would have thought possible. He still occupied a place on the Banking Council, but for several weeks he had not been in attendance.

A day came, approximately four weeks after her mother's death, coinciding with the end of Sheloshim, when Leah received a telegram from Markos that she was needed at home. The household routines were awry and he was required to spend most of his time at the import house. Now he had to go to Holland on business, and he did not feel comfortable leaving their sons alone in the care of the housekeeper.

Leah found Ephraim yet once more standing beside Elana's grave, his eyes dry, his face composed but withdrawn and strangely vacant. "I knew I'd find you here," she said softly, reaching out to embrace him.

Ephraim looked down at her, seeing there the image of her mother and being reminded anew of how alike they truly were. With a faintly rueful smile, he asked, "Have I grown so predictable?"

Leah nodded.

"Yes," he said, "I suppose I have. It's part of growing old. I can scarcely believe so many years have passed since we first came here." He took her face in his hands and studied it searchingly. "You were a child then, and now you have young sons of your own."

"So much has happened since then, Papa," she remarked.

"When one is young, time walks with leaden feet; when one is old, it runs with the quickness of the tiger." When she looked at him in surprise, he smiled and shook his head. "The words are not mine. They're from the Talmud." He took her arm and drew her away from the cemetery. They had gone but a few paces when Leah stopped and turned to face her father.

"It's not good for you to spend so much time with the dead. You belong to the living."

"I know," Ephraim said, "but it's hard to let her go. We were together for so long. I feel more at home with her here. Yet one must accept the will of Adonai."

They walked on in silence until they were within sight of the main house. Then, Ephraim stopped once more.

"You must go home now, Leah. You belong with your husband and your children." He said these words with more feeling than she had heard in his voice for weeks. She had come to tell him this very fact, and yet, he had sensed it without her putting it into words.

"I can't leave until I know you'll be all right," she said. "I'll be forever thinking of you spending hours in this cemetery."

"And letting the house fall down about my head," Ephraim remarked with the first levity he had employed since Elana's death.

"I didn't say that," Leah objected.

"You don't have to. A man's obligations speak louder than words, but I seem to have no heart to fulfill them. This is a large estate, too large for one old man." As he spoke, Ephraim scanned the expanse of his property, and Leah's eyes followed his gaze.

"You once said to me that you acquired this place so that all your children and their children would always have a home to which they could return at need. A place of refuge. Land that was truly theirs, because once our people could not own land." As Leah repeated her father's words, the memory of that earlier occasion brought the sting of tears to her eyes.

"That time may come again," Ephraim said. "We are not safe anywhere outside our own country, and as yet we still have no country. But you're right, my child. I owe the preservation of this land to my family for as long as I can hold it. Don't be troubled on my behalf. I'll find ways to work and to survive. And your Aunt Judyth will have a home here for as long as she wishes." With that, he answered the pleas Leah had addressed to him in the days immediately following her mother's death, when she had thought he was paying no attention.

"I'm glad of that," Leah said, much relieved. It was the first time since Elana's funeral that she had heard her father speak of the future instead of the past. It was a good sign. "I'll come back to see you often, Papa. And I'm glad Michael is home now."

Ephraim nodded. "It's good to have a son to depend on at such a time. In these past weeks, I've let everything go, but Michael has taken care of them."

"He still longs to write," Leah said almost absently.

"He can do that here," Ephraim remarked. "There's much to write about. The plight of his people, their need to become a nation once more, to be free of the stigma of 'wanderer' and 'foreigner.' Were I younger, I'd leave the estate in his hands and go to Palestine to work and help build a new home for us there. But my pioneering days are past."

Looking at him, Leah felt instinctively that all would be well with him now, that he had crossed the chasm from the shadows of death back into the realm of the living. "Even if you can't join the colonists in Palestine, Papa," she said, "you can still help them from a distance with some of the revenues from the crops and the produce of the mills."

"True," Ephraim agreed. "Interest in that cause has been rekindled throughout Europe. I'll join with that effort. After all, giving together is more effective than giving alone."

In that moment, Ephraim could feel a plan forming in his mind; a plan that would give meaning and direction to whatever years of life were left to him. In company with others similar to himself, in background and ideals, he would work to forge a Jewish nation, a heritage of hope and freedom for his family and his people. He felt certain Elana would know and would be pleased.

## CHAPTER FIFTY-ONE
## NEW BEGINNINGS

By late summer of 1885, life at Plaz Marjzendiak, while it would never truly return to normal in the absence of Elana, was beginning to achieve some semblance of order. An element of coherence had revived and the remaining members of the family seemed to have begun reconstructing their lives. This was especially true of Michael who, though he missed his mother's guidance, her encouragement and counsel, was also most susceptible to the attractiveness of the opposite gender, which for him she symbolized.

Michael not only missed Elana, he also missed Leah, the sister in whose house he had made his home more or less continuously for eight years. Now with Leah returned to her family in Zurich, Michael's loneliness knew no bounds. The brief, bittersweet interlude with Reyna Jheungwhold only contributed to the problem. He felt no desire to return to Berlin despite the excellent opportunity he had enjoyed as a member of the <u>Berlin Observer</u> staff. Albrecht Hoffmeyer was an admirable editor and journalist, a sympathetic friend, and he had been a congenial employer. Yet, Michael could not ignore the fact that Hoffmeyer had seemed relieved when Ephraim's letter, requesting his youngest son's return home as soon as possible to be with his dying mother, had compelled the young man to resign abruptly from his post.

Perhaps Hoffmeyer had felt responsible for Michael's safety, especially after the catastrophic vandalism that had followed the Consortium Loan Vote. In any case, as instructive as his Berlin sojourn had been, Michael had no wish to go back to the German capital. Certainly not at the present time.

Like Ephraim, Michael found himself visiting Elana's grave with disturbing frequency. At least twice per week he would walk from the main house to the cemetery to visit the site and spend time there remembering Elana, thinking of their times together. On some occasions he would remember her last request and bring flowers, sometimes one rose, sometimes a bouquet. Judith Mylinski aided him in this since she too was a frequent visitor to her sister's burial place. It was she who gathered flowers every other day to enhance the beauty of the main house's spacious rooms. Mindful of Michael's unassuaged grief, she formed the habit of setting aside a deftly arranged assortment of colorful blossoms for him to take with him to the family cemetery if he chose to do so.

On some days, he would stand and pray; at other times he would sit on a nearby rock and talk to his mother as they had talked together during her stay with Leah on the occasion of Frederick's birth. More often, however, he would sit quietly, once he had placed the flowers as attractively as he could, and relive all his memories of Elana from his earliest childhood to the day he had come home earlier in the year to find her on what had proved to be her deathbed.

"If only you were still here," he said aloud on a warm, late August afternoon, and was startled to realize he had received an answer.

"I'm here," said a warm contralto voice close behind him, and almost immediately a small, pale oval face, flanked by cascades of wavy chestnut hair appeared at his shoulder.

Michael was shocked. He had not been aware that he had spoken aloud. Certainly he had not suspected that he had been overheard. The girl who stood there beside him was young, barely twenty, and beautiful in a delicate, finely-chiseled fashion with a long graceful neck that called to mind a vision of swans floating on a lake. She was simply attired, but this only added to her beauty. On the bodice of her dress she had embroidered a gold-hued six pointed star, but since the fabric of her dress was a muted green, trimmed with bands of the same shade of gold at the neck and sleeve, the obligatory emblem did not detract from her ensemble. A matching bonnet of the same muted green color as the dress, tied with strings beneath her chin, completed her costume.

Embarrassed at his gaucherie in staring at her, Michael remembered his manners.

"Forgive me, but have we met before?" he asked.

"Not formally," she answered, "but I've watched you come this way on several occasions, often with flowers in your hands. Yet, I hadn't guessed there was a cemetery on the grounds, not until today." What she did not say was that until now, aware that her coreligionists did not routinely decorate graves with flowers, she had imagined he might be calling on a young lady, but knew of no dwelling on this part of the estate. She smiled self-consciously and Michael, in that moment felt the sunlight's warmth and he noted strangely that the day seemed suddenly brighter than it had before.

"Who are you?" he asked. "I don't recall seeing you about the estate before."

"I came here with my father," she responded. "His name is Moises Lindemann."

"The new estate agent?" Michael asked. "I didn't know he had a daughter. I thought he was a widower."

"Yes," she said. "He is. My mother died eight months after I was born. My father took me to Lithuania to be raised by my aunt. She was a second mother to me."

The young woman glanced about the graveyard. Her eyes lingered on the fresh flowers arranged on Elana's grave. She felt self-conscious at having betrayed so much about herself on such slight acquaintance.

"A recent loss?" she asked.

Michael could scarcely reply. Suddenly he felt choked by tears. He nodded. "My mother," he answered. "Just over six months ago."

Elana's grave was located close to Rachel's. The chestnut-haired girl's attention was caught by the dead infant's grave stone. She knelt and ran her fingers over the inscription.

"Her name," she said, her voice hushed, "was Rachel. The same as mine."

"Coincidence," he said, seeking to distract her. "It's a common name among our people."

"She lived for only a day," Rachel Lindemann observed. "How tragic!"

"Yes," Michael said, "it was. But at that time, my family was steeped in tragedy. The rebellion was in progress then. No one's life was safe." He stooped and took her hands in his, and helped her to her feet. "Adonai is to be praised that <u>that</u> time is past," he added.

"Yes, but my father has told me in many letters about all the upheaval that has followed. He wanted me to stay with my aunt in Lithuania. But once I was grown up, I insisted upon joining him." She paused thoughtfully. "Until I did, we had known each other only at long distance, by exchange of letters. I wanted to know my father in the flesh."

"Moises Lindemann, from what I've observed, is a fine man," Michael affirmed. "Honest, likeable. A pleasure to work with."

She asked, "Then you know him well?"

"I haven't known him long," Michael answered. "Only about two months. But yes, I've been favorably impressed. He's been a great help to me in trying to manage all this." His gesture took in the estate that surrounded them. "I find myself wondering how my father ever managed to work at the bank, run the factory and the mills, and still keep this place on an even keel." He shook his head in wonderment. "It's beyond me. These past two months would have been impossible for me without your father's help. He's made himself almost indispensible in just the short time he's been here."

Rachel smiled. "It's reassuring to hear you speak so well of him. In these uncertain times, its comforting to know that his position is secure." Obliquely, she was thanking him for letting her know that, as Lindemann's daughter, her own future was secure as well.

"I'd better be getting back," he said. "There's still much work to be gone over today. Tomorrow I must spend at the lumber mills."

"So now you're as busy as your father once was" Rachel remarked.

"Almost too busy," he agreed. "It leaves me little time for what I really want to do."

"And that is?" she inquired, her curiosity aroused.

He paused and gazed thoughtfully at her, aware at last of how beautiful she truly was.

"I want to write someday," he answered. "I've worked as a journalist in Berlin, but only for about a year and a half. Here, of course, that's next to impossible. But if I can somehow organize my time, put my life together again, block out the distractions. I hope to write books one day, books that other people will want to read."

The sun shone in an aureole about his head because of the angle at which he stood, half turned away from her. She knew his name, and in that light she could almost imagine she stood in the presence of the great warrior angel Michael himself, so regal and so determined did he appear.

"I'm certain that you will," she answered him, reaching out to touch his hand in that moment of utter conviction, of complete faith in the fact that he would accomplish the goal he had set for himself.

Michael felt that gentle but electrifying touch throughout his being. And as he did, he fancied he could hear the sounds of his beloved mother's contented laughter ringing out through the graveyard like the bells of a church.

Walking back with Rachel in the lengthening shadows of afternoon, toward the office that Ephraim had set up on the ground floor of the main house, Michael felt at peace for the first time since Elana's death. He could not explain to himself exactly why this should be so, but he knew beyond question that a measure of peace, of relinquishment and resignation, had settled in his heart.

He glanced at the girl beside him and wondered what magic she had worked upon him, what power she wielded. But then, he was still a very young man. Whereas women, even those who are quite young, have wrought this peaceful magic, or its converse, since Eve first walked the paths of Eden. It did not occur to him then that he had met his destiny, that this slender, gentle, soft-voiced girl, with her tranquil manner and her poignantly expressive mode of speech, would soon become his life partner. Moreover, the last place he would have expected to find her was in a cemetery. But he had been visiting his mother's grave, and although she had mentioned it only to Leah, Elana's dearest wish, before she died, had been to see her youngest child settled and established.

As Rachel looked up and pointed to the sky, a lone white dove flew upward and away. She laughed as she watched it recede from view in the afternoon sunlight.

"How lovely," she exclaimed, and once again that mystical laughter echoed through the air. Was it Rachel's laughter he had heard after all, or was it Elana's echoing back to her son from beyond the grave?

*  *  *

As summer ripened into fall and fall gave way to winter, Moises Lindemann further established his place in the workings of the running of the estate and the related commercial enterprises that were the mainstay of the Marjzendiak fortunes. He and Michael, though far apart in age, worked well together. Ephraim was relieved to know that he could lay aside much of the burden that had been his for so many years.

And Isaak, despite the demands of his office as Wola's mayor, was a frequent visitor to the estate office. He had felt bound by duty to his younger brother to ensure that he received the education he so deeply desired. And now that the academic process had been completed, he still felt obligated to watch over Michael, to run interference for him, as it were.

Far from resenting this attitude, Michael was grateful for it. He felt that he needed all the help he could garner. Business, after all, was not his bent. The calculation of appropriate quantities of grain and feed for livestock, of seed for planting, of hired labor for harvesting, was like a foreign language to him. And the running of the mills and the factory seemed at first as great a puzzle as a Chinese box.

Isaak, however, had run the mill on the Wrepz River when he was younger than Michael was at present. He knew the secrets of dealing with wood, and had learned the hard way the intricacies of dealing with people.

On an early October morning in 1885, Isaak stopped by Plaz Marjzendiak to talk with Michael about a personnel issue at one of the mills. When he entered the office expecting to find Michael, he instead met Rachel Lindemann, who was awaiting her father's return from an errand on the estate.

"Good morning," Isaak said cordially. "I hadn't realized that my brother had hired a secretary."

Rachel smiled quizzically. "I don't know that he has," she said.

"Oh, forgive me," was Isaak's response. "I shouldn't have assumed."

"It's quite all right. In fact, it might be a very good idea." She glanced critically about the office, obviously assessing the stacks of papers and ledgers arranged somewhat haphazardly on desks, tables and file cabinets. "While I'm waiting for my father, I may as well make myself useful." She promptly removed her bonnet and set about arranging the multiplicity of invoices and receipts in a more orderly, chronological fashion.

"You must be Mer Lindemann's daughter," Isaak stated. "We haven't met before. I'm Isaak Marjzendiak, Michael's brother."

Rachel reached out in response to his extended hand.

"I'm honored," she said, "to meet the mayor of Wola. You're quite the celebrity, from what I've heard."

"Hardly that," Isaak responded. "It's a difficult and demanding job, not at all glamorous, and often thankless."

"Rather like most jobs when one really examines them," Rachel remarked.

"You're quite perceptive," Isaak said, gazing appraisingly at her.

"Perceptive," she echoed, "for a woman."

"You mistake me," Isaak countered, "I've known some rather remarkable women, my mother and sister among them. I think my mother would have been pleased to know you."

She smiled and nodded as she transferred yet another stack of receipts to a less precarious location.

"I'll take that as a compliment," she said.

When Michael and Moises returned a quarter of an hour later, Isaak was seated comfortably in one of the two "guest chairs" and Rachel, having significantly transformed the controlled chaos of the voluminous papers into a semblance of order, was determinedly reorganizing the file drawers.

"Thoughtful of you, my dear," was Moises Lindemann's pronouncement.

"And may I stay, and do more?" Rachel asked, her glance fluctuating between her father and Michael.

"It would be a blessing if you will," Michael responded. "But I wouldn't have dared presume to ask you."

"Then it's settled," said Rachel. "You do have a secretary." She smiled at Isaak and proceeded to resume her task.

* * *

When the time of the High Holidays arrived, the business aspects of Plaz Marjzendiak had been reorganized and streamlined to such a degree that Michael was able to rejoice in the newfound hours of freedom he was afforded in the early mornings to embark upon the early stages of his life's work, writing. Writing in earnest. Filling one journal after another with copious notes of his observations, and setting a time line, a plot structure, and a tentative cast of characters for what would become his first novel. He even had a title: The Cauldron. The story line would involve a fictional reworking of his life experiences in Berlin, and a predictive projection of the ominous future which those events foretold.

He discussed his ideas at length with Isaak one evening over dinner while Luvna conversed with Judyth, and Rachel and her father Moises held a lively conversation with Ephraim. The Lindemanns, while not awkwardly intrusive, had made a place for themselves in the family constellation. Thus, it came as no surprise when following the family's return from the solemn services of Rosh Shosanah, Michael proposed a toast to his able estate agent and then, taking him aside, formally requested Rachel's hand in marriage.

Moises Lindemann seemed slightly embarrassed by the request, but he recovered quickly, smiled and consented, stipulating only that Rachel be in agreement for the consent to be binding.

* * *

At the end of January, 1886, the time had come to set Elana's headstone in place. The rabbi Hiram Wecheler conducted the ceremony and all the Marjzendiak family gathered in the family cemetery to pay final tribute. Moises Lindemann and his daughter were also there, and Franz and Mira Pietrowski attended together with their son and daughter and their respective families. Elana's sister Miriam made the journey from Amsterdam in response to a letter from her other sister, Judyth, reminding her of the approaching event.

Miriam came straight from the railway station to the cemetery, praying that she was not too late. Her prayers were answered. The heavy headstone still stood beneath its covering of canvas awaiting the moment when it would be unveiled, lifted by the stonemason and his helpers, and set in place at the head of the grave.

Today, despite tradition to the contrary, Elana's resting place was covered with a blanket of roses. Between them, Judyth, Ephraim, Michael and Rachel had each made this gesture in honor of this occasion of final tribute to the departed family member.

When the sun finally shone on the carefully carved marker, the words were spelled in large, raised letters:

IN LOVING MEMORY OF ELANA GROJEC MARJZENDIAK

CHERISHED WIFE, REVERED MOTHER AND BELOVED SISTER

APRIL 10, 1817 – JANUARY 29, 1885

Miriam silently nodded her thanks that Ephraim had thoughtfully included the sentiments of Elana's two living sisters. But to Judyth, the carved words meant something more. They were mute testimony to the fact that Ephraim had truly welcomed her as a member of his household.

* * *

Michael and Rachel were married in the spring of 1886. They chose as the site for their nuptials not the Great Synagogue in Warsaw but rather the more modest synagogue on the family estate from which Elana had been buried. The choice was Michael's, but Rachel readily agreed, knowing the basis for his reasons. That site, within view of the Marjzendiak cemetery, would allow them to exchange their vows, pour the ritual wine and welcome their guests close to the place where lay the mortal remains of Elana and baby Rachel. They spoke their vows in Hebrew, and the marriage contract, or Ketchubah, was written in the same language and beautifully adorned along its borders with scrolls, flowers and birds. It would later be framed and occupy an honored place on the wall of their living room.

Afterwards, the reception was held in the formal gardens below the rear veranda of the house. Elana's gazebo was literally covered with roses and other flowers from that same garden. Once the wedding couple was inside, and the trellis-like portal, equally adorned, had been closed; no eyes could intrude on their period of Yichud, the ancient custom of leaving the bride and bridegroom "alone together" immediately after the wedding ceremony.

The weather was cool, but in the full sunlight there was a comfortable warmth. For this event, all Michael's siblings and a few close friends had gathered. Adam and Meyhra had closed both their offices at noon in order to be present. And Jotyl and Batavnia traveled from Zurich along with Leah and her family, so as to pay respect to his and Michael's long-standing friendship.

When finally the festivities concluded and most of the guests had left, Michael and Rachel walked hand in hand to Elana's grave. They knelt facing her headstone, and Rachel took the white roses she had saved from her bridal bouquet to strew over the site.

"You brought us together here, Mother," Michael said softly. "It's only fitting that we come here for your blessing on our marriage and our future life together."

They stood then together in silence, not expecting an audible answer, but somehow aware of a gentle presence around them, and of the heightened fragrance of roses, Elana's favorite flower, even though the roses Rachel had carried with her had already begun to show signs of fading, and their frangrance should have lessened rather than have grown in magnitude.

In their minds they knew that Elana's true essence was no longer there. Her spirit did not inhabit her decaying flesh, nor did it haunt her gravesite. Yet her youngest son knew, and his young bride agreed, that she had somehow managed, despite death, to bring them together, and that she would always be alive in their hearts.

# CHAPTER FIFTY-TWO
## POLITICS AND PRESENTIMENTS

Nothing so frustrates and at the same time entices the human imagination as the contemplation of an alternative reality, the elusive charm of what might have been. A few hours prior to his assassination, Tsar Alexander II had signed into law the plan proposed by his Minister of Interior, Count Michael Loris-Melikov. This proposal did not suggest legislative government nor the formulation of a constitution. It did propose that elected representatives of the Russian people should meet on an advisory basis with members of the Council of State to discuss extension of the Tsar's earlier reforms and to have input into subsequent administrative policies. At best it was a radical departure from existing governmental tradition though it was a far cry from the constitutional reforms demanded by large segments of the citizenry. Upon the ascension of the new Tsar Alexander III, the plan had been suppressed and its author discredited and subsequently forced to resign.

Perhaps the advisor whose influence most strongly governed the policies of Alexander III's reign was the Procurator of the Holy Synod, Konstantin Petrovich Pobedonostsev. This man had been one of Alexander's tutors; he had shaped his character and bolstered his personal prejudices. And he, in conjunction with Count Dmitri Tolstoy (who had become Minister of the Interior in 1882) and other conservative ministers, encouraged the Tsar's domineering approach to government. Thus, they supported a return to the doctrine of "official nationality," first advanced under the reign of Nicholas I. The ruling principles of this doctrine were autocracy, orthodoxy and nationality, yet none of these ieologies could be comfortably applied to the widely extensive empire that Russia, by its expansion, had grown to be. Her multiethnicity clashed with the prevailing Slavophile philosophy. Her varied citizens worshipped in many different churches, including Eastern Orthodox, Roman Catholic and Uniate Catholic, not to mention the Jews, the Muslims and the Orientals who had, by the current administration, become subjects of the third Alexander's domain.

Unlike his father Alexander II, the currently reigning monarch distrusted difference as synonymous with dissent. He viewed dissent as a threat to autocracy. And he looked upon the Orthodox Church as a vital pillar of a stable empire. This narrow view of the world in which he lived was diametrically opposed to change. Yet change, in the form of forward progress, is not only a natural result of human endeavor, it is a law of Nature itself. Failure to acknowledge and adapt to this law constitutes a fatal flaw in any regime. In the case of Russia's autocracy, it embodied the seed of the empire's ultimate destruction

Censorship of the press, restriction of the universities, surveillance of even primary schools, unrelenting persecution of dissenters, embarrassment of the Roman Catholic clergy and violent anti-Semitism became the order of the day. The Melikov plan that might have formed the basis for a cooperative relationship between the Tsar and his people was buried in the reactionary fear that not to reject the Loris-Melikov proposal might be interpreted by the revolutionary elements as a sign of weakness to be further exploited. This policy which characterized the inception of his reign proved to be characteristic of the whole of Alexander III's regime. With the resignation of Loris-Melikov and of Milyutin*[8], the liberal War Minister, and the appointment of Konstantin Pobedonostsev's operatives in their places, the tone of the next administration had been set. But despite the repressive character of

---

[8] *Dmitry Milyutin, War Minister responsible for reforms in the Army during the latter years of Alexander II's reign.

domestic policy and the complexity and ineptitude of foreign policy, especially in the Mid and Far East, the reign of Alexander III has come to be known by Russian historians as the 'reign of the Tsar of Peace'. The application of this euphemistic title in no way lessened the fact that the aftermath of that administration, leaving in its wake a host of unresolved problems at home and abroad, proved to be anything but peaceful.

Throughout the later years of Alexander III's reign, the fortunes of the Russian empire waxed and waned as repression, strict regulations at every level, and reprisal gained ascendancy. The forces of domestic dissent in Russia itself and in her western provinces were weakened, but they could not be destroyed. They were based on too strong a core of disenchantment and disgust at administrative blindness and ineptitude.

Nonetheless, thanks to Alexander III's appointment of able Ministers of Finance such as Nikolai Bunge, Ivan Vyshnegradsky and subsequently Sergei Witte, its economy did manage to prosper, and by 1892, the country's trade deficit was converted into a surplus that benefitted, at least temporarily, the entire empire. However, this advantageous increase in revenues was largely attributable to the increased export of grain. In a nation plagued by low agricultural productivity, this strategy entailed considerable risk.

Just how much of a risk became apparent during the famine that resulted and persisted from 1891 to 1892. Because Vyshnegradsky unwisely delayed the banning of grain exports even as food supplies throughout the empire were running low, a wave of epidemics of typhus and cholera spread throughout the empire

In the rural districts, the sight of peasant farmers stripping layers of thatch from the roofs of their houses is commemorated in paintings and sketches of the period. This was done in order to feed their horses, so that the horses would survive to plow the fields the following year, and it became a not uncommon phenomenon.

In the urban and rural areas, the practitioners of medicine found themselves overwhelmed as they sought to combat the epidemics. The press was forbidden to use the word famine in their publications, and were advised to downplay the seriousness of the situation in order to avoid wholesale panic.

Against this background of domestic crisis, Alexander III called for the formulation of charitable organizations whose mandate was to provide food, medical assistance and, where necessary, shelter to those in need. The pattern was set in the Russian capital by an aristocracy-led and funded Commission for Social Aid.

The Vistula Provinces were no less vulnerable to these disruptive forces than were the other parts of the Russian Empire. It fell upon the members of the educated and affluent classes of society to implement the Tsar's urgent appeal for assistance.

In Warsaw and in nearly Wola, the Marjzendiak family rose to the challenge. At an unconscionably early hour on the morning of September 12, 1891, Ephraim, Franz Pietrowski, Michael, Bronislav Evelevski, the mayor of Warsaw, Isaak Marjzendiak, mayor of Wola and all the members of the Banking Adivsory Council of the head office of the Bank of Poland met in the board room of that institution to draft documents of incorporation for the Association of Public Charities of Greater Warsaw. The meeting lasted for four hours. At its conclusion, the hour had arrived for the bank to open its doors to begin the day's business.

It had been decided that the bank would set the example by designating a sizeable sum of money to finance and charter the early operations of the Association. It's first board had been appointed. All three of Ephraim's sons as well as Erik Pietrowski; Gerhardt Oslowski, son of Wola's former mayor, and Myles and Samuel Marks would serve on that body.

Thanks to Ephraim's foresight in managing the farming methods of Plaz Marjzendial, and thanks also to the abundant harvest those grounds produced, the grain silos on the estate were full to capacity. It was one of the few large farms that was able to contribute significantly to the grain distribution which the Association's charter proposed.

At his father's urging, Adam organized the senior members of the Medical Academy staff into an effective team with practical mandates on how to deal with the health crises, including a triage approach to separating those afflicted into categories according to diagnosis, stage of disease, and likelihood of recovery. Meyhra assumed the leadership of the nursing staff in order to help implement the doctors' instructions and assure the smooth running of the medical processes that would mean life or death for the people of Warsaw and its environs.

Many citizens did indeed succumb to their illnesses. And the combined plagues of typhus and cholera were not the only forms of illness that were prevalent. As winter approached, and with the rationing of food supplies, influenza grew rampant, and the elderly became especially vulnerable to this and other pulmonary disorders and related heart malfunctions.

Only the efficacy and leadership of those who served on the Association's board and planned its strategies prevented widespread panic from adding to the woes that walked the streets of Russian Poland's capital city. Warsaw's example and pattern of organization in meeting the crisis set the standard for the remainder of the Vistula Provinces. And realizing that no worthy outcome could be expected from subversive and revolutionary activities at such a critical time, the revolutionaries, with rare and sporadic exceptions, lay low. The underground press even praised the energetic manner in which the health and famine threats were being dealt with. But they did not accord any of their praise to the Tsar who had called upon the populations' leadership and intelligentsia to find a solution to the problem which his ministers had helped to create. The upsurge of civic activity had laid the foundation for ongoing and broadening benevolent efforts in the future. Greater numbers of more specific charities would emerge from the nucleus of the Association of Public Charities of Greater Warsaw. But a wider group of dissenting activists would also arise among the survivors of that horrific period.

* * *

Even as the deadly internal crises of famine and infectious epidemics were playing out throughout the Russian Empire, the ineptitude of her foreign policies were bearing bitter fruit. The refusal of the German ruler, Kaiser Wilhelm II to renew the Reinsurance Treaty with Russia, which German Chancellor Bismarck had secretly negotiated in the last months of 1887, left Russia in a position of diplomatic isolation.

Embarrassed and terrified that war with Germany and/or Austria-Hungary might ensue, Alexander III conferred with those among his ministers who favored forming close ties with France. By 1894, in return for a pledge to support the French in the event of an attack launched against them by Germany, Russia gained a French guarantee of support if she should be attacked either by Germany or Austria, the latter most likely resulting from

Germany's instigation. For the first time since the dissolution of the failed Three Emperor's League, Russia's Tsar breathed a sigh of relief. His diplomatic policies had secured French support and opened a rich source of French investment capital. His treaty with China in 1893 had secured a portion of Chinese Turkistan for Russia. The construction of the Trans-Siberian Railway was progressing rapidly and smoothly, and the country's economic growth, though intrinsically shaky, was still expanding. Assured by his advisors that this euphoric state of peace, won by treaties and closet diplomacy, and prosperity purchased at the cost of famine and pestilence, would continue, Tsar Alexander III began at last to view his reign as a successful one.

* * *

The summer of Abrahm Marjzendiak's thirteenth year was the most eventful of his life to date. Everything he had done, thought and read had been leading up to this year, this very special year, this magical year that would transform him from a boy into a man.

Of course he would still be subject to his father's authority in temporal matters; he would still perform his share of chores about the family home and grounds. He would continue to rely on his parents, Adam and Meyhra for food, shelter and allowance money. But in the realm of personal responsibility, moral integrity and self determination, and in matters of spiritual growth and ethics, Abrahm would become an adult on the Sabbath morning following his thirteenth birthday. Thereafter, he could participate in religious ceremonies as a member of a Minyan. And he would be solely responsible to Adonai for the performance of his religious and prayer obligations. He would put on his tallit or prayer shawl to recite morning prayers, and on special days of observance he would also wear the teffilin, the cords tied around the forehead and left arm, to remind the adult male Jew that his mind, heart and strength must be constantly dedicated to Adonai.

Given the historic background and belief structure of Abrahm's antecedents, there is little wonder that as the momentous occasion of his Bar Mitzvah drew nearer, the boy felt as though he walked on air. The sunlight imparted a special glow to the daylight hours, and on moonlit nights, the sky was filled with an effulgence that seemed mystical and, for him, of personal significance.

Abrahm did not discuss his unique perceptions and unusual feelings with Adam at this time. Not that he was reluctant to do so. He felt close to his father, and they had shared several prior spiritually meaningful experiences, both at home and at the synagogue. However, in recent months, indeed since before his grandmother Elana's death, Ephraim had come to fill a special place in the boy's life. More than six decades of living and experience stretched between them. Such a chasm of time might seem an almost insurmountable barrier, but in the case of these two men, one old and one quite young, no such obstacle existed.

Abrahm had stayed at Plaz Marjzendiak on many occasions while Adam and Meyhra worked endlessly to fight the succession of epidemics that had for so long besieged Warsaw and ultimately claimed Elana's life. In the course of that tumultuous series of events, Abrahm's grandfather had come to symbolize for him stability, serenity and sanctuary in the boy's life.

Conversely, for Ephraim, struggling to maintain his own equanimity despite the chaos and upheaval that surrounded him, Abrahm had been his touchstone, his rallying point, the motivation that had enabled him to project the strength and reliability that he had always symbolized for his family. He stepped willingly and gratefully into the role of his eldest grandchild's spiritual mentor. Inspired by the burgeoning inner awareness and mental and spriritual receptiveness that Abrahm had begun to demonstrate to him so openly in that all-important period of preparation, Ephraim conscientiously assumed the role that Adonai seemed to have appointed for him. He gave his grandson a schedule of study assignments and readings and deliberately set aside on his behalf time for periods of discussion and interpretation of the sacred scriptures, the Talmud and the Midrash.

Abrahm's academic training had, up to this time, been attended to by tutors whom Adam had hired from among the Jewish scholars who flourished in Warsaw in the 1870's and 1880's. These men, barred from teaching in the government-managed primary and secondary schools, were always eager to obtain private employment from the Jewish families who could afford to compensate them for their services. This was reminiscent of the way in which Maria Borowska had taken over the education of Pola and Erik Pietrowski when the Tsar's Russification program had displaced so many Polish school teachers from their posts and had replaced them with Russian instructors.

Normally, that time, from earely summer to fall, when formal academic training was in hiatus would have been the logical time for Adam to appoint for his son a biblical scholar and tutor to oversee his preparation for Bar Mitzvah. When at last Adam encountered a welcome break in his grueling schedule of medical practice, teaching and research, he had time to feel guilt for not having thought earlier about this necessary paternal duty. He was relieved to learn that his father had already taken the necessary steps to repair his oversight, but he was also somewhat embarrassed.

When father and son unexpectedly met one afternoon in late August and Adam broached the subject of obtaining a religious tutor for Abrahm, Ephraim smiled reassuringly at his first-born son.

"Fortunately, Adam, our minds have been working in tandem on that problem."

"In what way?" Adam asked in surprise.

"Abrahm has already acquired such a tutor. Me."

"You?" Adam asked, puzzled. "I don't quite understand."

"Do you doubt my qualifications for the task?" Ephraim's tone was somewhat aggrieved.

Adam shook his head in denial. "No, not at all," he answered, "it's just that I hadn't thought to ask," He left the sentence unfinished. "I should have consulted with you much earlier."

"With me, or with the rabbinical counsel, perhaps," said Ephraim. He then hastened to add. "But the past months, indeed, the past two years have been a nightmare for you. I've seen how hard you've worked, and that able wife of yours has been a God-send."

"Meyhra's been indispensible to me. I wouldn't have gotten through that time without her."

Ephraim touched Adam's arm.

"I know," he said simply. "I've understood. It was for that reason that I intervened as I have, and I began tutoring Abrahm every time he came to stay at Plaz Marjzendiak. It kept him occupied when the two of you couldn't watch over him."

"It kept him out of harm's way, what with so much contagion in the streets of Warsaw," Adam added by way of subtle justification.

"And it has been a great pleasure for me to have an opportunity to burnish my own religious acumen, using the tutoring of my grandson as an excuse. I'm honored to be able to perform this service for you both."

"What can I say?" Adam interjected.

"There is nothing you need to say" Ephraim responded. "Thanks to your son, I have kept my sanity. The loss of your mother threatened to overwhelm me. For a time, I floundered. I nearly sank into the pit of despair. But then, I looked at him, and I recognized the favor Adonai had shown me, the blessing he had granted to me, and the obligation I had almost failed to acknowledge. I can only extend to you my thanks that you sent Abrahm to me, entrusted him to my care when I needed him most."

Adam was silenced by this admission from his father. He was almost moved to tears by it. Father and son embraced, and Adam, in an effort to dissipate the mutual embarrassment that both men felt at such an open display of emotion, persuaded his father to join him at a nearby restaurant for a light meal.

At the table, over food and drink, they spoke of other things, of lighter subjects that did not call forth such deep and difficult-to-express feelings. The conversation calmed them both and relieved the tension that Adam especially had begun to sense when he had first realized that his father had perceived his paternal shortcomings and had acted to repair that deficit.

Finally, the two men addressed the details of when, where and how Abrahm's Bar Mitzvah would take place. Ephraim wisely and considerately allowed Adam to assume the dominant role in that planning process, so that he could feel that he had not, after all, failed as a parent.

It was decided that Abrahm's Bar Mitzvah service would indeed coincide with the Sabbath morning service on the first Saturday following the celebration of the boy's thirteenth birthday. It would take place in the Great Synagogue in Warsaw. On that occasion both Adam and Meyhra would accompany their only son to the synagogue sanctuary and, in conjunction with Ephraim, Isaak and Michael, would ascend the Bimah and take part in the rituals of passing and undressing the Torah scroll. They would each participate in the sacred readings, chantings and songs appropriate to the season. In accordance with time-honored custom, Abrahm would deliver the D'Var Torah, the interpretive sermon explaining to the assembled congregation the meaning of the torah and haftarah readings and their significance and applicability to daily life and current times. Afterwards, the rabbi would formally welcome Abrahm into the congregation as an adult, would recite the prayers of final blessing, and would bring the service to an end with the recitation of the Mourner's Kaddish, with Abrahm joining in this ritual as an adult for the first time.

The choice of which of his deceased ancestors would be singled out for special honor and dedication would be left to Abrahm. Then, with the formalities and solemnity of the event behind him, Abrahm would be free to enjoy the Kiddush, the collation of braided bread and wine that traditionally follows the service, and would be a prelude to the reception in his honor.

It was during the final month of joyously frenzied preparation for his son's all-important rite of passage that Adam received a letter from Sarah Krakowska. They had not communicated with each other for many years. The letter's only predecessor was the note that Isaak had carried from Krakow to Warsaw on the occasion of Adam's wedding.

Unaware that Isaak and Sarah, having become comfortable friends after he, Adam, had left Krakow, Adam was surprised and disconcerted. He could not imagine why his erstwhile beloved should choose this of all times to contact him, and he found himself between anticipation and dread at the prospect of reading this unexpected epistle. What would she have to say to him after all these years? How would he explain the letter to Meyhra? Tormented by such questions as these, he folded the letter into the pocket of his vest and postponed even opening it for a week after its arrival.

When finally he summoned the courage to break the seal and read Sarah's words, he was overwhelmed with nostalgia tinged with a wistful regret. Moreover, he was filled anew with appreciation and respect for the uniquely gifted woman whom family obligation had compelled him to renounce:

> Dear Adam,
>
> I know that you will wonder why, after so long and absolute a silence as has existed between us, I have elected to write to you at this time. Know that, as always, my prayers and best wishes go with you. Know also that I am content with my life as Adonai has chosen to order it. I revel in my teaching career and I feel honored to participate in opening the eyes and the minds of my students to the wonders and glories of the biological sciences that only reflect, after all, the wonders and glories of Adonai.
>
> From afar, I have followed your career with interest, and I am delighted to have met one of your former students, Dr. Felix Myles, who has taken over a medical practice here in Krakow. He speaks of you in glowing terms, and I am gratified to know how admirably you have fulfilled, as a mature physician and professor, the promise you so ably demonstrated in your students days here.
>
> Felix has told me that you have a son, Abrahm. Though mathemathics was never my subject, it has occurred to me that, based on Felix's anecdotes, and on a line from a hastily-composed letter from Isaak, which I recently received, your Abrahm must be at the age for his Bar Mitzvah. What a glorious occasion that will be for him, for you, and indeed, for your entire family.
>
> Please believe, as you approach that celebration of your son's coming of age, that I am in complete accord with the decision you made long ago, mutually painful though it was then. You could not have done otherwise, and your son's mounting of the Bimah to claim his rightful place in the timeless community of his religious peers could not have come to pass had his father been a weaker, less committed man.
>
> May Adonai bless you, guard you and guide you always,

Sincerely,

Sarah Krakowska

Reading those words, especially the closing paragraph, left Adam on the verge of tears. Yet he was grateful to Sarah for having written to him. She had restored his faith in his own integrity and in his own judgement. And she had done much to make him feel that he had not failed as a father after all.

* * *

As memorable as the day of his Bar Mitzvah would always remain for Abrahm Marjzendiak, it was the birthday party which he attended later that fall in honor of one of his distant cousins that was destined to be the real turning point in his life.

Her name was Judyth Marks. She was the daughter of Samuel Marks, who was one of Ephraim's associates on the Banking Advisory Council, the son of Adah Meinen's nephew. He was younger than Ephraim by some years, but he had all but despaired of ever becoming a father by the time his daughter had finally made her appearance. Understandably, his daughter quickly became the central focus of his life. He lavished upon her every luxury and by the time she was approaching her fourth birthday, he hired for a her a tutor, a religious teacher and a musical instructor, the latter step inspired by the unprecedented success of Leah Marjzendiak Kolvner's musical career.

Judyth was a child of many gifts and graces. Despite her father's almost idolatrous treatment of her, she was even tempered, loving, and more given to sharing than the average boy or girl of her age. Added to that, she was beautiful in a way that few little girls are truly beautiful before the age of six or seven. She was possessed of a smooth cameo complexion, violet eyes and wavy ebony-black hair. Her eyelashes were so thick that they seemed almost artificial, and her smile, frequent and spontaneous, was so beguiling that it called to mind the radiance of angels. The musical laughter that often accompanied it was a sound to delight the heart.

Judyth's mother Esther was the pattern on which her daughter was modeled. Blessed with not one but two phenomenal beauties in his family, Samuel Marks felt himself to be supremely favored by Adonai. Being an observant and deeply religious man, he frequently and freely expressed his thankfulness in his daily prayers, morning and evening.

For Judyth's fourth birthday party, all the family members, near in degree of kinship or distant, were invited. Thus it was that thirteen-year-old Abrahm Marjzendiak was in attendance. He was somewhat tardy for the dinner, having been delayed by his gardening chores. His mother had waited patiently for him, and had brought him to the Marks' home just as the main course was being served. Adam came straight from his medical office to join them.

Feeling awkward and conspicuous, Abrahm could hardly enjoy his meal. He was, therefore, pleased when the party adjourned to the living room, and Judyth was sat at the oversized coffee table, surrounded by presents, and the huge birthday cake was set before her, crowned with four giant candles. She hardly had breath to blow them all out since she was diminuitive for her age. When she succeeded in this momentous endeavor, she smiled broadly and her lyrical laughter filled the room.

Abrahm stared at the doll-like child in fascinated wonderment. He did not quite understand his feelings then, but as the years passed he would come to realize that in that moment, she had captured his heart.

* * *

The People's Will that had successfully encompassed the murder of Alexander II ultimately ceased to exist as its survivors became active in other political organizations. The single serious assassination attempt directed against Alexander III miscarried and as a result five university students, including Lenin's elder brother Alexander Ulianov, were hanged. But the memory of the wave of assassinations preceding the death of Alexander II continued to affect the policies of both his son and those of his later grandson with predictably adverse results.

The year 1894 made its advent quietly, ushered in by a gentle fall of snow. It was the first relatively mild winter to visit the Vistula Provinces, and indeed all of Eastern Europe, in almost a decade. Even the usually tumultuous winds seemed tame in that winter season when compared to their predecessors. The brutal famine had passed. Thanks to the establishment of the peasant's banks throughout the Russian Empire in 1892-93, and the ongoing work of the now well-established charitable organizations that were educating the peasant farmers in more efficient agricultural methodologies, last summer's harvests had been abundant. There was finally enough grain not only to feed the citizens, but to export and sell as well. The Trans-Siberian Railway now extended over an area of hundreds of kilometers, and was still under construction. Russia's land mass had expanded eastward and her political influence had spread to the borders of Turkey, China and northward to Latvia. French investment capital swelled the government's coffers. Prosperity seemed to have been achieved, although the empire's people had paid a high price for it. Many had perished from starvation, pestilence and attendant disability. Some had been obliged to sell all or parts of their land in order to survive. The Tsar may have felt pleased with the positive effects of his reign, but among the citizens and subjects under that reign there persisted an element of frustration, of dissatisfaction with the status quo that could not be assuaged simply by more money and fuller harvests.

Ephraim Marjzendiak and his friend and superior Franz Pietrowski had held many discussions in recent weeks about this very subject.

"Times are definitely better," Franz remarked as they sat in his office at the end of a particularly busy banking day in late February. "Deposits have increased. More savings accounts are being opened, and there are fewer withdrawals."

"True," Ephraim agreed. "But when you look closely at the faces of the people making those transactions, you cannot fail to notice that they show little satisfaction and no joy. When they talk, there's no humor, no levity in their manner or their speech. I've seldom seen such a glum lot. It reminds me of the days of the revolution."

"Oh, surely not," Franz responded. "Thank God those days are long past!"

"I only hope you're right," was Ephraim's rejoinder. "I hope the calm surface that we see is not merely a mask for latent violence lurking underneath."

"Like a volcano quietly rumbling until it builds up enough pressure to erupt." Franz responded, voicing the concern that both men felt.

"Precisely!" Ephraim exclaimed. "On the surface, we seem to be making progress. Even the secondary schools and universities have begun to ease their stringent quotas. The grandson of one of my Jewish friends has been accepted at the University of Warsaw. None of my sons was able to do that. And yet, most of the reforms that Alexander II either initiated or permitted have been seriously undermined or else surreptitiously reversed."

Franz nodded.

"The world," he said, "has turned upside down. It's become a maze of paradoxes."

"It's become a swamp," Ephraim said bitterly, "with pools of quicksand waiting to engulf the unwary. The people know it, too. They watch each other as though they expect to be denounced by friend or stranger. The dissidents haven't disappeared. They've simply gone underground, to await their best opportunity."

"And there are more rival dissident groups than ever." Franz noted. He shook his head. "Our world isn't the one we used to know, is it, Ephraim?"

"No," Ephraim agreed. "But I wonder if that world was truly any better."

"Perhaps, at a distance, we see it as having virtues that it didn't really possess. And we see the present, perhaps as worse than it really is, because it's still unfamiliar."

"You're becoming a philosopher as well as a banker," Ephraim remarked, and stood to take his leave.

At that moment, Franz was seized with a fit of coughing. It was a dry cough, Ephraim noticed.

"Perhaps you should take something for that cough," he suggested, but Franz shook his head dismissively.

"It's nothing," he said. "I had a bad cold late last year. The cough has hung on to a degree ever since. I'm sure, in time, it will pass."

Ephraim said nothing further. It was not his nature to pry, or to press an uncomfortable subject. But as February progressed into March, followed in due course by April, and as his friend's cough had not subsided but, in fact, seemed at intervals to be growing worse, Ephraim's concern deepened.

# CHAPTER FIFTY-THREE
## THREE DEPARTURES

Although he had noted a gradual decline in his energy level over the past few months, Franz Pietrowski had made no mention of that fact either at home or at work. Of the staff currently employed at the main office of the Bank of Poland, only a few of the "old guard" of long standing members remained. Few, aside from Ephraim, would notice the changes in appearance and manner that accompanied this decline. Ephraim did remark one day that his friend was coughing but no phlegm was forthcoming.

At home, however, Mira was growing more and more concerned. She did not like to ask probing questions; her husband had never been a man to complain of aches and pains or to raise the subject of his health unprompted. She had noted his occasional cough and worsening pallor. Eventually the day came when Franz awoke, feeling unable to get out of bed.

He noted a gnawing pain in every joint and muscle. His head ached unbearably and he was shivering from chills. Beside him, Mira had lain awake for hours, making every effort to remain still and not disturb her husband's sleep, yet keenly aware of his recurrent restless tossing and murmuring unintelligibly. At last, she could bear it no longer. When she saw that Franz's eyes were open, she sat up in bed and drew on a robe.

"I'm sending for Doctor Zarafiel," she said, "whether you agree or not." She put a hand to his cheek and drew back in shock. "You're burning up with fever!"

Franz mumbled an answer she could not decipher and turned away, pulling the bed covers more tightly around him. His teeth were chattering, and the shaking chills were growing worse before her eyes. What, she wondered, could this illness be? It had begun like a cold, but then had apparently resolved. Franz had seemed better for a few weeks; then he had begun to cough frequently, his appetite had gradually failed, and he had grown increasingly more sensitive to cold.

Mira hastily awakened Julius Petrov, the eldest grandson of the Petrov who had been her coachman during the rebellion of 1863. He had met a tragic and untimely death when she and Ephraim Marjzendiak had rescued Ephraim's family from the riot and fire in the Stare Miasto ghetto. Now, his grandson, yielding to the urgency in his mistress's demeanor, disdained to hitch the horses to a carriage and consume precious time. Instead, he saddled the fastest stallion of the matched team he generally used to take Franz to the bank in Warsaw, attached reins, bit and bridle and sped down the road at a gallop.

In twenty minutes he was back at the stable, the doctor's coach, in quick pursuit, arriving close behind him. Dr. Felix Zarafiel was a graduate of the prestigious Medical Universitat of Krakow. He was not a native of Poland, but was of Austrian and Turkish descent. He had lived in Warsaw throughout the past decade and numbered among his patients the elite of the city. Franz Pietrowski, however, was more to him than a patient. In the course of their acquaintance, the two men had become friends. Franz had given the physician sound advice in his financial dealings, and Zarafiel was a non-voting member of the bank's Advisory Council.

When Mira met him at the front door of the Pietrowski mansion, she was in tears and obviously extremely distressed, though she tried to maintain a tight rein on her emotions.

"Thank you, Felix, for coming so quickly," she said, holding out both hands to welcome him. "Franz is very ill. I've never seen him like this."

The doctor greeted her hastily and then turned toward the stairs.

"He's in his room?" he asked.

"He's not able to get out of bed," Mira answered. "He's having chills. He's barely conscious."

Without delay, both of them ran up the stairs, the doctor in the lead with Mira at his heels. Franz lay supine on the bed, tossing restlessly and shivering visibly despite the warmth of the room. His face was flushed and streaked with sweat. His hands were clenched into fists.

"I'm cold," he murmured. "I'm so cold!"

Despite the patient's complaints, Dr. Zarafiel commenced his therapeutic regimen with an order for cold compresses to be applied to Franz's face and chest in an effort to lessen his fever. Three hours later, that goal had been achieved. Franz was asleep and apparently resting comfortably, having swallowed two teaspoonfuls of a dark, overly sweet syrup to suppress his coughing. Once again, he seemed on the mend.

But despite the outward improvement, and the syrupy medicine notwithstanding, the cough grew worse, and now Franz was indeed coughing up copious quantities of watery phlegm. He spent fewer hours at his bank office, excused himself early from banking council meetings, and noted with mounting alarm that his energy and his enthusiasm together with his libido were all at low ebb. Franz Pietrowski, who had throughout the majority of his life looked forward to every morning with joyful anticipation, to every day's challenges with curiosity and confidence, and, since his marriage, to every night with passionate expectation, now plodded through his life in a miasma of dread and depression with little delight or hope. His main concern was to get through his days without unexpected complexities, and his nights without unbearable drains on his declining strength.

His wife Mira was as beautiful, vivacious and seductive as ever. Indeed, her beauty had ripened and matured, much as a tea rose will seem to grow in perfection of form and fragrance as it progresses from bud to half-bloomed rose to full bloom, luxuriating in the sun and distributing its perfume on the gentle breezes of spring and summer.

Franz loved her still, now more than ever. In the evenings they would sit together on the veranda, holding hands and reminiscing about all they had shared throughout the years, all they had done, and all they had meant to each other; yet the romantic adventurousness of their love had somehow subsided. As his strength waned, she clung to him the more. For her, there had never been any other man. When he was gone, there would be no other. Both knew this to be true, although they never spoke of it. For Franz' heart was failing. The origin of this failure was not in his coronary arteries, but in his lungs. He had developed a slowly growing tumor that was taking over the alveolar sacs throughout his right lung; this was the source of the increasing phlegm, and of the coughing that strove in vain to rid him of it.

Amid these altered circumstances, the pattern of the banker's life was changing, and routine practices within the bank were changing also. Ephraim took over more and more of his superior's duties, assuming them almost without thinking, and certainly before being asked. Ephraim was reading the handwriting on the wall, and its message filled him with sadness. What, he wondered, would his own life be like when his dearest friend and ally lived no more? Already, he had lost Elana, his soul mate, his life partner. Now, he was losing Franz, his dearest friend, as well. Both were irreplaceable losses.

Life, after all, is a litany of loss from cradle to grave; loss of security within the womb, loss of the sense of comfort and belonging which that environment engenders. As one grows older, there is loss of innocence. For some this brings a loss of trust in one's fellow beings, but for some fortunate few, innocence is replaced by fulfillment, and for them, life blossoms and bears the cherished fruit of children, few or many as they may be. The children grow and change, and leave to find their way in the world outside the family, but if all goes well, they return from time to time, often bringing their own families to gain strength from the root source of home and parents and the nurturing spirit of ingrained values, mores and customs from which they have sprung.

In a sense, Pola had never left home. Pierre had made every concession possible so that he and she and their three children, Paul, Victoirine and Matthieu could remain in Warsaw, close to her parents and her friends. Except for the brief interlude when Philippe had lived with them, Pierre had allowed no disrupting force to disturb his wife's equanimity. But now, she saw and sensed the imminence of her father's departure from life. Only the need to bolster her mother and give back some moral support to her father compelled her to maintain a tight control over her feelings and not give way to the hysterical weeping and wailing that raged just beneath the surface of her enforced calm.

Erik and Magda had also founded a family and Magda no longer worked at the bank. She had resigned shortly before the birth of her first child, Etienne. Three years later, the young Polish attorney and his bride had welcomed a second child, Suzanne, who was in every way the image of her mother. Both these satellite families proved, as the time of parting drew nearer, an indispensable bulwark to Franz, and even more especially to Mira.

In the last few months of his life, Franz was no longer able to go to the bank, even for Advisory Council meetings, so the bank obligingly came to him. The members would assemble in his dining room, and Mira made certain that they were served a sumptuous meal although her husband consumed very little. Ephraim began to make it a habit to load the master ledgers into his carriage and bring them for the commissioner's review. No longer were the daily ledgers handed out at random. Instead, the same ledger was issued to one teller daily until it was filled. Then it was signed, sealed and stored so that, at need, it could be summoned and every entry verified against the master ledgers. Since Ephraim's trial, no major deficit had ever been noted, no sums of money had ever been found missing. The system was still a cumbersome one, but the inefficiencies were no longer an issue. Every transaction was closely watched and recorded, reviewed and surveyed to eliminate the possibility of error.

Two years almost to the day from the time when Franz had admitted to himself the serious and final nature of his illness, Mira sent for their children and grandchildren. She also notified Ephraim. The day was a Sunday and he was at home. Julius Petrov, who had ridden to bring the doctor to his master's bedside now rode to summon his master's friend. On both occasions, the young coachman's mount was the same, the handsome chestnut colored stallion named Zenith. So that no time might be lost, Ephraim, without regard for his years or the advancing stiffness of his aging joints, climbed onto the horse's back behind young Petrov, using the garden bench by his driveway as a mounting post. Off they sped into the waning afternoon sunlight. Thus did they reach the Pietrowski estate in record time.

Both dismounted quickly, Petrov to stable and tend the horse, Ephraim to reach his friend's bedside without delay.

Franz, at this point in time, moved intermittently in and out of coma, one moment barely aware of his surroundings, the next, alert and gazing fondly from one familiar face to another. He knew the moment Ephraim entered the room, keeping to the background in deference to the family members. Franz raised his head.

"Come close, my old friend," he called out, his voice a mere shadow of its former authoritative resonance.

Erik made room for Ephraim at his father's bedside. Ephraim knelt on the carpet and took Franz's hand, cringing inwardly at the wheezing sound of the younger man's breathing. He wondered if it had sounded this ominous before and he had failed to notice.

"I'm glad you're here," said Franz. "I hoped you'd come." He paused for breath, a breath he drew with difficulty. "I wanted to say good-bye."

"Goodbyes are hard," was Ephraim's comment. "Why not borrow from the German custom and say 'til we meet again? As I'm sure we shall."

Franz nodded, and was silent for a moment.

"Tread carefully, my friend," he said softly. "I shall worry about you and yours. I'll not be here soon. But you can always depend on Mira."

"Both of you have always been true friends, always there in time of need." Ephraim's glance rested on Mira, who sat holding Franz's other hand. "No man could ask for better on this earth."

A deep sigh escaped Franz's lips. He gripped Ephraim's hand, then his head sank back on the pillow.

"You cannot imagine," he said, scarcely above a whisper, "what an effort it is just to breathe. I am so tired."

"Then you must rest," Ephraim whispered. "There's no need to try to talk just now."

"My time is short," Franz responded. "There is much I would say and do, but I've no strength for it." His voice faded into silence.

It was only a few minutes later that young Julius Petrov appeaered at the door and ushered into the room the black clad priest from the Cathedral of St. John in Warsaw. The reverend father was young for his post as assistant to the local arch-bishop. His name was father Josef Karolynski. He was thirty-four years old and had lived his entire life in the Polish capitol. His superior had sent him to administer the church's last rites to one of its most illustrious sons. Beyond question he knew all the elements of his assignment. He simply felt unsuited to the task. To attend to so crucial a service for a man of Franz Pietrowski's status, so the young priest thought, the arch-bishop himself should have come, and it should have been done much sooner.

Madam Pietrowska had made the request two days before and had waited in vain for the arch-bishop to make his appearance. Normally, she would have gone in person to voice her concern over the delay, but Franz had been so ill that she had been reluctant to leave his side. Now, she rose and held out both hands to the young cleric.

"Thank you for coming, Father," she said, and bowed her head for his blessing.

"I trust I am in time," he began, but she silenced him with a finger to her lips and led him to her husband's bed. Now was not the time for either apologies or recriminations. Franz's body was dying, but the salvation of his immortal soul was at stake, and nothing must jeopardize that.

Ephraim had never witnessed the administration of the sacrament of Extreme Unction, as it was then entitled. He wondered whether he should excuse himself, at least for the duration of the ritual.

"Perhaps I should leave," he said softly. "This is a time for the family."

Mira looked up at him and smiled reassuringly despite the tears in her eyes.

"You've been part of this family for many years," she said. "I sent for you because he wanted you here now. Truly, I think we all did."

And so Ephraim remained. Magda brought him a chair so that he would be more comfortable, and from it he watched as the young priest draped the alb across his shoulders, lighted the tapers and set them in their holders, placed the crucifix between them, and intoned the Roman Catholic prayers for the dying.

Franz's final confession was brief and whispered because he could scarcely speak. Father Josef bent close to the bed, his ear on a level with Franz's lips in order to hear his words. Then he granted absolution, made the sign of the cross, and anointed the dying man with oil on the forehead, eyelids, lips, hands and feet. The rite concluded with the giving of communion as bread, of which Franz could swallow only a small portion, and wine of which he could swallow scarcely a teaspoonful. Fortunately, for those few moments, the cough that had so disrupted his rest recently was in abeyance.

In less than two hours after the priest had given his final blessing to Franz and had blessed the family members and taken his leave, Franz Pietrowski closed his eyes and sighed quietly. He lapsed into a coma once more, and from this sleep he did not awake.

Mira sat by the bed, holding Franz's hand and crying softly; Ephraim held his other hand. It was he who noted that the flesh beneath his fingers was growing cooler.

"Good bye, old friend," he whispered. Mira looked across the bed at him, tears swimming in her eyes.

"I can't believe that he's no longer here," she said brokenly, and then she fell across her husband's body, weeping inconsolably. Pola, who had been kneeling at the foot of the bed, arose and lifted her gently and led her from the room. Mira glanced back at Franz, then turned away.

Pierre Rebaumme came and knelt by the bed. "You were always honest with me," he said, addressing a Franz who could no longer hear nor respond to his words. "You were always kind, even though I knew you didn't always approve of me." He glanced up and his eyes met those of Ephraim. "You didn't approve of me, either," he said quietly, feeling guilty and somehow isolated from those around him.

"That was not my place," Ephraim said almost fiercely, "and this is not the time. The needs of this family take precedence over every other consideration now. Do what you can for them. It's only Adonai's approval, or the converse, that matters."

Pierre Rebaumme reddened in response to that verbal directive. He had been thinking primarily of himself instead of his relatives by marriage. Belatedly, he turned to Erik, who was now head of the Pietrowksi family.

"I'm willing to do whatever is needed," he said, taking Erik's hand. "You have only to ask and it will be done. You know where to find me." With that, he made a hasty exit.

When Rebaumme had left the scene of his father-in-law's demise, Erik came to stand by his father's body. He did not weep openly, but his face bore the marks of such unassuagable grief that Ephraim looked away, so as not to intrude upon the privacy of the younger man's pain.

Magda stood apart for a few moments longer. Then she crossed the silent room and stood beside her husband. Erik reached for her hand, and the two stood, bidding a silent farewell to the revered and beloved Franz Pietrowski, Erik as an only son, Magda as a grateful daughter-in-law. On this day of parting, she knew in her heart that Franz had never betrayed the promise he had made to her on another day years ago when she had told him of her origins, and of the life of subterfuge she had been forced to lead in order to survive. There was no record of her birth, since gypsies in the Russian Empire did not file records of birth or death in the public archives as did other citizens. As far as could be traced, Magda Laskowska Pietrowska had come to life on the day of her marriage to Fyodor Laskowski. Prior to that date, the records were mute. She breathed a sigh of relief and thanks for Franz's lifelong silence. Only Erik knew the truth, and silence for him worked to the benefit of his children. Mira also knew the truth from her son, but she felt a strange kinship with her daughter-in-law that had nothing to do with ties of blood or heredity. Magda's secret was safe and would so remain for many decades, until the German National Socialist military forces invaded Poland and the search began for non-Aryan elements among the conquered populations of Europe.

Mira Petrowska had not slept nor eaten for two days. She moved like an automaton; her dress was creased, her hair pinned up haphazardly. She was barely recognizable as the leading hostess and trendsetter of Warsaw society. And no wonder. She had known for those two days that Franz was dying, though even now she was in partial denial. She could not accept his death as fact, but she was nonetheless oppressed by it.

Pola, who had always looked to her beautiful, glamorous mother for guidance and strength now guided her to a guest bedroom, helped her to undress, unpinned and brushed her hair, and put Mira to bed, promising to sit with her and holding her until she fell asleep. Both women were like rudderless ships at sea in a storm. There was no compass, no sextant to guide them now. Franz, who had been husband and partner to one and parent and protector to the other, was gone beyond recall. His wisdom, his patience and his tenderness were no longer there to be relied upon and the absence of these valued traits had left a terrible void.

Insecure, frightened and irreparably alone, Mira lay fitful and sleepless, her eyes haunted, her mind in turmoil, and her heart overwhelmed by grief. For the balance of that day, she would weep intermittently and sleep hardly at all.

A long day passed before Mira was able to marshal her personal resources and take up the reins of responsibility to face the rites and events that must now take place. Her son Erik would be invaluable to her in these efforts, as would her daughter Pola. Their respective spouses would also play essential roles in the process that must follow Franz's death. But Mira, as the widow, would be called upon to play the major part in her dead husband's funeral preparations. It would be she who must consult with the undertaker, she who would choose the coffin, the music, the religious readings, even the officiating clergy. None of these issues, as is too often the case, had been discussed previously between husband and wife, even during Franz's last painful days of terminal illness.

Inevitably, Mira sent for Ephraim, feeling the need to call upon his innate strength and his knowledge, for he had dealt with a similar bereavement. Uncertain of the customs surrounding a death in a catholic household, Ephraim, in his turn, was obliged to consult Mira prior to the funeral ceremony regarding what he should do, or more precisely, what she needed him to do. Dressed in unrelieved black, her hair carefully coiffed, Mira looked the model of a widowed matron, although the vivid dark beauty of the woman could not be dimmed by her mourning attire. Ephraim was moved to admiration for his friend and former business ally. To her ingenuity he owed the fact that he had been able to acquire the Zelinsky estate that was now Plaz Marjzendiak. But she called upon him now, not in the spirit of collecting a long-owed debt, but as a woman faced with unbearable tragedy. Having met with similar tragedy himself, he gave her the benefit of his experience. Having been close to her husband for more than four decades, he sought to advise her with respect to what Franz might have wanted done if he were still present to express his preferences.

The two old friends spoke again at some length in the drawing room of the Pietrowski mansion three days before the funeral was scheduled to take place. Ephraim had dutifully brought the records of Franz's accounts and holdings so that Mira could review them with her attorney at her convenience. Out of consideration for her feelings, he wished to spare her the necessity of coming into the bank and enduring the awkward exposure which that errand would entail. He sought to avoid subjecting her to the well-meant but offensive pity of the staff members who had been Franz's subordinates. A new commissioner now occupied Franz's office, a man Ephraim had been obliged to hire and groom to assume a part that rightfully should have been his. Mikhail Palavetski was a middle-aged Polish aristocrat of medium height and build, who appeared to have mild manners that concealed an astute mind, but was endowed with few of the social graces. Mira had disliked him on sight when he came to her home to consult with Franz, but had disguised well her aversion. Ephraim, who knew her tastes and sentiments from long acquaintance, realized that at this painful time in her life, the less she was reminded of all she had lost in terms of status and ready access to her assets, the more smooth the period of transition from wife and reigning social grand dame to secluded widow would be for her.

To that end, he summarized the total value of her estate in liquid assets, bonds and commercial holdings. The sum was impressive, much more than even she had known. Franz had ensured her financial future even if she lived into advanced old age. That was the one encouraging aspect of the situation.

Now came the part of their meeting both had dreaded; the final details of Franz's funeral service. The archbishop and his clergy had overseen the procedural arrangements. The undertaker had taken charge of preparing the body for viewing and burial. Franz would lie in state for the day preceding the service and would be interred in the Catholic Cemetery of the Resurrection near Wola.

Mira had requested that Ephraim present the eulogy and that Erik speak for the family as she felt too overcome with grief to be able to speak at a public gathering so soon after her bereavement. Ephraim would ride with her in her carriage to and from the ceremony and Ephraim and her son Erik would stand with her at the graveside during the final benediction. It was a difficult role for Ephraim to play, but he felt that he owed his friend no less than to carry out his widow's wishes.

The funeral of Franz Pietrowski, held in the same ornate gothic cathedral where he and Mira had wed, where he had seen each of his children married and where he had faithfully attended mass for most of his life, was a scene of muted grandeur and generous tributes that would have done credit to a king. The banking community of Warsaw and its suburbs was present en masse. The Governor-General and his staff were present, as was the Tsar's emissary, the young Grand Duke Mikhiel Romanov. The leading businessmen, politicians, merchants, educators, physicians, attorneys, journalists and landowners were in attendance. The pews of St. John's Cathdreal were filled to overflowing by the district's elite so that Franz's friends among the common people of Warsaw and its environs were obliged in many instances to stand inside the church and on the expansive steps leading to the main entrance. Filled as it was, almost beyond its intended capacity, the church's atmosphere seemed warm and oppressive, though the great doors of the edifice stood open to permit fresh air to circulate freely. Fortunately, the acoustics of the building were excellent. The tolling of the bell as the service commenced proclaimed the solemnity of the occasion as well as the hour, which was ten o'clock in the morning.

The sky was clear, bright blue with hardly any clouds or mist. Franz would have fair weather for his day of departure. Inside the cathedral, the Archbishop of Warsaw, His Eminence Fyodor Frederick Dubidnyk, offered the mass in Latin. However, the Russification process that had for so long pervaded every other area of everyday life within the Vistula Provinces had not deleted the Polish translations from the missal, and the sermon was presented in the classical Polish language that all present could easily understand.

When the Eucharist had been blessed and distributed in both forms, the time had come for those who would speak to come forward. Mikhail Palavetski delivered his comments first. They were succinct and complementary but, since he had scarcely known Franz, were also superficial and uninspired.

Ephraim arose next and made his way to the sanctuary. He did not ascend to the pulpit as Palavetski had done. He felt a stranger in this setting although he had been here before, for the weddings of both the Pietrowski children. He stood at the foot of the stairs leading up to the altar. He had composed some notes to prompt his presentation, but once he had begun to speak, he scarcely referred to them.

"Franz Pietrowski," he began, "was my superior from the day I joined the staff of the Warsaw Office of the Bank of Poland. I worked with him as clerk-teller, as chief teller, as associate director and then as assistant director. In all the years we worked together, I never knew him to be guilty of an unfair, mean or spiteful action, nor a belittling or demeaning word. He was a generous and a gracious man who perfectly fulfilled the definition of a gentleman.

Yet, above and beyond these laudable attributes, Franz was more than this. He was a loyal friend. My family and I have all benefited from his graciousness and his generosity. I would not be alive today were it not for him. My family would have had no home to which we could go when tragedy struck years ago in the Stare Miastro had Franz Pietrowski and his wife not befriended us. When our new home was set afire, again the Pietrowskis came to our aid. They afforded us shelter and helped us rebuild.

It is not possible to enumerate in detail all the countless ways in which Franz Pietrowski has shown the grandeur of his character, not only to me, but to many others. There are those among you gathered here who could, if called upon, recite a similar litany of his kindness and good will.

Franz and I came of different backgrounds and different faiths, but I would have been proud to call him brother. In many significant ways we were brothers. My own older brother died years ago. It does not matter to you how. But he died, and years later, I have come to realize that Franz Pietrowski took the place in my life that my brother Joshua left vacant by his death.

Now, Franz, too, has gone, and we are all the poorer for his absence from our company and our lives. May God and his angels welcome him into their midst in recognition of all his years of faithful service to his God, his family and his community."

Ephraim stopped there. He could not have said anything more even if he'd meant to do so. He had stopped himself in time before saying Adonai. God was the name by which these people called the author and creator of all things, and so he had substituted their terminology, though it came awkwardly to his tongue. When he had finished and stepped out into the center aisle en route back to his seat, there was not a dry eye in the assembly, including his own.

Erik spoke next. His tribute was that of a loving son who spoke for his family. He, too, praised his father's virtues and he emphasized the role model Franz had provided for him as a child and as a young man. He spoke of his father's gentleness, his concern for others, his dedication to his work and his devotion to serving the banking public with honesty and idealism. Finally, he touched on the unselfish love that had existed between his father and his mother and the shining example that love had embodied for himself and his sister. It was an example impossible to surpass or to forget.

When the Archbishop had imparted the final blessing, the pallbearers took up the coffin and conveyed it out into the courtyard where the black-draped carriage waited to transport it to its final resting place. Even the horses were black with black reins and harnesses, and black plumes on their heads. Ephraim and Mira followed close behind and then the other mourners fell into place one by one, in solemn procession.

At the cemetery, the grave had already been prepared and from the mound of earth beside it Mira and each of Franz's children and grandchildren took a handful and sprinkled it over the flower-draped bier. Ephraim was the last to carry out this ritual, the final respects paid to the dead. Then, the archbishop, draped in his gold vestments, sprinkled holy water into the tomb and the family and other mourners took their leave.

Ephraim had agreed to escort Mira home to the Pietrowski estate, but he could not bring himself to eat any of the food at the funeral reception. His stomach felt uneasy at the thought of consuming any solid nourishment. Absentmindedly, he took a goblet from a tray he was offered and took a sip of the wine. It was a fine vintage, but he took no more. After a brief interval, he found Mira and took her aside. He had brought her dishes prepared by Judyth Mylinski immediately after Franz's death. He offered to do that the next day if it would help, but she declined.

"The cook has prepared enough food to last a week, but I, for one, don't feel inclined to eat very much at present." She glanced about the hall where they stood and added, "I wonder how I shall manager to live in this house all alone except for the staff. The thought terrifies me," she said with a shudder.

"I know the feeling." Ephraim said. "I shall be right next door if you should need me."

She was tempted to ask him to stay but she could think of no reasonable excuse for such a request. The house was full of servants who would readily fulfill her every wish. And Ephraim's presence could not drive away her fears nor summon Franz back from the grave. She looked critically at him then and saw how tired he looked.

"Are you all right?" she asked.

"As all right as one can be on such a day as this," he responded. With a twisted smile she nodded.

"Indeed. Will anything ever be all right again? Well, our respective faiths teach us that it will. Now we must begin to work out what to do with the rest of our lives. You have a head start on me," she added somewhat bitterly. "I'm new at this, so forgive me if I call upon your wisdom and your strength from time to time."

He took her hand in his and asked, "What else are friends for?"

"I'll send for Petrov to take you home," she offered, glancing toward the bell-pull.

Ephraim shook his head. "Let the young man rest. He, too, has had a wearing day. Besides, the walk will do me good." With that, he turned and left, content to walk the distance back to Plaz Marjzendiak, alone with his thoughts and his memories.

\* \* \*

On October 20, 1894, the man who had ruled over "all the Russias" for thirteen years, his strength depleted by prolonged ill health that seemed to take its origin from a railway accident and consequent injury six years before, succumbed at last to the rigors of renal failure. By the time his attending physician had arrived at the correct diagnosis, Bright's Disease, it was too late to save the ailing monarch from death. Like the loving family man that he was, he died surrounded by his family, the family he had saved in the railway crash at Borki by using his magnificent stature and muscular strength to support, for nearly half an hour, the collapsed roof of the royal railroad car until help arrived to extricate them from the wreckage. Yet his health had never been the same thereafter.

As befitting his rank and station in life, Alexander III's funeral was one of great pomp and circumstance, attended by the heads of state and/or their ministers from many different countries. However, few of these dignitaries were his friends; many of them were his detractors. They called him the Tsar of Peace because no major military confrontation had transpired during his reign, but some who accorded him that title used the term in the satirical sense. The third Romanov Tsar to bear the name of Alexander had, during his reign, faced upheavals at home and diplomatic conflicts abroad. Yet, through secret agreements and hard-won treaties he had managed to keep the country out of open war, and had seen it through starvation and plagues without incurring revolution. But the people of Russia and its provinces were restless and dissatisfied. The cauldron was ready to boil over. This was the legacy he left to his son, Nicholas II.

One month after the death of Alexander III, the Dreyfus Affair burst upon France reviving in that heretofore liberal nation a new wave of militant anti-Semitism. The Dreyfus trial was covered by a wide variety of journalists including a young Hungarian-born Jewish playwright, lawyer and man of letters named Theodor Herzl. He had been brought up in Vienna, but at an early age had been strongly attracted to the charms of Paris. He had moved to the city of lights and ultimately settled there with his bride. He thus became the permanent Paris correspondent of the famed Austrian daily Neue Freie Presse. Herzl embodied the beau ideal of the young cosmopolitan; he frequented the literary salons of Berlin, Vienna and ultimately of Paris. He was an aficionado of the theatre, an acquaintance of Zola, Flaubert, Proust and Anatole Franz. His plays ran successfully in Vienna, Berlin, Paris and in theatres as far distant as New York. No man could have been more dissimilar to the average Eastern European Jew of his day than was Theodor Herzl.

Nonetheless, a dramatic break occurred between him and his friend Herman Bahr over a violently anti-Semitic speech Bahr expounded as part of a pro-Wagner demonstration. This event initiated the upsurge of Herzl's "Jewish consciousness," and the Dreyfus affair the following year completed the reorientation of Herzl's entire life focus. The cry of "Down with the Jews" had earlier begun to echo throughout France cutting across political barriers of conservatism, liberalism and outright socialism as it had through other parts of Europe. In response to his perception of these growing sentiments Herzl wrote the play, "The New Ghetto." In 1894, the Dreyfus Trail signalled the culmination of this regrettable trend, seriously threatening France's image as the repository of liberty and the sacredness of the rights of man.

The Dreyfus incident involved the illicit transfer of military documents to the German military attaché in Paris by a profligate officer named Walsin Esterhazy in order to secure funds to repay his gambling debts. The ascribing of this criminal act to Captain Alfred Dreyfus was traceable to the vindictive anti-Jewish sentiments of Colonel Henry, aide to the Chief of French Military Intelligence. Henry disliked Dreyfus for his Jewishness, his background of affluence and his preference for social isolation from his gentile fellow officers. This attitude was due to the predictable reticence of a Jew living and working amidst the Jesuit-trained aristocrats at military headquarters. Unfortunately, this was incorrectly interpreted by Henry and by others as snobbishness.

Despite equivocal evidence, the influence of Colonel Henry and of prominent bigots such as Edouard Drumont, author of <u>La France Juive</u> and president of the National Anti-Semitic League, convinced the presiding officers of an "international Jewish conspiracy" and persuaded them that Dreyfus' conviction would serve the cause of political expediency. The affair came to symbolize the duplicity of the royalists and of the dominant conservative elements of the French Catholic press. It also dramatized the depths to which the military could sink in its efforts to safeguard its image at the expense of truth and justice. Evidence of Esterhazy's guilt was suppressed and Captain Dreyfus of the French Artillery was summarily adjudged guilty of treason and exiled to Devil's Island. There he was incarcerated under such dreadful conditions that when four years later he was abruptly recalled to the French mainland and retried on the basis of new evidence[9], he had suffered irreparable psychic derangement and had aged almost twenty years.

---

[9] A repetition of the earlier document theft and of the written memo affirming the transfer of documents to the German attaché while Dreyfus was imprisoned had led to the second trial. The circumstances stated above meant that the earlier verdict was suspect and that the second verdict was totally absurd.

At thirty-nine he appeared in court stooped and emaciated, his face was deeply lined and he was totally bald except for a fringe of white hair. Even then he was found guilty. He was subsequently pardoned to quell the international outcries against the obvious injustice of both verdicts. Europe had unknowingly witnessed but the prelude to worse extremes of racism in the following century. And in Theodor Herzl, the Zionist movement had just recruited its most unlikely, most prophetic and most famous champion. Though he would not live to see the fulfillment of his dreams, Herzl's tireless efforts in striving to bring about a modern Jewish state would form the foundation on which the modern state of Israel would ultimately be built.

Between the first and second Dreyfuss trials, the year 1896 announced its advent on the world stage by a series of notable events. Perhaps the most notable of these were the establishment of the Nobel Prize and the holding of the first modern era Olympic Games in Athens, Greece. These would prove to be world-changing in their scope and influence, and would persist in focusing international attention for decades to come. On the literary front, the famous author Thomas Hardy published his novel <u>Jude the Obscure</u>. In the world of music, Giacomo Puccini premiered his immortal opera La Boheme, and on May 20 of that same eventful year, the incomparable pianist Clara Vieck Schumann succumbed to the ravages of her second and final stroke. This latter event sent shock waves through the musical firmament. Now, two of only three women musicians who had achieved success, fame and fortune as performers and composers in a realm that had previously been reserved for men, were no longer alive. First Marie Moke Pleyel had died, and now Clara Schumann was gone. Only Leah M. Kolvner remained.

Leah had been on tour earlier in that year, and had appeared in St. Petersburg, Krakow and Warsaw, where she had paid a visit to her family estate, and then had gone on to Paris. She had not concertized in Germany since her successful but tumultuous visit to Berlin. But now, upon hearing that her aging friend, mentor and fellow musician was seriously ill, she quietly travelled to Frankfurt, accompanied by her younger son, Frederich, himself already a budding musician and painter. There were no headlines, no fanfare, no public attention whatsoever. That was precisely the way Leah wanted it. This was a personal and private errand and no public intrusion would have been welcome.

She was with Clara just hours before she died. The older woman was wasted and emaciated, having been unable to eat for weeks. Her consciousness level was variable, but she recognized Leah immediately when Eugenie, the youngest of Clara's daughters, ushered her into Clara's room.

Leah embraced Clara, sat with her and held her hand throughout most of the two-hour visit. Conversation was impeded since Clara could scarcely speak coherently. Her last two years had been saddened and frustrated by the fact that she could no longer concertize. In early March, she had played for some students at the Frankfurt Conservatory where she had formerly served on the faculty. But then, her health had rapidly declined. A small stroke had ensued, but from this she had recovered. On May 10, a more massive vascular catastrophe had occurred. On May 19, 1896 Leah Kolvner and Clara Schumann took their leave of each other, quietly as old friends often do. A wealth of feeling passed between these two women, an understanding that required few words but was filled with meaning. In a sense, it was the passing of the torch. Now, there remained but one outstanding woman pianist still recognized in the world of classical music. That woman was Leah Kolvner.

When Clara was buried in Bonn Cemetary, near her husband Robert's imposing memorial, both Johannes Brahms and Leah Kolvner hastened by train to attend her services and pay final respects. Both missed their connections, but both arrived in time because the interment was postponed by the family until Sunday, mainly to allow for Brahm's attendance. Prior to that day, Brahms and Leah Kolvner had met only once. They would not meet again, as Johannes Brahms died less than a year later. However, both musicians did participate on different days in the four-day memorial concerts in Clara's honor that were held following the funeral.

Leah and Frederich returned to Zurich immediately after the memorial concerts, subdued and deeply moved by all that had transpired during their eventful week in Germany.

# CHAPTER FIFTY-FOUR
## THE TIDES OF CHANGE

Nicholas II, last of the Romanov Tsars and by far the weakest and least diplomatic of the lot, repeated his predecessor's errors by dismissing as "senseless fancies" an appeal by moderate liberals at the outset of his reign to set aside the old reactionary policies and bureaucratic whims of the autocracy and replace them with a code of constitutional law. Nonetheless, in the early years of his administration, Russian economy prospered. Foreign capital poured into the country as production increased, employment burgeoned and foreign trade expanded. The undisputed author of this rise in the Russian economy during the 1890s was Sergei Witte, who had ascended from the post of a railway station master to that of the head of the Southwestern Railway Lines and finally to Minister of Finance. This tireless statesman put Russia on the gold standard and thus encouraged foreign investors to put their capital to work in Russian industry. Witte also created the state monopoly on vodka sales, the stated objective of which was reduction of liquor consumption. Then when liquor sales increased, the financial ministry channeled the revenues into the treasury. Witte utilized trade tariffs to protect Russian industry while welcoming agricultural and complex metal machinery which his country was unable to manufacture. Under his auspices, the Russian railway network was expanded across Siberia to the Middle East and even the western railroad system extended its scope and efficiency. It is not surprising that within ten years Witte had attained the office of Prime Minister despite temporary career setbacks in the course of Russian attempts at expansion in Asia.

Russia became an industrial power though exporting primarily raw materials and importing finished manufactured goods. Unfortunately, the largesse inherent in this state of affairs did not find its way into the realm of the working class, which had helped to make it possible. Wages, benefits and working conditions lagged far behind those in Western Europe. The urban proletariat, frustrated and stifled by continuing hardship, began to develop political as well as social goals. In order to divert them from these interests, the administration finally fostered the implementation of labor unions, but only those led by government-appointed officials and directed toward achieving solely higher pay and shorter work shifts. The leaders of these unions were entirely oblivious to the more far-reaching political aims and aspirations of the working class. With their immediate financial needs addressed but their social objectives ignored, the laborers were amenable to ideological appeals from abroad, and there was no lack of such appeals both in terms of periodicals smuggled across the Russian frontier and in the form of overtures from socialist political groups based in Germany, France and especially from Switzerland, to which the Polish Socialist leadership had fled to escape persecution.

Meanwhile, though industry prospered and expanded, agriculture stagnated since the farming methods of the peasants, in whose hands was now concentrated more than half the arable land in Russia, had shown negligible progress from the 1870's and would advance very little until the end of the nineteenth century. The reasons for this lamentable situation were obvious. The members of this class lacked education and resources and the government, directing its major efforts towards industrialization and the financial measures calculated to support that goal, did little to assist the peasants in utilizing their relatively recently acquired land. Only the volunteers of the charitable organizations had even thought of trying to educate the peasants in farming methods, and there were not nearly enough of them to affect the entire empire. As the peasant population grew, a greater number of people were producing less yield per unit of cultivated land than in any other European country.

Despite apparent improvement, this polarization of its resources rendered the Russian economy basically unstable and set the stage for the political explosion that would follow Russia's ignominious defeat by Japan in 1905.

During the remaining years of the final decade of the nineteenth century, following the death of Alexander III, several seemingly unallied events took place whose underlying interrelationship would only become apparent with the passage of time. One such instance was the conversion to the Eastern Orthodox faith of Princess Alice of Hesse-Darmstadt, betrothed wife and emotional choice of Nicholas II despite parental and ministerial opposition. The adoption by the Princess of the traditional religion of the Russian autocracy was viewed as a mandatory prelude to a royal marriage between the two. The Princess, as sentimentally attached to the young heir-apparent as he was to her, took the matter seriously to heart and adopted the more conventionally Russian name of Alexandra Fyodorovna. She followed rigidly the tenets and attitudes of orthodoxy and rigorously supported the sacred nature of the autocracy following her conversion. While at first she took little interest in political matters and devoted herself almost exclusively to domestic and family affairs, the Empress subsequently assumed a dogmatic and inplacable stance on crucial issues, advising her husband to implement harsh and oppressive policies which served ultimately to alienate him from the sympathies of his people.

An affectionate and devoted couple, Nicholas and Alexandra soon produced a large family composed of four beautiful daughters, none of whom could secure the royal succession.

Finally, the Empress's fifth pregnancy was rewarded by the birth of a son, an heir-apparent to the House of Romanov whose health and very survival soon proved to be threatened by an incurable malady inherent in his mother's genes: Hemophilia, the so-called Hapsburg curse.

Simultaneously, events in the Far East were building into an inflammatory situation which would ultimately sharpen the conflict between Russia and Japan, between France and England and between the Franco-Russian alliance and the Prussian-Austrian alliance. Added to this was the expanding Russian market for Polish goods such as textiles, wood and wood products and raw material including metal in the form of "pig iron" for the manufacture of tools and machinery. On the political scene the phenomenon of urban expansion, prominent throughout the Russian empire, was no less active in the Vistula Provinces. The urban proletariat gradually lost its ties with the agricultural proletariat. The industrial middle class grew almost as rapidly as the laboring class. The intelligentsia became more heterogeneous and progressively more disenchanted with the unyielding rigidity of the new Tsar's adherence to the old dogmatic principles. The educational efforts of "Warsaw Positivism" (the ideological offspring of the organic work concept) began to materially lessen the burden of illiteracy and expand the horizons of the peasant class resulting in a general raising of social and political consciousness in both urban and rural areas. Schools and libraries arose in the villages paralleling the establishment of the peasant banks and popular translations of Karl Marx's <u>Das Kapital</u> became more widely accessible. Polish thought crystallized into separate sociopolitical concepts giving rise to conflicting ideologies and organizations that reflected those ideas.

* * *

Isaak Marjzendiak had served as Wola's mayor for six years in 1892. Throughout the period of his administration he had exerted every effort to remain scrupulously unaligned with any of the competing socialist political parties. At the same time, he had governed in as unbiased a manner as was possible under the prevailing circumstances. He was continuously aware of the scrutiny of the Russian Governor General stationed in Warsaw.

In addition, there was the viceroy, the Tsar's personal representative, to be placated and, on occasion, appeased if he fancied that the slightest infraction had occurred. In reality, no such infraction had occurred. Nonetheless, on one pretext or another, the viceroy's emissaries had made it a habit to present themselves at the mayor's office every few months, demanding to review the minutes of Council meetings, the ordinances recently signed into law, the budget reports, and occasionally, the mayor's public correspondence.

This campaign of ongoing harassment was beginning to take its toll. Isaak's patience was wearing thin; yet he dared not lower his guard. He dared not allow himself the luxury of betraying his true feelings. This was the aspect of a career in politics that Isaak most abhorred. The positive balance, however, was the capability to accomplish at least some of his cherished goals. These included the introduction of safer practices into the workplace, the factories and mills of Wola that reminded him poignantly of his own early employment at the Wishnieski Mill that now belonged to his family. In addition, he had succeeded in broadening the scope of the local labor unions and strengthening the bargaining power they wielded in negotiating with employed associations. He had encouraged and supported working condition reforms for agricultural workers as well, and had been invited to speak at some of the union meetings.

Isaak and Luvna were also drawn into the social life, not only of Wola, but of Warsaw itself, and that of its other suburbs and nearby neighboring cities. Certain aspects of this they enjoyed. It gave them an opportunity to visit with friends in a relaxed setting. But even here, the ever-watchful eyes of Mother Russia were upon them.

It was in the autumn of 1892, at a soiree hosted by the aging former mayor or Wola, Vladimir Zygmunt Oslowski and his gracious, perennially youthful wife Sophia, that the host's successor made the acquaintance of the man who was destined to profoundly influence his thinking and ultimately the course of his life. That man was Josef Kiemens Ginet-Pilsudski, an ardent patriot, a dedicated advocate of Polish independence, whose family had participated in the revolution of 1863, and whose mother had secretly maintained a private family library of forbidden books on Polish literature, language and tradition in defiance of the forceful Russification tactics of Poland's foreign overlords.

Born in Zulow in the Russian Northwestern Province that was formerly part of Lithuania, Pilsudski had been accustomed to affluence. His parents had owned a large picturesque estate, not unlike Plaz Marjzendiak. Unfortunately, when he was seven years old, fire had devastated the family estate, forcing them to move to much more modest living quarters in Wilno. Josef and his elder brother Bronislav had attended the Wilno Gimnazjum which was housed in the former Polish University of Wilno, and there had formed a Polish learning circle known as Spojnia, meaning "union", acquiring and distributing to interested students books that paralleled, in content and spirit, those that their mother had encouraged them to read. Madam Pilsudska's unexpected death, one year prior to Josef's graduation, caused young Josef to alter his plans, and leave Wilno and the bosom of his family to study medicine in Krakow. Here again, Russian bureaucratic interference intruded upon the young student's life. Trifling irregularities in the documents essential for his acceptance for the second year of his medical training blocked the continuation of his studies.

After that, both the Pilsudski brothers had immersed themselves in clandestine nationalistic and "subversive" endeavors. Although they were not directly involved in the assassination attempt against the life of Tsar Alexander III at the beginning of 1887, both young men were arrested. Sentenced to five years in the Irkutsk Prison in Siberia, Josef had just returned to Wilno. His life and career at that point were a question awaiting an answer. He had begun to seek that answer in the Polish Socialist Party or PPS, but he at first kept his association with that underground group secret by using an alias, Comrade Wiktor or Victor.

As Josef Pilsudki, he accepted the retired politician Oslowski's invitation, dressed appropriately for a formal social evening, and attended the gathering in the company of a party of casual acquaintances who were not associated with him in the Socialist political group. By far the most intriguing guest of the evening, and one who would come to exert a deep and far reaching effect on Josef Pilsudski, was Madame Maria Juszkiewez, whose father, Konstanty Koplewski, was a prominent Wilno physician. Maria had recently returned from St. Petersburg where she had attended the Bestuyhev Courses, a university for women. Even then, she had been an ardent activist in certain revolutionary circles. It was in this connection that she had met and married Marion Juszkiewez, a young railway engineer with whom she had produced a daughter, Wanda.

Unfortunately the ill-fated union had failed; Maria was at once too energetic, too intelligent and too sophisticated for her temperament and taste to blend well with those of the more passive and pedantic Juszkiewez. Maria had always been beautiful and dynamic. Upon her return to the scene of her girlhood, her beauty and poise had ripened into full blossom, and she quickly became know in elite social circles as "the Beautiful Lady."

All the ladies in attendance were colorfully gowned and decked with sparkling jewelry The one exception was Maria Juszkiewez, who was dressed in unrelieved black from her stylishly cut full-skirted dress to the jet beads at her throat and the matching jet ornaments that dangled from her earlobes. Not for nothing did she enjoy the title of "the Beautfiul Lady." Despite the ripe youthfulness and nubile allure of the younger women in the hall, none commanded the interest nor attracted the attention that Maria was able to ensnare seemingly without conscious effort. Within five minutes of her entering the assembly, she was surrounded by an impressive array of admirers. But the one guest who commanded Maria's attention was a tall, broad-shouldered, ruggedly handsome black-haired young man standing opposite her, Josef Pilsudski. Their eyes met and each recognized in the other a kindred spirit. Both were intelligent, gifted, articulate, passionate, patriotic and determined. And both possessed great physical appeal, a commanding presence and a quick wit.

Pilsudski raised his glass of wine in tribute to the black-gowned beauty, and she returned his silent, eloquent gesture with a seductive smile and a receptive nod of the head.

He waited and watched for his opportunity. When the swarm of drones had somewhat thinned, Pilsudski gathered up his courage and approached the queen bee, or so he thought of her, outshining as she did all the other women in the room. She was two years his senior, but that was irrelevant. Attired all in black as she was, he thought she must be recently widowed and said so, but she disabused his imagination gently but firmly.

"You are astute," she commented. "I am in mourning, but for a broken marriage, not a physical death."

"All deaths are regrettable," Pilsudski said sympathetically. "Even the death of a once warm relationship. Hopefully, you've been able to salvage some cherished memories to ease your sorrow."

"One fond memory survives in the person of my daughter Wanda," Maria said. "She makes it all, well, bearable. Without the marriage, I could not have had her. As it is, she was allowed to choose which parent she wanted to live with." She shook her head sadly. "I was very young on my wedding day."

"The young," Josef cited, "often make mistakes." He was recalling a failed romantic liaison of his own that had not progressed to marriage. A smile of understanding passed between them.

"You too, have made mistakes?" she asked.

"Not in my work," he answered. "That belongs to Poland. But privately, yes. The future is not open for us to know. That seems unfair, and yet…"

"And yet," she continued for him, "much that we dare to risk, much that has the power to inspire might go unaddressed if we knew the cost beforehand."

"You are wise," he responded, "as well as beautiful." He glanced toward the opposite end of the hall where musicians were taking their places on a raised dais draped like a stage. "Do you care to dance?" he asked, "Or is that an awkward question?"

Maria raised her eyes to meet his. He was half a head taller than she. Standing close to him, she had to tilt her head back.

"Not at all," she replied, and dropping her fan so that it hung from her wrist, suspended by its slim black cord, she reached upward and placed her hand upon his shoulder. "The waltz is my very favorite dance," she remarked. "That, and the Mazurka."

And so the beautiful divorcee and the dashing young socialist launched what would be their joint future on the wings of a waltz at a quasi-political ball. They would later that evening dare another waltz, and then a mazurka, but when they paused at this time with the conclusion of the music, they were standing before the Mayor of Wola to whom Pilsudski had been introduced upon his own arrival. Luvna, standing by her husband's side, graciously acknowledged Pilsudski's introduction of Maria Kaplewska Juszkiewez and smiled warmly at both the woman and the younger man. But despite her warm smile she suddenly felt cold inside. Were her instincts warning her that one of this pair meant trouble for her and her family, or was she slightly put off by the powerful personalities that both manifested on close contact?

Isaak, though not well acquainted, had met Maria Kaplewska before she had left Warsaw for St. Petersburg. He had not attended her wedding, but he knew her father moderately well. Pilsudski he had met tonight and had felt immediately drawn to him.

"You," Luvna had been saying, "are the most striking woman here tonight. Black deadens the complexion of most women, but it becomes you well. You fairly sparkle."

"Thank you," Maria responded. "I was admiring you from a distance as we finished our waltz." She turned to Isaak. "And you are the man of the decade. Your election was truly a tour-de-force. We heard about it even in St. Petersburg."

"It's kind of you, Madam, to so honor my achievement." Isaak said deprecatingly. He earnestly hoped that his becoming mayor of Wola had not attracted too much notice in the distant Russian capitol.

"I shall be expecting to see you build upon it," Maria said, gazing directly into his eyes. "Poland needs men like you!" And then she turned back to Josef Pilsudski. "And you," she added, "I expect great things of you both."

\* \* \*

In the months that followed that occasion, it was difficult for Isaak to openly seek contact with Josef Pilsudski. The name of PPS was becoming widely known; this group was gaining preeminence among the nationalist/socialist political parties. Its newspaper, Robotnik (The Worker) was the object of intense speculation and persistent pursuit. A reward was offered for information leading to the discovery of its printing press and the capture of its editor and staff.

Interestingly enough, the periodical was produced by only two men, Pilsudski and his typesetter, who also obtained the paper and ink for its printing. The PPS, in late 1894, assigned the entire project to Pilsudski who was then obliged to constantly move both his domicile and the party's press, in order to avoid detection. It seems almost incomprehensible to imagine that romance could flourish in this setting. Nonetheless, the young socialist/journalist and the Beautiful Lady managed to nurture the seed of erotic love so that finally on July 15$^{th}$, 1899, having renounced their allegiance to the Catholic Church because that institution would not accept Maria's divorce, Pilsudski and Maria Juszkiewez were married as Protestants in the village of Paprod Duza, near Lomza.

In order to have a brief honeymoon, the newlyweds were obliged to dismantle the press, conceal it in several pieces of luggage, and ship it by train to Lodz, where they called for it upon their return. And mixed with the parts of the press and the type were their wedding presents – pots, pans, linens, porcelains and what remained of Maria's trousseau. Shortly thereafter, Maria's daughter came to live with them, and the domestic trio resided in that location for the remainder of 1899.

\* \* \*

The seeds of dissent had taken root mostly in exile and under the title Polish Socialist Party (PPS). Founded in Paris in 1892, it became the first group to unite the concepts of social justice with national liberation and to work actively toward this joint goal both on Polish soil and abroad. This nucleus attracted similarly inspired groups in St. Petersburg, in Warsaw and in Wilno to which Jozef Pilsudski had earlier returned from exile to rebuild his life. Following an abortive involvement in the study of law even more brief than his attraction to a career in medicine, Pilsudski became active in the Lithuanian section of the PPS, traveling frequently between Wilno and Warsaw. When Stanislaw Wojciechowski arrived in Warsaw from London late in 1893, he had established the Workers' Committee, later the Central Workers' Committee (CKR), as the leading body of the PPS and Pilsudski remained an active member of this committee until 1914.

The initial publication of this group, based in London, entitled Przegsuit (Pre-Dawn) was smuggled across the Russian frontier through 'holes' in the border patrol. But the objective of the Polish based membership was the acquisition of a printing press and the publication of a periodical at home. This dream was fulfilled in Robotnik ('The Worker') the initial edition of which was printed in Lipniszki, fifty kilometers from Wilno, appearing July

12, 1894. Pilsudski became its editor, publisher and initial typesetter. Wojciechowski subsequently joined him and funds for the venture were solicited from activist university students or were surreptitiously supplied by affluent sympathizers, among them Isaak Marjzendiak, who favored the work being done and even occasionally attended meetings but preferred for the present to keep his association with the party "sub rosa". Though "The Worker" was directed towards the working class, the periodical's editor did not actively appear before laborers' assemblies at this point in his career. Pilsudski's role for the present was an underground one that facilitated the honing of his journalistic skills and the evolution of political concepts which would one day dominate the administrative policies of the revitalized Polish state.

Jozef Pilsudski had attended the first General Congress of the PPS in July of 1893 in the Ponar Forest outside Wilno in conjunction with other distinguished Polish socialists. These included Jan Kozakiewicz, Stanislaw Grabski, Maria and Stanislaw Mendelson, Rosa Luxemburg and Julian Marchlewski. It was at this meeting that delegates were selected to represent the group in Zurich at the International Congress of Socialists. From that point onward, Luxemburg and Marchlewski deserted the ranks of the PPS charging that its insistence on national Polish independence ran counter to the interests of the Polish laborers which were better served within the framework of the markets of Prussian, Austrian and Russian economy. They proclaimed that Nationalism diluted the major goals of class struggle and revolution. This then was the origin of the Social Democracy of the Kingdom of Poland (and later of Lithuania).

A third and larger rival political group arising out of the old Liga Narodowski (National League) began to pursue a new and independent course under the leadership of Roman Dmowski, a learned offspring of the landed class who attained the equivalent of a doctorate in the natural sciences and initially considered pursuing an academic career. However, his patriotic sentiments and his early involvement in Zet, the Union of Polish Youth, during his student days in Warsaw, inclined him in a totally different direction. Following arrest for his student socialist activities, Dmowski sustained a brief period of exile from Russian Poland and upon his return joined forces with Jan Ludwik Poplawski and Zygmunt Balicki, an old acquaintance and founder of Zet who had subsequently been awarded a doctorate in law at the university of Geneva. These three men became the triumvirate of the National Democratic Party. Like the PPS, it was militantly Polish in its ideals and aims and focused upon the attainment of Polish national independence and political reunification. Unlike the PPS, it emphasized an "all Polish" flavor that prohibited the inclusion of non-Polish elements such as gypsies and Jews within its ranks since Dmowski viewed these groups as 'internationalists' and 'pro-Germans'. For this reason the Polish Jewish socialists became united to some extent with Rosa Luxemburg's Social Democracy of Poland and Lithuania.

While Russian art and literature were reaching the culmination of their golden age as exemplified by the works of Ivan Turgenov, Feodor Dostoyevski and Leo Tolstoy, and symbolist writers, led and exemplified by Dmitri Merezhkovsky, were coming into prominence, socialist leaders such as Pilsudski, Poplawski and Drnowski were expressing their respective political philosophies through the medium of the underground press. These consisted of <u>The Worker</u> and <u>Pre-Dawn</u> representing the PPS, and first <u>Glos</u> (Truth) and then the <u>All-Polish Review</u> in the case of the National Democratic Party. The Social Democracy group depended less on the printed word and more on the mechanism of socialist assembly and oral presentation of policies to the laborers whose allegiance they sought to attract.

Throughout the four years in which the Russian Polish militia doggedly hunted the location of the PPS headquarters in Wilno,, in which its periodical The Worker was printed, the press resided in a homey apartment which was rented under the name of Adam Wojciechowski and was subsequently subleased by Mer "Wiktor Dabrowski and his bride," none other than Jozef Pilsudski and Maria Juszkiewicz.

Throughout this period, Pilsudski, alias Wiktor Dabrowski, traveled secretly to Warsaw and its suburbs of Praga and Wola where he continued to solicit funds for the publication of his periodical and to cultivate the friendship of Wola's Jewish mayor. Isaak Marjzendiak's political ascendance at a time of strong anti-Semitic sentiment in Poland impressed Pilsudski as something of a coup. He admired Marjzendiak who symbolized in his opinion the Jewish intelligensia which Pulsudski wished to ally with the PPS in order to counteract the 'Pan-Russian Labour Union' (known as the Bund) which at that time opposed unity with the Polish and Lithuanian proletariat in their struggles to overthrow the Tsarist regime. With Isaak's help, financial and political, Pilsudski was influential in implementing the publication of "Der Arbeiter" in London as an organ of the Warsaw Jewish organization. He later assisted the initiation of a Jewish press in Poland primarily for the printing of propaganda leaflets and proclamations.

A brilliant conversationalist endowed with great personal charisma, Pilsudski became the undisputed leader of the PPS, representing them in London and later at the Congress of the Second Socialist International in Paris in 1895 and 1896. While the resolution which he proposed at the Congress stressing the importance of Polish independence to the proletariat and to the international labour movement did not pass, Pilsudski made several important contacts with French, American, German and Russian Socialist leaders that would later prove extremely valuable to him and to Poland.

* * *

It was in 1896 that the concept of founding a Jewish state underwent significant ideological revision with the publication in Berlin of Der Judenstaat by Theodor Herzl. A storm of controversy, particularly at the rabbinical level followed this event. One consequence of this reaction was the refusal by Edouard de Rothschild and his banking associates to fund or lend moral support to Herzl's efforts. Herzl had already been rebuffed by Baron Maurice de Hirsch, the eminent Parisian Jewish philanthropist who considered the proposed Jewish state alternative shockingly at variance with the traditional national affirmative of the Sanhedrin's Principle of Western Life. Abandoned by the distinguished and wealthy elements of European Jewery, Herzl and his supporters turned instead to the Jewish masses and determined to convene a World Zionist Congress. This dream was realized on August 26, 1897, in Basel, Switzerland, when two hundred and four delegates from all parts of the world gathered in the Concert Hall of that historic city to publish openly the "treasonable" principle that the Jews were rightfully a separate nation rather than merely a religious community. Fired with a sense of historical mission, they unanimously elected Herzl President of the Congress, voted overwhelmingly in favor of his platform for the founding of a Jewish homeland in Palestine, established a World Zionist Organization under his leadership, and adopted a Jewish flag and a national anthem: Hatikvah. An Action Committee was permanently based in Vienna and at the conclusion of the Congress Herzl recorded in his diary the prophetic words: "In Basel I created the Jewish state." Thereafter he embarked upon the crucial step of opening diplomatic negotiations to lend substance to the basic machinery that had now been set in place.

Among the delegates to that history-making Congress were at least a few affluent members of Eastern European Jewry, among whom was Ephraim Marjzendiak. At eighty-three he was still tall, spare, unstooped by time and the hardships of his early years and the sorrows of his maturity. His beard was generously sprinkled with gray, but his hair maintained most of its pristine blackness even now and his eyes were bright and sharp behind the lenses of his glasses. By day he was a representative to this first-of-its-kind gathering, having traveled at some hazard from his home near Wola. Michael had been reluctant to remain behind and let his father make the long unfamiliar journey to Switzerland alone. But Rachel had persuaded him that someone was required to oversee the estate and take ultimate responsibility for the running of the mills and factories in his father's absence. And attending the Congress was the fulfillment of a cherished ambition for Ephraim, one he had been obliged to substitute for the older but less easily attained goal of personally visiting the Jewish settlements in Palestine. By night he enjoyed the sights of Basel with his lovely gifted daughter Leah, now a mature woman, as guide and companion.

She had received enthusiastically the news of her father's visit to the country she had made her home and had hastened to meet his train upon its arrival in Zurich. He was deliberately a week early for the Congress to afford his constitution the opportunity to acclimate to these intensely different surroundings. He also wanted to allow time for a visit to the home of Leah and Markos, before whatever unexpected rigors might ensue during the Congress could exhaust his gradually diminishing strength.

Zurich in August of 1897 was a center of culture as well as industry. Having failed to override Bern in its campaign to become federal capitol of the Swiss Confederation, the city at the source of the River Limmat had then concentrated on developing its role as the nation's economic and educational capitol. Leah Kolvner, who had completed her professional education there, was justly proud of her adopted home city and of the precious political neutrality which Switzerland had managed to nurture and preserve.

In the days preceding the opening of the Congress, Leah welcomed her beloved father with all possible festivities. The time of the three weeks of traditional Jewish lamentation, culminating in Tisha-Be-Av, had passed. Now celebration was in order. Ephraim watched with an access of love and pride his only daughter's preparations of the traditional kosher dishes for special occasions at this time of year. Equally encouraging for him was the sight of his grandsons Samuel and Frederick, both young men now, the older one following his father's mode, entering the arena of business to join the Kolvner importing enterprises; the younger, Frederick, already an accomplished musician like his mother, was also equally talented with brush, charcoals and canvas. In the three days that Ephraim spent in Zurich it was with Frederick that he spent the majority of his daytime hours watching in delighted fascination as the young artist, sketch pad in hand, animatedly described the colorful history of one landmark after another, sketching each in turn. These sketches became for Ephraim prized mementos of this visit. Whenever afterwards he felt lonely or depressed, he would consult his grandson's renderings of the old town hall, the guild houses, the Waterchurch and the ancient bridges spanning the Lake of Zurich and the Limmat River. And, of course, there were also the great glaciers to the north that by their stature and pre-eminence silently impart to those of discernment the proper place of man and his affairs in the larger framework of nature.

On Ephraim's last night in Zurich, Leah Kolvner was scheduled to play a concert in the newly constructed Tonnhalle in conjunction with the Tonnhalle-Gesselachast, Zurich's symphony orchestra. It was a pleasure he had long awaited. She chose for her program works of Chopin and Liszt: The Piano Concerto No. 1 of the former, Liszt's famous Hungarian Fantasia and two works of her own composition, the earlier and longer one dedicated to her family and entitled significantly "Images from Childhood." The other briefer composition, called simply "Rejoicing", she had written very recently in honor of her father's visit and the occasion of his coming to Switzerland to participate in the First World Zionist Congress, truly a cause for every Eastern European Jew to rejoice did they but recognize it.

For Ephraim and for Leah this proved to be a landmark experience. She was uniquely inspired by her father's presence, by his eager receptiveness and by her own exultant joy in at last being able to demonstrate to him before this prominent assembly a measure of her love and gratitude for all he had done for her, had meant to her from the time of her earliest perceptions. He was amazed to learn the scope of communication of which music is capable when performed by a truly intuitive artist. There was much that had never passed between daughter and father in words before that night, though some of it could be intimated. At the conclusion of Leah Kolvner's concert, words were no longer necessary to express what she had always felt and what he had accepted on faith. The storm of applause that greeted the final work on the program was repeated following the encore, the Chopin "Fantasy Impromtu" which was one of Leah's favorites.

Ephraim found his eyes wet with unshed tears and felt no shame at this unusual show of emotion. He had not wept since Elana's death. But these tears were of a different variety, an origin unrelated to grief or sorrow. They sprang from a sense of fulfillment. He was glad he had lived to know this moment and to experience it fully. Despite Leah's invitation, he did not come backstage to meet her musical colleagues, though he was pleased to hear her discuss their comments later. He had needed the time alone with his innermost thoughts and feelings before submitting himself to the company of others.

When Leah was almost alone he joined her in the small intimate room reserved backstage for artists of stature to receive guests and family. He embraced her tenderly, wordlessly but with an expressiveness of which he had not believed himself to be still capable, no matter what his feelings. In Leah and her sons he perceived the future not only of his family but of his people.

"Papa!" exclaimed Leah. "Oh, Papa, you saw, you heard?"

He nodded. "Yes, my little one," he said. "I saw, I heard! You were magnificent! Transformed! I've never seen you as you were tonight."

"I've never felt as I did tonight," she answered. "Perhaps because always when I played concerts before, I wished you were there to hear me. This time you were. You are here."

"Would that it could always be so," said Ephraim wistfully. "And that I could always feel as if you played each note solely for me. You have given me such joy tonight, my daughter. I have known little joy since your mother left us."

"I know, Papa," Leah responded. "It has been very lonely for you these past years. I have felt very guilty living peacefully miles away from all the strife and turmoil that has become routine for you and my brothers. Word reaches us here of the restrictions, the new laws imposed, the recurrent pogroms. I would ask you to leave Poland and come here to live where I can watch over you. But I know how much Plaz Marjzendiak means to you. "

"It is the symbol of the whole meaning of my life, as much a part of me as my blood." he mused. "And your mother's buried there." Leah looked searchingly at him then.

"Do you still visit her grave every day?" she asked softly, shyly. Ephraim shook his head.

"Not every day, no," he replied. "Not nearly as often as I used to. But it is comforting to know that she is nearby. That some day I will be there beside her, that we will one day be reunited. I have moved her portrait to my study where I can see it when I work. She still inspires me even though I can no longer talk with her or ask her opinion."

"It must comfort you though to have Judyth," offered Leah encouragingly.

"Judyth fills a place that is uniquely hers. But she is not Elana," answered Ephraim. "And now that Elana is gone, we both miss her very much. It is good to have Michael there with his family. His son Daniel is nearly eleven now. It hardly seems possible. And at last I have a living daughter named Rachel." Leah squeezed his arm affectionately.

"And the one named Leah had better take you home," she interposed. "The train to Basel leaves early in the morning. And I have a surprise for you, Papa," she added archly. "I'm coming with you to Basel."

"That's not necessary, my dear," he assured her. "You worry too much about an old man. I have taken care of myself for a long time. I shall be fine."

"You don't understand, Papa. I *have* to come to Basel. I have been asked to play at the Concert Hall on the opening and closing nights of the Congress. It is a very great honor."

"Indeed it is!" Ephraim agreed. "A great honor and a great pleasure for those in attendance at the Congress to hear my beautiful daughter play. I couldn't be happier."

Thus it was that Ephraim Marjzendiak and the famed and gifted concert pianist Leah Kolvner traveled together to Basel, called there by the same history-making event, the First World Zionist Congress. Markos followed later, for he too had a role to play in the proceedings, having agreed to contribute generously to the fund that would form the economic basis for the planned World Zionist Organization, and to act as one of its founding officers, a duty he would come to share with his father-in-law by the conclusion of the Congress. Leah, concerned for her father's welfare was greatly encouraged by the active interest he took in this latest phase in the evolving cause of Zionism. Before this visit she had feared that advancing age and loneliness might have robbed him of his characteristic zest for life. Seeing him once more in person under these circumstances reassured her that despite the loneliness occasioned by Elana's death and the difficulties raised for all Polish Jews by the policies of the Tsar and his ministers, Ephraim was still the strong, thoughtful, quietly courageous man she had always loved and looked up to for as long as she could remember. She felt deeply indebted to Theodor Herzl, not only for his leadership of the Zionist Movement, in which she believed as strongly as Ephraim and Markos, but for the salutary effect he seemed to exert upon her father's spirit and well being from his opening words:

"We are here to lay the foundation stone of the house which is to shelter the Jewish nation." Indeed, the physical resemblance of the younger Herzl to Ephraim was striking, allowing for the difference in age; both were tall, slim, imposing of bearing with dark flashing eyes, abundant dark hair and a full beard. They were also similar in ideals, character, sensitivity and the persuasiveness of their enthusiasm and dedication to an ideal. However, despite advanced age, Ephraim's constitution was the stronger of the two.

When during the course of deliberations, controversy arose regarding where to base the headquarters of the Action Committee, Zurich or Berlin, it was Ephraim, prompted by Markos, who had business interests in many cities, who suggested Vienna as a compromise location. For personal reasons Ephraim did not favor Berlin or any other German city. Yet a significant majority of delegates represented the Jews of Prussia and Austria-Hungary. And though the second largest delegation came from various provinces of subdivided Poland and the Baltic nations, the representatives from Switzerland were the most affluent, the most assertive and the most independent. The political climate in that country was the most conducive to personal independence and ethnic freedom. Because of their historic partly Germanic derivation, they favored Berlin but accepted the suggestion of Vienna as an alternative.

France was less well represented than either Theodor Herzl or Ephraim Marjzendiak might have expected despite the lingering bitter aftermath of the Dreyfus trial. And only a few delegates had journeyed from England, though America had sent a sizable contingent, and Amsterdam, geographically small, was numerically prominent in terms of its part in the gathering. Enthusiasm was contagious; the atmosphere was charged with hopeful anticipation and a sense of achievement. There was an aura of strong purpose and determination about these men, and somehow, despite their varied countries of origin, their disputes and the multiplicity of their accents, there was among them an unmistakable unity, a kinship that transcended family ties and nationality. It was rooted in the covenant that bound them to their historic ancestors, their prophets of old and all their descendants yet unborn. The solemn vows they made in that distinguished hall were testimony to that covenant, a pledge of faith with all the future Jews whose lives would be enriched by the consciousness of restored nationality. When afterwards Leah and Markos returned with Ephraim to Zurich, still exhilarated by all they had seen and heard in Basel, the breathtaking scenery on the return trip, the majesty of the Rhinefalls and glaciers as well as the stirring rhetoric of the Congress, and still mesmerized by the commanding presence and compelling enthusiasm of its President, they agreed wholeheartedly with Eprhaim's comment:

"It is good to have been there, almost as if one had been visited by the Messiah or His emissary."

\* \* \*

September of 1897 witnessed an official visit to Warsaw paid by the young Tsar. Margrave Zygmunt Wielopolski, a descendant of that earlier Wielopolski on whom Alexander II had placed such high hopes, chose this occasion in his role as leader of the Conciliationalist Party (forerunner of the Party of Realpolitik) to make a speech in Russian praising Tsar Nicholas and the virtues of the Russian autocracy. He further offered to him the tribute of a million rubles collected in honor of the imperial visit. The Tsar graciously donated the gift toward the construction of a Warsaw Institute of Technology to be modeled on the Russificated lines of the University of Warsaw. The PPS used this opportunity to publish a proclamation authored by Pilsudski and printed on the secret Polish Jewish press. This proclamation condemned the servile posture of the Polish Conciliationist Party, and it promised a future uprising of the common people.

The recently appointed Governor-General Prince Alexander Imeretrynski sought to ease the tension in the Vistula Provinces, attendant upon and following the imperial visit, by relaxing the censorship of the press and allaying the ongoing conflicts between the state and the Polish Catholic Church. Further concessions were urged upon the Tsar by this representative in a lengthy memorandum outlining a policy of leniency, the just and appropriate addressing of private grievances and the implementation of a civilian advisory body, all without lessening the policy of Russification. The intent of this memorandum was to encourage in the Polish-Russian citizenry a perception of union with the Russian population as a whole. Had the measures it contained been adopted, the fate of the Romanov Dynasty might have been different, but neither the Tsar nor his immediate advisors accepted any of Imeretrynski's proposals. Under the circumstances, their subsequent clandestine publication by the PPS in London, Moscow, St. Petersburg and Wilno with editorial comments and introduction by Pilsudski, served only to embarrass the Tsar and the Governor General. Neither of them were ever able to learn how a secret official correspondence had fallen into subversive hands.

* * *

Early in the following year, 1895, Mathieu Golovinsky, a discredited Russian attorney, opportunist and journalist who had fallen into disfavor at the court of Tsar Nicholas II, found himself exiled in Paris. He has been allowed to select this place of his exile. There, he went to work for the Okrana, the Russian secret police agency based in France, and while employed there, he was recruited by Ivan Gorymikine and Pyotor Rachikovski, sworn enemies of Sergei Witte and his modernistic reform programs. (Witte, because of his able statesmanship and proven positive achievements, enjoyed the confidence of Tsar Nicholas II.) Golovinsky's assignment was not a simple one; he was required to produce an irrefutable document that clearly branded the Jews as the originators of an international plot to overthrow the Christian monarchies of Eastern and Central Europe through "modernization," political maneuvering and financial exploitation and domination. Nor was this man allotted much time in which to achieve his objective which was intended to discredit Witte. Driven by a combination of greed and fear, Golovinsky discovered, in an old and largely forgotten manuscript written by a radical French journalist and author named Maurice Joly, the blueprint he needed to construct his libelous document.

Ironically, the forgotten book bore the unprepossessing title <u>A Dialogue in Hell Between Machiavelli and Montesquieu</u>. It had been written in 1864 as an indictment of the repressive administrative policies of Louis Napoleon, who had himself crowned Emperor Napoleon III of France. In its original form, it bore no connection to the Jews and in no way addressed international revolution or conspiracy. What it did explore was the acquisition and corruption of power in the hands of a desperate ruler. Readers of Machiavelli's original treatise <u>The Prince</u> would find this somewhat distorted fictional conversation no surprise, and its location in Hell would seem an appropriate fate for the wily political manipulator.

Golovinsky's manuscript was printed in serial form first in the French newspapers and subsequently in the Russian press where it would come to the attention of the Tsar. When Golovinsky had completed his plagiarism of Joly's work, the original author would no doubt have been appalled by the result. His protest against the abuse of imperial power had been transformed into a grandiose, pretentious self-proclaiming testament of an international Jewish conspiracy for world domination.

First published as a pamphlet in 1898, it ws then presented in serialized form in 1902. It would later surface in book form as part of a publication by an eccentric mystic known as Sergius Nilus, entitled <u>The Great and The Small</u> in 1903 and would, in 1905 be published separately by Nilus as <u>The Protocols of the Elders of Zion</u>. This fraudulent manifesto, despite repeatedly being discredited, even withdrawn from publication, would in the future arise, like the fabled vampires, to repeatedly enjoy new life.

The timing of the original pamphlet, which purported to represent the records of a series of meetings held by leaders of the twelve tribes of Israel in a cemetery in the city of Prague, was deliberate and demonic. It followed, by only a matter of months, the conclusion of the First World Zionist Congress. Furthermore, its publication in France served to reignite anti-Semitic sentiments initiated by the Dreyfus Trial and rekindled in the early 1900's when Dreyfus was finally pardoned. Modernization in Russia was equated with Westernization by the Slavophile ministers of Tsar Nicholas II, and was therefore viewed as "anathemic." Golovinsky had carried out his assignment well. Just how well would not be truly apparent for three decades. Nonetheless, even at the time of their inception, the Protocols effectively contributed to Tsar Nicholas II's distrust and fear of the Jewish subjects within his realm and, despite his able statesmanship, served to undermine the influence of Sergei Witte, a man who, himself, was a confirmed enemy of the Russian Jews.

# PART SEVEN: DENOUMENT

I will lift mine eyes to the mountains
From where shall come my help?
My help comes from the Lord,
Maker of Heaven and Earth…

(Psalms 121: 1-2)

**CHAPTER FIFTY-FIVE**

**TURNING POINTS**

The end of the year 1898 signaled another milestone in the unending conflict between the PPS and the Tsarist administration in Poland and Lithuania. Two monuments were scheduled to be unveiled at that time. November 21st was the date set for the official presentation of a statue of Michail Muraviev who had served as Governor of Wilno in the years 1863 to 1865. He was popularly known as "The Hangman" for his cruel and oppressive policies. Pilsudski's proclamation and his editorial, appearing in The Worker pursuant to this event described it as a slap in the face to every Polish citizen. Of the unveiling of the monument to Adam Mickiewicz in Warsaw on December 24th, Pilsudski wrote that this event must be an occasion of public demonstrations in an atmosphere of hostility and unrest in order to honor the spirit of the poet-patriot of Poland whose works had consistently extolled the sentiments of national solidarity and freedom, and the recognition of the efforts of all the nation's citizens on her behalf. Speeches were forbidden on this occasion and Cossack militiamen were imported to enforce this mandate and maintain order. Nonetheless, despite the administration's best efforts, the PPS prevailed, the demonstrations did take place and the demonstrators, aided by sympathetic workmen, for the most part eluded capture and incarceration.

The holiday season that year was one of restrained though sincere celebration in Warsaw and throughout Russian Poland. The militia struck with renewed vigor seeking the strongholds of dissent and propaganda. A Conciliationist informer had hinted to the local authorities that the mayor of Wola had ties with the subversives and that he had entertained known dissenters and political activists in his home. When surprise visitations to the mayor's residence and offices and the homes of his near relatives proved decidedly unfruitful, the informant's credibility suffered serious reverses. And when no less formidable a figure than Madam Mira Pietrowska complained to the Governor-General about the inconvenience these investigations had caused for her friend Mer Marjzendiak, whose exalted position on the Bank of Poland's Advisory Council should have placed him above such petty disturbances, Margrave Wielopolski received a letter of reprimand from St. Petersburg. That document is still preserved in the historical museum in Wola in company with other personal and official documents illustrative of memorable events of that period in the history of the district.

Despite his deep involvement in the affairs of the World Zionist Organization, Ephraim had managed to maintain a politically unobtrusive façade, allowing his monetary and intellectual contributions to speak for him. A sudden bout of transitory ill health intervened to prevent his attendance at the Second World Zionist Congress in August of 1898, but did not prevent his forwarding his report of the activities and achievements of the Jewish Warsaw Commission, the local branch of the World Zionist Organization (WZO) which he had worked to establish, to his son-in-law in Zurich, so that a member of the family could make the formal presentation.

The High Holidays that year were observed with strict formality and reverence in the Marjzendiak family, as was the custom. However, it was the observance of Hannukah that afforded the occasion for a family gathering of the Marjzendiak clan and allowed Ephraim and Markos to confer on the proceedings of the Congress in Basel the preceding summer. Markos remarked on the comments of Vice President Max Nordau who had introduced for the first time the Dreyfus affair into the discussions as a consequence of the second trial, its shocking verdict and that verdict's dramatic reversal earlier in the year. Leah, upon her arrival, was relieved to find her father fully recovered from his earlier indisposition, and enjoying his characteristic vigorous good health. His tireless enthusiasm for the cause he favored so ardently made him seem younger than he had in recent years. And the family reunion of his children and grandchildren contributed still further to his exultant joy and well being.

The solemn family prayers Ephraim intoned on that first night of the eight-day celebration paid tribute to the blessings Adonai had deigned to grant to his seed, allowing him to fulfill the promise of his name.[10] He had four living children of whom any father would feel proud. And through them, there were five stalwart grandsons. Abrahm, now 20, was assisting Michael in overseeing the running of the lumber mills. Samuel at 21 was already his father Markos' able second- in-command, a junior captain in the importing industry. Frederick at 19 was a violin virtuoso of considerable stature, a member of the Tonnhalle-Gesselachast, and a frequent soloist with that group. Furthermore, he was now a renowned artist whose paintings had been exhibited in Zurich, Geneva, Basel and Paris. Daniel at 18 already displayed his father's genius for words and his propensity for

---

[10] Ephraim means fruitful.

comprehending and utilizing a wide variety of languages. His poems in both Hebrew and Russian had elicited favorable comment and approbation within the respective circles toward which they were directed. Johann, youngest of the five at fourteen, was still undecided as to his future career. One year past his Bar Mitzvah, he was academically equipped to enter Warsaw University. The Russian quota system, once relaxed under Alexander II, had been re-imposed against Jewish students seeking higher education. Because the places were limited and the competition for them was fierce, Johann entertained little hope of his acceptance at that institution. His father Isaak was now seriously considering sending him to Krakow to attend his own alma mater.

Sarah Krakowska still lived there and the two had maintained a friendly correspondence over the years, devoid of any hint of their former quasi-romantic attachment. She was now a respected senior faculty member in the Biology Department of the University of Krakow. She maintained a modest but well appointed home on the campus, and she had made clear in her letters the fact that she would welcome Isaak's son into her home with all the affection of a "maiden aunt". Her faculty appointment, she added, would prove instrumental in assuring Johann's acceptance, despite his youth, and the unique charm of the city itself would help to make him feel at home much as it had done for Johann's father and uncle years ago. Indeed, as Ephraim conceded, conversing enthusiastically in the course of dinner, the family had much for which to be thankful as they approached the new century soon to begin.

* * *

March of 1899 brought with it many noteworthy events. Isaak Marjzendiak stood for re-election as Mayor of Wola, and, despite intense efforts by the Concilationist forces to unseat him, won the popular vote. This was a clear demonstration of the power now wielded by the Workers' Union as a result of the coalition recently formed between the Polish and Jewish contingents so actively encouraged by the PPS. As a result of this victory, Isaak became even more closely affiliated with the PPS movement; his friendship with Jozef Pilsudski deepened and his younger brother Michael, inspired by Pilsudski's daring, his charismatic appeal and his concise, vivid journalistic writing style, composed a series of articles for <u>Pre-Dawn</u>, the London periodical of the PPS which was directed to the intelligentsia of all three divisions of the Polish nation and of the exiles throughout Europe. In contrast <u>The Worker</u> published in Poland now served as an organ of the still illegal Socialist Labor Movement as well as the PPS.

Toward the end of March, Tsar Nicholas convened a peace conference in The Hague to discuss the growing divisiveness of elements within the Russian nation. At this meeting Theodor Herzl, the "uncrowned King of Zion" as he was becoming known, made contact with Nouri Bey, Secretary-General to the Turkish Foreign Minister. As a consequence of that contact, the framework was laid for the opening of negotiations with the Ottoman Empire. Herzl hoped to obtain a modest strip of Palestinian land which was to become the home of the New Israel. Unfortunately, these negotiations were ultimately doomed to failure. Nevertheless, they helped to strengthen Herzl's determination regarding the political necessities of a Jewish state, a concept which he continually introduced at subsequent World Zionist Congresses. His efforts to establish a German protectorate for the proposed new Palestinian state had already met with indifference. Now his attempts to win approval for a separate state on Turkish-held soil encountered evasion and subtle but definite rejection, not to mention open hostility in the ranks of Orthodox European Jewry. This latter group favored a policy of piously awaiting emergence of the Messiah to lead the Jews of the

Diaspora back to Palestine. They held to the view that any premature action on their part directed towards this goal constituted a presumption and an affront to Adonai.

Throughout the Summer and Fall of 1899, Russia pursued her expansionist policies for advancement of her power in Manchuria, further extended the railway system in that area and grew steadily more evasive in her dealings with the other European powers. The Tsar was equally evasive in his communications with the United States which had just annexed Hawaii and acquired the Philippines from Spain, thus achieving the status of a Pacific power. Secretary of State John Hay's proposed "Open Door" principle of trade in China contradicted the Russian Empire's objectives in Asia.

Against this background of internal and international instability, the Jews of Eastern Europe were departing the scenes of their youth and childhood in ever increasing numbers and seeking asylum elsewhere. Their goals of settlement were in Northern Europe, in the Zionist settlements in Palestine, and primarily in America where they had heard opportunities for advancement were numerous and persecution on the basis of religious conviction was forbidden by the nation's Constitution. That persecution can be subtle as well as overt was not, under the circumstances from which they fled, a significant consideration to the Jews of every social class and intellectual level who emigrated from greater Russia and from the western segments of the Prussian empire in the decade preceding 1900. In earlier years the emigrants of Jewish derivation had been primarily German. The records of the United States Immigration Service at Castle Garden, at the tip of Manhattan, clearly documented this German prevalence in the Jews processed through that edifice.

However, after 1881, the worsening political climate in Russia and her subservient provinces caused a sharp change in the pattern and character of Jewish emigration and of Eastern European emigrants in general. Many Russian and Polish dissenters, who felt either unsafe or unwelcome in large numbers in the other nations of Europe, undertook the long ocean voyage to the New World of freedom and opportunity that the United States of America had proved to be for their more adventurously inclined ancestors and contemporaries. The facilities of the U. S. Immigration Service moved in 1890 to Ellis Island and were soon almost overwhelmed by the swelling tide of Eastern Europeans seeking sanctuary on American soil.

Closer to home, the Winter of 1899-1900 proved to be one of the worst in Eastern European history. A relative drought in the months preceding the traditional harvest time had led to a diminution in staple crops. Starvation reared its threatening head in a setting already jeopardized by social unrest, administrative oppression and political conflict on an ever widening scale. Poor nutrition led to decreased immunity. The physician population of much of Eastern Europe found itself frequently working without respite and constantly depressed by the magnitude of its defeats in dealing with the situation. Adam frequently brought home stories of these events as did his former colleague Dr. Jedewreski, who had come out of retirement to assist him in this extremity. Meyhra, who attempted to assist them both, shared their feelings of frustration that so little in the way of effective drugs was available in this time of dire need.

Added to this was the fact that the economic boom of the preceding decade was now giving way to almost world-wide depression. The dawning of the twentieth century to which Ephraim Marjzendiak and his family had looked forward so hopefully only a year before, now presented a bleak and frustrating prospect. Work orders for the mills steadily declined. Fortunately, this was balanced by an increased demand for produce which on the well run

Marjzendiak estate was mercifully plentiful. But this year funds for the Action Committee of WZO had to be curtailed. Johann had offered to give up his plans to go to Krakow and begin his advanced studies in the Fall of 1899, but Ephraim would not hear of it. The estate, he argued, could survive without the voluntary help of his youngest grandchild and education for his people had never been more critical.

Thus Abrahm traveled with his young cousin that Fall to Krakow in order to see him safely settled in the home that would be his throughout his attendance at the university there. Isaak had wanted to make the trip himself, but was prevented by the political unrest that currently afflicted all of Poland including the relatively quiescent Warsaw suburb of Wola. He would have appreciated an opportunity to see Sarah once more after all these years. However, he reasoned, he could never forget the way she had looked when they had said their farewells in the railway station at Krakow, where he had left his friend's law practice to rejoin his family and to be close to Luvna. Perhaps it was best to retain that treasured memory and resist the strong temptation to seek the experience of a more poignantly emotional reunion. Instead, he composed a letter to be transported by Abrahm and given to Sarah upon the arrival of Johann and himself.

Abrahm was indeed grateful for the opportunity to make this journey. The necessary passes and documents that would allow for travel between the Vistula Provinces and Austrian Poland were difficult to acquire in these times, especially for Jewish citizens. Once more there was cause to be grateful to Madam Pietrowska and her influence with the Governor-General as well as to the preeminence of his Uncle Isaak, whose glowing accounts of Krakow filled both Abrahm and Johann with pleasurable anticipation. In this mood of excitement and adventure it did not occur to Abrahm to wonder why his father Adam's reaction to the proposed excursion of his son and his nephew to the scenes of his own academic triumph had not proved more enthusiastic. Unaware of the bittersweet nature of Adam's memories of Krakow, his son had no foundation on which to base an assessment of his father's restrained acceptance of the news that Johann was going to that famous city to study, and that Abrahm felt duty-bound to accompany him there. Intellectually, Adam was in agreement with this plan; emotionally he was in turmoil. Apprised of Isaak's intention to correspond with Sarah, to whose care he was entrusting his only son, Adam, unaware that the letter Isaak proposed to write was but the most recent in a series of such letters, entered into a serious and soul-searching dialogue with himself as to whether he should follow his brother's example. The note which he finally sent by Abrahm, brief and understated, restrained in keeping with its author's nature, was a compromise which did not fully satisfy him, but it did conform to his strict code of ethics and to his loyalty to Meyhra. It read as follows:

"Dear Sarah:

I find myself hardly able to express my gratitude for your kindness to my beloved nephew Johann, whose academic advancement you have so generously taken to heart. Naturally, knowing the depth of your feeling for others and the nobility of your spirit, I do not find this action on your part surprising. It simply confirms what I have always known of you, what I have admired and respected from our earliest acquaintance.

I can only hope at this extremity of time and distance that life has dealt kindly with you, more kindly in these latter years than it did in the days of our youth, and that you have found a measure of contentment and fulfillment in your work, even as I have managed to do.

Your interest in biology and environmental influences has inspired in me a passion for research which has proven most rewarding. I have recently submitted the results of my humble efforts to the Polish Academy of Science for their evaluation. Of course I do not dare to hope for more than the most cursory response to my correspondence on the subject. But perhaps the work will provide some useful insights, for other more able scientists, into the causes and workings of human inheritance as it relates to disease processes. You I know will understand my feelings in this regard as no one else can.

It is my constant prayer that Adonai will grant to you his loving kindness and care. I send this to you by one whom I regard as my life's treasure, my only child, my son Abrahm who owes his existence as much to you, in a very special way, as he does to his mother and to me.

My deepest and most sincere regards always,

Adam Marjzendiak

September 3, 1899

Sarah read this epistle in the privacy of her bedroom on the evening of Johann and Abrahm's arrival in Krakow. In her mind's eye she could see Adam painstakingly composing it, carefully weighing every word to be certain it conveyed just the proper shade of meaning without overstepping the bounds of propriety, or betraying too openly the full measure of his feelings. Adam had always been so, even as a very young man. That had been one of his major attractions for Sarah. She had much preferred his gentle reticence, his devotion silently expressed to the more flamboyantly direct approach of other young men of her acquaintance. In all her life she had loved only two men; one she had finally dared boldly to seduce because she knew it would be their only time together, their one opportunity for physical intimacy. To the other she had not dared too boldly to confess her love for fear that despite his dedication to his brother, he might have given a positive response with lamentable consequences. And the name of both these men had been Marjzendiak. How strangely intertwined their lives had been and still were, she mused as she read and reread Adam's dear sweet carefully worded letter that told her more in what it left unsaid than in all the cautious phrases it employed, trying so hard not to say too much.

And now the son for which they both had made so great a sacrifice was grown to manhood. He was the image of his father, so like the young Adam that Sarah's first glimpse of him took her back in time to her student days in her father's house, now long empty, the last in a procession of students needing a home departed years ago. Sarah had kept the house more out of inertia than any other conscious motivation. But tomorrow, she determined, she would visit it once more. Visit Jakob's garden and the Summer house where his ill-fated namesake had been conceived. For once she would allow herself to relive the past and then she would seal that past away once and for all and send young Abrahm back to his father with her blessing and the silent assurance of her undying love.

* * *

Thanks to the unstable economic situation and to his waning strength, Ephraim Marjzendiak had not planned to go to Basel that Summer for the Zionist Congress, but waited impatiently for word from his son-in-law concerning the progress that had been made in the ensuing year. President Herzl's report had been as stirring and inspiring as usual, detailing his audience with Kaiser Wilhelm II in Constantinople and his visit to Palestine, where he had been enthusiastically received by the Zionist colonists. Wider political issues had also been discussed, most controversial among which had been the policies of the Jewish Colonial Trust and the political methods to be utilized in the interest of world Zionism; the promotion of Zionist goals in all the countries of Europe and of the Americas as well. At this Congress too, Palestine was reiterated as the one appropriate site for the founding of the Jewish state. The relatively meager attendance of only one hundred and fifty-three in contrast to the three hundred and forty-nine delegates the preceding year was partly attributable to worsening political and economic rwide. To a lesser though important degree, it was also due to rabbinical opposition to the Zionist movement and its "denial of the Messianic Principle in modern Jewish life."

Ephraim's reaction to the lengthy communication from Markos Kolvner, which contained this information, was one of frustration and disappointment. Frustration that there was still such active opposition to the manifest necessity of Jewish political independence within the Jewish community itself, and disappointment that more in the form of tangible objectives had not yet been achieved. Despite his dedicated commitment to the Zionist cause, Ephraim was also frustrated and disappointed at his own lack of tangible achievements. But Warsaw in the Winter of 1899-1900 was hardly a setting conducive to exalted philosophical, political or economic accomplishment, even by a man of Ephraim's gifts, background and experience.

Russian national self-awareness, fostered by the period of economic and industrial growth and affluence that was just ending, had two less appealing ingredients; defensiveness and intolerance. All three had been accelerated by the results of the census of 1897, the first truly reliable survey of the Russian population mix. It had shown that of the nearly one hundred and twenty-nine million people then living under Russian rule, forty-one million, nearly a third, were non-Russians, and of these nearly five million were Jews, a figure representing approximately half the world's Jewish population at that time. This group, even more than the traditionally rebellious Poles, were increasingly viewed as "separatist," non-assimilatable and subversive. This view had little factual foundation and the classical autocratic reaction of increasing Russification only served to increase separatism and nationalism among the nations forced to dwell under Russian dominion. Thus the policy of "dry pogrom," continuous harassment and intimidation of the Jews stopping just short of bloodshed, prevailed even when the more violent upheavals and actual massacres were in abeyance. And with the growing privations of "creeping depression," cultural, religious and political animosity directed against the Jews of Russia and its satellites became a swelling tide as the twentieth century opened.

* * *

Early in February of 1900, Jozef Pilsudski under the name of Wiktor Dabrowski was again visiting Warsaw despite the ever present danger of arrest and detention. During this period, Pilsudski's letters to friends and colleagues in London and Zurich detailed the nerve-racking atmosphere prevalent in the city. Militiamen, mobilized by the Ministry of Police, arrested and detained more and more private citizens suspected of subversive activities and even of subversive sentiments. Most of the unfortunate victims were ultimately released after varying periods of incarceration and interrogation. A few would disappear permanently. A mood of paranoia seized the city. Against this background, the urgent note received on the morning of February 12, 1900, by the mayor of Wola assumed ominous overtones though couched in deceptively prosaic terms. It read as follows:

> Dear Sir:
>
> Because of urgent circumstances, I would deeply appreciate a moment of your valuable time this afternoon. I shall be at the University Library in Warsaw after lunch, until mid to late afternoon.
>
> Regards, W.D.

What it did not convey in obvious terms was the basis for the urgency of the errand to Warsaw, nor the fact that the author of the message felt himself to be under surveillance. The term "urgent circumstances," in the existing context of the times, referred to the need for funds of which Isaak Marjzendiak was well aware. He had a luncheon meeting with the town council that commenced at 11:00 a.m. and would probably continue until 2:00 p.m. If he was prompt, he could still make a stop at the main office of the Bank of Poland in Warsaw and keep his appointment at the University Library well before 4: 00 p.m. That would enable Pilsudski to avail himself of the last train from Warsaw to Lodz at 6:00 p.m. if indeed that was his intention.

The Town Council meeting lasted until nearly 3:00 p.m. and Mayor Marjzendiak was obliged to cut short his last-minute instructions to the Council Secretary Erena Skoldowska, promising to supply further details the following morning and to peruse at that time the completed notes of the meeting. He left almost immediately, and the driver of his carriage, Samuel Meyer, a distant cousin by marriage, would later recall that his mood was one of unaccustomed impatience bordering on agitation. The carriage could not seem to move fast enough to suit the urgency of Isaak's errand to Warsaw. Upon his return, Isaak mentioned to Meyer, he was scheduled to pay a visit to his father at whose home he was to meet with his wife for a family dinner that would include his brothers, their families and a family friend and neighbor, Madame Pietrowska. For the present, they passed the Marjzendiak compound without slackening their pace. Isaak seemed driven, compelled by an apprehension whose origin he was unable to explain even to himself. Preoccupied, for once Isaak failed to notice the imposing western gate of the city elegantly embellished in recent years and opening into Chlodna Street, which joined Elecktorety Street as it passed eastward toward Senatorska Street and the commercial section of the ancient Mazovian capital.

At the bank a surprise awaited Mayor Marjzendiak in the person of his father. Ephraim's errand was in a way as unexpectedly urgent as Isaak's. An altercation dividing the members of the Advisory Council had risen as a consequence of the economic pressures that were drawing the nation steadily into depression. A sudden rush of cash withdrawals was causing panic and Ephraim's vote proved to be the deciding one in determining the course of action to be taken by Russian Poland's major financial institution in dealing with this emergency situation. Cash assets were frozen until the first business day of the following week. Bonds and securities could be liquidated only after an advance notice of three working days, and a substantial minimum balance was instituted in order to insure maintenance of an active account. These measures were calculated to stem the tide of panic withdrawals without closing the bank entirely. The protracted debate which preceded the vote had lasted for most of the afternoon. Isaak was on the point of departing when he saw his father moving slowly toward his office, fatigue evident in every line of his spare frame. Despite his haste, the younger man followed that familiar figure through the door, surprising Ephraim in his turn.

"Isaak!" exclaimed Ephraim warmly. "This is indeed an unexpected pleasure. I hadn't anticipated seeing you until tonight. "

"I know," replied Isaak. "I had to come here to make an unplanned withdrawal."

"You, too?" remarked Ephraim, obviously disappointed.

"It's not what you might think, father," Isaak hastened to assure him. "It's only a small emergency loan to a friend." Ephraim nodded wearily. "I've long since ceased to ask about your friends, son," he remarked, moving towards his desk. "I often think the less I know of some of them, the better."

Isaak smiled a trifle ruefully.

"You may be right at that," he said. "But I make it a point not to involve myself too deeply in their overt activities. Fortunately, money, despite its influence, enjoys a certain anonymity."

"True," agreed Ephraim thoughtfully. "Spoken like a true politician. You've learned their ways."

"I've also learned the pitfalls of those ways. Thus far I've managed to avoid them," was Isaak's rejoinder.

"I pray your good fortune will continue, son," said Ephraim, his voice conveying a depth of meaning beyond the sense of the words he employed. He added, as Isaak drew closer to him, "In these times none of us is safe!"

"I worry about you!" said Isaak. "With Franz gone, they demand so much of you."

"It goes with the gray hairs," remarked Ephraim with a flash of his characteristic wit. "In almost every culture, age is assumed to impart wisdom. After today's proceedings, I'm none so certain that's a valid assumption."

"What was it this time?" asked Isaak, a note of deep concern sharpening his tone.

"The panic! The threat of depression! The people are afraid the bank will fail," replied his father candidly.

"Will it?" was the unexpected query.

Ephraim turned to face his son. "Not for a while. Not at all if we can control the panic and stem the withdrawals. Even in times of economic reverses, money is safer in the bank than stored in some makeshift cache in a private home. Theft becomes an epidemic under such conditions, whereas the bank is obliged to make good the deposits at least up to a specified level. That's what panic makes people forget. Facts, logic, reason," Then his tone changed. "This friend, is he in some type of trouble?"

"I don't know, father," answered Isaak honestly. "I won't be certain until I see him. But I'd better be going now. It's growing late."

"Youth is always in a hurry," said Ephraim philosophically, aware that his second son had now achieved the age of 59 years. "Take care! Judgment is inclined to take its time." And then he added earnestly, "May Adonai guard you in all your ways, my son." He reached out to Isaak and embraced him tenderly.

"May He bless you as well, father," said Isaak, deeply moved by his father's obvious concern. "Until this evening!"

Ephraim nodded in acknowledgement and then Isaak was gone leaving his father strangely troubled, burdened by a dread he could neither explain nor dispel.

* * *

The University of Warsaw stands within an impressive setting of wooded grounds and terraced accesses. It is graced with a remarkable library that even at the turn of the century could boast of a collection exceeding 400,000 volumes including a rich natural history division. Its botanical gardens were adorned with gently flowing fountains which were illuminated at night and its astronomical observatory is still one of the finest in Eastern Europe. On many prior occasions, Isaak had observed these embellishments with a distinct sense of pleasure. Today, he barely noted them in passing. His gaze, his whole attention was concentrated on the human elements in his immediate environment. After several anxious moments the object of his search appeared within his line of vision. A tall, broad-shouldered figure, stockier of build than Isaak, moved swiftly towards him across the main foyer of the library. The two men shook hands, glanced guardedly in all directions, and exchanged hurried greetings.

Pilsudski asked, "You understood? You brought it?"

Isaak nodded, withdrew a slender gray-hued envelope from the breast pocket of his jacket and handed it to the younger man.

"I hope it is enough," he remarked soberly. "The bank is taking measures to control withdrawals in order to stave off a panic."

"I'm not surprised," answered Pilsudski. "Everyone struggles to survive, even banks." With that he slipped the envelope into his pocket, not taking time to reckon its contents, a measure of his trust in Isaak's friendship and devotion to the cause for which Pilsudski worked so energetically. "You are a good friend," he remarked, clapping the Mayor on the shoulder. "Too good a friend to be endangered further." As he spoke Jozef Pilsudski's eyes scanned the building and the grounds just beyond the entrance, every movement and gesture betraying his apprehension despite his efforts to the contrary.

Infected by his friend's mood, Isaak asked, "Are you being followed?"

"That's hard to say," answered Pilsudski. "Last time I was in Warsaw I could have sworn I'd be arrested, but nothing came of it. The two men were probably thieves seeking a likely quarry. I don't dress the part. With you, it's another matter, my friend." Cautiously they walked toward the door, Pilsudski clutching a book he had checked out for the sake of appearances. "In about a week, I'd appreciate it if you could see this is returned. I don't expect to be back in the area quite that soon."

Isaak smiled, nodded and took the book from him.

"Of course," he answered following Pilsudski towards the door.

"It's just as well I go out alone," the journalist cautioned. "You follow in a few minutes."

Isaak said, "Good luck!" He was still unable to rid himself of the apprehension he had felt since first reading Pilsudski's note that morning. The Polish socialist leader nodded and moved away. Isaak's eyes followed him.

A group of students walked nonchalantly towards the library across the terraced quadrangle. Further away two Russian police officers, their uniforms covered by long fur-trimmed coats, loitered near a stand of chestnut trees. Pilsudski saw them almost at the same instant that Isaak did. He paused, momentarily irresolute, and Isaak, ruled by concern for his friend, stepped through the outer door of the library building and walked briskly towards him, calling out as though his greeting were the impetus that had arrested Pilsudski's progress.

"You almost left this!" he exclaimed loudly, holding up the book as he walked forward. The sudden radiance of the late afternoon sun, glinting redly on metal, quickened his pace. He ran forward without knowing for certain what it was he sought to avert. That metallic glint seemed to presage an ominous threat to his friend although he had not seen clearly what the object was. In his haste he nearly overshot his intended destination and was obliged to turn about to address his friend. He turned and reached out towards Pilsudski as though to transfer the slender cloth-bound volume to his possession. The gesture was arrested in mid-flight. Instead, Isaak lurched almost convulsively against his friend, his body shaken by a sudden spasm. The sharp report of the firearm seemed almost an afterthought.

The sudden stream of blood welling upwards spattered the burgundy-colored book as it fell from Isaak's grasp into the clump of snow that lined the cement balustrade of the library entrance stairs. Jozef Pilsudski caught Isaak as he fell, his eyes searching in vain for the origin of that fateful shot. The two darkly-clad figures were no longer visible. They had faded into the shadows of the ancient walnut trees out of range of the sound of Isaak Marjzendiak's painful spasms of coughing, and his final words to the man whose life he had just saved. Pilsudski knelt by his side, shocked and devastated.

The only word he could say was, "Why?"

Isaak's answer, barely audible, was an echo of words Pilsudski's wife had spoken to them both eight years earlier.

"Poland needs you."

# CHAPTER FIFTY-SIX
## GRIEF AND DESOLATION

In the music room of the Marjzendiak home Mira Pietrowska sat before the Pleyel piano that was its central feature, her long graceful fingers striking the concluding chords of Chopin's Piano Concerto #1. Ephraim stood by the window recalling the Tonnhalle in Zurich and Leah's concert there on the night before their departure for Basel. He would always associate the composition Mira played with that memorable occasion. The thought occurred to him that he had not realized until now just how accomplished she was. They had never discussed her frustrated musical ambitions, nor the basis for her ability to recognize Leah's budding talent when the family's wealthy neighbor had first invited her to take music lessons in her home. He was about to broach that subject when the carriage approaching the house caught his attention. It was Isaak's and Samuel Meyer was driving, and yet there was something strangely ominous in the scene before him or in Ephraim's perception of it that stilled his tongue and drove the thought of Mira and her musical facility from his mind.

The carriage halted, Meyer dismounted the driver's box, and another man emerged from the passenger section, but not Isaak. As Ephraim watched, these two men reached into the luggage box of the carriage and, with obvious effort, drew forth a third man who lay supine and still upon a litter. The man who walked beside Samuel Meyer as they bore the inert human form between them was unknown to Ephraim and his family. His manner was respectful without servility, and he was obviously shaken and saddened by the role he was called upon to play. Explanations at such times are awkward, even superfluous. Whatever the causes that eventuate in death, their revelation cannot reverse their effects. Jozef Pilsudski, also known as Wiktor Dabrowski and currently identified by the papers he carried as Ernest Witowski, was ill-prepared to address the grief of a Jewish family, especially when that family was faced with the sudden, unexplained and violent death of one of its members under circumstances that were mysterious as well as tragic. That this stranger was somehow involved was readily apparent. That his involvement was unintentional and deeply regretted became rapidly evident as he spoke with the family's eldest son.

"But how did it happen?" Adam asked. "Who was responsible?"

"There were two men.Militia officers, I think. They were gone before I could be certain."

Adam looked strickenly at his brother's lifeless body. "Did he say anything? Did he know?"

"I asked him that," Pilsudski replied. "He seemed to place himself between me and the bullet. He ran toward me just before the fatal shot.

"Did he answer?" Adam questioned, perplexed and anguished, appalled by the quantities of blood that covered Isaak's corpse.

"He said only three words," was Pilsudski's answer. "Poland needs you."

The implication was obvious. In that last fateful instant, Isaak had honestly believed that his country needed the man who stood before his father more than it needed Isaak himself. He had sacrificed his own life to preserve that of his friend.

Adam could not but wonder why Isaak had thought as he had, but the action he had elected to take was irrevocable, final. No discussion could alter it. Quietly, he directed Pilsudski and Samuel to place the body on the sofa in the music room.

When Ephraim saw it, he led Mira Petrowska out of the room. He could not, for the present moment, face either his son's corpse or the men who had brought it here. He could not yet face the fact of Isaak's death. They had spoken together, had embraced each other less than two hours earlier. Now, one of them was no longer alive. He had been torn out of the fabric of the living by an assassin's bullet. It made no sense to Ephraim. He could not accept it, he could scarcely believe it. He had heard the words that passed between the stranger and his eldest son, but he could not yet place them in a coherent context.

He directed Mira to take a seat in the living room, and she followed his directions silently, tears raining down her face, sobs issuing from her lips. Ehpraim's own eyes were wet with tears, and deep sobs choked him, oppressed his breathing. He went back into the music room, knelt beside the sofa and tore the lapel of his coat, the traditional mark of the Jewish mourner. The act was instinctive. Ephraim did not think about it beforehand. He simply tore the fabric, leaving in it a deep, unsightly rent. He leaned his forehead to the floor, and moaned in the extremity of his grief.

Meanwhile, Adam had led Pilsudski into the small salon adjacent to the living room. It was furnished with a desk and chair near the window. An informal table and matching chairs occupied the center of the room. It was Adam's intention to make the man feel as comfortable as he could under circumstances that were anything but congenial. His brother had obviously thought very highly of this man. When Pilsudski said that he wished to complete a note to Ephraim that he had begun composing in the carriage, Adam led him to the desk and bade him to complete the writing of his note there.

In an effort to behave civilly, Adam conferred with Samuel Meyer. There were practical tasks to attend to. The horses needed to be fed, their coats dried. They would need to be stabled and the coach put inside out of the weather. Perhaps, if he lost himself in such details, Adam thought, he could temporarily hold himself together, hold his grief at bay. Intense emotions had always troubled him, left him at a loss to express them and to deal with them. Today was no exception. He could hardly think and yet there were things that he must do, actions he must initiate. He was the eldest, the first born. His father, his whole family was depending on him.

When he returned to the music room, Ephraim still knelt there by Isaak's body, prostrate with sorrow. Adam went to him and helped him to his feet.

"Where is he?" were Ephraim's first words. "Where is the man for whom my son died?"

Gazing at his father's face, streaked with tears and contorted by grief and rage, Adam resisted the impulse to answer that query immediately. He thought it best not to let these two men be together too soon.

"I've left him to himself to deal with his own grief," Adam answered after a momentary pause. "They were friends."

"Friends," Ephraim echoed, and then he covered his face with his hands. "One can do without such friends!"

"We can't know what was between them, Father. But Isaak must have had good reasons for what he did. It's not our place to question those reasons now."

Ephraim glanced about the room, and then, steadying himself, he went to the windows and closed the drapes. Then, he and Adam wrapped the body, for the present time, in the fringed throw that covered the sofa, and placed it on the floor so that Isaak's feet were toward the door. It was the custom with the newly dead, so that the spirit could find its way into the next life, away from the world of the living.

Ephraim's first impulse on learning from Adam that Isaak had sacrificed his life to shield that of the man who had brought his body home had been to complete the assassin's task himself. Fortunately, the impulse was short-lived. However, he was distracted by grief at the thought that his son, barely past the prime of his life considering the normal longevity of his family, had been suddenly struck down by an anonymous and apparently indiscriminate slayer. That Isaak might have been the intended target was a thought even more painful, one that Ephraim preferred not to entertain.

* * *

Luvna sat by the low cot in the music room where Isaak's body lay, still covered by the fringed throw. Her eyes were unseeing, her mind unfocused, aware only of a searing psychic pain which had no physical component and was therefore all the more unendurable. Pilsudski, uncertain whether he would cause more suffering by remaining or departing, remained in the salon, fingering the few personal possessions he had retrieved from the snow where his friend had fallen, debating with himself to whom he should surrender them. Seated at the desk near the window, he hastily completed the letter he had begun, addressing it to Ephraim, the one to whom he felt he most urgently owed an explanation. Just as he was folding the paper with its neatly written script into the envelope, its intended recipient entered the room, glanced absently about him and became suddenly aware that he was not alone, that his unexpected companion was the stranger about whom he had but lately harbored such bitter thoughts. The goal of his errand to this room was momentarily forgotten.

"You're still here?" asked Ephraim somewhat belligerently.

Pilsudski nodded, getting to his feet.

"Yes," he replied. "Still here. I was writing you a letter. I hadn't expected to see you personally again. There are some things of Isaak's that I found. They must have fallen from his pockets." The tall stocky young man handed to Ephraim the items he had been about to enclose with the letter, watching his face for some sign of recognition. But Ephraim had not seen most of these particular objects before. They included a small square section of polished wood, the first Isaak had cut and dressed as a new and inexperienced workman in Wishnieski's lumber mill just outside Warsaw. There was the delicate floral pendant on a slender chain that had fallen from around Mariska' s neck so many years ago, a folded worn leather pouch containing the last few coins from the store Ephraim had given Isaak the night before he and his elder brother set out for Krakow. Here, too, tucked into the self-same pouch was a handful of earth from a garden in Krakow, adjoining the building where Isaak had shared for a short but blessed period of time a home with Sarah, the fair mysterious young girl he had loved but dared not touch and to whom years later he had sent his son in trust to receive the education that was denied to him in Warsaw. Neither his father nor his friend would ever fully understand the meaning of that precious store of humble treasures Isaak had kept always near him, keepsakes of times remembered. Ephraim stared dully at them now and then looked up to study the craggy, rough-hewn but handsome face of the man before him.

"You," he said, "whoever you are, I only hope you're worth the sacrifice that my son has made for you today."

"I hope so, too." answered Jozef Pilsudski. "I certainly intend to try to be. Your son was a good man, Mer Marjzendiak, and a good friend. Probably the best I shall ever know." He turned to leave, then faced his reluctant host one final time. "I'm sorry to have met you under such circumstances as these. Perhaps one day if we should meet again it will be in better times."

"It could hardly be in worse!" remarked Ephraim. "Who are you, anyway?"

"Pilsudski is my name," the stranger answered. "Jozef Pilsudski, though I have from time to time been known by others."

Ephraim studied the man a moment longer. "I'm not surprised," he said. "Pilsudski. Not a name one would easily forget."

Pilsudski offered Ephraim his hand but was not offended when the older man did not return the gesture. Jewish mourning customs were unknown to him but he assumed this might be a part of them.

"Goodbye, sir," he said simply.

"Go with God," said Ephraim solemnly after a brief pause. He had heard Christian acquaintances use this form of farewell salutation. "You meant much to my son, enough that he was willing to die that you might live. His driver will take you wherever you wish to go. You will forgive me if I do not hope we meet again."

Pilsudski nodded wordlessly. There was a look in Ephraim's eyes that silenced speech. The younger man turned and left the salon, found the main entrance and departed with one final glance around the foyer with its array of paintings to which a few, unknown to him, had recently been added: Michael's, Abrahm's, Johann's and Daniel's. The style was slightly different from that of the older portraits. It was that of Pierre Rebaumme's second son Matthieu. Elana's portrait was no longer there in its old place. The wall looked bleached and barren there, and Pilsudski wondered absently whose portrait had been taken down. He could not know it now hung in a place of greater honor. He closed the door behind him and descended the stairs to where Samuel Meyer awaited him. He had missed the last train to Lodz but there was another scheduled through to Wilno. From there he could find means to get back to his new home at 19 Waschodnia Street, apartment 4.

\* \* \*

Word of Isaak Marjzendiak's death spread like a blight across the Jewish community of Warsaw and its suburbs. For many he had symbolized the hope of his people, the tangible proof of their innate ability to rise above the adversities to which as aliens in a conquered land they were constantly subjected. This was especially true of the younger generation and the fact that Isaak's father had quietly, unobtrusively but steadily risen to achieve a place of prominence in Warsaw's banking community had endeared Isaak to the Jewish elders as well. Now suddenly and inexplicably he was gone and the furtively violent manner of his death struck terror into the hearts of all. If such a fate could overtake even the mayor of Wola, none of them was safe.

This latest family catastrophe depressed all of its members almost equally. Added to the terrible burden of grief was the fear that without Isaak's influence, the family estate might now be in jeopardy. Harsh laws restricting the rights of Poland's Jews continued to be enacted and property rights outside the Pale of Settlement were being more strenuously curtailed. Still, strictly speaking, Plaz Marjzendiak was part of the town of Wola, within the Pale, and had not changed ownership in more than thirty years.

The funeral service was to be held in the family synagogue on the estate grounds. Rabbi Janowski had died eight years earlier. His post on the rabbinical council had been assumed by Rabbi Abel Kreschner, a leading Talmudic scholar and theologian widely known and respected in Galicia as well as the Vistula Provinces. His willingness to journey from Warsaw to Plaz Marjzendiak in order to perform this final service for Isaak was an earnest of the esteem in which the mayor and his entire family were held.

Adam Marjzendiak found himself cast by this tragedy in the role of head of the family. Isaak's death, coming so unexpectedly after he and his father had met and conversed less than two hours before, had quite overwhelmed Ephraim. Though he had tried valiantly to treat the Socialist leader Pilsudski with the respect and civility due to an honored guest, Ephraim had not yet found it in his heart to forgive the man for his role in Isaak's murder. The burden of that bitterness had proved as incapacitating to the aggrieved father as would a physical illness. Thus Adam had taken the initiative in utilizing the still novel and rather expensive telegraph system available in Warsaw's commercial section to notify Leah and especially Johann of the events that had transpired and of the impending funeral which must take place as promptly as possible. Since Orthodox Jewish religious observance forbade embalming, the body was being preserved in the estate's refrigeration building but kept separate from the Kosher-killed and dressed meats stored in another compartment. Fortunately, it was winter. Nonetheless, tradition and practical considerations urged that the funeral ensue with all possible dispatch.

Isaak had met his death late in the afternoon of Monday, February 12, 1900. Even allowing time for the absent family members to reach Wola, the funeral could not be delayed beyond sunset of Friday, February 16, the Sabbath. The members of Chevrah Kadishah had already completed the ritual cleansing and preparation of the body. The water had been poured and the words of blessing recited. Isaak lay wrapped in the tallit he had worn for prayer, and in the all-encompassing shroud. The sealed plain wood coffin was covered with a black cloth. Outside the door to the 'cold room' stood two metal holders, bearing lighted black tapers to honor the dead.

Ephraim and Luvna seemed to take turns by mutual unstated agreement in keeping vigil outside that door. Ephraim stood dry-eyed and withdrawn, his grief for his son too profound for verbal expression despite the traditional encouragement of lamentation. Luvna wept constantly but silently, unable to seek or derive any consolation from the knowledge of all her deceased husband had achieved for the honor of his family and the benefit of his people. Could his relatives have known the future ascendence of Jozef Pilsudski, the good he was destined to accomplish for Poland and the spirit of toleration his administration would ensure for Poland's Jewish citizens, their wrenching grief might have been somewhat assuaged. Pilsudski's influence would have far reaching positive effects with the resurgence of Polish nationhood in the early twentieth century, because Isaak had so generously preserved his life.

As it was, Pilsudski did not return to Warsaw at this time even to attend his friend's funeral. For the present the avowed leader of PPS was maintaining a low profile, privately indulging his very real grief and endeavoring to plan future strategy.

Leah reached her ancestral estate on Wednesday evening, February 14th accompanied by her husband and her younger son Frederick. Samuel had been obliged to remain in Zurich to attend to family interests there. He looked upon his inability to attend his uncle's funeral as a great personal sacrifice and had composed a letter to Ephraim detailing his feelings and attempting to offer what consolation he could in this time of grief. Johann arrived from Krakow early the next morning. Sarah came with him, having cancelled her classes for that week as soon as she had learned of Isaak's death.

The decision to travel from Krakow to Warsaw had been for her a rigorous one, jointly dictated by personal inclination and a sense of responsibility for the welfare of her sixteen-year-old charge. Even with bona fide papers, the crossing from Austrian to Russian Poland was fraught with dangers, the most awesome of which was the uncertainty of military and political policy as practiced by the border authorities. Once that hazard was successfully addressed, the overland journey by railway was still subject to repeated document verification and interrogations. Such an ordeal occurring under such circumstances would have been almost unendurable for the grief-stricken youth recently notified of his father's tragic and untimely death. Though both Sarah and Johann were burdened by a keen sense of loss, together they were stronger than either would have been alone and Sarah's greater maturity had served throughout their travels as a brake upon the young man's readily aroused temper.

Johann resented so many of the external circumstances of being a Jew in Eastern Europe: the wearing of the yellow star which seemed superfluous, in view of the manner of dress, the obligatory beard and the yarmulke which distinguished the adult Jewish males of his day. Likewise he resisted the logic of requiring an additional border pass for Jews and extra documents to afford them passage from one precinct of the Vistula Provinces to another. On the train they were constrained to a vegetarian diet since Kosher meat was unobtainable. And only certain cars on the train were open to Jewish occupancy; the dining car was available for their convenience only on a very limited schedule. Had he, Johann wondered, been that young and unobservant earlier when he and Abrahm had traveled on this same railway in the opposite direction? Had the freedom of Krakow sharpened his sensitivity to the injustice of his people's position under the autocratic oppression of the Tsarist regime?

Once they had arrived in Warsaw, political and philosophical considerations were put aside in deference to the family situation. According to custom, Johann would not be allowed to look upon his father's face in death, but its features were etched upon his memory for all time. He joined his mother in her vigil outside the door behind which Isaak's coffin rested until the time appointed for the funeral; three hours before sunset. In that scant few hours Sarah chanced to meet Adam for the first time since he had left Krakow. Time, as it inevitably does, had wrought many changes in each of them, but recognition was instantaneous and they shared a kindred grief.

"In all my fancied versions of this moment," said Sarah apologetically, "I had not thought it would be on an occasion such as this." She went to him, touched his sleeve in tentative greeting. "Please accept my condolences. No!" She shook her head as if in protest.

"That sounds so stiff, so formal. It would be more honest to say permit me to share my grief with you."

"Your presence here says that, Sarah," answered Adam. "On Isaak's behalf, I cannot properly thank you for bringing his son home."

"Except for that necessity, I probably wouldn't have come." Sarah's tone was sharp with grief. "I don't think I'd have dared. I've never been to Warsaw until now."

"And now is not the best of times," was Adam's response. "Not for any of us."

Sarah nodded. "I know! And I've heard there is revolution in the air again, and the threat of international war. We never learn our lessons, do we?" She ended ruefully.

"Only temporarily," remarked Adam.

"Have you any idea how it happened?" she asked, taking him momentarily by surprise.

"Isaak?" he wondered.

She nodded in assent.

"He saved a friend's life."

"That sounds a fit epitaph," she remarked. "So like him! A generous impulse acted upon without thought of the consequences to himself. The ultimate mitzvah!"

Adam stared at her in wonder, amazed at the sense of peace her words brought him. She had traveled hundreds of kilometers to add her love and her grief to all of theirs, and had in this brief span of time put Isaak's death into perspective commensurate with his life. It did not lessen Adam's brotherly grief, for he would miss Isaak until the day he himself died. But it did allow him to accept the fact of that death as a logical conclusion to his life instead of the jarring travesty it had seemed to Adam until now. "I can only hope that in this tragic time," Sarah added, "the knowledge that both you and Isaak each have sons to carry on your name brings you some measure of comfort. They are fine young men of whom any father can feel proud."

Gently, Adam took Sarah in his arms and kissed her brow. It was a kiss of gratitude having no hint of passion in it. She had expected nothing else. But she felt deeply grateful to have brought a measure of consolation to him whom she still so deeply loved.

"Thank you, Sarah," Adam said, his voice barely above a whisper. But she heard every word including the ones he did not say.

The family synagogue was too small to contain the crowd that sought to pay final respects to Isaak. The eulogy delivered by Adam summarizing his brother's attributes and deeds was silently seconded by those present. And Ephraim, too, spoke a few words in summation.

"My son was a man," he said haltingly, his voice laden with the weight of his grief. "Like all men he was imperfect. But he upheld the laws of his people and always he sought to walk humbly in the ways directed by Adonai. There were issues on which we did not agree. But no father could be blessed with a more worthy son." There was more he would have said, but could not bring himself to continue. He stood silently, the bitter tears coursing down his face. Adam and Michael went to him to help him to his place, but he shook his head and moved instead to the sacred table on which the ancient scroll of the Torah rested. It was securely fastened within its case for it had been determined to be beyond repair. It would be buried within Isaak's coffin as a mark of the esteem he had earned within the community. Adjacent to it lay the new Torah scroll which Rabbi Kreschner had brought for the funeral ceremony. By a strong effort of will Ephraim mastered his feelings. Finally raising his eyes to look out at the assembled mourners, he intoned the traditional words that close the customary eulogy for the dead. The words of Job.

"The Lord has given, the Lord has taken away. Blessed be the Name of the Lord."

# CHAPTER FIFTY-SEVEN

## LIFE GOES ON

Amidst the sorrow and anxiety that his family had endured as a consequence of his Uncle Isaak's death, young Abrahm Marjzendiak now faced, in the events occurring in his extended family, another cause for personal concern and loss.

Ever since his thirteenth year, he had made excuses to visit the home of Samuel Marks for one reason or another. He had borrowed books from the Marks' library. He had volunteered to perform outdoor chores ranging from mowing their extensive lawn to planting beds of bushes to relieve the tedium of the land. He had exercised the horse that Samuel had bought for Judyth on her tenth birthday, and he had subsequently taught her to ride it. The horse had been a filly with a beautiful chestnut coat and white leggings. Judyth had named her April because that was the month in which she had been born.

Abrahm had even helped to tutor Judyth in mathematics, which she had formerly disliked, and in logic and Hebrew literature. Under his tutelage, she had not only learned to appreciate those subjects, she had come to excel in them.

In the years since the two had first met, Abrahm, fascinated by judyth's blossoming beauty and naïve charm, had been drawn still closer to her by the quickness of her mind. She learned easily and retained information with a tenacity that was remarkable in a young girl. She became an accomplished equestrian, thanks to Abrahm's attentive instructions, and she learned to sing and play the piano with a deftness and skill that, while not sufficient to cause her to aspire to a career in music, would certainly be enough to make her a sought after guest at social gatherings when she had matured for a few more years.

On her part, she grew to admire and look up to Abrahm, to seek his advice on a variety of subjects and to respect his opinions. Though nine years separated them in age, they became inseparable friends. Therefore, when at age sixteen, Judyth was ready to complete her education, and her father decided to send her to Paris where his younger sister and her family lived, Abrahm was torn between joy for the opportunity which that prospect presented for his young cousin, and a deep sense of loss for the years that she would be absent from his environment.

This dilemma troubled the young man, and it was because of it that he came to understand and to acknowledge the true depth of his feelings for his young cousin. He began to fret over her safety. After all, France, that had seemed so liberal a few years earlier, had been the scene of the Dreyfus trial and scandal. He found himself wondering if Judyth would be safe there, despite the watchfulness of her aunt.

Judyth herself had no such fears. Her Aunt Annelle had visited with her brother on several occasions, and a closeness had developed between aunt and niece. Annelle was coming to stay with the Marks family for several days and would then accompany Judyth back to Paris. She would attend to her enrollment and oversee her life there.

Though somewhat reassured by these arrangements, Abrahm insisted on driving the two ladies to the railway station in his grandfather's coach. He had a keepsake that he wanted to give Judyth as a parting gift. He also wrote her a letter assuring her of his continued esteem and concern for her. And to her aunt he entrusted a package from his youngest uncle, Michael. Abrahm did now know at the time exactly what the bulky package contained. However, Samuel Marks did know, for Michael had taken him into his confidence.

At long last, Michael had completed his first manuscript. It still bore the title <u>The Cauldron</u>, but its scope had expanded considerably since the time when he had first conceived it. The story's setting ranged from Berlin to Paris to Warsaw, and its fictional characters were members of a Jewish family that specialized in the import-export trade. Michael hoped to have his first book published in Paris by the House of Belin on the Rue Sarow, an established publishing house, founded originally in 1777, and specializing in educational texts as well as historical and fictional publications. And Annelle Peletier had agreed, through her brother Samuel, to be his messenger and his contact person. She had even agreed, at Samuel's request, to contact a Paris-based lawyer on Michael's behalf to ensure that the publication arrangements went smoothly. Michael was especially desirous that this project was speedily and successfully concluded, as one of his goals was to provide, through this novel with its thinly veiled political significance, a counter weight in opposition of the damage being done to the reputation and safety of Europe's Jews through the wide distribution of Sergei Nilus' infamous book <u>The Protocols of the Elders of Zion</u>.

Within this context, Annelle had taken on a complex assignment. Henceforth, she would be guardian of a vivacious teen-aged girl who unknowingly possessed a legendary and disturbing beauty, destined to inspire a poet, a portrait painter and a historian to celebrate her pulchritude in their respective fields of endeavor. Annelle was also about to become the means of launching the career of Michael Marjak, as he would come to be known, as a writer of controversial and prophetic historical fiction. Perhaps it is fortunate that none of us can read the future. Certainly, it did not occur to Abrahm as he set off in his grandfather's recently repainted carriage, that by transporting Judyth, whom he looked upon as his childhood sweetheart, and her matron Aunt Annelle to their train, he was setting in motion a train of circumstance that would dramatically alter the course of their lives and his own.

Pierre Rebaumme had sent his widowed younger son Matthieu to Paris the year before to further his studies and his artistic career at the Sorbonne. He also hoped Matthieu's time away from Warsaw would dim the memory of his loss. In the eventful four years he was to spend there, he would not only meet the young Judyth Marks and be moved to paint the most famous portrait of his career, but he would also learn from her the tragic and mysterious details of Isaak Marjzendiak's death and the momentous news, for him, of Luvna Meyer Marjzendiak's bereavement and widowhood.

In Paris, Judyth was destined to meet three famous men; young Rebaumme (whose image of her would one day hang in the Louvre under the title "Girl with Violet Eyes"); Catulle Mendes, who would immortalize her in a poem entitled "Youth on the Threshold of Life"; and the historian Henri Hauser who would compare her unusual beauty to that of the Empress Josephine, whose good looks she actually outshone, even at so early a stage in her development. She was also destined to meet in passing the former Serene Princess Katerina, who had voluntarily accepted banishment of herself and her children to Paris. The widow of Alexander II still had relatives living in that city. Understandably, it was to them she had turned in her bereavement when Alexander III finally took the time to address his attention to the matter of the woman who had supplanted his mother in the affections of his father.

"You won't forget me," Abrahm said earnestly, "in all the glamour and sophistication of Paris?"

"Oh, Abrahm" Judyth responded. "I could never do that! You've taught me so much. You're so wise, so learned."

"That's what you think now," said Abrahm. "In Paris, you'll meet many people, perhaps very famous ones. Warsaw and I may pale by comparison."

Judyth shook her head, and the tassels on her pale pink hat shook with the movement. She was a vision in pink, a dazzling vision that Abrahm would keep in his heart and treasure all the while she was gone.

"You've no idea how much I think of you," she said. "I almost wish I weren't going away. I feel as though if I stayed here, you could teach me all I'll ever need to know."

Abrahm laughed. "You do me too much honor," he said humbly. "You'll soon be learning things I've never dreamed of. And you'll see sights I'll probably never behold. I almost envy you this chance, and yet I want it for you, too. I want all that is best in life for you. You do know that, don't you?"

She smiled shyly. "I've guessed as much," she said, and glanced away toward her Aunt Annelle, who stood a few feet apart from the two young people, giving them an opportunity to say their good-byes in relative privacy.

"And you know that I care for you, don't you?" he asked.

"Yes," she answered, her eyes meeting his. "We care about each other, Abrahm. And that won't change. I promise. Paris is just a place, a city on the map. I'll learn all the genteel things there that my family thinks a lady should know. But Warsaw will always be my home. And you'll be here waiting to welcome me back."

"Of course," Abrahm said, and handed her the small packet that contained a gold mezuzah on a chain to wear around her neck. "Meanwhile, wear this, and think of me every time you see yourself in a mirror. Know that my love and my prayers are with you always."

Judyth was moved to tears by his words as well as by his gift. She reached up and embraced him, standing on tip toe, and gently kissed his cheek. He turned his head slightly and kissed her tenderly on the lips. It was her first real kiss, and for a moment she felt giddy from it.

Her aunt moved to her side and gently touched her shoulder.

"We must board now, dear," she said softly.

"Yes, Aunt Annelle," Judyth agreed, with a little shake of her head to clear away the momentary dizziness. "I know, but it's hard to say good-bye to those we love, even if it's only temporary." She looked up at Abrahm standing so tall and straight before her, and smiled. "Write to me," she said, and turned from him to follow her aunt aboard the waiting train.

Abrahm waved to her from the platform, his heart torn by ambivalent feelings of love, longing, hope and pride. This girl had crept into his life and made a place there that no one else, so he thought, could ever fill. How changed, he wondered, would she be by her years of schooling in Paris? Would she still count him among those she loved when she returned?

He watched the train pull away from the platform, the grinding sound of its metal wheels on the track seeming to bore into his soul.

"I love you," He whispered to her departing visage through the train windows. "I love you. Never forget that."

\*\*\*

After the nerve-racking experience through which he had lately passed, Jozef Pilsudski was ill-prepared for further trauma to follow so quickly in its wake. Nonetheless, tragedy befell ten days after his return home. The task of obtaining sufficient quantities of paper to carry on the printing of The Worker had always been logistically difficult. Now, with the depression growing gradually but steadily more pressing, supplies of ink, paper and the metal pegs used to create and set the type were all in short supply. Aleksander Malanowski whom Pilsudski had visited briefly in Warsaw prior to keeping his ill-fated appointment with Isaak Marjzendiak, arrived on February 19 in Lodz to confer with his colleague and to transport a supply of the precious paper to the Dabrowski apartment. It proved to be a costly tactical error. Malanowski was followed by members of the militia who had been instructed to take no decisive action until the results of their observations had been reported to the Ministry of Police in Warsaw. Since anonymous assassination had failed in its intended object, it was determined to ensnare as many victims as possible in the net that was closing around the leadership of the PPS in Russian Poland.

Fortunately, Wanda Juszkiewicz was at that time visiting Pilsudski's aunt Stefania Lipman in Wilno. Throughout the bitter months that followed the events of the next few days, Pilsudski was deeply grateful for that fortuitous circumstance. Malanowski, suspecting that he might be under surveillance, declined the Pilsudsi's generous offer of hospitality. He obtained instead a single room in the building where Kazimierz Roznowski, Pilsudski's current typesetter for The Worker, resided. Within two days Malanowski's consultations with Pilsudski and his closest colleagues were concluded. Within that same time span specific instructions were received by the Ministry of Police in Warsaw from its headquarters at St. Petersburg: Malanowski was arrested as he boarded a train for Warsaw at the railway station in Lodz. Roznowski had escaped the militia by minutes, having taken an earlier train to Wilno. At 3:00 a.m. the Pilsudskis, under the names of Maria and Wiktor Dabrowski, were awakened by the local militia, arrested and transported to the prison at Lodz where they remained for a period of two months. Roznowski too was captured in Wilno shortly after he had transmitted the news of Pilsudski's arrest, of which he had only then learned, to Stefania Lipman. The PPS had been struck a severe blow. The thirty-sixth issue of The Worker stood half completed in the press which had been confiscated from the apartment on Wschodnia Street. The end of that week saw the major members of the local PPS leadership in custody.

Of all those arrested only Maria Pilsudska had little to fear except the physical inconvenience of imprisonment and the psychic stress of prolonged separation from her daughter Wanda. On April 17 Jozef and Maria were transferred to the citadel at Warsaw where Jozef Pilsudski was sequestered in the infamous X Pavilion reserved for political prisoners. An ordeal of intensive interrogation soon followed. The members of the militia, working directly with the Ministry of Police, were skilled in their task. They would ask the same questions in several different ways, cross-checking for inaccuracies and concealments and correlating unintentional revelations regardless of how minor they might seem. Nevertheless, their efforts in this instance revealed little new information. Pilsudski succeeded in conveying the impression that his apartment had been primarily a collecting station for journalistic articles and party information. This material was duly recorded in the periodical he published and was then transferred to other sources for ultimate distribution. His wife Maria, he insisted, had known little of his political efforts and had cared for them even less. The rearing of her daughter had been her chief concern. Under existing Russian and therefore Polish law she could not be held responsible for her husband's activities and would ultimately be released essentially without sentence. Pilsudski's own fate was far more precarious and the time for hearing and sentencing was drawing near.

Few visitors were permitted for political prisoners and these were usually limited to close relatives. Stefania Lipman, Pilsudski's aunt, fitted this category and so was allowed to visit the prisoner Dabrowski, also known as Pilsudski, shortly before the date of his formally scheduled hearing before Governor-General Imeretynski. She arrived armed with a charming though forceful personality, a clever wit, a honeyed tongue and a wealth of valuable and encouraging information from the headquarters of the "Legal Society for Helping Prisoners"[11] where Maria Paszkowska, a close ally of Aleksander Sulkiewicz[12], was a diligent and trusted employee. The plan she had outlined to Pilsudski's resourceful and charismatic aunt appealed to that lady's vivid imagination. By the time it was transmitted separately to Pilsudski and to his spouse, detained in a lower-security section of the prison, it had undergone a few embellishments of Stefania's own.

Her first action upon arriving at the ancient Citadel of Warsaw was to distribute handsomely wrapped parcels of fresh baked kichlen[13] for the Commandant of the prison, his junior officers and for the militia members most immediately concerned with the confinement of her nephew. The recipients of these sweet meats consumed them eagerly with no knowledge of their Judaic origin deriving from Stefania's unusual childhood spent in a Jewish foster home after the death of both her parents. Pilsudski's family had always fared well in their dealings with Poland's Jews. His aunt had married a Jew and their relationship, now terminated by the husband's death, had been an eminently successful one. Had Pilsudski's later colleagues studied his background more closely they might better have understood their leader's policy of tolerance and fair dealing in regard to the recurrent "Jewish problem" in post World War I Poland.

Thus introduced, Pilsudski's aunt could have stayed as long as she wished, but being judicious as well as witty, the lady knew how best to discharge her assignment and depart before she had outstayed her welcome. Smiling maternally at the young militiaman who admitted her to the X Pavilion, Stefania Lipman swept regally into her nephew's cell, waited until the door closed soundly behind her and then moved towards Jozef with all the energy and enthusiasm of a woman half her age, embracing him affectionately. She then stepped back and studied his face with frank appraisal.

"So, Jozef! You look pale and thin. What do they feed you in this dungeon?" she asked in some alarm.

"Mostly words!" he replied crisply. "Questions, endless questions."

"To which they do not like the answers," remarked Stefania nodding her head sagely. "I am not surprised."

"What do they expect?" wondered Jozef.

"They expect sooner or later to wear you down. To trap you into betraying others. Friends, colleagues, sympathizers. But," She looked about her significantly. "It is not to be

---

[11] Anglicized literal translation
[12] Dedicated PPS member and functionary of the Russian Customs Authority. This post which he held for many years facilitated distribution of PPS publications across the border into Poland.
[13] Traditional sweetcakes of Eastern European jewish origin.

so simple after all." Jozef put his fingers to his lips and shook his head. His aunt nodded in understanding, reached modestly inside the bodice of her dress and extracted a single sheet of thin paper closely written in small neat characters. She unfolded the sheet and held it for Pilsudski to read while she continued speaking. "What can you really tell them that they cannot already guess? You are a journalist. You publish a newspaper. An underground news paper, it's true. But that they know! So what else is there?" Stefania shrugged her shoulders expressively while her nephew completed his perusal of the paper she held out to him. When he signaled his understanding of the plan thus presented, she folded it and replaced it within its silken hiding place, smoothing her bodice coyly. She looked disapprovingly about the cell, her tilted nose wrinkled in disgust. "Really!" she exclaimed. "How do you stand this place? It's dark, damp and chill even in the spring. You cannot stay here much longer. It is too depressing! I should have nightmares staying in this place." She threw up her hands in mock horror. "It's enough to drive one mad!" she remarked expressively and then winked. Pilsudski nodded in agreement.

"Indeed!" was his succinct remark, and then in a more mundane and practical vein he added, "I trust you've remembered to bring some of your home-baked bread. The food here is scarcely fit for pigs. And the guards seldom bother to wash their hands."

And so it had begun. The elaborate, oblique plan to free the revered PPS leader commenced from that moment with an issue as simple as the prisoner's aversion to food distributed with less than optimal sanitation precautions. It soon progressed to a decided almost pathological distrust of uniformed personnel and ultimately became manifest as a self-imposed fast since the prisoners in the Citadel were fed exclusively by militia members. Aunt Stefania was soon recalled to the prison by the urgent pleadings of Maria Pilsudska who distractedly expressed her wifely concern for her husband's failing health and strength as well as her perfectly credible fear for his mental stability.

Maria Paszkowska, pursuing the strategy already agreed upon, received Stefania Lipman's impassioned plea on her nephew's behalf with warmth and sympathy and promptly consulted Dr. Ivan Shabashnikov, director of the Jan Bozy Mental Hospital in Warsaw. This was upon the recommendation of the prominent psychiatrist, Dr. Rafal Radziwillowicz who had authored the program for achieving Pilsudski's escape in the first place. It was not without peril but Radziwillowicz had chosen well. Shabashnikov was not only a noted specialist in fixations and obsessions but was of Buriat extraction. He considered himself a native Siberian rather than a Russian. Armed with this knowledge, Stefania Lipman paid yet another visit to her ailing relative in prison in order to remind him of his earlier days spent in exile in Siberia. She recalled to his mind the beauties of that country which he himself had vividly recounted to his family upon his return to Wilno.

As fate would have it the consultant called to minister to Pilsudski's physical ills was Adam Marjzendiak who had replaced his friend and colleague Samuel Jederwreski as prison physician. He recognized his patient immediately but was careful not to reveal this fact to the prison guards. Adam was not directly involved in the escape plans. But as a skilled medical practitioner he recognized a well established case of self- instigated malnutrition fueled by a spurious mental illness when he saw it. He determined to treat the prisoner to the best of his ability and to keep his private curiosities just that: private. Marjzendiak was present at the initial visit of the noted psychiatrist. He consulted with his eminent colleague regarding the prisoner's physical and mental status. Considerable physical deterioration was clearly manifest. Both physicians attested to the extremity of Pilsudski's condition and the urgency of his transfer to the Nicholas the Miracle Worker Mental Clinic in St. Petersburg under the direction of Dr. Bronislaw Czeczot. This choice was a fortunate one from every point of view. The hospital was neither a political nor a penal institution but an outstanding center for psychiatric research and therapy. Its director was of Polish origin and sympathies who readily agreed to accept on his staff Dr. Wladyslaw Mazurkiewicz, a PPS member who had just recently taken and passed his final examination at the Military Medical Academy in St. Petersburg. It was through this man that the final phase of the escape plan was implemented.

It was now April of 1901. Pilsudski had languished for several weeks in a closed ward with other mental patients. His one source of solace during this period was the fact that his wife Maria had been set free at the end of January of that year under a bond of five hundred rubles and ordered to live in her native city of Wilno. There she awaited news of her husband's fate. She did not have to wait long. On May 14, 1901, Jozef Pilsudski and Wladyslaw (Walter) Mazurkiewicz walked out the back door of the mental clinic during the night shift to which Mazurkiewicz was then assigned. With the help of Sulkiewicz and other friends they reached the Lewandowski estate where Maria Pilsudska had gone ostensibly for a brief holiday to recover from the effects of her eleven month imprisonment. Within the month the Pilsudskis were in Kiev where the thirty-sixth edition of The Worker was finally completed. By late June they arrived in Lwow and were met by Dr. Mazurkiewicz to whom they owed so much. His recommendation to Pilsudski was a period of rest and relaxation, especially after the nerve-racking episode in the mental clinic where he had been confined among truly mentally ill patients and compelled to simulate mental illness himself.

The next few weeks were spent in Krakow and in the mountains of Zakopane which Adam and Isaak Marjzendiak had each described to Pilsudski in glowing terms under radically different circumstances, the one as a friend, the other as a doctor endeavoring to calm and cheer a nervous patient. Now at first hand Pilsudski could appreciate both accounts. Krakow was and is an awesome and impressive city filled with tradition and history in every edifice and street. The mountains outside its walls are majestic and arresting and yet provide a soothing setting in which to recover one's physical well being and peace of mind. By November, Maria and Jozef had arrived in London. A chapter had closed in the life of Comrade Wiktor and the "Beautiful Lady" of Wilno society. Henceforth, the publication of The Worker would be assigned to others. The real leadership of PPS was now Pilsudski's goal and he was prepared to undertake it in earnest. The sentence of Governor-General Imeretynski of five years exile in Eastern Siberia was never to be carried out.

* * *

December of 1901 heralded the onset of yet another tumultuous winter in Warsaw. Not since his early youth could Dr. Adam Marjzendiak recall a more inclement season. His practice flourished but under circumstances he abhorred and many of his patients did not survive that winter. Unexpectedly, though he did not succumb to a chill or a fever, one of its victims was Adam's father Ephraim. The aging patriarch of the Marjzendiak family, who had withstood so many trying winters, so many hardships and adversities and had managed heretofore to rise above them all and find fresh strength, fresh challenges and new meaning in his life had never fully recovered from Isaak's death. It had come so suddenly with no opportunity to prepare for it. At first it had seemed that the presence of Luvna in the house would have offered a source of consolation since Ephraim had asked his daughter-in-law to come and live at the family estate. It was obvious that she could not abide the house in Wola where every room reminded her of Isaak. And with the election of a new Mayor she would have had to find other quarters anyway.

It had seemed the ideal solution for both father and widow, but time was to prove otherwise. Ephraim grew more depressed, Luvna more restless. And Adam, all but overwhelmed by the growing magnitude of his medical practice, could not oversee events at Plaz Marjzendiak as he would have wished. Michael, his time and energies consumed by running not only the factories but also the estate, could neither predict nor avert the tragic chain of events which was building steadily to a climax. Perhaps if Johann had been at home instead of having returned to Krakow and his university studies, Luvna Meyer Marjzendiak would have felt less unsettled, less at odds with her environment. Her life with Isaak both before and after their marriage had been one of excitement and challenge, one that appealed to her highly evolved and disciplined intellect, stimulated her imagination and afforded her ample opportunities to exercise her considerable talents. Suddenly, after having finally emerged from her protracted period of mourning, Luvna found herself deprived of even the stimulus of tears, the involvement of grief and its demonstration. With her husband dead and her son away at the university, her home vacated in favor of her husband's successor and even her role as chatelaine of a great house now supplanted by Judyth Mylinski, time weighed heavily upon her. Her life seemed to be at an end at the age of fifty-one. In desperation, she resumed temporarily her love of painting, abandoned with Johann's birth. For several months, this exercise of her long-dormant artistic talent sustained her. She filled the small salon, the morning room, the summer parlor and the solarium with canvasses that were colorful and varied. Birds, flowers and outdoor scenes were all represented. Scenes of storms were also prominent. It was thus that she filled her time and finally laid to rest her grief. And there were occasions when she regretted that Isaak was not there to see these glorious fruits of her talent, for he had encouraged her often to revive and pursue her art.

With the resurgence of her natural energies, Luvna inwardly rebelled against the confines of her widowhood, and in that rebellious mood she resented Ephraim's continuing indulgence of unending grief. Youth, even relative youth, is more resilient in this context than is age, which has endured more slights, more grief, more traumas and more adversities. There comes at last in the affairs of men that day when one more hurt, one further tragedy is one too many to be borne.

Values were changing at the turn of the century throughout Europe and even in the new world thousands of miles across the seas. Traditional religious values were being questioned and this was true alike of Jew and Gentile. Economic depression, social deprivation and denigration of individual worth were rampant. In this setting Luvna Marjzendiak's personal rebellion was but a sign of the times. At first it took the form of altered habits of dress, a more flamboyant mode of attire and manner than had been her custom in recent years. Or perhaps within the current setting of bereavement, her natural exuberance seemed somehow out of character.

Luvna's interest in the theater and opera revived. She began to attend these events in the company of less recently widowed women friends. Inevitably, she attracted the attention of more than one unattached man and her fair, delicate beauty, which had withstood the onslaught of time extremely well, ultimately drew the notice of younger men not all of whom were Jewish.

Years earlier, the artist Pierre Rebaumme had been commissioned to paint the portraits of the Marjzendiak family by Ephraim. Rebaumme's younger son Matthieu had painted later portraits of the third generation members of the family except for Samuel and Frederick who lived far away in Zurich. All the while Matthieu had painted the sons of the Marjzendiak children, he had admired the strength of character they had inherited from their parents and especially from their grandparents. When later Isaak requested that the younger Rebaumme immortalize the images of his wife and young son, he had not realized he was introducing his wife to his own successor in her affections. Nor had Luvna nor even Rebaumme himself any idea of future events and what they held in store. Thus does destiny weave its complex pattern from the simplest of threads.

* * *

The St. Petersburg State Opera was visiting Warsaw for a festive season honoring Tsar Nicholas and his Empress Alexandra. The opera first chosen for presentation on that program was a heroic and grandiose tale set to glorious music by Glazunov and, therefore, its premiere performance in Russian Poland was superlatively well attended. Madam Mira Pietrowska came out of seclusion and virtual social retirement at the invitation of the Governor-General in order to be present. Against the expressed wish of her father-in-law, Luvna arranged to accompany her without troubling to acquaint Mira with Ephraim's sentiments on the subject. It was a thoughtless omission on Luvna's part, and one that was destined to have far-reaching consequences.

One result was immediately apparent. The revered Madam Pietrowska was helped to alight from her carriage by the Governor-General's Aide Colonel Vladymir Vytepkin who likewise assisted her guest Madam Marjzendiak, widow of the martyred former Mayor of Wola. Vytepkin was discomfited by the revelation of that lady's identity but managed to maintain an outward veneer of calm decorum and to escort the two ladies to their box in the lower mezzanine section. A short time later they were joined by Matthieu Rebaumme who was Vytepkin's guest. The artist, now in his late 30's, was a great favorite of the Governor-General and had obtained several valuable commissions as a result of his patronage. Rebaumme's professional career was in full flower and he had been for some time contemplating the possibility of either relocating in St. Petersburg, which was the cultural center of the Russian empire, or returning once more to Paris where he had taken advanced artistic training following his wife's death. While Russia's poor grew steadily more impoverished, her privileged aristocracy continued to enjoy an enviable affluence which was a constant affront to those less fortunate. The conversation of the four occupants of the Governor-General's box soon turned toward the subject of current events as the audience awaited the overture and the raising of the first act curtain.

"Surely," opined Rebaumme to his friend Vytepkin, "you must be aware of the tension of the masses. It is evident everywhere! This society is like a volcano waiting to erupt. I'm often torn between curiosity and dread. Should I remain in Poland and record events on canvas as they occur or should I leave while I can and escape to France? To Paris with her legendary lights?"

Luvna had always been fascinated by the stories she had heard of France and especially of Paris. She turned to Rebaumme with evident interest.

"What does Madam Rebaumme say to that?" she asked mischievously. The artist studied her face for a long moment before he replied.

"At present there is no Madam Rebaumme," he said at last.

"At present?" said Luvna, both mystified and embarrassed.

"Mer Rebaumme is widowed, my dear," Mira intervened smoothly. "In that he is akin to each of us in this box. Even Colonel Vytepkin has lost his partner to the rigors of mortality."

"You put things so well, Madam," Vytepkin responded. "It is a major part of your charm. A charm which is quite considerable."

"The Colonel can afford to be wildly complimentary without commitment in the company of a lady who could well be his mother," answered Mira archly.

"Would that I had so gifted and beautiful a mother!" Vytepkin responded. "My origins are less than illustrious, Madam. I have achieved my present rank and status through sheer hard work and fortunate recognition."

"As did my own father," said Mira with a hint of nostalgia. "We were burghers. Industrialists. My own present station I owe primarily to my late husband."

These reminiscences were interrupted by the entrance of the conductor. The overture began. Soon the performance was in progress. Throughout its course, Matthieu Rebaumme watched not the diva on stage but the beautiful blond woman at his side who embodied a much more fascinating enigma for him than the mythical heroine of the opera. His interest followed her throughout the evening and came to full flower at the reception given by Governor-General Imeretrynski in honor of his guests. The leading members of the opera company were also in attendance, conducted thither to be displayed as a symbol of the government's munificence and cultural awareness. Little heed was paid to the groups of laborers who clustered about the tree-lined access ways leading to the recently renovated governmental palace, silently expressing their disfavor. Cultural awareness indeed, thought Luvna! The volcano of which the artist Rebaumme had spoken seemed imminently on the point of eruption, much like Luvna's own highly wrought emotions striving for release from their self-imposed bonds.

She still missed Isaak and all they had shared. But Isaak was gone. That period in her life had ended. Surely there must be something to take its place. Beside her stood the dashing, talented artist who had painted her portrait ten years earlier, his eyes as they gazed upon her mirroring his recollection of those enchanted hours set apart in memory when he had admired her in silence, over-awed by her exalted station, by the power her husband wielded, and by the preeminence which her family had achieved. Now she stood within his reach, lovely, vulnerable, undeniably appealing. And they shared a bond of which until now he had not dared to speak. Luvna was openly Jewish.

The Rebaumme family had come originally from Provence, the center of a highly cultivated Jewish community. When Matthieu's grandfather Moises had moved to Paris to pursue a career in art, he had neither concealed nor flaunted his religious convictions. France had then been the cradle of liberty where every Frenchman was equal before the law. One stood or fell according to his merit and individual achievements were credentials enough. Moises' son Pierre had followed that example and his grandson Matthieu continued the family tradition. Ephraim had learned of Pierre Rebaumme's background only after he had given him the commission for his family's portraits. His efforts had been rewarded. His protege's future had been assured. But Pierre's younger son was a secular Jew. He had broken with his father and elder brother on the subject of religion, for they were Catholics, though indifferently devout ones. Matthieu, by contrast, celebrated none of the religious feasts and holidays either of Catholicism or of Judaism and went to Temple only once a year on Yom Kippur. Jews of his stamp were still somewhat rare in 1902 but they were becoming an active minority. In future generations they would constitute a sizeable segment of world Jewry.

Tonight such thoughts were very far from the mind and heart of the artist and his companion. They dined and danced in an atmosphere of delightful abandon and Madam Mira Pietrowska looked on approvingly, pleased to see Luvna happy and fulfilled for once since Isaak's funeral. She would have felt less pleased had she foreseen the storm that would break within a matter of weeks when Ephraim learned the outcome of tonight's events.

The revelation could hardly have been less auspicious. Ephraim Marjzendiak awoke late on a morning in February to find his daughter-in-law departed from the house, her residual luggage stacked in the hall awaiting transport. As it happened, Mira Pietrowska had chosen that same morning to pay a social call upon her friend and neighbor and erstwhile business partner. She was met by a storm of disfavor whose origin she was at first unable to comprehend.

'Gone?' Ephraim exclaimed, his still powerful voice hushed with shock. "Gone where?"

"She said to Paris, sir," answered Philene LeClaire, the French maid Judyth had engaged some months earlier to assist with the housework she could no longer manage by herself.

"Whatever for?" wondered Ephraim.

"She didn't say, sir," answered the French woman, "but I envy her. Even in winter Paris is the loveliest place to be on earth."

"Home is the place to be!" was Ephraim's response. "Home! Not running off to some strange city alone. She doesn't know a soul in Paris." This thought filled Ephraim with considerable alarm concerning the welfare of his daughter-in-law.

"If you please, sir, I don't believe she went alone. The gentleman who came for her." The woman attempted to elaborate but was struck dumb by the unmistakable wrath of the master of the house.

"Gentleman?" said Ephraim acidly. "What gentleman?" For answer Philene pointed towards the main foyer with its array of portraits. This gesture conveyed little intelligible meaning to Ephraim but to Mira it spoke volumes. She moved resolutely forward to confront Ephraim and thus divert his attention from the intimidated maid.

"Ephraim, my old friend," she said placatingly. "I think I understand. Come into the parlour with me." Ephraim stared at her in some surprise and did not move from where he stood.

"To what do I owe the pleasure of this visit, Madam?" he asked with some asperity. He was too distraught by Luvna's unexplained departure to don a guise of instant civility with a long-term friend like Mira Pietrowska.

"Personal inclination," the lady replied. "If you must know, I awoke this morning overwhelmed by boredom. That house empty of all save the servants and myself seems to grow larger daily." She was thinking of her children Pola and Erik whose recent visits together with their respective families had just ended, leaving the house emptier than ever. Ephraim nodded.

"Indeed! I find myself faced with the same problem. And now that girl Luvna has taken it into her head to go off on holiday with some stranger." Mira took his arm and led him toward the salon off the foyer. When they were both seated she turned to the man before her, looking at him appraisingly.

"We've known each other a long time now, Ephraim. I feel I can be frank," she began. "Luvna is not a girl. She's a woman, and by modern standards not an old woman by any means." Ephraim stared at her for a long moment, mystified by her tone as well as by her words.

"She is a widow, Madam," he pronounced solemnly. "My son's widow."

"Yes, of course," Mira agreed. "Isaak was a fine man. His death has impoverished all of us. But Luvna is still alive. She still has a life to live, Ephraim. She has a right to choose in what manner she will live it."

"A widow's behavior is prescribed by law," said Ephraim.

"I've heard of that law, my old friend. It is harsh and unyielding and very, very old," said Mira as painstakingly as if she spoke to a child instead of the revered patriarch of a large family.

"Our laws are all very old, Madam. Our traditions are sacred."

"Ephraim, Luvna has lived by that law. She has been widowed for more than a year. The monument for her husband's grave is already in place. It is time she rejoined the living. It's time you did, too." The truth of Mira's words was indisputable but the old rebellious grief would not be denied. Ephraim sat silently before her, the bitter tears forcing their way between his eyelids.

He said at last, "What life is there left for me now?" Bitterness and grief were heavy in his voice.

"Life is what we make of it," answered Mira. "Luvna has gone to build a new life in a new setting."

"You know of this then?" asked Ephraim with dawning suspicion.

"I know something of it. The rest I can guess."

"You knew! And you didn't tell me?" And now the old man stood and came towards her, a cold anger in his voice and in his eyes.

"What was to tell?" she wondered. "They had met years ago. But then they were both married. Now they are both alone. It is good that they met again at so opportune a moment."

"Opportune?" Ephraim thundered. "What are you saying? Who is this man?"

"The artist, Matthieu Rebaumme. You were his father's friend and patron. Surely you cannot disapprove?"

"I do disapprove!" Ephraim's voice rose with the force of his emotion. "He's several years her junior and almost a Gentile. What sort of match is that?"

"The one she's found, Ephraim. The one she needs. Wish her joy and let her go," said Mira soothingly. But Ephraim would not be soothed.

He wanted to know. "When did she leave?"

"I gather she left this morning," Mira responded.

The old man questioned further. "By what route?"

"Probably by train. There is a train to Paris via Berlin later this morning." And as Ephraim turned and left the room Mira realized his intent and followed him, determined to divert him from his efforts to prevent Luvna's flight.

Ephraim drove the carriage himself, too goaded by anger and frustration to wait for the coachman he paid for the service of driving him on the rare occasions when he traveled outside the estate. Now that he had retired from his post on the Banking Advisory Council, those occasions were rare indeed. All the way to the railway station Mira tried in vain to dissuade Ephraim, to show him the futility of his errand. Holding on to Luvna would not bring Isaak back. But Ephraim would not allow himself to hear the truth of her words nor would he accept the surrender of his convictions which the acceptance of her sentiments would entail.

They reached the station just in time to see the train begin slowly to move away along the track. Ephraim saw Luvna standing on the rear observation platform and shouted her name, running after the train as it slowly gathered momentum. Luvna, clasped in the arms of her new-found love, was oblivious to all other sights and sounds. She never even heard her father-in-law's frantic cries nor saw him sink to the ground, overwhelmed by grief and by the blinding pain that suddenly filled his head, making him feel as though it would burst momentarily.

Ephraim Marjzendiak at age 88

# CHAPTER FIFTY-EIGHT

## THE ENDING OF AN ERA

It was a subdued and saddened Leah Kolvner who emerged from the train arriving from Zurich to alight upon the same passenger platform on which seventy-two hours earlier her father had collapsed, spent and ill. Modern means of communication had enabled her to reach her native city in so brief a period of time. With her traveled her husband Marcos and her younger son Frederick. Samuel, as had often been the case in recent years, had remained in Zurich, not out of lack of respect for his grandfather but in order to ensure that the family business interests would survive the absence of the owner, no matter how protracted that absence might prove to be. The message had stated simply that Ephraim had been stricken by a sudden violent illness which he might not survive. Further details were lacking; definitive plans were, therefore, difficult to formulate.

As Leah scanned the railway station for a familiar face, her nephew Abrahm came into her line of vision. He was the eldest of her brothers' children and the most restless, the most rebellious against the inequities and injustices that beset his family and his people in the setting of Russian Poland. Like his Uncle Michael, Abrahm was sensitive to the subtler socio-political aspects of the current situation. He chafed at the relative helplessness of the people, the despotism of the Russian overlords and the apparent acceptance of these inequities by his father Adam and his grandfather Ephraim, whose lives seemed to him, at least on the surface, dedicated to getting on with the job of every day living without striving to effect important changes. He had not yet realized that the two could be inter-related, or that the contributions made by both his father and his grandfather to the Zionist movement symbolized their efforts to bring about changes in the hardships of Jewish life. Abrahm could not yet fully appreciate how great a role those contributions would ultimately play in the future of the Jewish people.

Yet the young man loved his family. His grief over Ephraim's illness was evident in his face as he approached. His eyes were dry but reddened; his tall spare frame, so like Ephraim's, seemed somehow shrunken and crumpled by the burden of his sorrow. One glance at him confirmed his aunt's worst fears. Her father would not recover from this illness.

Plaz Marjzendiak as they approached it seemed to Leah a setting of desolation such as she had never known before. All her prior homecomings, even the occasion of her mother's final illness, had brought her a measure of comfort and calm. This was home, the land that belonged in a special way to her family. Even though under Russian rule their hold upon the land seemed at times precarious, Leah had always felt a special sense of belonging whenever she returned here. Now she realized with devastating certainty that the source of those feelings centered not in the land nor the home built upon it, not even in the family synagogue nor the crops and livestock which the land supported. It was attributable almost totally to the man whose vision and energy had transformed his dream of a home for his family, despite all the formidable odds against its fulfillment, into this flourishing reality. With the waning of his life force, even the land that he had held in trust all these years for that family seemed overwhelmed and in mourning despite the fact that the master of the house still breathed.

When Leah reached her father's bedside she was uncertain what she would find. The beloved face with its traditional beard streaked with gray, the character lines etched deeper than she remembered, all these she expected. Ephraim's hair was still predominantly the brown-black hue it had always been. Touches of gray outlined his temples and strayed down his sideburns; yet his beard was now the color of pepper mixed with salt. The luxuriant growth of dark hair through which his daughter had twined her infant fingers on his head and face still remained as thick as ever. But his eyes were dull and sunken now; they contained no sign of recognition. His right hand and arm lay motionless at his side. His left hand searched the coverlet seeking some undetermined objective. Leah took that searching hand in both her own and drew it silently to her lips. Her tears fell upon it and her father responded to those tears. His eyes closed fitfully, then opened and sought her face as she sat beside his bed bending close to him.

"Leah?" he asked hesitantly.

"Yes, Papa," she replied soothingly. "I'm here."

"My beautiful Leah," said Ephraim. "I'm glad you've come."

She noted with concern that the right side of his face drooped and that the muscles of that side lagged behind their partners on his left when he spoke, giving his mouth a downward twist.

Shaking his head, he asked, "Where is Isaak? I can't find Isaak."

"You'll find him soon, Papa," Leah reassured him and added under her breath, "or he'll find you."

"I never seemed to know him well enough," mused Ephraim distractedly. "Somehow, of all my children, Isaak was the one I failed."

Leah objected. "Never, Papa! You never failed any of us. We couldn't have had a better father than you. No one else could have worked harder or cared more."

"I loved him," said Ephraim sadly. "But there was so much to understand about him, and never enough time. And I never gave him back the mills."

"He no longer wanted the mills, Papa," Leah assured him. "He wanted a political career. And you gave him the means to achieve that."

"And it killed him," whispered Ephraim brokenly.

To that Leah could make no reply. In her heart she agreed. If Isaak had pursued some other occupation, he might never have known Jozef Pilsudski and he might still be alive. But then he might have met death in some other way even earlier and more tragically.

"Luvna is gone," said Ephraim from the depths of desolation. "I could not stop her."

"Perhaps its best, Papa," offered Leah in an effort to relieve her father's guilt. "Everything here reminded her of Isaak and all she had lost."

Ephraim looked at her in silence for a long moment, his mind clear and concentrated upon her words, his eyes alight now with new understanding.

"You really think that's why she left?" he asked.

Leah nodded. "Yes, Papa. I think she had to go to survive!"

Ephraim considered that for a time and seemed at last to accept it. Then he looked about the room.

"Where are the rest of my children? And their children?" he asked. Leah smiled warmly at her father, patted the hand she still held and nodded agreeably.

"Nearby," she said and turned to call softly. "Michael!" Michael entered his father's room, glanced at the drawn draperies and shook his head.

"It's too early to darken the room," he said with feeling. "Let the afternoon sunlight shine in! Darkness will come soon enough." And it was obvious that his words encompassed more than the end of the day. A smile crossed Ephraim's face as his youngest offspring opened the drapes flooding the room with red-gold light.

"Yes, Michael," he said, his voice growing slowly weaker. "Darkness comes too soon for all of us."

Adam entered behind Michael followed by Abrahm and Daniel, the latter still dusty from inspecting the fences that bordered the estate. Markos and Frederick Kolvner hovered just outside the door awaiting a sign from Leah, who nodded and beckoned for them to enter. Last of all followed Johann, breathless, tired and disheveled after a hurried journey from Krakow. At eighteen he had declined Sarah's generous offer to accompany him on this occasion as she had done two years earlier. Instead, she had sent a letter borne by him for Adam, assuring Ephraim's eldest son of her sympathy and her prayers. In that letter she had included a message for his father, if he could still be told, that she planned within a few months to resign her teaching position in Krakow and was gradually preparing to move to Palestine to teach science there to the children of settlers in one of the larger cities. Currently she was awaiting her assignment and she had leased the house to Johann for as long as he wanted to use it. When it was sold, the proceeds would go to the Zionist fund as had the sale of Sarah's father's home more than a year before. Not included in that farewell letter to her lost love, because it was unknown to her at the time, was the fact that in the Holy Land she would find at last a companion for her later years, one who taught the young as she did. And since her childbearing years were past, they would no longer need to worry that their progeny would harbour a life-threatening disease.

"You are my jewels," said Ephraim as his family gathered around him, each striving to restrain their tears. "My fortune! Better than all the gold of Solomon and more precious even than his wisdom."

In the doorway stood a familiar figure half in shadow, her dress a model of perfection as was her custom, her hair perfectly groomed and still almost totally unmarred by gray. Ephraim raised his eyes and acknowledged his old friend.

With a flash of the old mischief that had lurked for decades beneath his confrontations with Mira Pietrowska, he asked her, "Since when, Madam, have you stood in the shadows?"

"One does not hasten to intrude upon a family reunion," said Mira with feigned formality as her full-skirted garments swept across the floor.

"You have always been like an adopted aunt, Madam," said Leah, graciously relinquishing her seat to the older woman.

"You have seemed almost as much a daughter to me as my own. I could not be more proud of all you have achieved," said Mira.

"I've accomplished so little compared to what I wanted to," answered Leah earnestly.

"For you, my dear," said Ephraim, "there is still time. Not so for me! What I leave undone others must complete." Looking deeply into her father's eyes Leah knew to what task he alluded: The dream of a new Israel as Herzl had predicted at that first Zionist Congress in Basel and as he still preached in every public presentation which he gave. Someday a new flag would fly over the promised land and one day, if Adonai willed, some of Ephraim Marjzendiak's descendants would walk in the shadow of that flag.

"The men in my life," complained Mira lovingly, "have all been so ungallant, hurrying away to leave me alone. First my father, then Franz, and now you, my old friend."

"You will never be alone, Madam. You have too many memories," said Ephraim, his voice scarcely above a whisper.

"I could have welcomed a few more," said Mira so softly that only Ephraim's ears could hear, only Ephraim's fading consciousness could divine her meaning. He smiled fleetingly; his eyes opened momentarily for one last glance at all whom he loved. "The Lord giveth, the Lord taketh away." he said softly. They were the last words he spoke. His eldest son Adam completed the quotation from Job for his father.

"Blessed be the Name of the Lord!" he said reverently.

Together the family watched the sunset, Leah holding Ephraim's sentient hand in hers, Mira holding the lifeless one. When the last golden rays had faded from the room, so had the living spirit of Ephraim Marjzendiak. His sons and grandsons chanted the prayers for the dying, closed the dead eyes and positioned Ephraim's body on the floor with his feet towards the door in the ancient tradition of his people. Afterwards, the Hevrah Kadishah cleansed and dressed the body, draping it in the tallit that Ephraim had used in life for prayer. Lighted tapers would be placed at the head and foot of the plain wood coffin when it was finished and the body confined therein.

*** 

The funeral took place the following morning just before midday. It was attended by many dignitaries from the Warsaw banking community, by the current Mayor of Wola, Andreas Gdelewski, by Governor-General Imeretynski to honor his friend Madam Pietrowska and by the local leaders of the Jewish community. The family synagogue adjacent to the house could scarcely contain them all.

The service was presided over by Rabbi Kreschner who had now assumed the continually rotating role of senior rabbinical advisor for the Jewish Community of Warsaw. His words extolling the attributes of the deceased were simple and sincere.

"Truly he showed us a way out of darkness and in times of trouble he was as a brother extending the hand of help. There is not one among us who will not miss Ephraim Marjzendiak."

Adam eulogized his father, holding back tears which he felt might bring shame to the family name. There was little after all that could be added to the Rabbi's heart-felt sentiments and what Ephraim had meant to his family could scarcely be put into words.

"My father," he said haltingly, "has set an example for his children and their children which will be difficult to equal and impossible to surpass. May each of us be worthy of him. Now and in future." The others had nothing to add individually. The traditional prayers for the dead followed. Ephraim was buried later that day in the family cemetery next to Elana. His wish of ten years earlier was at last fulfilled.

There was a sense of emptiness about the estate, a perception of loss too keen to reckon, too painful to mention aloud. Leah wandered vacantly from one room in the house to another, her eyes burning with unshed tears, her mind assailed by a tumult of conflicting thoughts and feelings. Uppermost was the awful conviction that these familiar scenes known to her since childhood had become strangely alien or that she had somehow subtly changed. She came to her old bedroom at the end of the upstairs hall and opened the door, overwhelmed with uncertainty, expecting it too to be changed beyond recognition. It had remained unused since her last visit at the time of Isaak's death. For this she felt saddened and guilt-ridden that it had required her father's final illness to once more recall her home. But here at least was a haven of welcome. The bed retained its lace-trimmed canopy that Elana's industrious fingers had woven and decorated. The crimson carpet Leah had coveted as an adolescent girl visiting Lodz with her father still screened her feet from the chill of the hardwood floor. Her schoolgirl treasures stood enshrined in the niche above the window seat from which she had watched on countless occasions for her beloved father to come home from the bank at Warsaw. Her combs and brushes graced with seashells were arrayed upon her dressing table just as she remembered them on her wedding day when Ephraim had come to escort her to the ceremony that would join her life with that of Markos Kolvner.

So much had ensued since then; so many joys and sorrows. Here in this room filled with memories she could rejoice at the happy recollections and for the sorrows she at last felt free to weep. She found the bed and fell across it and cried herself to sleep as she had sometimes done as a young girl. But when she awoke, her eyes smarting from the tears and from the red glow of the afternoon sun across her face, she felt stronger and calmer, and Ephraim seemed quite close instead of divided from her by the barriers of death and the cold austerity of the grave. Leah stood, giving herself a moment to overcome the instant of giddiness that followed. She splashed her face with water from the basin and moved resolutely to the door.

With well considered purpose she found the music room and the piano which her father had caused to be installed there especially for her visits and at other times to provide himself with a link to his absent daughter. Leah Marjzendiak Kolvner sat at the imposing instrument and ran her fingers over its smooth finely grained wood surface. She opened the keyboard cover and was soothed by the touch of the black and white keys. The tenets of her faith warned against the playing of music or indulging in any other pleasurable activity so soon after a parent's death, for though the week of shivah had passed, the period of sheloshim was still in progress. But the music she chose now was not intended for pleasure. It was the requiem composed by Gounod in 1873 on the occasion of the death of his grandson Maurice. It seemed to the bereaved artist an appropriate means of easing the bitterness of her grief.

To her elder brother Adam, paying a professional call on Judyth Mielinski, who was confined to her bed by a fever, the peals of solemn music filling the house seemed terribly inappropriate. He hastened toward the room which was the music's source, intent upon silencing it but was intercepted by Michael emerging from his office at the sound of footsteps in the lower rear hall.

"What does she think she's doing?" asked Adam angrily.

"What she must!" was Michael's reply, moving to block his brother's passage. The older man frowned, puzzled.

"What does that mean?" he wondered.

"Leah is different from us," explained Michael. "She feels things differently. She responds differently. She pays tribute to father in the way most appropriate for her and we must not interfere!" He emphasized the last words. "Do you understand?" Michael asked as Adam shook his head.

"Music is forbidden at this time!" he said solemnly.

"The enjoyment of music is forbidden," corrected Michael, himself an artist in words rather than music. "Listen to what she's playing. Does that sound as though she's enjoying it?"

"It sounds like a dirge," replied Adam.

"Gonoud's Requiem," supplied Michael, who recognized the theme and funereal variations echoing throughout the hall. "She plays it in honor of Father, who gave her the means to study and become a musician. As he afforded to each of us the means to achieve our individual goals and ambitions despite all the chaos around us. We are all very fortunate to have had him for our father. Only a few are so blessed."

"I know," said Adam, his voice tinged with the sadness of loss. "We are the exceptions that prove the rule. I wonder how long our Russian conquerors will allow us to remain so exceptional."

* * *

As it had been at the time of the Tsar's assassination in 1881 and in the famine of 1891-92, the ills of the Russian Empire tended to be in some fanatical way projected upon the Jews who dwelt within its borders. Pogroms had erupted at those times which were either fomented or at least supported by Russian dignitaries who had conveniently looked the other way while Jews by the hundreds and even thousands were attacked, assaulted, dispossessed and in many instances slaughtered. Russia's latest Tsar, Nicholas II, was currently engaged in a policy of vacillation and injudicious foreign intrigues which was fraught with peril and foredoomed to ignominious defeat. The nation's recent period of prosperity had been followed by depression, deprivation and once more near-famine in several of the urban areas. The Boxer Rebellion of 1900 with its aftermath of Russian expansionism in the Far East had laid the foundation for political unrest and upheaval in that quarter which was only now coming to fruition. Bloody rebellion waited in the wings as 1902 drew to a close and 1903 dawned with its burden of turbulent alliances, conflicts and plagues.

Early in 1902 the Anglo-Japanese Alliance had become a settled reality whose terms purported to insure protection of England's interests in China while also safeguarding the commercial, industrial and political prerogatives of Japan in Korea. The attempts to incorporate Germany into this agreement had of course failed, although unofficially Germany's monarch Kaiser Wilhelm II kept in close attunement with events at the Russian court. There was no unanimity of opinion among the Russian ministers regarding how best to respond to this state of affairs, and Tsar Nicholas tended to express agreement with each of his ministers in turn while surreptitiously following the fanciful advice of a rather unscrupulous former cavalry officer named Bezobrazov. This man's economic explorations of the forest along the frontier region between Manchuria and Korea were a monetary failure which cost the Russian treasury in excess of two million rubles. His efforts did contribute materially, however, to the Russo-Japanese tensions which surfaced in the course of the years 1903 to 1905.

Paralleling those events of international import were serious upheavals in the evolution of the Zionist Movement. Events had not run smoothly for its leader Theodor Herzl as he vainly pursued first one haven and then another as a place of asylum for the beleaguered Jews of Eastern Europe. Yet, ironically enough, it was the leadership of Russian Jewry which came to be his bitterest opponents, mistaking his desperation on their behalf for treachery. As he had endeavored to impress the Sultan with the prospect of economic resurgence for Turkey through establishment of a Jewish settlement on Turkish lands, he had subsequently tried to interest the Kaiser in the advantages of a German protectorate in Palestine. Herzl now turned with renewed zeal to England and that nation's wealthy influential Jews led by Lord Rothschild who held a seat on the Royal Commission on British Immigration.

As the lot of Russia's Jews grew steadily worse, greater numbers of them sought entry into Britain. If these would-be immigrants to Britain could instead be settled as colonists under British sponsorship in the Near East at the crossroads of three continents, Britain's position in that sector would be appreciably strengthened. To this end Herzl had' met with Lord Hereford, President of the Commission, with Lord Rothschild and with Joseph Chamberlain, the colonial minister. All three agreed in spirit with Herzl's proposals. Unfortunately Lord Cromer, the Viceroy of Egypt, though initially neutral to the project, was turned against it by the uncompromising opposition of Egypt to a Jewish colony on its land, even land that was essentially desert. Furthermore the technical and economic problems inherent in the irrigation project necessary to render the lands in question even marginally habitable worked against the proposal. Thus, Herzl's proposal, at first so favorably received, was ultimately rejected.

Failure after failure was slowly but inexorably depleting Theodor Herzl's physical and emotional resources. Meanwhile, the Zionist forces which he had mobilized were split by schisms on ideological and operational grounds. The practical Zionism to which Eastern European Jewry had given birth under the aegis of Hoveve Zion (the Lovers of Zion), and of which Dr. Pinsker had been the founder and first President, found itself frequently at odds with the ideals of political Zionism of which Herzl was founder. Yet both were right and future events would prove that both were essential to the establishment of a Jewish nation.

* * *

On the eve of Passover in 1903 there erupted in Kishinev one of the worst pogroms in the history of the Diaspora. Forty-five deaths were recorded though more probably occurred. In excess of one thousand Jews were injured, fifteen hundred homes were leveled and lootings were rampant throughout the Jewish community. The Tsar's Minister of the Interior, V. K. Von Plehve, who could have intervened to limit the severity of these assaults at their inception, waited for two whole days before implementing efforts to put a stop to them.

The Jews of Kishenev had offered no resistance. They fell like sheep before their assailants. In Odessa, where similar forces were at work, the sentiments and actions of the intended Jewish victims were totally the converse. As is so often the case, it was primarily the efforts of two men which made the difference. One was the twenty-three-year-old activist Vladimar Jabotinsky who was destined to become Herzl's successor as Zionism's most powerful spokesman. The other was Meier Dizengoff who would one day become the founder and first mayor of Tel Aviv. Together these men organized a self-defense corps which effectively forestalled the proposed Odessa Massacre.

Nonetheless, the events at Kishenev which triggered the militant resistance movement in Odessa precipitated less effective but more tragic efforts on the part of Theodor Herzl, efforts for which he would be subsequently condemned and castigated despite his obviously altruistic intentions. K. T. Von Plehve, who had formerly been Chief of Police and was now Minister of the Interior, was a confirmed anti-Semite who had instigated or abetted every anti-Jewish atrocity in the Russian Empire since 1880. The "Black Hundreds" and other similar groups had operated freely under police protection, pillaging and victimizing scores of Jewish citizens. Admittedly, Von Plehve was an unlikely avenue of appeal but the power he wielded and the influence he possessed led Herzl at last to make a desperate overture on behalf of his people, much as Moses had appeared before Egypt's Pharoah to obtain the liberation of the ancient Hebrews.

The remarks on the part of Von Plehve and Witte, the Minister of Finance, should have warned Herzl that here, as with the Sultan and the Kaiser, his efforts were fated to prove futile. Both ministers must have recognized that the pogroms were besmerching Russia's reputation in Europe and that the massive Jewish emigration which Herzl proposed as an alternative could have favorable effects in restoring the nation's good name abroad.

In the course of these meetings Witte stated with bitter humor, "Naturally we encourage Jewish emigration, with kicks."

And Von Plehve dared to offer as a jest, "If it were possible to drown six or seven million Jews in the Black Sea, that would be the perfect solution."

It is a terrible and horrifying irony that only forty years later, an Austrian expatriate named Hitler, with the indispensable assistance of leading members of Germany's medical profession, found means to solve the 'impossibilities' and to implement Von Plehve's "perfect solution" without recourse to the Black Sea. The one negotiated effort which bore fruit for Herzl in these final years of his life led to the offer on the part of the British government of a territory to colonize in Uganda. Here at last was a sincere offer of concrete help from a Western nation prepared to back its goodwill with concrete results. Irony of ironies, it came at a time of greatest schism in the Zionist Movement and when Herzl himself was most vulnerable to attack, thanks to his ill-fated efforts with the Russian ministers.

When Herzl made his proposition at the Sixth Zionist Congress in Basel that the Uganda territory be accepted as an interim asylum for the endangered Jews of Eastern Europe, the spokesman of the Mizrachi, the religious 'right' of the Zionist Movement, announced their support. The essentially Russian 'left' including the survivors of Kishinev were bitterly opposed. Absent from the Jewish delegation from Poland were the moderate leaders who had formerly accepted as their spokesman Ephraim Marjzendiak. Absent too was Markos Kolvner of Zurich who had played so active a role in establishing the financial security of the movement. Such Eastern European leaders as Yehiel Thlenov of Hoveve Zion hailed the offer of Uganda as the first historic event in the long struggle of the Jews of the Diaspora since the destruction of the Temple. But they were opposed by the dissident Russian majority.

When the Congress finally passed the motion to send a committee of investigation to study the proffered Uganda territory, the vote was two hundred ninety-five in favor, one hundred seventy-eight opposed with one hundred abstentions. Embittered by this defeat, the Russian delegates left the room, retired to a nearby chamber and wept for 'lost Palestine' intoning the prayers for the dead. Herzl must have felt like Daniel entering the lion's den when he walked into that chamber determined to win back the defecting faction. It required hours of rhetoric and reassurance to convince those stubborn and disenchanted delegates that he was not the traitor they had called him, that there was no intention to abandon the ultimate goal of a Jewish state in Palestine. At last the protestors relented. They returned to the final plenary session of the Congress. They even applauded Herzl's impassioned closing speech. But the conflict they had implemented had helped to insure that Herzl would not be present at the Seventh Congress to hear the Uganda proposal finally rejected following the report of the commission. By July 3, 1904, Herzl would be dead of cardiac failure and exhaustion.

\* \* \*

Exhaustion had almost overwhelmed Adam Marjzendiak in the late Fall of 1903. The spring thaw of that year had been tumultuous and treacherous following a fierce storm-filled winter. Summer had been unseasonably humid for the Vistula District and had seemed to magnify and multiply every conceivable human ill. Now winter was about to return, replete with its quota of respiratory infections, injuries and deaths. An endless panorama of human suffering seemed to fill the doctor's waking hours and to torment his sleep with nightmares punctuated by his memories of the death of his old friend, mentor and former partner Samuel Jedewreski who had scarcely outlived Adam's father Ephraim by a month. It barely seemed possible that Adam had lost two such major forces in his life within so brief a span of time.

And now, within a matter of days, came news of yet another death. This one took place in Zurich and its victim should by all known standards have been too young to die. His health had been excellent at least until very recent months. He was a man of energy and initiative and immeasurable charismatic charm, knowledgeable and extremely capable in business and finance, dedicated to his family and beloved of his friends. But death is no respecter of such considerations. Markos Kolvner had decided not to journey the relatively short distance to Basel that year because of a variety of business demands upon his time and energies coupled with a persistent upper respiratory disorder that had begun late in summer. This affliction lasted throughout the time of the Sixth International Zionist Congress, and had remained with him through most of September and October, growing if anything worse rather than better.

Leah wrote to her elder brother near the end of September requesting his help and advice. He responded by sending a letter of reassurance and a package of medications which he hoped might prove useful in alleviating his brother-in-law's symptoms. The science of microbiology has progressed amazingly since the early 1900's. Had it been as advanced at that time as it is currently, Markos Kolvner might have survived to recover from the viral infection that caused his untimely death in early November of 1903. Leah would never have thought of blaming her brother for this tragic loss. She welcomed his presence at her husband's funeral and his heart-felt words eulogizing Markos' life and work.

"We can scarcely reckon the measure of benefit tohis people, his community and his field of work that is owed to the Kolvner family, and especially to Markos, who was its most astute and active member. He has brought to the museums and private collections of Europe and North American so much beauty, such timeless art, such reverence for the creative wonders of which man is capable that we shall all be ever in his debt. And for his personal attributes of graciousness, generosity, patience and perseverance under duress, we shall miss him for as long as memory endures."

But Adam, the research scientist as well as the physician, never ceased to chastise himself inwardly for failing to appreciate the seriousness of the illness Leah's letter had tried vainly to describe. He felt, whether validly or not, that had he been able to summon the energy to go to Zurich himself to examine and treat his friend and relative by marriage, he might have been able to save Markos' life. A letter and bottles and boxes could not substitute for his personal diagnostic acumen. Adam's guilt was unending and unendurable mainly because it remained internalized and unexpressed.

In the winter and spring that followed, Adam Marjzendiak exhausted himself still further by relentlessly pursuing his research as well as his active and almost overwhelming medical practice. His letters encouraged his young nephew Johann to continue his studies in Krakow. Fired by his uncle's example, the young man qualified to attend the Medical Academy of Krakow where he was destined to distinguish himself both as a student and, much later as a full professor in the rapidly evolving field of embryology and heredity. That was the area of endeavor which had piqued Adam's interest in the early days of his own medical career, and which now occupied many hours of his nights. Nights which should have been devoted to rest and sleep. Guilt is a hard taskmaster. It can spur a man to achieve beyond his normal expectations, but in so doing it exacts a heavy penalty. In Adam's case the forfeit was his life. By May of 1904 he had finalized the current phase of his self-imposed research project and had mailed his notes to Johann in Krakow. In the young student's senior year they would form the foundation for his thesis.

When Johann returned to Warsaw in the late spring at the end of his current curriculum, it was to attend his Uncle Adam's funeral. Abrahm and Meyhra were particularly grateful that Johann arrived in time for the ceremony. Leah, still in mourning for her husband's death, brought Frederich with her, feeling too overwhelmed by this double loss to attempt the journey alone. Both Abrahm and Johann spoke at the funeral. Abrahm extolled Adam's fulfillment of the role of father, of his having served as a role model for his son in a time of social and politicl upheaval, as well as the occupational stresses of wave after wave of contagion and illness through which he had tirelessly worked. Johann praised his uncle's farsightedness in striving to uncover the secrets of the hereditary ailments that plague mankind. Because in that era, Warsaw's medical community was dominated by its Russian physicians, hardly any other doctor attended the service, but a multigenerational array of grateful patients filled the Great Synagogue almost to capacity.

Of Ephraim Marjzendiak's children, only Leah and Michael remained. Of Ephraim's grandchildren four, Samuel and Frederick Kolvner and Daniel and Johann Marjzendiak seemed to have found their respective paths in life. Samuel had fallen heir to his father's importing business and was already enlarging its scope and influence both on the European continent and in the New World where he had established contacts in the United States and in Canada. Daniel, while less esthetically inclined than his father Michael, had inherited his father's way with words and was destined to distinguish himself as a journalist during World War I and to play a role in bringing to his fellow Jews residing in Germany at the time some consciousness of future peril that would lead to the survival of several hundred thousand of their number, though it would not save the life of his own daughter. Frederick, Samuel's brother, had already become a distinguished musician and painter whose canvasses hung in the famous art galleries of Europe and whose skill as a composer was only now bearing measurable fruit.

Johann, youngest of the new generation, was totally determined upon a career in medicine and the biological sciences, following in the revered footsteps of his uncle Adam. Johann was fortunate in being able to benefit from the experiences of both Adam and Isaak in receiving their education in Krakow, where the spirit of Polish independence still burned brightly and intellectual freedom enjoyed an exalted status almost comparable to religious fervor. These four young men envisioned their future as intimately united with the future of Eastern Europe and hoped to contribute meaningfully to the significance of the Jewish presence as the Old World adjusted to the demands of the new century.

Nonetheless, his father's death exerted a profound effect upon Abrahm Marjzendiak. All the bitterness and frustration that had smoldered within his young soul as he contemplated the tragic situation of his people, their hardships, and the pogroms to which they were subject made his presence in Warsaw progressively more painful. The inability of the majority of his contemporaries to study at the universities and thus achieve their noblest objectives and aspirations because of the enforcement of educational quotas and vocational restrictions now erupted in an emotional storm that manifested itself initially as profound depression. The fact that, by a peculiar quirk of numbers, he himself had been accepted to study at the University of Warsaw did not alleviate his feelings of frustration and grief for his less fortunate coreligionists. The loss of his grandfather, his uncle by marriage and his father in relatively rapid succession left Abrahm in the unenviable circumstances of a ship without a rudder. He and Ephraim had grown quite close in the course of the older man's declining years. Indeed, Ephraim had come to depend upon his eldest grandson in many subtle ways of which even he himself had not been fully aware. Thus an understanding had grown between them. More than once Ephraim, who had desired passionately to be a part of the colonization of Israel, had spoken of the world outside Poland, beyond the dominion of the Russian Empire and the Tsar's anti-Semitic policies.

Markos Kolvner had written enthusiastically of the opportunities for immigrants to America who possessed the initiative and energy to avail themselves of what was offered. Of course, Markos had made it clear, the adjustment to a totally new culture could be difficult and demanding, but it could also prove to be quite worthwhile. As events brewed to a boil in the geopolitical cauldron of 1904, Abrahm found his frustrating depression fusing into something far more tangible: a settled resolve to get away from the crushing burden of arbitrary restrictions that was strangling Eastern Europe and to seek abroad the opportunities which were so patently lacking at home. He began to study articles describing France where Judyth was completing her education. He had learned from her mother that Judyth loved the French language and culture. Was there, perhaps, an opportunity for Abrahm in Paris, or perhaps in London?

* * *

The climactic events that were even then determining the future of the Marjzendiak family were also shaping the course of Russian history. On February 8, 1904, Japanese forces had carried out a surprise attack on the Russian warships anchored at Port Arthur, an act that followed by only four days the disruption of diplomatic relations between the two countries. Open war was now a "fait accompli." The much larger Russian nation was totally unprepared for war despite the martial stance it had assumed all the while negotiations for an agreement of peace and mutual understanding had ostensibly been carried on, a period of several months. Korea had been and remained the point of contention since both countries argued that they had rights and interests there that must be safeguarded. Japan, though small, had insured her preparedness and was in a position to establish her mastery of the seas between Port Arthur, Russian's prized eastern port, and Vladivostok.

Throughout 1904 the Russo-Japanese conflict raged unabated. It was a series of ignominious disasters for Russia. From May to late August her land forces suffered one defeat after another, losing in October the Battle of Cha-Ho which was fought primarily to relieve Port Arthur. Instead, in January of 1905 Port Arthur surrendered. Shortly thereafter the Russian Army was forced to evacuate its position at Mukden. The burden of retrieving Russian honor now fell once more upon her fleet, the majority of which was barred by the Straits Convention from leaving the Black Sea where it existed mainly as a merchant fleet. In Baltic ports the fleet was re-equipped and recommissioned as a war fleet. As such, it reached the coast of China in May 1905 and toward the end of that month was soundly defeated by the Japanese Navy but not before it had provoked a nearly explosive confrontation with the British Government. This event, occurring as the re-equipped Baltic fleet sailed toward its fatal encounter, caused several deaths and severe damage to British commercial ships, requiring the payment of reparation by the Tsar's government in order to avoid war.

Nor were these foreign conflicts without parallel on the domestic front. The ongoing hostilities, with their attendant conscriptions and mobilizations of peasants and laborers engaged both in industrial and agrarian pursuits, ultimately disrupted the economy, the food supplies and citizen morale. The war, at first supported by the common people, became an extremely unpopular enterprise as one defeat after another assailed public pride and destroyed the confidence of the Russian masses in their leadership. Von Plehve was assassinated in July of 1904 by a Soviet revolutionary known as Sazanov.

Less than a year earlier, Von Plehve's old rival Count Witte had been dismissed as Minister of Finance thanks mainly to Von Plehve's instigation. Yet the fall of these two powerful anti-Semitic statesmen did little to better the position of Russia's Jewish subjects. And Witte soon regained some degree of pre-eminence through his brilliant handling of the peace negotiations into which Russia entered with Japan in August of 1905 at Portsmouth, New Hampshire. These negotiations took place under the sponsorship of U. S. President Theodore Roosevelt whose nation was now showing an increasingly greater interest and influence in international affairs.

Meanwhile, even before hostilities had ended and peace was being sought abroad, labor disputes had already erupted throughout Russia as the Congress of Zemstzo[14] representatives met with conflicting policies on the part of Von Plehve's successor as Minister of the Interior Prince Svyatopolk-Mirskiv who had previously been perceived as something of a liberal. Obviously, whatever his personal views, he was unprepared to deal with the widespread dissatisfaction that existed. Publication of an imperial ukaz (proclamation) promising various administrative reforms of benefit to the Russian peasants failed to address the widespread demands for representative institutions and only succeeded in further alienating both the Slavophiles and the labour unions which over recent years had acquired a strongly Social Democratic flavor. In January of 1905, a deputation of workers led by the activist priest Gabon, founder of the Assembly of Russian Workers, marched to

---

[14] provincial and district assemblies

the Tsar's Winter Palace to present a petition for redress of grievances on the part of the nation's labor force. These men were unarmed; they expected to be peacefully received and had no intention of opening the door to overt violence. Nonetheless, the Tsar's troops fired upon them. Several hundred were killed or injured. This was the "Bloody Sunday" massacre which is held by most historical authorities to be the opening event of the 1905 revolution.

A rash of strikes followed in St. Petersburg, Moscow, Saratov, Riga, Lodz, Warsaw and Wilno. Faced with such violent opposition to his administration, Svyatopolk-Mirski resigned to be replaced by a professional bureaucrat named Bulygin. Numerous peasant revolts ensued and the Tsar's uncle, Grand Duke Sergei, was assassinated. For a short time this act of murder seemed to exert a sobering effect upon the Tsar. Nicholas announced through Bulygin his intent to create a constitutional assembly. Unfortunately, this somewhat pompous announcement proposed too little in the way of concrete acknowledgement of the public will. Even the moderate elements of the opposition remained unimpressed. Strikes spread throughout the Empire like a plague, affecting industries and trades hitherto uninvolved in the general upheaval. The peasant revolts continued and led to the formation of a Peasants' Union. In the Armed Forces riots and mutinies abounded.

Regrettably, the constitutionalists could not agree among themselves. The liberal group led by Prince Sergei Trubetskoy insisted upon an assembly which would be representative of the entire Russian people without distinction of class. The conservative elements, opposed to this resolve and led by Count Bobrinski, attempted to curry favor with Nicholas by directly attacking the liberal platform. Given the choice, Nicholas opted to comply with Brobrinski's proposals. In mid August Bulygin published the Imperial Decree creating an assembly virtually in name only, having the right merely to submit requests to the Council of State for their consideration.

Given the instability of the domestic situation, it was not surprising that agitation for a truly representative constituent assembly increased rather than subsiding. Strikes multiplied; production declined. In October a railway strike was declared which paralyzed the entire Russian railway system for several months and laid the foundation for the first Soviet Council of Workers' Deputies. This body soon contained representatives from the professional groups such as lawyers, doctors and teachers, all of whom formed unions in response to Imperial apathy and duplicity. Finally, as a result of the widespread chaos in his country, Tsar Nicholas began to realize the extent of the disaffection of his people. The October Manifesto contained his response. It provided for the election of the Legislative Duma and gave the Russian nation the hope of a constitution with a Counsel of Ministers and a President thereof comparable to a Western European Prime Minister. More importantly from Tsar Nicholas' point of view, it split the ranks of the opposition and quenched temporarily the fires of revolution. The radicals remained dissatisfied but the liberals believed that progress was at last being made. The land owners ceased to support the peasant and worker groups and the "Black Hundreds," partly at the instigation of the latter, became once more active attacking not only Jews but Russian intellectuals as well. The group which gained least from the revolutionary activities of 1905 and early 1906 were the Jews. Under the original terms of the Bulygin Duma project, they did not even receive franchise since their 'civil disabilities' disqualified them from the full rights of citizenship. Under the October Manifesto, however, the right of the Russian Jews to vote was granted. That was the sum total of relief afforded to the Russian Jewry. The Pale of Settlement remained in force and the Numerous Clauses with their educational restrictions were not rescinded.

Furthermore, Count Witte was appointed President of the Counsel of Ministers. The League for the Attainment of Equal Rights for Jews attempted to unite those Jews who were outside the Bund. The Russian Liberation Movement elected a number of Jews to the Duma Council, a body that was formed to cooperate with the Duma, all to no avail. So little was accomplished that the Jewish activists became as divided as the other components of Russia's citizenry; the Zionists with their factions, the anti-Marxist liberals (the Jewish People's Group) and the moderates (the Jewish People's Party) all came into active existence by early to mid 1906. The most effective unity at this time was between the PPS and Rosa Luxembourg's Social Democracy Party of Poland and Lithuania whose aims were based on a common ground against the Imperial policies expressed in the October Manifesto.

Michael and Daniel Marjzendiak became active for a time in the Jewish People's Party which championed the ideals of moderation and strove to weld all Jews into one political entity. Abrahm stood with the dominant Zionist group, but failing to see any real progress being made, he abandoned that affiliation. With Michael and Daniel overseeing the management of the family estate, with Ephraim dead and buried and Abrahm's erstwhile hope for meaningful governmental reform for Jewish citizens deeply disappointed, there was little to detain him in Warsaw. Now, there was only one thing, one event to which Abrahm Marjzendiak looked forward. That was the return to Warsaw of the one person who still anchored him to his homeland, the return of Judyth Marks from Paris.

# CHAPTER FIFTY-NINE
## HOMECOMING

Judyth received Abrahm in the living room of her family home. This room held many reminders for Abrahm. He and Judyth had first met here when he had been a teenage boy and she the birthday girl at her fourth year celebration in the fall of 1887.

His most cherished memory of her, seated at the commandeered coffee table, surrounded by family members, contemplating the candles on her birthday cake, had remained vivid in his mind for ever after. Each detail of her face, framed in dark shiny curls, sparked a poignant train of memories, flowing forward as she grew from curious toddler to awkward pre-teen and then to radiant, graceful young girl. And with each succeeding year, Abrahm's attraction to his beautiful cousin had grown deeper and more intense.

He realized he had been waiting all these years since age thirteen for Judyth to mature enough to decide to share his life. It seemed as though, unknowingly, he had been holding his breath, waiting for circumstances to coalesce and free him from his self-imposed prison sentence. He had attended school, had graduated and had returned to Plaz Marjzendiak to assist his grandfather. He had raged silently at the inequities rampant in Russian Poland and had even attended an occasional "opposition" meeting. But he had not taken an active part in the activities of those attendees around him, even when his friends like Matthieu Holtmeyer and Jacob Oberman had tried to enlist his aid. As things worked out, that was just as well. Even being numbered among their circle of acquaintances had proven to be a liability for Abrahm. Despite his non-involvement, he had been seen at one of the meetings just before the nationalists had mounted an assault on a lesser Russian diplomat named Vashily Sparskov. When, after four days the man had died, every name and face the authorities could possibly implicate had led to an arrest and detention.

Only because Abrahm could prove his whereabouts at the crucial time had he been released. That had occurred only after hours of interrogation, asking the same questions over and over in an effort to confuse him and wear down his resistance. Once he had regained his freedom, Abrahm had vowed to dissociate himself from any connection that might endanger his family. In the case of Matthieu, that was an extremely painful sacrifice for Abrahm. They had been friends since boyhood.

If he had ever been tempted to undertake an active part in the political activism of his friends, that experience had laid to rest any such inclinations. Even now, he could not suppress a shudder at the thought of what his involvement in any of the anti-Russian demonstrations that were currently taking place in the Vistula Provinces could mean to his family. The recent pogroms in Odessa and Minsk were graphic illustrations of the lengths to which the Russian authorities were capable of going to enforce their power and proclaim their enmity against the Jews, even without overt provocation.

Now, as Judyth moved forward and reached out to welcome him, he understood at last the basis for his former sense of unreality. For in this long-awaited moment of reunion, he at last felt fully alive. Time took on new meaning for him. Impelled by his enthusiasm, he took Judyth in his arms and drew her close against his chest, surprised and at the same time pleased to find that even grown up to age nineteen, the top of her head came barely to his chin.

They stood thus, clasped in each other's arms for a moment, and Abrahm had never known such bliss, such perfect peace in his entire life. The restlessness that had plagued him since the death of first his grandmother, then his uncle, his grandfather and then his father seemed strangely stilled. The peculiar apathy that had left him unresponsive to the contagious militancy of his friends and acquaintences in the opposition also lifted from him. Everything he treasured, everything he longed for he held now before him in the person of this small, slim, violet-eyed dark-haired girl.

"It's so good to see you again," she said, gazing up at him with near adoration in her eyes. "It seems like decades since we've been together."

"I know," he answered reverently, "I've missed your presence more than I can say. Your sunny smile, your lyrical laughter, the sound of your voice. I was afraid you'd decided to stay in France.

"And not come home?" Judyth scoffed. "How could I? Everything I love is here." She moved away from him a short distance, then turned back to face him, her eyes shining. "Everyone I love is here as well," she added. "In spite of all the negatives, Warsaw and its surroundings are still home. It made going away to school more worthwhile, knowing that I had all this to come back to."

"All this?" he asked, hoping to pin her down, wishing she would say she had missed him specifically as much as he had missed her.

"The house, the garden, family and friends." She beckoned to him to join her on the broad divan that faced the picture window. "You don't understand because you haven't been away."

"Maybe, my dear, you're seeing Warsaw through a rose-hued mist," he said sadly. "I'm glad you were away when all the bad things happened. You have no memory of them. And that's good." He sat beside her and took her hand into his.

"Oh, but I heard about them," she answered him. "Mother wrote to me. I'd hoped you'd write to me too. I waited for your letters."

"But you know how poor I am at putting thoughts into words. I've always felt awkward about writing letters. You and I could always talk in person, even though I'm so much older. But with letters," he admitted, "I'm a total loss! Now that you're home, I can tell you how I feel."

"I should have written you directly," said Judyth contritely. "Not using mother as a go between, asking her to tell you how I was doing. It was just that I felt gauche. I was afraid you'd think me forward."

"Why would I think that?" Abrahm wondered.

"Convention. Social limitations. And, I'm nine years younger than you are. That makes a difference."

"Not to me," he said, taking the plunge. "You found a warm place in my heart the moment I saw you."

"And I've looked up to you all the time since," she responded. "You've always been my hero. Always so tall and strong. So wise."

"That I'm not," he admitted with a wry smile.

"Don't say that!" Judyth pleaded. "Not now, when I so need your wisdom."

"Why is that?" He wanted to know, a puzzled frown creasing his brow.

"I need your advice," she said. "Something has happened, and I don't know what course I should follow." Her voice trailed off into an awkward silence.

"Did something happen at school?" He asked, faintly alarmed.

"Yes, in a way," she answered. "Of course, I put off doing anything about it then. But now that I've come home, I'll have to make a decision."

"What decision?" Abrahm asked uneasily, noting the way in which she looked away from him as she spoke.

"I know I can count on you to give me your honest opinion," she said. "We're true friends. We've always been honest with each other, haven't we?"

"Why yes, of course," Abrahm answered, uncertain where this conversation was leading.

And now she did indeed look directly at him. "You've known Cousin Johann all his life," she said. "Being a man, you understand him in ways to which I would have no access." She paused, uncertain how to continue.

"We were friends as children," he said, "if that's what you mean."

"That's part of it, yes." Judyth asserted. "And lately, since he's been older, you're still close, aren't you?"

"Yes," said Abrahm. "Sort of. What is it you want to know about him?"

"What do you think of him as a person?"

"He's my friend," Abrahm answered. "My relative. We don't see each other as much lately, though. Our lives have sort of gone in different paths. Why are you asking me this?" And when her silence persisted, he turned her to face him. "I came here for a totally different conversation," he said. "I came today to talk about us, about you and me."

"We've always been friends," said Judyth, flashing him a dazzling smile. "I think I've loved you forever."

Abrahm stared at her in surprise. He asked, "Do you mean that?"

"But of course I do!" Judyth responded. "I'm amazed you have to ask."

"Then how," said Abrahm, "does Johann fit into it?"

Judyth grinned sheepishly. "Because," she explained, "last month Johann wrote me a letter."

"Why would he do that?" Abrahm wondered. "He knew you'd be home soon."

"Anxiety sometimes makes people impatient," said Judyth. "It causes them to behave rashly."

"And did he?"

"Did he what?"

"Behave rashly?"

"Well, that's precisely what I wanted to ask you," Judyth answered. "You're older and wiser than I; older than both of us."

"Nine years," said Abrahm. "Five with regard to Johann."

"But that gives you such an advantage, the perspective that comes with maturity."

"Judyth," said Abrahm, striving to keep the exasperation from showing in his voice. "What is it you want to ask me?"

"Marriage," she began, "is such an enormous step."

"Yes, I agree," said Abrahm, and then he realized what all these circuitous statements were about. "Is that what Cousin Johann wrote to you about?"

"There! You see? You knew! I didn't even have to tell you."

"He wrote asking you to marry him?"

"Yes! And of course I'm flattered. But how does one know what to answer?"

Abrahm could scarcely believe his ears. He had planned to ask Judyth's parents for permission to court her now that she had graduated. Decorum dictated that course of action for a young man with honorably serious intentions toward a young lady. He had felt, since they were so well acquainted with each other, that he owed her the courtesy of informing her of his plans. And unwisely he had assumed she already suspected the depth of his feelings for her.

Now, he was embarrassed to broach the subject to her at all. His gauche, naïve younger cousin, ignoring all the proprieties of custom and convention, had beaten him to the prize. If he were to press his suit now, it would seem petty, spiteful, the product of a mean-spirited jealousy. Yet how could he not tell her of his feelings?

"What should I say, Abrahm? How should I respond?"

"What do your parents say?" Abrahm asked. "How do they view the situation?"

"I don't know," she replied. "I haven't told them."

"Why ever not?"

"I'm afraid my father will laugh," she said. "And Mother will say Johann's prospects aren't promising because he's so young."

"Do you love Cousin Johann, Judyth? Because that's the crucial question."

"We've not seen each other for years," she answered. "How can I be sure?"

"You said you'd loved me forever!" Abrahm exclaimed.

"But that's different!" Judyth almost shouted.

"How is it different?"

"It's a different kind of love. It's respect, and admiration. You're a tower of strength to me, a refuge in time of storm."

"Yes, that's exactly what love should be," Abrahm said heatedly. "That's the kind of love all of us search for, the kind that can be relied upon when trouble strikes."

His eyes searched her face, seeking some sign that beneath the shallow youthful shell of her picture-perfect prettiness there resided a warm, tender woman who simply needed more time to emerge.

In desperation, he reached out and drew her once more into his arms. His lips found hers and clung to them, his hands gently stroking her hair. When she relaxed in his arms, silent and safeguarded, he whispered, "Has it never occurred to you that I love you? That I've waited years for you to reach the time in your life where you are now?"

"You've always been like a big brother to me, Abrahm." Judyth said in a puzzled voice.

"You've always come to me for advice, I know. But could you learn to think of me as more than a big brother? As something more permanent than a safe port in a storm?"

"If that's what you want," she answered in a small breathless voice. Nonetheless, her answer conveyed little conviction. Judyth Marks was nineteen years old. To her, Abrahm Marjzendiak occupied a place somewhere between father figure, older brother and resident local hero. Such idealized icons as Judyth's mind had created out of her child's view of her eldest cousin are not easy to fondly embrace as flesh and blood men. She had said she would try if he wished, and try she would. But such efforts seldom guarantee success, especially when confronted with an eager and determined adversary.

Johann Marjzendiak had not failed to follow conventional protocol merely due to naivete. He was aware that he had a rival, a formidable one; one with a close and favored relationship with the object of his affection. He reasoned that unconventional strategies are often resorted to by desperate, inexperienced campaigners. Such warriors have no choice but to attempt to break new ground. One might cite young David's unusual strategy against Goliath as a case in point. Except of course that David of Bethlehem, later to become David, King of Israel, had not been totally inexperienced in fighting off rivals. It was simply that, in the past his rivals had been mainly wolves seeking to steal and eat his sheep, rather than giant men seeking to capture and subjugate his people. He had employed a time-honored strategy that had served him repeatedly. That practice had refined his aim, trained his eye, and steadied his nerves. Only as he aimed and hurled his stone missile at the giant's brow did it dawn upon him that Adonai, through his prophet Samuel, had chosen and anointed him in preparation for that moment. Undoubtedly he saw before his mind's eye a long procession of feral wolves who had fallen victims to his sling, schooling him to meet his greatest foe of all, the champion of the Phillistine hosts.

Johann had no history of past triumphs to call upon. He had never won a fight, and had in fact gone to great lengths to avoid physical strife and conflict. He would never knowingly have attended a militant political meeting even on a dare. Yet, he was not a moral coward. He held, despite his youth, strong convictions and patriotic sentiments. He was convinced that the pen was mightier than the sword and that peaceful protests can be stronger than armed assault if well-timed and coordinated, and persistently carried out.

It was thus, without consulting any kinsman, Johann, deprived of fatherly advice by an assassin's misdirected bullet and of motherly counsel by an amorous artist, had set out to plot his own course on the intimidating sea of erotic adventure.

His letter, sent to her at school, was a paean to Judyth's numerous physical perfections, from her violet eyes and ebony-colored hair to her tiny high-arched feet that he had often seen in childhood, before the mandates of social correctness intervened. He had rhapsodized her beauty, extolled her matchless virtues and confessed his enslavement to her innumerable charms. Then he had stated that his life would be barren and unlivable without her as his life's companion.

Indeed, the plethora of poetic images Johann had called forth had left Judyth faintly embarrassed and exultant, but confused. She had never received a correspondence like this before. Quite simply, her cousin had swept her off her feet.

And while she had told herself and Abrahm that she feared her father might laugh at Johann's suit and her mother might dismiss his proposals because of his youth, Judyth knew better. She could not be unaware that Johann's soon-to-be-completed medical training would enable him to carve out a respectable place in the world. Doctors can almost always find work. Illness in some form afflicts mankind universally from birth until death, and the men who know how to alleviate the ravages of disease are uniformly welcomed in every society.

Judyth found herself backed into a corner, forced to make a choice she had not planned to make so soon after graduation. She was intelligent, discerning and possessed of a strong will and an independent turn of mind. She did not, however, harbor a specific ambition as had some of the other women of her immediate and extended family. Leah had become a famous musician, despite tremendous odds. Meyhra had undertaken nursing and had excelled at it. Judyth Marks could lay claim to none of these gifts. She played the piano moderately well as a young women of her day and social station often did. But she would never set a concert audience afire with her genius, for she had none. She could cook, sew and embroider well, she had a flair for style, she was well read, and could hold her own in a conversation. Her imagination was fired by the stories of women in England and America who sought to gain the right to vote for their gender. But in her own land, even her male co-religionists had only recently won the right to vote. They could own property for the present, and a few had achieved public office, but the majority of common rights of citizenship that many took for granted were still beyond their grasp.

Judyth Marks looked about her world and felt dissatisfied; she wondered what path she should follow. She debated within her own mind what partner would be her best guide in following that path. If it was difficult to be a man in this time in the Vistula Provinces, especially a Jewish man, it was no easier to be a woman of Jewish faith and heritage, faced with the prospects of bearing and raising children in a society that tended to categorically restrict and reject them before they had even shown the world of what they were made.

Between them, in different ways, Abrahm and Johann had placed Judyth on the horns of a dilemma. Had she been a vain, light-minded creature, she might have enjoyed playing her two suitors against each other, toying with their feelings and causing them to squirm. She might have relished pretending to favor first one rival and then the other, inspiring each to try to outdo his opponent in plotting ways to win her heart. But had she been such a person, neither of these two young men would have loved her, and both indeed loved her very much.

\* \* \*

Abrahm, in his role as general manager of the Marjzendiak Mills and factories, was obliged to keep abreast of the political forces at work around him. It was for this reason that he had consented to attend with Matthieu the two opposition meetings he had gone to in the first place. But he had been there only as an observer, not as a participant. Nor was he the only spectator in the audience. Plain-clothed Russian militia members had also been present.

Militia officers made it a point to learn the times and locations of as many meetings of dissidents as they could and to make certain that some among their members were in attendance.

As fate would have it, on March 14th of 1906, a meeting of the Polish Freedom League was scheduled to take place in the once fashionable but now seldom used Marlionevzki Theatre at 6:00pm. The time had been chosen deliberately to coincide with the dinner hour of the upper class, the wealthy, the influential and the Russian administration. Hopefully, those people would be engaged in social pursuits while their subordinates and "inferiors" met to lay plans to oppose them.

Judyth was too shocked to ask how Johann had learned about this rally. She was appalled that he wanted her to accompany him there, but relieved that he had brought with him drab, commonplace clothing for both of them to wear. And they would sit in seats at the rear of the balcony where they could hide on the floor if necessary. What Johann did not tell her was that he suspected that Abrahm had decided to attend.

This was to be a meeting to discuss recently enacted changes, promulgated by the newly-appointed Duma, meeting in St. Petersburg and ratified by the Tzar, that would have far-reaching effects on the outlying Russian provinces. Such information, warning the provincial subjects of things to come, was almost never made available by local administrators. It was only through clandestine sources that those likely to be negatively affected were able to learn what to expect in the future and how to prepare for it.

"Jan Janowksy has just returned from Russia," Johann had overheard Abrahm's foreman at the old Wishniewski mill reporting to him. "He'll be one of the main speakers tomorrow night. I'd go in your place, but my wife is ill, and her sister can't stay with her just now. She has to work at night."

"This is just the sort of thing in which I've been warned against participating," Abrahm had objected.

"I'm told Jan's speaking at 6:30pm," the foreman, Stanos Cruzych, had responded. "Why don't you slip in through a side door after the rally starts, and then leave when his talk is over? That way, you'll know if any of your family's business interests are threatened."

Abrahm had pondered that question for a moment. "I may do just that," he finally said. "But I'll have to go disguised. I'll have to be very careful."

It was this exchange that had planted in Johann's mind the idea of the nondescript clothing, and the unobtrusive vantage point from which to listen and watch unobserved.

None of Abrahm's friends in the Polish Freedom League were expecting to see him at the meeting. Instead, they assumed that he would scrupulously avoid any entanglements with them and their associates, as he had stated was his intention.

As daylight slowly dimmed and faded into dusk, Abrahm had still not fully committed to going to the Marlionevzki Theatre. He felt certain all entrances would be watched. He could not guess how to gain access to the place without attracting notice. Reluctantly, he walked the eighteen kilometers from the perimeter of Plaz Marjzjendiak to the Barbizon gate of Warsaw, his mind still divided between continuing his trek and turning back toward home.

The theatre was on Sygisimundt Street, and as he turned along that thoroughfare, he noted a few familiar faces in passing. None recognized him. No one made any sign of greeting. Good, he thought. His disguise, contrived of old clothes, a shapeless hat pushed down over his face, darkened glasses and a false theatrical beard, was effective. Encouraged by this, he gradually accelerated his pace and circled around to the rear of the theatre. He noted with some surprise that the stage door stood slightly ajar. He glanced cautiously up and down the street. It seemed to be deserted. It was still almost an hour before the assembly was schedule to convene. Assuming a shuffling gate, Abrahm Marjzendiak moved toward the door, paused to listen for voices or other sounds, checked that the key was inserted in the door on the inside, and then slipped through, closing the door behind him. He paused in the semi-darkness to accustom his eyes to the dim atmosphere surrounding him. Then, impelled by a self-protective impulse he could neither justify nor deny, he silently removed the key from the lock and slid it into his pocket. Unless there was a duplicate key handy, the stage door could not be locked. Even if it was locked, he had a key that would open it, and the bolt was located on the inside. Sooner or later, Abrahm could gain access to the street, even if he was obliged to conceal himself for a period of time within the theatre in order to avoid detection or capture.

With time to spare, he explored the backstage area. He looked into several empty dressing rooms, he briefly scanned the property room filled with props. One shiny stage knife caught his attention. The blade was rigged to collapse backward into the handle when pressed against a solid surface. In one large room, he noted a long mirror covering the length of the wall opposite the door. Arrayed before it was an equally lengthy table with closed jars of makeup laid out as if in readiness to accommodate a large cast of performers.

Yet, no one was here to use these supplies; no company had engaged the Marlionevzki Theatre in years. To Abrahm, it seemed a sad waste. The place was well equipped. He dared not risk turning on a light, the better to explore. Leaving off his curious probings, he ventured out from the backstage area and soon heard muffled voices. Uncertain to whom they belonged, he paused to listen and observe.

Three men dressed in dark fur coats devoid of insignias and wearing large hats not unlike his own stood in the prompting box below the stage. They could see the audience clearly from that vantage point, and they could hear whatever was said on stage. Conversely, those on stage, if anyone in the box spoke, would be able to hear them, for that was the purpose for which it was intended.

Abrahm crouched behind a desk set a few feet away from where the three men had stationed themselves and waited. He could hear diverse sounds as the group began to assemble within the theatre. They filled the seats at the forefront of the ground floor. The balcony level was apparently empty for the present. For a gathering of this sort, the lower level seats were preferable. There would be speaking with very little movement such as might be used to enhance a dramatic performance. There would be no dancing, no marching and no music.

Quietly, the four men waited, three together, one apart. The group on stage took their places as if on cue. The man designated to coordinate the proceedings, one Jacob Gamien, opened the assembly with a brief prayer to God for guidance and enlightenment. This was followed by applause from the audience, and during the noisy interval one man of the three whispered to his companions, "Perfect! We can hear every word."

A second man hastily put his forefinger to his lips for silence.

Onstage, Gamien set the scene for what was to follow. He spoke of the unrest in St. Petersburg and the repressive changes being wrought by the new Tsar. He mentioned the contrasts between the prior and current rulers and stated that Tsar Alexander II's assassination by the People's Will had not proved to be a benefit for the subject people of Russia; that despite the reactionary advice of many of his ministers, Alexander II had governed with moderation and a measure of justice.

This presentation met with mixed responses from the audience. Some obviously agreed, but others booed. And it was during that distraction that Abrahm noticed movement in the balcony. Apparently there were late arrivals who had decided to go upstairs in the hope of gaining a better view of the stage and its occupants.

Now, having aroused a mixed response, Jacob Gamien introduced the keynote speaker of the evening, Jan Janowsky. His entrance provoked enthusiastic applause, followed by silence as he took possession of the podium.

"People of Warsaw," he said solemnly, "I stand before you the harbinger of good news and of bad news. The good news is that I have at last seen with my own eyes a faithful copy of the statutes our departed monarch Alexander II signed into law on the morning of his death, a scant few hours before he was assassinated. If I could, I would have brought it with me to show you, but I could not do so; it is closely guarded. Those who now wield his power dare not permit the original document to come to light. For all I know, by now it may have been destroyed. But in it, the former Tsar promised the most far-reaching reforms of his entire administration."

Now, hysteria reigned, and Janowsky was forced to strike the gavel several times upon the podium to reestablish order so that he could go forward with his address.

"The paltry concessions that this latest Tsar Nicholas II has made are but a token of what his grandfather envisioned. The calling forth of a new Duma is a ploy to put in power men who share Tsar Nicholas' plans and prejudices. And they will favor the rich of central Russia. The provinces will be used to serve the empire's soaring economic needs. The subject people will be conscripted to replenish the empire's armies that have been sorely depleted by costly and ill-fated foreign campaigns. Our future looms bleak indeed!" he said sadly, "We have little to hope for, and much to dread. Alexander III was a dreamer despite his impressive physique, and his son is without vision or statecraft. We have exchanged a lion for a jackal, a leader for a buffoon. No foreign ruler respects him, no king or prince relies upon his promises. How can we?"

Janowsky paused dramatically.

"What are we in the Vistula Provinces to do to better our sorry lot? If we do nothing, we will be divided, conscripted, enslaved! If we rebel, our families will be imprisoned or shot, our property confiscated. And the foreigners among us? Their favor will be sought to make them rise against us, and then they too, will be made victims so that in fighting each other, we cannot mount an effective force against our real enemy, our overlords."

"We dare not act precipitously. We must lay our plans carefully, logically, without rash emotion or distorted judgment. Premature rebellion will only be crushed as it has been in the past. But Mother Russia has multiplied her foes. We now must watch to see which of those foes stands the best chance to defeat her. Then, when the fatal blow falls, we must strike and regain our freedom!"

The crowd was not certain he had finished. There was a momentary silence, then a tremendous cacophony of raucous noise. There was shouting, screaming, stamping of feet, clapping of hands as the audience responded to the speech it had just heard.

The three men in the prompting box moved restlessly.

"We've heard enough!" exclaimed one.

"No, wait! Let's see what happens next," said the second.

"We'd best get out of here," said the third, and with that they converged on the corridor that led to the stage door.

Abrahm remained still and silent, his attention divided between the three men whom he suspected of representing the militia, and the belligerent crowd in the theatre. He noted that the people he had observed in the balcony earlier were no longer to be seen. Who were they, and where had they gone? What would happen next? What was his best course of action, to remain in hiding where he was, or to make his exit as the other three clandestine observers had done?

* * *

Out in the streets surrounding the theatre, peasants, tradesmen, private citizens and uniformed militiamen combined in a mass as wildly disorganized as a swarm of bees lost from their queen. They seemed to follow no predetermined purpose. They were rowdy and undisciplined, and it was uncertain whether most of the people there had been inside the building during the speech or not.

Inside, the rally tried to continue, but the noise outside threatened to drown out the voices of those on stage. The crowd rose from its seats, alarmed by what they were hearing in the streets.

In the balcony, Judyth and Johann cowered on the floor behind the last row of seats, afraid to venture outside, and equally afraid to remain where they were lest they be trapped and possibly arrested. They had seen no sign of Abrahm's presence and Johann was overwhelmed with guilt at having brought Judyth here and placed her in jeopardy to no purpose. He had hoped to discredit his elder cousin in Judyth's eyes, and thus gain for himself an advantage. Instead, he had betrayed his own poor judgment and achieved nothing that justified his behavior.

Even as the two young people hid, trying to resolve their dilemma, a detachment of uniformed militiamen entered the theatre and began to disperse the crowd, barking orders and in some cases, seizing men and women by the arms, dragging them out of their seats. This action provoked loud protests and sporadic violence as militia officers responded to blows with answering blows, and then threatened people with detainment, possible arrest and serious charges if the violence continued. No one saw Abraham Marjzendiak emerge from the back stage area, climb the narrow stairs to the stage boxes and thus gain access to the upper balcony without mingling with the crowd below. Something about those furtive figures had roused his curiosity. He was determined to find out who they were and why they were there, assuming of course that they still were there. If not, perhaps they had left some clue.

Dropping to his hands and knees, Abrahm crept quietly to the rear of the balcony section, his attention divided between the objects of his search and the events evolving below on the ground floor of the theatre. He suspected that the figures he had seen were children; one had looked quite small. If that was true, they must by now be totally terrified. He was twenty-eight years old, and the sounds of wave after wave of arriving militia sounding trumpets and shouting at the people in the streets struck fear in his heart as well.

Moving slowly and silently, Abrahm reached his goal, the back row of seats from which the view of the stage was partially obstructed by tall columns and access to the seating area was afforded by a steep set of stairs that were precarious and forbidding. These seats, when the theatre had flourished, were seldom sold and commanded only a modest fee. Peasants had occasionally occupied them. Tonight they were empty. Behind them, Judyth lifted her head and froze. She barely restrained a scream by clapping her hand over her mouth. Her eyes seemed enormous in her face as she recognized Abrahm, despite his disguise.

He put his finger to his lips and warned her to keep silent.

"Don't move!" he mouthed, exaggerating the workings of his lips so that she could read them. He sidled over beside her and crouched down behind the seats next to her and Johann. He had not as yet recognized her companion, but as he stared at the downward bent head, a fleeting suspicion dawned upon him. He took hold of a handful of dark curly hair and raised the head. His eyes met those of his youngest male cousin and again he signaled for silence.

"Stay put!" he whispered, "This will soon end. I know a way out." Abrahm's mind was seething with conflicting emotions, but now was not the time to express them, and he made no attempt to do so. The three Jewish cousins crouched in the shadows of the last row of balcony seats watching and listening while chaos reigned below them.

Despite Abrahm's assurance that the drama would soon end, they remained trapped where they were for more than an hour and a half. At one point they were obliged to lie flat under the seats while a lone militia officer climbed the steep stairs, shining his torch across the rows of cheap seating, looking for stragglers. What he saw from his vantage point halfway up the stairs was emptiness. His calls to come out if anyone was there elicited only silence. It was an eerie setting at best. The man turned away, descended the stairs and extinguished his torch. The echo of his footsteps died away, but Abrahm still refused to let either of them move. They stayed hidden for another quarter of an hour. Then, following his lead, they crept cautiously down the stairs, into the stage boxes on that level, and down the narrow stairway that led backstage.

The hall was deserted now. No one remained but the three cousins. All felt frustrated beyond belief. Abrahm had learned very little of what he had come to discover. Johann had failed utterly to discredit him, and Judyth was still undecided between them.

Cautiously, Abrahm, led them to the stage door. It was bolted now from the inside as he had expected it would be, but he held the key in his pocket. He slid the bolt back as softly as possible, then paused to listen for several heartbeats. When no sound arose outside, he inserted the key in the lock, turned it, and opened the door a crack. The street outside, a side street, was almost empty. Two lone figures passed each other moving in opposite directions, making no sign of recognition or collusion. Still, Abrahm waited until they had gone before he opened the door enough to permit their egress. He had left the key inside as he had found it, but he tightly closed the door. When he tried reopening it he found that it was equipped with a third lock, a spring lock, apparently placed to keep unwelcome intruders from disturbing the cast.

* * *

The homeward journey was a silent one. When they were near the Barbizon gate, Abrahm hired a carriage to take them back to Wola.

When they were seated inside, Abrahm turned to his cousins. "You'll both stay at Plaz Marjzendiak tonight." He said this in a voice that, while low-pitched enough so the coachman could not hear him, brooked no argument. "In case they're searching and asking questions, you were our guests for the evening. That will be your reason for being away from home. Is that clear?"

Two heads nodded in unison, two voices answering as one in the affirmative.

In the front hallway, before they mounted the stairs, Abrahm had a few more words to say to them.

"Tonight never happened! Should any of us be questioned, we never left these premises once the two of you arrived. We enjoyed a quiet frugal meal and a pleasant social visit. Then, noting the lateness of the hour, we said our good nights and retired to bed. Hopefully, Judyth, you can find a change of clothing in my aunt's closet that you will feel is appropriate to wear. Perhaps, after a restful night's sleep, one of you will have something to say to me that will explain why I was obliged to rescue you from a potentially dangerous, possibly lethal situation."

* * *

That night, Johann, exhausted by a host of conflicting emotions, uppermost among which were dread and embarrassment, slept like a proverbial log without regard for unaccustomed surroundings and a strange bed. It had been three years since he had stayed at his grandfather's house. The abrupt departure of his mother with her new love had placed him in an awkward position. His grandmother's sister had rescued him from that situation by taking him to live with her when she had moved to a modest house in Wola. The house was registered in Johann's name. When Judyth Myliska died, it would be Johann's property, provided Russian law was not radically revised by that time.

On the other hand, Judyth Marks, who had in the past been a frequent visitor at Plaz Marjzendiak, went to rest in Leah's old room at Abrahm's suggestion. Once there, she found herself strangely restless. Her mind was filled with disturbing images inspired by all that she had seen, heard and experienced tonight. Foremost in her mind was the image of her older cousin Abrahm coming to the rescue of herself and Johann without stopping to consider the possible peril to himself.

It had been he who had made them lie flat under the seats when the militia officer had searched the balcony. Fortunately, it had been a cursory search that had failed to disclose their hiding place. It had been Abrahm who had then led them to safety, shepherding them through the tumultuous Warsaw streets and ensuring their safe passage away from the city and its perils of the night.

Judyth could imagine many people being arrested as a result of the interrupted freedom rally. The rough treatment by the militia of those in attendance seemed a preamble to much worse to come. And Judyth had seen Jacob Gamien knocked down on the stage by one of the uniformed Russian officers as he tried to restore silence and order in the auditorium. What, she wondered, would have been their fate had they been seized and taken into custody? What would her father have said? What indignities and punishments might her family have endured because of her thoughtless adventure? Tormented by these questions, Judyth tossed and turned in Leah's bed until nearly dawn before she finally lapsed into a fitful slumber.

Because at the last minute Stanos Cruzych's sister-in-law had not had to work that night, the foreman had changed his plans. He had indeed attended the rally, had noted with mounting alarm the dark-clad ominous looking men entering the auditorium by several doors at once, and had made an attempt to follow his own advice and slip away unseen. At first he had congratulated himself on his own foresight. He had reached the foyer of the theatre without mishap, his eyes scanning the area in search of an unguarded exit. But as he had moved towards what he thought was a clear way to safety, a tall, stocky militia officer had stepped into his path, seized his arm and dragged him away.

As a result of the interrogation that followed Stanos Cruzych's arrest and detention, two men in long frockcoats arrived early the following morning at the main house of Plaz Marjzendiak. To their credit, they knocked discreetly, expecting to be greeted by a servant. To their surprise, the front door was opened by Michael Marjzendiak, still dressed in robe and slippers.

"To what do I owe the honor?" He asked in a voice of thinly veiled sarcasm.

"To his supreme majesty Nicholas II's pleasure," was the openly sarcastic response.

Michael looked about the porch as if seeking to find the august ruler physically present at his door.

"I do not see his supreme majesty," Michael remarked. "My humble dwelling would be honored to welcome him."

"Welcome us, his representatives, instead," said the senior officer, attempting to force open the door.

Reluctantly, Michael stood aside and allowed the two men to enter.

"You have business with a farmer at this hour?"

"Are you Abrahm Marjzendiak?" the officer inquired.

"No sir, I'm not," Michael answered. "My name is Michael Marjzendiak." He did not bother to inform them that he was better known under his nom de plume of Michael Marjak, since some of his newspaper articles and essays were known to be activist and somewhat controversial.

"You own and operate the Marjzendiak mills?" was the next question.

"The mills are owned by the family," Michael informed them. "My nephew Abrahm currently manages them. May I ask, has there been some trouble at one of the mills?" He was barely able to conceal his sudden alarm.

"Not yet, as far as we know," said the officer. "But one of the employees has been taken into custody."

"For what reason?" Michael asked, his voice hushed with concern.

Behind him, at the top of the stairs, Abrahm emerged from his bedroom, fully dressed and equally a prey to concern, even to anxiety.

"Which employee?" He wanted to know as he hastily descended the winding staircase above which Ephraim's portrait still hung. Both officers were immediately struck by the strong resemblance between the older face depicted in the painting and that of the younger man who had just entered the hall.

"The man identified himself as Stanos Cruzych, a foreman in your employ," said the senior officer in response to Abrahm's question. "And who are you?" There was a distinct note of menace in the man's voice.

"I?" Abrahm responded. "I'm Abrahm Marjzendiak."

"Ah!" said the junior officer. "So you are in charge of the mills and factories. Mer Cruzych answers to you."

"That's right," Abrahm conceded. "What is he accused of doing? Why is he in custody?"

"We're asking the questions, Mer Marjzendiak. It's your place to answer." The senior officer, whose name was Bronislav Kresske, moved closer to where Abrahm stood. "Your man had some interesting things to tell us about you."

"Really? What sort of things?"

"He said you attended the rally of the Polish Freedom League last night at the Marlionevzki Theatre."

Abrahm almost chuckled. Michael glared at him in shock.

"Did he really?" Abrahm said. "Perhaps he misspoke. Perhaps what he meant to say is that he suggested I attend that meeting. As it turned out, I had already made other plans for the evening. I was obliged to decline the suggestion, however well meant it may have been." He did not dare smile overtly, but inside he felt a certain ironic amusement. He was quite sure Cruzych had made the statement under duress.

"Is there anyone who can corroborate your story and confirm your other plans? A lady, perhaps?"

"Yes, of course," said Abrahm. "My plans did include a lady, and a gentleman."

"And who might they be, this lady and gentleman?" Kreskke asked with mock politeness.

"My two young cousins. Judyth Marks, who has only recently returned home from school in Paris, and Johann Marjzendiak, who will soon graduate from the Akademy of Medicine at Warsaw. He's completing his practical training there. They visited with us last night. We dined and socialized until rather late. I invited them to stay the night."

Abrahm turned to Michael, his uncle, separated from him in age by less than a generation. "My uncle was very tired as a result," he offered. "I assume your early visit awoke him." A meaningful glance passed between them.

"Indeed it did," said Michael, joining in Abrahm's fabrication, although he had been working on the estate ledgers rather than sleeping when the two militia officers had knocked. He had hastened to answer the door in order to avoid allowing other family members to be disturbed.

"These two cousins," Kreskke said. "Are they still asleep, too?"

"I assume they are," Abrahm answered.

"Would you call them?"

"Is that necessary?" Michael questioned, uncertain whether or not the two young people were really in the house.

"I'm afraid it is," he was answered. "We wish to question them separately."

That last statement sent an uneasy shiver through both Marjzendiak men.

"My cousin Johann you may question alone," said Abrahm, relying on the young man's rigorous medical training to guide whatever testimony he might be called upon to give. "However, it is unseemly that a sheltered young woman such as my cousin Judyth should be questioned without another family member being present."

Kreskke considered that for a moment, and then decided to relent.

"Very well, bring the cousins to your drawing room." He gestured towards what he assumed to be the main salon, just visible from the hall. "We'll interview them there. You two may be present, but you must not speak or interrupt."

Michael walked towards the stairs; the junior officer followed him. Abrahm, moving quickly, intercepted them. He knew which rooms each of the cousins occupied.

"I'll go," he said, and bounded up the stairs, the junior officer at his heels. He knocked first on the door of his aunt's old room.

"Cousin Judyth?" he called softly, knocking discreetly as he did so.

A stifled sigh answered him, followed by a few sleep-garbled words. Soft footsteps echoed in the room, and the door was opened marginally.

"Yes? What is it? What time is it?" Judyth said sleepily. When she recognized her cousin Abrahm, her eyes betrayed concern. Then the other man stepped into her line of vision and the color drained from her face. Her eyes sought those of Abrahm. "Why is he here in the house?" she asked indignantly. "What's happened?"

"This officer has some questions to ask you, I believe, regarding our dinner last night. I'm sure it's a purely routine matter." He tried to look reassuring to calm his cousin's obvious near panic. "I think he wants to make sure I was a proper host and never left your presence."

Judyth's face begin to regain its customary rosy hue. "But of course," she said with spirit. "You were, as always, an ideal host. After all, you did invite me." Then she faltered. Normally, another female family member should have accompanied her. "As well," she added, "as Cousin Johann. We were both delighted to visit the family compound again, and see Emily."

The officer cut her short, which Abrahm would have done at that point anyway. Emily Vroska was now confined to her room and could no longer run the house. Her duties had been assumed by the brisk and business-like Bertine Montefiore. But all this domestic politics was of no concern of the Russian militia.

The officer asked, "What time did you arrive, my lady?"

Judyth seemed to consider that matter for a long moment.

"I'm not exactly certain," she said, striving to recall what time she and Johann had reached the theatre the preceding evening. "I think it must have been shortly before 6:00pm. Dinner was scheduled for – wasn't it 6:30?" Her voice, her eyes, her very soul all combined to ask that question of her elder cousin.

"That's true," said Abrahm in response. "It was about that time."

Hearing voices down the hall, and recognizing that of his beautiful cousin's among them, Johann hastily threw on a respectable change of clothing from the closet, noting that the fit was acceptable. The garments he had cast aside the night before he crammed into the bathroom hamper and set an ornament from the sink counter on its lid. Then he quickly walked to the door and threw it open.

His trained physician's eye took in the scene at once. He rightly guessed that Abrahm and Judyth were being questioned, though he wondered why.

"Good morning," he said civilly, his glance encompassing both his cousins, as well as the uniformed officer. "Cousin Abrahm, I'd no idea you were on such familiar terms with the militia that they visited you at such an early hour." He pointedly consulted the wall clock. "It's an ungodly early hour!"

"May I present my other dinner guest last night, my cousin Johann Marjzendiak?" Abrahm said by way of introduction.

Johann joined the group outside Judyth's door.

The officer asked, "You had dinner here last night?"

"Why, yes," answered Johann. "But then my cousin has already informed you of that."

"You were all here for the entire evening?" Asked the officer, aware that his superior was observing him from the hall below.

"That's correct," Johann affirmed. "It was an intimate family gathering. That hardly seems a matter that would be of interest to the militia."

"You were aware of the seditious assembly at the Marlionevzki Theatre on the same evening as your family gathering?" This was the junior officer's inquiry.

Johann looked puzzled. He was uncertain how much he could logically be expected to know about the underground. He tried to remember where he had learned of the rally, and realized that he had been told of it by a student who said he'd seen it announced in a newspaper he had found discarded in the street outside the Akademy. Reluctant to implicate the other student, he pondered the question for a long moment.

"Is that the rally mentioned in the press?"

The officer asked suspiciously, "What source did you consult to read of that?"

"Well," said Johann, "I didn't exactly consult it. I stepped on it going down the stairs outside an Akademy lecture hall. It looked to be the front page of a periodical. There was only the one sheet, and it was crumpled and dirty as though it might have blown away. None of my colleagues recognized it or claimed it. I glanced briefly at it, and then threw it into a trash bin. I'd forgotten about it until you brought it up just now."

The officer looked carefully from one family member to another. None of them moved or spoke further. All presented a united front of surprised, innocent silence. The story they told was plausible, and each had told it separately without hearing what the other had previously said.

Judyth, clad in bedgown and wrapper, shivered in the morning draught in the hall.

"Are you satisfied?" Abrahm asked. "Cousin Judyth was awakened from sleep; she's not warmly dressed. Have you anything further to ask of her?"

The officer responded by a slight shake of his head.

"You may retire," Abrahm directed Judyth who promptly withdrew and closed the door. She, he knew, was the most vulnerable of them all. She, under close interrogation, might have cracked, might have betrayed some small detail that could trap them. He felt relieved that she was now safe behind the bedroom door, which he had heard locked.

Abrahm turned to the officer. "You've still not told me why Stanos Cruzych is in custody."

"That's not your concern," said the officer as he turned to descend the stairs.

"I beg your pardon," Abrahm insisted, "but I am much concerned. The man's my foreman. If he's not at work this morning, the day's run of lumber will be delayed. His duties must be reassigned. Was all this done because he's a Pole working for a Jewish firm?"

It was a valid question. Christians employed by Jews had been a sore point in the past in Russian-dominated Poland.

"Stanos Cruzych was arrested exiting the Marlionevzki Theatre when the rally was broken up. I seriously doubt he'll be at liberty to report for work in your mill this morning or any other morning in the near future."

The senior officer Kreskke, who had broken off his questioning of Michael, the other vulnerable party, in order to observe the questioning of the younger family members, just as Abrahm had hoped he would, stepped forward to meet his colleague at the foot of the stairs. It was he who made the ominous pronouncement.

"I think we've finished here." He said, then added, "It seems the employee sought to buy his freedom by involving his employer. Too bad he didn't know about the dinner party. He might have tried another ploy if he had."

"Perhaps," said Abrahm, "he went there out of curiosity. I've never heard of his being implicated in anything against the state."

"Mer Marjzendiak, I advise you to use greater care in your hiring practices in the future," said Kreskke. "I would suggest you warn your staff that you and they will be closely watched in the future. Don't be surprised if we call on your mills and your factories from time to time."

"Yes, sir," Abrahm responded. "I'll be expecting you."

When the officers had gone, Abrahm watched their horse-drawn vehicle disappear down the driveway of his home, his thoughts dark and bitter. Even though he had escaped detection at the theatre last night, and had safely extricated his two younger cousins from their foolhardy escapade, he was still in jeopardy. For that matter, every Jewish businessman and property owner in the Vistula Provinces was in jeopardy. Premises of Jewish ownership were subject to search and possible seizure at any time. Such painful uncertainty and harassment was becoming unbearably repugnant to him. How much longer, he wondered, would he be able to endure it?

Upstairs, Judyth waited for Abrahm to return. She had washed and dressed in one of Leah's youthful outfits. It was of a pink filmy fabric and emphasized her youthful slimness and flawless complexion. Her eyelashes were thick and long and her lips a deep rose pink. Her dark wavy hair cascaded over her shoulders. She had never looked more appealing. She had never been more frightened in her life.

It was Johann who knocked hesitantly at her door, but it was Abrahm she needed to see.

Johann asked, "Are you all right?"

"No, I'm not," Judyth answered petulantly. "Do you see what your little adventure has caused?"

"But that's not true," Johann objected. "Those men weren't here because of us. They'd no idea we were there."

"Thanks to Cousin Abrahm," Judyth retorted. "He got us out of that terrible place. He even invented that story about our being his guests at dinner. Thank the Lord they didn't question us about the menu!"

At that moment Abrahm appeared at the door. "The menu, had they inquired, was roast lamb and sprouts, chopped vegetable salad and home-baked bread," Abrahm said in response to Judyth's remark. "So I would have told them, but at that point, I doubt they cared. They could not prove any of us attended the meeting so they quickly lost interest. It's too bad my foreman changed his mind about going and then sat in the audience where he was readily visible. Fortunately, you two knew you had no business there and hid in a dark corner where you were difficult to see."

"Yet you found us, Cousin Abrahm. How was that?" Judyth asked.

"I saw you from backstage," Abrahm answered.

"How did you know it was us?" Johann wanted to know.

"I didn't," Abrahm admitted, "but I suspected you were two frightened children playing with fire. In that I was right. What, in the name of all that's holy, were you doing there?" He looked at each of his young cousins in turn.

Judyth blushed furiously.

"I followed him," she finally said, pointing to Johann.

Johann in his turn admitted hesitantly, "I heard about the rally as I said, almost. A fellow student saw it in an underground newspaper discarded on campus." He paused uneasily. "I went to the Vistula River Mill to talk with you about what I'd learned. Then, as I entered your office, I heard you talking with a man dressed in overalls about the meeting. He said he wasn't going. Something about his wife being ill. And you said you'd go instead."

"I said I <u>might</u> go," Abrahm objected.

"You knew Cousin Abrahm would be there?" Judyth asked in amazement.

"Well, I thought…"

"You thought I'd be there," Abrahm interrupted, "and you'd hide in safety and show cousin Judyth how reckless and unwise I could be."

"And instead," Judyth said, "Abrahm acted wisely, concealed himself backstage and ended by getting us out without being caught."

"Have either of you any idea how serious this could have been? I may have lost the best foreman our mill has had in six years because he was guilty of the momentous indiscretion of being seen in the wrong place at the wrong time. I'm afraid he may have thought he was being loyal to me."

"Why should he think that?" Asked Judyth, seating herself on the lounge across from her bed.

"It was believed that the main speaker would bring back valuable information regarding Tsar Nicholas' latest policies about liberalization, and particularly about Jewish rights in Russia and Poland. That might have happened later, but the militia staged their attack and broke up the meeting before anything new or meaningful was said."

"So it was all a waste of time!" Judyth exclaimed, a strong tone of disgust in her voice.

"More or less, yes," Abrahm agreed. "But I must confess that I'm very disappointed in some of the members of my own family. I would have expected better from you, Johann. I'm sure Uncle Isaak would feel the same if he were still alive."

Johann demanded indignantly, "Leave my father out of this discussion!"

"Your father died saving the life of a man whose policies he passionately endorsed," Abrahm countered. "He was himself a politician, but he never in his life did anything underhanded." He stared hard at Johann. "I know he'd be ashamed of what you did last night, and especially shamed by your motives for doing it."

"Was that really why you took me there, Johann? To put Abrahm in a bad light?" There was bitter disappointment in Judyth's voice.

"And you went along with him," said Abrahm accusingly. "Where was your discretion? What became of your common sense?"

"Johann made it sound so exciting." she began.

"Substitute dangerous, even potentially lethal, and you'll have it right. Maybe the two of you deserve each other." Abrahm turned angrily away, leaving his two younger cousins to comfort and console each other. At this moment he felt betrayed by them both. He wondered if he had wasted years waiting for an empty-headed child to achieve a maturity of which she was inherently incapable. He had allowed his youth to stagnate in a country that he no longer felt proud to inhabit. This morning he knew in his heart that he would prefer to be almost any place other than here in Russian Poland, under the rule of a sovereign who was little more than a poseur and a fop. Easily swayed between the rival factions among his ministers, with essentially no grasp of the principles of statecraft, Nicholas Romanov was probably the poorest excuse for a national leader on the entire European continent. His only son was too sickly to rule even if by some fluke the boy's father managed to hold the Russian Empire together until the young Tsarevitch reached his legal majority. Most of his sisters, all older than he, were better equipped to serve as reigning monarchs than either their father or their brother. But thanks to the father's ineptitude, none of them were destined to get that chance.

## CHAPTER SIXTY
## EXODUS

Stanos Cruzych, along with three hundred other ill-fated citizens of Warsaw arrested at the Marlionevzki Theatre on that fateful March evening, never returned to take up his normal employment. His family inquired after him in vain. He, like the others, was made to serve as an example of what might be the fate of those who openly defied the authority of the new Tsar. Those members of the Polish Freedom League who had escaped from the theatre and eluded the militia fled westward into France and Switzerland. A few traveled south to Italy. The other private citizens who had been fortunate enough to depart early said devout prayers of thanksgiving to God and vowed to avoid involvement in such activities as oppositionist gatherings in the future.

For three weeks, Judyth Marks and Johann Marjzendiak were barely on speaking terms. Throughout that period of time, Abrahm sought to explore his feelings toward Judyth even as he struggled to maintain order in the lumber mill without the assistance of his foreman. Abrahm was a troubled and divided man. He no longer took pride in his work. He did not exult in the beauties of his home. He was unable to feel deeply about the future of his nation. More than anything, he wanted to absent himself from his surroundings. He was constantly reminded of all he had lost, of the people in his life who had meant most to him – his father, his uncle, his grandfather and grandmother. He wondered if he had also lost Judyth.

Two events occurred almost simultaneously that propelled Abrahm towards a decision. One was the appearance at the Vistula River Lumber Mill of Bronislav Kreskke. True to his promise, he arrived at an unexpectedly early hour, just after the mill had commenced operation on a Friday. Abrahm was acting as foreman, guiding his crew in the preparation of a run of finished wood for shipping.

"So," Kreskke remarked without preamble, "I find you hard at work, a man of business rushing to meet a deadline."

Abrahm glanced at the intruder, his face devoid of emotion. He asked formally, "What can I do for you, sir?"

Kreskke failed to answer. Instead, he noted brusquely, "I see you've not replaced your foreman."

"I'd hoped I wouldn't have to," Abrahm responded.

"I would suggest that you do so without delay," Kreskke countered. "Stanos Cruzych won't be coming back to work for you."

The finality of the Russian's words chilled Abrahm profoundly.

"Are you saying that he's dead?"

"I'm saying you shouldn't await his return. It would be a waste of time. Now, I'd like you to show me through your mill."

Abrahm stared at the militia officer in shock. He had chosen the most inopportune time for his visit, and now he proposed to carry out an inspection when Abrahm was under tight time constraints to supply a client with a large order of lumber. Reining in his anger, Abrahm led Kreskke to his office.

"What exactly do you want?" he asked as soon as he had closed the door.

"I wish to see your operation," Kreskke answered. "How much volume of business do you conduct in a week? In a month? Who are your suppliers? Where do you find your clients?"

"That could take hours," Abrahm stated, aghast.

"I've plenty of time," he was reminded by his unwelcome visitor.

And so Abrahm Marjzendiak was obliged to show the man his books, knowing all the while that the Russian militia officer knew little or nothing about bookkeeping and business. The task consumed the bulk of the morning, and then Kreskke demanded that Abrahm show him through the mill's physical plant.

Standing on the porch at the rear of the mill, the Russian looked down into the swiftly flowing river and remarked cryptically, "An ideal place to dispose of incriminating evidence!"

Abrahm stared at the man in wonder. "What sort of evidence?" He asked.

"Who knows?" he was answered. "Perhaps clandestine documents, or a body!" Kreskke smiled at Abrahm's obvious discomfort, noting with satisfaction the slight shiver that the young Jewish businessman tried vainly to conceal. It did not occur to him that the origin of Abrahm's discomfort was not a current situation but a past one. He had learned from Ephraim long ago that it was at this site that a young woman's body had been found by Abrahm's uncle Isaak, and that Isaak had later admitted to his father that she had been his first love.

The aura of sorrow and despair still permeated the place, rising up from the river like an invisible miasma of grief. Even the Russian shuddered.

"It's not a prepossessing place, I must say." He turned toward the entrance. "Is there more?" He asked the question to cover his own sudden discomfort.

Abrahm shook his head. "No," he said, "you've seen it all." Abrahm watched as the Russian shrugged.

"Thank you," he said. "You've been most gracious." He then departed, mounting his black horse with a flourish and galloping off down the winding road that led away from the mill. He would not soon come back to this site. There was something subtly ominous about it, the after-image of death. But then Abrahm could not know the other man's reaction. He was left wondering how often he was destined to be harassed again by this meddlesome officer.

Despite the delays, they did manage to meet the deadline. Abrahm was even able to get away early from the mill. By the time he reached the Marks home, he had managed to put Bronislav Kreskke and all he represented from his mind. He had determined to ask Judyth's father Samuel Marks for his daughter's hand in marriage.

Samuel received Abrahm cordially in his spartanly furnished study. The older man respected his young visitor, had watched from a distance as Abrahm had stepped into his grandfather's shoes and taken over the management of Marjzendiak Enterprises, maintaining and gradually expanding the business.

"I'm honored by your visit," Samuel said, his eyes warmly receptive, his smile approving. "What can I do for you, Abrahm?"

Abrahm cleared his throat. In the pocket of his coat, which he had changed at home before leaving to pay this visit, there rested a small square royal blue box from the Insbruk Jewelers. It contained the diamond engagement ring he hoped to place on Judyth's finger.

"I would be honored," Abrahm said, "if you would grant me permission to wed your daughter Judyth. I've waited several years for her, watching her grow and develop into the lovely young woman she's now become." In his mind's eye, he could still see the vivacious, violet-eyed four year old Judyth had been when he first met her. He smiled at the memory. It took him a moment to note that the smile of approval had faded from Samuel Marks' face.

"Oh, but I did not realize," Samuel was saying apologetically. "You never mentioned. Does my daughter know how you feel?"

"I have told her," Abrahm replied. "I mentioned it to her just recently."

Samuel shook his head. "Why did she not tell me?" he asked.

Abrahm sensed that a barrier had arisen between the two men. He did not know its origin, but it seemed to him insurmountable.

"This poses a problem," Samuel said softly. "Had I known, I would not have accepted the other suit."

"What other suit?" Abrahm asked, fearing that he already knew the answer.

"You are more mature, more seasoned, well established in business," Samuel lamented. "You're the more preferable candidate."

"What does this mean, Mer Marks? Tell me in plain terms. Have you, then, already given Judyth to someone else?"

Samuel nodded. "Only this morning," he said, "your cousin Johann came to me, asking the same question. Unfortunately, I have only one daughter."

"Have they spoken together since?" Abrham asked. If Judyth had not yet consented, there might still be a chance. Abrahm suddenly realized that he had allowed valuable time to slip by while he had been deeply involved in the details of managing his family's business. Three weeks had elapsed since the fateful night when all three cousins had met at the Marlionevzki Theatre. Prior to that, Judyth had told him of Johann's letter, but she had pleaded uncertainty as to how she should respond to it. Was she, he wondered, more certain now?

Samuel endeavored to answer his visitor's question. "I think they may be speaking about the matter even now," he said almost apologetically.

"Are they here, in the house?" Abrahm inquired.

"I believe they took the carriage," Samuel answered. "Johann mentioned driving in the park."

"They went alone?"

"No," Samuel replied hurriedly. "That would not be appropriate. My widowed sister went with them. You've met her, I'm sure."

"Judyth introduced me to her Aunt Sophie," said Abrahm, striving to recall the face that matched the name. Samuel Marks had two sisters, both of whom had played major roles in Judyth's life. One lived here in the family home, the other resided in Paris. He felt awkward, intensely ill at ease, as though he were suddenly a stranger in this house that had been like a second home to him throughout his teen years and his early and mid twenties. Now, at twenty-eight, he felt old for his age. And worse yet, he felt superfluous.

"I guess I should have put two and two together when you spent so much time here paying attention to a child so much younger than yourself. I confess to having been obtuse," Samuel admitted, "and you haven't come around as often since my girl came home from school." Samuel looked the younger man in the eye as though excusing himself for his earlier inattention to important details.

Abrahm returned the other man's stare. "I saw your daughter just three weeks ago," he said, and then he stopped, uncertain how to continue. He had no idea how Judyth had explained her absence from the house on that fateful March night. Had she said she had stayed at Plaz Marjzendiak? Had she mentioned Johann's presence, or why they had been together? What role had she assigned, in her explanation, to Abrahm? Those questions tied his tongue. Until he had clarified them, he dared not risk aggravating what was already a hopelessly entangled situation.

"Have you then, given my cousin Johann your word that your daughter Judyth will be his, or have you given him permission to court her?" Abrahm asked.

Samuel hesitated momentarily, seeking to recall to his mind exactly what their conversation had entailed. Johann had been quite emotional, even slightly incoherent at times.

"I believe what I told him was that he might visit my daughter, escort her to social events, and seek her accord with his wishes. If she is agreeable, I said I would welcome him as my son-in-law."

"Then it's not finally decided," Abrahm said, relieved.

"It all depends on Judyth's wishes," Samuel asserted.

Abrahm asked, "Then will you grant me the same privileges?"

"That would be very unusual," Samuel responded. "A father seldom allows two different men to court his daughter at the same time."

"Would you then ask her if she would agree to consider us both?"

Samuel Marks experienced a moment of desperation. He felt trapped. He felt manipulated. He had given into Johann's histrionics in a moment of weakness. He would prefer to give his daughter to the more mature business man before him. Still, Johann had asked first, and was about to complete his post graduate training at the Medical Akademy. While he pondered this dilemma, the front door burst open and a deliriously joyful Judyth swept into the hall followed by her Aunt Sophie.

Judyth rushed to her father and threw her arms around his neck. Then she let him go and thrust her left hand before his face.

"Papa!" she exclaimed. "Just see what Johann has given me!"

Samuel glanced from his daughter to Abrahm and it was only then that Judyth became aware of her older cousin's presence. The brightness of her smile did not diminish. She moved swiftly to Abrahm and embraced him in turn, obviously expecting him to be happy for her as well.

"For three weeks," she said, "I've refused to speak with him. He came to visit, but I sent him away. And then, today he enlisted my father's help. He took Aunt Sophie and me to the park, and there he gave me this ring and asked to marry me."

"And you agreed," said Abrahm, struggling to smile despite his inner turmoil.

"He's made me very happy," Judyth answered. "I suppose I was waiting for a demonstration of forceful determination."

Abrahm took her left hand in both his own. "There could hardly be a more forceful demonstration than this," he said, touching the ring on her third finger. "So when will the wedding take place?"

"Oh, not for a while, I suspect," Judyth replied. "Not until after Johann's finished his training. He's not yet certain just where he wants to practice, but it won't be far from here. I hope Warsaw will be home to us both."

"Indeed, yes," Abrahm said graciously. "My congratulations to Cousin Johann on the successful conclusion of his suit. I gather he was able to set your mind at ease regarding whatever dispute there was that made you angry with him?"

Their eyes met, and Judyth's looked away first. "I think we were both at fault," she conceded. "Johann made me see that."

Abrahm took her very gently in his arms and kissed her cheek.

"I wish you every happiness," he said sincerely. But in that moment he silently resolved that Warsaw, that had been the center of his life for as long as he had known life, would be home to him no more.

He had for a time worked with the Zionist organization, inspired by his grandfather's efforts in that group, but with Theodor Herzl's death and that of Ephraim Marjzendiak, his enthusiasm had waned. There were connections that he would miss, friends he would regret not seeing again. But Judyth would soon have Johann. His cousins, Frederich and Samuel had already forged their paths and had found their life partners. Undoubtedly Daniel would soon follow suit. He, Abrahm, had waited a long time only to lose the one he sought to someone else.

The only person left alive with whom he could share his feelings was his mother Meyhra. Her life had come to center around Abrahm's father Adam. She had seemed cast adrift by his death. She no longer pursued a career in nursing. In recent months, once she had come to terms with her loss, her house and garden had become the focus of her days.

Abrahm had gone to live at Plaz Marjzendiak when Ephraim had asked him to run the family's business, and for a time, until Michael's return, he had helped run the estate.

\* \* \*

Abrahm was surprised to find how torn he felt upon leaving the mill for the last time. He lingered over terminal chores, showing his nephew Daniel yet again the various routines that had become second nature to him over the years. The many stages of initial cutting, cording, pressing, finishing and packaging the different sizes alone could fill a thick ledger. And then there were the different grades of wood, the sorting according to whether it was hard like oak or soft like pine.

Some woods would be used to manufacture furniture in the Marjzendiak factories, while others would go to the makers of coffins and still others would be purchased by contractors to go into the construction of homes and other buildings.

Abrahm's uncle Isaak had explained to him the intricacies of wood working long ago. After all, Isaak had worked here as a young man. It had been his first job after leaving the flour mill. He had been full of details about processing and selection, but it had been from Ephraim that Abrahm had learned the sad details of his uncle's first love, and then only in part. The elderly patriarch had never divulged the girl's identity nor the name of her family. Abrahm would leave Warsaw unaware that the dead body that had once been found in the Wrepz River beside the mill was that of the former mill owner's daughter.

* * *

Leaving the mill, Abrahm paid visits to a few old friends; it was painful to think that he would probably never see them again. He had recently resigned from the local Zionist association. He wished them well, but he had found that his path led in another direction.

Judyth was delighted that Abrahm had come to visit her. As always, he was her hero, her living icon. She has always looked upon him in that way. That was precisely why she could not think about him as an ordinary man, a man with whom she could plan to build a life and a future.

"I'm glad you're here!" She exclaimed when she saw him in the hall. She ran down the stairs and threw her arms around him.

Abrahm smiled and returned the embrace. But then he saw the ring on her finger and it reminded him that she would never be his in the way he had hoped and dreamed for so long.

"I've come," he said solemnly, "to say goodbye."

"Goodbye?" She repeated in surprise. "Why goodbye? Where are you going?"

"I'm moving away from Warsaw," he answered. "I'm going very far away, to America."

Judyth shook her head in dismay. "I don't understand," was all she could think of to say.

He took her hands into his. "You and Johann are going to be married," he said. "That's wonderful! It gives you something to look forward to with joy."

"I'm so glad you understand, Cousin Abrahm," Judyth said. "It is a joyful thing."

"I've always wanted your happiness," he said. "But…"

She gazed into his eyes. "But, what?"

"But knowing that your life will soon be changing has given me the impetus to go and seek changes in my own life." He paused, uncertain how to continue.

"But you're not leaving right away," said Judyth, seeking to reassure herself. "Not today or tomorrow."

"Next week," Abrahm said.

She cried out in shock, "But you'll miss our wedding! You can't go that soon. You mustn't!"

"Judyth," Abrham said, "Listen to me. I've watched you grow up from a bright-eyed child to a lovely young woman. All those years, I nurtured in my heart a fantasy that was never meant to be. I realize that now. I know that you and Johann make an ideal pair. But I'm not part of that. I can't be part of that. I still love you."

"But not the way that he does." Judyth protested.

"Yes," Abrahm said, "Exactly the way that he does! That's why I can't stay and watch you stand beneath a canopy exchanging vows with someone else, even someone I care about, like Cousin Johann. I can give you up, knowing it's what you want. But I cannot be there to see it!"

There were tears in Abrahm's eyes as he spoke the last words. He tried to hide them from her, but he failed.

"Oh, Abrahm," she said, understanding at last, "Why did you say nothing? Why did you not tell me?"

"There were times I nearly did. But then you were too young. When you came home a few months ago, I wanted to. I tried to tell you, but you were asking my advice on how to answer Johann's letter. I told you then, but somehow you didn't hear me. And now it's just too late. I would have asked you to wait until I could send for you. I would have met you at the dock in New York and taken you to the home I had found for us. But now, I will go alone."

"Oh, Abrahm," Judyth whispered sadly. "I never knew. I never truly understood. Not until now." She looked up at Abrahm. "And now, as you say, it's too late."

She glanced about the room. Her eyes fell upon the coffee table where she had sat so long ago, blowing out candles, because this was the largest room in the house, the only one that would hold all the family at once, and all the many gifts they had brought for her birthday.

"I gave Johann my word" she said with a catch in her voice. "I accepted his ring. What sort of woman would I be if I backed out of my promise?"

Abrahm could not possibly answer that question for her; he would not have asked that she do that.

"What am I to do?" The words seemed to be wrung from the depths of her being.

"Only you can answer that," he said softly. He had taken the ring he had bought back to Insbruk Jewelers only last week. With the refund, he had purchased his passage on a German passenger ship that would sail from Sweden. "Only you know what you want from life," he went on. "With Johann, your life will be as you've always known it. Not much will change except your name and address. If you were to wait for me, it might be a year or more before we could finally be together."

"Do you have to go so far away?" she wondered.

"It's better that I do," he said wistfully. "The last few years have been so depressing. And now, with you ready to be married, but not to me, there's very little for me to look forward to in Warsaw. Between them, Michael and Daniel can run the estate and the business. They won't need me. Only Mother will miss me, and she says it's too late for her to pull up roots and move to the other side of the world."

"But I shall miss you, Abrahm," Judyth said. "I'll miss your wisdom and your strength."

"Now, you'll have Johann. Despite his youthful impulsiveness, he's a good man, Judyth. And he loves you. Each of you can learn from the other. You will come to depend on each other as husband and wife should." He leaned down and kissed her cheek. "I wish you every joy, Judyth. And since I'll be gone by the wedding day, I'll say it now. May you be mother to thousands!" It was the traditional tribute to a new Jewish bride on her wedding day. The practice went back to the time of Abraham and Sarah. Judyth clung to him for a moment longer, unwilling to say a final farewell, reluctant to see the precious chapter of her girlhood that he symbolized close forever.

"God bless you, Judyth," he said with a sad smile. "Remember me, as I shall you."

She nodded and smiled, too full of emotion to speak.

He drew away from her then, and he was gone. He had other leave-takings to conclude, but this had been the hardest, the most wrenching. It is always difficult to say farewell to one's most cherished dream.

When he closed the front door of the Marks home, Abrahm felt suddenly old. In years, he was only twenty-eight, but the last fourteen years had been spent awaiting the realization of that dream, and now he knew it would never be realized.

*** 

Meyhra helped her son pack for his journey. She had laid out many rolls of unused yarn and had, in the past few weeks, woven two jackets of sturdy wool, one dark green with a blue stripe, and one mahogany brown. She had also made three fleece caps with flaps to cover his ears, and several pairs of socks. Furthermore, she had sat for hours in the arbor by the back door of the house she had shared with Adam, darning underwear that her husband had once worn. Abrahm and his father were almost identical in height and build. She knew the items she had so carefully mended would serve her son well as winter approached in the foreign new world to which he was going.

For warmer weather she included cotton garments, some newly purchased especially for this trip. To Meyhra, her son was young while it was she who was old. In two more years, she would be sixty. He had asked her if she would like to travel with him.

"Yes," she had said in answer, a twinkle of mischief in her eyes. "I should love to, but not on so long a journey as you propose, my son. My home is here. I was born in Warsaw. I've watched it grow and change, not always for the better." She smiled and patted his hand. "But here is where my roots are. If you dig up an old tree, you damage its roots, and the tree will die." She had shrugged then. "Everything dies in time, anyway. Best to leave me here where I can flourish for a little while longer." She gazed about the arbor and the garden beyond, noting each familiar tree and shrub. "And if things don't go the way you hope they will," she added, "you still have a home here to come back to."

Abrahm smiled noncommittally and kissed Meyhra's cheek. If the thought that he might one day return to Warsaw made her acceptance of his departure easier, then so be it! He would say nothing to the contrary. Who knew what the future held in store? Perhaps one day he would return to pay a visit to his family, bringing with him a family of his own and the evidence of his success in the new world.

Almost all of his living relatives saw him off at the Warsaw railroad station. That landmark that had been the site of so many emotional episodes in the history of the Marjzendiaks was witness to yet one more momentous occasion, the departure of the only offspring of Ephraim's eldest son, to initiate what would become the American branch of his family. Only Aunt Leah was absent, and Abrahm had timed the journey so that he could stop in Stockholm, where Leah owned a home overlooking the harbor, and enjoy a visit with his beloved aunt to thank her for all her encouragement and support. He had saved each of her letters, not only those she had addressed to him, but those she had sent to his father. In the latter she had described vividly the places she had visited in Switzerland where she had studied and made her home, and in the other countries wherein she had concertized. A close bond had formed between Leah and Abrahm, and it had grown stronger with Ephraim's death. Aunt Leah, after all, had been a pioneer, a woman who defied boundaries and broke down barriers. She had soared into a realm where women ordinarily did not go. And she had been a Jewess who was too proud of her roots to dissemble or deny her origins. That courage had nearly brought her to disaster in Berlin. Thank Adonai for Madame Schumann's intervention.

There were times that Abrahm would take out the letter she had written to him about that experience and reread it to bolster his own resolve. It had begun almost as a memoir:

"Dear Abrahm,

To you, the eldest and most mature of my nephews, I wish to write about the most trying and most instructive event of my life thus far.

I write this from a vantage point of time and geographic distance from the period and the circumstances that I desire to relate. That passage of time, that barrier of distance affords a measure of comfort and safety without which I would probably not dare to commit this experience to paper."

After that unusual preamble, Leah had gone on to describe the ambivalence of her conflicting emotions upon her return to Berlin for the first time since her student days at the Konservatory. She had known a sense of triumph upon her arrival in that tumultuous city, but it had been mingled with an aura of dread.

"I knew there would be those who, because of my faith and my ancestry, would be disposed against me. Then, too, there was the added handicap of gender. It did not matter that I had been hailed in most of the great concert halls of northern Europe, and that a veritable army of critics, prepared to be prejudiced and hostile, had, with very rare exceptions, favorably reviewed my performances, comparing them to those of my revered mentor, Madame Schumann. The very air in Berlin was laden with conflict, and much of that conflict centered on the issue of the Jews.

Why, I debated with myself, had I accepted a commission to concertize in that place at that time? Of what was I thinking? Well, one thing I was thinking was that I would see my old friend and mentor once again. And this time we would meet as equals. That thought sustained me right up to the moment when I stood backstage and waited for the conductor to escort me out and introduce me to the capacity crowd in the Berlin Philharmonic Hall.

That was the moment when panic struck, when all my fears and uncertainties assailed me anew. My heart pounded in my ears, my breathing became labored. I was ready to turn and run from the theatre, a thing I had never before considered doing in my career up to that point.

But then, Herr Willner took my arm and led me forth. He spoke my name, and a wave of thunderous applause greeted me, and made me feel welcome. Once I was onstage, the lights, the orchestra, the unmistakable exultation that always comes over me just before a concert, all these began to work their magic. The fears and doubts faded into the background. I entered into that mystical bonding that comes to exist between the performer and the audience, a bond that builds and grows stronger as the performance progresses.

Once more, I knew with certainty that this was my destiny. This was who I am, who I was meant to be.

And then, much later, my mentor Madame Schumann led the standing ovation in my honor. She caused them to pay me tribute even despite the undercurrent of hostility that threatened to dilute the generous expression of enjoyment and acceptance within that vast auditorium.

She was there also to rescue me from the threat of the angry crowd of Christian Democrat youth outside the stage door. Faced with their abusive attack, your 'brave' aunt Leah tried to run away in earnest, but there again, Clara Schumann came to the rescue. She showed me that nothing is gained by running away from your fears. Yet, she also showed me that there is a time for orderly retreat to regroup one's resources."

At the letter's conclusion, it had evolved into what might have served as a valedictory address. "Belief", she wrote, "is the conviction of the mind. But faith, the faith that leads one to where one's destiny truly lies, that is the certainty of the heart; that is the gift of the Creator. It is a presumptuous mistake to confuse these two forces. But when they coincide, one is truly blessed by Adonai. And then, you should allow nothing and no one to distract you from your preordained path."

"Madame Schumann has lived her life guided by that principle, and from her, I have learned to do the same.

It is my hope and prayer for you that Adonai will always bless you, guide you and prosper you in whatever endeavors you undertake. Be direct and forthright in all your dealings, and be guided by Him who knows what lies ahead for all of us. Know that He will never lead you astray.

Love always, to you and yours,

Aunt Leah."

\* \* \*

On June 20th Abrahm took ship from Konigsberg on the Baltic Sea, having traveled thence by railway from Warsaw. Both Judyth and Johann had been among those who had seen him off at the railway station. Johann was puzzled and a little hurt by his insistence on so urgent a departure. The reasons Abrahm gave his young cousin, though logical and valid, relating to weather and climate and a desire to be settled in his new environment in New York well in advance of winter were not the most pressing ones. Dread of even greater persecutions which might provoke him to some rash and futile action arising out of his emotional frustrations and disappointments supplied the spur to Abrahm's haste. Awkwardly embracing both erstwhile beloved and fortunate cousin, Abraham Marjzendiak, at the age of twenty-eight, departed the scenes of his childhood with no intention of ever returning there again. Whatever future awaited him across the sea, it seemed vastly more desirable than the buried hopes and dreams he was leaving behind.

As fate would have it, the Russian Railroad Workers's strike and the various mutinies of Russian sailors, remnants of which actions still persisted, all seemed to conspire to slow Abraham Marjzendiak's progress toward his destiny. Despite the fact that, unlike many of his fellow emigrants, he possessed the means to pay foe his passage, three times he was obliged to change ship. But even the complexities of life can often bring unexpected pleasures. In Stockholm where his third conveyance, the Rhine Maiden, docked and remained in poet for three days, Abrahm was able to meet with his beloved aunt Leah who was scheduled to play a concert on the evening of June 25th. This afforded them both a rare treat. Abrahm had never before attended a professional concert given by L. M. Kolvner. Indeed, except for her husband and sons, only Ephraim of all her family had previously enjoyed that distinction. And only in the past few months had Leah officially resumed her musical career that had been put on hold due to the death of her husband.

On the afternoon following the concert, the artist and her nephew sat at ease on the terrace of the modest estate Marcos had acquired long ago through his business dealings in this famous city. The house and grounds overlooked the port. Today the afternoon sun was warm and the air was delicately scented with blossoms. Leah's mood was pensive and subdued as was often the case after a concert; by contrast, Abrahm could scarcely contain his excitement.

"I didn't realize you composed as well as performing," said Abrahm, his voice hushed with admiration. "That was wonderful, Aunt Leah! The composition about your childhood made me see home anew. The entire program was inspired."

Leah smiled wistfully at the young man before her, so like and yet unlike his father as she remembered him shortly after his return from Krakow. Adam, too, had been recovering from a frustrated romantic attachment, one that, despite her extreme youth at the time, Leah had been able to understand and to commiserate. As on that prior occasion, she refrained from overtly discussing the matter she knew to be uppermost in her kinsman's mind. Instead she confined her reply to the subject of music.

"Indeed, I was inspired last night," she said thoughtfully. "It's been a long time since I've felt that magic spark. Not since your grandfather died."

Abrahm nodded. "I know," he remarked. "He was a very impressive man. He could describe something to you and make you see and feel it as though you were really there. And he could make you aware of yourself, your own value, your potential. He made you realize that there is no one else in the world quite like you. No one with exactly what you have to offer."

Leah nodded enthusiastically. "I remember the first time he made me feel that way," she reminisced. "I was still very young then. He had just been promoted and assigned an office at the Bank of Warsaw. He took me with him one morning when he was required to work only half a day. I was overwhelmed by all the elegant furnishings in his office. He told me how many rubles each was worth. And that the wonders of one human mind were infinitely more valuable."

"I loved that old man," said Abrahm sadly. "My world seemed to come to an end when he died."

"I know," said Leah, reaching out to brush an unruly lock of thick dark hair away from his brow. "But he wouldn't want you to view his death in that way. His was the spirit of the pioneer. He always encouraged his children to seek out new frontiers, to attempt new achievements." She handed Abrahm a fresh cup of tea faintly flavored with mint. "Ephraim would be highly approving of what you're doing now," she added.

Abrahm asked mischievously, "Drinking tea with my gifted aunt?"

"No, you silly brat!" Leah teased lovingly. "Going to America. Striking out on a totally new track. Something none of us has ever done before."

"Well of course, it's not Israel," admitted Abrahm almost shyly.

"It doesn't matter!" Leah said emphatically. "It's somewhere away from Warsaw and all the terror and threats and political maneuverings." She leaned forward in her chair, intent upon her nephew, compelling his attention like an inspired prophetess from the ancient days of their people's history. "It's a new beginning for us, for our family, Abrahm. You're unique, as Ephraim always said, a limited edition. You're going to make a contribution that no one else could possibly make." She paused for breath and rose to come and stand beside his chair. "Think of it," she exclaimed. "Now there'll be Marjzendiaks on the other side of the world, thousands of miles from where we started, and all because of you!" She knelt impulsively before him. "Promise me you won't let anything dim that marvelous pioneer spirit Ephraim has bequeathed to you. I expect great things from you, Abrahm!"

Abrahm smiled a trifle ruefully. "I'll do my best not to disappoint you," he promised. Almost as an afterthought Leah Kolvner sprang to her feet and went back to the table, bending to retrieve a slender white envelope from its stone surface.

"One thing more," she added turning to face her nephew.

He stood and walked toward her, mystified and strangely moved by the intensity of her mood. She smiled mysteriously and handed him the envelope. It contained a single sheet of paper, very official looking, adorned by a seal. Abrahm glanced from the paper to his aunt.

He remarked, "A letter of credit!" It was a statement rather than a question.

Leah nodded solemnly but the brilliance of her smile belied the solemnity.

"My farewell gift," she said, striving for a lightness she was far from feeling. "Markos made some important friends in New York. That letter is addressed to one of them: Jacob Schiff, President of Kuhn, Loeb and Company. His firm is a major one among the banking houses of New York City. In a new place you'll need money and connections to get started."

Abrahm was overwhelmed. "Aunt Leah," he asked, "what can I say?"

"Nothing at the moment," was her amused reply. "But later, when you've arrived, keep in touch. I don't look forward to a long barren transoceanic silence. I want to know how the American branch of the family is doing. Understood?"

Abrahm embraced Leah warmly, poised midway between tears and laughter.

"Perfectly, Aunt Leah," he answered. "I'll be an absolute flood of information. The Warsaw Gazette of New York."

"Good!" Leah said, returning his embrace and adding a motherly kiss on the forehead of this charmingly adventurous young kinsman. "I plan to hold you to that! Now you'd better be off or you'll miss your Rhine Maiden."

With a glance at his timepiece, Abrahm was forced to agree. The idyllic visit into the world of music and Northern European culture was ended. Now it was time to embark in earnest on his new life. He would never forget these days in Stockholm, or his aunt's prophetic words.

* * *

Abrahm stood on the deck of the German passenger ship as it was being prepared for departure. His mind still held a vision of his aunt's mystically beautiful, still strangely youthful face as his ship steamed out of the harbour. And from her vantage point on the terrace of her Swedish estate, Leah Kolvner watched as the fancifully named vessel that bore her nephew to his undisclosed future sailed forth into the sunset.

# HERITAGE Bibliography

Bank, Richard D. (2005). *101 things everyone should know about Judaism.* Avon, Massachusetts: Adams Media.

Carroll, James (2001). *Constantine's sword: the church and the Jews.* New York: Houghton Miflin.

Cohn, Norman (1996). *Warrant for genocide: the myth of the Jewish world conspiracy and the Protocols of the Elders of Zion.* London: Serif.

Crankshaw, Edward (1976). *The shadow of the Winter Palace: Russia's drift to revolution, 1825–1917.* New York: Viking Press.

Fellner, Judith B. (1995). *In the Jewish tradition: a year of food and festivals.* New York: Smithmark.

Gaster, Theodor H. (1955). *Festivals of the Jewish year.* New York: William Morrow Company.

Gefen, Nan Fink (1999). *Discovering Jewish meditation - instruction & guidance for learning an ancient spiritual practice.* Woodstock, Vermont: Jewish Lights Publishing.

Heilman, Samuel C. (2001). *When a Jew Dies.* Berkeley: University of California Press.

Hirsch, Jonathan (2001). *The woman who laughed at God: the untold story of the Jewish people.* New York: Viking Press.

Hoffman, Laurence A. (Ed.) (1977). *My people's prayer book: traditional prayers, modern commentaries. Volume 1 – the Sh'ma and it's blessings.* Woodstock, Vermont: Jewish Lights Publishing.

Morrison, Martha and Brown, Stephen F. (1991). *Judaism.* New York: Brown Publishing Network.

Radzinsky, Edward (2005). *Alexander II, the last great tsar.* New York: Free Press.

Robinson, George (2000). *Essential Judaism: a complete guide to beliefs, customs and rituals.* New York: Pocket Books.

Roth, Norman (2005). *The daily life of Jews in the Middle Ages.* Westport, Connecticut: Greenwood Press.

Thubron, Colin. (1976). *Jerusalem.* Amsterdam: Time-Life Books.

Tripp, Leo (1980). *The complete book of Jewish observance.* New York: Behrman House.

Warnes, David (1999). *Chronicles of the Russian tsars.* London: Thames and Hudson.